AN UNEASY ALLIANCE

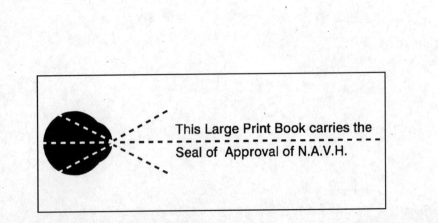

This Large Print Book carries the
Seal of Approval of N.A.V.H.

THE DEVIL'S OWN, BOOK 2

An Uneasy Alliance

JD March

WHEELER PUBLISHING
A part of Gale, Cengage Learning

GALE
CENGAGE Learning·

Farmington Hills, Mich • San Francisco • New York • Waterville, Maine
Meriden, Conn • Mason, Ohio • Chicago

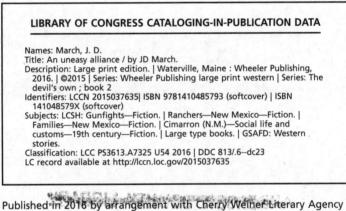

LIBRARY OF CONGRESS CATALOGING-IN-PUBLICATION DATA

Names: March, J. D.
Title: An uneasy alliance / by JD March.
Description: Large print edition. | Waterville, Maine : Wheeler Publishing,
   2016. | ©2015 | Series: Wheeler Publishing large print western | Series: The
   devil's own ; book 2
Identifiers: LCCN 2015037635| ISBN 9781410485793 (softcover) | ISBN
   141048579X (softcover)
Subjects: LCSH: Gunfights—Fiction. | Ranchers—New Mexico—Fiction. |
   Families—New Mexico—Fiction. | Cimarron (N.M.)—Social life and
   customs—19th century—Fiction. | Large type books. | GSAFD: Western
   stories.
Classification: LCC PS3613.A7325 U54 2016 | DDC 813/.6--dc23
LC record available at http://lccn.loc.gov/2015037635

Published in 2016 by arrangement with Cherry Weiner Literary Agency

Printed in the United States of America
1 2 3 4 5 6 7 20 19 18 17 16

Writing this series has been an epic journey, and I could not have done it without the support and friendship of Whistle, Shelley and CC. I owe them more gratitude than I can ever express. Their generosity of spirit shines through their every gesture.

I dedicate this series to them and to my other two staunch supporters, John and Mark.

CHAPTER ONE

There were no guards.

No bars.

No cuffs.

But it was still a prison — with his father as chief warden.

Hell! If someone had a gun to his head it would make sense. But no, Johnny Fierro had simply picked up a pen and signed his life away.

Or at least the only life he'd ever known.

He shook his head slowly. What the hell had possessed him? He'd been all set on heading back to the border, back to his old life, but it was like an invisible force dragged him back to this ranch. And now he'd signed some crazy partnership agreement with two men he barely knew. Loco. That's what he was, plain loco.

A gunfighter like him, owning a chunk of land like this.

He rested his arms on the corral fence and

stared across to the mountains behind the hacienda. Stands of aspens splashed color on the steep slopes, and wisps of cloud shrouded the craggy peaks.

It sure was pretty.

He sighed, because there it was. If he was honest with himself, the ranch had gotten to him and the thought of owning a piece of it was too tempting. He shook his head again. Who was he kidding? It would never be his because he sure didn't believe his old man would let him stay. The fact that they'd signed a piece of paper didn't mean a thing. No, it was only a question of time before his father figured Johnny Fierro was all trouble and threw him out. Nothing lasted; he knew that, he'd learned that the hard way.

He'd left them all in the house, his so-called family, the doctor, and the lawyer, who'd shown him where to sign. He'd needed to get away from them to get his thoughts in some kind of order. And even that had caught a look of disapproval from his old man, who'd been busy handing out drinks to everyone. Hell, everything he did garnered him a black look from his father.

A cloud of dust drew his eye. Squinting, he could make out someone riding in from the east. His hand went to his gun. A man couldn't be too careful. He eased himself around for a better look as the stranger reined in his sorrel horse and trotted into the yard.

Heavily built and maybe about the same age as Johnny's father, the man had the look of a cattleman. The stranger raised his hand in a greeting, calling out to a vaquero working at the far end of the corral. Yeah, definitely a rancher.

The man glanced toward Johnny as if aware he was being watched. Johnny bit back a grin as the fellow stiffened and took a second look, focusing in on the gun that he wore low and tied tight to his thigh.

He rode slowly forward, his brows drawn close together. "Fierro?"

Johnny hesitated, thinking of the partnership deal he'd just signed. The ink would barely have had time to dry. "Sinclair, now," he said softly.

The man's frown edged into a scowl. "Thought you'd left. You're not wanted in these parts, Fierro."

Johnny smiled. "My old man seems to want me. He offered me a piece of this." He gestured toward the bunkhouse and the Sinclair land stretching off into the distance.

The man's face hardened. "We don't need the likes of you in Cimarron. No one will do business with Sinclair if it means dealing with you."

Johnny allowed the smile to broaden. "Now, that ain't too friendly, Mister . . . ?"

The man puffed his chest out. "Donovan. Joe Donovan. Maybe you'd better remember because my hands will shoot you down if you step on my land. And I reckon most of the ranchers in these parts will feel the same. You're just a paid killer, a threat to good law-abiding folk. And I'm warning you; stay away from our women unless you want a lynching. We don't want no breed like you anywhere near our families."

Johnny raised an eyebrow. "Hell, Donovan, don't hold back. Why don't you say what you really think?"

Donovan hissed in a breath. "Think you're real smart, don't you? You won't think that when someone's stringing you up. Or putting a bullet . . ." Donovan swung around at the sound of footsteps.

Johnny nodded to his brother, who was striding across to the corral. "Hey."

Guy looked hard at Donovan. "It's Mr. Donovan, isn't it? I think we met briefly in town a few days ago."

Donovan flushed. "Aye, lad, we did. I'm here to see your father. Is he about?"

Guy nodded. "You'll find him in the hacienda."

Donovan swung his horse away and headed toward the house, even as Guy turned and looked at Johnny curiously. "What were you talking about? He didn't look too friendly."

Johnny shrugged and stared back at the mountains. "Just passing the time of day is all."

Guy snorted. "Didn't look like it from where I was."

Johnny glanced at him. "Was there something you wanted, Harvard?"

His brother sighed, kind of like he was giving in on asking about Donovan. "I guess . . . I suppose I wanted to say I'm glad you decided to stay. Or maybe I should say come back. Even if you did cut it a little fine. I'd just about given up on you when you walked in. What decided you in the end?"

Shit, why did Harvard always want to know about everything? Always asking questions.

"The horse was being mule-headed. Wouldn't turn toward the border, that's all."

His brother grinned at that. "Ah, so at least one of you has some sense. But really, why?"

11

Johnny shook his head. "I don't know! Figured I'd give it a try. Doesn't mean I'm staying long. You got a lot to learn, and you might feel different when someone turns up looking to gun me. You'll wish I was gone then."

Harvard shrugged. "That might never happen. You can't be sure that anyone will come looking."

"They will. Believe me, they will."

Harvard stared at him, kind of thoughtful and serious. "Doesn't that scare you?"

"No. If I was scared, I'd be dead a long time ago. It gives me my edge."

"So why do they challenge you?" Harvard's brow was furrowed, like he had a headache or something.

Johnny sighed. "You sure ask a lotta questions." He paused, trying to figure how to put it so that his brother would understand. "Look, Harvard, life ain't been too hard for you, I guess. But for some of us, people who got nothing, gunfighting is a way to make your mark. And the faster you are, the more people will pay you."

"To kill."

"To do their dirty work for 'em because they ain't got the guts to do it themselves."

"So other gunfighters will come looking for you because you're the best? And they can earn more by killing you?"

"I never said I was the best," Johnny snapped.

"It's what all the ranch hands say," Harvard said, waving his hand toward the bunkhouse. "And you looked awfully fast when you took down Chavez and his —"

"Well, it ain't what I say." Johnny glared at him.

"So who is the best?"

Madre de Dios! "I dunno, it's whoever's fastest on any particular day. Who knows? You get dust in your eye, you're dead. Anyone who says they're the best is dumb."

"OK. So you're one of the best?"

Harvard just didn't know when to quit. "Yeah, OK, I'm one of the best. Happy now?"

His brother frowned. "But the fact remains that someone really is the fastest . . ."

"Oh, hell! Just leave it. If it shuts you up, I'm the best, OK?"

"So I can say I have a famous brother." Harvard grinned at him, like he'd won a contest or something.

Johnny gave him the coldest look he could. "Yeah, you got a famous half-brother. Famous for killin'." He watched as the smile faded. "Now, if you don't mind, I'd like to be left alone."

But instead of leaving, the man just stood with his head bowed.

"I said I'd like to be left alone now. Maybe you don't hear too good?"

His brother lifted his head and looked at him. "I'm sorry, it's not a game. I shouldn't have asked you about it. The trouble is . . . I want to get to know you again. We're brothers and yet we know nothing about each other. Aren't you at all curious about me? My past?"

"Nope. Ain't my business." The man did like to make a meal of everything. He still didn't look like he was leaving, just stood there. This rate, the only way he'd get Harvard to leave would be to pull a gun on him. After all, he'd done it before. He tried not to smile at the memory.

"It is our business. We're brothers and that should mean something. It does to me. I suppose it's why I went to help you during the fight with Wallace."

"An' I seem to remember telling you, I wouldn't have done the same for you. Being brothers don't mean nothing. We're partners in this ranch, that's it." He knew he was being hard, but no way was he getting over friendly with anyone. Wouldn't be here too long and he didn't want it to be any harder to leave when he had to go. He was already regretting his decision to sign that damn paper.

"Partners?"

"Yeah. Partners."

His brother sighed and turned slowly toward the house. "I'm sorry to have disturbed you then, partner."

There was something in the tone of his voice. Offense taken? Hurt? Johnny felt guilty.

He spoke softly. "Harvard?"

The man glanced back.

"I'm . . . This ain't easy for me."

"I don't think it's easy for any of us, Johnny. It's a daunting prospect, finding a brother I thought was dead years ago. And trying to adjust to living here after so many years back East, and learning about ranching. At times it all seems too much. Overwhelming. I feel as though I'm stumbling around in the dark. But if I don't try, I know I'll be missing out on something. A chance at a totally different life."

"Thought you had it all back in Boston. Fancy house, fancy school, money . . ."

"Those things aren't everything. They don't mean much if there's nothing else. I was discontented in Boston. All I did was socialize and womanize."

Johnny perked up at that. "Womanize?

15

Hey, that's more like it, Harvard. Maybe we got something in common after all." He paused. "You ever been to a bordello? I mean, you do know what a bordello is, right?"

"I am familiar with the term."

Why couldn't the man just say yes? "Ain't you never been to one?"

His brother narrowed his eyes. "I have been known to venture into one, yes."

"Well, when the doc says I can ride again, I was going to pay a visit to the one in Cimarron. Maybe we could ride into town together."

"There's a bordello in Cimarron?" Harvard sounded surprised at that bit of news.

"Yeah, I know. Don't seem very likely, but yeah. An' they're real pretty girls too."

"I take it that you've already paid the establishment a visit?"

Johnny shuffled uncomfortably. No way would he admit that he'd been thrown out, and by a woman too. But the doc had said he'd talk to her, seeing as how she was a friend, so doubtless she wouldn't throw him out next time. "Yeah, I paid it a visit. So, if you want to ride in with me, that'll be OK."

"I would like that. Thanks, Johnny. And now I will leave you in peace." Guy turned to walk away and then swung around again.

"Damn, I almost forgot. I thought I'd best tell you that Peggy is planning a celebratory meal for tonight." He smiled and shrugged. "She's delighted that you and I are staying. I think she thought I'd hate this life and return to Boston, and that you'd go back to the border."

Johnny groaned. "I don't want no fancy dinner." He hesitated. "Just say I'm still feeling rough from opening up my gunshot wound again."

Guy shook his head. "I give you due warning, if our new foster sister doesn't have the pleasure of your company this evening, she'll delay the whole thing until you're feeling better. If it's any comfort, Ben will be here. One of the hands will drive the lawyer back to town. Would that make it more bearable?"

Seemed Harvard wasn't as stupid as he looked. It would be easier with an outsider there. And Ben would keep the old man in check. Johnny nodded slowly. "Yeah, OK. I'll come."

Guy grinned. "Good. I'll tell Peggy you'll be joining us for dinner."

Johnny watched Guy stride back to the house. He swallowed hard. He had an uneasy feeling he'd made another mistake, let his guard down too much. Must be get-

17

ting soft or something. Why did he keep doing these things? But hell, Harvard wasn't so bad. And there was something about his brother that said perhaps he was more than just a Fancy Dan. And the man could fire a rifle. That had been some shooting the day of the showdown. Maybe, just maybe, he was worth getting to know.

CHAPTER TWO

He'd removed his spurs, put a clean shirt on. But he couldn't go down without his gun. He felt naked without it even though he knew the old man would hate it. He stared down at his boots. Maybe if he'd cleaned them . . . No, his father wouldn't notice the boots, but he'd sure as hell notice the gun. Well, tough. The old man would have to get used to it.

No doubt Harvard would be wearing fancy clothes. And he'd know which knife and fork to use, though Johnny couldn't figure out why anyone needed more than one. It'd matter to Guthrie Sinclair, though. And this big thing they made of talking at the table. Why did they do that? He could never think of anything to say. If he just ate, they stared at him like he was doing something strange. But no one ever said what he was doing wrong. Hell, why was life so complicated?

He huffed out a breath. No way was he going down without the gun; they'd have to put up with it. At least Ben would be there, and that would help. Fuck it. What did any of it matter? He didn't care what any of them thought, damn them all. Simply go on down and get the whole thing over with. Slamming the door shut behind him, he headed downstairs.

He stopped dead in his tracks at the door to the dining room. Candles flickered and the lamps around the room were lit, all glowing softly. The table was laid with flowers and silver. Lots of flowers, and even more knives and forks than usual. Shit!

"Johnny, aren't you going to change for dinner?"

He turned to see Peggy standing in some fancy dress, not at all like the things she usually wore. The fabric looked shiny, and kinda rustled when she moved. And her hair was all piled up on her head. What the hell did she mean? Change for dinner? And just as he was thinking it couldn't get any worse, the old man walked in, dressed up in a suit and string tie.

Guthrie looked at Johnny, his lip curling slightly. "You are changing for dinner, Johnny? You'd better hurry up."

Change into what, he wanted to shout.

Fancy clothes? And just where did they think he had these fancy clothes? In his fucking saddlebags? But he didn't shout. He just turned and trudged back upstairs to his room.

He was standing by the window when someone knocked on the door. "Yeah?"

Harvard came in and looked around the room, casual like. "I wondered if you had everything you needed for tonight. Peggy's putting on a grand dinner and you didn't seem to have much luggage when you arrived so I thought you might not have suitable clothing."

He stared at his brother, trying to see if the man was making fun of him. But that wasn't Harvard's style. More likely he knew Johnny didn't have much of anything and was trying to help. Kinda nice, really. He'd noticed before that Harvard tried to put people at ease.

He shook his head. "No, I ain't got anything suitable! I went down there a minute ago, and they're all dressed up like they're going to a wedding or something. I reckon they're really pissed at me."

"They just didn't think, Johnny. Come on, I'll loan you a shirt and tie. Or perhaps you'd prefer a cravat?"

What the hell was a cravat? Johnny sighed

21

heavily but followed him.

He perched on the side of the bed as Harvard rummaged in a cupboard and fished out a shirt and tie. "Put these on and hurry up; otherwise Father will be mad at both of us."

Johnny pulled the shirt on but stood holding the tie. "I ain't never worn one before. How the hell do I put it on?"

Harvard's eyes widened at that, but he took the tie. "I'll tie it for you. I could loan you some trousers . . ."

Johnny shuddered, thinking of some of the strange Eastern clothes he'd seen his brother wear. Shit! "No! I'm wearing my own pants. And tough if they don't like it."

Harvard looked him up and down like he was sizing him up for a coffin or something. "You can't wear the gun belt, you know."

Johnny glared at him. "I ain't going down without my gun."

"It's not done to wear a gun at this sort of dinner. And it's not like you'll need it. It's only us and Ben."

He glared again at his brother. "I ain't going anywhere without my gun."

Harvard huffed, kind of like a horse might. "Fine. How about a derringer? If I lend you a jacket, you could have a gun inside it and no one will know. That could be a compromise."

He nodded slowly. It did seem like it might be one way to stop the old man getting mad. "OK, I'll wear a jacket."

A few minutes later Johnny stared at his reflection in the mirror. Nobody would be able to see the gun, he had to admit, but he looked real odd. Harvard was giving him a strange look too.

"I never thought I'd say it, Johnny, but bizarre as your Mexican clothes are with all that embroidery, they suit you more than that. Still, it means you've made an effort to conform and that will please Peggy and Father. Come on, before he gets really mad at both of us. He's very good at getting mad — it seems to be what he does best!"

And with a broad smile, Harvard opened the door and led the way downstairs.

It was an awful evening. He never did figure out which fork he was supposed to be using at any given time. He tried to copy what his brother did but there was so much of the stuff, he got confused. And when he wasn't staring at the damn knives and forks, he was trying to resist the urge to pull the tie off. It felt so damn tight. It was probably what a noose felt like, just before they hanged you. He swallowed, trying to push away the

23

memory of the gallows in the courtyard in Mexico. Damn, but he'd come close to swinging . . . He pulled at the tie again before dropping his hands back to the table. He had to stop fiddling with the thing. The others all seemed to be enjoying themselves, though, talking and laughing and sipping their wine.

God, he wanted a tequila, or a beer. They were one hell of a lot better than wine. Damn grape juice!

And he still couldn't think of anything to say. They talked about all kinds of things he knew nothing about. Ben did his best to include him but Johnny was past caring. All he wished was that the evening was over. Maybe he could say he was tired because of his wound? But Ben would see straight through that one. Shit! Now they were talking about galleries in Europe for God's sake. What was a gallery? Who cared? And how did they know all this stuff anyway?

"Johnny?"

He looked up at Ben. The doc was watching him, except his eyes were warm, not cold. "I think you should call it a night, Johnny. You opened that wound up and you really shouldn't be overdoing it. I'm sure your family will forgive you if you turn in, since it's doctor's orders."

He tried to stop his face breaking into a grin. "Well, if you really think so, Ben, I'll head on up. G'night all." Trying to stifle a huge sigh of relief, he headed to the door. He'd forgotten something, he was sure he'd forgotten something. Shit! Then he remembered. "Thanks for the dinner, it was real nice." And then he fled to the security of his room.

He ripped off the jacket and fumbled with the tie, desperate to get rid of the thing before it choked him. How could people eat wearing the damn things? He went and stood at the open window and breathed in the scented evening air. Deep breaths, trying to calm himself. He wished he was camped out somewhere under the stars, away from everyone. Someplace where the only sound was a coyote howling and the crickets chirping. When did life get this complicated? He didn't belong here; he couldn't imagine ever belonging here. Hell, he was used to stirring his coffee with a stick, not some fancy silver spoon. And a bed was fine occasionally, when he needed some comfort from a woman but not every night like this. He felt more at home in his bedroll than this fancy bed with its clean, crisp sheets.

The bedroll was stashed in the corner of

his room. It looked comforting and familiar. He looked at it for a second and then stretched it out on the floor next to the window. Blowing out the lamp, he wriggled in and lay with the breeze ruffling his hair. It helped — a little. And curling up, he settled down to sleep.

CHAPTER THREE

Guy gave his brother a surreptitious glance across the table. Johnny looked very uncomfortable and he hadn't stopped fidgeting with the tie since Guy had tied it.

He'd been amazed when Johnny admitted he'd never worn one before. How could someone reach that age without ever wearing a tie? But of course, his brother's life had been so different from his own. He'd been shocked to find that Johnny was a gunfighter but now Guy wanted to know what had pushed his younger brother into such a life. Why had he turned to a gun? What had his childhood been like? Certainly, the scars on Johnny's back bore testament to the fact that life had not been kind to him. He didn't appear to have had any sort of schooling. But despite his lack of education, he was very sharp, and was one hell of a chess player! Guy grinned. This long-lost brother was certainly an enigma, but he was looking forward to getting to know him better.

He tried to pay attention to the questions that Peggy was firing at him, wanting to know what Europe was like and which cities he'd visited. Father had as many questions as the girl. And all the while Johnny looked more and more uncomfortable. But try as Guy might to steer the conversation to territory where Johnny might join in, it seemed that their father was not to be thwarted.

He could see Ben was doing his best to engage Johnny in conversation but his brother was becoming more withdrawn with each course. Guy ground his teeth. Surely their father wasn't so insensitive as not to see how out of his depth Johnny was? But now the man was regaling the table with stories of Scottish clans and Scottish poetry. Yes, he was that insensitive.

He tried to catch Ben's eye and was in despair of doing so, when Ben gave Johnny his excuse for escape. Guy saw the relief flood his brother's normally impassive face as he excused himself and left the room. But Guthrie seemed irritated by Johnny's swift departure.

"Ben, I'm sure he could have stayed up longer. It's good for him to join in family occasions."

Ben smiled blandly across the table. "Johnny has had a very close call, Guthrie, and he's opened the wound up again. He needs plenty of rest, and he was looking tired."

"He was looking bored," snapped Guthrie. "He makes no effort to join in conversation at the table."

Guy sighed. "I think, sir, he would be more inclined to join in if the conversation related to something he knew about. Quite frankly, talking about art, politics and literature is akin to excluding him."

Guthrie snorted derisively. "He made no effort. He's going to have to knuckle down and try to fit in, now he's decided to stay. I hope he isn't thinking this is going to be an easy ride. He's going to have to learn to do an honest day's work and pull his weight."

Guy looked across at Ben who just shook his head, almost in exasperation.

Guy glanced back at Guthrie. "It's going to take time. He hasn't had the advantages of a proper education. And he's been on his own for a very long time. You can't expect him to fit in instantly."

"All the more reason for him to take an interest in our discussions so he'll learn how to behave in civilized company. What happens when we have people for dinner?" Guthrie took another sip of his wine.

Ben cut in. "Guthrie, give him a chance, he's only just arrived. Unless, of course, you really do want him to leave, because if you aren't careful, that's exactly what he will do. He might have signed the partnership agreement but it doesn't mean that he won't still throw it in if you push too hard and don't give him some time to settle. Have you even read the Pinkerton Agency reports yet to find out more about his childhood?"

Guy looked up sharply. Damn. He'd overlooked that. Of course the agency would have provided a report to Father when they traced Johnny . . .

"No, Ben, I haven't read it. It sickened me when they told me he was Fierro. I . . . I don't think I want to know."

Ben shook his head sadly. "Guthrie, the only way you'll ever understand that boy of yours is to find out what happened to him after Gabriela took him away. There's a story there and you need to hear it. Until then, you might as well be strangers."

"That's all done, Ben. It's now that matters."

Guy shook his head. It was ridiculous to dismiss the past as though it had no bearing on the present. God, what a stubborn, difficult man Father was at times. And remote. But then, it couldn't have been easy for his father, alone for so many years. Of course, there'd been letters between his father and himself. And his father had visited Guy in Boston occasionally but the fact remained that Guthrie must have been lonely. But surely now he had his family reunited, the man would unbend a little? Become more approachable?

He smiled his thanks to Peggy as she poured him a cup of coffee and tried to drag his attention back to the conversation. He suddenly envied Johnny his early escape. The long days and backbreaking work were taking their toll. He'd have given anything to head upstairs to bed. Instead, with a fixed smile, he started asking Peggy questions about the local families he could expect to meet. It was going to be a long evening.

It was several days before Ben gave Johnny permission to ride, an event which caused the entire household to heave a collective sigh of relief. As Johnny had become more bored, everyone had tried to find ways to occupy him but with limited success. Guy had been amused by their father's efforts to show Johnny how to do the accounts. The man had obviously been unsure as to how to find out if his younger son could read or write.

Guy had enjoyed watching Johnny, who, with narrowed eyes, listened impassively as Guthrie tried, not very tactfully, to raise the subject. Johnny had surveyed their father coolly, watching him become more and more uncomfortable, before finally saying, "Why don't you just ask, Old Man? Yeah, I can read and write. And yeah, I can even add up. If you want me to do the fucking books, I will. But they won't be as pretty as if old Harvard had done them."

Guthrie turned an interesting shade of puce. "I will not tolerate that sort of language in the house. You're living with civilized people now, and it's time you started acquiring some manners."

Johnny had merely shrugged, picked up the ledger and stalked over to the desk. Then, looking at Guthrie again, he'd said, "Well, you going to stand and watch or will you let me get on with the job?"

Guy dragged a reluctant Guthrie outside, leaving Johnny slouched in the chair at the desk.

Much later, a thunderous-looking Guthrie had gone to inspect the ledger, which had been discarded on the floor. Picking it up, he proceeded to check the figures, pen in hand ready to correct the errors. But Guy was interested to see that not once did his father have to alter the entries. He couldn't resist commenting. "So Johnny did a good job on the accounts?"

Guthrie looked at the ledger. "There are spots of ink everywhere; they're a dreadful mess."

"But they added up right?"

"Yes." Guthrie sounded grudging. And Guy wondered for what felt like the millionth time quite what Guthrie wanted of Johnny. Why couldn't the man ever give him a single word of praise?

As soon as he heard he was cleared to ride, Johnny had reminded Guy of their planned trip to town. "We'll go Saturday night, unless you're chickening out, Harvard."

"On the contrary, I'm all agog." Johnny had looked at him and asked if that was catching.

And so, on the first Saturday night of Johnny's freedom, the two of them saddled up and headed to town.

CHAPTER FOUR

Johnny breathed a sigh of relief as they rode out toward town. It felt good to be away from the ranch, away from his father's disapproving gaze. Hell, whenever he caught his father's eye, the man was watching him, kind of like he expected his newfound son to make off with the family silver.

He shook his head, irritated with himself. What did he care what the old man thought? It wasn't like he'd be around for long. At some point his father would throw him out. Or he'd walk out before the old man could show him the door.

He glanced across at Harvard, who was riding alongside. Damn but his brother was a puzzle. What the hell was he doing here when he could still be living in comfort back in Boston with his mother's people? What was the man running from? Or looking for? It seemed crazy to swap that life for the ranch. Ranching was damned hard work —

up before dawn and backbreaking labor until nightfall. Yeah, hard labor.

And Harvard was so . . . so fussy. He never got his hands dirty — he always wore gloves. And on the rare occasions he took them off, he was always fiddling with them, or tucking them in his belt. Then two minutes later he'd take them out and pull them back on again. And then there was his hat. He never seemed able to decide where to wear the damn thing, always pushing it back on his head or pulling it forward.

But Harvard was a hard man to read. Those eyes didn't give much away. Johnny could read most men, but not his brother. If Harvard was running from something, that wasn't anyone's business but his own. But what the hell did *agog* mean?

He could hear the town now; laughter, singing and raucous music were coming from the saloon. How could anyone live there? Towns were fine, now and again, when a fellow needed a woman or a drink. But the rest of the time it would wear him out to be around people all the time. It meant he had to be continuously alert, watching his back, watching dark alleyways, never able to relax. Even this far out of town, he was getting ready. And it was always best to avoid saloons on a Saturday night; there was always some jerk who thought he could take Fierro. Killing someone tended to put a damper on a night out. Unless he'd planned to kill someone, which was another matter altogether . . .

His brother's voice broke his thoughts. "What's the matter?"

Johnny frowned. "What d'you mean?"

"You're acting differently now we're near town."

Johnny shrugged. "Just lookin' out for trouble, that's all. One of us needs to be sharp and seeing as you ride along in a dream half the time, I figure it best be me."

Harvard rolled his eyes before tilting his head and staring at him. "Do you always expect trouble?"

Johnny shifted in his saddle, and huffed out a breath. Were there really men who went through life without expecting trouble? What would that feel like? He glanced at Harvard. "Yeah, I always expect trouble. And you know something? I usually find it. Or it finds me. But tonight, I ain't looking for trouble, just a woman to fuck."

His brother raised an eyebrow. "A woman to fuck? My! I bet the women find you really charming, brother. You have such a romantic turn of phrase. So eloquent, so . . ."

Johnny narrowed his eyes. "Just shut up.

Brother!"

Guy grinned. "Well, I suppose that's an improvement on Harvard."

Johnny leaned forward on his saddle horn, easing his back. "What?"

"You called me brother, albeit somewhat sarcastically, but still a vast improvement on Harvard. Unless, of course, Harvard is a term of endearment."

Johnny glared. "Quit yapping. At least one of us needs to watch our backs."

They rode through the center of the town while Johnny scanned the street, holding his reins lightly in his left hand and resting his gun hand on his thigh, close to the Colt. Johnny reined in outside the bordello and almost laughed out loud at the expression on Harvard's face.

His brother frowned, taking in the handsome building and the ornately carved oak door. "You sure this is the right place, Johnny? It doesn't look like a bordello."

"Yeah, kinda funny, ain't it? It looks real respectable from out here. I guess people could get a bit of a shock if they went in." He walked to the door and cocked his head, listening to the sound of music coming from inside, before turning and looking at his brother. "Coming?" And he pushed open the door and walked in.

His gut clenched, and he almost faltered as the damn woman who ran the place spotted them and walked toward them. She had that same icy look on her face that she'd worn when she threw him out on his first visit. Shit. Surely she wasn't going to throw him out again? Not in front of Harvard . . . Fuck!

But Ben had said he'd fix things with her. Damn. He should have come alone on this visit, just to check that Ben had cleared it, like he'd promised he would.

But if Harvard thought she didn't look none too friendly, he didn't show it. He'd already whipped off his hat and was greeting the woman with a charming smile.

She inclined her head and held her hand out to shake Guy's hand. "Mr. Sinclair, I assume. How nice to meet you. Ben has told me so much about you. I imagine you find things rather different out here after spending so many years in Boston. It's a little more uncivilized here." She turned to Johnny, her face hardening again. "Mr. Fierro, it seems we meet again. Please, Mr. Sinclair, help yourself to a drink. I want a quiet word with Mr. Fierro."

Johnny's heart sank. Surely she wasn't going to throw him out again? Shit, shit, shit! Maybe a smile would work on her. He tried to pull his lips into a smile. She didn't look impressed.

"Mr. Fierro, let me make myself very clear." She narrowed her green eyes and spoke very softly so that no one could hear her words other than him. "You are here under sufferance, as a special favor, because Ben is a good friend of mine. I do not like gunfighters, I despise them. I think they are the lowest form of human life and quite frankly I would love any excuse to throw you out of here. So I give you due warning that if you wish to visit my premises, there are some rules, and they are not negotiable. I will not tolerate any gunplay in here. I will not tolerate drunkenness. I will not tolerate brawling. And if you hurt any of my girls, or insult them, or lift a hand to them, I promise that you really will wish you had never been born. Do I make myself clear?"

He felt the blood rushing to his face and fought to bite back a furious retort. "Crystal clear, ma'am." But he couldn't stop himself. "And let me tell you, ma'am, I've never hurt a woman in my life. I've never felt like hitting a woman in my life — until now!" And he stalked to the back of the room and settled himself in the corner with his back to the wall. He could feel her gaze, boring into him. He lifted his eyes and stared straight back at her across the room. Damn woman, and, God, she was ugly. It was strange though how she sounded real educated. She didn't sound like women in her line of work.

"I got you tequila, was that right? Do you really want to sit all the way back here?"

He dragged his attention back to Harvard, who was standing with two glasses in his hands.

"I always sit in the corner."

"Why always in the corner?"

Johnny shook his head slowly, barely able to believe what an innocent his brother was. "So I can watch the room, and keep my back to the wall. That way no one can shoot me in the back."

Harvard looked shocked, and sad too. "Is that really how you live? All the time? Don't you ever relax?"

He thought about that. Did he ever relax? He smiled briefly. "Why d'you think I like bordellos, Harvard?"

"And that's it? The only time you let your guard down is when you're with a woman?" Harvard sounded like he found it hard to believe.

"I didn't say I let my guard down. I never let my guard down. How d'you think I lived this long?"

"It's a pretty sad way to live your life, Johnny."

The words stung. He'd never really thought about it before. He stared down at his tequila, swallowing the sudden lump in his throat. When he spoke, his voice was very soft. "It's the only way I know, Harvard; the only way I know."

They sipped their drinks in silence. Then Johnny looked around. "The girls don't seem too friendly in here. You must be putting 'em off. I never have trouble getting girls. They always swarm over me."

His brother cocked his head and gave an exaggerated sigh. "Me? Putting them off? I think not. It's far more likely that it's your terrifying reputation that's making them keep their distance. I never have a problem, in or out of a bordello, brother. And let's face it, attracting girls in a bordello isn't exactly difficult, so this must be your fault." He set his glass down with a smirk.

Johnny raised an eyebrow. "My fault? I spend half my life in bordellos, and believe me, I never have no problems. This is your fault. It has to be your fault. It's that fancy accent of yours, an' all those fancy words. And fancy clothes and manners. That's what's putting 'em off." Or was it that damn woman? Shit, had she ordered the girls to stay away from them, to try and humiliate him? He stared across at her, what was it Ben had called her? Delice? Yeah, that was it, Delice. She was standing at the bar talking to some of the customers. As he looked, she glanced across and caught his eye. She raised an eyebrow, and looked amused, like she knew all the girls were avoiding him. Bitch. She must have told the girls to keep their distance. It was the only explanation.

Harvard had got up and was smiling at some redhead, acting all smooth. Like he needed to bother! The girl would go upstairs whatever he said. Yep. There they went now.

Johnny glanced again in the direction of a pretty, raven-haired girl he'd noticed when he first walked in. She immediately looked away, avoiding his gaze. He sighed, and stared down at his tequila. Maybe he should just go, leave Harvard to his redhead and head back to the ranch. Sure as hell didn't fancy the saloon on a Saturday night. And he didn't want some rough saloon girl either. Seemed, though, if he was staying in these parts, that was all he was going to get.

He watched as Delice beckoned the raven-haired girl over. He had sharp hearing and he strained his ears to hear the short exchange.

"Sadie, honey, I'm sorry but it looks like

you've drawn the short straw. Mr. Fierro seems very interested in you; he can't take his eyes off you." She frowned. "But why are you all avoiding him? You're all acting as though he's got the plague or something."

The girl pulled a face. "Well, he's famous, isn't he? I mean, everyone's heard of Johnny Fierro and well . . ." She flushed. "He's kind of scary. We ain't never had a gunfighter in here before. You always told us you wouldn't have them in here."

"Honey, he's only a customer, same as all the rest. Brains in his balls. And believe me, he's only got one thing on his mind tonight and it sure isn't his gun. So go do your job, there's a good girl."

The girl walked slowly toward him, dragging her feet. As she looked at him, he could see the fear in her eyes. Damn! Had he really got to that stage, sunk to such a level where his reputation, instead of thrilling girls, just scared them?

"Would you like another drink, Mr. Fierro?" Her voice trembled slightly.

"You don't need to call me Mr. Fierro. My name's Johnny. And no, thanks, I don't want another drink."

"Was there . . . was there anything else you wanted, Mr. Fi . . . Johnny?"

He pushed his glass in circles on the table

43

for a few seconds, looking at the damp marks it left. Then he looked up at her. Her dark hair cascaded onto her shoulders and she licked her lips nervously. Full, pouting lips and she had a dimple in her chin. He nodded slowly. "Yeah, there was. How about you and me go and get better acquainted?"

She swallowed. "Upstairs?"

"Yeah, upstairs."

She turned and slowly led the way up the stairs and along to a large room all done out with velvet and lace. It seemed real fancy for a small place like Cimarron. He closed the door behind them and watched as she swallowed hard again. She smiled, a little too brightly. "So what do you fancy, cowboy?"

Poor kid. She really was scared. "How about we talk?"

She looked puzzled now. "Oh, you mean you want me to tell you what I want to do to you? Talk dirty-like?"

He shook his head. "No. I meant, talk. Tell me about yourself, Sadie. It is Sadie?"

She nodded, slowly. "Yeah, Sadie."

"Why are you so scared, Sadie? I ain't gonna hurt you."

"I've never met a gunfighter before."

"Well, you met one now, but there's no need to be scared. I don't bite, you know.

An' if you'd rather, we'll only talk, OK? And I won't tell that sour-faced old cow that you were too scared to do anything else."

Sadie gave a small smile. "She's fine, really. She's good to us girls. Looks after us."

He raised a disbelieving eyebrow. "If you say so. Now, tell me, Sadie, where you from?"

It was some considerable time later that he headed back down the stairs, feeling rather pleased with himself and a lot more relaxed. Harvard was deep in conversation with the old cow. Yeah, that figured — they'd get along real well. They both sounded like they'd had fancy educations. He paused in the doorway. They hadn't noticed him and he was curious to hear what they were talking about.

"I really don't know why you don't head back, Mr. Sinclair. It's obvious from the time he's taking that although Mr. Fierro is very good at firing his gun, it's probably all he can fire."

Harvard smiled at the jibe. "Well, Miss Martin, I think I ought to stay and wait for Johnny. He's still recovering from getting shot and I think I should be around to keep him out of trouble."

"If you really think you can keep Johnny Fierro out of trouble, you have a lot to learn about gunfighters, Mr. Sinclair. Particularly one as infamous as Mr. Fierro." She turned as Johnny stepped through the doorway and looked at him with that damn superior look again. "Mr. Fierro, we were just talking about you."

"Yeah, I heard. And for the record, ma'am, I don't have any trouble firing my gun." He gave her the ghost of a smile. "Or anything else. I like to take my time, particularly over the second and third ones." And he put his hat on and sauntered toward the door. "Coming, Harvard?"

His brother followed him to where they'd tethered the horses. Johnny swung himself onto Pistol and headed out of town, leaving Guy trailing behind.

He settled into a steady trot until Harvard drew level with him. His brother jerked his head in the direction of the town. "What you said back there? Three times? Did you really . . . ?"

"Yeah. Doesn't everyone?" And with a snort of laughter, he spurred his horse into a gallop.

CHAPTER FIVE

Guthrie stood in the rose garden sipping his Scotch, enjoying the solitude. He never had any time to himself these days. How would it all pan out? And why was Johnny so good at irritating the hell out of him? He couldn't understand the boy. He was surly, his language was truly appalling and he seemed to take off at every opportunity. What had made the boy decide to stay? And how long would he stay? It just wasn't going to work. The boy was wild. Boy . . . Trouble was he wasn't a boy. He was a man. A very dangerous man.

He'd never believed that danger could be tangible, but sometimes he'd look at his son and feel it emanating from him. Those eyes might as well have shutters over them for all the emotion they gave away. He could never tell what Johnny was thinking; he always seemed cool and remote. Untouchable. And then there were mealtimes. He dreaded mealtimes now. Guy and Peggy would chatter away but Johnny would sit looking tense, like some wild animal ready to run at the slightest crack of a twig. A dangerous wild animal. There it was again — dangerous. Had he done the right thing in encouraging Johnny to stay? Maybe he should have just let Johnny leave? But then, what would have happened to the young man? He'd have ended up dying a bloody death in a hail of bullets . . . Guthrie clenched his jaw, and shut his eyes, trying to blot out the image. But hell, it would probably end that way anyway. Guthrie couldn't see him staying long. Johnny was too far down whatever road he was traveling to change now.

And then there was the damn Pinkerton report. It sat in the bottom drawer of his desk, unread. He'd started it so many times, but he hadn't read beyond the first page. It turned his stomach — a catalog of killings. It was impersonal with no effort to put the events in any sort of context. Merely a report, which was, after all, what he'd paid for. He knew it probably contained information about the boy's childhood. He knew he should read it. But if he was honest, he was afraid to. He kept thinking about the gunfight he'd heard about, when his son had apparently stood smiling, watching as a man died slowly in a dusty street. He hadn't found the courage to ask Johnny about that gunfight. To try and discover if gut shooting someone was something his son made a habit of.

He took another sip of his Scotch. He had to read the damn thing. Maybe it would help him understand the bitter young man. Maybe there'd be some clue as to why the hell Johnny ever picked up a gun in the first place. Because one thing was for sure, he couldn't ask Johnny and it was obvious that Johnny wasn't going to volunteer any information. The boy barely said anything at all, ever. Conversation, it appeared, was not one of his son's talents. He swallowed the last of his drink and headed back into the house to his desk.

He sat down heavily in the chair and fumbled in the bottom drawer for the report. God, he needed another drink. He poured himself a large Scotch, slumped back down, and opened the large document. It was divided into various sections: there was a list of gunfights and killings, a list of range wars, the suggestion of some robberies that his son might have been involved in, another very scanty section on his childhood which seemed to show that the agency had found next to nothing on that, and a list of associates in his early teens who were known to have schooled him in the art of gunfighting.

He didn't know if he had the stomach for it. Perhaps it was better not to know. But then he'd be constantly wondering. He considered throwing the document into the dying flames of the fire in the hearth. But that would be like burning money — look how much this damn report had cost. And he ought to read what the report said because he had a duty to protect Peggy. Perhaps Johnny was a danger to her, to them all. Johnny was always cold with them. He didn't call any of them by their names. What went on behind that impassive expression? The boy was impossible to read. Sometimes, he'd seen a brief flicker of emotion in his son's eyes. But then it would disappear, leaving Guthrie wondering if he'd imagined a fleeting expression of pain or interest before the mask of indifference was back in place.

And then there was that damn gun. Johnny was never without it. It was like a festering sore between the two of them. Guthrie told him time and again that it shouldn't be worn in the house. And Johnny would just spit back venomous words about how he was "no fucking kid" and would do what he "fucking liked." His insolence and arrogance left Guthrie speechless at times, with no idea of how to counter it. But although Johnny's language was foul, Guthrie had noticed it improved dramatically when Peggy was around. Out of deference to her? Or because he feared what Guthrie would do to him if it didn't?

Guy was such an easy ride by comparison. His manners were impeccable — he was the perfect gentleman. Pity it didn't rub off on his brother. Guthrie knew he should be pleased that Guy and Johnny appeared able to get along; they'd even gone out together that evening. They were heading into town, Guy said. Just as long as that didn't mean trouble. With Johnny there, God only knew what could happen.

He stared down again at the report. He should read it before the two of them got back, or lock it away again.

He fingered the pages, scanning the list of gunfights. Gunfights all over the place including Santa Fe, Abilene, Nogales, Sonora and far too many more. Written next to the names of the towns were details. Santa Fe, November 1869, killed three men in a shoot-out — self-defense. Santa Fe, November 1869, killed two men in a shoot-out — self-defense. As he read he noticed

51

that many of the gunfights listed had self-defense posted by them. But it also said to see notes at the start of the report. He turned back to the beginning and found the appropriate place. It stated: "Although many of the gunfights listed are technically self-defense, we understand that Mr. Fierro is very skilled at goading his opponents to become so angry that they move to draw first, enabling him to plead self-defense. It is a ploy used so frequently that it seems to be beyond coincidence. One witness is reported as saying that 'Fierro knows how to play on his opponents' weak spots.' We have a report from another witness, although uncorroborated, which says that on one occasion Fierro used the ploy in a man's house and then gunned him down in front of his wife and children."

Guthrie swallowed hard. God almighty. In front of a man's family . . . He tried to push away the recurring image of his son standing smiling, watching a man die. Guthrie had spent hours brooding over that gunfight, even dreamed of it. Now there'd be another nightmare image to haunt his dreams — his son killing someone in front of a sobbing family.

And yet Ben said how much he liked Johnny. And Ben was no fool. Had Ben seen another side of the young man or was his son just playing Ben along? And Peggy had warmed to him too. Guthrie had occasionally heard them laugh together, but as soon as he walked in, Johnny's face would turn impassive and he would stalk off. What did Johnny and Guy talk about? Guy was about as forthcoming as Johnny when it came to volunteering information. Guy would generally answer questions, but somehow, it didn't seem quite right to ask what the two of them talked about.

The sound of galloping hooves startled him, and he quickly fumbled with the report and pushed it back into his desk. He could hear voices — two voices. Thank God they were back. He'd feared trouble in a Saturday-night saloon. The combination of Johnny Fierro and drunken ranch hands could all too easily have led to a fight. Was this what it would be like every time they went out? Fearing that his younger son would either get himself or his brother killed in some drunken fight?

He could hear Guy now, saying, "Three times?" And Johnny replying, "If you don't believe me, you can always come and watch. You might learn something."

He wondered what they could be talking about, but at least they sounded cheerful.

Even so, he knew that as soon as Johnny saw him, the good cheer would disappear like an early frost in the first heat of sun.

"Still up, Father?" Guy stood in the doorway. "I thought you'd have gone to bed hours ago. Johnny and I were just going to have a drink. Will you join us?"

He found himself fumbling for an answer. "A drink? Um, well, yes, why not?"

Johnny stood framed in the doorway, no trace of a smile now. "On second thought, Harvard, I might just turn in."

Well, no surprise there, then — taking off as usual. But it seemed Guy wasn't going to let the boy off so lightly.

"No, you don't, Johnny. You said a drink, and a drink we'll have."

Johnny sullenly accepted the glass of tequila that Guy thrust into his hand.

Guthrie forced a smile. "Well, boys, good night out? Was the saloon busy?"

Guy started to say something but Johnny interrupted. "We didn't go to the saloon. We've been whoring. Even old Harvard, here." There was a challenge in the statement.

Guy closed his eyes and shook his head briefly as if in exasperation.

Guthrie slammed his glass down. "Whoring?"

"Yeah, Old Man, whoring. We might have got into trouble in a saloon on Saturday night. Figured you wouldn't want Harvard here caught up in no brawls or gunfights, so I took him whoring."

There was a self-satisfied smile now on Johnny's face and Guthrie felt an urge to knock him across the room.

"Another Scotch, Father?" Guy fumbled with the bottle and waved it around in an obvious attempt to cause a diversion even as Johnny prowled around the room, pausing momentarily by the desk to stoop and pick up a couple of sheets of paper.

Guthrie swallowed hard. It felt like his heart plummeted into his boots. Surely those weren't pages from the report? He'd put it away safely in the drawer. Hadn't he?

Johnny was engrossed in what he read, biting his lip and running his hand through his hair. He turned toward Guthrie. "This what you been doing, Old Man, while we been whoring? Sitting here reading about all the bad things I'm supposed to have done? Makes me look a real mean hombre, don't it? And this ain't the bad stuff."

Guthrie felt poleaxed by the accusing look in his son's eyes. And there was something else . . . anguish?

"Yeah, real good to know that you can

trust your family," Johnny sneered contemptuously. "An' everyone telling me how great it is to have family. You wanna read it, Harvard?" His voice cracked slightly as he waved the sheets toward Guy, who just shook his head.

"At least he didn't need one of these for you, Harvard. He knows all about you, don't he? But I bet this is just a tiny bit of a report he's got on me. Hell, I bet it's got pages listing all the things I've done. Does it tell you how many men I've killed? I know you been just dying to ask that since I first got here. Or how old I was when I first killed a man? Tell you that, does it? Hell, you didn't even know about the prison. Shows what shit your report is."

Johnny walked toward him, crushing the papers into a ball and stopping just inches from him. He could feel the heat of his son's breath, he was so close. Guthrie tried to look him in the eyes. To not show the fear he felt. Or the sudden sense of shame. And he tried to read the strange expression in his son's eyes, which were glistening. "You know, Old Man, I should take your damn report and ram it down your throat. Lucky for you I got myself fucked tonight, kinda puts me in a good mood. So I'm gonna do you a big favor and give you some advice.

You got questions, ask 'em instead of believing every story you ever heard about me. Trouble is you ain't even got the guts to ask me, have you? You'd rather believe your fucking report." And as his voice seemed to break once more, Johnny suddenly pushed the crumpled ball down Guthrie's shirt and turned and walked toward the stairs.

Guthrie swallowed and found his voice. "If I ask, will you answer me?"

Johnny paused at the foot of the stairs, smiling wolfishly. "Well, partner, I might. But on the other hand I might just leave you wondering." And with that he climbed the stairs.

CHAPTER SIX

Guy watched Johnny walk upstairs. Lord, was this what it was always going to be like? What he really wanted to do was knock their heads together. Johnny and Guthrie were as stubborn as mules and both far too quick to make snap judgments. Throw in Guthrie's temper, and the two of them really were a recipe for disaster. And they both seemed to say whatever came into their heads, without ever weighing the consequences of their words. The irony was how alike they were.

"Well, that went well," he commented as he watched his father stumble across the room and pour himself another drink. Guy couldn't help but wonder how many drinks he'd had already.

Guthrie emptied his glass in one swallow. "Now, do you see why I wasn't easy about him being here? You can see what he's like — wild and dangerous."

Guy considered Guthrie's words before answering. "He wasn't wild or dangerous the night I played chess with him. The two of you seemed fine that evening. And I've found him fairly amenable. Not forthcoming, I grant you, but hardly wild or dangerous. It seems to me that you almost go out of your way to annoy him. Or to hurt him. Are you trying to make him leave?"

Was there a momentary hesitation, he wondered, before his father snapped, "Of course I'm not trying to make him leave. But I don't see how he'll ever fit in here. God only knows what our neighbors will make of him. There'll be trouble, mark my words."

"Ben likes him," Guy responded coolly. "In fact, Ben seems remarkably fond of him. He seems to think there's far more to him than just Johnny Fierro, gun for hire. And, as I'm sure you'll agree, Ben is no fool."

He watched as Guthrie seemed to reflect on the words. When it didn't look as though he was going to respond, he thought he'd goad him a little more. "And what on earth were you doing with that report on Johnny? Were you really sitting here reading up on him?" Guy shook his head in exasperation. "No wonder he was so angry and I can't say I blame him. If you have any questions, why don't you ask him? Look at the other day when you were trying to find out if he could read and write. If you'd asked him outright, he'd have been fine. I mean, I know he's not easy, but you just seem to make him even worse, even more reticent. I can't help but wonder if you're doing it deliberately."

Guthrie snorted angrily. "I can't talk to him. He's as cold as ice. You can see the way he looks at me and the way he clams up whenever I'm around."

"He's not exactly talkative with any of us so I wouldn't read too much into that, if I were you. But you're avoiding the issue. Why were you sitting here reading up on him? That is what you were doing? Correct me if I'm wrong. Has that report really been sitting in your desk, unread, all this time?" Guy leaned against the liquor cabinet. He had a suspicion that his father had drunk enough and that blocking the cabinet might be a wise move.

Guthrie glared at him without respond-ing. But Guy didn't feel inclined to let him off the hook. "Well, has it?"

Guthrie threw up his hands. "Damn it! Yes. It's been sitting in the desk all this time. I couldn't bring myself to read it. I've tried, but it turns my stomach. And believe me, every time I look at it, I seem to find something even worse than the last time I looked at it. And if you saw it, you'd know exactly what I mean."

"So you're focusing on the bad parts?"

His father banged his fist down on the desk. "You don't get it, do you? There aren't any good parts. Fierro is a cold and calculating killer."

Guy raised an eyebrow. "Fierro? Not Johnny? And it seems to me that if you haven't read the entire report, how can you know that there aren't any good parts? The fact is he was prepared to sacrifice his life for the sake of the women on this ranch, women he didn't even know, because he knew what would happen to them if Wallace and his men had overrun this place. That doesn't sound like a cold and calculating killer to me. More like a man with a core of decency running through him who tries to do the right thing."

"Well, tell me this, Guy," Guthrie said, sounding defeated, "would you call gunning down a man in his own home in front of his wife and children the act of a decent man?"

He felt as though his father had hit him in the stomach. Surely Johnny couldn't have done that. Could he? He tried frantically to remember things Johnny had said to him.

Warning him, maybe? Johnny telling him once that Guy would never want to see him in action — that he was dangerous. That Guy shouldn't make the mistake of underestimating him. God in heaven, could his brother really have gunned someone down in front of their family?

"Now maybe you see what I mean," his father said. "And something else, I know of at least one gunfight where he gut shot a man and stood smiling while he watched him die in agony. That's Johnny Fierro."

Guy tried to quell the feeling of nausea. "You can't be sure that isn't just gossip. How do you know that?"

Guthrie looked at him steadily. "One of our hands, Buck Lee, saw him do it. That's how I know. Ask him yourself if you don't believe me."

God almighty! What sort of world had he come to? Life out here seemed so totally alien after all those years in Boston. Could Johnny really have done these things? Surely not. Could he? He shut his eyes briefly, struggling to remember more details of conversations he'd had with Johnny. What was it Johnny had said? How he never let his guard down and always expected someone to be gunning for him. Well, no wonder people were gunning for him if he went around shooting people in front of their families. But no . . . somehow that just didn't fit. He was sure that Johnny wasn't all bad, that there was a decent man hiding behind that cold, cynical exterior. Wasn't there?

"You haven't asked him about the gunfight?"

"No." His father sounded very tired. "I haven't asked him anything. I . . . I suppose, I'm afraid of what he might tell me."

Guy felt a stab of sympathy for him. He could understand Guthrie's fear if Buck's story was to be believed. And presumably there was no reason for the man to lie. But to gun down a man in front of his children, what sort of man did that? He shook his head slowly. "Father, it doesn't make sense. I mean, the report doesn't say that he's wanted by the law does it?"

"It would seem not."

"And leaving aside the gunfight that Buck saw, how can you be certain that the Pinkerton report is accurate? Because I still think there's a decent man in there."

"Guy." Guthrie's voice was gentle. "Don't you think that's because it's what you want to believe? I have to be honest here; Johnny's reputation is fearsome and long established. Even if he does sometimes do the decent thing, you don't get a reputation like his by being nice. We have to be realistic and assume he has a murky past, to say the least, and that he has committed some appalling acts."

Again, Johnny's words echoed in his head, telling Guy not to underestimate him, telling him how dangerous he was. Was Guy being naive? Did he really only want to see the best in Johnny because of his memories of him as a young child? Was he deluding himself? If only he could raise the subject with Johnny, but even if he did, the chances were Johnny wouldn't reveal anything. Johnny never seemed to give anything away, never showed any emotion. He kept everything well hidden . . . Even when he'd been so ill after being shot, he'd fought to hide any emotion. A proud man . . . But this evening, for a few brief seconds, Guy had seen pain in Johnny's eyes.

Hell, this wasn't getting him anywhere. He looked at Guthrie, who stood watching him with an expression of what, exactly? Compassion?

"I still think you should speak to him, Father. Maybe he'd respect it if you simply asked him outright." Guy shook his head again as he stifled a yawn. "I don't know, I think I'll head on up, maybe things will seem better in the morning. I'm sorry. I don't think I can handle all of this right now. Good night."

He heard his father bid him good night as he trudged up the stairs to his room. Walking along the passage he saw a glow of light under the door to Johnny's room — he was still awake. Guy hesitated, and then rapped on his brother's door.

"Go away."

The tone of the voice gave no quarter, but damn it, things couldn't be left as they were, so Guy opened the door and walked in. Johnny was standing by the window, staring out into the night. He turned and stared coldly across the room. "Exactly which part of go and away didn't you understand?"

"I saw your light. I . . . I wanted to check that you were OK."

"OK? Why shouldn't I be? Sure there wasn't something else you wanted? Brother."

God, he sounded colder than ever now.

"The old man show you my report, did he? You been reading up on your bad brother? Because you look kinda pale. Even paler than usual."

"No, no, I didn't read your report. But . . ."

"But the old man filled you in." Johnny

gave a mirthless laugh, but the smile didn't touch his eyes. There was something else there. Shame?

"He mentioned a couple of things." He stumbled over the words, not sure what to say.

"Oh, yeah, I bet he did. So, what dreadful deed have I done that's scared the shit out of you?" Johnny sounded defiant but the look in his eyes wasn't.

"I didn't say I was scared."

"No, but you sure as hell look it. He been telling you what I'm really like? Telling you I'm a real bad hombre?"

Guy shook his head, suddenly doubting the wisdom of trying to talk to Johnny in his current mood. "He doesn't know what you're really like. None of us does and we won't if you don't talk to us."

Johnny laughed again. "So, do tell, Harvard, what exactly is it you want to talk about?"

Why did Johnny always revert to sounding so damn cocky? He was so irritating with that superior smirk.

"OK, how about a gunfight where you apparently shot someone in the gut and stood smiling while they died." Guy couldn't believe he'd said it out loud, but damn it, he wanted to know. Surely Johnny couldn't have done something like that. He'd deny it.

Johnny stood motionless, with a strange smile playing around his mouth. "I been in a lot of gunfights, but I believe I do remember that one. It was down in Santa Fe if I remember right. What about it?"

Guy felt the color drain from his face. It wasn't meant to go like this. Johnny was meant to deny it, but instead he sounded so casual. "What do you mean what about it? Is that normal for you, to shoot someone in the gut? To stand smiling while they die? That couldn't have been you, you're not like that."

"Harvard, I told you before, you don't know what I'm like. You know nothing about me. And yeah, it was me, OK? I was wondering when the old man would ask me about it, but I guess he just ain't got the guts."

Guy was puzzled now. "Why did you think he'd ask you about that gunfight in particular? How did you know that he knew about it?"

Johnny was silent for a few seconds, as if deciding what to say. "Well, maybe I knew it would be in his report, or maybe, just maybe, it's because Ben asked me about it weeks ago. So I figured if Ben knows about it, chances are the old man does, too."

Guy felt a surge of relief. If Ben knew about it and seemed so fond of Johnny, there must have been a reason or somehow the story had got muddled. Whatever it meant, it must be all right. "What did you tell Ben about it?"

"That ain't none of your fucking business, Harvard." And then he smiled again, "Maybe I told him a pack of lies to shut him up."

Guy shook his head, disbelieving. "Ben's no fool. And I don't believe you'd lie to him."

"You got a lot to learn about me. You don't know what I'm capable of."

And that was the trouble. He didn't know what Johnny was capable of; he only knew what he wanted to believe and what his instincts told him to believe.

"So what else did the old man tell you about me?" Johnny's tone was casual, but Guy could see concern in those cool eyes.

"What makes you think he told me anything else?"

"It's written all over your face. And I figure it's something much worse than that gunfight. So I'm just dying to hear what it is." Johnny rubbed his hands together. "Hell, this is fun, ain't you having a good time? Think of the stories you'll be able to tell your fancy friends when you run back to Boston. All about this evil gunfighter called Johnny Fierro you ran into when you visited New Mexico." He paused briefly and glanced down before looking back up with a strange, challenging look on his face. "Bet you won't tell them we're related though, will you? Brother."

Guy stared at his brother's face, trying to read the expression, before saying slowly, "His report says that you gunned down a man in his own home in front of his family. The man's children were there."

Johnny glanced down at the floor briefly before looking back at him with a totally impassive face. Putting his mask in place — the strange thought flashed through Guy's mind even as Johnny said, "I'd need a few more details than that, Harvard, to narrow down which one they're talking about in the report. I mean, there've been so many killings . . ."

Guy shook his head slowly. "I don't believe you did that, Johnny. Not in front of his children. I know I don't know you, as you're so fond of reminding me, but I do know you wouldn't do that. In fact, I've never been more certain of anything in my life. You didn't do it." And as he said the words, he knew they were true. Whatever his brother might be, this story just didn't fit.

A ghost of a smile passed across Johnny's face. And something else . . . Relief? Gratitude? "Well, you sure got a lot of faith. Misplaced, maybe, but a lot of faith. Tell you one thing, I bet there's a whole lotta shit in that report." Johnny sounded very tired. "Never fails to amaze me how I can be in two places at once. You know, there I am thinking I'm in Sonora but I see something in the paper saying I'm in Abilene or Tucson. Hell, sometimes I'm in all three. I guess I got a real talent for spreading myself around." He shrugged. "Now, if you don't mind, I'm dead on my feet and I'm turning in."

Guy frowned as Johnny picked up his bedroll. "Where are you going?" He raised his eyebrows, surprised, as Johnny shook the roll out and laid it down by the window without answering. "You sleep in your bedroll? What's wrong with the bed?"

"A man don't want to get too comfortable, Harvard. Makes it harder when you have to move on."

"You don't have to move on, Johnny. You live here now."

Johnny looked at him bleakly. "I'll have to move on sooner or later. The old man'll want me gone. He'll believe his report, all of it, whether it's true or not. And let's face it, some of it's true. And the only person who knows which bits are true is me and somehow I don't see him asking. Do you see that happening?" Johnny laughed, but there was no mirth in it. "Fact is I've done some things I wouldn't want no one to know about. Including you. When I was starting out I was more concerned about getting me a reputation than what kind of reputation it was. And I guess now I got to live with that. I told you before, I'm dangerous and you'd better remember that."

Guy walked to the door before pausing and turning back. "And I remember telling you, Johnny, that I don't think you're nearly as bad as you want us all to believe. I believe you have plenty of redeeming qualities. Strange as you may find it, I have faith in you, and you'd do well to remember that. Good night, Johnny."

He was just closing the door when he thought he heard his brother reply. He could have sworn he heard Johnny say, "Good night, Guy."

CHAPTER SEVEN

Guthrie trudged down the stairs with a sick feeling in the pit of his stomach. He dreaded facing Johnny at breakfast. Would Johnny mention the previous evening? Or would it be just another thing to hang, unresolved, between them, another thing eating away at their relationship. Relationship? That was a joke, they didn't have a relationship. And right now, he couldn't see them ever having one — wasn't sure if he wanted one. Not after reading about that man gunned down in front of his family. How could any son of his do such a thing? But it wasn't like he could ask Johnny about it; after all, the two of them seemed unable to have even the briefest of civil conversations. Johnny was taciturn at best and mostly monosyllabic.

He paused and stood in the doorway to the kitchen, watching Peggy bustling around cooking eggs and chatting to Guy, who was leaning against the cabinet laughing at something she'd said. They were both dressed up, ready for church. It looked a happy scene. And it could be like this all of the time if it wasn't for the other one.

"Uncle Guthrie, come and sit down." Peggy smiled at him, and poured him a cup of coffee. "Come and have your breakfast, otherwise we'll be late for church."

"How are you this morning, sir?" He met Guy's cool gaze and muttered a reply about being fine. God, fine. That was what Johnny always said. The boy would doubtless say he was fine as he drew his last breath. And where the hell did that thought come from?

"Have you seen your brother this morning?" Easier to call him *your brother.* It was easier than saying his name.

"No. He was up and out early. Anyone would think he was trying to avoid us. I wonder why?" Guy's tone was sarcastic.

"It's a pity that Johnny won't come to church with us. I mean I know he's Catholic, but I don't see why he couldn't come sometimes. It's not as though he goes to the Catholic church, either." Peggy sounded puzzled.

"I wouldn't worry about it, Peggy." Guy's tone was smooth. "It's Johnny's choice. And it's not as though our church is his religion. You shouldn't expect him to come. Now, are we all ready?"

Guthrie swallowed the last of his coffee and followed the others out to the buggy. He barely noticed the journey there or paid any attention to their idle chatter. He had a vague impression that it was a sunny day. But he felt anything but sunny.

He tried to concentrate on the sermon. And then wished he hadn't, as the minister pontificated on the nature of evil. He could swear that some of the congregation was looking at him, reflecting on the latest addition to the neighborhood. The prodigal son? Or was it Cain and Abel?

After the service he followed the throng of people out into the sunshine and waited patiently for Guy and Peggy to join him. He bit back a smile as he watched Peggy enthusiastically introducing Guy to some of her friends. His son's manners were impeccable; Guy smiled and bowed and shared a personal exchange with each of the blushing, fluttering girls.

"Guthrie."

Guthrie turned to greet Dan Mitchell. The man had a small spread a few miles east of the town and was a stalwart of the Cattlemen's Association, although Guthrie suspected that the man's work for the association was designed to further his own interests rather than any concern for the community as a whole.

"Dan." He shook hands and smiled politely, hoping that Guy and Peggy would get moving and rescue him from conversation with the most boring man in the territory.

"I see that other boy of yours never comes to church, Guthrie." Dan Mitchell smiled, but it didn't touch his eyes.

Guthrie forced another smile. "No. Johnny was raised Catholic, so he doesn't come here with us."

Guthrie turned abruptly as a second voice butted in. "From what I hear, he doesn't go there either. Can't believe they'd want someone like him, anyway."

Guthrie sighed. Joe Donovan. Well, no surprises there. Joe had been vociferous in questioning Johnny's presence in the valley.

"If you've got something on your minds, why don't you just spit it out," snapped Guthrie, losing his battle with his temper.

Joe's jaw jutted out. "Just this, Guthrie. There's decent folk living in these parts. The sort of folk who don't want someone like Fierro around. The fact he don't go to church shows he ain't changed. People are scared. A man like that! Who knows what he might do. I tell you, folks are scared to sleep in their beds because of that boy of yours. You keep him at your ranch; otherwise he's likely to end up with a bullet in the back."

"Is that a threat, Joe?" Guthrie asked coolly.

"You better believe it, Guthrie, there'll be no shortage of people prepared to do it. No one wants his kind near their daughters and no one wants to mix with him. He's scum, an' we both know it. Not saying it's your fault. You're not to blame, we know that. You didn't raise him so you don't owe him nothing. You'd be better worrying about keeping your own family safe. Especially with a nice girl like Peggy in the house." The man suddenly noticed Guy, who'd walked across to join them. "So, young man, how you settling in?"

"I find some of the neighborhood is not to my taste." Guy looked very aloof.

"Probably thinking of that half-brother of yours, I imagine." The man was smirking now.

Guthrie thrust his hands deeper in his pockets. It wouldn't do to hit the man outside the church.

"On the contrary," Guy said smoothly. "I'm very taken with my brother. It's some of the neighbors I find hard to stomach. Ready, sir?" He glanced across and Guthrie nodded.

Guy tipped his hat at the ranchers. "Gentlemen." Something in the tone of his voice seemed to imply he thought they were anything but.

As the two of them walked toward the carriage, Guy said, "Well, you did warn me what the neighbors would think about him. But I can't say I think much of your friends."

Guthrie snorted. "They're not friends, Guy. But, given some of the tales you've heard, you must at least have some understanding of why he's not welcome."

Guy sighed. "Yes, I do, but they're not even prepared to give him a chance. I'm certain he's essentially a good man. There's far more to Johnny than meets the eye."

Before he could answer, Peggy came hurrying up, grabbing at her flowery bonnet to stop if from falling. "Sorry, I didn't realize you were ready to leave."

As they headed back to the ranch, he mulled over Guy's words. The young man really did seem to have faith in his brother. So did Ben. Could they both be wrong? Was their faith in Johnny misplaced, or was there more to him than the Pinkerton report suggested? Well, only time would tell, always assuming Johnny stayed around long enough for anyone to discover the truth.

As Guy put the buggy away, Guthrie walked with Peggy toward the house. Johnny was sitting outside in the sun, surrounded by cleaning paraphernalia and his saddle and his guns. Easy to see how he'd spent his morning. But cleaning guns on a Sunday? Guthrie knew it was a challenge, that Johnny would expect him to be angry. Why else would he do it in full view of everyone? Well, this was one challenge he wasn't going to rise to. If Johnny was hoping to see his father lose his temper, he was going to be disappointed.

"Hi, Johnny," called Peggy. "Isn't it a lovely day? You should have come with us. All my friends are longing to meet you." She looked at him critically. "You're a mess! You're covered in gun oil. And just look at those boots! Don't you dare wear them in the house. Go on, you've got half an hour to get yourself looking respectable."

He watched as Johnny grinned at her, a relaxed open smile. "You really are a nag, you know. Pity the poor man who ends up with you."

She flicked Johnny across the head with one of the oily cloths. "Go on with you, Johnny Sinclair. Half an hour!"

Johnny hauled himself to his feet and

gathered up the guns, sliding one back into the holster on his hip. His face was expressionless as he looked at Guthrie. "Fun sermon, was it?"

"It was about the nature of sin." He tried to keep his voice neutral.

A ghost of a smile passed over Johnny's face. "I should have come, then. I know a lot about sinning." And with a laugh, he hefted his saddle over his shoulder and sauntered toward the barn.

Guthrie sighed. Well, at least they hadn't started another argument. He didn't think he could face that at the moment. No, they'd have a peaceful day. He would bite his lip and not rise to anything. And filled with resolve he headed into the house.

Johnny made it to lunch on time, and in a clean shirt, too, much to Guthrie's amazement. The boy seemed to have made an effort. But damn it, it seemed that there was always something to upset the even keel. This time it was, of all people, Peggy, who looked at Johnny critically and said, "I asked you to change your boots, Johnny."

"I cleaned them." Johnny looked down at his feet and kicked at a bit of mud still clinging to one of them. "Sort of."

"But I asked you to change, Johnny. Couldn't you have just done as I asked for once?" Peggy sounded plaintive.

"I couldn't," Johnny said irritably. "They're the only boots I got."

"Well, you'd better get another pair, next time you're in town," she said, sounding just as irritated.

"Why would I get another pair of boots? I only got one pair of feet."

Guy let out a snort of laughter. "He's quite right, Peggy. He can only wear one pair."

"Well, what happens if they get wet?"

Guthrie had to smile at the note of triumph in her voice. Even so, he found himself sympathizing with Johnny. A new and unusual experience.

"I just wear 'em until they ain't wet." Johnny looked exasperated.

"Well, you shouldn't. You can catch a chill doing that. Didn't your mother ever tell you that?"

Johnny looked at her coolly. "No, she didn't ever tell me that, but then I never had any shoes so maybe that's why she never mentioned it."

Peggy flushed bright red while Guthrie tried to stifle a sigh of irritation. All he'd wanted was a nice peaceful lunch. Was it really too much to hope for?

"I'm sorry, Johnny. I put my foot in it,

didn't I?" Peggy looked apologetically across the table.

"I think that's enough discussion of feet, Peggy," Guy said with a grin. "Leave the poor man alone. If he only wants one pair of boots, it's up to him. Now, how about passing some of those potatoes around?"

Guthrie cleared his throat. "I thought it would be a good idea if you two boys shadow Alonso this week. With Johnny laid up sick, he hasn't had a chance to see the whole spread. It would be a good way of getting to know him, and the men."

"You mean it will be a good way of trying to get back on good terms with him after me pulling a gun on him on the way to Bitterville." Johnny smiled thinly. "Why don't you ever say what you mean?"

Guthrie gritted his teeth. He was not going to rise to it. "I'm sure that's water under the bridge."

Johnny laughed sardonically. "Sure. If that's what you want to tell yourself."

"What else is happening this week?" Guy cut in, his voice artificially cheerful.

"The Cattlemen's Association is having its monthly meeting in a few days' time, but I don't think there's anything interesting to discuss. I suggest the two of you give it a miss and come to the next one."

"And save you some embarrassment for another few weeks." Johnny's voice was soft, but the same sardonic smile pulled at his mouth.

Guthrie counted to ten under his breath. Then he made a supreme effort to sound friendly. "As I said, there isn't anything of interest on the agenda. Another month will do no harm."

"We should have a party," said Peggy suddenly. "So you can both meet all our neighbors."

Guthrie shuddered inwardly, thinking of the comments of two of their neighbors that morning. He noticed that Guy looked slightly alarmed too.

"I don't like parties." Johnny's tone was sullen.

"Oh, you'll like ours, Johnny, and we have such nice neighbors and they'll all want to meet you and Guy," Peggy said happily.

"They might want to meet Harvard, but I can promise you they won't want to meet me. And I sure as hell don't want to meet them." Johnny put down his fork and looked mutinous.

"But of course they'll want to meet you, too, Johnny. Why wouldn't they? I know all my friends are dying to meet you."

"Sure, just before their fathers shoot me."

Johnny sounded very sarcastic.

Peggy's face fell. "Uncle Guthrie, tell him he's wrong. Everyone will want to meet him, won't they?"

He thought briefly of that damn report, his son shooting a man in front of his family . . . He looked across the table at Johnny, who looked at him expectantly. "I'm sure there's plenty of time for parties later in the year, Peggy, when both the boys have had a chance to settle in." Johnny threw him a look of contempt. Well, what the hell did the boy expect him to say to her? All he'd wanted was a peaceful Sunday dinner. He wondered if he'd ever be able to enjoy a meal again. Was it always going to be like this? Worrying about what to say, avoiding certain subjects, having an image of his son killing someone hovering in his mind?

Guy came to his rescue, asking Peggy how she'd prepared the sauce and complimenting her on her cooking, telling her about meals he'd eaten in Europe. It was comforting to know that Guy would always cover any awkwardness, always knew what to say. So different from Johnny. He couldn't imagine ever being able to rely on Johnny. He looked up to see his younger son watching him and had the unpleasant feeling that Johnny knew exactly what he'd been thinking. How the hell did the boy do that?

They were drinking coffee when Alonso came in, apologizing for interrupting. The man looked embarrassed and asked to speak with Señor Johnny. Johnny narrowed his eyes and got slowly to his feet. Guthrie frowned. "Alonso, what's this about? Why do you need Johnny?"

Alonso flushed and threw a worried glance toward Peggy before shaking his head. "Sorry, Señor Sinclair, but I need to speak to Señor Johnny."

Guthrie watched with growing irritation as Johnny left the room with the segundo. "This is ridiculous." He threw his napkin down and followed them outside.

"Now, what's this about, Alonso?" he demanded, only too aware of Johnny looking at him coldly.

Alonso twisted his hat in his hands. "There are two men, Señor Sinclair, in Cimarron, looking for Señor Johnny. They are asking for Fierro. One of the hands just came and told me. He thinks they are gunfighters. He was worried they would come here looking for Señor Johnny. That there would be trouble."

Guthrie snorted. "I think that's a given, Alonso, where my son is concerned." He turned to look at Johnny, who met his gaze, unflinching, with not a trace of emotion showing. "Well, what are you going to do? We can't risk men like that coming here."

"I told you this is what it would be like, didn't I, Old Man? And this is only the start. What was it you said? We'd deal with it as a family? Well, I got news for you, we ain't a family and the only person who'll deal with this is me. But don't worry. They won't come near your precious ranch. I'll deal with it in town."

"You can't take them both on."

Johnny stared at him in disbelief. "Didn't your fucking report teach you anything? Two's nothing. I faced two lotsa times."

"What if they're faster than you?" What a damn stupid question to ask, he thought as he said it.

Johnny rolled his eyes. "Well, if they're faster, I wind up dead. If I'm faster, they wind up dead. That's how gunfights tend to work, in case you didn't know that, Old Man."

"Why are we talking about gunfights?" Guthrie jumped. He hadn't heard Guy's soft footsteps.

Johnny grunted in irritation and pushed past his brother to go back to the house.

"Where are you going?" Guthrie felt a knot of fear in his stomach, the bile rising in his throat.

"I'm going to get my gun and then I'll ride into town, OK?"

Guthrie looked at him in confusion. "You've got your gun on."

"The other gun." Johnny paused, and gave him a chilling smile. "The killing gun." And with that he went into the house.

"Would someone tell me what's going on?" demanded Guy.

Guthrie shrugged, wondering what to say. But there was little point in sugarcoating it. "There are two men in town looking for your brother. Alonso says they're gunfighters."

"Gunfighters. Looking for Johnny." The color drained from Guy's face. "Father, we can't let him face this alone. Two to one isn't fair. He's been laid up, he's still not recovered. And he's had no chance to practice or do whatever it is he needs to do."

Guthrie shook his head, feeling compassion for his son. "Guy, you've got to understand, for Johnny Fierro two men is nothing out of the ordinary. And this really is something he has to do alone. We can't help him with this."

"But we should. At some point someone will be faster. We can't let him do this."

"Seem to remember telling you I was the best, Harvard."

Guthrie and Guy stared at Johnny as he came back out of the house. He was wearing a different holster now and a different gun.

Guy shook his head. "No, you said only someone dumb says they're the best. You can't do this alone, Johnny. You don't need to do it alone now. You've got family."

"Family?" Johnny sounded puzzled. "No, Harvard, I got partners and I sure as hell don't need 'em for this. I'll be back later." He lifted his thumb in a type of salute and walked toward the corral.

Guthrie reached out and grabbed Guy's arm as his son moved to follow Johnny. "Let him go. He has to do this alone. We'd only get in his way, possibly get him killed."

"Don't you care at all?" Guy turned furious eyes on him.

"Of course, I care," he snapped. "But we can't help him."

But Guy shook off his restraining hand and strode over to where Johnny was just swinging himself onto his horse. Guy grabbed hold of the horse's bridle. Guthrie hurried over to them. Damn it, he wasn't going to let Guy get killed. This was John-

87

ny's fight and Johnny would have to deal with it.

Johnny glared at Guy. "Let go of my horse, Harvard. I'll be back later."

"You can't be sure of that."

Johnny sighed heavily. "No, I can't be sure of that, but it don't matter none."

"It matters to me, damn it."

"Look, Harvard, I'm used to this. A gunfight don't bother me none. Someone wins, someone loses. None of it matters anymore. I guess you can only be scared when you got something to lose and I don't think I ever had that." He paused, and then grinned. "But, hell, I ain't never been beaten yet."

"There's a first time for everything, Johnny."

"I guess, but what the hell, this is what I do." He stared intently at Guy for a few beats, almost it seemed to Guthrie, like he was memorizing his face. And then in a surprisingly gentle voice Johnny said, "Guy, let go of my horse now. I'll see you later."

Guthrie watched as Guy released the bridle and with a raised hand, Johnny spurred the horse into a lope and set off toward Cimarron.

Guy turned an anguished face toward him. Guthrie didn't know what to say to him. Nothing could make it better.

"I'm going after him and don't try to stop me. This is something I need to do. He won't see me; I'll stay out of sight in town. I just need to be there, in case . . ."

Guthrie sighed. "In case of what, Guy? What do you really think you can do to help him?"

Guy smiled, but it was a sad smile. "Nothing, nothing at all. But I want to be there in case he needs me. I couldn't bear for him to die alone."

Guthrie swallowed the lump in his throat as Guy saddled his horse. "I'll stay here with Peggy," he said gruffly. One thing he was sure of, he couldn't stand and watch his son die.

Guy nodded as though he understood, and turned and rode toward the town.

CHAPTER EIGHT

Guy rode to town at a gentle pace. The last thing he wanted was to catch up to Johnny — he'd be furious at being followed. But Guy couldn't, wouldn't, leave Johnny to face alone whatever he had to face. He might have to keep his distance, but he'd be there if Johnny needed him. How could Johnny be so blasé about the possibility of dying? Did he really not care? If Johnny was to lose this gunfight, the least Guy could do was be there to hold him, so he wouldn't die alone.

But if Johnny survived, was this what it would be like? Always waiting for people to come looking for him, to kill him? The thought sickened Guy. How could anyone live a normal life with that hanging over them? And what would the effect on the family be? No wonder Guthrie had voiced concerns — he'd realized only too well what Johnny's presence meant. If Johnny's past was half as bad as Guthrie seemed to think, the man was just being realistic. No wonder people would be looking for him. Johnny might travel light but he carried a lot of baggage.

Guy reined in as the town came into view. It looked strangely deserted, giving it almost the appearance of a ghost town. Despite the warmth of the sun on his back, he shivered, suddenly doubting the wisdom of his action. And now he was here, what was he going to do? He hadn't even thought about that when he'd taken off in pursuit of Johnny.

He leaned forward, resting his hands on the saddle horn while he tried to figure out his next move. Maybe the best thing was to approach the town from the side and slip in unnoticed. He stepped down from his horse and tied the animal to a hitching rail out of sight of the main street.

He was looking for somewhere to hide when he caught sight of Ben beckoning from the window of his house. He hurried over and Ben opened the door and dragged him inside.

"What are you doing here, Guy? Surely Johnny told you to stay away?"

Guy looked at Ben's worried face and smiled apologetically. "I couldn't. What if he needs me?"

Ben sighed heavily. "Exactly what use do you think you can be to Johnny out there?" He gestured toward the main street.

"He's there?"

"Yes. He's there, but answer the question, Guy. How on earth do you think you can help him, or are you trying to get him killed?"

"Of course I'm not." Guy glared. "I, I wanted to be here in case . . . I couldn't bear the thought of him dying alone." He stared at Ben, hoping that he'd understand. Ben shook his head in irritation.

"Are you sure, Guy, that this isn't partly about you wanting to see Johnny Fierro in action?"

He was silent. Guthrie had said the same thing. How much of his rash action was exactly that and how much was genuine concern for Johnny's welfare? He sighed and leaned against the table. "I saw him in action in Bitterville, or at least I caught the tail end of it. Except . . ." He hesitated. "I suppose that wasn't a proper gunfight. Those men had been drinking, and he had plenty of cover. But I saw him take down Chavez and his gunfighter." He flushed. "But you're right; I've never seen him in a proper stand-up gunfight. So, maybe I do want to see what all the fuss is about, but mainly I want to be here for him if he needs me. I saw too many men die in the war, calling out for someone, for family."

"Guy," Ben said gently, "are you sure that Johnny even sees you as family? And to be brutally honest, if he realizes that you're here it will affect his concentration, and that could cost him his life. Right now, he doesn't need any distractions and that includes you."

Guy hissed in a breath. He'd never even considered that aspect of his action. "Damn. I didn't think . . . just followed him. He told me to stay at the ranch. But, Ben, he called me Guy. Do you realize that's the first time he's actually used my name?"

Ben nodded, looking thoughtful. "I noticed he never uses any of your names. It's almost as if he's afraid to get too close. But possibly he just used it for effect, hoping that you'd do as he asked. Had you thought of that?"

Guy shook his head. "No, I think he said it last night too, when he said good night, but it was so quiet, I wasn't quite sure. But where is he now, what's happening?"

Ben shrugged. "He's sitting in a rocking chair opposite the saloon with his hat over his eyes."

"He's what?" Guy wondered if he'd heard right.

"You heard. Come and look, but don't get close to the window. We can't risk him getting a glimpse of you."

He followed Ben and looked out cautiously. Sure enough, Johnny was rocking, with one foot resting on his knee, lounging back, a picture of relaxation with his hat over his eyes.

"What the hell is he doing?" he demanded of Ben.

Ben shrugged. "I've no idea. I've never seen Johnny Fierro in action. But believe me, when he arrived in town people took cover. They know what's going to happen."

As they watched, the saloon doors swung open and three men emerged. They stood looking down the street and appeared not to notice the figure in the rocking chair. Just as they turned to walk toward the livery, Johnny pushed his hat back.

"Well, if it ain't Ed Shilo. Heard you was looking for me."

The men stopped dead and looked toward the figure in the chair. As he watched, Guy realized one of the three was barely more than a boy, just a kid really.

"Well, well. Johnny Fierro. Heard you was dead, hanged down in Mexico. Then I got

94

bad news. Heard you wriggled out like the slippery son of a bitch you are and were up here, alive and well all along. Well, you won't be living much longer, Fierro. Your time has come and I'm going to enjoy sending you to hell for what you did to my brother. I hear you been living it up on some ranch, but got shot up a while back. So I guess you're gonna be outta practice."

He heard Johnny laugh and say, "I'd have to be a lot more out of practice for you to stand a chance against me, Shilo. Who's your fat friend? Need him to help you, do you? And the kid there, barely outta diapers?"

"Don't underestimate the kid, Fierro, he's fast and looking for a reputation. Your reputation. And this here is my cousin, so you see the two of us got a score to settle over my brother."

Johnny pushed the hat back, and gave a strange half smile. "Your brother was shit, Shilo, and we both know it. He deserved what he got, so why don't you just get back on your fucking horses and get outta here, before your mother loses another son."

"We ain't going anywhere, Fierro, until you're lying in the dust."

Johnny smiled and glanced at the kid. "You'd better get outta here, while you still can, because I promise you, I will kill you. Hell, you don't even look old enough to shave, you sure you're ready to die? I'll tell you something, I won't make your killing clean. I think I'll make it real slow for you, kinda to warn off other dumb kids who think they can take me."

Guy hissed in a breath. Was Johnny that callous?

Johnny smiled coldly. "Believe me, you'll be begging me to finish you off. And you just a kid. I bet you never even had a woman yet, have you? Kind of a waste, to die before you've had your first fuck. There's a bordello down the street. Lots of pretty girls there who'd show you just what to do and how to do it. But I guess you'd rather stay here and die. Slowly. Might take your kneecap off to start with, while I do the other two, so you can see 'em die. Then maybe a bullet in the gut, now that is painful. I seen a lot of men die that way. Hell, I killed a lotta men that way, it can take a real long time, an' all the while they're screaming, screaming for me to finish it."

Guy watched in horror as a pool of urine spread round the kid's feet. "What's Johnny doing, Ben?" And as he said it, the young boy suddenly turned and fled, followed by Johnny's mocking laughter.

"Reducing the odds, Guy, that's what he's doing," Ben said.

"Think you're real clever, don't you, Fierro?" sneered Shilo.

"Well, I figure I'm a lot smarter than you. That kid's a lot smarter than you. Mind you, even my horse is smarter than you. Now if you'd got any brains, you'd get on your horse and ride outta here. You can't take me, Shilo, not even with your fat friend there to help you. I'll kill you both. Up to you, what's it gonna be?"

"We ain't going nowhere, Fierro, so let's get this over with."

Johnny stretched and got casually to his feet, yawning as he did so, and looking rather bored. Guy suddenly had an image of a cat playing with a mouse, and he felt the hairs on his neck stand on end. He suddenly understood what Johnny had meant when he'd described himself as dangerous.

"Well, Shilo, it's your funeral. I guess if you want to die, we might as well get this dance over, 'cos I want a beer real bad." Johnny sauntered to the middle of the street and turned to face them, with the sun at his back. Even now he seemed relaxed. But never had Guy felt quite so tense. How could Johnny be ready? He looked far too casual, surely he should be looking . . . well, something other than how he looked.

Then the fat man moved slightly and there was a blur of movement from Johnny. His gun was in his hand, firing, and as Guy watched, Johnny's assailants fell to the ground. And even as Guy thought it all over, Johnny whirled around in a crouch firing at the roof of one of the buildings. Almost in slow motion a man with a rifle teetered on the edge before he fell and hit the ground with a thud. Johnny straightened, still scanning the buildings as he walked toward the two bodies lying in front of him. He kicked at them with his foot, keeping his gun pointed at them and then, seemingly satisfied that they were dead, walked over to the man he'd shot off the roof, and again tested him with his foot.

It was over so quickly. Guy felt stunned by the speed at which it had all happened and now there were three men lying dead in the street. And how had Johnny known about the man on the roof?

Johnny strode toward Ben's house and flung the door open. His face was like thunder. He grabbed hold of Guy's jacket. "What the hell did you think you were doing? I told you to stay at the ranch. You trying to get me killed? What is it, a third of a ranch not enough for you?"

Faced with such fury, Guy felt defensive. "You couldn't have known I was here, I was really careful because I didn't want you to see me, but I wanted to be here in case . . ."

But Johnny cut off his words. "I heard you coming from half a mile away, Harvard. D'you think I'm stupid? You made as much noise as the fucking cavalry. Oh, but I forgot, you are the fucking cavalry aren't you, Soldier Boy." His voice dripped with sarcasm.

"Johnny." Ben sounded very calm. "Just simmer down. Guy shouldn't have come, but his intentions were well-meant."

Johnny rounded on Ben. "Well-meant!" Johnny grunted in derision. "No, he just wanted to see the great Johnny Fierro in action. Well, Harvard, did I put on a good enough show for you? Enjoy the entertainment, did you? It's what you wanted, ain't it? See the killing machine in action? Well, I hope I didn't disappoint you. Only three dead bodies, sorry it wasn't more."

He knew he deserved his brother's rage. He looked at Johnny's furious face. "Will you listen, Johnny, please? I saw so many men die in the war. Dying and calling out for someone . . . like children . . . Even now, I dream about that. I know you'll think I'm crazy, but I wanted to be here in case you needed someone, like they did."

Johnny closed his eyes briefly, before shaking his head slightly, as if in exasperation. "Look, Harvard, I know you don't know much about gunfights, but take it from me, the dying's usually quick. But the point is, a man's got to be able to concentrate. And, believe me, if there's someone you care about watching, well, it makes it harder." Guy could swear that a ghost of smile crossed Johnny's face as he allowed the implication of his words to hit home.

"Now, I'm going to the bordello to get myself well and truly fucked." And turning, he walked out of the house and up the street, not even glancing at the bodies of the men lying in pools of blood in the dusty street.

Guy hurried after him and followed Johnny into the bordello where the girls gathered around, chattering like a flock of starlings. "Aren't you riding back with me?"

Johnny turned to him, suddenly remote. "No, I ain't riding back with you. I'll be back tomorrow. I told you, I'm going to get myself fucked." He looked across at the girls, "Sadie, come on upstairs, honey, and bring a couple of your friends with you." And then he turned back to Guy. "Didn't you know? This is how I always celebrate a killing." And he walked upstairs.

Guy watched as the girl, Sadie, glanced across at Miss Martin, who'd watched the entire scene from the bar. She nodded slightly at Sadie, who immediately followed Johnny up the stairs with another couple of girls in her wake.

Guy walked slowly to the bar, surprised to find he was shaking now. The woman looked at him appraisingly and silently poured him a large whiskey, which she pushed into his trembling hand.

"Your first gunfight?" Her tone was cool.

He nodded. "You saw it?"

She laughed. "Honey, the whole town saw it. Everyone was watching from behind their shutters. Hypocrites. They condemn it, but don't they just relish the bloodshed."

"You don't mind him going upstairs with three of your girls, to celebrate?" Celebrate, God, what a notion.

"I'd heard that's what Fierro did. I was expecting him in here straight after."

"But . . . to celebrate?" Guy felt light-headed and nauseated. He took a large gulp from the glass, grateful as the whiskey tracked a burning path down his throat.

"Honey." Her voice was gentle now. "He didn't look like a man celebrating to me. More like a man trying to block something out. Trying to forget."

He considered the implication of her words as she topped up his glass. A man trying to forget. He thought of the bleak look in his brother's eyes. No, there'd been no look of celebration in those eyes, just exhaustion and pain. He realized that the woman was far more astute than he was and wondered idly what on earth an educated woman like her was doing running a bordello. She certainly seemed to understand Johnny better than he did.

"And this is what he's known for? Taking women to bed after shooting people?"

She nodded. "Oh, yes, people always say that Johnny Fierro celebrates his killings by going whoring. And, from what I hear, always the same number of girls as the number of men he's killed."

"And you don't mind him taking three up there?"

She shrugged. "Makes no difference to me, if he wants three girls, it's all money in the till." She looked at Guy thoughtfully. "You've got a lot to learn about life out west. And you've certainly got a lot to learn about that brother of yours. Boston rules don't apply out here and there are a lot of men like your brother, men who don't value life in the way to which you're accustomed.

You're trying to apply your code of behavior to him and that's as alien to him as his way is to you."

"You don't like him, do you?"

She shrugged again. "Honey, I sure as hell wouldn't trust him. But as long as he treats the girls OK and doesn't make trouble then I'll continue to let him visit, but it's only because it's a special favor to Ben. Ben and I are old friends and he asked me to make an exception to my rule and let this one gunfighter over the threshold."

Guy stared at her in surprise. "Does Johnny know he's here under sufferance?"

She smiled. "Yes, he knows and he's none too happy about it, either. But Ben seems to like him and I have to admit that puzzles me. Ben's a pretty shrewd judge of character and if he likes Johnny Fierro, well, I have to ask myself if I'm missing something. So for the time being, I'll give Mr. Fierro the benefit of the doubt. Now, I would suggest, Mr. Sinclair, you go on home and let your family know that their black sheep is alive and well. And I'll send him home to you in the morning. OK?"

Guy smiled wryly. "OK, Miss Martin, and thank you." He walked slowly toward the door, and then turned. "How did you get to be so wise?"

She smiled, raising a painted eyebrow. "Too many years in this business. Now go on home."

He raised his hand in a mock salute to her and walked out into the street.

CHAPTER NINE

Shafts of sunlight woke him, casting shadows across the room. At least the activities of the previous night had briefly blocked out the gruesome images of yet more ghosts to haunt his dreams. Three more men dead by his hand. At times he felt as though he was suffocating under the weight of the bodies of the men he'd killed. They were piling up on top of him, crushing the life from him as he sank into some black abyss . . . There was never any escape. There would always be more men he would have to kill or be killed himself. And he knew his soul was damned. There could be no redemption for Johnny Fierro.

He could feel the warmth of a girl pressed against him. She muttered as she rolled over but she still slept. It was Sadie. The other two had obviously left in the night when he'd eventually fallen asleep. He didn't even know their names.

What would it be like to have a woman of his own? He couldn't imagine that. A woman who didn't fuck any man who paid for it, a woman who wanted only him. His brother would have that. Harvard would get married and put the whoring behind him — like it had never happened, like he'd never paid for a quick fuck. But for Fierro? It wasn't a quick fuck, it was a little comfort and a man took it where he could find it, because he knew, in the end, that's all there would ever be.

He stretched his arm over the girl and cupped her breast in his hand, caressing it as he pulled her toward him. He needed her now, needed her to hold him so he could lose himself briefly as he possessed her once more. She squinted at him through sleepy eyes, her makeup, so carefully applied, smudged and grubby on her cheeks. He pushed himself, hard and erect, against her, muttering, "I ain't finished with you yet, Sadie," as he sought her lips once more.

The sun had risen higher by the time he walked downstairs. He hoped that the old cow wasn't around, that it would be one of the girls manning the desk to relieve him of his money. He was disappointed.

Delice was standing by the bar, wearing the same drab dress she'd worn the first time he saw her. None of the girls were there. Shit. And why did he always feel so uneasy with her? No one had ever managed to make him feel quite so unsure of himself before. Well, fuck her, but then, who'd want to? Imagine waking up next to that. He forced himself to look relaxed, but she looked at him with one eyebrow raised, like he'd crawled out from under a stone.

She pushed a piece of paper toward him. "Your bill, Mr. Fierro. Three girls, all night."

He glanced at the bill as he fished some money out. "They didn't all stay all night."

She looked at him without a flicker of emotion. "Honey, if you aren't man enough to keep them all night, that's not my problem. You took three girls upstairs, and you leave in the morning, that's the bill."

He clenched his jaw, biting back a smart retort, and pushed the money across the counter.

"Did you want breakfast before you leave?"

The question surprised him. He raised an eyebrow. "Is it included?"

Her lips twitched, like he'd said something real funny. "It's a dollar."

He managed to stop his mouth dropping open. "A dollar? One whole dollar? That must be some breakfast."

"Oh, it is."

He leaned forward, resting his elbows on the bar. "Ma'am, I just been screwed upstairs. I don't need to be screwed downstairs as well."

There wasn't a flicker. She stared at him without any expression. "Do you want coffee?"

He laughed. "How much is coffee?"

She looked him up and down, sizing him up it seemed. "You look like shit, so you can have the coffee on the house."

"You're all heart."

"Oh, don't I know it." She took a coffeepot from behind the bar and poured him a cupful. "Milk? Sugar?"

He shook his head. "No, just black." Like his soul. The thought flashed briefly in his mind that the woman was thinking the same thing. He wondered again why he found her so disturbing.

He took a quick swallow. It was good coffee, strong enough to stand a spoon in. "Did Harvard stay long?" It seemed easier to try and make conversation.

"Harvard?" She furrowed her brow, puzzled. "Oh, you mean your brother. I calmed his shattered nerves with a couple of whiskies and sent him on his way. He seems like a man out of his depth out here."

Johnny looked at her sharply. Those green eyes were surveying him coolly. Impossible to read. He shrugged. "I guess it's pretty different from what he's used to. Our old man sent him to some fancy school out east."

"While you were educated in the school of life?"

He smiled at that. She was pretty shrewd. "Yeah, something like that."

She topped his coffee up before asking, "Are you jealous of the life he had?"

The question surprised him. Gave him pause to think. And although it was none of her business, he found himself answering it seriously. "No," he said slowly, "I guess everyone gets dealt a hand and you play your cards the best you can. And, hell, can't imagine that I'd ever have wanted to go to some fancy school. Poor devil, I wouldn't wish that on anyone." He shrugged. "He's OK. But you're right; he sure finds life different out here."

"He cares about you, you know." Her words were casually spoken, but he looked at her sharply. And found himself shrugging again.

"I dunno why he should."

"Neither do I," she replied smoothly as she polished the glasses stacked by the bar.

"But oddly, Ben seems to care about you, too. Why is that, do you think?"

Her eyes were fixed on him now. He felt as though she was looking inside his head, at his thoughts, at his soul. And he felt ashamed because he didn't want anyone to know what he was like, especially her. Though why the hell he should care what she thought of him was beyond him.

"I like Ben," he said, knowing he hadn't answered the question. Her mouth twitched slightly, like she was amused that he was avoiding the question. "He's a good man," he muttered.

"So you can recognize a good man, then?" Her tone was cool.

He glared at her. But she didn't seem bothered. Just poured more coffee in his cup and went out the back leaving him alone. She was back after a few minutes with a big plate of pancakes that she set down in front of him.

"On the house. You look like you'd better eat something." Again, her mouth twitched slightly, and he found himself wishing she'd just smile at him.

He looked again into those green eyes that he couldn't read. "Thanks, they look good. And, yeah, Ben's one of the few good men I've met. I can recognize one when I meet one. And for what it's worth, Harvard seems like a good man too. Deserves a better brother than me, I reckon." He tried to concentrate on the pancakes, feeling her gaze resting on him, considering him.

"Well, I suppose he'll have to make the best of what he's got." She sounded amused now. "I have to say, Mr. Fierro, you're not quite what I expected."

He looked at her now. "It ain't Fierro now. Not here, at any rate." He chewed on his lip. "I'm trying . . ."

"To change? Until I believe different, you'll be Mr. Fierro."

He wondered how to explain that it might not be wise to use the name. But she really did seem able to read him, for she said, "For what it's worth, I won't use the name if there are strangers in here. But let's face it, all the locals know exactly who you are. And what you are."

Again, he felt a stab of shame. He tried to change the subject. "Sadie seems like a nice kid. Don't deserve to be in this kind of game."

"Honey." He looked up at her as she spoke. "None of us deserves to be in this kind of game."

"Ain't that the truth." He shook his head sadly. "I bet there ain't any whores who

111

dreamed of doing that for a living when they were little kids."

"Whereas you dreamed of being a gun-fighter?" She raised an eyebrow.

He nodded slowly. "All I ever wanted. I grew up the hard way. And I spent every spare minute practicing my draw and teaching myself to use this gun." He slipped the gun from the holster and laughed softly. "Yep, all I ever wanted was this gun and to be the greatest pistolero. Wanted everyone to know my name."

"And now they do." Her tone was cool.

He slid the gun back, the weight against his thigh a sudden unexpected comfort. "Yeah, now they do." He paused and sighed heavily. "And a bunch of girls in a bordello are so scared of my name they don't even want to fuck me. Yeah, everyone knows my name."

"Except your brother. I suspect that even the legend of Johnny Fierro hasn't quite made it to Boston."

Johnny smiled. "No, not quite. But it seems like I'm working on it."

"And what does your father make of having Johnny Fierro for a son?"

Johnny pushed the last pancake around the plate, his appetite suddenly gone. Her eyes were on him, watching his every move.

Shit, wasn't none of her business, nosey cow. He looked up angrily, ready to insult her. But the steely look in her eyes stopped his retort. And he dropped his gaze down again. Dios, how did she do that to him?

He sighed heavily. "He ain't none too impressed, I guess. He sure as hell don't trust me."

"There's no reason why he should, is there?"

"I took a bullet in the back saving his fucking ranch for him."

She tilted her head to one side, surveying him through those damn cool eyes. "From what I hear, he gave you a third of his ranch. Seems to me that's probably more than you've ever had before — for all the money you must have made from your killings. What have you spent that on? Have you saved it all up for a rainy day? Or squandered it all? Somehow, I suspect the latter."

"Not much point in saving it," he snapped. "I don't expect to live long enough to retire."

"So, what did you spend it on?"

He knew that she guessed the answer already. But he might as well own to it. "Getting myself fucked, as often as possible, OK?"

"Your father must be so proud!"

113

He had to laugh. And he found himself wishing she'd laugh with him. She might be as ugly as sin, but there was something about her that he kind of liked. And that was odd given how much he thought he disliked her. "Yeah, real proud." He shook his head slightly. "Only a matter of time before he kicks me out, I reckon. It's like he can't stand to have me around. I dunno, maybe I remind him of her, or maybe he figures I'm gonna be too much trouble. Or bring trouble, like yesterday."

"Her?"

"My mother. Ben says she ran off with someone when I was a kid. I guess that must hurt a man, losing his woman to another man."

"And losing his son, too."

He nodded slowly. He'd never really thought about that. But from what Ben said the old man had tried hard to find him. But he knew he couldn't ask the old man about it. The man was so damn cold.

"So, Mr. Fierro, you ever had a woman of your own?"

He set his cup down with a clatter, laughing. "Who the hell do you reckon would want a gunfighter?" He shot her a quick glance and grinned. "Although, if you must know, there was someone once. Hell, I even

114

got myself engaged. But we were way too young. She was a real lady, too good for me. But I guess I fancied myself in love for a while, never had a lady before." He took a gulp of coffee. Memories flooded his mind. He could see her creamy skin and fine bones, the way she ducked her head when she laughed. He sighed softly. "And I guess if I'm honest, it was probably the only way I was going to get to fuck her, by getting engaged. And I sure wanted to fuck her."

She raised a painted eyebrow. "Such a gentleman you are, Mr. Fierro. So you took her virginity and dumped her?"

Hearing it put so bluntly, he felt embarrassed. But he shook his head slowly. "No. She dumped me. I guess . . ." He hesitated, recalling the look in her eyes when she'd seen his first gunfight. She shouldn't have been there. He'd never meant for her to see that. "I guess she saw through me. Couldn't cope with the killings. Can't say as I blame her. Like I said, she really was a lady. You know, educated, fancy accent, been all over the place, too. Funny thing is, she and Harvard would get on real well. I ought to introduce them."

"Yes, I'm sure your brother would love your castoffs."

He smiled at that. The idea rather appealed to him, but he sensed her looking at him disapprovingly. "So, what about you? Do you and Ben . . . ?"

"Fuck? No, honey, we don't. Odd as it may seem to you, it is possible for men and women to enjoy a platonic friendship, and Ben and I are old friends. That's all."

He wondered what plonic meant, but he kind of got the message.

"Your family will be worrying about you. You ought to be getting back."

"Worrying? Why the hell would they worry?" He felt puzzled. "Harvard knows I'm OK."

She shook her head at him like she couldn't believe what he'd said. "You really are clueless, aren't you? Worrying is what families do. You were in a gunfight, the first one they've had close contact with. They will be concerned about the effect on you."

"Don't see the old man worrying about me."

She looked at him levelly. "Don't you? Funny, I didn't take you for a fool."

He pushed his cup away and glared at her. "Told you, he don't trust me at all."

She picked up the cup and looked at him like he was dumb or something. "We're not talking about trust. We're talking about the natural reaction of a father when his son is

116

in danger. Just because he doesn't trust you doesn't mean he doesn't care. Now, why don't you go on home and try and keep your temper when they ask you lots of damn fool questions. Which we both know they will."

He smiled, in spite of himself. "You mean, play nice?"

"Yes, play nice. Otherwise, you'll end up having some big fight and walking out in a huff. And that might be kind of a shame, as it seems this is the first chance of a different life that you've ever had. You're not stupid, so don't blow it." Her mouth twitched again. He could have sworn she almost smiled.

"Because, you know, honey, I think you do want a different life, don't you?"

The sudden question rocked him. He felt a lump in his throat. Bit his lip, hard. "I think," he spoke very softly, "it may be too late for that."

The expression in those green eyes was softer now. "Doesn't have to be. If you want something badly enough you should grab it with both hands. Now, run along home, and play nice." And carrying his cup and plate, she walked through the swing door into the kitchen, giving him a wave of her hand.

Play nice. Well, maybe it was worth a try.

He really didn't feel like a fight today. He'd bite his tongue just this once. And putting his hat on, he headed out into the sunlight.

CHAPTER TEN

A light breeze ruffled his hair as he rode out of town, basking in the warm sunlight. It felt like the distant mountains beckoned him with the promise of freedom. He could picture himself on the buckskin, galloping flat out across the range to those far lavender peaks where no one would question him or doubt him. Where no one would care about his past. Where no one would care . . . And that was what it boiled down to. Where no one would care. Because, although he found it hard to believe, it seemed that here people did care. Ben seemed to care about what became of him. Though God only knew why he should. And that woman, Delice, had commented on how his brother cared about him.

A brother!

He couldn't come to terms with the fact that Mama had known all about Guy and never told him. Hell, she'd been a mother to Guy for a couple of years . . . How could she not have told Johnny he had a brother? Still, it hurt too much to think about that.

If only the old man would talk to him about the past. Johnny sighed heavily. He'd give anything to hear his father's telling of it. But it would be a cold day in hell before that happened. The old man's lips were closed as tight as an old maid's legs. And he was damned if he was going to ask.

If he was honest, he knew he was making it tough on his father, testing him. He just kept pushing him to see how far he could go before the old man snapped. But that way lay danger and there was the rub. He liked danger; it gave him a buzz, made him feel alive. Perhaps if he just knuckled under, said yes, sir, and no, sir, the old man would accept him. But he had too much pride for that. Couldn't be less of a man than he was. Wasn't changing for nobody. And if Harvard and Ben could accept him, then the old man would have to accept him too. Or not.

He reined Pistol in as he rounded the ridge overlooking the ranch and slid from the saddle. He let Pistol graze and settled down on a mossy knoll, with his back against the hillside. He gazed at the plains to the south. That way lay freedom. It stretched all the way to the far border. But down in the valley was the hacienda and it felt like that could lead only to disappointment. At some point he'd push the old man too far. He didn't seem able to stop himself. Why did he do that? Like throwing the whoring in his face when common sense dictated it would have been more sensible to let his father think they'd only gone out for a game of poker and a beer. But to find the old man had been sitting reading up on him, well, that had hurt. No one would want Johnny Fierro for a son. He didn't blame his father for that. But he wished the man would come right out and ask him about the past, instead of blindly accepting everything in that damn report. Trouble was most of what was in the report would probably be true . . . A lot of men had died at the hands of Johnny Fierro and that was the problem. When the old man found out the scale of the killings, he wouldn't want Fierro anywhere near his precious ranch.

Even so, the thought of owning something, if only for a short time, kind of appealed. And it was real strange to have a brother, but that was kinda good, too. And yet he knew he wasn't making it easy on Harvard, either. But it still seemed like the man wanted to get to know Johnny Fierro. God only knew why. What was it Harvard had said? Something about having faith in him. That felt good, too, even though he knew the faith was misplaced. He didn't deserve that level of belief. Presumably it was only a matter of time before Harvard saw through him, just like their father did.

If Mama had sent him back here when he was young, life could have been so different. But wondering why the hell she hadn't sent him back hurt like hell. It tore at his guts, like it was eating away at him. And thinking like that didn't do any good. He couldn't undo the past, like he couldn't undo what some of Mama's men had done to him. He sucked in a breath. Don't start thinking about that, it was bad enough to relive it in his dreams. The old man would be disgusted if he knew . . . Shit. He had to stop thinking about it.

The sun was climbing higher and a heat haze shrouded the land, so the grazing cattle seemed to shimmer in the dazzling light.

He tilted his hat forward, shielding his eyes, squinting down at his new home. If he rode on toward the ranch, what would his father say about the gunfight? The man would go crazy when he heard there were three more dead men.

But there'd been no choice, it was kill or

be killed. And trust Shilo to have someone hiding on the roof, to put a bullet in the back of Fierro. As soon as he'd seen it was Shilo, he'd been scanning the roofs, knowing there was probably someone up there. The three of them deserved what they got. They'd come for a killing, well, they got three. But he couldn't see the old man seeing it in the same light. Johnny Fierro would be the talk of the town, and that wasn't going to please Guthrie Sinclair.

What was it Delice had said? That they'd ask him a lot of damn fool questions. But she also said his father would be concerned. He snorted. Couldn't believe that. But she'd seemed pretty sure of herself. Play nice. Maybe it was worth a try. If only because he was kind of curious to know more about his brother. Find out what the man was running from. Might as well enjoy owning something for a little longer. It wouldn't last, but it would be good for a while. Yeah, play nice.

Nice-ish.

He scrambled to his feet and caught hold of Pistol's reins. He swung himself back into the saddle and rode toward the ranch.

He hoped that maybe no one would see him coming, but he should have known better. The old man and the girl were standing outside, watching his approach. He stopped at the barn and slid off as Peggy ran toward him, flinging her arms round him, almost knocking him over. Startled, he grabbed at his hat to stop it falling to the ground.

"Johnny, we were so worried. Thank God, you're safe." She clung to him, like she was afraid he'd disappear in a puff of smoke if she didn't hold on real tight.

He thought of saying that God had nothing to do with it, that it was down to his fast draw, but didn't think she'd appreciate the humor. "Harvard told you I was OK, didn't he?"

"Yes, but I was still worried. You didn't come home. He said you just needed a little time alone, but I was scared you wouldn't come back."

He tried not to grin at Harvard's explanation of his absence. Time alone — well, yeah, him and three whores. "I told him I'd be back and I'm here, so quit fussing."

He could feel the old man's eyes on him. Just look straight at him, don't matter what he thinks. Fuck him. Stare him straight in the eyes. "Well?" He knew his own voice sounded like a challenge. But it was odd, the old man didn't look angry. He looked . . . what exactly? Tired? And kinda sad.

"Are you all right?" There was a look almost like concern now on the old man's face. Why? Why should he care? What was it Delice had said? Something about a father's natural reaction when his son was in danger.

"I'm fine. Why shouldn't I be?" He could have bitten his tongue off. Why did he always have to be so prickly with the old man?

"Guy said there were four of them." The old man sounded like he was fishing for more information.

He shrugged his shoulders. "I've faced more than that before. Anyway, one of 'em vamoosed, too damn scared to face me." He saw the old man clench his jaw at the expression and then remembered that the girl was there and wished he'd not said that.

"Sorry." He muttered the apology, and the old man's expression seemed to soften.

"But you are all right?" His father sounded real insistent now. Anyone would think the man really was worried about him or something. Hell! Maybe Delice was right after all.

"I said I'm fine. What's another three dead men to me? They came looking for a killing and that's what they got. I didn't ask 'em to come, you know. But if they come looking, I'll kill 'em. Or would you rather I just stand there and let 'em gun me?" He felt guilty as he spat out the words.

Saw a look of something like pain in the old man's eyes.

Play nice.

He took a deep breath. "Look, I'm fine. It's over. They drew first, it was self-defense." As he said the words he saw a strange flicker of emotion in the old man's eyes.

"You didn't goad them into drawing on you?" The old man sounded real nervous.

Johnny threw his hands up. "No. I didn't. What the hell gives you that idea? I gave 'em plenty of opportunity to leave. And believe me, there's plenty of witnesses to that. But don't worry, I put on a real good show for the town." Yeah, he'd certainly done that. People were shit. They said how they hated gunfighters, but boy, didn't they just love to watch someone wind up dead. Sick, really. Hell, he should sell tickets, he could get rich.

"Johnny." The girl stretched her hand out and touched him gently on the face. He tried not to flinch away. "We were worried about you. Don't be angry with us for that. We were so frightened you'd be hurt."

He felt an unfamiliar pricking sensation in his eyes as he tried to avoid meeting her concerned gaze.

"You see, Johnny, we really do care about you."

He swallowed the lump in his throat. "Look, I'm fine, really. Now, I'd better go and get my stuff together if I'm working with Alonso." He pushed past them both and headed into the house and the sanctuary of his own room.

He hesitated over which gun to take, staring down at his modified gun as he caressed it. He felt safer with it and closed his eyes briefly as he felt how it molded to his hand, loving the smoothness of the wood against his skin. It felt so good to hold it and he rested his face briefly against the cool metal barrel. God, he loved this gun, it was the one thing in his life he could rely on. People, they let you down, disappointed you in the end. But there was something honest about a gun. It was better than any friend. And probably better than family too. It was odd though, how Guy had come rushing to town after him, saying he was worried. Still, he was sure that some of that had been a desire to see the famous gunfighter in action. But Guy couldn't have faked that look in his eyes. The eyes didn't lie and there had been fear and real concern in them. Still, Johnny would trust his gun before he trusted any gringo and, making a decision, holstered the fighting gun. The fight was too recent, too raw. This was the gun he wanted. Slinging his bedroll over his shoulder he headed back outside.

He spotted Guy, standing talking to Alonso, and went to join them. "You ready? I got everything I need, so I'm ready to ride when you are."

Guy frowned. "You sure you're up to this, Johnny? I mean, after that gunfight and everything?"

Johnny stared at Guy in amazement. "What the hell are you talking about? Why wouldn't I be up to working? Gunfighting is what I do, just like reading books is what you do. I told you, it don't mean nothing. So quit fussing, and get mounted up."

As he turned he almost ploughed into his father, who had come up behind them. Shit. Now he'd be in for it. He shut his eyes briefly and waited for the fury.

"Johnny." Strange, his father didn't sound mad, just kind of sad. "A gunfight might be nothing out of the ordinary for you, but for us it's different. Odd as it may seem to you, we were worried. We can't take the possibility of your death as lightly as you appear to take it. You might as well start getting used to the fact that you've got people around you now who care what happens to you.

"I might not like your past, but I care about your future. And I happen to want you to have a future." The man turned to walk back toward the house, before turning briefly again. "Now get on that horse, young man, and be sure to do what Alonso tells you. And try to stay out of trouble. Otherwise you'll have me to answer to."

Johnny stood watching the man's departure in amazement. Dios! He couldn't think of a damn thing to say. Not a single smart remark. And oddly, that felt kinda good. He realized he was grinning like some dumb kid. So just for once, he did what he was told and mounted up. He looked across at Harvard, who had his mouth open like he was planning on catching flies. Johnny grinned at him. "You heard the man. What's keeping you?" And with that he spurred Pistol into a lope and set off after the rest of the men who were already heading out.

CHAPTER ELEVEN

Guthrie swiped away the beads of moisture trickling down his neck. The room was stiflingly hot and the air was heavy with the smell of sweat. A fly was buzzing as it pushed against the window searching for a way out. And who could blame it? He'd give anything to be out of this damn room and back in the fresh air. And all the time their voices were droning on, talking of inconsequential things instead of getting down to the reason they were all really here.

He'd told his sons there was nothing of interest on the agenda, used it as an excuse to stop them from coming with him. But the hairs on his neck were standing on end. There was an undercurrent of tension in the room. There had to be a reason for this meeting, of that there was no doubt. But no one had told him what it was. These days he felt excluded. Over the past few weeks he'd tried to close his ears to the gossip but it was all but impossible not to hear some of the cutting remarks or catch the looks of disapproval on people's faces.

Well, he'd always known it would be like this, so really, he shouldn't be surprised but it still hurt. He looked at the faces around the table. Men he'd known for thirty years and yet, now, it seemed that the Cattlemen's Association had turned against him en masse and all because Johnny had finally come home. What the hell did they expect him to do? Turn his son away? But of course that was exactly what they expected him to do. And they'd told him so frequently. It felt like the whole community stood against him and he was helpless in the face of their implacable opposition to the presence of Johnny in their valley. Nothing he said made any difference. And, if he was honest, Johnny's behavior didn't help matters. The boy had gone into town twice since the gunfight. Gone whoring . . .

Will Turpin's voice broke into his thoughts. "Now, gentlemen, we come to the main reason for our meeting today: the future arrangements for the transfer of funds. I know in the past we've all known exactly when money would be moved by stage. But, as previously agreed, in future it will be best if only one man is responsible for those arrangements. It will reduce the possibility of the information becoming common knowledge. We can't be too careful when it comes to protecting our money."

The men sitting at the table all nodded in agreement. "Aye, well said, Will. We can't be too careful these days." Matt Dixon's voice was louder than the others and as he spoke he looked directly at Guthrie.

Guthrie clenched his jaw. So this was the reason for the meeting. "I wasn't a party to these discussions. This is the first I've heard of it and I consider it a totally unnecessary precaution."

Will glanced across at him, smiling smoothly. "Oh, didn't we mention it to you, Guthrie? We must have overlooked you in the pre-meeting discussions. Sorry about that."

"You know damn well you didn't consult me." Guthrie glared at him, trying to resist the urge to smash his fist into the man's smug face.

Matt Dixon cut across him. "You can hardly be surprised, Guthrie. Do you really think that there's a man here who wants Fierro to know when we're moving large sums of money? You think we'd trust a man like him? He's not wanted here and I for one will warn you — if he sets foot on my land I'll be only too happy to put a bullet in him."

Guthrie bit back an angry retort as he listened to the murmurs of agreement from all round the table. Henry Carter nodded, saying, "No one wants Fierro here. He's a threat to us all. Good people are afraid to let their womenfolk drive into town now because of him. No one's safe anymore."

"My son proved his loyalty to this community and his family when he took on Wallace. And if Wallace had managed to take my land and Steen's old place, it would only have been a matter of time before he set his sights on your spreads too. You know law has broken down since Maxwell left. You owe my son your gratitude, not your condemnation."

Carter snorted. "I bet he only got rid of Wallace so that there'll be more for him when he makes his move."

Guthrie shut his eyes briefly in exasperation. "And do tell me, Henry, exactly how you think my son is going to seize control of this valley single-handed? I've never heard anything so damn stupid in my life."

Carter banged his fist down. "Never thought you were a fool, Guthrie. That boy of yours has probably got a gang all ready to move on this valley. He's scum and he's not wanted here."

Guthrie smashed his fist down on the table, easily outdoing Carter's force. The glasses on the table rattled from the impact. "Don't you dare talk that way about my son. He risked his life saving my ranch, and almost died doing so. He's got more guts in his little finger than you have in your entire body."

Will Turpin held his hand up. "Gentlemen, gentlemen! Let's all calm down. This matter can be easily resolved. I suggest we take a vote on it. All those in favor of making our financial arrangements the responsibility of just one man in future, raise your hands."

Guthrie watched as the men raised their hands. Every hand, barring that of John Dove, one of the older ranchers, was raised.

Will Turpin smiled thinly. "Well, that's carried, then. Now all we have to do is decide who will have the responsibility."

Guthrie shoved his chair back from the table with a clatter, and got to his feet. "Sinclair will make its own arrangements. The rest of you can do as you damn well like. Good day to you." He turned on his heel and strode out of the room. God, how could he have not seen this coming? Once the association had insisted on having its meetings anywhere other than Sinclair he should have been prepared for this sort of ambush. Well, damn them all. They could all go to hell.

He was stepping into the saddle when he heard John Dove call to him. "Sorry about that, Guthrie, but there was no stopping them and I didn't have a chance to get word to you before the meeting. They kept me in the dark until the last moment."

Guthrie sighed. "They knew you'd back me, John. But I'm grateful for your support." He shook his head sadly. "They won't give Johnny a chance even though he's earned it. They've made up their minds and that's it. All I can hope is that over time they'll ease up but I'm not expecting it any time soon."

"Guthrie, you need to warn that boy of yours to stay away from their ranches. I wouldn't put it past any of them to put a bullet in him. They've got it in for him."

Guthrie felt a cold clutch of fear. "You really believe that, John?"

The other man nodded sadly. "They're blowing it out of all proportion, I know, but they mean business, Guthrie. And let's face it, your boy has got himself quite a reputation and that scares a lot of folks. And that gunfight in town on Sunday, well, it didn't help matters."

"That wasn't Johnny's fault. Those men came looking for him. What was he supposed to do? Stand there and let them gun him down?"

Dove shrugged. "The fact that people came looking is exactly what some folk are worried about. We've had very few gunfighters in this territory but your son comes home and suddenly there's a big gunfight in town. That's what scares them. And yes, maybe they're overreacting, but the fact remains that they've already seen trouble and that don't make them none too happy." The man rubbed his chin, and flushed. "And let's be honest here, Guthrie, your son don't go out of his way to be too friendly. Comes into town wearing that gun of his low and he's been seen going into the whorehouse. It don't go down too well."

He knew John Dove was right. Johnny didn't go out of his way to be friendly but if Guthrie was honest with himself he knew that even if Johnny made more effort it probably wouldn't make any difference. People had already made up their minds and there seemed to be little prospect of anything changing. "Well, thanks again for your support in there. It's appreciated, John, and I'll warn Johnny about riding on anyone's land."

"He's always welcome on mine, Guthrie. He's your son, that's good enough for me." And with a wave, the man walked back into the meeting.

Pity more people weren't like John Dove. At least he was willing to give Johnny a chance. But he was in a minority. Guthrie sighed. Minority? Hell, John Dove was the only one prepared to give Johnny a chance. Although doubtless his old friend, Edith, would too, if she ever got to meet Johnny. On the one occasion she had come for lunch, expressly to meet the two boys, Johnny had sloped off saying he was damned if he was going to be inspected like some prize bull. The incident had embarrassed Guthrie. He'd tried to explain Johnny's absence by claiming that some cattle had got caught in a gully and that Johnny was out with a work party. But he suspected that Edith hadn't believed him. It had been the raised eyebrow that had given her away.

If only Johnny wasn't always so damned awkward. God only knew what went on in the boy's head, though. He couldn't figure Johnny at all. Still, Guy seemed to get on well enough with him. Ben obviously liked him and at least the boy was courteous to Peggy. Perhaps that was the most he could hope for at present.

He didn't want to ride back to the ranch yet. The boys would wonder why he was back so soon. He wasn't far from Edith's place; it was only the other side of the hill. And making a decision he turned toward her ranch. A glass of lemonade would be welcome on such a hot day and maybe she'd have a few words of wisdom to offer her old friend.

She was standing on the porch when he rode in. She raised a hand in greeting and beckoned him into the cool of the house. "Guthrie! What a lovely surprise. I thought you'd be at the cattlemen's meeting." She patted a big leather chair. "Come and sit yourself down and I'll get you a nice cold drink."

"That would be wonderful, Edith! It's as hot as Hades out there and not a breath of wind. God knows, we need some rain."

She smiled, reaching for a pitcher of lemonade and poured him a generous measure. "So, Guthrie, are you going to tell me why you're not at the meeting and why you've ridden out here on such a hot day? I know you too well, Guthrie Sinclair, there has to be a reason."

He gave her a rueful smile. "That easy to read am I? To tell the truth I was at the meeting, but I left. And I knew if I went straight home the boys would want to know why I was back so soon."

"And you didn't want to tell them?"

He shook his head. "No. Not till I've thought things through."

"Would I be right in thinking that this has something to do with Johnny?"

He looked at her sharply. What the hell had she heard? And if she'd known of the association's plans, why didn't she warn him?

She laughed. "Don't look so suspicious, Guthrie. I'm not privy to the inner sanctum of the association, but I guess from your reaction that I'm on target."

Guthrie sighed. "Sorry, Edith, but, yes, you are of course right." He quickly described what had happened at the meeting and then sat back waiting for her response.

She shook her head slowly. "The trouble is how I can offer an opinion when I haven't even met Johnny? On the one occasion when I came over to meet him, he was conspicuous by his absence."

Guthrie cut in. "I did explain why he wasn't there."

She laughed. "Guthrie, you didn't really believe that I fell for your story that he was out with a work party! It was obvious to me that he was avoiding me and I have to wonder why. But I can't judge whether people are overreacting to his presence when I haven't met him. I certainly hear enough about him. The people in town are constantly discussing him. They monitor his every movement and if what I hear about him is correct, he's not exactly doing himself any favors. Can't you talk to him, ask him to be friendlier? And while you're at it, suggest he spend less time in the bordello. It's behavior like that which doesn't sit well with the people of Cimarron."

"I can't tell him how to spend his spare time, Edith. He's a grown man, not a child."

She smoothed her skirt down and settled back in her chair. "He's living under your roof; therefore you can lay down some ground rules."

Guthrie shuffled uncomfortably. "We already did."

She raised an eyebrow. "So? What were they? What are you afraid of? Are you afraid of him?"

Guthrie stared at the floor and shook his head slowly. "No, I'm not afraid of him, but I am afraid he'll leave if I push things. He more or less told me he would. Our agreement is that he works hard on the ranch but I don't tell him how to spend his spare time.

Apparently that condition is not negotiable."

"Well, it seems you've backed yourself into a corner. I really don't know how to advise you. But you'll have to tell him and Guy about the cattlemen's decision. They're your partners and have a right to know. I thought you were rather rash offering him a share. It wasn't at all in character. You're normally far too canny to do anything so reckless." She looked at him thoughtfully. "I would like to meet Johnny. Form my own opinion. Perhaps I should pay you an unexpected visit. If he doesn't know I'm coming, he won't have the chance to perform a disappearing act."

"My God, but you're devious, Edith! Still, I do want you to meet him so perhaps that would be a good idea. You'll have to think of some pretense for dropping in. Make it a mealtime. That's always a good time. Johnny rarely misses out on food! He has a very healthy appetite."

Edith sniffed, before adding primly, "And not only for food if what I hear is correct."

Guthrie spluttered on his lemonade, felt the liquid going up his nostrils. "Edith!" He coughed again as the lemonade caught his throat.

She laughed. "Ah, it's good to know I can still shock you, Guthrie! Anyway, I will pay you an unexpected visit over the next few days so that I can form my own opinion of the scourge of the valley. The way people have been describing him, I have visions of an evil cutthroat wearing a vast sombrero with a knife clenched between his teeth and firing off his gun at everyone. I daresay, I'll be disappointed. Reality rarely lives up to our expectations."

He had to laugh. "Edith, you're always good for me. Thank you. I suppose I'd better go and face the cutthroat and his Brahmin brother!" Still laughing, he gave her a kiss on the cheek before heading back into the blistering heat.

CHAPTER TWELVE

He breathed a sigh of relief when he made it home without being spotted by either of the two boys. It would give him some breathing space to decide how to tell them about the meeting. He suspected that Johnny would be far from impressed when he heard about it. And Guy could be hot tempered at times. Hell, they were all hot tempered. The only calm person in the family was Peggy and he supposed that as she wasn't really family, she didn't count. Poor Peggy, she did have a lot to put up with. Three grumpy men. Family. But not family. Because, more often than not, it was all too apparent that they were just strangers to each other, bound only by blood.

Still, in time they would become used to each other, always supposing Johnny stayed. He still couldn't believe that his younger son would stay for long. He could see how quickly Johnny became bored by the more mundane work on the ranch. Sometimes Johnny's pent-up frustration would bubble over and the two of them would end up having words over something inconsequential — certainly never anything worth fighting over. Guthrie had spent many sleepless nights worrying over what would become of Johnny if he didn't stay at the ranch. And in all his imaginings, there seemed to be only one alternative for the boy, a bloody and pointless death in a hail of bullets.

Guthrie sighed as he unsaddled his horse. This latest development could only bode ill for the family. All he could do was hope that it wouldn't be the last straw for his impatient and unruly son. Damn Cattlemen's Association. After all he'd done for them over the years, this was how they repaid him. Well, damn the association. Sinclair would manage without it. They needed Sinclair more than his ranch needed the association. Damn them all to hell.

But despite his bravado, it was with some trepidation that he outlined the events of the meeting to the boys after dinner that evening. He had delayed the news as long as possible, hoping that they would be more mellow and receptive after a good meal. And he had parried Guy's questions about the meeting, saying they would discuss it after dinner. Now he waited nervously for their reactions. But he was surprised when his younger son made no response. Instead, Johnny sat hunched staring into the bottom of his glass of tequila. His face gave nothing away. God only knew what he was thinking.

Guy stood in front of the fireplace, swirling the Scotch around in his glass. He got straight to the point. "So, how much is this going to cost us if we have to pay for guards when moving funds, without sharing the overhead?"

Guthrie shrugged. "It depends on the amount of money we shift. The greater the amount, the more protection we'll need. It could cost up to ten percent of our profits. It's a hefty amount but we'll have to carry the cost and hope that eventually the Cattlemen's Association asks us back in. Some of the smaller ranchers can ill afford extra costs at the moment, so maybe it won't take long for them to come to their senses."

Johnny looked up. "And what if they don't? What if they carry on like this for years?"

Guthrie met his son's eyes. "Then we carry the cost. We'll survive. It just sticks in my craw that they're behaving like this."

Johnny stared into the bottom of his glass again. "It ain't right that you and Guy should be out of pocket because of me. You should make up the difference out of my cut."

"Johnny, we're partners. Equal partners. We're in this together. And there is no question of Guy or me taking anything from your share. We stand together as partners and as family."

He thought for a minute that Johnny wasn't going to reply. The boy still seemed intent on studying the contents of his glass. Then, without looking up, Johnny muttered, "Maybe it would be best if I leave. I said I'd bring you trouble and I have. You think I don't know that there are people who won't do business with us, because of me? Times are already hard and the ranch doesn't need the extra expense. And let's face it, this is my fault."

Guy shook his head. "Sorry, Johnny, but you're not escaping that easily! I'm voting with Father and we outnumber you. We're equal partners and you're staying right here, brother. Hell, I'd have to work even harder if you left."

Johnny flashed Guy a brief smile, but shook his head. "I dunno. This is my fault. If I wasn't here everything would be fine and none of this would have happened."

Guthrie sighed. It sometimes seemed that

Johnny held himself responsible for the entire woes of the world. "Son, if you weren't here everything wouldn't be fine. It would be anything but. And, whether you believe this or not, I would far rather have you here than kowtow to the damn cattlemen's prejudices. This is where you belong, Johnny, and if some of the neighbors don't like it, well, quite frankly, they can go to hell."

Johnny's head jerked up in surprise and Guthrie saw a brief flash of relief in the boy's eyes. And gratitude?

"And I second that," said Guy with a grin. "It also gives us a wonderful excuse not to have the party that Peggy is constantly nagging us to hold. After all, most of our neighbors are very dull company."

Johnny gave Guy a brief grin. "And we're not?"

Guy laughed. "Johnny, I think I can honestly say that I have never met anybody remotely like you and you are far from dull! Still, we will have to plan a campaign of revenge. If the Cattlemen's Association wants to make life more difficult for us, I think we should think of ways of making their lives more difficult."

Guthrie held his hand up, shaking his head. "No. We're not looking for a fight. In fact, I think we should just keep our heads down —"

"You mean roll over and let them walk all over us?" Guy's tone was scathing.

"No, that's not what I mean. But I think we should act with dignity and not lower ourselves to their level. And Johnny, I think you should stay well away from the boundaries of the neighboring ranches. John Dove thinks they're really out to get you and I don't want you to end up with a bullet in the back."

"Surely, they wouldn't do something like that? Is that what life in the west is really like?" Guy sounded horrified.

Johnny gave a short laugh. "I told you before, it's a tough life out here. Still" — Johnny paused and gave a chilling smile — "I'd like to see them try and take me out. Make a clean fight of it."

"Johnny, a bullet in the back is not a clean fight." Guthrie shook his head in exasperation. "Neither of you seems to be taking this seriously. They mean business and that is precisely why we won't give them any cause to come after us." He paused, wondering how to phrase his next remark. He didn't think it would be well received. "I think it would be for the best, Johnny, if you don't go into town for a while. It stirs people up."

Johnny stared at him. "Nobody tells me what I can or can't do. And if the people don't like me going into town, that's their problem. I'm not going to sit here on Saturday night just because a bunch of folks don't like me riding in."

Guthrie tried again. "It doesn't help that you spend so much time in the bordello. People talk."

Johnny raised an eyebrow. "Well, I got healthy appetites, you know."

Guthrie gave an exasperated sigh. "You're getting a reputation —"

"Dios!" Johnny ran his hand through his hair in irritation. "I already got me a reputation in case you didn't realize it. You don't get it, do you? It doesn't matter what I do, folks will talk. That's how it is. And I seem to remember warning you that's how it would be. And let's face it. Me and a saloon on a Saturday night with a bunch of drunken cowhands would lead to trouble. Believe me, I know that once they've had a drink or two, they all think they can take Fierro. Then the people would have something to complain about if I had shoot-outs in the saloon every Saturday night. I ain't doing anyone any harm. I ain't causing anyone any trouble and it's far better that I go and have a drink in the bordello than in any town saloon. And there's nobody who's going to tell me I can't. Including you. And in case you've forgotten, Old Man, we got a deal. My time off's my own and that's how it's staying."

Johnny's fists were clenched tightly by his sides but Guthrie could see him trembling with barely repressed anger. Guthrie counted briefly to ten in his head; it would be prudent not to lose his temper. One unruly person in the room was more than enough. "Johnny, I haven't forgotten our deal. But I am concerned about your welfare and I was simply suggesting that you avoided town until things have calmed down. That's all I was doing. Even my friend, Edith, who rarely ventures into Cimarron, has heard the gossip." He could have kicked himself. He hadn't intended to mention Edith for fear that her "surprise" visit would be interpreted by Johnny as something she had planned with Guthrie in an effort to meet his elusive son. Still, Johnny probably wouldn't give Edith a second thought.

Johnny looked singularly unimpressed by his father's words. "A deal's a deal. And if I want to go into town, I will. Ain't nobody going to stop me. And if all the old biddies want to gossip about me, well, let them. Give 'em something to think about instead of jam making and coffee mornings. Probably just jealous that the girls in the bordello have the pleasure of my company and they don't."

Guy gave a barely repressed snort of laughter. Guthrie glared at him. "This is not a matter for levity, Guy. This situation lost its entertainment value when the association started costing us money."

"I offered to leave, didn't I?" snapped Johnny.

Guthrie shut his eyes briefly, and offered up a silent prayer for patience. "You did indeed, Johnny. And I have made it very clear that I don't want you to leave, and neither does Guy. All I am saying is that discretion is the better part of valor."

Johnny stared at him, looking puzzled. "What the hell does that mean?"

Guy grinned at him. "It means, brother, that sometimes keeping a low profile gives you an edge and you come out the winner."

Johnny gave a dismissive grunt. "Well, why the hell doesn't he say that?"

Guy grinned at him again. "Well, we're determined to increase your vocabulary so that you're less inclined to use some of your more colorful expressions."

Guthrie bit back a laugh. It was good to see his sons getting along so well and it amused him that Guy seemed to be able to get away with saying anything to Johnny without getting his head bitten off.

"There ain't nothing wrong with my colorful expressions," said Johnny loftily. "I don't use 'em around Peggy, so it don't matter."

"Boys, can we get back to the matter in hand? I suggest we start thinking about what economies we can make at the ranch to help us ride out the storm. The accounts had better be brought right up to date so that we can go through them this week. Johnny, as you seem to hold yourself responsible for our situation, you can do the books."

There was another muffled snort of laughter from Guy. Johnny glared at them both. "I don't feel that responsible. Anyway, you always complain that I make a mess of the books, that there's ink spots everywhere, so it would be much better if one of you did them."

Guthrie narrowed his eyes and looked his son square in the face. "Oddly enough, Johnny, I wasn't born yesterday. And I know damn well that you sit there shaking the pen so that you can make as much mess as possible in the vague hope that I'll stop asking you to do them. It won't work. You'd find it would be a much quicker job if you just got on with them." Guthrie stood up. "And on that note, I'm off to bed. Good night."

As he left the room he heard an explosion of laughter from Guy, and the words, "I think your ruse has failed! He's on to you."

Guthrie smiled as he headed up the stairs. The neighbors might not like Johnny, but at least on evenings like this he allowed himself the hope that, given time, they would meld together as a family and have a future. Unless the damn Cattlemen's Association put them out of business first.

Chapter Thirteen

Edith Walsh watched Guthrie ride away before pouring herself another glass of lemonade and sinking into her favorite chair. She always felt that it was a comforting place to sit when she had any serious thinking to do. And the truth was, she was worried about her old friend. Ever since she'd heard that Guthrie's long-lost son was Johnny Fierro, she'd been worried. And even more worried when she heard that he'd come back to live at his father's ranch. There couldn't be anyone in the state who hadn't heard of Fierro or who didn't feel a pang of fear at the mention of his name.

She and Donald had settled in the valley shortly after the death of Guthrie's first wife. They'd seen him at his lowest, grieving and seemingly inconsolable, and had tried their best to offer what comfort they could to him and his baby son, Guy. Edith had frequently invited him for dinner or week-ends and he and Guy even spent one Christmas with them. But then it had all changed. Guthrie had suddenly arrived back from a trip with a new wife in tow.

Edith's lip curled as she thought about Gabriela Sinclair. She had tried to like her, really tried. But Gabriela Sinclair was not a woman's woman. Even now, all these years later, Edith felt angry when she thought of Gabriela. The woman — or girl, for that's really all she had been — had been totally shameless. She'd flirted outrageously with Guthrie's male friends and they'd all loved it. Even Donald. She set the glass down violently on the table next to her, spilling the lemonade. God, she'd hated Gabriela. Really hated her, if she was honest.

Now she cast her mind back, remembering Gabriela's beauty. She'd had wonderfully silky dark hair that all the women had envied, and dark flashing eyes and a very voluptuous figure. Edith ground her teeth as she remembered how Donald had always been eyeing Gabriela, and how his hands had lingered on her shoulders a fraction too long when he greeted her with a kiss. Her only consolation had been that all the other local husbands had been equally guilty of that crime. The baby had arrived remarkably soon after the wedding, less than nine

155

months, and the local female community had enjoyed rebuffing Gabriela Sinclair's claims that it was a honeymoon baby. It was all too obvious to everyone that Guthrie Sinclair had done the decent thing by marrying her. More's the pity, thought Edith, somewhat sourly.

The local women had all hoped that the arrival of the baby would calm the young bride down and make her less likely to flirt with their husbands, but it had been a vain hope. Nothing, it seemed, could keep Gabriela in her place. Least of all her husband. And so, when she'd run off, which came as no surprise to anyone other than Guthrie, all the women had breathed a sigh of relief and hoped that was the last they would ever hear of the woman.

Edith sighed sadly, as she remembered Guthrie's grief at the disappearance of his new bride and their young son. Although Gabriela was no great loss, the child had been an enchanting little boy with a smile to melt the sternest matron's heart. Edith had always wondered what would become of John, saddled with Gabriela for a mother and without his father's influence. Well, it seemed her fears had been well founded. Although shocked when she had heard what Guthrie's son had become, she wasn't surprised that the boy had turned out bad. No, not surprised at all.

But she was puzzled at Guthrie's apparent readiness to have the boy back, never mind making him a partner in the ranch. She wondered about that. Guthrie was a good, law-abiding man whom she greatly admired, but it seemed that he had thrown caution to the winds to take this wild desperado under his roof. The thought of Fierro living in that beautiful house made her blood boil. She had long harbored hopes of eventually becoming the third Mrs. Sinclair, of being the wife that she felt Guthrie deserved and mistress of his home. But now, with the arrival of his two sons, Guthrie had less time for her and she feared she'd missed her opportunity.

She had enjoyed meeting Guy again. He was well mannered, charming company and, all things considered, a welcome addition to the neighborhood. He wouldn't be a barrier to an eventual union between herself and Guthrie. No, the trouble lay with Guy's elusive younger brother. And he was already causing trouble for his father. She appreciated only too well how the latest development with the Cattlemen's Association could affect the profitability of Guthrie's ranch. But she couldn't blame the association for being wary of Johnny Fierro. Certainly no one in town seemed to have a good word to say about him. She wished she could meet him, form her own opinion, because surely the boy must have some redeeming qualities if Guthrie was prepared to let him stay. All she heard was the gossip. The local women said when he rode into town he was always wearing his gun. They relished recounting that he spent all his spare time in the bordello and expressed great shock that he had apparently gone straight to the bordello after a gunfight and spent the night with not just one, but several women. That had certainly caused the tongues to wag and given rise to much speculation at the sewing circle.

She could only presume the boy took after his mother; that he was as wild and ill disciplined as Gabriela had been. Well, time would tell. But in the meantime she wanted to meet him and, judging from his previous disappearing act, her visit would have to be unannounced. Tomorrow, she decided. Tomorrow would do very nicely. And then she could finally meet the infamous Johnny Fierro.

She set off the next day, intending to arrive at the ranch late in the afternoon so that she would be invited to dinner and probably to stay the night. That should provide ample opportunity to study Johnny Fierro at close quarters.

She wasn't far from the ranch when the buggy jolted over a particularly uneven bit of ground and one of the wheels dislodged from the axle, throwing her violently to one side. She just managed to stop herself falling onto the stony ground, muttering a few curses as she made a grab at the side panel.

"Damn." Climbing out, she aimed a kick at the wheel which lay on the ground. It was another swelteringly hot day, and the prospect of walking the rest of the way to the Sinclair ranch was not a pleasing one. She stooped to lift the wheel but knew she wasn't strong enough to lift it back to its axle. "Double damn!" She was about to kick it again when the creak of leather made her spin around to see a cowboy watching her.

There was a curious stillness about the way he sat on his horse which unnerved her. He tipped his hat to her. "Ma'am, looks like you got a spot of trouble." He was softly spoken with a slight drawl, and although his words were polite she felt a pang of fear. She was out here alone and there was something about him . . . She couldn't put her finger on it, but an air of . . . menace?

He slid gracefully from his horse and

walked toward her. "I'm . . . I'm Mrs. Walsh." She knew she sounded nervous. "I'm on my way to visit my old friend, Guthrie Sinclair. Are you from Sinclair?"

The cowboy looked at her through slightly narrowed eyes. "That's right, ma'am, from Sinclair."

She watched as he stooped to lift the wheel. "I'll get it back on the axle for you, ma'am. They expecting you at Sinclair?"

The question made her feel more nervous. Why should he care if she was expected? "Yes. Yes, they are. I told your boss I would be coming by."

The cowboy glanced up at her, a slight smile seeming to play around his lips. "Is that so, ma'am?" He bent to his task, putting a shoulder against the buggy as he strained to lift it from the ground. He was obviously strong. And very masculine. She could see the muscles straining through the fabric of his shirt as he maneuvered the buggy into a better position.

"Your boss is an old friend of mine. You're a fortunate young man to have a job with such a good employer." She knew she must sound foolish, but she had to say something, trying to cover her nerves. She thought she heard him give a small laugh at her comment, but maybe she was mistaken. "I don't believe I have seen you at Sinclair, perhaps you haven't been there long?"

"No, ma'am, not long."

"I knew that my old friend has had to take on a lot of new hands recently. He lost a lot as a result of trouble in this valley. I know that he has always employed a lot of you people."

The cowboy looked up at that. "You people?"

She felt herself flushing. "Well, Mexicans and suchlike."

"Ah, Mexicans and suchlike." His voice was still soft but there was something in his attitude that seemed slightly insolent. Really, Edith, she said to herself, you're being ridiculous. He's being very helpful and has been nothing if not polite.

"I have a ranch of my own. A little way from here, perhaps you have heard of it?"

He continued to push against the wheel before speaking. She could hear her heart beating.

"Yes, ma'am, I believe I've heard tell of it." She had to strain to catch the soft drawl when he spoke.

"It's lucky you came along. Mr. Sinclair will worry if I'm late. He'd send someone to look for me."

The cowboy looked at her through narrowed eyes, and again a smile seemed to hover around his lips, as if he guessed she was nervous of him and trying to create the impression that people would be searching for her if any harm should befall her.

She tried not to breathe an audible sigh of relief as he finally secured the wheel.

"That should be fine now, ma'am. But it might be an idea to have one of Mr. Sinclair's other fortunate workers to check it for you."

She knew he was laughing at her. She fumbled in her purse for a quarter. She held it out to him. "For your trouble. I am very grateful to you."

The cowboy looked at the coin. "That ain't necessary, ma'am. Glad to be of service." He tipped his hat and moved over to his horse and swung himself into his saddle. But he didn't ride off. He sat watching her as she picked up the reins and urged her horse onwards. She was aware of him watching her until she finally made it over the ridge and she could see Sinclair ahead. She gave a sigh of relief.

As she drew closer, she could see Guthrie. He was calling out to the hands driving some cattle into the main corral. He waved his hand to her as he strode over to help her from the buggy.

"Well, Edith, you didn't let the grass grow under your feet, did you? Come on inside. Peggy was making some coffee."

She followed him into the house, thinking how safe he always made her feel. Protected. He was a good man who didn't deserve the latest misfortunes to befall his ranch. What a pity that his younger son had ever returned home.

Edith took a seat. The cool house was a welcome relief after the suffocating heat on the long drive over. She smiled as Guthrie handed her a cup of coffee. "Thank you, that's most welcome. I'm afraid I had a little trouble on the way here so the journey took far longer than it should have done." The door opened and she smiled with pleasure as Guy walked into the room. "Guy, how nice to see you again. How are you settling in now?"

"Very well, thank you, Mrs. Walsh. I'll have a cup of that too, Father, if there's enough."

Guthrie smiled. "Plenty. But Edith, what do you mean about a little trouble? Nothing serious, I hope."

"The wheel came off my buggy. It was quite a jolt and it shook me up slightly."

Guthrie frowned. "Thank heavens you're all right. Who helped you with the wheel?"

Edith hesitated. "One of your hands, I believe. Or at least he said he was from here."

"He didn't introduce himself? I hope he was courteous."

"Ye . . . es." She flushed at her hesitancy, knowing she must sound foolish. "I mean, yes, he was polite, it was just . . . Oh, I don't know, it's just me being ridiculous. He was polite, he put the wheel back on and he wouldn't take any money. There was just something about him that puzzled me."

"Well, can you describe this hand? If he was rude, I'll be having words with him."

She shifted awkwardly in her seat, embarrassed now at having mentioned it. "No, Guthrie, please don't. He really wasn't rude. I'm being foolish. Although I must say, I'm surprised to see you equipping your Mexican hands with such fine horses."

Guthrie frowned, puzzled. "Fine horses?"

"Well, the young man was riding a fine buckskin and had a very ornate saddle. At first it crossed my mind that perhaps he had stolen it."

"An ornate saddle?" Guy's head jerked up as she spoke, and he looked amused. "Could you describe this ranch hand? What was he wearing?"

"Oh, really Guy, I barely noticed. But his

164

saddle was decorated with very showy silver conchos."

Guthrie gave an exasperated sigh and banged his cup down as Guy started laughing. She stared at them both, wondering briefly if they had both taken leave of their senses.

Guthrie finally explained. "That wasn't one of the hands, Edith. That was Johnny. He should have introduced himself."

"Oh dear, and I told him that I was expected here. I am sorry, Guthrie."

Guthrie sighed. "I don't suppose he'll be gracing us with his presence at dinner now. But as to why he didn't introduce himself, well, I really don't understand that boy at times."

Edith gave an inward shudder as she recalled the things she had said to Johnny Fierro and her comments about Mexicans. And it wasn't as if he was even a Mexican; his mother was a half-breed Indian. Damn. She would not have endeared herself to him but no wonder he had frightened her. She must have sensed what a dangerous man he was. Poor Guthrie. But she hoped that Johnny Fierro wouldn't repeat her comments about Mexicans to Guthrie; she wouldn't want her old friend thinking she was prejudiced.

Guthrie was pacing up and down the room. "I'm sorry, Edith, I really had hoped that you could meet Johnny over dinner, but it seems our plan has been thwarted. He's going to guess that I planned this."

"Are you saying you and Mrs. Walsh planned this visit so she could meet Johnny?"

Edith flushed again. Guy didn't sound very impressed.

Guthrie nodded. "You know perfectly well that Johnny disappeared deliberately last time she came for lunch. It's only natural that as an old friend of mine, who knew him as a baby, she would want to meet him. Particularly in the light of recent developments."

Guy ran his hand through his hair. "Do you really think Johnny wouldn't have guessed if she had just turned up unexpectedly? Anyway, you can be certain now that he won't be home for dinner this evening. You know what he's like. He likes to do things on his terms and you'll only have succeeded in annoying him." Guy paused and then gave Edith an apologetic smile. "I'm sorry, Mrs. Walsh, we shouldn't be having this discussion now. I don't mean to cause you any embarrassment."

"Guy, there's no need for you to apologize. The fault is mine. It was a silly plan and it seems to have gone wrong, like all the best-laid plans tend to!"

Later, as Edith stared out of the guest bedroom window, she reflected on the events of the day. She had made herself seem ridiculous to Johnny Fierro. He still hadn't turned up at the ranch by the time they'd all turned in for the night and she had a suspicion that he wouldn't be around at breakfast time either. She'd simply have to leave after breakfast and put the whole debacle down to experience. Still, at least she had met Johnny, albeit briefly and, if she was honest with herself, she now had an idea of why people felt nervous. It wasn't fanciful, he really did seem rather dangerous and she couldn't see him ever being welcome in the valley. No, he was definitely not a welcome addition to the neighborhood.

CHAPTER FOURTEEN

Johnny watched as Mrs. Walsh disappeared
over the ridge, obviously in a hurry to get
to the ranch as quickly as possible. He
grinned to himself, satisfied he'd ruined
what appeared to be a plan to surprise him
with an unexpected visit. He had no desire
to meet her socially. His mother had told
him frequently that all of Guthrie's friends
had looked down on her when she arrived
at Sinclair. And his mother had been particularly scathing about a certain Mrs. Walsh,
accusing her of hating half-breeds in general
and Gabriela in particular.

And even though Mama had usually been
drunk when she told him the stories, having
met Mrs. Walsh, he figured there was probably a grain of truth in his mother's accusa-
tions. "You people." He gritted his teeth as
he thought of the words Mrs. Walsh had
used. He'd heard far worse over the years,
but even so . . .

But now he had an evening to fill because he sure as hell wasn't going home for dinner. He grinned. The girls in Cimarron could have an unexpected weekday visit from him. Seemed Mrs. Walsh had done him a favor after all.

He turned Pistol toward the town. He knew his father would be mad at him for not introducing himself to Edith Walsh. Still, maybe the old man would calm down by tomorrow. Probably best to keep out of his way. And he sure didn't fancy an evening listening to Mrs. Walsh sucking up to Guthrie and Guy. He knew there was gossip about her and his father. He'd overheard some of the hands talking about how much bigger the ranch would be if the two of them married. Well, fuck that. He sure as hell wasn't going out of his way to be friendly to some woman who'd treated Mama like dirt. "You people and suchlike." Surprised she didn't say Mexicans and breeds — but she'd sure been thinking it. He'd seen it in her eyes.

Cimarron was quiet when he rode in. He was aware of a few people staring out at him from behind the drapes at their windows. Seemed like folk here hadn't got enough to keep 'em busy if all they could do was gawk and gossip about him. It was almost tempting to do something to really shock them, but he figured the old man would be pissed off with him if he did that, and it didn't seem worth the fight. They were getting along better, but it still felt like he had to watch every word. The old man was sure good at getting riled and it seemed he got riled with Johnny a hell of a lot more often than with Guy. He wondered if his father realized how hard Johnny was trying to fit in. Johnny huffed out a sigh. He was trying but ranching was so damn boring. Felt like his head was going to explode and at times like that he just had to get away. But whenever he lit out all he did was piss off his father.

And this latest stunt of the Cattlemen's Association didn't help. Not that he was surprised. No, not surprised at all. Folk were pretty much shit whichever way you looked at 'em. They were quick enough to hire him when they wanted his gun but then wouldn't give him the time of day after he'd done their dirty work. It was kinda surprising that the old man didn't want Johnny riding shotgun on the shipments. But maybe his father figured that would cause more trouble than it was worth. Or just wanted him where he could keep an eye on him and make sure he was pulling his weight.

He'd warned the old man to expect trouble once the locals knew Fierro was staying. Still, at least his father had said again that he wanted Johnny to stay, even managed to sound as if he meant it. Yeah, it sounded real good when he'd said about how they'd stand as a family and how he'd rather have Johnny there than kowtow to his neighbors. Really sounded like he meant it — for the time being. But Johnny didn't believe it would last. In his experience, nothing ever lasted and in the end people always let you down. It was only a matter of time. Shit, Fierro, quit thinking like that. What was that fancy word Harvard used? Positive? Yeah, that was it, think positive.

Well, right now he figured that the most positive thing to think about was Sadie and her friends. He left Pistol at the livery stable before strolling to the bordello.

He paused momentarily at the door, scanning the room. All was quiet apart from the girls who all started chattering when they caught sight of him. He grinned. Yeah, Mrs. Walsh had done him a favor after all.

As the girls crowded round him he spotted Delice coming out of her office at the back. He grinned across, tipping his hat to her. She didn't smile back, just raised an eyebrow and shooed all the girls away.

"Miss Martin." He smiled, hoping she would catch his sudden good mood. She didn't seem to get the idea though. She just folded her arms and tilted her head to one side.

"And what mission of mischief brings you into town midweek, Mr. Fierro?"

"Figured I'd pay you all a visit." He grinned again. She didn't. Maybe she wasn't buying into this.

She narrowed her eyes as he sat down at his usual table. She put a bottle of tequila and a glass down in front of him, and pulled up a chair across from him.

"Figured you'd pay us a visit. In the middle of the week?"

"That's right." His smile faltered. Why should she be bothered by his coming in midweek? Didn't make no sense.

"Strange." Her voice was soft. "I can't imagine that your father approves of you taking time off in the middle of the week."

"I don't need his permission for anything." He fired out the words like bullets from a gun.

Her lips twitched, like she was amused by his outburst. "I didn't say you did need his permission. I'm simply curious as to why you're in town midweek when it seems the sort of thing that will annoy him and spark a fight between the two of you. I thought you were trying to make a go of this new life?"

"What's it to do with you anyway?" He knew he sounded angry, but hell, it wasn't her business. But she still didn't look too bothered by his words.

"Oh, nothing, honey, nothing to do with me at all. But it would be kind of a shame to fall out with him over something so foolish. So, why the sudden visit to town?"

Her voice had a steely edge to it, like she wasn't going to give up on this line of questioning.

He sighed. Tried to look her square in the eyes but dropped his gaze again. "I'm trying to avoid someone, that's all."

"Who?"

"Oh, some woman who owns a ranch, a friend of my old man's. Mrs. Edith Walsh. She seems mighty keen to meet me and was planning a surprise visit because last time she came I avoided her."

"How did you find out she was planning a visit?" Delice sounded curious now.

So he told her how he'd come across Mrs. Walsh stranded with her buggy and fixed the wheel.

Delice was looking at him now like he was really dumb. "And you think that not bothering to introduce yourself is going to impress your father?"

Johnny glared at her. "No. I know it's going to piss him off, but I don't want to spend an evening with her."

"What have you got against her?"

"You mean besides the fact that she hates Mexicans and breeds? My mother told me about Mrs. Walsh. Let's just say I don't want to meet the woman."

Delice nodded her head slowly. "I take your point, if in fact that's true. But if your father likes her and values her friendship she might not be all bad. Presumably your mother must have been very young when she met her. Perhaps they just didn't get along. People don't always get along and often it's nothing to do with the color of their skin, simply differences in personality."

Johnny shrugged. "I dunno, but I saw it in her eyes when I fixed her wheel. She don't like breeds."

Delice smothered a laugh. "Maybe you just made her nervous, out there all alone. And you do have a very wild look in your eye."

Johnny started laughing. He was really starting to like this woman. She didn't let him take himself too seriously and she knew how to make him laugh.

"Anyway, from what I hear you've got more serious things to worry about than Mrs. Walsh. The Cattlemen's Association, for example."

Johnny stared at her. "How the hell d'you know about that? I mean do you know everything that goes on in these parts? I don't see you or the girls out and about in town. How come you always know everything?"

For a moment he thought she wasn't going to answer but then she gave a slight smile. A kinda sad smile.

"Well, honey, me and my girls might live behind these walls not mixing with the town folk, but it doesn't mean we don't watch and listen to what goes on. Not much gets past us in this town." She paused and then added, "We're like children with our noses up against the windows of the candy store, wishing we could go inside."

Johnny looked at her. She was studying her hands now. He felt a lump in his throat suddenly. He spoke softly. "Hell, we both know that most people are shit. There ain't many worth knowing, that's for sure."

She smiled at that. "What a wonderful cynic you are, even more of a cynic than me."

He wondered what the hell she was talking about but it seemed like she was more cheerful again. He rubbed the back of his neck and leaned back in his seat. "Tell you one thing, those cattlemen are making life damn awkward for us. And it's all my fault."

She frowned. "I don't see why this is your fault. You've given them no cause to act like that. I grant that you have a less than enviable reputation. But you didn't start any of the trouble in town. And you saved your father's ranch."

Johnny shrugged. "Yeah, well, maybe it would've been better if I'd left then. Just taken my money and got the hell out. Quit when I was ahead. Now there's some people won't do business with us and we got the cattlemen being damned awkward and they're a mighty powerful bunch of men."

"More powerful than Sinclair?" Delice had raised an eyebrow in a kind of questioning way and was looking at him real hard.

"Well, Sinclair might be the biggest ranch but at the moment it feels like it's us against the world. I offered to leave."

Delice gave him a sharp look. "And what did your father say to that?"

Johnny grinned. "It was real strange, but he said he wanted me to stay. Said it like he meant it too. Said he'd rather have me here

176

than kowtow to all those folk. Said we'd face it together."

She smiled at that. Her eyes looked a lot softer. "So?" She sounded real gentle. "That should surely tell you something, honey. When you go back tomorrow, just remember he's trying. Don't go losing your temper. Try and remember you're on the same side. Play nice. Remember."

Johnny sighed. "Yeah, I guess. But shit, sometimes I feel like I ain't never going to fit in. It's like everything's closing in on me and I can't breathe. And there's no end to the work and I get like I have to escape and ride free. I mean mending fences or rounding up strays, it's so boring. It drives me crazy. And now I feel trapped."

She shrugged. "Well, no one ever said it would be easy for you to adapt to such a different life. But let's face it, do you want your old one back?"

He thought about it. Would he want to go back to being a gunfighter? If he was honest he knew he'd tired of that life long before he came home. He shook his head slowly. "No, I guess not. But I sure miss the freedom. And it's like my past is right here with me so I haven't gotten away from it. Don't suppose I ever will."

"Give it time, honey, just give it time.

Now, which of my girls has caught your wandering eye this evening?"

He grinned. "Well, I was kinda wondering about that redhead . . ."

She narrowed her eyes and gave him a real stern look. "You know perfectly well that she's the girl your brother favors. No! I do not think that's a good idea."

"You spoil all my fun."

She raised an eyebrow. "Oh, I don't think you could really accuse me of that. But if you want Sadie, you'll have to be quick. One of her regulars always comes in on a Wednesday evening."

Johnny grinned. "Yeah, she's mentioned her regular. Jeb Lutz. Says he's got real bad breath. And he don't take a bath too often."

Delice smothered a laugh. "I couldn't possibly comment. I never discuss my customers. But, you would be doing her a big favor. And it would put her in a much better mood tomorrow. She and Polly have had a major fight and aren't speaking and she's going around like a bear with a sore head."

Johnny grinned. "So, which poor girl ends up with her regular if Sadie ain't around?"

Delice pulled a face. "Damn, I never thought of that. It would be Polly. Perhaps my suggestion isn't such a good one."

"So come on, give, who's his third pick?"

"Guy's redhead."

Johnny grinned. "Well, I'm going to do you a real big favor. Tell you what I'll do, seeing as how all your girls love me so much and I'm their favorite customer."

She interrupted him. "And what makes you think that?"

"They all tell me that."

Her lips twitched. "They're paid to tell you that. It's what they tell all the customers."

Johnny grinned again. "Yeah, but in my case they mean it."

"You're an arrogant man, Johnny Fierro. And a favor? I shudder to think what that may be."

"I'll take Sadie and Polly, and I promise they'll be friends by the morning." He winked at her as he stood up. He called out to the girls. "Come on Sadie, before Jeb Lutz gets here." The huge smile that broke out across Sadie's face made his decision worthwhile. As did the other look on her face, when he grabbed Polly by the hand and pulled her upstairs as well.

He didn't hurry in the morning. Figured he'd let Mrs. Walsh leave before he headed back to the ranch. Instead he enjoyed a leisurely cup of coffee while Delice dished him up some pancakes. As he left, Delice called out to him. "Don't forget what I said. Play nice when you get home. You're on the same side."

He tipped his hat and headed out to collect Pistol from the livery stables. Hell, leastways now if he avoided town for a couple of weeks to keep the old man happy, he'd had a good night with the girls. He was halfway back to the ranch and still grinning about the previous night's activities when the crack of a rifle shot echoed across the valley.

A bullet traced its way across the sleeve of his jacket.

CHAPTER FIFTEEN

He threw himself off Pistol and dived for cover in a ditch by the side of the road, cursing himself for daydreaming about girls instead of keeping an eye on his surroundings. Getting soft, Fierro! But where the hell had that bullet come from? Shielding his eyes against the bright light, he scanned the hills opposite and thought maybe, just maybe, he saw the sun glint off something metallic. He kept his eyes fixed on that spot, hoping the sun would stay shining. And then there it was, the telltale glint again. Leastways he knew where the bushwhacker was now. Keeping very low, he ran into the brushwood behind the ditch. Wasn't no one going to shoot him in the back. He dodged through the trees, knowing he was well screened now.

He figured if he followed the side of the road up around the far bend, he could double back and creep up on the son of a bitch from behind. Whoever he was, he wasn't a bad shot. The bullet had almost found its mark. Almost, but not quite. And that bastard would be regretting that real soon. Johnny grinned, relishing the familiar sensation of the blood pumping through his body. It felt like all his nerves were on fire and every sensation seemed stronger than it had ever been before.

He sprinted between the trees, following the line of the road, and then crouched as he saw movement on the opposite hillside. He could see a man carrying a rifle, clambering down over the loose rocks, grabbing occasionally at the ground as he almost lost his balance. Sure looked in a mighty hurry to get the hell out of there. The man must have left his horse tethered nearby. Be kind of a shame not to be by the horse ready and waiting for the man . . . Johnny grinned again. Yeah. He'd be sure to welcome the man. All he had to do was find the horse. It had to be close.

Moving slowly now, he edged forward to where the trees thinned out. A skinny sorrel mare stood forlorn, tethered to a spindly aspen. Her ribs showed up starkly in the dappled light. Johnny bit his lip. Seemed like this fellow didn't look after his animals too well. Another reason for disliking him and they hadn't even met yet. Boy, he was looking forward to this meeting.

He crouched down. He figured the man would be so desperate to get on his horse and away he'd never notice the small shadow at the side of the road that was the only giveaway to Johnny's presence. The blood was really pounding round now and Johnny shut his eyes briefly as he relished the buzz.

He could hear the sound of the man's running feet. The bastard was panting from having run so far. He was obviously out of condition. Johnny smiled. That would make his job even easier. He watched as the man hurried to his horse, pausing briefly to try and catch his breath while he tried to shove the rifle into its sleeve on the saddle.

"G' morning." Johnny spoke softly.

The man whirled round to face him. He had a weaselly sort of face, with eyes a touch too close together and a weak mouth. And he looked very, very frightened as recognition dawned.

"W . . . what do you want?" The man was shaking slightly.

Johnny tilted his head, as if considering the question. "You." He motioned with his gun for the man to move away from his horse.

The man looked even paler now and stumbled slightly as he moved a step away from his horse. "What d'you mean, you want me?"

"Oh, I just don't like people who try and shoot me in the back." Johnny spoke very softly. "I don't like it at all. Kinda cowardly, don't you think?"

"I don't know what you're talking about. I'm out to shoot some game. I was after an elk. Saw it on the hill opposite where I was."

"An elk?" Johnny raised an eyebrow. "An elk, huh? Well, I have to say no one's ever tried that one on me before. Maybe 'cos I don't look much like a damned elk." Johnny stepped closer, and grabbing hold of the man, shoved the barrel of his pistol into the man's throat, causing him to gasp.

Johnny smiled thinly. "You know, I get this urge sometimes to kill someone and I got a real urge right now."

"I didn't do nothing. I told you, I was trying to shoot an elk. Never even saw you."

Johnny narrowed his eyes. And pushed the gun harder into the man's throat. The fellow was sweating now. Any minute he'd be pissing himself. And the urge to pull the trigger was getting stronger. And so was the feeling of power. No one fucked with Fierro. "You know, I'd be doing everyone a favor if

I pull this trigger. Because I'd lay money that you've tried this stunt before and if I let you live you'll do it again. Sooner or later."

The fellow was shaking all over now. "A man like you is bound to have made enemies. It could have been anyone."

"But you and I both know it wasn't anyone. It was you up there with a rifle trying to put a bullet in my back."

"Fierro, you can't kill me. That'd be murder."

Johnny laughed softly. "Well, that's kinda what you were planning for me. But I just turned the tables. And you know, that makes me feel real good. It takes more than some lily-livered son of a bitch like you to get the better of me."

He cocked the hammer of the gun, enjoying the strangled gasp of fear that the man made. "So, any last requests?"

The sound of wheels on the rough road echoed through the valley. Johnny eased the hammer back into place but kept his gun jammed against the man's throat. He whispered in the man's ear. "Looks like it's your lucky day."

A buggy came round the corner. Shit. Edith Walsh. She reined in her horse, staring at Johnny with a shocked expression.

"What's going on here? What are you doing? Mr. Porter, are you all right?"

Johnny raised an eyebrow, gave a short
laugh. "Porter? Is that his name? Well,
ma'am, your friend, Mr. Porter, was trying
to put a bullet in my back. You know, I don't
take too kindly to that."

Mrs. Walsh gave a snort. "Rubbish, Mr.
Porter is a local rancher, a respected member of this community. He wouldn't do a
thing like that."

"You calling me a liar, ma'am?"

Well that sure shut her up. Briefly. She
flushed a deep red. "No, all I'm saying is
you must be mistaken."

Porter tried to speak but it came out more
as a croak. Maybe 'cos the gun was still
jammed in his throat. "Thank God you
came along, Mrs. Walsh. Fierro here was
going to kill me —"

"Let him go this minute." Boy, she sure
looked riled up.

With one arm around Porter's throat,
holding him fast, Johnny reached into
Porter's holster for the man's pistol. Then,
thrusting the man to one side, Johnny
emptied it. Keeping his own gun trained on
Porter, he stepped up to the mare and slid
the rifle from its sleeve, enjoying the looks

of fear on the faces of Porter and Mrs. Walsh.

"What you doing?" Porter's voice came out more as a squeak.

Johnny didn't answer. He took the shells out of the rifle and threw them into the thick undergrowth.

Then he shoved Porter toward the skinny mare. He leaned forward to speak softly in the man's ear. "Now, Porter, just get the fuck out of here. But I warn you, try anything again and I really will kill you. That's not a threat, that's a promise. Better men than you have tried to kill me. It don't work. Now, make yourself scarce before I change my mind."

Porter clambered into the saddle, clawing for leather, before kicking the horse into a gallop and riding off.

Johnny turned to Mrs. Walsh. She had a look on her face that said she didn't think too much of Fierro. No surprise there. He tipped his hat to her. "Ma'am, did you have a nice evening at the ranch?"

She glared at him. "Never mind my evening at the ranch. What were you going to do to Mr. Porter if I hadn't come along when I did?"

"Well, ma'am, to tell the truth, I hadn't really quite decided —" He got no further.

187

"The truth? I'm surprised you know what that is."

Johnny kicked at the stones around his feet, gave a slight smile. "Ma'am, if you ain't going to believe anything I say, why ask?"

"Because I am hoping to find some redeeming qualities in you. You have quite a reputation, you know."

Johnny laughed softly. "Oh I know. But that don't mean what everyone says about me is all true. Wouldn't you say so, ma'am?"

"I really have no idea. But your father is an old and dear friend of mine. I knew him long before you were born and it grieves me to see people turning against him because of you. Not that I'm surprised. You didn't even have the courtesy to introduce yourself to me, yesterday."

Johnny grinned. "Well, ma'am, truth to tell, I kinda thought that you'd have figured out who I was. But, if I may say so, you're exactly how my mother described you to me."

Her eyes widened. "Your mother mentioned me to you?"

Johnny paused, let her think about that one. "Oh yes, more than once. Told me all about how welcoming people were."

Mrs. Walsh looked at him sharply. "When your mother first arrived here, I, and many of the other local ladies, tried very hard to make her feel at home and help her to adjust to life here."

"I didn't say that you didn't." Let her chew on that one.

She didn't chew for long. "I really have no idea what your meaning is, but I will tell you that your mother rebuffed many attempts to befriend her. She didn't seem very interested in joining the sewing circle or any of the other social groups we have here."

Johnny bit his lip to stop himself from laughing. His mama in a sewing circle. Boy, that would have been worth seeing. But if she had joined she'd sure have livened things up. He tried to put the mental picture out of his head and concentrate on what the damn woman was talking about now.

"We tried to teach her how to cook many of our local dishes but she wasn't interested in that either." Mrs. Walsh paused. "But she was a good horsewoman." She sounded grudging when she said that. "It gave your mother more to talk to our husbands about than it did the ladies of the community."

Ah! Now that had the ring of truth to it. What would the old hag say if she knew exactly how much Mama had preferred the company of men? But if Mama had carried on with Mr. Walsh, no wonder the widow hadn't liked her. Could Mama have been fucking all the local men? Somehow, he suspected not. Flirted, more like. The fucking had come later. After she'd left Sinclair with the fellow Ben had mentioned. But Mama had probably tried him on for size before she left.

"Well, ma'am, fact remains I'm home, and as long as Guthrie wants me here I'm staying, so the likes of Porter better get used to it."

"From what I hear, your presence is already costing your father money."

"Ma'am, seeing as how my brother and I are equal partners in this ranch, I'd say it was costing us all money. And really, that ain't anyone else's business. I'd say it's between my partners and me. I'm sure you agree."

The woman flushed red as a brick and looked real flustered. "Your father was very disappointed that you didn't return home yesterday evening."

Johnny gave a short laugh. "Is that so? Well, I'm sure if he's got a problem with it, he'll mention it. Now, ma'am, if you'll excuse me, I've got work to do." He tipped his hat again and went to retrieve Pistol who was grazing at the side of the road.

Johnny swung himself into the saddle.

"Oh, I almost forgot. Did you have one of our fortunate workers check that wheel? Or do you want me to have another look at it?"

She looked taken aback at the question. "Um, no, one of the hands checked it. But . . . thank you for asking."

Johnny looked her straight in the eyes. "You see, ma'am, I do have some redeeming qualities." And tipping his hat once more, he spurred Pistol into a lope and headed toward the ranch.

He slowed to a walk as he approached the house. It didn't take no genius to figure that his father was going to be mad at him about the previous evening. Maybe he could divert him by telling him about the back-shooting Porter. But the old man weren't going to be none too happy about that either. Johnny sighed softly. It looked like he wouldn't be visiting town any time soon. His father would want him to stay around the ranch until things calmed down. Shit. His whole life was a fucking trap whichever way he played it. *Play nice, you're on the same side.* The words echoed round his head along with a mental picture of those searching green eyes. Play nice. It was easy for her to say.

His stomach lurched as he spied his father waiting outside for him.

"Johnny, I want to talk to you inside. Now, please."

Fuck.

CHAPTER SIXTEEN

He followed Guthrie into the house, his spurs jangling as he walked. He tried to stop himself from clenching his fists, but damn it, if the old man wanted to make a song and dance about this then he was more than ready for a battle. He wasn't taking orders from no man, including Guthrie Sinclair.

Remember you're on the same side. Shit. Damn woman. Felt like he couldn't get her voice out of his head. How did she do that? Fucking easy for her to say.

He tried to take a deep breath to calm himself down. But bushwhackers always put him in a foul temper. A man couldn't do anything much lower than that. He hated cowards. And bullies.

Guy was leaning against the wall with his arms folded. Kinda like he was waiting for the two of them. Felt like he was being bushwhacked on all sides today. But then Guy winked at him and leaned over to whisper, "Not coming back last night was probably not the smartest thing you've ever done. Just don't lose your temper."

Another one who figured he knew what was best for Fierro. Johnny sighed and turned to look at Guthrie who'd sat down at his desk. The man was drumming his fingers on the polished wood, like he was trying to make up his mind what to say.

"Spit it out, Old Man, instead of beating on that desk like it's a war drum." He regretted his words as soon as they were said. Why did he do that? It would only rile his father even more. And out of the corner of his eye he saw Guy give a shake of his head, like he couldn't believe what he'd heard.

The old man just continued to drum his fingers, but now there was a tightness around his mouth. Shit, why did Fierro always fuck up or put his foot in things?

"Johnny." He sounded like he was having a struggle to stay calm. "I have to say that I was very disappointed in you yesterday. Disappointed that you didn't introduce yourself to Edith and disappointed that you failed to join us for dinner. And for the life of me I can't think why you have to be so rude. Edith is an old friend, she knew you as a child and it's only natural that she

194

wanted to meet you but it seems you're going out of your way to avoid her."

Disappointed. He hated it when the old man said things like that. Like Fierro could never get anything right. He'd rather his father just yelled at him. "I fixed her wheel for her. What more do you want?"

"For you to start behaving like a member of this family, that's what I want." The old man took a deep breath, kinda like to stop himself going off. "So why are you avoiding her?"

Johnny shrugged. "I ain't some prize bull to be inspected by her."

The old man huffed out a sigh. "It isn't a case of inspecting you, she wants to meet you. Meeting, getting acquainted, it's what civilized people do. God knows what she must think of you after your rude behavior."

Johnny shrugged again. "Won't make no difference what I do, she don't like Mexicans and she sure as hell don't like breeds."

His father stared at him, his brow furrowed. "What the hell gives you that idea? And, I hate the term breed."

Johnny gave a short laugh. "You should have thought of that before you fucked my mother, because it's what I am, ain't it?"

Guy sighed heavily and shook his head. The old man turned a very funny color —

sort of purple, and gritted his teeth. Didn't look none too happy.

Probably wasn't the smartest thing he could have said just then.

"I'm not going to rise to that one, John." Shit, he hated it when the old man called him John, probably like he had when Johnny was a little kid. When he was safe. Before Mama left. "Suffice it to say that I never gave it a thought. And why you think Edith would think it mattered is beyond me."

"I saw it in her eyes and my mother told me how much your friend Edith hated her." He stopped abruptly. Could have bitten his tongue off. He hadn't meant to mention Mama again. Shit.

"Your mother talked to you about Edith? Edith Walsh?" His father frowned.

No way was he getting into any talk about his mother. He figured the best thing he could do was try and get the old man's mind onto something else. Like bushwhack-ing.

"Anyway, I saw your friend this morning when I was coming back from town. She came along just after someone tried to bushwhack me."

Well, that sure stopped the man in his tracks. "Someone tried to bushwhack you? On the road? You hadn't strayed onto someone else's land?"

Johnny narrowed his eyes. "No. I had not strayed onto someone else's land. I was on the road and I was kinda under the impression that anyone is free to use the road. Even me. Anyhow, I was riding along and someone fired a rifle. Only just missed me, too." And he held his arm up so the old man could see where the bullet had traced its way along the sleeve of his jacket.

"Where did this happen? I mean, on the road, you say? No one would have . . . Maybe you imagined it . . ." The old man trailed off as he continued to stare at the mark on Johnny's jacket.

Johnny rolled his eyes. "Well, I didn't imagine this, did I?" He held his arm up again and glared at his father.

Guy strode across and peered at Johnny's jacket. "Hell, Johnny, that was a close call. Who on earth would do that to you when you're riding along minding your own business?"

"Man called Porter, that's who."

"Porter?" Guthrie's mouth was working and he shook his head repeatedly. "Porter! The rancher? That's ridiculous. I've known Porter for years. He wouldn't do a thing like that."

Johnny narrowed his eyes. "You calling me

a liar?" He spoke soft, guessing his father would sense the menace behind the question.

His father gave an exaggerated sort of a sigh. "No, Johnny, I'm not calling you a liar. All I'm saying is you must be mistaken. Porter's no bushwhacker."

Johnny gave a soft laugh. "Yeah, he is. Tried to tell me he was shooting at an elk. Do I look like a fucking elk? No. He was out to get me, whether you like it or not. Like all your rancher friends warned you they would. Anyway, your friend, Edith, came along just as I was deciding what to do with Porter. Kind of spoiled my fun."

His father paled. "What do you mean, spoiled your fun?"

Johnny leaned back against the bookcase. Stared down at his boots for a second before looking his father square in the eyes. "Well, I was deciding whether to kill him before he tries the same game again."

Guy muttered something half under his breath, but it kinda sounded like he said shit. And the old man looked even paler.

"And Edith came along in the middle of this?"

Johnny grinned. "Yeah. She didn't seem too happy about it. Anyway, I let him go. Which I'll probably regret, because I tell you, he'll try it again. Maybe not on me, but he'll try it again on someone. And, for what it's worth, I'll lay money it ain't the first time he's done it."

His father was running his hand through his hair and pacing up and down. "I can't believe you threatened him. How could you be so foolish? There has to be some other explanation for all of this. He must have been shooting at some game and didn't see you. That must be it. And now he's going to go round telling everyone you threatened him, which is going to make this whole situation even worse."

"Seems I should have shot him, then. Would have saved a lot of bother."

Guthrie glared. "This is not funny, Johnny."

"I wasn't joking." Johnny paused, to let his words sink in. "Anyhow, seems like you prefer to believe his story to mine. Doesn't say much about what you think of me, does it? Maybe you'd rather that I just leave. Make your life a whole lot simpler and keep all your friends happy. Make this valley a safer place for decent folk. Isn't that what they say?" Even as he said it, Johnny felt his gut clench. They always seemed to end up back at this. He tried to look his father square in the face, but the man's head was down so Johnny couldn't read his expression.

He couldn't stand the silence. Or the sight of his father's bent head, like he was too ashamed of his son to even look at him. "That's it, then? You'd rather I just leave? Fine, I'll go get my things and be out of here." Johnny turned on his heel, feeling sick inside. It wasn't supposed to go like this. He always screwed up. On the same side? That was a fucking joke.

He didn't get to the door before the old man banged his fist down on the table, so hard Johnny was surprised that the desk didn't split in two. "We've discussed this before. I told you I don't want you to leave." His father took another deep breath, looked at Johnny. "This is your home. You were born here. You belong here." The old man sighed. "I just want you to try and fit in. Make more effort."

Johnny tried to stop his mouth dropping open. "Make more effort? Make more effort! Have you got any idea how fucking hard I'm trying? This ain't easy but I'm trying and you don't . . . I mean I mend fences, I round up strays, I mend chicken runs, I swill out the pigs, I fix broken gates, and I even do the fucking books. But it seems like whatever I do, it's never enough."

He ran his hand through his hair. Maybe it would be better if he just turned and walked out. Be his own boss again instead of jumping to someone else's tune, because it sure felt like whatever he did was never going to be enough for his father.

"Can I suggest that everyone calm down." Guy sounded very calm. Too calm, maybe. "Johnny, before you go any further, I think Father has made it perfectly clear that he wants you to stay, and so have I. Father," he continued, turning toward the old man, "siding with Porter, whoever he may be, is not showing much faith in your son. And we can't deny that someone has taken a shot that could easily have killed Johnny. Personally, I feel that if you were aiming at an elk you would be bound to see a man riding a horse on the road in your sight line."

The old man threw his hands in the air. "I know Porter, damn it. I've known him for years. He's a little hot tempered but he's no bushwhacker."

"Sir, I think you should rely on Johnny's judgment. He was there, we weren't."

Johnny looked across at Guy and nodded his head in acknowledgment of the support. Good old Harvard, he always seemed to back Johnny. Probably wouldn't if he knew what Fierro was really like, but even so, it felt good at times like this.

"All I'm saying is that I can't believe Porter intended to shoot at Johnny. I'm not doubting what happened."

"With all due respect, sir, I think you just don't want to believe that someone you've known for years could behave in such a way. And Johnny, before you go getting all lathered up, the reason Father was so concerned, and thus so irritable, is because of all the trouble in town last night."

Johnny stared at Guy. What the hell was he going on about?

Guy returned his gaze without flinching. "I assume, from your bemused expression, that you didn't know about the trouble."

"No, Harvard, I ain't got a clue what you're talking about. I was tucked up all nice and cozy with two girls last night."

His father gave another irritated sigh. Johnny glared at him. "I can't help it if I got healthy appetites, you know."

Guy jumped in real quick at that. "I think how many girls you had last night is totally irrelevant. We heard that a group of saddle tramps rode in to town yesterday and were causing a lot of trouble in the saloon. There was some gunplay, and they were a nasty bunch by all accounts."

Johnny shrugged. "Didn't hear nothing.

Kind of had my hands full." He looked at his father. "Maybe you'd like a blow-by-blow account . . ."

Guy tried to muffle a laugh.

Guthrie glared at them both. "No, I do not want an account of your activities. I do want you to stay and become a part of this family. I happen to care about your future. But, by the same token, I'd also like to see you make more effort to get along with our friends and neighbors."

"Edith Walsh ain't no friend of mine. And as for your neighbors, well, they don't seem too welcoming so I don't see why I should put myself out."

"Johnny, I don't know anything about your childhood or how your mother raised you, but making an effort to get along with people, whether we like them or not, is what civilized people do. It's a great pity that your mother never taught you that lesson."

"Leave my mother outta this, Old Man. She took care of me. That's all you need to fucking know." Except she hadn't taken care of him. Or protected him. Or stopped some of her men friends . . . Shit. Keep calm, Fierro. Don't let him see he's got you riled. Dios, his gut was churning. Blank face. Keep the mask on. Never let 'em know when they've scored. If only Guy would say

203

something. Hell, it was what his brother was good at.

"Can we all calm down again?" Good old Harvard. He always knew when to step in. "I think the best thing would be for Johnny and me to go up to the north pastures and check our fence lines up there. We're short-handed and haven't been able to check that section and it would probably be better if things can settle down around here for a few days, in case Porter decides to make trouble."

"He won't." Johnny kept his voice soft and calm. Like nothing the old man said could have gotten to him. "I tell you, he was out to get me and I reckon he'd rather let this drop. I told him what I'd do if he tried anything. I think he got the message."

Guy chewed on his thumb before shaking his head slowly. "Maybe, but the fact remains that Mrs. Walsh knows what went on and there's a fair chance she'll talk. Wouldn't you think so, Father?"

The old man sighed. "I suspect Edith will talk to me first. I'll ride over to see her. Try and smooth things over. But it would be a good idea if the two of you check those fences. It's a job that needs doing and, as you say, it'll allow things to settle down around here." He lifted his head and looked

Johnny in the eyes. "Always assuming you're not walking out on us?"

Johnny shrugged. "I warned you about this, didn't I? Sure you really want me to stay?" Hell, why did he keep asking that? All it did was give the old man a chance to kick him out.

"You know the answer to that. The two of you had better get your gear together and head straight out. I'll deal with things at this end."

Johnny looked at the man, trying to see if there was any emotion there. But his father turned away and stared out of the big window behind his desk. Johnny shrugged again and turned to Guy. "Come on, then, let's get going." He swung on his heel and walked upstairs, trying to squash the desire to puke all over the floor.

CHAPTER SEVENTEEN

Johnny had hardly spoken a word since they'd left the ranch. Now he was gazing into the distance, seemingly lost in thought. And the expression on his face certainly didn't invite questions. Guy sighed, wishing he could understand what went on in Johnny's head. Johnny kept pushing their father to the breaking point, didn't seem able to stop himself. One of these days he'd push too far. And Guy had a feeling that day wasn't too far off.

He shivered. The past few days had been excessively hot, as though summer was having one last fling before burning herself out. But now there was a chill in the air. An ominous bank of clouds was building in the north and he hoped they'd make it to a line shack before nightfall. He still hadn't become accustomed to sleeping rough and the thought of spending a night in a bedroll in the open had little appeal if the weather was apt to change. He'd done enough of that in his army days and when the war had ended he'd made a mental promise to himself to never sleep rough again. He smiled wryly. So much for that promise. He'd expected to remain in Boston. The thought of returning to the family ranch in New Mexico hadn't appealed. But now he'd made the move, he knew nothing could induce him to return to Boston. He relished the hard work here and although he was very much a greenhorn, he enjoyed the challenge of mastering this new life. He still found the west incredibly uncivilized but he reveled in the beauty and wildness of the region. He just wished that Johnny could settle. Life had dealt his brother a poor hand. Despite all the disadvantages, he'd clawed his way up from the bottom, but at what cost?

Guy still found it hard to believe that his brother had made his living with a gun. Killing for money. He couldn't in his wildest imaginings think what could have been so bad that Johnny was driven to choose that life. Because, if he was certain of one thing, Guy was certain Johnny had made his decision about his future at a very tender age. By Johnny's own admission he had started practicing before he was ten years old. Guy shuddered, thinking how different Johnny's life had been in contrast to his own life of comfort and privilege. If he was honest, it made him feel guilty. He'd had so much, every luxury money could buy while Johnny had nothing. Even now when Johnny ate, Guy could see the hunger. The way his brother hunched over his food, almost as though he expected it to be taken from him. Johnny had been fighting for survival while Guy had enjoyed picnics and parties.

He tried to shake himself out of his introspection. Maybe a few days with his brother would lead to some more revelations about his past. He hoped so. At times he felt like a man dying of thirst in the desert, desperate for some droplet that Johnny would let fall. Some clue as to what made his brother tick. But Johnny was the most guarded individual he'd ever met. And certainly the deadliest.

"Looks like rain." Johnny reined in and reached for his slicker tied with his bedroll. "And it's getting fucking cold. If it's this cold when it's only September, what the hell will it be like in the winter? Dios, I hate the cold. And the rain. Should've stayed in Mexico."

Guy felt a cold clutch of fear. "You don't mean that." He tried to make his tone light.

"Heck, Johnny, you'd miss all this. Riding for hours, rounding up strays, fixing fences. Now admit it, wouldn't you miss all of that?"

Johnny grunted, screwing his eyes up as he peered into the distance. "It's already fucking raining over there. Shit." And he pulled his slicker up round him, shivering as he did so.

Guy pulled his own slicker on, looking at the heavy bank of cloud. "Have you any idea how far we are from the line shack, always assuming we're going in the right direction?"

"We should make it in an hour or two by my reckoning. It would be a hell of a lot quicker if the ground wasn't so rocky. But if it's any consolation, I reckon we're on target. I've been up this way before so I have a pretty good idea where we're headed."

"What were you doing this far north?"

Johnny ignored the question and urged Pistol on, leaving Guy in a cloud of dust. Guy cursed under his breath. Johnny had to be the most irritating man he'd ever met. He'd lay odds that his brother had been a very difficult child. He felt a brief pang of sympathy for Gabriela. She must have had her work cut out trying to deal with him. But the sympathy was gone as quickly as it came. If she hadn't walked out, taking Johnny with her, doubtless his brother would have grown into a very different person.

The first drops of rain were carried by the rising wind, stinging his face. He pulled his hat lower and huddled down into his slicker. Johnny had a point. It was cold. Resigned, he pushed on, following Johnny, who did give the appearance of knowing which way he was heading. It was a good thing one of them did.

It was closer to two hours before they spied the shack. But although it was spartan, Guy thought it was as welcome a sight as the most exclusive hotel. They settled their horses and fed them from the supplies stored under the eaves before pushing open the battered door of the shack and taking shelter.

Johnny searched the cupboard to scrape together a semblance of a meal while Guy lit a fire. He cursed as the damp wood spat sparks but it looked as though it would catch. Thank heavens. At least there was a chance they'd be able to dry out and get warm again.

Later, after their meager meal, they both huddled at the fire. Johnny had his arms wrapped round himself and there was a bluish tinge to his fingers. Guy reached into his saddlebag and pulled out a flask. "I liberated this from the liquor cupboard before we left. Fancy a snifter?" He held it out to Johnny, who seized it gratefully and took a short swig of whiskey.

"The old man would kill me if I did something like that." Johnny fell silent again.

"Not coming back for dinner was bound to aggravate him. You knew he wanted you to meet Edith."

"I don't jump to no man's tune. And like I said, she sure don't like breeds."

What would it be like to be disliked just because of the color of your skin? Guy thought of the circle he'd mixed with in Boston, remembering the barbed remarks some had made about Negroes. Most of the people who'd made the remarks had never even met a Negro. They were just ignorant and bigoted and doubtless they would have the same opinions of Mexicans, Apaches, or anything outside their personal experience.

"It's strange. When I've met her socially she has been very pleasant and quite entertaining company. But of course in that sort of social setting one would never have an inkling of what prejudices may lie under the surface. It's like the comments of some of the ranchers. At first glance they seem perfectly affable and one wouldn't guess what they really think. I met all sorts in the army and people never fail to surprise me."

"Well, that's the difference between us, Harvard. You're always surprised if people are shit, and I never am." Johnny held his hand out for the flask. At least his fingers didn't look so blue now.

"You really are very cynical."

Johnny grinned. "That's what Delice told me. Said even more than she was." There was a slight ring of pride in Johnny's voice as he spoke. Guy couldn't help but wonder if Johnny knew what cynical meant.

"I was afraid you were going to walk out on us this morning." There, he'd said it, voiced the fear that had been nagging away at him all day.

For a moment he thought Johnny wasn't going to reply. His brother's face was almost entirely hidden in the shadows, out of reach of the light cast by the flickering flames. When Johnny finally spoke, his voice was little more than a whisper. "It's like I can't help myself. I keep pushing and pushing. Sometimes I think maybe I want him to throw me out. And then I get sick inside thinking that's exactly what he'll do. I tell you, I'm finding all this shit so fucking hard. And it don't matter what I do, because I nearly always fuck things up. And the way he looks at me sometimes . . ." Johnny fell silent again. The only sound was from the wood crackling in the hearth.

Guy waited.

"I mean, I wouldn't blame him if he did kick me out. I know that no one really wants Fierro around. The things I've done . . . Things I wouldn't want anyone to know about. Hell, things I wouldn't even tell a priest. And the worst part . . ." He shot an intense look at Guy. "The worst part is, well, I miss it. I like how it made me feel and sometimes all I want . . ." Johnny trailed off as though reluctant to say what he really wanted. Assuming he even knew what he really wanted.

Guy sighed and tried to figure out quite what to say. "It was never going to be easy. I mean, three totally disparate individuals . . ."

"I don't see you and Guthrie as desperate." Johnny looked puzzled.

"No. Disparate, not desperate. It means fundamentally different. We have nothing in common, except of course, blood. We have no shared background. Or not since you were very young. And I spent all those years in Boston. And we're suddenly thrust together as though we can become an instant

213

family. It was always going to be a slow process as we all get to know each other again." Guy paused, wondering how to phrase his next remarks. "But it does seem, sometimes, that you say things you know will irritate him. Like telling him when you've been whoring. It's probably not the wisest approach." He paused again. "It's almost like you're goading him and I don't understand why."

Johnny huddled closer to the fire, his arms wrapped tightly around himself. Guy waited. Sometimes, it seemed, you just had to be patient with Johnny. He'd answer when he was good and ready.

"Hell, Guy, I don't understand why. Like I said, I just can't stop myself. It's like there's a part of me that wants to keep pushing. See how far he'll bend before he breaks. And I guess that I miss the freedom to do what I want. Go where I want. When I want. And, I mean, I know you won't be able to understand this, but I kinda miss . . ." Johnny paused again, kicked at the fire with his foot. "I kinda miss the gunfights, not knowing if I'll walk away. Makes me feel really good. I love that feeling, almost like a woman makes me feel." He trailed off again. "I don't miss the killing. I mean, that had really gotten to me. I told you before I get real bad dreams. I guess if the old man knew what I was really like he wouldn't want me around. An' he's got that fucking report on me and I don't know what's in it."

Guy interrupted. "Is there something specific that you're afraid is in there?"

Johnny stared at him, furrowing his brow as he tried to figure out the question. "You mean one particular thing?"

Guy nodded.

Johnny shook his head. "No. It ain't only one thing. It's a whole load of things that could be in there. I dunno what he knows about me and what he don't. And he sure as hell ain't going to tell me and I ain't asking."

"Johnny, I honestly don't believe you're as bad as you seem to think. OK, you might have done things you regret, but you've done a lot of things you can be proud of, too."

Johnny gave a humorless laugh. "Regret. I've got a shitload of regrets."

"What you need to do is concentrate on the aspects of ranch life that you enjoy. Sure, some of it's boring but a lot of it isn't. Look on it as a new challenge. Hell, you cracked gunfighting, so try something new!"

"It's easier for you," Johnny said softly.

"You might not have lived here in years, but you kept in touch with letters an' all. And you saw him when he went to Boston to visit with you. He talks to you different. He listens to what you say but he never seems to believe me. Like over the bushwhacking."

Guy thought about Johnny's words before answering. His brother had a point. Their father did treat them differently. "I don't think it's that he didn't believe you. I think he was shocked and because it was someone he's known for a long time he didn't want to believe Porter could do such a thing. Human nature, I guess. And as to how he treats you at other times, to be honest, I don't think he has a clue how to deal with you. I think," Guy hesitated, "I think he's terrified you'll leave, go back to your old life, get yourself killed and I think he's so scared of that happening that he won't allow himself to get too attached."

Johnny remained silent for a few moments, as though weighing up Guy's words. "I dunno, I think that he don't trust me and he don't really want me around. I'm already causing trouble for you all. And this trouble in the saloon you told me about. Well, I'll bet he thought I was behind it."

"No, he didn't appear to think that at all. I got the impression that his main concern was that you would have got caught up in it simply by being there. More a case of being in the wrong place at the wrong time." Guy grinned. "We should have known you were tucked up with a girl."

"Two girls, not one, two."

Guy couldn't help but notice that Johnny looked rather pleased with himself as he emphasized this point.

"And which two girls had the dubious pleasure of your company?"

"Sadie and Polly." Johnny looked across at him. "I left your redhead for Jeb Lutz."

"I'm sure she's very grateful," said Guy, drily. "Anyway, it's as well you were there and not in the saloon. They were a nasty bunch by all accounts and giving the impression that they're figuring on staying a while. That town needs a sheriff."

Johnny shrugged. "Folk get what they deserve for the most part. If they're too damn mean to put their hands in their pockets to pay a sheriff, they shouldn't complain when saddle tramps settle and start making trouble. Serve 'em right. They're only concerned for their own skins and treat outsiders like shit."

"Meaning you?"

Johnny shrugged again. "Oh, I don't care what they think of me. And I sure as hell don't expect them to be different. Just pisses me off that folk treat me like shit but expect to use me when it suits 'em."

"You think they'll want you to sort this out? I can't see that happening. I'm sure the men will move on and that'll be an end of it."

"Maybe. Anyway, the people of Cimarron can go hang, because even if they ask, I wouldn't lift a finger to help them." Johnny gave a humorless laugh. "Besides, they couldn't afford me. I'm an awful expensive gun to hire."

Guy raised an eyebrow. "Anyway, I'm sure they're the least of our worries. I'm far more worried about your bushwhacker and the rest of our neighbors."

"Porter won't try nothing else on with me. I scared the shit out of him. And the others, they can go to hell. I'm staying. Or at least until the old man throws me out."

Guy felt a pang of sympathy for his brother. Johnny really did seem to believe that Guthrie would throw him out at some stage. "So even though you miss your old life, you will stay?"

"Didn't say I missed my old life. Just the rush I get when I'm facing someone down. It feels so good. I feel more alive. Like my blood's pumping faster and stronger and it's real exciting. Can't explain it really. But it's a feeling almost like when you're fucking." Johnny tilted his head to one side, listening. "Anyway, it's stopped raining, so maybe we'll stay dry tomorrow. And warm. I'm sacking in now. Didn't get much sleep last night." And with a wink he went and tossed his bedroll in the corner and settled himself down.

"Johnny," Guy spoke softly, "give Father time. It will get easier, I promise. Between us, we'll make the old goat unbend and become more human." His words were rewarded by a laugh from Johnny.

"OK, whatever you say. Just keep the old goat off my back otherwise I might shoot him one of these days. Or take to the bottle. G' night, Harvard, don't snore."

CHAPTER EIGHTEEN

Guthrie watched the two of them ride off before returning to his desk. Nothing was going smoothly. Occasionally, he'd allowed himself to hope that now he had the two of them home, where they belonged, that the ranch would go from strength to strength with everyone pulling their weight. New blood, new ideas. But right now, that prospect seemed far away.

He'd felt a stab of fear earlier that Johnny would actually walk out, but even then he'd been unable to voice it. He hadn't a clue about how to handle his younger son. And it seemed that whatever he said, he put his foot in things.

It was so much easier with Guy. Partly because Guy's upbringing was such that they could have a rational discussion of issues. But mainly because Guy had lived with him until he was seven, and even when he went to stay with his mother's family in

Boston to go to school, they'd corresponded. He knew all about Guy.

But Johnny had been lost for so many years. All Guthrie had were distant memories of holding Johnny in his arms or lifting him onto a horse, or pursuing him through the barns before collapsing in a pile of hay with the toddler, the two of them laughing uproariously together at the chase. Johnny had been such a happy child. But now, try as he might to look for some remnant of that child in the man, it seemed there was nothing left. Instead, Johnny was so remote that Guthrie felt powerless to break through that hard exterior. And Johnny seemed to have no idea how to behave in company or pass the time of day with their neighbors. God only knew what the boy's upbringing had been like for it appeared that Gabriela hadn't taught him even the rudiments of civilized behavior. She had failed their son.

But he was determined that he wouldn't fail Johnny. He'd do everything within his power to keep him safe. He sighed. Safe. That was a joke, with half the local ranchers threatening to shoot him and now the business with Porter. Could Johnny be right? Had Porter tried to bushwhack him? He didn't want to believe that. He wanted to think the whole thing was a dreadful accident. Because he knew, if he did believe it had been deliberate, then anything could happen. And by keeping his son here, he was putting him in as much danger as Johnny faced in his old life.

And what the hell had Johnny meant when he said Edith didn't like Mexicans or breeds? Was Johnny just being extra sensitive because he must have seen so much prejudice around the border? But somehow, he didn't think Johnny had sounded as if he was merely touchy about his mixed parentage. No, he'd sounded as if he was stating a fact.

Edith. Guthrie poured himself a drink. It was odd, but now he came to think of it, Edith didn't employ Mexicans on her ranch. That was very unusual, nearly everyone in the territory employed Mexican vaqueros. Everyone except Edith.

He cast his mind back trying to recall the things Gabriela had said about the neighbors when they'd first been married. She'd complained regularly that all the "gringo women" looked down on her. Gabriela would throw things in rage after coming back from various social mornings, spitting venomous comments about the wives of their neighbors. He'd always tried to calm her down, afraid that she'd injure herself or their unborn child, and she would accuse him of not standing up for her. Of not believing her. Being a typical gringo. And the incidents would usually end with her hurling heavy objects at him and locking him out of their room.

But all of his rancher friends had been so complimentary about Gabriela . . . He wondered now if he'd been blind. If he was honest, he'd known all his friends wanted to bed her. What man wouldn't? But maybe that was the only reason for the compliments; they'd only seen her as someone they'd like to bed whereas he'd always imagined they liked her for herself even if they were attracted to her. He'd been so proud and he knew they all envied him. But he had believed that they and their wives liked her. Could he have been so wrong? Had Gabriela been right when she said the women hated her because she was part Apache and part Mexican? He'd thought maybe the women envied Gabriela her beauty, but he'd never thought they were prejudiced. Maybe, he'd failed her too.

He buried his head in his hands. God! He was a huge success in business but right now it seemed like he was a failure on every other front. If only he knew more about Johnny's past. Maybe it would help him understand the boy. He'd finally plucked up the courage to read the Pinkerton report but it was surprisingly scanty, given all the money he'd paid. It was full of the sort of snippets reported in newspapers, and unsubstantiated reports but it seemed very thin on solid facts. Whoever had compiled it appeared to have relished painting Johnny Fierro as a desperado, but had skimmed over incidents where Johnny's behavior did seem to stand up to closer examination.

What was it Johnny had said to him about that report — something about his father being "robbed?" He could only assume that the report was a mishmash of true and false but there was damned little about the boy's childhood. The Pinkerton men had failed to dig up any information on that. And if Gabriela had died when Johnny was only about ten, what the hell had the boy done after that? Where had he been in those missing years before he started to make his name? He wouldn't bet on Johnny filling in the gaps at any time in the near future. It seemed the past really was past and no questions were permitted on that front. He had the distinct impression that if he tried to press Johnny, the boy really would just up and leave. Hell. What a stinking mess.

And what should he do about Porter? Or

Edith? The last thing he wanted was yet more gossip about Johnny. Because, if he was honest with himself, he didn't know how much more Johnny would take. And if he was certain of one thing, it was that he wanted Johnny to stay.

The rattle of wheels broke into his thoughts. Looking out of the window he could see Edith drawing up outside in her buggy. Well, her arrival would save him a ride. And maybe he'd even learn a thing or two from her. Or about her.

He left the cool of the house to go out and welcome her. "Back so soon, Edith? Come on in out of the heat. It's so sticky there's bound to be a storm before the day is out."

Edith smiled her thanks as he poured her a glass of lemonade from the jug placed there earlier by Peggy. It had sat untouched while he drank whiskey and he knew that Peggy would be upset if it wasn't drunk.

"You must be wondering why I'm back so soon." Edith's tone was tentative. Like she was fishing to find out what he knew about the morning's incident.

"Johnny told me about the business with Porter. It must have been very alarming for you to drive into the middle of it." He kept his comment deliberately neutral. No way would he be condemning his son to outsiders — friends or not.

"Yes, it was. I was in half a mind to continue on my way home but I changed my mind. I wanted to know if he even told you about it. I worry about your safety, Guthrie. I feel that he's a very dangerous young man."

Guthrie smiled at that. "Well, I daresay that he is a very dangerous young man — when he's threatened. But he's no danger to his own family. He's trying to start a new life, Edith. I hoped that you would be able to get to know him."

"Guthrie, I saw him with Mr. Porter, and you didn't. He had his gun to his throat and it looked as though he intended to pull the trigger. If I hadn't come along when I did —"

"Edith," Guthrie interrupted. "As Johnny was under the impression that Porter was trying to bushwhack him, I think we can excuse his reactions. He wanted to know what Porter was up to, that's only natural."

"Bushwhack him!" Edith's tone was scathing. "Guthrie, we both know Mr. Porter. Is it likely that he would do something like that?"

Guthrie looked at her thoughtfully. "I wonder if we ever really know anyone."

She threw him a dubious look. "I'll tell you one thing; we've known Mr. Porter a lot longer than we've known Johnny Fierro."

Guthrie set his glass down sharply. The whiskey spilled over the desk. "Are you seriously asking me to doubt my own son? I may not have known him for long, but I think there's a good man under that hard exterior. He risked his life for the women on this ranch, women he barely knew, simply because he knew what Wallace's men would have done to them if Wallace won. He sought revenge for the murder of two good family men, killed on the cattle drive in the summer. And he did it because he was appalled at what happened to them. Oh, he's a mystery to me, I'll admit that, but he's my son and I trust him." His vehemence surprised him. But oddly, he found he meant his words. Johnny was many things, an enigma, but Guthrie believed that at heart there was a good man hiding in Fierro. A proud man.

Edith looked taken aback by Guthrie's vehemence. "My, my, it seems that Johnny really has wormed his way into your affections."

Wormed. What an unpleasant way of putting it. "I wouldn't say wormed. No one could accuse Johnny of having made it easy for me. But Guy and Ben have both taken to him. And as I'm sure you'll agree, neither of them is a fool."

"No, neither of them is a fool. But I worry for you. His being here is affecting the ranch. Everything you've worked for is threatened by his presence."

"Edith. Don't you realize, everything I worked for, I did so that one day my sons would inherit it? And now they're home. And I intend for it to stay that way. Sinclair will survive. The ranch has faced hard times before and I daresay it will again in the future. But for the time being, people are just going to have to get used to the fact that Johnny has come home."

She flushed. "Well, maybe it's a shame that you didn't see him today, with his gun at Mr. Porter's throat. I can't believe Mr. Porter will just let the matter drop."

Guthrie looked out of the window, pondering her words. "Actually, I think it's rather telling that he hasn't already been to see me to complain. Unless, of course, he's got something to be ashamed of and Johnny was right."

She didn't reply. She sipped her lemonade. It was strange, over the years she'd always made the right noises when he'd discussed his search for Johnny. He wondered about

Johnny's words. She didn't like Mexicans or breeds.

"Why don't you employ any Mexican vaqueros on your ranch?"

She looked startled by the sudden change of topic. "Mexican vaqueros? What on earth made you think of that? Well, I'm not very good at Spanish and it's much easier to deal with people who speak English."

"A lot of them speak excellent English so that shouldn't raise any communication problems. You should employ some. They're loyal workers and very good with stock. I owe the success of my ranch to having such good vaqueros."

Edith sat silently for a few seconds, her hands restlessly turning the glass in her hands. "Well, Guthrie, that's quite a vote of confidence in your Mexicans."

Guthrie raised an eyebrow. "My Mexicans? They're my employees. I don't really give any thought to their bloodlines. But we shouldn't forget that this was their territory originally. To them, this is home. We're the newcomers."

Edith shifted, as though uncomfortable in her chair. "Has Johnny vouchsafed any information about poor Gabriela? It was so distressing for you when she left; I've always wondered what became of her."

"I understand that she became sick and died when Johnny was still very young. Too young to be left to fend for himself. I feel that I failed him by not finding him years ago. I don't intend to fail him again."

"No one forced a gun into his hand." She flushed, as though regretting the tart remark.

Guthrie eyed her thoughtfully. "No, I don't suppose they did. But perhaps as a young boy of mixed blood growing up on the border, faced with prejudice because of the color of his eyes or the color of his skin, he may have felt it was the only way to survive. Prejudice is rife at all levels of society, wouldn't you agree, Edith?"

She slid a dainty fan from her pocket and fanned her face. "I really wouldn't know about that. I'm so busy with the running of my ranch. And my charitable activities with the church amongst some of the poorer families hereabouts take up a great deal of my time, so I really don't know much at all about those sorts of things. I suppose we ladies really don't understand the minds of men."

Guthrie suppressed a smile. "It's not just men who hold prejudices. Women do too. Even my Gabriela apparently met with prejudice in this locality. Surprising, don't you think? The wife of a rancher like myself, fairly successful even in those days, but she faced a great deal of prejudice."

"Well, that really is very unfortunate. I know that myself and my friends all tried to make her welcome when she arrived. But there you are, what would I know about such things?"

"What indeed!"

"Now, I really must be getting back. As you say, it looks as though a storm could be brewing. Do thank Peggy for the lemonade. Such a good girl she's turning out to be. She's a credit to you."

Guthrie stood to escort her to the door. "Well, I'd say she was a credit to her father. Now, Edith, head straight back. I'd avoid the town if I were you. I heard there have been some saddle tramps in, stirring up trouble."

"Why thank you for your concern. I had heard about the trouble. I was worried that your Johnny might have been involved."

Guthrie opened the door and walked with her toward her buggy. "No, Johnny was not involved. Don't worry yourself on that score."

He waved good-bye before walking slowly back to his desk. With a guilty look at the remains of the lemonade, he poured himself another whiskey. And then he started to laugh. Well, well, Johnny Fierro. No education at all. But Johnny could certainly read people. Because he knew now that Johnny's reading of Edith had been spot on. Johnny had seen in two minutes what Guthrie had missed during years of acquaintanceship. His laughter faded. Hell, if Johnny was right about Edith, then maybe he'd been right about Porter. And if Porter had indeed tried to bushwhack him, who else might try the same thing? Was Johnny ever going to be left alone or were they going to spend their lives looking over their shoulders and fearing for his safety?

Chapter Nineteen

The rain had set in again by the following day, and Johnny swore as he tightened another fence line. He hated rain. In the past he'd deliberately stayed south. If he had to sleep rough, it was a damn sight warmer down round the border. But no, here he was with rain dripping down his neck, finding every way it could inside his slicker. He gave the wire a savage twist. Fucking rain. Why was he here? Just pack the whole thing in and head south. He bowed his head briefly, and all the rain cascaded off the brim in front of his face like a veil of tears. And where the hell did that thought come from? A veil of tears? He must have been spending too much time with Harvard.

Head south to the sun. It was odd, but the idea didn't have as much appeal as he thought it would. If only he wasn't so torn up over everything. Felt like he didn't know which way to turn. He was so fucking confused. And Fierro was never confused. Which was why he couldn't handle all of this. This was what drowning must feel like. Everything he felt secure with was sinking under some great wave caused by Guthrie, Sinclair and his ranch and all the demands he made of his son. And if Fierro wasn't careful, there'd be nothing left. He wouldn't exist — he'd be a broken and hobbled beast of burden.

But the alternative was no better. Then he'd felt he was drowning under a sea of bodies of the men he'd killed. And that life would bring even more nightmares. That life was no life at all. The living death of a damned soul. Shit, Fierro. Just mend the damn fences and quit thinking at all.

There were a hell of a lot of fences to mend. He and Guy worked flat-out for the next three days, so tired by the evenings that they both fell asleep almost as soon as they'd finished eating. It was easier that way. Harvard never asked awkward questions when they were eating so leastways he'd managed to avoid any of the man's demands for information about Johnny's past. And Johnny felt he was running out of stories to tell Guy. Most of it he'd never repeat to a living soul. And certainly not to this educated, refined brother. Shit. What the hell would Guy think if he knew the worst of it? Like how Johnny's mother had died and what he'd done. Or the things he'd done when he was starting out to make a name for himself, or what some of Mama's men had done. Or the prison. Oh, God, the prison. Never, never that, not to a living soul. Not even to himself. That was a step too far. He could feel his hands start to shake. With a shudder he took a swig from his water bottle. Then he breathed deeply, trying to slow his heartbeat. Damn it, none of it was anyone's business. They could all fuck off. He wasn't telling no one anything so why was he getting so twisted up about it all? He must be loco, always worrying away at things. Like a dog with a damned bone.

The sound of hooves jerked him back to the present. It was Harvard, back from checking the fences to the west of where they were working.

Guy grinned, an open, easy smile. "I'm delighted to report that this appears to be the end of it. That next stretch was obviously already checked by an earlier line crew and looks good and sound. So, in order to show what a generous and thoughtful soul I am, I shot us a couple of rabbits and I intend to cook us a delicious supper. I even secreted a rather fine Chateau Margaux in with the supplies. I found it in the wine cellar and liberated it because I felt that our father's rather dour, Presbyterian tastes probably don't extend to appreciating the finest of French wines."

Johnny stared at Guy expressionlessly, trying to figure out what the hell the man was talking about. Still rabbit and wine sounded pretty good so he nodded and tried to look like he understood. It would be so much easier if they just spoke the same language. He sometimes wondered if Guthrie understood everything that Guy went on about. But yeah, he probably did. It was only Fierro who was too dumb to figure it all. Well, Fierro and Peggy. But she didn't count, being a girl. She sat openmouthed at times listening to old Harvard like he was some sort of god or something. She'd be catching flies at that rate. Still, she was pretty good at stopping the old man getting too worked up over things. Seemed to know how to calm him down so she was kinda handy to have around. But she made fucking awful tamales. Thank God they had Carlita in the kitchen. Now there was a woman who understood tamales.

"Are you listening to me, Johnny?" Guy

shot him a piercing look. "I asked you if you thought we should try and catch some fish. Then we could have a fish course and it would almost be like a civilized meal."

"Fish? I was thinking about tamales. And chicken mole. And salsa. Now that would be a civilized meal."

Guy grinned. "I'm sure you can talk your way around Carlita when we get home. In the meantime you'll have to make do with my lapin á la moutarde. You'll like it, I promise."

Johnny laughed. "Anything you say. And it has to be worth celebrating if we can head back tomorrow, out of this rain."

Surprisingly, Johnny found he did like Guy's fancy way with rabbit. It tasted a whole lot better than some of Peggy's plain cooking. All those dreary roasts.

"So where didja learn to cook like that? Thought you wouldn't have been allowed near the kitchen. Not with all them servants."

"I learned from a very obliging young lady when I was in France."

"Obliging?" Johnny grinned. Now that was more like it. "I guess when you say obliging, you mean obliging in more than just the cooking department?"

Guy raised an eyebrow. "A gentleman

never talks about his conquests."

Johnny stared at him, what the hell was he talking about now? "Well, I don't know about your conquests, what I meant was did you get to fuck her?"

Guy gave an exaggerated sigh and poured them both another glass of wine. "In answer to your somewhat crude inquiry, yes, I got to fuck her. As well as learning how to cook rabbit."

Johnny thought about that. "Tell you something — I'd have skipped the cooking and spent more time fucking. You got a lot to learn. Sometimes I worry about you." He took a sip of his wine. Real slow, like Guy did, so the man wouldn't accuse him of not "savoring the aroma" whatever that meant. Funny thing though, he found he enjoyed the wine more when he drank it slow, so maybe Harvard had a point.

"Do you ever think about anything other than women?"

Johnny decided to answer seriously. "Yeah. Gunfights. And these days I find myself thinking about fences and alfalfa. I mean, shit, Johnny Fierro trying to calculate how much fucking wire we need or how many acres of alfalfa to plant. I should stick to thinking about fucking."

Guy was laughing now. "One of these days

238

you're going to surprise us all and fall in love. And all the whores in Cimarron will go into mourning. Always assuming that you really are as good at it as you're always telling me."

"Oh, I'm good. And it would be kind of a shame to keep myself for just one woman. Wouldn't be fair on the rest of 'em. Hell, I got 'em lining up for me."

Guy snorted with laughter. "Can't say that I've ever noticed that."

"That's 'cos you go round with your eyes closed. You never notice half of what's going on around you. That's going to get you killed one of these days. You're out west now and you need to smarten up."

Guy shrugged. "Good thing I've got you to watch my back, then."

"What makes you think I'll watch it for you?"

"Apart from the fact that you watched it when we were in Bitterville? Let's just call it a hunch. And I, in my own incompetent eastern way, will watch yours."

Johnny tried to stop the smile spreading. "I ain't sure that knowing you're watching my back will help me sleep better."

Guy leaned over and got another bottle of wine out. "Afraid we've drunk the good stuff, but this should be passable." He

239

poured a hefty amount into Johnny's glass. "How did you start as a gunfighter?"

Johnny furrowed his brow, puzzled. "What do you mean? I got myself a gun and started hiring out. I told you how I used to practice."

"Yes, but did someone help you start out? I don't understand how you managed at the beginning."

The beginning? When the hell had that been? Long before he'd ever picked up a gun. It was just part of him. Like the dream had taken control of him. And becoming a gunfighter had been his destiny. Yeah, that was the word. Destiny.

"There was someone . . ." He paused. Didn't know if he wanted to go down this road. Didn't want anyone to know too much about him. But shit, seemed like Guy always wanted to know things. And he knew he could trust him not to blab to anyone.

"Who?" Guy's voice intruded into his thoughts.

Johnny shrugged. "Oh, just a man."

"You can't leave it there. That's no way to tell a story."

"Didn't know I was." He looked across at Guy, who simply raised his eyebrow in a kind of questioning way. "It was after I'd been in prison." Shit. Not the prison.

"Where they sent you for stealing bread? I still can't believe they sent a boy of twelve or thirteen to prison for stealing bread."

"Yeah. Well, the bread was only the start of it. They threw me in jail and I knocked out the sheriff when I was trying to escape. I guess that was the part they didn't like."

Guy grinned. "I don't suppose they did. So, you met this person later?"

"Yeah. I moved around, looking for work, trying to earn enough to buy bullets so I could keep practicing. And I had this scruffy old horse I'd found. Didn't seem to belong to no one so I used to ride him and travel about."

"Bareback?"

"Well of course fucking bareback. Where d'you think I'd get a saddle from?" Johnny ran his hand through his hair. "Anyhow, I was always hungry and sometimes I'd hold up a traveler if they looked like they could spare some supplies. I'd relieve them of their load." Johnny grinned at the memories.

"Very considerate of you."

"Yeah. I thought so. Anyway, I saw three men coming along the road and they had a mule. I figured they could spare something so I just rode right out in front of them with my gun drawn. I told them I was going to take some of their food. But I must have been fucking hungry and not thinking straight because when I took a good look at them I realized they'd got their guns tied down, like professionals. Almost shit myself, but figured I'd have to bluff my way through.

"But their leader looked kind of amused that I was holding them up. Must have looked pretty funny. I was a scrawny kid, barefoot with old raggedy clothes and an old raggedy horse. And a gun that was so heavy it used to take all my strength to hold the damn thing straight. Anyhow, he said I was welcome to some of their supplies, but they were making camp about a mile farther on and if I wanted I could join them for a hot meal.

"A hot meal." Johnny shook his head. "I hadn't had one of those since the prison. But I figured it was a trap and asked if they thought I was dumb or something." Johnny took a sip of his wine. "Their leader, this big gringo, said they'd ride in front of me and keep their hands on their saddle pommels and I could follow them with my gun out, so I knew they wouldn't try anything. But I figured they probably thought I didn't know how to use it, so I told them I'd killed before and I wasn't afraid to do it again."

Guy's head shot up. "Killed before? You

were just telling them that, right?"

Shit. That was the trouble with talking, you could give yourself away. Especially after wine. It's why he hardly ever drank. It left you open. Tripped you up. "Well, I didn't want them thinking I was a push-over." That was it. Not actually telling a lie to Harvard but sidestepping the question. "So I followed them because I had a real hankering for a hot meal." That and the need for company. He'd never realized quite how lonesome it could be when it was only him and the horse for weeks on end. Not that he'd ever admit to being lonesome.

"This gringo made the others take their guns off so that I could trust them to build a fire. I was a real innocent back then. Never occurred to me they'd have guns in their jackets too."

Guy jerked forward. "Hell! Did they pull their guns on you?"

Johnny laughed. "No. But they could have. They just built the fire and cooked the meal. And asked what I was doing out there and where I got my gun. I told them I was going to be the fastest pistolero anyone had ever seen. They looked like they thought that was kind of funny but they didn't really laugh at me. They told me they were gunfighters and their leader said if I wanted, I could stay the night and they'd have a look at my draw in the morning. Tell me if I was any good."

Johnny fell silent. Remembering how the hope had welled up at their offer. But how he'd also wondered what price they'd make him pay. How he'd wondered if all three of them would . . . "So I said I'd camp at the edge of their camp, but if any of them came to take my gun in the night, I'd kill them." He'd told them something slightly different to that, but there was no way he was telling Guy what he'd suspected, or what he'd said.

"And did they try to take your gun?" Guy sounded curious.

Johnny felt a sudden lump in his throat. "No. Instead of sitting on guard, I fell asleep. When I woke in the morning some-one had put a blanket over me and tucked the gun in next to me." He was silent for a second. Hadn't known what to make of that, but back then he'd figured it must have been some kind of a trick. "Anyway, after breakfast, they set up some cans and told me to shoot them. Not draw, just see if I could hit them. Which I did. So they put up some bottles and said see if I could draw and hit them. Got each one through the neck. Then their boss asked if I could hit them with his gun. So although the first was a bit off, I got the feel of the gun and hit all the others."

"Through the neck again?" Guy sounded impressed.

"Yeah. Through the neck. They each made me try their guns. And then the boss wanted me to draw again. And all the time, all I wanted to know was what he thought. But he was kinda quiet at first. Then he said my draw was crap." Johnny shook his head. Damn but those words had hurt. "I got mad and said he could go fuck himself. Said they'd see in time, I would be the best. And I started to leave but he told me to shut up and just listen. Then he said they needed a fourth man, and he said I had a smart mouth which would come in handy. He said they'd teach me all the tricks. Then he said something strange. He said if I agreed to join them, I had to promise that when I went solo I'd never draw down on any of them. Hell, I was still real mad and asked why the hell he would worry about that when he thought I was crap."

Johnny paused again. It was all flooding back like it was yesterday. "And he looked at me and said, 'Son, your draw's crap because you're wearing your gun all wrong. But I know real talent when I see it. And my guess is that you will be the fastest pistolero any of us has ever seen and I sure as hell don't want to be facing the wrong end of your gun when that day comes.' Shit, I couldn't believe it. It was all I'd ever wanted and here was this professional telling me I really did have what it takes."

Johnny fell silent. No way would he tell Guy that he'd then demanded to know what else the men would want to do with him. Or that deep down, he'd known he'd have put up with anything to learn his trade. But the men weren't like that. The leader had looked kinda sad at Johnny's words. Said their tastes ran to whores and all that was required from Johnny was to keep a civil tongue in his head and get along with them all.

"Were they kind to you?" The wording of Guy's question surprised Johnny and he looked at Guy sharply, wondering if his brother suspected. But he thought not. Guy was seeing him as a young kid, not realizing how very old Johnny had been even then. Hell, he'd been old for a very long time.

"Yeah. Luke — his name was Luke — tried to give me a bit of schooling. Told me where different countries were, how to add up so I could handle deals, that kinda thing. Tried to teach me table manners too but he said I was beyond hope. He only ever hit me once."

"What for?"

"They took me to a whorehouse, and I was lippy with one of the girls. Luke asked them to excuse us, took me outside and then hit me really hard across the mouth. Said didn't I know that none of those girls wanted to be there. Wasn't their dream when they were growing up. But when you're a girl and you're cold enough and hungry enough, you'll do anything to survive. Said how it was easier for boys, they could always find work, and he said how if I'd been born a girl that's where I would have ended up. And he was right. And I've never fucking forgotten it either."

Guy shuffled across to grab the bottle and top up their glasses. "So how long did you stay with them?"

Johnny frowned. "I dunno. Maybe eighteen months. But I wanted to go my own way and make a name. Luke knew that. Night before I was due to leave, we had a meal around the campfire and drank too much whiskey. But he said he wanted me to promise him something. I told him I hadn't forgotten my promise not to draw on them. But he said he wanted something else as well. Said if I ever tracked down my old man, he wanted me to listen to him. He said if I found out that it was like Mama said, then shoot him and good riddance. But he said there're two sides to every story and he thought I should hear my father's side. Shit. Everyone could tell what a liar my mother had been, everyone except me."

"That other gunfighter said the same to you, didn't he? The one who helped you when you were whipped?"

"Yeah. I wonder what the old man would say if he knew he owed his life to two gunfighters." Johnny sighed. "I'm turning in. These bedtime stories wear me out. Still, least we get to ride back tomorrow. I must be getting old, I want a proper bed."

Guy grinned. "It will be very welcome, I admit. No wonder Father wanted us around. He doesn't have to go out and do things like this anymore. He can sit by the fire, in his favorite chair, drinking his best Scotch."

Johnny snorted. "Yeah, in the dry. And not getting cold. Lucky bastard. G'night. Try not to snore."

CHAPTER TWENTY

Guy snored but that wasn't what woke Johnny up. It was the dreams, as always. Faces of men he'd killed, fields of blood, and the prison . . . Long before dawn, he gave up trying to sleep, angry with himself. Should never have told Guy about how he started out. Should have known it would give him a bad night. Hell, he got little enough sleep as it was, he didn't need to lose even more.

He wriggled out of his bedroll and wrapped it around him before shuffling to the window. The rain had stopped but a heavy layer of cloud blocked the moon. Moonlight was pure and clean, which he always found soothing. But on nights like this, the darkness could be suffocating. It was like being buried alive. He could almost feel the darkness like dirt in his mouth and his throat.

He looked east, hoping to see the early

traces of dawn, but there was no soft warming glow. It just looked slightly less black that the other blackness, like it was an omen. Shit. Where did these thoughts come from? How dumb did that sound? A dark dawn as an omen. He really was loco.

He chewed on his lip, wondering if he should check his saddlebags. That would calm him. It always calmed him. A man couldn't be too careful . . . Sighing softly, he grabbed his saddlebags and went through them methodically. It was like a ritual as he checked each bag for bullets, and shells for his rifle. Then he checked his knives, and the threaded needle he kept in his jacket, always to hand if he got shot up. He rubbed at an old scar on his shoulder, remembering the times he'd had to find somewhere to lie low and try to heal up. It was the motto he lived by — never let anyone see him at his weakest.

What would Guy say if he knew the number of times Johnny Fierro had dug bullets out of himself? Guy probably thought Johnny carried that bottle of tequila for drinking. But it had other, more important, uses, although it stung like hell when he sloshed it over a wound. Still, it did the trick.

He peered over to the window, hoping again for a glimmer of dawn. Damn but he felt old. He was too young to feel this old but he was worn out from years of fighting to survive. Deep down he'd hoped life would be easier at the ranch. It sure was different, but not easier. And just like he'd always expected, no one wanted him around. The ranch was going to suffer because of him.

Should he leave? It was the hundredth time he'd asked himself that in recent days. Hated to think Guy and Guthrie would be out of pocket simply because of his presence. It wasn't fair to them. But then, when was life ever fair? Life was a bitch whichever way a man looked at it. He would have left, but back at the ranch, just for a second he'd seen a glimmer of something in the old man's eyes, something that said his father wanted Fierro to stay. Johnny ran his hand through his hair, trying to figure it out. But yeah, the old man had looked as though he'd meant what he said, before the shutters came down again and Johnny hadn't a clue what he was thinking. Shit, the old man was hard to figure.

His father irritated the hell out of him sometimes, like the way he'd listen to Guy but was quick to yell at Johnny. But all the workers liked him. The old man treated his men and their families fairly and he paid good wages. He expected a lot in return but when a man was sick or his family was ill, Guthrie Sinclair always did what Johnny considered the right thing. That said a lot about a man. Most ranchers were only concerned about how much work they could get out of their vaqueros, caring only for their profit. But Guthrie seemed to have different values. Even faced with the ranch taking a hit because of the latest stunt by the cattlemen, his father had said they'd deal with it as a family.

Family. He couldn't figure that at all. Still didn't know what was expected of him and it sure felt like he was on trial. Why would they want him? That was what he asked himself most and it was a question he couldn't answer.

The sound of Guy stirring dragged his thoughts back to the present. "You're up early." Guy peered blearily at Johnny. "I think perhaps I should have had a little less wine last night."

Johnny grinned. "Thought you said good wine doesn't give you a hangover."

Guy winced as he sat up. "I think the damage was caused by the second bottle. It wasn't a good vintage."

"Ah." Johnny kept his face straight and his tone neutral. "So nothing to do with the whiskey after dinner and the tequila we drank while you were cooking?"

Guy gave a half smile. "No. Nothing whatever to do with that."

"Well, you'd better get moving, because I think there's more rain coming and we should try to keep ahead of it."

They'd packed the night before, so after a quick cup of coffee they mounted up and hit the trail.

Johnny could feel the rain in the air, and the heavy cloud still blocked out the real signs of dawn. He pulled his slicker up around him, shivering as he did so. Pushing his hat forward, he urged Pistol into a lope.

They kept up as fast a pace as possible but frequently had to slow when the going became too rocky. Johnny looked across at Guy. "I'll be glad to get home. I'm going to have a good long soak but right now it feels like I'll never be warm again."

Guy grinned. "For a hardened gunfighter you really do like moaning about the cold. Doesn't do your tough-guy image any good at all."

"That's OK. If you tell anyone, I'll just shoot you."

"Do you think Porter will have made trouble in our absence?"

Johnny thought about it briefly. "No, I

don't. I think I scared the shit out of him and he won't want to push his luck." He gave a short laugh as he remembered how Porter had been shaking with fear. "I still think I should have finished him off. He's trouble. And I'd bet he'll try that trick again on someone. But not on me. I bet dear Edith's kicked up a stink, though."

Guy glanced across. "Father said he'd try and smooth things over. Keep her quiet."

Johnny shrugged. "I dunno. He'll listen to her story over mine any day. Don't matter none. She didn't really see much. I wasn't breaking any law so she can think what she damn well likes."

Guy pulled his hat lower. "She seems very anxious for our father's good opinion so I expect she'll leave well enough alone. Anyway, we're going to be too busy planning the fall roundup to worry about what anyone thinks. I think Father sees it as our first legitimate test. It gives him a chance to see what we're made of and something tells me you won't moan about the cold when he's around."

Johnny had to laugh. Harvard was too smart at times and he was right. No way would he be griping in front of the old man. To hell with that. Guthrie was more than quick enough to find fault with Fierro and he had no intention of making that easier for the man. "No, I guess I won't. But the fall roundup will be straightforward. It's not like a real big drive. Taking herds through swollen rivers, now that's dangerous. But the roundup to move cows and calves closer in for winter? Well, that's easy."

"You've done it before?"

Johnny shrugged. "I've helped out when money's been short or I've been lying low. And they always like someone to camp away from the main herd so it suited me. Meant I could usually stay on my own. It was better that way. Now quit talking, and let's get moving." He spurred Pistol on. All this talking. Didn't his brother ever run out of things to say?

But give the man his due, Harvard took the hint and for the next few hours they pushed hard, figuring they could be back at the ranch that night. The rain was chasing their tails but at least they weren't riding into it and somehow, the thought of home was comforting. Strange, but it was good to think of his own room waiting for him. And a hot meal.

They finally paused on a ridge where they could see the ranch nestled in the valley below. Lights glowed in the hacienda as dusk settled. It looked like it was welcoming them back. And it felt good.

Johnny took off down the hill. Pistol took on a new lease of energy, doubtless scenting a warm stable and a bran mash. And Guy followed close on their heels as they galloped into the yard by the big barn.

Johnny's gut clenched as he saw Guthrie coming out of the house toward them. Shit. What now? He was bound to be in trouble for something. And he was too tired for a fight. Maybe he should have gone to town instead of coming straight home.

"Good trip, boys?"

Well, he sounded cheerful, and he was smiling. Johnny realized he'd been holding his breath, expecting trouble. But it seemed at least this time he needn't have worried. The old man looked quite friendly, almost like he was pleased to see them back.

Guy was talking cheerfully. Telling him they'd been working hard and had fixed all the weak spots in the fence lines. And the old man was nodding happily. So why couldn't Fierro think of something to say? How come it was so easy for Guy? He wished he could do that. "Guthrie." He spoke softly. Tried to think of something else to say. "Everything been OK here?"

"Absolutely fine, Johnny, but it's good to see you both back. And good to hear it went well. One job less for us to worry about."

Johnny didn't mention Porter till after dinner. Figured he might as well enjoy some peace while the old man was in a good mood. But the question was eating away at him. He slumped on the couch, trying to figure out how to raise the question.

"Has Porter paid you a visit?" He blurted the words out.

Guthrie cocked an eyebrow, but didn't look too pissed with him. "No, he hasn't and I found that quite telling. Seems he's not talking about it, either. There hasn't been any gossip so I guess he doesn't want people to know about it. One could almost think he has something to hide."

Johnny's head jerked up. Almost sounded like the old man had decided Johnny's version of events might be the truth. "And your friend, Mrs. Walsh?"

Guthrie smiled. "Oh yes, she came to see me, not long after you two boys left. That was interesting too." The man fell silent for a minute, and then looked at Johnny, almost like he was embarrassed. "And I think I owe you an apology, Johnny. You said she didn't like Mexicans and in all the years I've known her, I'd never noticed that. But I think you're right. Seems I didn't know her half as well as I thought. All these years I

257

thought of her as a good friend. But I never noticed that."

Johnny couldn't believe what he was hearing: the old man apologizing to him? He tried to think of something to say; to get it right for once and not put his foot in it. "Guthrie, it don't matter none. She's no different from a lot of folk. It doesn't bother me. There's a lot of people hate breeds more than she does. I mean, what I'm saying is, I wouldn't want you to feel bad about seeing her."

Guthrie smiled. "Let's just say, then, that I will see her differently from now on. The scales have fallen from my eyes."

Johnny raised an eyebrow. That was one he hadn't heard before, but he kind of got the picture. "And have those saddle tramps moved on?"

Guthrie shook his head. "No. I've told the hands to avoid Cimarron for the time being. There've been too many fights in the town and a lot of gunplay and I certainly don't want anyone from here caught up in it. We're getting our supplies from Elizabethtown, but Cimarron needs a sheriff if it's to continue to thrive."

Johnny shrugged. "You can't force law onto people. They get what they deserve if they ain't willing to put their hands in their pockets."

Guthrie rubbed his chin, and shook his head. "Sometimes things need a helping hand. If things were better with the Cattlemen's Association at the moment I'd suggest we share the cost of a sheriff until the town sees the benefits, but this is probably not the time to raise the subject. So, for the time being, we'll avoid town until those tramps have moved on."

"What you're saying is you want me to stay away from Cimarron for the time being?"

Guthrie nodded. "We discussed it before and it would mean a lot to me."

It would mean a lot to him. Johnny stared at him. The words sounded so strange. Like the man cared. Johnny pulled at a loose thread on his shirt. His mouth quirked into a grin. "OK. For a week or two, if it keeps you happy." Johnny hauled himself to his feet. He wanted his bed.

Guthrie smiled. "Thanks, it would keep me happy. See you in the morning."

Chapter Twenty-One

Johnny tried hard over the next few days to keep the old man sweet. Worked his guts out, kept his head down. He even went through the books to see if he could find ways to save money. They were only in this mess because of him. But it felt good not to be butting heads all the time. He knew it wouldn't last but he was going to enjoy it while it did. Guy had headed out with the crew to the eastern pastures to start roundup while Johnny took a bunch of men and moved the bulls away from the ranch. If they were bringing cows and calves in, they didn't want the bulls around.

He'd wondered about his father sending Guy off with the men and keeping Johnny closer to home — maybe the old man just didn't trust him. But Guthrie had seemed OK, friendly even. Maybe, just maybe, he could still make this work. And by working so hard he found he didn't miss the rush that his old life had given him. Or least-ways, didn't miss it as much. Seemed the best way to deal with it was to wear himself out during the day so he fell into bed at night and didn't have the energy to think about anything.

Didn't stop the dreams though. But hell, he was used to those and he guessed they wouldn't ever stop. He sometimes wondered what it would feel like not to be haunted by the past. If life had been different and if Mama had never left Sinclair and he'd grown up here, would he have still ended up as a gunfighter? Was he born bad? Or could it have been different? He huffed out a sigh. He really had to quit worrying over these things. He couldn't change the past. Things were what they were and he had to live with it.

He was clearing out the big barn when he heard the clatter of hooves. Peering from the gloom into the sunny yard, he saw a bunch of men from the Cattlemen's Association. Six of them. He watched as his father came out to speak to them and wished he could hear what they were saying. They followed his father into the house.

Damn it. He wanted to hear what the hell they wanted. Because all his senses said the men were here to see him and not the old man. Something to do with Porter, maybe? No, that didn't feel right. This was something else.

Making a decision, he darted across the courtyard and slipped in the side door to the house. He could hear them talking in the living room.

"Not here on ranch business, Guthrie. We need to talk to Fierro."

"Fierro? I believe you mean my son, Johnny Sinclair. He's working at the moment. And why the delegation?"

"There's an important matter we need to discuss with him. Can't you call him in?"

Johnny stepped into the room. "I'm listening." He spoke softly, enjoying the looks of startled surprise on the men's faces. Good. He had the edge now. But Guthrie looked worried and pretty pissed off as well.

Donovan slapped his hat against his thigh. "There's been a lot of trouble in town, Fierro. Saddle tramps causing trouble. We can't let our womenfolk near the place because of those men. They've been causing fights, even smashed up a couple of stores yesterday."

Johnny raised an eyebrow slightly. "Is that so? Well, it ain't really my concern, is it?"

"We could make it your concern." A thin-faced man chipped in. He had nervy, darting eyes, the sort of fellow who never had no balls for anything.

"What is it you want with Johnny?" A vein was pulsing in Guthrie's temple.

"We need him, Guthrie. There's been a load of trouble in Cimarron and we need someone to straighten it out before it gets totally out of hand."

"We'll make it worth your while, Fierro." The thin-faced fellow gave an oily smile. "Say, five hundred dollars worth your while."

Guthrie turned an interesting shade of red.

Johnny figured he'd better say something before the old man had a seizure. "You want me to deal with some trouble?"

"That's what you do, isn't it?"

Johnny let his gaze wander over them, a smile playing around his mouth. "But I thought you didn't want the likes of me in your valley. What was it you said, something about me being a threat to good law-abiding folks? Something about me being scum? And yet, here you all are, asking for my help?"

"We're prepared to pay you a fair price to deal with those troublemakers. Five hundred dollars is a lot of money, Fierro."

"Five hundred dollars? Well, trouble is,

I'm an awful expensive gun to hire. And, I tell you, five hundred dollars just wouldn't be enough to buy my gun to sort out a bunch of saddle tramps. Seems to me there's a crowd of you. Get together, deal with it yourselves. I guess you outnumber them. You don't need no hired gun."

The nervy fellow paled. "We're not gunmen, Fierro. We're law-abiding ranchers. We wouldn't have any idea how to handle a bunch of troublemakers like these."

Johnny bowed his head briefly. He scuffed the floor with the toe of his boot before looking back up at the man who was chewing on his lip. "Law-abiding ranchers? But I guess you all know one end of a gun from the other. It's your town, your problem. Seems like none of you got a set of cojones."

"OK, Fierro. Seven hundred and fifty dollars. Dealing with those men would be nothing to you. There's only five of them."

Johnny stared back, not letting any expression show on his face. "Only five of them. And one of me. As opposed to a whole town of menfolk."

Donovan slapped his hat against the wall. "Seven hundred and fifty dollars, Fierro. That's an awful lot of money. Particularly to a man like you."

"Think so?" He shrugged. "Don't matter

'cause I don't hire out no more. My old man there don't like it. So, if you take my advice, you'll grow some balls, deal with it yourselves and then get yourselves a sheriff. Now if you'll excuse me, I got some real pressing business to attend to. It's my siesta time." He turned and walked out of the room, his spurs jangling as he headed toward the stairs.

He laughed softly at the outburst of voices. "Guthrie, call him back. Make him see sense."

"You tell that boy of yours to do his duty by the town."

"Tell him he's got to help us. It would be an easy job for someone like him."

Johnny paused at the foot of the stairs, listening as his father spoke, louder than the lot of them. "My God! Look at you all. Listen to yourselves! You've one hell of a nerve coming here and demanding Johnny risk his life to help you out. You've all told me how you resent his presence here. Told me I should send him packing because you didn't want the likes of him in this valley. Those were your words, I believe. Well, I've got news for you all, he's staying. This is his home, where he belongs and he's here to stay whether you like it or not. He doesn't owe any of you anything. And neither does he hire out anymore. So, I suggest you take his advice and deal with your problems yourselves. If you hadn't all been so tight-fisted, and had paid for a sheriff, then maybe you wouldn't have this problem. I have work to do, so get out, now!"

Johnny's eyes widened. He stood frozen to the spot, too stunned to do anything for a few seconds . . . Damn! His old man was standing up for him. It was almost as if his father actually cared about his no-good gunfighter son. Although why the hell Guthrie should care was a mystery. Even so . . . The man had backed him . . . Why?

Because they were on the same side, maybe?

Johnny bowed his head, remembering De-lice's words. Hell, maybe she was right.

He unbuckled his spurs and slipped quietly up to his room. He wasn't surprised that the men had wanted to hire him. It was always the same. They treated him like dirt until they needed him. And then, once he'd fixed things, they wouldn't want to know him again. People were shit. Wouldn't matter where a man went, folk wouldn't be no different. So no surprises there. But Guthrie had surprised him. And not for the first time.

Footsteps echoed along the passageway.

There was a knock on his door. And all he wanted was to be left alone to think a while. He sighed. "Yeah."

"Johnny." His father pushed open the door, slow like maybe he expected to be yelled at. He looked at Johnny, his brow furrowed. "You all right?"

Johnny frowned. "I'm fine, why wouldn't I be?" He gestured toward the window. "They gone?"

Guthrie nodded. "I couldn't believe their nerve coming here to ask you that."

Johnny bit back a laugh. "What else would they do? They got trouble. They figure the best way to deal with it is to pay someone to do their dirty work for them. That way they don't get their hands dirty or risk their own skin. It's what folk are like. It's an ugly world. Full of small-minded, ugly people." Johnny shrugged and let out a long sigh. "They don't bother me none. I'm used to it. Hell, it's how I made my living. People are quick to use me when they got trouble, and as soon as it's over, they want me gone."

He locked eyes with his father and shrugged again. "It's how it is."

His father was silent for a moment, like he was trying to decide what to say. "I suppose I've never really thought how difficult this is for you. This different life. For what it's worth, Johnny, I was proud of you down there. You handled it well." Guthrie gave him a brief smile. "I'll leave you, um . . ." His father suddenly laughed. "To have that siesta."

As the door closed, Johnny fell back onto his bed, his gut churning and his heart thumping like it was going to bust out of his chest. Couldn't believe what the man had just said. Proud of him! And said it like he meant it. Proud. Johnny shook his head and tried to swallow the lump in his throat. Couldn't figure it at all. All he'd done was tell them he wasn't buying into their game.

He didn't think anyone had ever been proud of him. Mama sure hadn't been proud. Told him often enough he was just a burden. A load of fucking trouble. Blue-eyed trouble. More trouble than he was worth, she'd said.

Proud?

How could anyone be proud of him? If his father knew what he was really like, he wouldn't be proud. Not if he knew Fierro.

But his father had told those men his son was staying. That he was home. Where he belonged. Shit. Where he belonged? Could he belong here? He eased himself off the bed and padded to the window. Looking across at the mountains that rose steeply behind the ranch, his favorite peak caught his eye. It always did. He must have spent hours staring at it since he'd been back. He loved it when it was flushed pink by a fiery dawn. Or when, swathed in cloud, the tip would peek out, seeming to call to him.

He turned away, overwhelmed suddenly by a torrent of emotions.

Proud.

Where he belonged?

But surely the old man would see through him at some point? No one could want Fierro, could they? No, at some point the old man would see him for what he was. A priest had told Johnny he was a damned soul. And priests knew about things like that.

He pushed the thought away. He just wanted to enjoy the warm feeling. His father had said he was proud of him. Him. Johnny Fierro. Shit. Never thought he'd hear anyone say that — let alone his father, who looked like he could carry the world on his shoulders. He shook his head again. Turning, he glimpsed himself in the mirror. He had a silly grin on his face.

That barn still needed clearing. There was a lot of work to be done over the next few days before Guy returned with the cows. And hell, it wouldn't do to piss off the old man by not pulling his weight. He strapped his spurs back on. They jingled as he hurried down the stairs and he realized he was whistling.

CHAPTER TWENTY-TWO

Peggy could sure drone on when she had a mind to. And she had a mind to right now. Going on about how she couldn't see her friends because the old man wouldn't let her go into Cimarron. She'd been stomping around the house like a bear with a sore head since she'd been confined to the ranch.

Not that Johnny could see why it mattered. All she and her friends did when they got together was giggle and whisper. If they had a drink and game of poker he could understand it. But no, they simply huddled together whispering. Some of her friends had come to call at the ranch in the past. He'd tried to be friendly. Well, maybe not real friendly, but he'd tipped his hat to them. An' all they did was turn bright red like they'd been in the sun too long.

He forked another mouthful of Peggy's stew. He'd rather be eating that fancy rabbit with mustard. And by the look on Guy's face, he was thinking the same thing. Poor old Harvard. He'd been moving cows for days and he had to come back to a meal like this. Pity it was Carlita's day off. Least-ways then they'd have gotten a proper meal. Not stew.

"Peggy, you're not going into town, and that's final."

The way the old man said it sure shut her up. She turned bright red and her lip trembled.

He thought maybe, just for once, he'd try and start some talk. "When Guy and me were checking those lines up north, he cooked some rabbit real fancy, Peggy. You should get him to teach you."

"And what's that meant to mean?" Her face turned a deeper shade of red, and her lip wobbled even more. "Are you saying my cooking's not good enough, Johnny?"

Hell! He'd only mentioned the rabbit. An' Guy was raising his eyes like Johnny was dumb or something. This was why it was safer not to start any talk at the table. He always said the wrong thing. Johnny shook his head. "No. I just said you should get him to teach you. It was real good. I thought you could add it to all them dishes you do."

"To her repertoire." Guy said it soft. Like he was scared.

"Uncle Guthrie, tell them to stop complaining about my cooking. It's not fair. I do my best."

The old man gave a big sigh. "Peggy, Johnny was not criticizing your cooking. He was simply telling us that Guy can apparently cook rabbit 'real fancy.' " The old man said the last bit like he was copying Johnny.

Johnny bit back a smile. Peggy would probably throw something at him if he laughed. And it never paid to piss off the person who cooked your food. Guy had once pissed off Carlita and the chili verde had been so hot that night that even Johnny had found it hard to eat.

Peggy started banging the dishes around, carrying them off into the kitchen.

"That rabbit was real good." But he said it soft so only Guthrie and Guy heard.

"Drink, boys?" Guthrie went to the liquor cabinet and poured himself a good measure.

"I'll join you in that. I think we deserve it." Guy walked over to take a drink, wincing at the sound of splintering glass in the kitchen. He proffered a glass. "Johnny?"

Johnny shook his head. Drink loosened a man's tongue. And that was never a good thing. Especially with the old man around. And although they were getting along better, he liked to keep a close watch on everything when Guthrie was there. Never give anything away. It was safer that way.

"You know," Guy hesitated, "I think we should do something about a sheriff for Cimarron."

Guthrie sank into his favorite chair and shot Guy a quick glance. He nodded slowly. "That's an excellent idea. You could ride to Santa Fe and advertise in the newspaper, and maybe send a couple of wires to other towns. If we carry the cost for a few months, the town folk would see the benefit and could then take on the responsibility."

Guy perched on the arm of the couch. "I think that's a good plan. What say you, Johnny?"

Johnny shrugged. "Don't see why it's our problem. We're already down because of the cattlemen and the shipments. Let them pay."

Guthrie leaned back in his chair and rubbed his chin. He shook his head. "No, I think it would smooth things over with the neighbors. And it's in our interests to clean up Cimarron. The hands like to go there on Saturday nights. It's closer than Elizabethtown. And it's a thriving place and we should encourage that."

"And it will put Peggy in a good mood again and the cooking may improve." Guy winked at Johnny.

Guthrie smiled. "Well, that too."

Johnny kicked at the floor with his boot. Mud still clung to the heel. Just as well Peggy hadn't noticed. She'd have tipped the stew over his head. He shook his head. "No sheriff will want to come in and deal with five men."

"Maybe they'll move on. They'll get bored, and want some new entertainment."

Johnny grunted at Guthrie's words. In his experience, people like these saddle tramps tended to stay put when they were getting things their own way. And it didn't look like the cattlemen had the balls to deal with them. He had the feeling at some point he'd have to take care of it. Still, the town could sweat a while longer. Johnny wasn't hurrying for no man, especially a bunch of gringo cattlemen. He shrugged. "Whatever you think best."

"I'll head off in the morning, then." Guy looked happy. Dios, the man had a lot to learn about life out west. Problems tended to need real men, not some new sheriff or some smart-ass lawyer. But then again, maybe Guy had a woman stashed in Santa Fe. Now that would make more sense and sure explain him being in such a hurry.

"Yeah, you go tomorrow. We can manage fine." Johnny grinned. Shit, he was tired.

"I'm turning in. I'll see you before you leave."

He was thankful the evening was over. He still never said the right thing at meals, but if he didn't say anything, that pissed off everyone. Why couldn't they concentrate on eating? That's what they were there for, after all. And life would be one hell of a lot simpler.

The moon cast a comforting glow around his room. He stood by the open window listening to the lowing of the cattle. There was a chill in the air at night now, signaling the end of summer. What would the ranch be like in winter? Damn cold probably, considering how close they were to the mountains. But he'd rather it was cold than wet. A man could wrap up against cold but at least the sun would still shine. He hated the cold, but he hated rain even more. It seemed to seep into his soul. And gray skies dragged him down, making him feel he was sinking into a deep pit.

He shrugged his clothes into a heap on the floor, but placed his gun carefully under his pillow before crawling into bed. He was beat. He'd never worked so hard in his life. There had to be easier ways of making a living than getting kicked by mule-headed cows or breaking his back clearing dammed-up streams.

Why did Guy stay? He had an education. Man like that could do anything. Become a lawyer or a banker, maybe. Not that he could imagine anything more boring than being a lawyer. But even so . . . Guy seemed to find the strangest things interesting. Like he'd always got his nose stuck in a book. Same as the old man. He was always reading something. Newspapers. Books. Even Peggy was always reading — except when she was darning clothes or doing that gawd-awful broidery. Was that the right word? Didn't sound right. Well, whatever it was called, it looked a real mess. You could see all the stitches, sort of like crosses and things.

Shit. He needed a woman. Must need a woman if all he could think about was books and sewing. And he couldn't even go into Cimarron. Fuck. Shivering, he pulled the covers round himself. At least a girl would warm him up. Sensible thing would be to close the window. But it was too damn cold to get out of bed. Snuggling down farther, he settled down to sleep.

The ranch felt quiet after Guy left for Santa Fe. But there was so much work Johnny hardly had any time to call his own. Felt like all he did was work, eat and sleep. Peggy was still in a foul temper but at least Carlita was doing the cooking. She even made him some tamales. Spicy tamales. Better than fancy rabbit any day.

He was fixing the big gate into the corral, making it swing right on its hinges, when he saw the rancher John Dove ride in. Johnny waved his hand in greeting. Dove was always pleasant to him. He'd made it clear he had no problem with Fierro. He always passed the time of day and seemed a nice fellow. Not like the rest of the ranchers in the area. Johnny gave the hinge a savage swipe with the hammer. No, the other ranchers were pretty much shit. He eased the gate back onto the hinge and checked its swing. Made sure it was clearing the ground again. He still had to mend the handle on the water pump. Damn thing was always breaking. But there was a real nip in the air, and his hands were cold so maybe he'd go warm up for a while. Surely it wasn't always this cold in September?

He snagged some coffee from the kitchen. Guthrie and Dove were talking in the living room. He knew he should go and say hello to John Dove. It would please his father. The oddest things seemed to please him. He couldn't figure it at all. Couldn't see that any of it mattered. Still, it kept the old man happy. He ambled over, pausing in the doorway to listen to their conversation.

"It's got worse there now, Guthrie. A girl was raped yesterday."

Johnny stopped in his tracks. Felt like the blood was draining from every bit of him. He barely heard Guthrie's answer. Then Dove was speaking again. "No, no one we know. One of the whores from that bordello. But thank God Guy's gone to Sante Fe. Cimarron needs some law before things get even worse."

Numbly, Johnny turned and stumbled up the stairs to his room. Mother of God, no. This was his fault. How could he not have seen this coming? All the signs were there. And he'd known it would get ugly. He'd known he'd have to do something about those saddle tramps at some point. If he'd done it right away, this wouldn't have happened. But oh no, Fierro had wanted those ranchers begging for his help. Wanted them to sweat, them and all the rest of the people in that town who thought they were better than him. He'd wanted to show the people of Cimarron he was more of a man than the whole fucking bunch of them. Let the women see that their menfolk hadn't got a set of balls between them.

Which of the girls had it been? Shit. He banged his fist down hard. If he hadn't waited it would have been all right and none of the girls would have been hurt. They'd all be safe. And now, no one was fucking safe and it was his fault.

He took some deep breaths to get his heart beating normal again, instead of trying to bust out of his chest. He walked to the drawer where he kept the fighting gun and dismantled it quickly. He'd cleaned it the day before but he needed to check it. He spun the chamber and then loaded it carefully. He felt more in control now. The feel of the gun calmed him as he checked it again and then weighed it in his hand before sliding it into the cut-away holster. He fastened the belt tightly round his hips. And then tightened it again. The familiar action soothed him. He fastened the tip of the holster to a concho on his leather pants, checking it twice. He didn't want that holster moving even a fraction when the time came to draw. Then he checked his other gun and placed it carefully inside his jacket, along with a single black glove.

Next he bent to check the knives in his boot and as he straightened he glimpsed himself in the mirror. It was like Johnny Sinclair had never existed. The man in the mirror was Fierro. Cold, expressionless eyes stared back at him. No mercy there. Just the stare of an ice-cold killer. Who would have his revenge.

He shut the door of Johnny Sinclair's room and walked downstairs. No sign of Dove now. He must have left. Gone to tell others the news. But the old man was there, sitting behind his desk. He looked up. Saw the gun. Turned pale. "You overheard John Dove." It was a statement, not a question.

Fierro nodded. "I'm going into town."

The old man pushed his chair back and half stood. "Johnny, this is not your fight. We'll send for the law. It's up to them to deal with this situation."

"As long as those men are walking and breathing, there ain't a woman safe in that town. And I ain't waiting for no fucking sheriff."

"The men will make sure their wives and daughters stay inside. Thank God it wasn't some innocent young girl. At least it was only a whore."

"Only a whore?" Fierro's voice was at its coldest now.

"You know what I mean, it could have been worse."

"Only a whore? You know, I'm going to do you a very big favor and try and forget you ever said that."

Guthrie sighed heavily and sank back into his seat. "Damn it, Johnny, you know perfectly well what I mean. Of course I'm not saying that it didn't matter because it was a whore. I'm just saying it would have been worse if it was some innocent young girl."

"Like the daughter of one of your rancher friends, because they're more important than a whore? Well, I tell you, a lot of my friends are whores, and I'll take them anytime over stuck-up girls who think they're better than everyone else."

"I didn't say they were more important." The old man sounded tired.

"No. But you were thinking it. Now, I'm riding into town." He turned and walked to the door. His spurs jingled like a death march at a fancy funeral.

"Johnny. Be careful. And please, I know you don't usually, but can you come back tonight. Let me know you're safe."

He glanced across the room. Saw the pain in the old man's eyes. Shit. He gave a slight nod. "Yeah. I'll be back."

CHAPTER TWENTY-THREE

The town was quiet and shuttered when he rode in. Balls of tumbleweed blew along the deserted sidewalks and the only sound was the creak of wood. But then he noticed the drapes moving at some of the windows as people peered out, watching him ride in. He tethered Pistol at a hitching rail and strolled to the large mercantile belonging to the town's mayor. What the hell was the man's name? Something like Tandy? Whatever his name, he was a lump of lard and twice as useless.

He pushed open the door to see a group of ranchers deep in conversation with the mayor. Johnny paused in the doorway, enjoying the hush that fell as they all turned to look at him. "Morning." He spoke real soft, so they had to strain to hear him.

"Fierro. What do you want?" Matt Dixon eyed him angrily.

Johnny didn't answer for a couple of beats

283

before he shrugged. "Heard you had some trouble."

That got their attention.

"You've reconsidered our offer? You'll take care of this?" Henry Carter asked hopefully.

"Well, that depends, don't it?" He stepped into the room, letting the door bang shut behind him. The men jumped, startled by the noise.

"Depends on what?" An ugly, bullheaded man took a step toward him.

Johnny raised an eyebrow. The man hesitated and stepped back. Johnny smiled coldly. "Like I told you before. I'm an expensive gun to hire."

"We offered you seven hundred and fifty dollars. That's a lot of money, Fierro."

Johnny stared at them, letting his gaze linger on each one. "Like I said, I'm an awful expensive gun to hire. Question is can you afford me?"

"How much more do you want? Damn it, seven hundred and fifty dollars is a small fortune."

Yeah. He knew Henry Carter would be the first to get riled. Had a real short fuse.

Johnny narrowed his eyes, like he was considering things. "Five of them, you say? Well, I reckon at two hundred and fifty dollars a man, that makes twelve fifty."

"Are you crazy, Fierro? We're not going to pay you that kind of money," spluttered the mayor, puffing his chest out.

Johnny shrugged. "Fine." He spun on his heel and walked toward the door, only his spurs breaking the silence. Then there was a clamor of voices.

"You can't walk out, Fierro. You got to take care of this for us."

"Surely we can negotiate, Fierro."

"Where do you think we'd find that kind of money?"

Johnny turned and looked back at them. "I ain't negotiating. That's the price, take it or leave it. There's enough cattlemen and storekeepers to chip in and pay it. But then again, maybe you ain't worried about that pretty little daughter of yours, Mayor. And you, Donovan, ain't you got a couple of daughters? Might be them next. Still, ain't no concern of mine." And he pushed open the door.

"Come back, Fierro. I'm sure we can sort something out." The mayor took a couple of paces toward him, sweat glistening on his forehead.

"Like what?" Johnny spoke very coolly.

"How about half up front and the rest when you've done the job?"

Johnny smiled thinly. "That ain't how it

works. Hell, I might not live long enough to collect and think how sorry you'd be then. Tell you what, I'll go and sit outside a while, and you can talk it over. But it's twelve hundred and fifty. Up front."

"But we need time, Fierro. Even if we agree to your outrageous demand, we need time to raise that kind of money." A vein was pulsing in Carter's forehead.

Johnny closed in on Carter, so close he could feel the heat of the rancher's breath. "Outrageous demand? You want me to gun down five men. That don't come cheap. And if you piss me off, Carter, the price will go up to fifteen hundred. The bank's open. Think on it. I'll be outside."

He strode out, ignoring their mutterings and slack-jawed shock. Tilting his hat down over his eyes, he settled into the chair outside the store, pushing it back onto two legs against the wall.

He bit back a smile as the store door swung open and one of the cattlemen scurried down the street. Then another came out, hurrying in the other direction. And then Donovan emerged, heading toward the bank.

Johnny laughed softly. Yeah, he'd got them on the run — all sweating, trying to raise the money. They could easily afford his price if they all chipped in, wouldn't cost any of them much. But it could cost him a great deal. He pushed that thought out of his head. Instead, he concentrated on the buzz as his blood started to flow faster.

It didn't take long. He reckoned he didn't sit there more than twenty minutes before they were all back in the store. He waited. Whistling softly. This was his game and he'd play it his way.

The bullheaded man called him in. They were standing by the desk, and the mayor held out an envelope. "It's all there, Fierro. No need to count it."

Johnny took the money and perched on the side of the shop counter, thumbing the notes as he counted. He sighed heavily, shaking his head. "You can't count. It's thirty dollars short. So, the price just went up. We'll round it up to thirteen hundred, seeing as how you're really pissing me off. I'm sure if you dig down in your pockets, and the mayor empties that till, you'll find the extra."

Johnny watched, not letting any emotion show on his face, as they scratched together for the remainder.

They were all sweating. The mayor licked his lips nervously. Any minute now they'd be pissing themselves. Johnny held his hand out for the remainder of the money and ambled to the door. "I'd like to say it was a pleasure doing business with you, but I'd be lying."

"When will you take care of this, Fierro?" Carter's voice was hoarse.

Johnny turned, gave them all a cold smile. "Today. I keep my end of a bargain."

He let the door go with another satisfying bang, hesitating only briefly outside, before walking to the far end of town and the bordello. There were no folk on the streets. Just him.

He pushed the door open and scanned the room. A few of the girls huddled together in the corner. There was a heavy, dull sort of feel in the room. They smiled weakly but didn't get up. He tipped his hat and walked through to the back, to Delice's office. She was sitting behind her desk, looking at books of figures. She glanced up as he stepped into the room, closing the door behind him.

"What are you doing in town at this time of the day?" But there was no spark in her voice. And the look in her eyes was the look of a woman who'd had enough.

"Which of the girls was it? Which one?"

She sat back in her chair with a sigh. "Lizzie. She was out running an errand. An errand for me. She'd only popped out for a few minutes. Three of those saddle tramps grabbed her. People must have heard her scream but no one went to help. If only I hadn't sent her on that errand."

Johnny stared down at the floor, scuffing up the rug with his boot. If only. Life was full of if onlys. "And no one went to help." He kicked the rug, but savagely this time. "Well, they wouldn't, would they, 'cos there ain't one man in this town with any balls." He sighed. There was a real pain in his gut now, felt like it was ripping right into him. "She all right?"

Delice shrugged. "I guess it could have been worse. They knocked her around, but I think she'll be all right." Delice gave a humorless laugh. "All right. That's a joke. But what does it matter, we're just whores."

He saw the challenge in her eyes. Felt a lump in his throat. He reached into his pocket and took the envelope and dropped it on her desk.

She fingered the envelope curiously. "What's this?"

"It's for Lizzie. Tell her I'm sorry. This is my fault."

Delice opened the envelope, her eyes opening wider as she saw the large wad of notes. She looked at him, her brow furrowed. "There has to be over a thousand dollars here. What do you mean, that this is your fault? How in the world is this your fault?"

He grimaced, feeling the heat flush his face. "I should have taken care of it before it came to this." His voice came out more like a whisper.

Delice looked at him like he was stupid or something. "What do you mean, that you should have taken care of it? What does it have to do with you?"

"They asked me. More than a week ago, the cattlemen asked me. I knew those boys were trouble but I wanted the cattlemen to beg for my help." He couldn't meet her gaze. Didn't want to see the contempt. "Tell her I'm sorry."

She resealed the envelope and tapped it rhythmically on the desk. He wished she'd just yell at him and get it over with.

"What the hell am I going to do with you?" It was odd but she sounded irritated more than angry. "Johnny. This is not your fault."

He looked up. "Of course it's my fault."

She threw her hands up. "Oh, for God's sake! Did you hold a gun to the heads of those saddle tramps? Did you tell them to go find a girl and rape her? Were you there egging them on?"

"I should have done something sooner. I knew there'd be trouble." He seemed to have lost his voice again.

Delice raised her eyes like she was looking to heaven and sighed heavily. "This was not your responsibility. God! It was up to the town to look out for its own people. Deal with its own problems. They've been without a sheriff for some time, but they didn't want to pay for a replacement. They talk about it but nothing ever gets done. And if some of the lily-livered cowards came knocking on your door, you were right to turn them away. It wasn't your battle. In case you've forgotten, you are no longer a gun for hire. You've hung up your gun, remember? You're Johnny Sinclair — a rancher, not a gunfighter."

He looked at her, wondered how best to explain. She sure looked mad. He shook his head. "Johnny Sinclair? No, I guess he really did die a long time ago, if he ever existed at all. I'm Johnny Fierro and I guess I always will be. It's too late for anything else."

"Stop feeling sorry for yourself." She sounded real snappy.

Sorry for himself? What the hell was that meant to mean? "I'm not feeling sorry for myself; I'm just telling it like it is."

"Rubbish. You're an intelligent man, and you can be anything you want to be. Yes, part of you will always be Johnny Fierro but there's another man inside you struggling to get out — a compassionate man. If I can see that, it's certainly high time you recognized it too."

He frowned, unsure what she meant. "I ain't intelligent. I haven't had any schooling."

"Do not confuse intelligence with education." She sounded like a preacher or something.

"Johnny." Her voice was softer now, and so were her eyes. "Honey, believe me. You can be anything you want. It isn't too late. You're a good man. I do believe your heart is in the right place. Even if you were a gunfighter!" She said the last bit in a teasing kind of way. And that had him really confused.

He ran his hand through his hair. Tried to figure things out. He could feel her eyes boring into him. Maybe he'd better get off the subject of whether his heart was in the right place. He could think of far too many times when it hadn't been.

He nodded toward the envelope. "You'll give that to Lizzie?"

Delice gave a short laugh. "Yes, honey, I'll

give it to Lizzie. It's a fortune to a girl like her."

Johnny shrugged. "She'll be able to get a fresh start. Go somewhere new, maybe get a business going. Somewhere no one knows her."

"You see what I mean, honey? You are a compassionate man." She looked down at the envelope again. Her brow furrowed and then her eyes snapped wide open and she paled. "My God! This is your fee, isn't it? They've bought your gun . . ." She looked at him and he could see the fear in her eyes. "Honey, you shouldn't be doing this. There are at least five of those men hanging around. And in case you hadn't noticed, there's only one of you. And I don't see our mayor and his friends backing you up."

He shrugged. "I can handle it. I've handled worse than that before."

"Yes. I suppose you have." She sounded kind of sad.

She stared down at the money, chewing on her lip like she was nervous or something. "Johnny, will you come in here after?"

He thought about the reputation he had for whoring after a killing. But not after this one. This was different. "I don't think I'll feel like doing that today."

She looked puzzled for a second and then

bit back a smile. "No, that wasn't quite what I meant. I just meant, come and let us know you're OK. That you're safe."

He managed to stop his jaw dropping. It seemed that lots of folk were suddenly worrying about him. Which he sure as hell wasn't used to, but it was kind of nice. But it wasn't the time to think of that. He had a job to do. And he was going to do it, just like he'd always known he would.

He nodded. "Yeah, I'll come in after."

She smiled. "Thank you, the girls and I would appreciate that. And, I'll go and give this to Lizzie." She stood up. "Be careful, honey. Please."

Chapter Twenty-Four

He stood outside the bordello deciding how to play things. The street was deserted but he could feel the tension in the air. Like the town was waiting for something, for Fierro. He needed to distance himself now. Put the talk with Delice out of his mind. Let Fierro take control.

The men were probably in the saloon. He'd let them keep drinking — for now. It would make his job easier. But he didn't want them to know he was in town. And some big-mouthed rancher might say something. Shit.

It would suit the cattlemen very well if he got killed. He had no intention of giving them the satisfaction. Fuck that.

He wanted to see what he was up against. Size them up. Because even if they were only saddle tramps, there were still five of them and five was five whichever way you looked at it. But he had no intention of letting a bunch of saddle bums take him out. Fierro wasn't that obliging. He walked with slow measured steps toward the saloon. He could feel the buzz starting to build. He needed that. Needed to feel the rush that gave him his edge, made him feel he could take anybody. And he wanted revenge. Revenge for poor Lizzie.

He remembered her now. And he was going to make those men pay. Just like he'd made the town pay.

He hesitated in the shadows outside the saloon. The doors needed a coat of paint and hung lopsided on their hinges, swinging slightly in the breeze. Then he ambled on past, casting a casual glance inside. Or casual to anyone watching. But he didn't miss a thing. The men were standing at one end of the bar, talking loudly amongst themselves and ignoring the other drinkers. There weren't many of those. Even the town drunks were steering clear. He walked on, chewing on his stampede string. Glancing at the town clock on the church tower, he saw it was just after one. The men wouldn't be drunk yet. He'd give it a while longer.

Even so, he'd miscalculated badly on this one. He should have left it to later in the day. But no, Fierro had been all fired up, rushing into town for revenge. Instead, he should have stayed cool and waited a while. He was getting sloppy. Losing his touch. Now he was here, and half the town knew he was here, so he couldn't afford to wait too long. Didn't want the men getting wind of his presence. And he sure as hell didn't trust the townspeople to keep their mouths shut. They'd be only too glad to see Fierro taken down. He had no intention of giving them the satisfaction. Still, he'd wait until the men had enjoyed another round of drinks.

There was a rocking chair along the boardwalk so he sat down, tipped his hat over his eyes and waited. Rocking gently, he relished the feeling of his blood pounding through his body and the feeling of excitement growing stronger by the minute. Why wait any longer? Fierro was back in control. And it was time for Fierro to get even.

He stood, ready for this now and looking forward to it. He walked purposefully to the saloon, pausing only briefly in the entrance to scan the room. The men at the far end of the bar were sure having a bad effect on the saloon profits; seemed most folk were too scared to venture in. But that was a bonus. Leastways if things kicked off in the bar there wouldn't be many bystanders to worry about.

The men barely glanced at him as he walked toward the bar. Instead they carried on bragging and talking to one another. The barman's eyes widened in recognition and wiped his hands down the stained apron. "What will you have, Mr. F—"

Johnny cut across him. The last thing he needed was some fool of a bartender to call him Fierro. He'd do that himself when he was good and ready. "A beer."

The man pushed a beer toward him, his hands trembling slightly. Dios. This town was full of cowards.

Johnny leaned against the bar, his drink untouched. He watched the men in the corner, his gaze never leaving them, and waited for them to notice. It didn't take long.

"What you looking at, mister?" A skinny runt of a man was looking at him, like he wanted a fight.

Johnny smiled slowly. That would be fine by him, it just wouldn't be the sort of fight that this jackass had in mind. "I'm looking at you."

The man scowled, cracked his knuckles. "Well, unless you're looking for trouble, mind your own damn business. Else I might be tempted to make you wear that drink." His friends laughed loudly, like the fellow

298

had said something funny.

"You could try, but I wouldn't recommend it." Johnny kept his voice very soft.

The men laughed, louder this time. "You wouldn't recommend it." One of them tried to mimic him. "Hear that, Wade, he wouldn't recommend it."

Wade swung himself round to look Johnny square in the eyes. "You know, boy, I think we're going to have to teach you some manners."

"OK." Johnny smiled. "But it might be cleaner outside. I'd hate for the bartender to have to clean your brains off the floor when I'm finished with you. That's always supposing you got any brains between the lot of you."

Wade stepped forward, his face red and mottled. "You're going to regret that. Me and the boys are gonna teach you a lesson. And it'll be your brains on the floor."

Johnny sucked in his breath, and then shook his head. "Oh, I doubt that. I really do. I think I can handle five pieces of shit like you."

That did the trick. They were all getting steamed up. Yeah, real mad. And they thought it was going to be so easy. He was going to enjoy disappointing them on that score.

"You do, do you?" It was the runt again. He had a big mouth for such a small man. "Well, you got a shock coming, cowboy. And what name should we put on your tombstone?"

Oh boy, he loved this part. He narrowed his eyes and moved away from the bar. So they could see his rig real clear — all tied down like the professional he was. "My name?" He spoke real soft now. And smiled real slow. "My name? It's Fierro. Johnny Fierro."

Their faces showed a mixture of fear and disbelief. A couple of them backed off slowly, muttering to each other in low voices. But one of the group, with a gut which said he drank way too much, said: "He ain't Fierro. He's bluffing. Fierro's dead. I know he's dead. Heard all about it. Got himself hanged down Mexico way. This is just some fool cowboy who thinks he's smart."

"I dunno, Clint. That rig looks professional." The runt licked his lips, and his left eye twitched with a life of its own.

Good, once they got twitchy they screwed up. Made mistakes. Johnny leaned against the bar. He was running this show and he loved the feeling of power, of being in control. Nobody fucked with Fierro.

They were all staring at him. Not sure what to make of him. He raised his glass, like he was toasting them, a slight smile playing around his lips. And he knew that would get to them. It always got to people. Just the way he wanted.

"Nah." Wade was swaggering. Trying to look tough. "He ain't Fierro. Anyhow, what would Fierro want with us, even if he was still alive?"

"Yeah." Clint had to have his say. He was that type. "Like I said, Fierro's dead. So let's teach the breed a lesson. One he won't live to remember."

"OK." Johnny shrugged, like he didn't care either way. "In here or out there?" He nodded toward the doors. "Like I said, kind of a shame to make a mess in here."

The runt licked his lips again. "He's awful sure of himself, Wade. You sure Fierro's dead?"

Wade scowled. "You doubting my word, Hank? Of course Fierro's dead. And even if he wasn't — which he is — he don't come this far north of the border. And he wouldn't care about us. We ain't done nothing to piss off the likes of Fierro."

Johnny sighed and shook his head sadly. "Now, you see, that's where you're wrong." His expression hardened. "I hear you had a little party with a friend of mine, the only problem is she didn't welcome your attentions. I think the law calls it rape. And I don't take too kindly to bullies who make war on women."

"A friend of yours." Wade sneered. "Just some whore. So it ain't rape anyway. She was just giving us a free sample."

They all laughed, like it was a real good joke. "Yeah, just showing us the wares. Not that she was up to much. But we gave her a go anyhow."

Johnny stared at them expressionlessly. "Like I said, she's a friend of mine. So, I was planning on killing you all anyway, kind of like a free sample of my particular talents. And then, I got real lucky, 'cos the town fathers got together and paid me a whole lot of money to make the world a better place by taking you down. Now ain't that just the icing on the cake?" Johnny smiled thinly. "And, just so you know who's sending you to hell, it takes more than a bunch of rurales to finish me off. And if they couldn't manage it, I don't see a bunch of saddle tramps doing any better."

He jerked his thumb toward the doors. "You want to die in here or out there?"

They were starting to sweat, casting glances at each other, not sure whether to believe him. The saloon felt stiflingly hot and Johnny could smell their fear. He loved this. The scent of fear, the tension rising, and his blood pounding.

The atmosphere of menace had penetrated the alcoholic haze of the town drunks. They scuttled out of the saloon like cockroaches, all except one sunk in the corner, asleep in a drunken stupor. Johnny made a mental note to try and keep the shooting clear of the drunk if things kicked off in the saloon. And he intended to make sure they would. It would give him more cover. Perhaps now was the time to help things along a little.

"Ask the barkeep who I am." He nodded toward the man cowering at the other end of the bar, ready to duck for cover.

"You ain't Fierro." Wade puffed his chest out. He turned to the bartender. "Who is he? You ever seen him before?"

The barman looked at Johnny, his frightened eyes pleading for permission to speak. Johnny gave him the benefit of his broadest smile. "Yeah, go ahead. Tell 'em who I am. I don't keep it a secret."

The barkeep swallowed hard. "He's Fierro. Johnny Fierro." And he ducked below the bar.

"So?" Johnny smiled at them. "If you're done talking, can we start this dance?"

Before Wade could answer, the runt made a move toward his gun.

Amateur. The thought flashed through Johnny's mind as he saw the man didn't even have his gun tied down. With one fluid motion Johnny drew his gun and took out the runt with a shot to the chest. Fanning the hammer, he fired at the others, each bullet finding its target. As they fell, one by one, he felt a surge of power. But as the last one went down, a searing hot pain, like a fire deep inside, tore through Johnny's flesh. Fuck. Struggling to concentrate, he reached inside his jacket for the second gun. It had been Wade who got him. The man was down, but even now he was aiming again at Fierro. Finger on the trigger, Johnny flung himself sideways and fired again. Wade's head jerked back as his brains splattered across the floor.

The reek of cordite and piss filled the room. The barman was still hiding somewhere and the drunk still slept.

Johnny straightened from his crouch. Waves of pain were sweeping over him now. His side was sticky and wet. He grabbed a towel from the bar and thrust it inside his jacket, which he then fastened tightly to hold it in place. Tried to stand straight. No way would he give the town folk the satisfaction of knowing he'd been hit. But fuck, it hurt. He had to breathe in short bursts as each fresh wave of pain swept over him. He knew the bullet hadn't gone straight through. It was sitting inside him, eating into his core. It needed to come out. Fast.

The barkeep crawled out of his hidey-hole and peered cautiously around the saloon. His eyes widened with wonder as he saw the five bodies strewn like ragdolls across the floor.

Johnny tipped his hat to him. "Sorry about the mess." His soft drawl sounded steady. Not giving anything away. Not showing how bad he was hurting. "But I'm sure the town will pay for the damages." With a nod he walked out of the bar. Upright and casual, like he hadn't a care in the world.

He needed to get to his horse. Get out of town, deal with the bullet.

Delice.

Shit.

He'd promised he'd let her know he was OK. That was all he needed right now. But a promise was a promise. And he always kept his promises.

People were coming out of their houses now to gawk at him. He ignored the expressions of fear and awe on their faces. Just walked straight and steady toward the bordello. Never let people see he'd been hit. Never let them see the pain.

He'd never realized how long that street was. Felt he'd walked twenty miles by the time he reached the bordello. He pushed open the door. The girls were huddled in the corner, their faces pale and drawn. Delice stood at the door to her office, watching him with those cool green eyes.

"It's over." He spoke softly and was grateful that his voice came out steady. But shit, he was hurting now. Needed to get out. Fast. He turned to leave, just needed to get to Pistol now.

"I'd like a word before you go."

He paused, shut his eyes briefly. That was all he needed. "Some other time, maybe?" His voice still sounded steady but the pain was getting worse.

"It won't take a minute. Come into my office. Now." There was a hard edge to her voice. He tried to think how he could get out of it, but he wasn't thinking too good right now.

He sighed. Just get it over as quickly as possible. Then he could escape. Deal with the bullet. He walked across the room, managing not to sway, but it was taking all his energy to stay upright. He could feel her watching him, her eyes boring into him. She followed him into her office and closed the door behind them.

"What was it you wanted?" He tried to sound casual. If only she'd get it said and then he could leave. His side was burning up and the pain was getting worse. But she still didn't speak, just looked him up and down like she was searching for something.

"So what do you want?" His voice came out angrier than he meant it to. He tried again. "You said you wanted a word?" Yeah, that came out better.

"Take your jacket off."

CHAPTER TWENTY-FIVE

His chest tightened. Shit. Did she suspect something? She couldn't, could she? He was acting normal. She couldn't know. Just play it cool. He laughed. "Sorry, but I ain't in the mood for that sort of thing right now. Some other time, maybe."

He took a step toward the door, hoping he could stay on his feet long enough to make it to his horse.

She gave an exasperated sigh. "I said, take your jacket off." She sounded real hard, like she wasn't someone to mess with. She folded her arms and stared at him like she could see right inside him.

He clenched his jaw. Maybe he should just tell her to fuck off. Mind her own business.

"Johnny, take the jacket off."

There was no getting out of this. Slowly, painfully, he shrugged the jacket off, stifling a hiss of pain. His shirt was sodden with blood. Peggy would be real pissed off about that. Delice didn't look surprised though.

"And just what were you intending to do about that?" She sounded real cool.

"It's a flesh wound. I'll patch it up myself."

"A flesh wound?" Judging from the tone of her voice, she wasn't buying into that one. "You'll patch it up yourself?"

"It won't be the first time." He snapped the words out.

But oddly, instead of looking pissed, she looked kinda sad. "Not the first time? No, honey, I don't suppose it is." She sighed. "For God's sake, sit down before you fall down. Let me have a look."

"No! I said I'll deal with it and I will."

She looked at him like he was an irritating little kid. "Stop being so damn stubborn! I'll send for Ben. In case it has escaped your memory, we have a doctor in this town. I believe you're acquainted with him." She knew damn well he was acquainted with him.

"No. You ain't sending for Ben."

She rolled her eyes. "Why not? You need a doctor."

"Won't give people the satisfaction." His voice was weak. Shit, he was hurting bad.

Her brow wrinkled. "What on earth are you talking about? What satisfaction?"

"Them knowing I got shot. Don't want

anyone to know." He kicked his boot against the desk. Fought to stop himself showing how much pain he was in.

"You don't want anyone to know?" She seemed to be thinking about that one but didn't look too impressed. "Why? Because Johnny Fierro is invincible?"

Where the hell was Vincible? And why was he in it? Seemed easier to just shrug . . .

He shut his eyes as a huge wave of pain swept over him. When he opened them again she was looking worried.

"I'll send the boy from the kitchen for Ben. Don't worry, I'll say I'm not feeling well. No one will know it's for you."

"I don't want the girls to know." His voice came out as a whisper. "You know they talk. They'll let it slip to someone."

She paused at the door. "Trust me. No one will know."

She left him alone in the office. Even through the pain he couldn't help noticing how many books there were lining the walls. Everyone seemed to read damn books. And she sure had an awful lot of them.

He tried to lift his shirt to see how bad the wound was, but he hadn't got the energy. He'd try again in a few minutes. Maybe he'd feel better then. He closed his eyes, tried to clear his mind and block out the pain. He was getting too old for all of this. He was so fucking tired. And now, that buzz he loved so much had gone, leaving him empty inside. Same as always. But the pain was eating into him. He didn't think he could wait for Ben. The doc might not even be in town.

He struggled to reach into his boot for the special knife he kept for things like this. But the tequila was in his saddlebags. Shit. He knew he should slosh some alcohol over the knife. Luke had always drummed that into him. Alcohol on the knife first and then on the wound. He was reaching into his jacket for the needle and thread when Delice came back.

"He shouldn't be too long . . ." She broke off, and picked up the knife, examining it curiously. "That's a scalpel. A surgeon's knife." She gave him a long hard look. "You carry that around with you?"

"Oh, yeah. I'm real handy with a knife." He tried to sound casual. "Isn't everyone?"

She sighed and flashed him an irritated glare. "I've sent the girls upstairs to clean the rooms and do some mending. They won't see Ben come in."

Even as she spoke they heard Ben calling out for her. "Delice? Anyone around?"

311

She opened the office door. "I'm in here, Ben."

"I had a message you weren't feeling too good. What seems to be the problem?"

"That's the problem." She nodded her head in Johnny's direction.

Ben's eyes widened as he saw the blood-soaked shirt. "What the hell happened? I heard you strolled out of the saloon like you hadn't a care in the world. Why didn't you come to my office?" Ben sounded pissed with him too. Seemed like everyone was today. Before he could think of a smart answer, Delice chipped in with her two cents' worth.

"Apparently Mr. Fierro didn't want the people of Cimarron to know he was shot. He has his reputation to think of, you know. The invincible Fierro — untouchable, unfeeling and armor-plated." She didn't sound too impressed and Ben gave an irritated snort as he opened up his black bag.

"Take your shirt off, Johnny. Let me see what we're dealing with."

Johnny looked across at Delice. "Ain't you got something else to do? Someplace you'd rather be?"

She folded her arms and leaned against the door. "No."

Shit. He didn't want to take his shirt off

312

with her standing there. Didn't want her to see his scarred back. Though why he should care what she thought he couldn't even begin to figure. And he didn't want her watching when Ben dug the bullet out.

"Johnny." Ben sounded real snappy. "Shall I help you with the shirt?"

"Does she have to be here?" Johnny jerked his head toward Delice.

"Honey, oddly enough, I've seen men with their shirts off before. Don't be embarrassed on my account." He could have sworn that her lips twitched, almost like she was laughing at him.

Johnny sighed. He fumbled with the buttons but couldn't seem to manage them. Ben took over, pushing Johnny's hands away and easing the shirt off. Ben frowned as he saw the extent of the blood, and started swabbing it away. He gave a hiss of annoyance. "This is deep. And the bullet is still in there."

Johnny grunted. "I know that, Ben. I can fucking feel it."

"We need to get you down to my office so I can deal with this properly."

"No!" Johnny's voice sounded icy, even to his own ears. "You do it here or I deal with it myself."

Ben snorted. "And how would you deal

313

with it?"

"Oh, didn't you know?" Delice sounded very calm. "Johnny Fierro keeps a special knife to cover all eventualities." She pointed to the knife on the desk.

Ben's eyes widened. "Do tell me then, Johnny, just how would you put yourself back together after you performed your amazing surgery on yourself?"

"Got a needle and thread in my jacket." He said it casually, like it was nothing out of the ordinary. They stared at him like he was loco. But then again, maybe he was.

Ben sighed heavily. "OK, you win. We'll do it here. Delice, could you fetch a bowl of hot water, please? I need to wash my hands." He paused, then muttered to himself, "I should wash my hands of the whole thing. My God, you're a difficult man, Johnny Sinclair."

Delice paused in the doorway. "Johnny Sinclair? Oh no, Ben, this isn't Johnny Sinclair. This is most definitely Johnny Fierro."

He would have glared at her, but he hadn't got the energy. And anyhow, she was right.

Ben busied himself, preparing for his work, getting a knife and all the other stuff he seemed to need for what was a simple job. Dig it out and sew it up. Simple.

"I'll give you some morphine. This is going to be painful and you need something to help you cope. And so you stay still."

"Don't need no morphine, I'm riding outta here when you're done. And don't worry about me moving. I'll stay still."

Ben's mouth dropped open. He was silent for a few seconds. "Ride out of here?" Ben threw his hands up. "Ride out of here! That's insane. You'll be in no fit state to ride anywhere."

"Just cut the damn thing out." Johnny paused as Delice bustled back into the room with a bowl of steaming hot water. "Get it over with, OK? Then I'm riding home."

Ben shook his head, like he'd given in. He washed his hands and set to work. Delice stood close by, watching. Looking at Johnny all the while, her eyes boring into him. But her face was blank, showing no expression. Dios! What was it with this woman? He never knew what the hell she was thinking.

He gritted his teeth as Ben began. He knew how much this was going to hurt. Even more than it was hurting now. But no way would he let that damn woman see his pain. Even so, he let out a hiss as the probe entered his side, couldn't stop himself. He clenched his teeth again. Tried to freeze his expression and stared right back at Delice. He'd show her what sort of man he was.

The pain seared right through him. A red-hot poker in a mass of burning flesh. It was so intense he could see stars dancing. He wanted to cry out, but he clenched his jaw even tighter. He held her gaze, fighting the desire to pull away from the thrusting probe.

Don't puke. Whatever he did, he wasn't going to puke. Or pass out. Her face was blurry now, but he held on to looking at where he figured her eyes were. No way was he passing out. He wouldn't let anyone see him do that. Especially her.

He let out another hiss of pain as Ben gave a grunt of triumph. "I can feel it. Damn, it's deep. You were lucky, it's only missed the lung by a whisker."

"Just get the fucking thing out." His voice sounded strange, kind of strangled. And Delice's face was fading . . . Had to hold on. He could collapse later, when he was alone. Then there'd be time enough to fall into a welcome blackness. But that deep pit seemed too close right now. He gritted his teeth. He was damned if he'd pass out. But he felt so tired and the pain felt like it was in his soul, eating away at him. Consuming him like the fires of hell. Where he was headed. No redemption for Johnny Fierro. The words of a priest from another time echoed in his head. There'd never be any redemption. Never any peace. Just eternal damnation.

Ben heaved a sigh of relief as he dropped the bullet on the floor. And Johnny fought the rising desire to puke as Ben set about cleaning him up. Stitching him up. Sewing the demons back inside Fierro and sealing them in.

He tried to focus on Delice, but she looked like she was wrapped in some silver sparking cloth of stars. Shimmering, going in and out of focus. Just hold it together, Fierro. Never let them see beneath the mask.

"Ain't you done yet?" His voice was a croak. Dios. Should have kept his mouth shut. And now he wanted to puke. He fought to keep the bile down.

"Almost done." Ben's voice came from far away. Some distant place. Johnny could see the hacienda, its sprawling mass like a glimpse of heaven. He struggled to bring himself back. To hold on longer. Ben had to be done soon. Please, God. Please.

Ben's voice came again. "You're in no state to ride, but I don't suppose you'll take any notice of that."

He tried to focus on Ben's face. Why the hell couldn't the man stand still? And he knew Delice was still watching him, could feel her eyes.

"Very impressive." She didn't sound impressed. And what was she impressed about? Couldn't figure it. Too tired. "Your performance. Very impressive, Mr. Fierro."

He tried to quell the bile rising in his throat. He could taste it. God, no.

"Here, use this."

Just as he lost the battle, she passed him an ash bucket from the fireplace. He retched into it. And the action made him hurt more. And puke more. The sickly smell was in his nostrils. Filled the room. He couldn't look at them now. But he sensed their concern. Their pity. He didn't need nobody's pity. Fuck that. But he wished she hadn't seen it. Not his weakness.

"You're not fit to ride, Johnny. You'll kill yourself." Ben sounded very gentle and that made Johnny feel worse.

"I'm fine, just fine." He scowled at them. "Just need a minute or two and I'll be out of here, so mind your own fucking business." He knew his words were harsh and ungrateful, but he didn't need pity. Or help. He was fine. Do things his way. He'd look after himself, like he always had. For as long as he could remember.

Ben huffed and muttered something about Johnny being stubborn. And Delice just continued to watch him, those eyes giving nothing away. He wished he could just lie down and sleep for a very long time. Instead he tried to stand. Ben pushed him back down. "For God's sake, just give it a while."

"Mind your own fucking business."

"I could arrange to put that bullet back in you, young man, if you don't mind your language."

He tried to imagine Ben shooting him, and failed. He forced a smile. "No, Ben, you don't have it in you to pull the trigger."

"No, I don't suppose I do." Smiling, Ben squatted down in front of him. "Just give it a few minutes. Would you like some water?"

"I suppose tequila is out of the question?"

Ben muffled a laugh. "What are we going to do with him, Delice?"

"Well, to start with, we're not giving him any tequila. Although I might give him a bill for bleeding in my office."

Ben gave another snort of laughter. "The person I feel sorry for is Guthrie Sinclair. God knows what he did to deserve a son like this. Though come to think of it, maybe that's where Johnny gets it from."

Johnny hissed in a breath. "When you two have done laughing, I need my horse."

Ben sighed. "There's no stopping you, is there? You could spend the night here. Get a little stronger. Ride out in the morning."

"I'm riding out of here today. If I stay the girls will find out about this and I don't want no one to know. And besides." He paused, feeling suddenly awkward. "I promised Guthrie I'd go back after. Let him know I'm OK."

"Johnny, I could ride out and see Guthrie —"

"No. You ain't listening. I'm riding out and the whole damn town is going to see me ride out — in one piece."

"Ben, he's made his mind up. Don't waste your breath." Delice stared at him through narrowed eyes as if considering some sort of problem. "I'll have the boy bring your horse to the alley alongside the building. No one will see you struggling to mount. God only knows how you're going to do that." She held her hand up before he could say a word. "I know; you've had worse. And of course, you're just fine."

He had to smile. Not much of a smile but still a smile. "See, you understand me perfectly."

She made a sort of harrumph noise and walked out of the room.

He swallowed hard, wanting to puke again. Leastways now it was only Ben to witness it. Ben held the bucket as Johnny retched into it again before falling back in his chair. Even though the room was swaying he could see the concern in Ben's kind eyes.

"I'll come out to the ranch later. Sew you back together again." Ben shook his head. "It's all going to come apart on that ride. All my stitches will open right up. You should let me take you back in my buggy."

"Ben, let it go. I'm riding back. That's final." Johnny leaned back wearily in the chair. The burning in his side had become a stronger, pulsing throb. And his head throbbed too. But he knew, when he rode out, he had to look like he hadn't a care in the world. Someone had once told him he was a master of illusion. He wasn't totally sure he'd understood their meaning but he liked the sound of it. He was good at pretending. He'd had a lifetime to practice.

He jerked forward with a start as Delice came back. Had he passed out? No. Maybe he'd dozed off. He wasn't going to pass out. Not till later. Much later.

"You can leave through this side door and your horse is tethered in the alley. It's not overlooked and is always in shadow so you might just get away with it." She sounded real businesslike. Heck, she was good at this.

He tried to summon a smile. "Thanks. I owe you."

"No, Johnny." Her voice was softer now. "Me and the girls, we owe you."

He tried to shrug, but couldn't manage it. "Just give the money to Lizzie."

Delice smiled. "I did and she's already planning a new life. And, honey, I hope there won't be a next time, but in case there is, just remember you don't need to pretend in front of Ben and me. We're friends, OK?"

He tried to swallow the lump in his throat. Friends. It had a nice ring to it. And seeing as how they'd started out, it was kind of unexpected.

"And for God's sake" — her tone was crisp now — "try not to fall off on the way home."

She and Ben watched as he moved with agonizing slowness to the side door. Pushing it open, he peered out. Pistol was waiting patiently in the alley. There was a single stone next to him. Like it had been placed there on purpose. The stone was large enough to stand on. Good old Delice, she thought of everything. It was funny, but it seemed he'd made two good friends in this town. Everyone else might be shit but he had two people on his side. An unusual experience.

He soothed Pistol, who nickered in pleasure at seeing his master. Johnny gritted his teeth as he maneuvered himself onto the stone. A wave of pain swept over him and he clung to the saddle as the alleyway wavered around him. He waited for the pain to subside. "Stand still, amigo." He stroked Pistol's neck. "Stand very still."

As though aware of Johnny's distress, the horse stood rock steady while Johnny lifted his foot into the stirrup. Another wave of pain engulfed him and he sagged against Pistol. He hoped Delice and Ben weren't watching. He wanted his room, his bed. Wanted to lie down and sleep for a hundred years.

The stars in front of his eyes subsided and he was relieved to find his foot was still lodged in the stirrup. Grasping hold of the pommel and summoning up his last reserves of energy, he hauled himself into the saddle.

The shock from the pain almost pitched him right over. He clung to Pistol's neck. The pain was even worse than Ben's probe. He tried to take deep breaths but that hurt too much. His heart felt like it was going to bust right out of his chest, and sweat was pouring down his face. He sank forward onto the horse's neck as images swam in front of his eyes, faces from the past, and blood. Lots of blood.

He couldn't have said how long he stayed

there. It might have been just moments. It might have been an hour. He needed to get home. He needed to ride out in front of those people who'd like nothing more than to see him dead.

Raising his arm, he swiped the sweat from his face. Then he set his hat low on his head to cast a deep shadow over his face. His side was damp and sticky. Must have opened up some of the stitches already. No surprise there.

"Home, Pistol. You have to get me home." He gave the horse a light touch with his heels and turned him so they would follow the route home right down the main street.

He felt in control now. Wouldn't allow himself to feel anything until they were out of sight of town. His jacket was secured so no one would see the telltale signs of blood. Sitting bolt upright in the saddle, he clenched his jaw tight and rode out into the dazzling sunlight.

He looked straight ahead, ignoring the stares of the people who crowded the sidewalk.

The only time he paused was outside the mayor's store. The man stood outside, staring like the rest. Johnny looked him up and down like he was something unpleasant he'd stepped in. Then he rode on.

It felt like one of the longest rides of his life. But he'd had worse. It went with the territory. Live by the gun. Die by the gun. Sometime.

Out of sight of town he slumped forward again, trusting Pistol to get him home. He'd keep his energy for the ride into the ranch. His head was swimming and he rested his head on Pistol's neck. Leastways if he passed out he wouldn't fall out of the saddle.

A strange moaning sound brought him to with a start. But then he relaxed as he realized the noise was coming from him. He must have been unconscious because the ranch was in sight. He pushed himself upright. Didn't want anyone to notice anything unusual.

It took all his strength to hold the position until he finally rode Pistol into the deserted barn where he fell out of the saddle into a pile of straw.

CHAPTER TWENTY-SIX

It felt like an eternity since Johnny had left for town. Guthrie could have sworn he'd worn a path in the floor as he paced back and forth, waiting for his return.

Why the hell did Johnny feel he had to deal with things in this way? He was supposed to be a rancher, not a gunfighter, but it seemed Fierro wasn't going to leave in a hurry. All Guthrie wanted was Johnny Sinclair. It was a pity that life was never that simple.

Cimarron needed a sheriff but it had needed one for a long time. He'd had arguments in the past with the store owners and the other ranchers but they weren't prepared to back him and contribute to the cost. Maybe now they'd see he'd been right all along. Hopefully, Guy's trip would bear fruit and they would attract someone of the right caliber to restore law and order and bring a little peace to the growing town.

If only Guy was here now. Could Guy have talked Johnny out of this mad idea? No, probably not. Johnny was a law unto himself. Seemed to live by his own code and didn't look like changing any time soon. Johnny was as wild as the horses that roamed the vast Sinclair spread, and far more difficult to tame.

He paused in his pacing. Difficult to tame? In fact, if he was honest, they'd made progress. He could see it now. The atmosphere between them was less strained. Except when something like this happened and Johnny went charging off to impose his own brand of law and order. He felt an all-too-familiar fear. He needed to know Johnny was safe. There were five men. How on earth did Johnny think he could deal with that by himself?

He looked up with a start as Peggy came in. "Can I get you anything, Uncle Guthrie? A drink or maybe a sandwich?"

He could see she was trying to be brave, trying to act normally. But the tearstained face couldn't be hidden. Poor Peggy. He knew she was desperately worried so he tried to look relaxed and cheerful for her sake. Didn't want her to see how worried he was too. "No, no thanks. I'm fine." Fine? God, he even sounded like Johnny.

Peggy's lower lip wobbled and fresh tears cascaded down her cheeks as she threw herself into Guthrie's arms. "He'll be all right, won't he? Tell me he'll be all right. He's been gone so long. Surely he should be back by now."

Guthrie held her tightly and made soothing noises as she sobbed into his chest. He wished he could make things better for her. Hell, he wished he could wave a magic wand and make things better for all of them.

"Peggy," he spoke gently. "These things take time. He had to get to town, assess the situation and decide how and when to deal with it. And then ride home again. It could be quite a while yet."

"Why didn't you stop him?" Tears choked her voice. "You shouldn't have let him go. You should have stopped him."

Guthrie looked at her and held her slightly away so he could see her face. "Do you think I could have stopped him?"

She sniffed noisily as she thought about it. "No . . . I don't suppose so. He does exactly what he wants."

"He's a grown man, Peggy. He's been on his own for a long time. Too long." He paused, as the reality of his own words hit him, Johnny had been on his own for far too long, much longer than anyone his age should have been. "There's nothing I could have said that would have made any difference. He'd made his mind up."

"But what if . . ." She gave another sob. "What if . . . I mean there are five of them. He can't take on five men."

He couldn't think of anything to say to that. Because all she was doing was voicing his unspoken fear.

"Darling, why don't you go and help Carlita in the kitchen? It'll help to keep busy."

She sniffed. "And you're sure I can't get you anything? A sandwich?"

He shook his head. "No, thanks. I'll wait. We'll all have dinner together later, when Johnny's home." Again the cold dread. When Johnny's home. Please God, let him come home.

He limped to the window as Peggy walked slowly back toward the kitchen. The damage from his old injuries troubled him far more when he was worried. Looking out, he could see the hands getting on with their chores, talking to each other, enjoying the sunshine. He envied them their apparent contentment. He turned back to sit at his desk, swiveling the chair toward the window so he could start the long vigil which he hoped would end with the sight of Johnny riding in. Coming home.

He sat for some time, his eyes never wavering from the horizon. Surely the boy should be back by now? Unless . . . But he couldn't bring himself to think of the alternative. A cold, paralyzing fear clutched his guts. Johnny would come home. He had to.

It seemed that hours passed before he glimpsed a rider on the horizon. As the figure came closer he could see that it was a buckskin horse. For a second he wondered if he was imagining it. But no, that was Johnny. He sat back in his chair, suddenly exhausted. Totally drained and feeling as though he'd done the hardest day's work of his life. He looked again, feeling the weight fall from his shoulders. As he focused on the figure, he sucked in his breath. His son slumped over Pistol's neck. But no, Johnny must have been leaning forward to adjust something on the bridle for now he was sitting bolt upright. He'd kept his promise — he was coming home.

He watched Johnny ride into the barn, making the decision to wait in the house for his son. He suspected Johnny wouldn't want to answer a barrage of questions. He'd give him some time.

Peggy had heard the hooves and came rushing to the window. She was obviously set on running straight out but Guthrie put a restraining hand on her. "Just let him be. I don't think he'll want to talk to any of us right now. There'll be time enough for that later. I think he'd rather be alone right now."

She nodded, her face glowing with relief. "I was so afraid that he wouldn't be coming back. That he . . ." She broke off, unable to voice the thought.

Guthrie patted her reassuringly on the back as she turned back to the kitchen. He sat down again to wait for Johnny to come in. His son certainly wasn't rushing. He'd obviously decided to rub down his horse and have some time alone before coming to the house. But thank God he was safe.

He felt a surge of anger. Everyone wanted to use his son when it suited them and then cast him off again. The petty-minded bigotry of his neighbors made his blood boil. Their rank hypocrisy. No wonder Johnny had a low opinion of his fellow man. He'd little reason to like them. Even Edith, who he'd thought he knew so well, even she could only see the labels. Breed. Gunfighter. She wasn't interested in knowing the man.

Knowing the man? At times Guthrie despaired of ever getting to know him either. Johnny wore his freedom like a crown and wrapped himself in an impenetrable suit of armor.

The big front door creaked open and he heard Johnny's footsteps in the hallway. He paused at the doorway of the living room and looked in, meeting Guthrie's eyes. Guthrie swallowed hard. God! Johnny looked so pale and older somehow than earlier in the day.

"Kept my promise." Johnny's voice was very low. "Came back straight after."

Guthrie thought he detected a note of irony in his son's tone. He looked all in. Dead on his feet. And he wondered what the cost of all this was to Johnny. "It's over?" He had to know. He wanted the details but knew it wasn't the time to ask.

"Yeah. It's over. Don't want to talk about it. I'm going to bed. I won't want dinner." Johnny turned away and Guthrie listened to his son's slow progress up the stairs. The boy looked awful. Well, the whole town had been baying for blood and it seemed Johnny had finally played their tune.

Would it ever end? Would people ever leave him in peace? Somehow he thought not. He'd hoped people would accept Johnny's presence after a while, get used to him being around. But now that hope was fading. Johnny had warned him what to expect, said it would be like this. And he, fool that he was, hadn't believed his son. He'd thought Johnny was being overly dramatic. Hell, why did people have to be so damned unpleasant?

He stood up and paced around the room. What a mess. These were people he'd known for years, except it seemed he hadn't known them at all. He paused at the doorway, noticing a wet patch on the floor. Someone must have spilled coffee. He bent to mop it up with his handkerchief, but instead of the familiar brown stain he expected to see, his handkerchief turned red. Blood red. And then he saw the trail of stains continuing up the stairway — the stairs Johnny had just walked.

He raced up the stairs and along the corridor. The telltale patches led to Johnny's door. And there the trail stopped. He had a momentary flash of Johnny's exhausted and pale face. How could he have been so blind?

He pushed open the door to see Johnny sitting on the bed, pulling a blood-soaked dressing away from his side. Johnny stared at him, his mouth set in a hard line and his eyes flashing with rage.

"Don't you ever barge into my room again. You fucking knock, Old Man, before you come in here. You hear me? You fucking knock." Johnny's voice faded. His face was white and he looked dreadful.

"Why the hell didn't you tell me you'd been hit? I'll send someone for Ben."

"No." Johnny's voice was stronger now, and as sharp as the crack of a bull whip. "Ben knows. He'll be here soon."

Guthrie stared at Johnny in confusion. "What do you mean, Ben knows?"

"He got the bullet out in town." Johnny sounded exhausted.

"And he let you ride home in this state?" Guthrie felt a wave of anger toward his old friend as he spoke. "The irresponsibility. What the hell was Ben thinking?"

"He had no choice. I wasn't staying in town. I wanted everyone to see me ride out. And Ben'll be here soon to patch me up again. Had worse." There was a touch of defiance in Johnny's voice.

Guthrie shook his head in exasperation. He'd never understand this boy. And what did he mean by saying he rode out so that people would see him? It didn't make any sense. "But why couldn't you just stay put? Ben would have looked after you. This is total madness."

"None of your fucking business."

He gritted his teeth. Why did Johnny always resort to foul language whenever they argued? To shock him? But for now he'd ignore it. "Just tell me why you embarked on such a crazy ride when you could have stayed in town. Please tell me it wasn't because of your promise to me to come straight home." Could all this have been his fault? Had Johnny been worried about breaking his word?

"You wouldn't understand." Johnny's tone was sullen and his face was devoid of all emotion, liked he'd wiped it all away. He wasn't even showing his pain now. He was giving nothing away.

"Please, son, try me. I would like to at least try and understand."

Johnny was silent for a second, and then he sighed softly. "I wouldn't give them the satisfaction. OK?"

Guthrie furrowed his brow, totally confused. No, it wasn't OK. "Give who what satisfaction?"

"Told you that you wouldn't understand." Johnny's voice was barely a whisper, as though he'd run out of energy.

"Please, son, give who what satisfaction? I really don't understand. But I'd like to."

Johnny shot him a glance from eyes dulled with pain. He looked as if he was fighting to stay conscious. "The people in town — they'd like nothing more than to see me killed in that shoot-out. And me getting hit would come a close second. So I was damned if I'd let them see. They can all go to hell."

Guthrie thought over his son's words. He wanted to say Johnny was overreacting, but if he was honest, he knew the boy's words were true. God, the boy was proud. No wonder Fierro had acquired his reputation if Johnny had always been that proud.

He was aware of Johnny watching him through half-closed eyes, waiting for a reaction. "Thank you. Now I do understand, Johnny. I really do. Even though I'd rather you hadn't risked hurting yourself worse by riding home."

Johnny's eyes widened with surprise. "You understand?"

Guthrie smiled. "Yes. But it doesn't mean I approve of you riding back, though."

"I don't want anyone here to know, either. They're bound to talk."

"I'll go and get Peggy to bring you some soup or something."

"No." Johnny's voice came out stronger now. He looked distressed. "Please, I don't want her to know about this. You know how she chatters to all her friends. She's bound to say something."

"I can keep a secret, you know." Peggy stood at the door, her face a picture of shock at the sight of Johnny. And she also looked indignant, hurt by his words.

"Dios." Johnny ran his hand through his hair. "I don't want anybody to know about this, Peggy. Nobody. OK?"

Guthrie could see she was confused, but she nodded. "I'll keep it a secret, don't worry. Will you be all right? Can I get you something? Anything at all? I'm sure you should have something."

Johnny shook his head. His hand, which was clutching a towel to his side, was shaking as he tried to stanch the blood flow. He seemed to struggle to answer. "No. Ben'll be here soon."

"I'm already here!" The doctor walked into the room, easing past Peggy in the doorway. "I did call, but I got no answer so I let myself in." He eyed Johnny with obvious concern. "God, you're a mess." He turned toward Guthrie. "Can you and Peggy go downstairs, please, and leave me to deal with my patient." He was already opening his black bag. He shook his head, as though irritated. "I can see you're going to be my most difficult patient. Let me have a look at that."

Guthrie ushered Peggy out of the room, closing the door gently after them as he offered up a silent prayer of thanks that Ben had arrived so promptly.

He followed her to the living room, where she sank into a chair, her face pale and drawn. "Why doesn't he want people to know he's hurt? I don't understand."

Guthrie sighed as he poured himself a drink and turned to face her. "He's a very proud man. He knows that a lot of our neighbors will be delighted he's hurt. Many of them would have liked to have seen him killed. They don't want Johnny Fierro around, even though he came to their aid."

"But he's done them all a favor. Given them what they wanted. They should all be grateful." She sounded indignant. Her face was flushed and she was clenching her hands. "Poor Johnny risked his life and people are just downright mean."

Guthrie smiled ruefully. "People are strange, darling. And they often resent being indebted to someone who's done them a favor. I think we should go along with Johnny's wishes on this and keep it within the family."

He threw a log on the fire and sat down to wait for Ben while Peggy went off to brew beef tea for her foster brother. Thank God the doctor had turned up so quickly. But Johnny's ride home had been crazy. He could have killed himself. And the thought slid into Guthrie's mind that Johnny didn't seem to value his own skin at all. In fact the boy seemed totally reckless when it came to his own safety. It was as if he didn't care if he lived or died, and he was far too young to feel like that.

The sound of Ben clattering down the stairs shook him out of his reverie. "Is he going to be all right, Ben?"

Ben sank into a chair by the blazing fire, accepting the whiskey that Guthrie had poured for him. "Yes, I think so. It's deep but the wound is fairly clean, so provided there's no infection, he should mend. Judging by the scars on him, he's had worse. But he's too damn stubborn. What he did today was crazy, and unnecessary."

"He's very proud." Guthrie spoke softly. "I wish I knew what goes on in that head of his. But it's like living with a puzzle. And it seems that every time I think I've found an answer, the puzzle changes to something totally different."

Ben sipped his whiskey, looking thoughtful. He shot Guthrie a look. "I've told you before. You'll never understand him until you understand what his childhood was like. It's the boy that makes the man."

Guthrie shook his head, irritated. "He won't tell me anything. It's a forbidden topic. I know nothing of his past and I don't see him opening up any time soon." Guthrie paused. "I know nothing of his past! That's a hell of a thing to have to admit about my own son."

"Give him time, Guthrie. He needs to learn to trust you. This is a huge adjustment. I don't think he's had to explain himself to anyone in years, not anyone who cared, or live by a routine, or even have somewhere to call home. Beneath that very prickly exterior and cold demeanor, there's a good man. Even if he doesn't recognize that in himself, it's there." Ben paused, and then looked up with a smile. "You know, he might be my most difficult patient, even including present company, but I have to confess, just between the two of us, that I like him."

Later, after Ben had headed back to town, Guthrie sat reflecting on his friend's words. He felt a warm glow and it definitely wasn't attributable to merely the fire. No, Ben's words had soothed him. The boy had found an ally outside the family circle, one he could respect. Things could only get better.

CHAPTER TWENTY-SEVEN

He had a bad night. His side hurt like hell and he was afraid to close his eyes and sleep. His nightly tormentors invaded his mind. Whenever he dozed off, the demons took over. And now there were even more of them. Five more. It was better to stay awake.

He couldn't regret the gunfight in Cimarron. He'd done what he had to do. But he longed for some peace. A good night's sleep, a dreamless sleep. What the hell would that be like?

Still, he'd got the better of the people in town and he'd made them pay. It felt good to know he'd outsmarted them. And the old man had seemed to understand. That surprised him. He'd thought his father would just pitch into him, but instead he'd seemed more concerned that Johnny was safe. That felt real good.

Poor Lizzie. She'd been in the wrong place at the wrong time. He hoped she had the guts to make a fresh start. Leastways, she had the money to do that now. Maybe her luck would change. Maybe she really would take a chance at starting over and would strike gold. This was probably the first real chance she'd ever had. Maybe things would work out for her. Maybe . . . Shit, life was full of maybes and what ifs.

He wished Guy was home. It would be good to have someone to talk to — and that was an odd thing to want. Couldn't remember ever wanting to talk to a particular person before. He'd never let anyone get that close until he'd come home. Still, Guy should be back by the evening. But he'd bet that Guy would yell at him and tell him he was crazy, risking his life and all. Harvard didn't understand that he didn't care. Everyone died sooner or later. Didn't really matter at all.

The sun was coming up, casting a golden glow into his room, promising a fine day. He lay back against the pillows, watching the fingers of dawn spreading their soft light over the mountains.

He shut his eyes again. Maybe he could catch a little more sleep. It was easier in the light. It was the darkness that held danger. And too many damn ghosts.

When he awoke again, the sun was high

in the sky. He must have slept for hours. Easing himself up, he was relieved to find he could move without too much discomfort. There was a tray next to the bed so someone must have come in with it but he hadn't heard a thing. Normally he woke at the slightest sound.

He felt hungry so that had to be a good sign. He leaned carefully across to see what he'd got. The muffins and fruit looked good. There was a jug of coffee too. He stuck his finger in it to see if it was still warm, but it was cold. He really had slept for a long time.

As he ate, he figured out how to hide his injury. He could spin a yarn to the ranch hands to explain why he wasn't riding for a few days. Could say the old man was making him go through all the books and accounts for a few days as a punishment for his latest gunfight. That should stop any questions. And he could always drive the wagon if they needed supplies from town. Nobody would know there was anything wrong, so long as he played the part.

Looking through the window he spotted a couple of the local ranchers heading out toward their horses. They were walking close, like they didn't want anyone else to hear what they were saying. They'd obviously been to see the old man. But, strangely, he didn't feel worried. He figured that Guthrie wouldn't have given anything away. Would have kept Johnny's injury a secret within the family. Family? It took some getting used to. But somehow, deep down, he was certain that the old man wouldn't have let him down.

Guthrie had sure been pissed off by the locals lately. He'd backed Johnny. Even said the right things. Maybe Delice was right. She'd said they were on the same side. And hearing the old man support him against all the opposition had felt real good, like he mattered and he sure wasn't used to that.

Turning away from the window, he struggled into some clothes, taking care not to pull the stitches. Didn't think Ben would be too pleased if he had to stitch him up a third time.

He made his way very slowly down the stairs. Getting dressed had taken more out of him than he'd expected, and he hissed at each jarring step. He stopped halfway to get his breath and have a rest. Still, could be worse. And he'd try to be sensible and take things easy for a few days. Ben said he'd get better quicker if he did that. And Ben seemed to be good at his trade. So maybe he'd follow doctor's orders — just this once.

His father was sitting at his desk by the

window with his head bowed like he was lost in thought. Maybe chewing over whatever those ranchers had come to see him about. He looked up sharply as Johnny shuffled in, trying not to look as bad as he felt.

"Should you be up? Surely Ben told you to stay put for a while longer?"

Johnny shrugged. "Don't fuss. I'm being careful. Just ain't one for lying around. Figured I'd see if there was something useful I could do." Maybe that would please the old man. Keep him happy. But he looked real grumpy right now.

"I had a visit this morning from a couple of our neighbors, local ranchers."

"Yeah. I saw them ride off. What did they want? Making trouble?"

The old man was glaring good now. Like he was pissed off about something.

"They told me that you charged a very large fee for dealing with those saddle tramps. Thirteen hundred dollars."

The way the old man said it was like he couldn't believe it. Like he must have heard wrong or something.

Just play it cool, relaxed. Johnny shrugged. "They'd offered to pay so I figured they damn well could. I was putting my life on the line and that don't come cheap. If they'd any guts between them they could have handled it themselves. It didn't have to come to this."

The old man stood and started pacing back and forth across the room. If he carried on like that he'd wear a trench in the floor. "I didn't think you were going to demand money when you rode in yesterday. It's hiring out. I thought that was over. Thought you were starting fresh."

Yeah, the old man was pissed. Johnny shrugged. "I know it's hiring out. But they wanted the job done. Hell, the whole town wanted the job done. Well, they got it done. Why should I do it for nothing?"

"Because you're part of this community, damn it!" That vein was pulsing in the side of the old man's head, just like it always did when he got riled. "All you've succeeded in doing is reinforcing their opinions of you. Gun for hire."

Johnny clenched his fists and tried to keep the lid on his temper. Play nice. But fuck it, why should he? "They wanted a gun for hire so they fucking well got one. And do you really think I care what they think of me? People are all the same, and they all want to use me when it suits them. You think if I'd done their dirty work for nothing they'd have thought any better of me? Bullshit."

"You have to give the money back. All of it."

Shit. The old man was loco. But he had a steely look in his eye, like he meant what he said. "You got to be kidding!"

His father glared. "I am not kidding. You must give it back. It's not right to profit out of something like this."

Johnny fixed his iciest expression in place. Seemed the old man needed to hear some home truths. "It's what I do, didn't you know?"

The old man paused in his pacing. "I mean it, Johnny, give it back."

Johnny waited. Let the silence unnerve the old man. Yeah. That vein was pulsing faster now. Johnny smiled and then spoke real soft. "Well, that could be kind of tricky, Old Man." He paused, let Guthrie think on that. Then, in a soft drawl, he added: "You see, I ain't got it anymore."

His father's mouth dropped open, like he was lost for words. But not for long. "What d'you mean, you haven't got it anymore? You haven't had time to spend it. It's a lot of money."

Johnny fiddled with one of the conchos on his trouser leg. Kicked at the floor. Then looked up, met his father's eyes. "Well, thing is, I gave it to the girl. Figured the town

347

owed her and I owed her. So I really don't have it anymore."

His father's mouth had dropped open again. Was staring at him like he thought Johnny had gone loco. "You gave it to the girl? The one who was raped? The whore?"

Johnny narrowed his eyes. "The girl who was raped. Yeah."

The old man turned an interesting shade of purple. And didn't look none too impressed.

"You gave thirteen hundred dollars to a whore? Have you gone mad?"

"Nope. If I'd dealt with this when they first asked me, this wouldn't have happened. We all owed her." He knew his father wouldn't understand this. And that vein was pulsing even faster. Any minute it would explode.

"You're crazy. Nobody gives that much money to a whore. What the hell got into you?"

Johnny tried to unclench his fists. But he was itching to punch the old man.

Play nice.

No. Not this time. "Stop calling her a whore." The words came out like an explosion. "She's just a girl. A girl who didn't do anyone any harm. Maybe, just maybe, that money will give her a fresh start. A chance to go somewhere new, get away from all this. She didn't deserve what happened and the town . . ." He paused, tried to control himself. "I should have stopped it from happening. Could have stopped it. We're all guilty. So, yeah, I've made everyone pay. Hell, the town can afford it. Maybe now they'll pay for a sheriff."

His father threw his hands up. "None of this was your fault. You didn't need to ride in and deal with it this way. You should have stayed home and we'd have got the law to deal with it. Instead, you went charging off, almost got yourself killed and made the town pay out a great deal of money. What the hell do you think people are going to say if they hear you gave all their money to a whore?"

He bit his lip, really bit it so it hurt. But he knew it wasn't enough. Knew he'd really let rip if he didn't put a stop to all this talk. He shut his eyes briefly as he turned toward the door. "You don't get it, do you? I don't care what they say. That was my pay. What I do with it is up to me. Ain't nobody telling me what to do. And that includes you, Old Man."

"We haven't finished yet."

Johnny ignored him. His side hurt like hell now and it was all he could do to make it up the stairs back to the sanctuary of his room. Looked like that was where he'd be spending the rest of the day, 'cos he sure as hell wasn't talking any longer.

CHAPTER TWENTY-EIGHT

Guy sat slumped, listening to Guthrie's tirade about what Johnny had been up to while he was away on his trip to Santa Fe.

It had been a tiring trip but he'd come home optimistic that the advertisements would bear fruit and Cimarron would soon have a sheriff. He'd looked forward to an enjoyable evening back with his family. He certainly hadn't expected to find that Johnny had taken the law into his own hands, gone to town and killed five men. Five! God, it was like the dreadful business in Bitterville all over again. Except this time Johnny had caught a bullet and could have been killed. The thought of Johnny being killed gave him a cold, empty feeling in the pit of his stomach. And he found it impossible to understand how Johnny could behave so recklessly and with such apparent disregard for his own safety. Life out here was so strange, like living in a foreign country.

"But Johnny really is going to be all right?" He interrupted Guthrie's rant about his brother's shortcomings. He wondered how much of it was Guthrie's way of letting out pent-up emotions because he'd probably been terrified by Johnny's near brush with death.

Guthrie gave an impatient grunt. "Yes. Ben says he'll be all right, thank God. But he gave all that money to a whore. A whore! I think the boy's taken leave of his senses."

Guy sighed. "I think, sir, by Johnny's code, he would think he'd done the right thing."

"What do you mean, by his code?" Guthrie sounded very suspicious, as though he thought that Guy was privy to some closely guarded secret.

"Well, he obviously felt that if either he, or the town, had dealt with the saddle tramps earlier, none of this would have happened. I think he would have seen it as only right that the girl be compensated for the dreadful thing that happened to her because it could have been avoided. Don't you see, to him, what he's done is the honorable thing? Justice if you like."

Guthrie frowned and looked taken aback. "Justice?"

Guy nodded wearily. "Yes. Justice. He

might handle things differently than you and I would, but he has a strong sense of right and wrong. A strong moral center."

Guthrie raised an eyebrow. "A moral center? This of the boy who goes whoring at every opportunity and kills without any apparent sign of it affecting him?"

"Yes." Guy used his most authoritative tone. The tone he would use to the soldiers in his command when they were being particularly obtuse and thickheaded. "A moral center. To him, whoring is just a way of life, something he's probably been doing for years. He doesn't see anything wrong about it.

"As for his killings, I think he's very much affected, but he's far too proud to let you see that. He's very good at hiding his emotions. Look at how he struggled to hide his pain when he was injured in the battle with Wallace. And from what you say, because of his pride, he was determined to hide, from the people in Cimarron, the fact he'd been shot. He hides behind a mask of invulnerability, but it is just that — a mask. Make no mistake."

Guthrie sank down into a chair. "I never know what to say to him. I always put my foot in it, say something that makes him angry. I just don't have a clue how to deal with him."

Guy viewed his father curiously. "Why do you feel you have to deal with him? Just trust him. He usually does the right thing. It's just that his methods are somewhat unorthodox."

Guthrie gave a rueful laugh. "Unorthodox. That's one way of putting it."

"He's a good man. Trust me. And start trusting him."

Guy watched as Guthrie seemed to ponder the advice, before nodding slowly. Thank heavens he appeared to have finally calmed down.

"And the money? What on earth are people going to think about that when they find out that Johnny gave it all to the girl? Because one thing you can be certain of is that they will find out."

Guy grinned. "Does it really matter? They've treated Johnny appallingly and they won't think any better of him if he gives them their money back. Johnny once told me that the difference between him and me is that I'm always surprised when people behave badly, whereas he never is. I'm beginning to see his point of view. One of these days you will too."

Guthrie started to laugh and it seemed the years fell off him then. "OK. You win.

You're right of course. People haven't given him a chance." He paused, the laughter fading. He shook his head as though in sorrow. "Men I've known for almost thirty years have treated him like dirt. It seems I didn't know them at all. And Edith . . . I thought I knew her well but I never recognized her prejudices. Until now."

Guy shrugged. "She'll get used to him. Johnny doesn't want you to stop socializing with our neighbors. For a start, if you did, it would only make him feel guilty that he'd caused you so much trouble. And besides, he knows we have to get along with them. He's just not prepared to go out of his way to be friendly when he knows what they really think of him. And I can't say I blame him. Quite frankly, if this whole dreadful business has cost the town a lot of money, then that's fine by me. It'll make them appreciate a sheriff a lot more."

Guthrie nodded. "Yes, that's a good point." He paused, and flushed slightly as though embarrassed. "Thank you, son, for helping me see things a little clearer. I'll speak to your brother tomorrow. Try and mend fences."

Guy offered up a silent prayer of thanks that another potentially damaging clash between Guthrie and Johnny had been averted. He hauled himself to his feet, rubbing his aching back. "I think that would be a very good idea. I'll go and look in on him now to see if he needs anything."

He trudged upstairs feeling totally drained. Playing peacemaker was an exhausting business, even without a trip to Santa Fe. He knocked on the door to Johnny's room.

"Go away."

Guy smiled. He'd expected that response. "Johnny, it's me. I've just got back and I thought you'd like to hear about how my trip went."

There was a long silence. Guy leaned against the door and tried to stretch the crick out of his neck.

"OK. Come in."

Pushing open the door, Guy forced a cheerful smile, not wanting Johnny to see how very tired he was. "It seems as soon as I turn my back, you manage to land yourself in a load of trouble."

Johnny was sitting by the open window, his hair blowing in the cool breeze. His pale face was impassive. "Thought you wanted to talk about your trip."

Guy grinned. "I lied. Your exploits sound far more interesting than mine." He hoped Johnny would catch his mood, throw him one of his infectious smiles. But his brother bowed his head and fiddled with the gun which lay dismantled in his lap. It was only then that Guy noticed the bottle of gun oil and the cloths.

When Johnny spoke, his tone was very cool. "My exploits? It's not a game, Guy."

He'd misjudged this badly. Guy sighed. "I do know that. But I thought that you might appreciate some company." He paused, wondering how to phrase his next remarks. "And I thought you might like to know that Father's calmed down. He's not mad at you anymore."

That got his attention. Johnny's head jerked up. "He ain't?" There was a flicker of pleasure in Johnny's eyes.

Guy smiled, relieved his brother's mood had improved instantly. He really wished he could knock Guthrie's and Johnny's heads together. The irony was how alike they were in so many ways, but neither one could see it. "No, he isn't mad anymore. Let's just say he's looking at things differently now."

Johnny ducked his head and started fiddling with his gun again. Guy waited patiently. He was learning that when Johnny did this it was usually a precursor to an embarrassed admission. "That due to you, Harvard?"

Guy shrugged. "We talked."

"Thanks, Guy." Johnny hesitated, started fiddling with the damn gun again. "Look, I know . . ." He paused again. "I mean, I know it can't be easy. Being caught in the middle and all. But, well, I do appreciate it."

Another small step forward. He felt like cheering but contented himself with a smile of acknowledgment. "Which of the girls was it?"

Johnny gave a long sigh. He looked exhausted, like he hardly had the energy to stay upright in his chair. "I was wondering if you'd ask."

"Did you think I wouldn't care?"

Johnny took a few seconds to answer, just sat staring down at his gun as he fitted it back together. "I wasn't sure. Thought maybe in your world . . . I hoped you'd ask." Johnny hesitated again, loaded the gun and then weighed it in his hand before looking up at Guy. "It was Lizzie."

Guy frowned as he tried to recall Lizzie.

Johnny helped him out. "Blue eyes, brown wavy hair. Older than the others."

"Ah, yes. I remember Lizzie. She has freckles. Is she going to be all right?"

Johnny's expression was bleak. "I dunno, Guy. Is anyone ever really OK after that?

They were a bunch of brutes . . ." He trailed off and stared in silence out into the dark night.

"Johnny, what you did . . . giving her the money . . . it was a very kind gesture."

Johnny turned back to stare at him. "Kind? Don't you see? If I'd dealt with it when those ranchers first asked me, this wouldn't have happened. I owed her. This is my fault."

Guy shook his head gently, wondering how best to help and say the right thing. "It's not your fault. Why do you hold yourself responsible for other people's failings? You could say that we're all to blame. Or none of us. The guilty men are those who carried out the act."

His brother shook his head. "I knew there'd be trouble. And I knew nobody else would deal with it. That it would be up to me. But I thought I'd make the town wait. Wanted them begging for my help. And because I did that, Lizzie suffered. The sin is mine."

"Sin?" Guy was puzzled by Johnny's use of the word. He hadn't thought of his brother as a religious man. Far from it. But it seemed an incongruous word to use.

"Yeah, sin." Johnny's face was etched with pain. He should be lying down but Guy knew better than to suggest it. Yet. Better to wait until Johnny was too exhausted to put up a fight.

"I mean I know I'll go to hell. Nothing's going to change that. The things I've done . . . But sometimes I need to do something that I know feels right, just so I can go on living with myself."

He's serious. He really means it. Guy felt a wave of sadness sweep over him as he looked at Johnny's bowed head. And he couldn't think of a damned thing to say that would help. But he had to say something to try and ease his brother's suffering. Because suffering it undoubtedly was.

"Have you spoken to a priest?" He knew Johnny was notionally a Catholic so presumably a priest would be the right person to speak to.

Johnny gave a hollow laugh. "Not much point in that. They washed their hands of me a long time ago. Told me I'm beyond redemption."

Redemption. Never in his wildest imagination had he ever expected to be discussing religious doctrine with a gunfighter. "But I thought, in the Catholic Church, you get redemption when you repent. Isn't that all part of the process of confession?" Guy was a little hazy about the mechanics of absolu-

360

tion and repentance but he was sure that he recalled hearing about it in the army and at Harvard. But it was very different to the faith in which he was raised.

"Yeah, but that's it. You got to be repentant and I sure as hell ain't repentant about every man I've ever killed. Some maybe. But not all. So I'm damned."

"You really believe that?" Guy stared at Johnny in amazement. It seemed a very harsh and absolute approach. He was sure that good deeds could outweigh bad, a sort of heavenly ledger book with credits and debits.

Johnny's eyes were dulled by pain and he was shifting uncomfortably in his chair. "Yeah, I really believe that." He shrugged, and winced. "It's how things are. So, how did you get on in Santa Fe?"

It wasn't a very subtle way of trying to change the subject but it was as good as any. And because he could see how exhausted Johnny was, Guy thought it would be as well to go along with it. They could discuss religion and philosophy another day.

"I've arranged for advertisements in Santa Fe, Albuquerque, across into Colorado and down into Arizona. That should get some response and hopefully, somewhere in all that territory is the man we need for Cimar-

361

ron." Guy paused and decided to bite the bullet. "And now, could I help you back to bed? I mean, I know you're absolutely fine, but it seems to me a helping hand wouldn't do any harm."

He was rewarded by a soft laugh. "Yeah, well, of course I'm fine. Never been better. But OK, just this once I'll accept a helping hand. Wouldn't want you to feel that you're a waste of space."

Guy grinned and eased Johnny to his feet and supported him as he walked with agonizing slowness back to the bed.

He was turning to leave when Johnny spoke again. "And really? The old man's not mad at me no more?"

Guy smiled across at him. "No, he's really not angry anymore. He was even talking about apologizing to you tomorrow. That should be something to look forward to."

He turned away quickly, trying to suppress his smile at the look of happy confusion on Johnny's face. "Good night, Johnny." And as he softly shut the door, he found himself hoping that Johnny would have a good night, without any nightmares.

Chapter Twenty-Nine

Guthrie watched Guy trudge up the stairs and felt a pang of guilt. Guy had looked exhausted when he arrived home. He'd slid wearily from his horse instead of dismounting in his usual brisk manner. He'd probably been looking forward to a nice quiet evening at home but instead he'd walked into the middle of yet another battle between his father and brother. And yet again Guy had stepped in to play peacemaker. It was a role he had to play all too often. And Guthrie knew he was entirely to blame for the latest fight between himself and Johnny.

He'd been so frightened for his son the previous day. The thought that Johnny could be killed had terrified him. When he'd seen the boy riding home, seemingly unharmed, the sense of relief had been overwhelming. But it had been short-lived. To discover Johnny had been shot and could have died, had brought all his raw, unexpressed emotions flooding back. And then to have the visit from two neighbors complaining about the amount of money Johnny had demanded for his services, it had all seemed too much to bear.

He'd been caught off balance by the visit. He'd played his hand well, though. His visitors had left not realizing that Guthrie hadn't known about Johnny's fee, and he hadn't given them any hint that Johnny had been wounded. He'd been determined to hold Johnny's trust. But after they'd left he'd felt a totally irrational anger that he'd been left in the dark about the money. But now he'd calmed down he appreciated that Johnny had been in no fit state the previous evening to tell him anything about what had transpired. Now he felt guilty over the way he'd lit into Johnny earlier. Just when things had been going better between the two of them, when it seemed they were finally making some progress, he'd gone and messed it all up.

He shivered. The room was chilly as the fire dwindled in the hearth. He threw some logs on and watched as the flames caught the dry wood and went licking up the chimney. Pouring himself another whiskey he reflected on Guy's words. Justice. Was that really how Johnny viewed it? There'd been that business in Bitterville just a few weeks earlier. Then Johnny had ridden in to avenge the deaths of two vaqueros. Although Guy had insisted it had been a joint decision, Guthrie hadn't believed him. He suspected Guy had probably tried to keep the lid on the situation and failed. Johnny Fierro had taken the law into his own hands and dealt out his own brand of revenge. Or justice?

It certainly seemed that Johnny had been on the side of the angels then, even if his course of action was not one Guthrie could condone. But there was no denying that it had been a justice of sorts. Just as the latest gunfight could be called justice.

A moral center? Maybe Guy was right. Johnny had again chosen to exact his own brand of revenge, and was prepared to risk his life in the process. Just like he'd done when he'd taken on all of Wallace's men in the battle to save the ranch. Johnny's main concern then had been for the safety of the women on the ranch.

Guthrie laughed ruefully as the truth of Guy's words hit home. Johnny did usually do the right thing, but in an exceptionally unorthodox manner and without any regard for his own safety. He'd been viewing all of Johnny's actions from the wrong angle. But, hell, the boy was hard to fathom. Like giving all that money to the girl who'd been raped. He could see that it was a kind gesture but to give her thirteen hundred dollars seemed excessive. Quite why Johnny had felt it incumbent on himself to present her with that much money was beyond him. He shook his head. Would he ever understand what went on in Johnny's mind?

He took another sip of his whiskey as he reflected on what Ben was always saying. That he'd never understand his son until he understood the boy's past. Not much chance of that at the current time and he knew he'd only himself to blame. Johnny wouldn't be confiding in him any time soon. All he'd done was push the boy further away.

If only Johnny would spend more evenings at home, maybe they could get to know each other. But the boy went whoring at every opportunity and was certainly making a name for himself on that score. Guthrie grimaced as he imagined what his own parents would have said if they were still alive. And God knows what Gabriela would have said. She wouldn't have approved of her son's behavior. She'd always been very scathing about putas. But Guthrie felt it was probably politic not to point that out to

Johnny. It seemed that any mention of Gabriela just drove the boy even further away. Instead, he needed to mend fences and try to repair the damage he'd inflicted on those first early buds of progress in his relationship with Johnny.

He sighed and set his glass down firmly on the table. The easiest thing would be to leave an apology until the morning. But it wouldn't be the right thing. And while he was all too aware that Johnny needed his rest, perhaps he needed an apology from his father even more. He got wearily to his feet and limped toward the stairs with some trepidation. If only he knew how to handle Johnny . . . Handle him? What was it Guy had said? Just trust him. Guy seemed to, and he was nobody's fool.

He tried to ignore the tight knot in his gut as he made his way slowly toward Johnny's room with about as much enthusiasm as a man walking to his execution. The fact was that Johnny always unnerved him. It was that curious stillness the boy seemed able to achieve. It reminded him of an animal waiting to pounce on its prey. And then there were those cool eyes that gave nothing away but seemed to look straight into the heart of a man. Johnny Fierro would make a formidable opponent. He only hoped that under the tarnished suit of armor he would find Johnny Sinclair.

Gritting his teeth, he gave a tentative tap on his son's door. An apology of a knock in all honesty, and he still hadn't a clue what he was going to say.

"Yeah?"

His son's soft drawl didn't sound too welcoming, but he opened the door gently and eased his way into the room. Johnny was sitting on the bed, shirtless, with the bandages showing very white against his dark skin. He looked at Guthrie without expression and said nothing.

"Um, I was wondering whether you needed anything? A drink? Something to eat?"

"Harvard's already been and asked me that. And the answer is the same. I'm fine." His tone was neutral, giving nothing away. For heaven's sake, why did he always say he was fine? Guthrie had the feeling that Johnny would say he was fine if he'd been shot full of bullets and was bleeding his last in the street.

"Was there anything else, Old Man?"

The drawl was casual, but those cool eyes bored right into him. He could almost believe that Johnny could see his knotted gut and the thoughts somersaulting through his mind. Guthrie nodded reluctantly. "Yes, there was. I . . . I believe I owe you an apology. My behavior this morning . . . What I said . . ."

There wasn't a flicker in those blue eyes. Nothing. Guthrie swallowed hard. This wasn't going to be easy. But then, he'd never thought it would be. "I shouldn't have lit into you today. You were right, it's your money and it's nobody's business what you do with it. And . . ." He swallowed again, looked for some reaction, but Johnny sat motionless. "And you were right: people wouldn't think any more of you if you'd done their dirty work for nothing.

"I overreacted. I admit I hoped that your days of gunfighting were over. Wanted them to be over." Guthrie paused, looking through the open window briefly before looking once more at Johnny. "And when you rode into town, I was . . ." He paused again, this was so difficult. "I was terrified. Terrified that you'd be killed. Five men . . ." He trailed off, unsure of what to say next and embarrassed by the naked honesty of his admission. The silence filled the room like a thick fog. He wished Johnny would say something. Anything. But he still sat motionless, watching his father intently, no flicker of emotion in those eyes at all.

"Anyway, I wanted to apologize. And for what it's worth, I didn't let anything slip to those men this morning. Nobody knows you were hit."

Johnny shifted slightly, looked down at the floor briefly before meeting Guthrie's eyes. "I guessed you wouldn't let me down."

Guthrie started with surprise. "You did? You trusted me?" And he felt hope surging through him.

Johnny gave a slight shrug and just the hint of a smile seemed to play at his mouth. "Well, I figured you'd think I'd shoot you if you gave me away." The smile had spread now and Guthrie suddenly felt years younger.

"I really am sorry, son. I think we'd better put it down to the release of pent-up emotions."

Johnny grinned. "I'd say it was that you didn't like having two men turn up knowing more about what went on in town than you did. And the fact that you didn't know about the money. But if it keeps you happy we'll say it was pent-up emotions."

Guthrie narrowed his eyes and gave Johnny a long look. "You know, you always were too damn smart for your own good."

Johnny shrugged, wincing as he did so. "How d'you think I stayed alive so long?

Damn, I'm beat."

Guthrie wondered whether to offer Johnny a hand, but he bit back the question. Discretion was definitely the better part of valor and now that Johnny seemed in a good mood he didn't want to ruin the moment.

"Guy's trip went well." That seemed a good neutral subject to discuss.

Johnny gave him a quick searching glance, and raised his eyebrow a fraction as though guessing the reason for the change of subject. "Yeah, he told me. I guess now the trouble's over, you might get someone interested in the job." Johnny paused as he tried to maneuver himself into a different position. "But I wouldn't bet on the town chipping in to pay for a sheriff. They got short memories. When things are going well they don't want to pay for nothing. And now they'll be mad about paying me." Johnny smiled briefly. "They'll go back to treating me like shit and want me gone."

Guthrie gave Johnny a shrewd look. The boy was certainly cynical, but it was probably a realistic assessment of the situation. "But I trust you won't be giving them the satisfaction."

"Hell, no. It's much more fun pissing them all off." Johnny paused and stared down at the floor before looking back at

Guthrie. "As long as you're sure you really want me to stay. I mean, I'd understand if you didn't want me around. We both know I bring trouble, even if Harvard don't see it. And word's gonna get out that I'm here and I reckon there'll be people come looking for me. So, if you want me to go, just come right out and say it."

There was a touch of defiance in his son's voice, as though daring Guthrie to be honest. When would Johnny give up with this line of questioning? And what did he have to say to convince the boy that he really was wanted? God, he wished he knew how to say the right thing, but how could he when he didn't understand what Johnny needed to hear? Things were going well; he didn't want to mess it up again. And he had to admit that where Johnny was concerned he did have a talent for saying the wrong thing.

"Please, son, we've been over this ground before and I know you find it difficult to accept but I really do want you here. If people from the past show up, well, we'll deal with it, but we'll do so as a family. We haven't been together long and we're all still getting used to each other, but this is your home. It's where you were born, where you should have grown up and it's where you belong." He was rewarded by a brief flicker of surprise in Johnny's eyes. God, the boy really did have a hard time accepting that anyone could want him. Damn Gabriela. What the hell had happened to the boy in those missing years and why was he so sure no one would want him? He felt he should emphasize the point. "And as for the locals, they'll get used to you being around. It'll take time, I know that, and I know you find it difficult to adjust, but we'll get there."

Johnny appeared to be studying the floor, hunched over and not looking at him. Any minute he'd shrug again. Yep, there it was. He strained to catch his son's words.

"Well, if you're sure. But if you change your mind . . ." Johnny's voice trailed off.

"I won't change my mind. Now, I think it's time you got some rest." He hesitated before deciding to risk his next question. "You're sure you don't want anything? Peggy made some soup . . ."

"No, it's OK, I'm . . ."

"Fine?" Guthrie finished the sentence and felt like he'd won first prize in a contest when he was rewarded by a grin.

"Yeah, I'm just fine."

Guthrie was opening the door when Johnny spoke again, very softly. "Thanks, Guthrie."

Guthrie couldn't repress the broad smile

that spread over his face. "Good night, Johnny." And he had a spring in his step as he went on along the corridor to his own room to turn in for the night.

CHAPTER THIRTY

Johnny leaned against the corral rails and bitched. "I tell you, if the old man makes me do any more fucking books, I'm out of here."

The ranch hands didn't trust him, he knew that, but as long as they bought the story he was selling, he didn't give a shit. All they needed to hear was that his father was mad at him about the gunfight and this was how he was making Johnny suffer. Not that the hands would feel sorry for him. But that wasn't the point. Just as long as they believed it.

The two ranch hands looked uncomfortable, muttered some lame excuses and shuffled off. He smiled. He knew he was putting them in a tight spot having to listen to him bitching about their boss. Didn't matter none. It served a purpose. It grated though. Equal partners, but everyone knew Guthrie was the boss.

He was still sore from the bullet but he'd been good, followed Ben's orders and done damn little for days. He was recovering quicker than normal, so maybe following doctor's orders did pay off sometimes. Even so, he'd rather do things his way. Hated following orders. Even Ben's.

He knew his family thought he was crazy to hide that he'd been shot up. They didn't understand that in his business, reputation was everything. And so, whether they liked it or not, he'd play things his way. He'd come out of this with his reputation intact, maybe even added to it. Another gunfight where Fierro walked away without a mark on him. He knew he was supposed to be leaving that life behind but he had to protect his reputation. Couldn't just let it go, not even while he was here.

He was surprised at how the old man had backed down after their fight. Hell, Guthrie had apologized to him — said sorry. Could hardly believe that. Trouble was, now the old man was fishing. Fishing for information about the past. Johnny's past. Johnny's mother. Maybe not pushing hard, but pushing all the same and Johnny sure wasn't opening up that can of worms with his father. Shit, it was bad enough that he had to remember everything without fucking talking about it. But if the old man kept pushing, he would walk away. Walk back to a life he no longer wanted. It would be better than talking about his mother.

Turning away from the corral, he caught a glimpse of Ben driving up to the house. Come to check up on him probably. No one seemed to trust him, but, hell, that was nothing new. He walked over to greet Ben as the doctor hopped down from the buggy. "There ain't anyone here but me, Ben. If you wanted Guthrie and Guy, they went into town to look through all them letters that keep turning up from people wanting the sheriff's job."

Ben nodded. "I know. I saw them. It's you I wanted to see. Find out how you're doing."

Johnny scowled, glancing around quickly to make sure that no one could have overheard the doc. "Best come inside, then." He led the way into the house, where no one could see or hear them. He knew Peggy and Carlita were visiting one of the vaquero's wives who'd just had her first child.

"I'm fine now, Ben. Wondered if I could ride into town this week."

Ben just shook his head. "Take your shirt off and let me have a look at you first. Then I'll make a decision."

Johnny shrugged himself out of his shirt. "I got needs, you know."

Ben laughed. "Yes, I know. I think you might have mentioned your needs before."

"So?" Johnny leaned forward casually like it didn't hurt no more, hoping it would show how fit he was now. "When can I ride again?"

"Give it another four or five days."

Johnny stared at him. Surely Ben couldn't mean that. Four or five days — he'd go crazy. "You gotta be kidding. I told you, I'm fine. I've had worse than this, you know."

Ben didn't look too sympathetic. "I know, you've said that before as well. But I don't want to take any risks. It's not that long since you last got shot!"

"Hell, that was months ago. Come on, Ben, I need a woman. I mean, really need a woman, you hear what I'm saying?"

Ben raised an eyebrow. "I hear you. But you've waited this long and a few more days won't kill you."

"It might." Johnny glared at him but Ben didn't look bothered. "I'm getting desperate. Don't you care? You're a doctor; you're supposed to care about your patients. Take care of 'em and all that. I might not last a few more days."

"Tough." Ben was doing up his black bag.

"If it makes you feel better I'll give your best wishes to Delice and the girls. I'm sure they'll be thrilled."

Johnny snorted in disgust. "Not as thrilled as they would be by a personal visit." But Ben didn't look like he was listening. Was shuffling his feet now, looking kind of embarrassed and rubbing his chin like he was trying to think of a way to say something.

"Got something on your mind, Ben?"

Ben gave a soft sigh and nodded slowly. "Yes. You."

What was that supposed to mean? Johnny waited, watching Ben with narrowed eyes.

"Guthrie's a very old friend of mine, Johnny, and I don't like to see him hurting."

"What d'you mean, hurting?" Johnny frowned. Shit, he hadn't done nothing, but the way Ben had said it, it made it sound like it was Johnny's fault.

"He says you won't tell him anything about your past, that it's a forbidden subject. Now that the two of you are getting along better, why won't you talk to him?"

"He tell you to ask me that, did he?"

"No, he didn't. He didn't know I was going to raise the subject with you and no, before you ask, we haven't been discussing you. It was just a couple of things he said in passing. I've simply put two and two together. I care about this family and I'd like to see you settling in better."

"If you care so much, Ben, I suggest you mind your own fucking business." Johnny spoke very softly. "The past is done, so butt out. My past is just that — mine."

Ben snorted, like he wasn't going to take no notice. "Gabriela was his wife, and it's only natural that he wants to know about her. I understand you've told him she died but you've told him nothing else."

"Just leave it, Ben, OK?" Johnny spoke softly. He could see the sadness in Ben's eyes as the man shook his head.

"You're wrong, Johnny. You need to get some things off your chest. I know life's been tough on you. Harder than anyone should have to bear. But you're home now, with people who care about you. And you need to learn to start trusting them. What happened to your mother? How did she die?"

The blood started to pound in his head and he could feel his chest getting tighter. He had a cold feeling in the pit of his stomach and he wanted to puke. "Just leave it." The words burst out of him like bullets from a gun. "Just leave it alone. She got sick.

She died. That's all."

Except it hadn't been like that. Shit. Don't think about it. Block it out. Don't fucking think about it. All that blood and . . . He struggled to control his breathing. Look casual. Like everything is fine. Don't think about it. Think of something else. Anything else. Not her. Not him. Not how she looked. Or how he looked.

Why the hell did Ben have to start on this? Wasn't none of his business. It was bad enough having the old man fishing, without Ben joining him.

He swung away from Ben. Stared out of the window at his mountain in the distance, trying to block out the memory of her staring eyes and the blood. So much blood. His fault. All his fault.

His mountain looked hazy in the September sun. Like it was bathed in some soft purple and golden silk and was calling to him. Would there be good hunting there? It would be good to go there sometime. A hunting trip with Harvard maybe. He loved that mountain. It always calmed him. It was a link. A buried memory of another time that sometimes rode into view before disappearing in the mists of his mind. A time when he'd been safe. A reminder that there had been a better time. But things never stayed the same. That was life.

He could feel Ben watching him. Why couldn't the man just back off? Harvard would have known to back off. His past wasn't nobody's business.

Ben huffed out a sigh. "You've built so many walls around yourself no one can reach you and it's time to start letting people come closer. They worry about you. You must know that's what families do. Gabriela must have worried about you when you were a child."

Mama worry about him? That was a joke. She was always too busy worrying about where the next bottle was coming from. And the next man. Felt like that's all she ever thought about. Had it ever been any different? He sure couldn't remember a time when it had. She'd told him often enough that he was just a nuisance and no wonder his father hadn't wanted him. Told him it was all his fault they lived like they did. Everything had always been his fault. Just like the way she died. But it didn't do no good talking about that. Couldn't change things now. Trouble was, the memories never went away. They crept into his mind, filled his dreams, crowding in with his ghosts. No wonder he never got any fucking sleep. And if his family knew the truth they'd never get any sleep either. The past was past and that's how it was gonna stay — dead and buried.

"If being a family means talking about the past, I'm out of here, Ben." Johnny paused to let the words sink in. And then he spoke real quiet and cold, so Ben knew he wasn't bluffing. "I ain't telling nobody nothing. Ain't anyone else's business and it sure as hell ain't yours. You stick to doctoring and leave me alone or I might just have to do something about that. And I tell you something else, if you push it, I'll make damn sure the old man knows who to blame when I leave."

Ben's mouth dropped open, and he took a few seconds before he spoke. "Are you threatening me?" He said it like he didn't really believe it.

Johnny smiled slowly. "Well, I guess you could take it like that. I ain't bluffing. So mind your own fucking business and stay out of mine. I don't need nobody telling me what I should do. And I tell you, if I won't take it from the old man, I sure as hell ain't taking it from you."

"What is it that you're so afraid of?"

His gut wrenched. He leaned closer to Ben, spitting the words like venom. "I ain't afraid of nothing. Nothing. It's a long time since I been scared." And wasn't that the truth? Because when you knew you'd had things as bad as they could get, there was nothing left to be scared of.

Ben shook his head slowly, looking at him with something like pity in his eyes. "My God, but you're a hard one aren't you? What the hell happened to you? No wonder Guthrie's hurting if this is how you react to questions."

"Don't push me, Ben." He said it real soft. Most people sensed the menace when he spoke like that. "If you know what's good for you, you'll leave now. Go see to your other patients and keep out of my business."

Ben picked up his black bag and walked to the door before pausing. He looked across the room at Johnny. "You're wrong, you know. You've got to start letting people come closer before it's too late. You're hurting people close to you, but the person you're harming the most is yourself."

Johnny turned away, his fists clenched. Why did everyone think they could treat him like he was some little kid? He wasn't no kid no more. But he felt a twinge of guilt as he heard the door close behind Ben, 'cos he'd have sworn he'd seen tears in the man's eyes when he left. But real men didn't cry. Mama said so. So what did that make Ben?

Fuck. He kicked the door viciously, making it rattle on its hinges. He stood by the window, watching Ben drive away into the distance. And now he felt sick inside, like the anger had burned itself out leaving an empty shell. Maybe that's all he was, all he could ever be. If there'd ever been any good in him it had sputtered out long ago like a candle in the wind. He felt old and tired. So very tired. Too tired to leave and take up his old life again but too old to take all this shit too. And so here he was, back where he always found himself, not knowing whether to stay or go.

Guy and Guthrie rode into view, close together, laughing at something. Even at a distance he could see how easy they were together. God, he envied Guy that. To be able to relax, laugh, tell a joke, be happy. What the hell must that be like? Figured the closest he ever got to being happy was when he was fucking and it was all too brief. The rest of the time he felt like he was all coiled up like a goddamn rattlesnake waiting to strike. Yeah, that just about summed him up, a rattlesnake, and nobody loved them.

Guy and Guthrie were walking into the

house, still laughing together.

"Looks like we might have found the right man for the job, little brother." Harvard was waving some piece of paper around. "Out of all the no-hopers, we have one very promising applicant. Want to read his letter?"

Johnny decided not to rise to the little brother gibe. He'd had enough grief for one day. "Nope. Most sheriffs tend to be washed up 'no-hopers' who ain't worth passing the time of day with, so I ain't interested."

"I worked as a lawman a very long time ago." Guthrie's words shook him. Johnny started in surprise and looked at his father, who was watching him with a hint of amusement showing on his face.

"No kidding?" Johnny couldn't think of anything else to say.

"No kidding, son. But it was a very long time ago. I was just marking time."

Johnny gave a brief laugh. "Well, yeah, I guess it must have been 'cos you're real old now and you've been here since creation."

Guthrie and Guy both laughed at that. They sure were in real good moods.

"Father is going to interview the prospective sheriff next week. We've wired him to come to Cimarron." Guy sounded smug.

Johnny raised his eyebrow a fraction.

"Guthrie interviewing a sheriff. Hell, I might even come into town for that — this I gotta see."

CHAPTER THIRTY-ONE

Stoney stood at the cracked window looking through the dust and cobwebs at Cimarron's main street. The people strolling along the boarded sidewalks looked affluent and contented. Friendly, too. They stopped frequently and passed the time of day with each other. It seemed a pleasant town. He could do worse. And he couldn't be that picky. Decent jobs were hard to find.

He'd never been this far north before. He'd spent too many years in border towns. Places where law didn't exist. Except for the rich. They were always protected. Everything worked in their favor. He'd found that out the hard way. And now he was listening to another rich man droning on about the role of a sheriff. Like he didn't know what a sheriff's job was, for God's sake.

Now the broad-shouldered rancher was starting off on the "many benefits" of the town. Growing community. New businesses.

All the usual stuff. God, the man could talk.

"We did have some trouble a short while ago. A bunch of saddle tramps took over the town. A girl was raped. It was all very unpleasant but they were dealt with. It's all quiet and back to normal now."

He looked up at the words "dealt with." Chewed on his lip and eyed the rancher thoughtfully. Dealt with. Hmm. He'd heard that one before. Reckoned that the good upstanding people of Cimarron had gone out and hired a gun. In fact, it had to be more than one hired gun. He'd only ever known one gunfighter capable of taking on a bunch like that and he was dead several months now. He'd raised a glass to him when he heard about it. A glass? Hell, he'd drunk the whole bottle and the best part of a second.

He dragged his mind back to the present. The rancher was asking him something. "So, if we were to offer you the position, would you be interested?"

He glanced out the window. The town seemed as good a place as anywhere to settle. He was about to answer but the words froze in his throat as his gaze fell on a man walking up the main street. He shook his head and took a longer look. God Almighty. He must be seeing things. He had to be imagining things. That man was dead. But that swagger . . . A voice in his head hammered away, screaming that it was who he thought it was.

He shook his head in disbelief as he watched the young man stroll across the main street like he owned the town. So familiar. So foreign. The gun was low on his hip and his hat tilted down to hide his eyes. And he still had that swagger. No trace of the scrawny starving child. But it was him. The same man. And he sure didn't look dead.

Now he understood why this town was suddenly so fired up to get itself a sheriff. They must have hired this man to deal with the saddle tramps and now wanted to get rid of him, just like people always did after their dirty washing was taken care of. And now, he guessed, their gun wouldn't leave.

He turned angrily to the rancher, who stood waiting for an answer. "You couldn't even be straight with me, could you? You ain't no better than any other rich folk I've met in my time. You all want things your way. Want everyone dancing to your tune. But if you think I'm going to deal with him by running him out of town or killing him for you" — he jerked his head toward the street — "then you've got the wrong man. I got news for you, I ain't in the business of taking on gunfighters. I thought you wanted a lawman. I should have known better."

The rancher, what was his name? Sinclair? Yeah, Sinclair, made a good show of acting surprised. Looked confused, screwing up his face. "I'm sorry, I really don't know what you're talking about. You were asked here because you applied for the position of sheriff and on paper you appeared to be the most promising candidate. I really don't understand —"

He interrupted. "Don't feed me a load of bullshit. You think I didn't just see Fierro walking down the street? What happened, did you bring him in to take care of your trouble for you and now you're stuck with him? That it, is it? Well, I tell you, there ain't a sheriff alive who could take him on. And I sure as hell ain't trying for a lousy thirty-five dollars a month."

Sinclair had paled at the name Fierro. Yeah, well, he might now that he'd been caught out. Looked flustered. And had turned bright red. A pulse was throbbing at the side of the man's head.

The man seemed to struggle for words. But not for long. "I can assure you, that you were not invited here to run Fierro out of town or kill him."

Stoney interrupted. "Now you're not going to tell me that it wasn't Fierro who handled those saddle tramps, are you? Because I tell you, Sinclair, I won't believe you."

The rancher had turned a funny shade of purple now. "No. I wasn't going to tell you that. And let me tell you, I don't like your tone."

"You don't like my tone? Well, that's rich, because I ain't too keen on yours either. I think the reason I'm here is because the people of Cimarron want Johnny Fierro gone. But I tell you, there ain't a man alive who could take out Fierro in a straight fight. Only way they'll get rid of him is a bullet in the back, and that ain't my style."

"Damn it, man, will you just listen." The vein was pulsing hard. "You are not here because anyone wants to get rid of Johnny Fierro. Perhaps, before this interview degenerates any further, I should tell you that I am very proud to call Johnny Fierro my —"

The door of the office creaked open, rickety on its rusty hinges.

"How's it going, Guthrie?" And then the man in the doorway paused, stood stock-still, open-mouthed and lost for words, briefly. Very briefly. "Holy shit! Stoney? That really you? Damn! Don't tell me you're our new sheriff?"

And he couldn't think of a damn thing to say. Trust the kid to say plenty! And his language hadn't improved neither. Always did have a mouth on him. Someone should have washed it out with soap years ago.

"Shit! Stoney Rockwell as I fucking live and breathe. You offer him the job, Guthrie? You could do a lot worse."

Sinclair seemed as confused as Stoney. And looked embarrassed, which struck Stoney as odd. "Well, I, um, I was about to but he seemed to have some reservations. Um, he seemed to be under the impression that he'd been brought here to, um, run you out of town, or kill you."

Fierro started laughing like that was the best joke he'd heard in a month of Sundays. "Stoney? Stoney couldn't run me out of town or kill me, and I gotta feeling he wouldn't want to."

The rancher paused, looked at Fierro curiously. "I gather that the two of you are acquainted."

Stoney shook his head slowly. "You mean you ain't looking for a sheriff to deal with Fierro?" His head felt like it hadn't done so much thinking and been so muddled in a very long time.

Sinclair shuffled his feet and looked uncomfortable. "Well, no, actually. As I was just about to explain to you when he walked in, Mr. Rockwell, this is my son."

"Your son?" Stoney resisted the impulse to bang on his ears to check they were still working. He stared around the room to buy himself a second to gather his wits together. None of this made any sense. He knew exactly what Fierro intended to do to his father if they ever met. He'd spent very little time in Fierro's company but even so he'd told Stoney exactly what he was going to do when he finally hunted his father down. And yet here he was, seemingly on quite easy terms with the man. None of this made sense.

Fierro was grinning now, that really cocky grin that you didn't see too often. "Yeah, Stoney. Meet my old man. Guthrie." He turned toward the rancher. "You gotta give Stoney this job. He's OK."

Sinclair was silent for a second, viewed Fierro thoughtfully with just a hint of a smile pulling at the corner of his mouth. "He's OK." The man mimicked Fierro's words, but like he was teasing him. Shit, that was taking a risk. No one teased Fierro. But oddly, Fierro didn't look too bothered, just kept grinning.

Sinclair let loose the smile, so it took right

over. "It seems, Mr. Rockwell, that I have little choice in this matter. You seem to have my son's approval, so the job is yours, if you want it."

Fierro didn't give him a chance to answer. "He wants it. Hey, Stoney, you and me are going to go get a drink." He turned briefly toward the rancher. "Don't hold dinner. Me and Stoney gotta lot of catching up to do."

He threw his arm around Stoney's shoulders. "Come on, I want you to meet a friend of mine." He led him out into the street and started walking purposefully toward the far end of town, past the saloon.

Stoney still couldn't quite believe it was Fierro. He seemed different. Definitely different somehow. Not quite so tense. "You're dead." He couldn't think of anything else to say. "Hell, Johnny, I got very, very drunk because I heard you were dead."

"Takes more than a bunch of rurales to finish me, Stoney. They just weren't man enough for the job."

Well, some things never changed. Fierro still had a high and mighty view of his own abilities. "If we're having a drink, we just walked past the saloon."

Johnny paused briefly, gave him a slow smile and then said in that familiar drawl, "Well, I really ain't too popular in there right now. Kind of messed the place up a while ago and Mac, the barkeep, ain't overly fond of me."

"I'm guessing, when you say messed it up, you took out the saddle tramps in there."

"You know as well as me, Stoney, there's more cover inside." Johnny pulled him on toward a tall, imposing building at the far end of the street. "I thought we'd have a drink here. The owner's a friend of mine. Best whorehouse in town."

Stoney shook his head, exasperated now. What the hell was it with Fierro and women? No, some things never changed. Johnny Fierro was always a devil for the women. Never could get enough. Stoney wondered where the hell Johnny got his energy from. He'd never known a man go at it like that. Heck, he'd seen Johnny go upstairs with several women at a time and none of 'em had been complaining the next morning.

"You've got a lot of explaining to do, Johnny. Like how you ain't dead."

"When we've got a drink. Let's get that first." Johnny pushed open the imposing oak door and led him into the "best whorehouse in town." To tell the truth, Stoney was surprised that Cimarron had a whorehouse, never mind one as fancy as this. It boasted a gleaming zinc-topped bar, fancy iron tables, lamps with fancy shades with sort of tasseled things hanging down, and wine-red velvet drapes. He let out a low whistle. And the girls, heck, they were pretty, not rough like so many of the girls in their trade.

The girls came crowding round, crushing against Fierro as the two of them tried to make their way to a corner table at the back. Typical Fierro. Always had to have the corner table. No. Some things never changed.

Johnny was joking with them all. He could turn on the charm when he wanted to, that was for sure. A tall woman emerged from an office by the side of the bar. Dang, she was ugly. Her face was chalk-white and her scarlet lipstick seemed to make it look even paler. Stoney shuffled uncomfortably as she stood watching them, surrounded as they were by all the girls pawing at Fierro. She pursed up her lips and it was hard to tell if she was mad at 'em or maybe, just maybe, she was amused. "Ma'am." He had to say something, sure wouldn't want to rub her the wrong way. She gave him a kind of curt nod, looking him up and down like she thought she might have seen him on a wanted poster. He stood a bit straighter and hoped his boots weren't muddy.

"Back so soon, Johnny? I didn't expect you in today." Strange, she sounded like she had class, educated, a bit different to the usual madams he'd met over the years.

Johnny turned and glanced at her, smiling, easy. "Delice, want you to meet an old friend of mine, Stoney Rockwell. Stoney, this is Miss Delice Martin. She owns this place."

She didn't look impressed. "A friend of yours?" She raised a painted eyebrow fractionally. "And do tell me, is Mr. Rockwell in the same line of work as you?"

He watched Johnny's reaction with interest. Her words sure stopped him in his tracks. Johnny ducked his head down, a trait he remembered from old, before looking back at her and then talking soft. Real Fierro. "No, he ain't a gunfighter." Stoney could have sworn that Johnny's lips twitched at the very idea — like he was holding back a laugh. Cheeky bastard. Just because everyone wasn't as fast as he was . . . "Stoney is your new sheriff."

The woman looked kinda taken aback at that. Looked kinda thoughtful too. Then folded her arms, tilted her head to one side and looked at Fierro hard. "Our new sheriff?"

Fierro nodded. "Yeah, Delice, your new

sheriff."

She nodded like she was deep in thought. Nodded real slow. "Well, that's really going to impress the good people of Cimarron, knowing that the new sheriff is an old friend of Johnny Fierro." She paused. What the hell was coming next? "Because we know how much the town folk love you, Johnny, don't we? Oh my, they are going to be pleased."

Stoney gave a nervous swallow. Damn woman had a point. Probably the people of Cimarron weren't too keen on having Johnny Fierro for a neighbor . . .

Johnny looked thoughtful. Kicked at the floor with his boot, just like he used to when he was considering a problem. Then he flashed her one of those smiles. The kind that seemed to leave folk breathless, not quite able to believe that someone could smile like that when they had a mind to. "You might have a point there, Delice. Maybe, we'll play down exactly how long I've known Stoney. Maybe it's for the best."

She smiled then. A kind of indulgent smile, like a mother gives a kid who's always in trouble. "You wanted a drink? I'm not running a bar, you know."

Johnny grinned at her. "Yeah, I know, but Mac ain't too happy with me. You know

399

that. A bottle of tequila would be good." Johnny paused. "You got any good stuff? That stuff you usually serve is rotgut."

She narrowed her eyes, gave him a certain kind of look. "My customers don't normally come here to drink tequila. We have other attractions. In case you hadn't noticed."

Fierro started laughing. "Yeah, I noticed. But just this once, Delice, a good bottle? He is going to be sheriff, and you need to be nice to him."

The woman gave a loud sigh. "OK, but don't tell everyone. It could ruin my reputation."

That made Fierro laugh more. "What reputation?"

The woman turned and walked off laughing, calling at all the girls to leave Mr. Sinclair alone. Sinclair? Shit. None of this made no sense at all.

He sat at the table, where a bottle of damn good tequila was placed in front of him by a pretty, dark-haired girl, and wondered how to phrase the question that was playing on his mind. "So, Johnny, it seems you ain't dead. But what I want to know, if I take this job, is whether someone's gonna turn up sometime with a wanted notice for you. I'll be straight with you. If I take the job I'll do it right and if you're wanted somewhere, I will hand you over. So, I've been straight with you and now I want a straight answer. Are you wanted anywhere and is there anything you should tell me about?"

CHAPTER THIRTY-TWO

Johnny poured them each a generous measure of tequila, buying himself some time. He stared into the bottom of his glass. He could feel Stoney's eyes boring into him, waiting for an answer. Stoney. He could hardly believe it. Thought he'd have been long dead by now. Hell, the man should've been dead by now. He wasn't much of a gun. But then, that had never been Stoney's aim. He'd been looking for revenge. Maybe he'd found it. And now wanted to put the past behind him.

What would that be like? To turn your back on everything without having to worry about your past creeping up on you, all stealthy, like a big cat waiting to pounce, and you didn't even know it was there. A man's past could take him by surprise. Let your guard down just a fraction and . . . Never drop your guard. Even with old friends. No. Stoney wasn't never a friend.

Didn't know him well enough to call him that. But Stoney was a good man. And Johnny owed him. Yeah. Owed him everything, if truth be told. But then again, maybe not.

And maybe not the straight answer he was demanding. Because there was the business in Utah. He tried not to think about that too often. But it lay in the back of his mind, kind of dozing, and every now and then, it jumped up and bit him and he'd find himself watching his back even more than usual. Yeah, Utah. If he was wanted anywhere, it would be there. But if they figured he was dead, maybe there wasn't no wanted poster. He'd covered his tracks, hadn't he? He knew one thing for sure — he wasn't going to swing for it. Whatever happened he'd be damned if he'd swing for it. Hanging was possibly the only thing he feared.

He smiled, real easy, and tipped back his tequila. "Wanted? Me? You know me better than that, Stoney." And he sucked a piece of lime, looking all relaxed. Except Stoney didn't know him that well and Johnny sure as hell wasn't telling him about Utah. Wasn't telling no one about that.

Stoney looked relieved. "OK then. That's fine. So, how come you ain't dead? I heard you were sentenced to hang in Mexico, but you're the healthiest looking corpse I've ever seen."

Johnny smiled at that. Good old Stoney. Always called a spade a spade except when it was a shovel. "Tell you one thing, they damn well tried." He spoke softly. Yeah, it had been a close-run thing, and yet here he was. Sometimes he thought maybe he was dead, and all of this was just a dream to taunt him. And God would suddenly take it all away, to punish him even more, because he didn't deserve shit. Didn't deserve nothing. And certainly didn't deserve this new life, this promise of something better.

"So. Spill the beans."

Where to start? How to describe it? This lifeline thrown to a drowning man, sinking in the pit of blood and bodies and bullets. This sudden glimpse of heaven. It had to be God's joke. With the joke being on Johnny Fierro because it would all come crashing down like a building on shifting sand.

"I . . ." He hesitated, thinking of the young guard he'd killed when he made his escape. "I broke out, that's all."

Stoney frowned. "How didja manage that? They got their jails pretty much sealed tight."

Johnny shrugged. "There was a fiesta. They let their guard down." No way was he telling Stoney he'd stabbed a guard. "I made it across the border and then a Pinkerton man tracked me down." He smiled briefly at the memory of the man, in his scruffy suit and hat, so totally out of place in the border saloon. He laughed. It was all so crazy, so unbelievable. "One day I was waiting to be hanged. And then, just days later, I meet a Pink who sent me here."

Johnny paused, remembering the years he'd spent hating his father. It had been eating away at his soul. Devouring every bit of him. "I was gonna kill my old man. You know that. But I promised I'd hear him out. And when I got here, it turned out my old man had been trying to find me for years. Guess it's just as well I made that promise."

Johnny took another swallow of tequila, thinking hard. Plotting. Always plotting. "I guess the rurales might want me, but I figure maybe that don't count, being the other side of the border an' all. Especially since they didn't let on that I got away." Yeah, that would take Stoney's mind off wondering if there was anything else he could be wanted for.

Stoney shrugged. "It don't count, so don't worry about it. I'm more interested in hearing about you and your pa. Come on, I'm waiting."

Johnny raised an eyebrow, just a fraction. Some folk were so easy to play. Feed them a fat worm and then just reel them in. He'd sure got Stoney's attention and he wasn't thinking about wanted posters no more. Figured he'd played his hand well. It needed a touch more but he'd be careful not to overplay. "Thought I should mention the rurales. I'm trying to be straight with you here." He paused to let the words sink in. "Wouldn't want you finding out about that and thinking I hadn't been square with you."

Stoney gave a grunt of irritation. "I just said, if you'd open your ears and listen, it don't count. So forget it."

Johnny flashed him a smile. "Like I said, I remembered what you said, and I heard the man out." He paused again. This was the tough part. How to say his mother had been a lying whore who'd fed him a pack of lies all his life. How he didn't have to have lived the life he had. That there'd been some-where safe all along. Safe from the beatings and all the other things they'd done. Ben had to be fucking loco if he thought Johnny was going to talk to his old man about that stuff. Funny thing, though, he'd always figured that Ben suspected what his moth-er's men had done to him. He tried to drag his mind back to Stoney, but the argument with Ben was still raw. And it hurt. And he didn't know how to put it right.

Stoney gave a big sigh, real impatient like. "So?"

Johnny shrugged. "Seemed things weren't like I thought. Must have misunderstood my mother, I guess. Got things mixed up in my head."

Stoney gave him a look, like he knew exactly what Johnny wasn't going to admit, that his mother was just a lying whore. "You got things mixed up?"

"Yeah." Johnny shot him a defiant look, daring him to say more. But he knew Stoney would back off. He knew what Johnny's mother had been. A good fuck. What a thing to say about your own mother. But it'd been true. Hell, the men had queued up to give her one.

"So what happened when you met him?" Stoney's voice brought him back to the present.

Johnny smiled. "He offered me a share of his ranch."

Stoney's mouth dropped open. "Just like that? Damn, but you're a lucky son of a bitch. And exactly how big is this ranch?"

Johnny raised an eyebrow like it wasn't none of Stoney's business. But hell, anyone could find out how big Sinclair was. "A few hundred thousand acres."

Stoney let out a low whistle. "Shit, that's one big spread. And you own half of it?"

Johnny shook his head. "Nope, not half."

Stoney interrupted. "So your pa wasn't exactly divvying it up equal?"

Johnny ghosted a smile. "Yeah, he was. You see, I ain't just got me an old man." He paused again, playing Stoney, he'd got him on the line now. "I got me a brother too."

He sat back, pleased with the result of his little game. Stoney looked lost for words. Speechless. Opened his mouth to speak, and then closed it again. Then opened it again. "A brother? What kind of a brother? Did he grow up at the ranch? Does that mean you got a stepmother? Well? Don't just sit there smirking, like the cat that got the cream, damn it!"

Johnny pushed his glass in small circles on the table. He was enjoying this. He loved to string things out. He was in control, just the way he liked.

"Jesus, Fierro. You always were one irritating son of a bitch. An' it grieves me to say you ain't changed any."

Johnny sipped his tequila. Real slow. He eyed Stoney over the top of his glass, and raised an eyebrow like he was surprised.

"You want to know about my brother?"

Stoney narrowed his eyes and glared at him. "Well, as it happens, yes. I'm still getting used to the idea that you ain't shot your pa full of holes and now you got yourself a brother. So. What . . . is . . . he . . . like?"

Johnny leaned back in his chair. "Put it this way, you'll never believe we're related." Johnny had to laugh. Shit. Him and Harvard. Who'd have thought it? "He's older than me."

Stoney jerked forward and looked at Johnny. Then he nodded his head slow. "Your mama know about this brother, did she?"

The man was no fool. He'd cut straight to the chase. Johnny pushed his drink in circles again. "So I'm told."

"But she never mentioned him to you?"

Johnny shrugged. "Must have slipped her mind, I guess."

Stoney looked at him from under half-lowered eyes. "Yeah. I guess it must have slipped her mind." He reached for the bottle and poured them each another shot of tequila. "So, what's he like, this brother of yours?"

Johnny grinned. "He looks a real dandy. His ma died when he was born. He was sent east and lived with his aunt and uncle in

Boston. Went to some fancy school there. And he was in the cavalry in the war."

Stoney rolled his eyes. "So, you two don't get along."

Johnny stared down at the table. Funny thing was, he trusted Guy more than almost any man he'd ever met. "He's OK." Those simple words spoke volumes. And they weren't lost on Stoney.

"He's OK? A dandy?"

"Yeah. He's OK. His name is Guy. He was meant to be here today to interview you, along with Guthrie, but someone had to go to Santa Fe on ranch business so he went. I didn't want to miss out on Guthrie interviewing a sheriff. And besides." Johnny paused. Just this once he'd be honest. "I guess the old man would rather Guy handles business things, him being educated an' all."

Stoney pushed his chair back and eyed Johnny. "You know what your old man was in the middle of saying when you walked in earlier? He was giving me hell for suggesting that I'd been called in to get rid of Johnny Fierro. And he said that he was proud to call Johnny Fierro his . . . and then you walked in. And, you know what? I think he was about to say that he was proud to call Johnny Fierro his son. So maybe, he don't think you're as dumb as you seem to think he does, even if you do have a Fancy Dan for a brother."

Johnny was silent. There was a lump in his throat. Proud? The old man? Of Johnny Fierro? And yet the old man had said it before. Back when the ranchers had visited the house demanding Johnny deal with the saddle tramps. But he'd only said it to Johnny. Not to anyone else . . .

Johnny swallowed hard. The old man wouldn't be proud if he knew about Utah. No. He'd want to see Johnny hang if he knew about that. And he wouldn't be too happy if he knew about Johnny's recent fight with Ben. Funny how Ben had gotten to him.

And that brought him back to Stoney. He'd have to do something about Stoney. Didn't want anyone knowing about their past. In this game image was all. Image. Reputation. No. It wouldn't do at all.

Johnny sighed softly. "Thing is, when you meet Guy, I don't want you to tell him how we met."

Stoney paused from rolling a smoke. "What the hell does it matter how we met? I reckon they'd like to know. Especially since they're paying my wages."

Johnny bit back a smile. The man had just played right into his hands. "Well, yeah,

411

actually, I guess we are paying your wages. So, just keep quiet about where we met. Not too much to ask is it?" Johnny paused. How far could he push it? "I mean, I'd hate to have to tell them about some of the things in your past."

Stoney's face was a picture. Disbelief, indignation and anger, all mixed up. "Are you threatening me, Johnny?"

CHAPTER THIRTY-THREE

"Well? I'm waiting for an answer. Are you threatening me?"

He watched in growing irritation as Johnny pushed his glass of tequila around in circles on the table. That was something else he'd forgotten about Fierro. You went for drinks with him and he drank hardly anything. But Fierro always made sure his drinking companions got drunk. Manipulative, that summed him up. Devious. Always had been. Probably always would be.

Johnny sighed. "Seems like I been doing a lot of that lately."

Stoney narrowed his eyes. He didn't think Johnny's reply made anything any clearer. What the hell did he mean by that? "Is that a yes or a no?"

Johnny shot him a quick glance before staring back down at his glass. "No, Stoney, I ain't threatening you." He paused. "Just stating a fact. I don't want no one screwing things up for me. I do that well enough on my own."

Stoney leaned back in his chair. "Stating a fact? Sounded like a threat to me. And I don't expect that from you."

Johnny looked up at that. His eyes narrowed like he was angry. "Why? Because I owe you? I pay my debts."

Stoney shook his head. "No, not because you owe me. I happen to think you're a better man than that. The sort of man who don't threaten people who ain't never done him any harm."

Johnny laughed but it wasn't a happy laugh. "You don't know me at all. You don't know what I'm capable of."

Stoney looked at him sadly. Fierro might have landed himself a share of a damn big ranch but it wasn't making him none too happy. What line had Fierro spun his family? How much did they know about him? He had to ask. "Just what have you told your pa about the past?"

Johnny smiled. But the smile didn't reach his eyes. "Nothing. I ain't told him nothing. And that's the way it's staying." Johnny paused and drummed his fingers on the table. "He's got a Pinkerton report on me but I reckon it's got a lotta crap in it. Some of the stories in it . . ." Johnny shook his head. "And the stories that ain't!" The fingers were drumming faster now.

Stoney eyed him curiously. "What does he know about your ma?"

If he'd wanted a reaction he got one. Johnny's fists clenched and he banged them down on the table almost knocking the drinks over. The girls and Miss Martin were all staring at them, shocked, like they didn't normally see Fierro behave like that. They'd probably only seen the charming side. But there was another side to Fierro and he shouldn't be underestimated.

Johnny leaned across the table and his words sounded more like a snake hissing than a man. "He don't know nothing, Stoney, and that's the way it's staying."

"So he don't know how your ma earned her living?" Might as well push his luck and get things clear.

Johnny narrowed his eyes. Spoke quiet. Shit, he looked cold. And deadly. "No. He don't know how she earned her living. And there ain't no man alive going to tell him. Not if he wants to stay living. If you get my drift."

Stoney wondered what the hell Sinclair did know about his son's upbringing. Or lack of it. "What does he think she did to put food on the table?"

Johnny sighed. His shoulders slumped and he seemed calmer again. Less deadly. "I told him she worked in a cantina."

"Makes sense." Stoney kept his tone level. Last thing he wanted to do was piss off Fierro.

"Where's the point in telling a man his wife was a whore?" Johnny shook his head slightly. "Seemed better to say she worked in a cantina."

"Yeah. Much better." Especially when the woman in question had been a dirt-cheap whore. He'd asked around a bit after he'd first met Johnny. And everyone told him the same thing. The boy's mother was a half-crazy drunk. A damn good looker who was a damn good fuck if you weren't too choosy about the surroundings. By all accounts the place they lived in was a dirty hovel and the kid ran wild as an alley cat. How the hell had the wife of a wealthy rancher like Sinclair ended up in that situation? Maybe she'd gone loco. Might explain things.

Johnny was watching him. What the hell went on in that head of his? He was smart, that was for sure. Too damn smart. Stoney liked Johnny. Liked him a lot, if he was honest. Johnny usually ended up on the right side in range wars from what he'd heard. He seemed to have a strong sense of right and wrong. Even so, Stoney wasn't sure he'd trust him too far. But given the way he grew up, it wasn't surprising he was so screwed up. No, not surprising at all. The only surprising thing was that he'd survived this long. What the hell did Sinclair make of it all? Could almost feel sorry for the man. Might have a bulging wallet and a parcel of land, but he'd got himself one hell of a son to cope with.

"So, what you're saying is you don't want me to mention anything about how we met. Either to your brother or your father. Or else you'll mention some interesting little facts about me, kind of as payback."

At least Fierro had the grace to look uncomfortable. Shuffled in his seat, started fiddling with that damn glass again. Shrugged his shoulders and bit his lip. "Sorry, Stoney. It don't sound too good when you put it like that."

"Nope. It don't."

"Thing is, I'm trying to settle here." He raised his head and looked Stoney straight in the eyes.

Shit. He looked like a man who'd had enough. All wore out. Kind of bleak. Hell, who was he kidding? Fierro looked old. Old way beyond his years. And yet, he'd got a share of one of the biggest ranches in the state. And walked away from a hangman's noose. Any other man would be happy.

"Tell you one thing, Johnny." Stoney shook his head in disbelief. "Walking away from that noose. Ending up with all this." He waved his arm vaguely in the direction of where he figured the ranch was. "You got the luck of the devil."

His words seemed to amuse Johnny. He laughed and even had a swig of his tequila. "Yeah." Stoney had to strain to catch Fierro's words. "The luck of the devil. You know what they say? Only the good die young and the devil takes care of his own."

Stoney watched him. He figured it was best not to say anything. Fierro seemed to have retreated out of reach. Shit, he was in a state. On the edge. How the hell had he survived this long? Fierro was fiddling now with some sort of bead bracelet. His hands forever moving. Never still. What sort of man wore a bead bracelet, for God's sake? Had to admit though, Fierro got away with it. And even if he didn't, Stoney knew better than to mention it. Fierro wasn't a man to tangle with.

Fierro started pushing the glass around the table again. "Like I said. I am trying to settle."

It was kind of strange, but Fierro almost

sounded like he was pleading. Johnny Fierro pleading? If he hadn't heard it with his own ears he'd never have believed it, but it sure sounded that way. "Johnny, I ain't going to say squat to anyone. You and me, well, that ain't nobody's business I reckon. I ain't the sort of fellow to go chewing the fat over the past with no one. What's between you and me, well, it's just that. Between you and me. So, I won't be talking to your pa or your Fancy Dan brother, so quit worrying. And for God's sake, stop fiddling with that damn glass. You're gonna wear out the table." Stoney cast a glance in the direction of the classy madam. "And somehow, I don't think she" — he jerked his head towards the bar — "would be very pleased."

His words had the desired effect. Fierro grinned. Like he relaxed suddenly. "Delice? Now don't tell me you're nervous of Delice? Hell, she's as soft as butter."

Stoney narrowed his eyes, glared at Fierro. "I ain't a fool, so don't treat me like one. She's one tough nut. Not one I'd care to crack."

Johnny glanced over to where the madam stood talking to a couple of her girls. "To be honest, Stoney, I ain't sure anyone's ever had a crack at her. And there ain't a customer who'd dare even lay a finger on her arm." Johnny paused and leaned back in his chair frowning. "Got to say, she's a bit of a puzzle. But I like her. She's OK."

Stoney raised an eyebrow. That was high praise coming from Fierro. "So, we OK, Johnny? Or are you planning on shooting me?"

"No. I ain't planning on shooting you. Just want to give things here my best shot. I promised the local doc I'd give this life a go." Johnny trailed off. Looked tense again. And started drumming his fingers again like his words reminded him of something.

Seemed like a good idea to distract Fierro from whatever was playing on his mind. "So, the local doc, is he a friend of yours?"

Fierro drummed his fingers faster and ignored the question. Maybe asking about the local doctor wasn't one of the best ideas he'd ever had. Fierro sure looked tense. Something was bugging him, that was for sure. Something to do with the local doctor? Didn't seem likely, but who could tell. Fierro was a complicated son of a bitch. God help Guthrie Sinclair.

"What about you, Stoney? You still hunting for them comancheros?"

Stoney leaned forward over his drink. No way was he getting into that conversation.

"Let's just say I ain't hunting anyone no more."

He could feel Johnny's gaze boring into him but knew Johnny would back off. He'd always know not to press a man.

"Sure. Whatever you say." Johnny spoke softly. Seemed to hesitate slightly, and then spoke again. "Just so you know, if you'd ever needed my help with that, I would have come."

Stoney nodded, still couldn't look up, but he felt the start of a smile creasing his face. The kid had always had a good streak in him. "Yeah, I know, and I appreciate it."

Johnny grinned. "So, we're good, OK?"

"Yeah, Johnny, we're good."

The madam was looking across at them. Stoney tried to avoid catching her eye. There was something about her that scared the shit out of him. A woman to be reckoned with. And not one to cross. But she seemed mighty interested in him and Fierro. Watchful. That was the word. Looking out for Fierro, maybe? She seemed an unlikely ally for him. But, hell, Fierro needed all the friends he could get. And it seemed this woman was a friend. It would be interesting to meet the Fancy Dan brother. Fierro seemed to rate him and that was praise indeed.

A couple of the girls sashayed to the table. One of them, with a huge dimple in her chin, leaned across the table as she ran her fingers through her dark wavy hair, ensuring that he and Johnny got a good look at her cleavage. And, boy, what a cleavage. "Was there anything else you wanted, Johnny?" She chewed on her lower lip briefly and then slowly licked her lips, never taking her eyes off Fierro. How did he do it? Everyone knew whores would come on to any man, but it seemed that they enjoyed their work a whole lot more when Fierro was around.

Fierro shuffled in his seat as he watched her. Like he needed to get himself comfortable. No, some things didn't ever change. Stoney could guess what was coming next and figured he might as well sit back and watch the master at work.

Fierro leant back farther in his seat, making a big show of thrusting his hips up as he got more comfortable. Then he stretched a hand out, a smile playing around his mouth, and traced his finger very slowly down the girl's shoulder as she let out a low sigh and tilted her head back, like she was stretching her neck. Except she wasn't. How could any man take that long to run a finger over a girl's shoulder?

Fierro's finger paused, just before it reached her bosom. And he smiled real slow. "Now, Sadie, I'm having a drink here with an old friend. You trying to distract me? You got something in mind?"

The girl wriggled, chewed on her lip, and ducked her head slightly. "Well, Susie and me were wondering if you two boys wouldn't like a little entertainment."

Fierro left his finger where it was, and eyed the two girls, like he was considering a problem. "A little entertainment, huh?"

Stoney rolled his eyes.

"Just exactly what did you have in mind, Sadie?" Fierro grinned as the girl moved in closer and whispered in his ear. He nodded agreement to whatever she suggested. "What about you, Stoney? You interested in joining Susie there upstairs?"

Stoney sighed. "Well, tempting as that offer may be, I don't think it would look too good if the town's new sheriff spends his first night in town in the bordello. Probably wouldn't impress folk."

Johnny grinned. "Can't say I've ever worried about what folk will think. I just follow my urges." Johnny paused and pulled Sadie a little closer. "And I've got urges right now, Sadie."

The girl gave a huge smile, like she'd won

a pile of money at the card table. She pulled Johnny to his feet and turned to lead him away upstairs. He winked at Stoney. "Catch up with you later, Stoney. Got other things to see to right now." He made to follow Sadie, and then swung back and grabbed Susie too before heading up the stairs with an arm around each of the girls.

Stoney studied the contents of his glass. Seemed it was going to be just him and a bottle this evening. What the hell was it with Fierro? He always had to show off his prowess with girls. And it seemed like he hadn't changed any.

"Another drink, Mr. Rockwell?" Damn it. He hadn't noticed the madam walking toward him. Been too busy wondering what Johnny had in mind for the two girls. Embarrassed, he started to shuffle awkwardly to his feet, but she held up her hand to signal him back down. "Oh, please, don't stand on my account." Dang, she sounded icy. He sank into his chair as she poured him another drink.

"So, Mr. Rockwell, you're going to be our new sheriff." She didn't sound overly impressed.

"I've been offered the job, ma'am, and this seems a good place to settle."

"But you haven't held the position of

sheriff before?"

She was pretty shrewd. How did she know that? Lucky guess? "No, ma'am, but I've worked as a deputy here and there. I figure the time's come to put down some roots."

There was a slight furrow in her brow, and the way she was looking at him made him feel uncomfortable, like she was thinking hard about what he'd said. "So, have you known Johnny for long?"

Ah, so this was a fishing expedition. "On and off, ma'am."

"When you met, were you in the same line of work?"

"I wouldn't say that."

She narrowed her eyes slightly and gave him a steely look. Then she cast her line again. "But you appear to know Johnny well. He welcomed you like a very old friend."

He thought he'd throw her a bone. "It's always good to meet an old friend."

"So, where did you and Johnny meet?" That had encouraged her. He was going to enjoy returning her hook empty.

He screwed up his face, like he was trying to remember, then shook his head. "Well, ma'am, you know, it's kind of slipped my mind. Maybe Johnny would remember but for the life of me, I can't recall. Reckon you'd best ask him."

She tilted her head to one side, pursed up her lips and gave him a piercing look. "Mr. Rockwell, it appears that despite your somewhat disheveled appearance . . ." She paused, and looked him up and down with what he felt was a very critical eye, making him wish he'd done a better job of cleaning his boots. "You're a lot sharper than you appear at first glance."

He held her gaze. "So it would seem, ma'am. Whereas, you, if I may say so, are exactly what your appearance would suggest."

Her lips twitched like she was biting back a laugh. "You know, Sheriff Rockwell, I think you and I will get along splendidly." She made to walk back to the bar, but paused and turned back to him. "In your case, I will make an exception to my rule about this not being a bar. You'll be welcome for a drink anytime."

He tipped his hat. "Well, thank you, ma'am. That's very friendly."

He turned his attention back to his drink and considered his options. Being sheriff of this town could have something going for it. It was a quiet enough place and was starting to prosper. He could enjoy the odd drink with Johnny, as long as the fellow didn't get distracted by girls. There was a small house that came with the job. He could do a lot worse. And he knew he could do the job. Upholding the law and bringing outlaws to justice was a cause close to his heart. He felt easier too now that Johnny had assured him there weren't any wanted posters out on him. That had set his mind at rest. There were only the rurales to worry about and they had no jurisdiction here. So, he could accept the job with an easy mind and concentrate on doing a good job. He downed his drink. Yeah, everything would be just fine.

Chapter Thirty-Four

One thing was certain, the office needed a damn good clean. But at least it was an office. And he'd never been too bothered about neatness. Stoney ran his fingers through his hair trying to smooth it down. If anyone came calling, he didn't want them to think he was a slob. He shuffled the papers around on the desk, hoping to create the impression that he was a busy man. Yes, the office would do just fine. All it needed was a few wanted posters of some desperados and bank robbers, and it would do very well.

He sat back in the chair to plan his first day in the job. Then he spun round in it, just like a kid would do. Couldn't believe how easily he'd landed this job. He spun the chair again, hoping nobody would see him through the window. God only knew what people would think if they saw the town's new sheriff acting like a dumb kid.

He supposed he should watch the stage come in, check out the passengers. Always paid to know who was coming into town, in case it spelled trouble. That way you could usually stop it from developing. Sort of nip it in the bud. And having Johnny Fierro around could attract trouble. There'd always be some dumb kid who'd want to go up against Fierro. Cocky enough to think they'd be faster. Had ending up with a share of a big ranch blunted Johnny's skills? Somehow, he thought probably not. He'd bet that Johnny practiced his draw as often now as he ever did. His gun was too much part of him to let it go. And the one thing he'd noticed about Johnny was he still had that certain look about him. Nothing a man could put his finger on, but leaving no doubt that he was as tough as a man could be. Someone not afraid of dying and not afraid of killing. Johnny might be using the Sinclair name, but Fierro was still there, just under the surface. God help Guthrie Sinclair.

The clattering of wheels and the pounding of horses' hooves announced the arrival of the stage. His office window gave him a good vantage point to watch the passengers clambering out. A couple of old biddies were given a helping hand by the driver, while an overweight businessman almost tripped getting down. Stoney grinned. He'd like to have seen that one face down in the mud. The last passenger was some fancy fellow, the type who never had a hair out of place. He was dressed sort of Western style, but his hat didn't sit quite right on his head, and he had fancy gloves. Stoney shook his head. The lengths people would go to in order to make it look like they fitted in. Who was the fellow trying to kid? Hell, he'd probably even got clean fingernails.

Another man was strutting along the sidewalk. Short and fat and puffing hard from the effort of walking. Looked a big tub of lard and full of his own importance. Stoney sighed as the fellow walked purposefully toward the office door. He figured he probably didn't want whatever this fellow was selling.

Stoney quickly moved back to the desk in an effort to look busy just as the door opened. The man walked in, wheezing hard. Stoney waited while the red-faced fellow caught his breath. Had to be some big noise in the town; he had that look about him.

"I wanted to come and introduce myself. The name's Tandy and I'm the mayor."

Yeah, that figured. "Mayor Tandy." Stoney moved to shake hands. "Rockwell. Stoney

Rockwell."

The man removed his hat. "A pleasure, Sheriff Rockwell. The town needs a good sheriff."

Stoney raised an eyebrow and cocked his head to one side. "But the town didn't want it bad enough to pay for it."

Tandy flushed a brighter shade of red. "I was going to appoint one but that Guthrie Sinclair took matters into his own hands and went directly to the council with an offer to bring someone in and pay the salary for a time. Thinks because he's got a big ranch, he can do whatever he likes."

Stoney shook his head. He really didn't need this crap today. "Mr. Sinclair didn't strike me as that type of man. Seemed a pleasant fellow, and concerned about the well-being of this nice town of yours. Told me you had some trouble here a while back."

"Ah." Tandy shuffled uncomfortably. "Well, yes. A bunch of drifters."

Stoney scratched his chin. "And from what I hear, you folk got a hired gun to deal with them."

Tandy's color turned closer to purple. "Well, that wasn't exactly like it was . . . ."

"Well, Mayor Tandy, why don't you tell me how it was."

The man puffed up his chest. Looked like a rooster strutting around a farmyard. Stoney suppressed a smile.

"We did ask a fellow to deal with them. We didn't do anything against the law. In fact that's what I wanted to talk to you about. Johnny Fierro, here in our nice little town."

"I hear he's Guthrie Sinclair's son."

"Well, yes, Sheriff, supposedly." The mayor snorted. "Fierro didn't grow up here. Could be anyone really. He appears out of nowhere after all these years and says he's Sinclair's son. He certainly doesn't favor his supposed father. No resemblance at all."

Stoney sighed. "I reckon Mr. Sinclair is smart enough to have checked it out. Now is there a point to this, Mayor, and are you ever going to come to it?"

Tandy glared. "No need to take that sort of tone, Sheriff. I'm doing my civic duty here. Trying to warn you of the undesirable element we have in this town."

"Well, you warned me. Was there anything else?"

"I want to know what you're going to do about Fierro. He's got to be stopped."

Stoney furrowed his brow and leaned back in his chair. "Stopped from what?"

"We don't want the likes of him around

432

here. Nobody wants him. Decent people aren't safe to walk the streets with him at large. And it's your job to get rid of him." The mayor's color really couldn't be healthy.

Stoney shook his head slowly. "Well, they really did put the donkey in charge of the henhouse when they picked you as mayor. You don't mind paying Fierro to do your dirty work but once it's done, you want him gone. Now that don't sound too decent."

"I'm telling you, Sheriff, he's not safe to be around respectable folk."

"Well, unless he's broken the law, he's as entitled to walk the streets of your town as you are. Now, if I catch him smashing up the saloon, or drunk in the street, or robbing the town bank, then I'll lock him up. But unless that happens, or he breaks the law in some other way, he's a free man. Comprende?"

"He's a desperado. Shouldn't be allowed near decent folk."

Stoney rolled his eyes. "Seems to me, Mayor, that Johnny Fierro did this town a big favor. Did what you didn't want to do yourselves. Any rate, I've got a lot of work to do, so unless there's anything else, good day to you." Stoney walked to the door and swung it open. "I said, good day to you, Mayor Tandy."

The man put his hat back on. His lips were drawn in a thin line and his cheeks puffed out even more than before. "I can see that you and I are not going to get along. I'm very disappointed by your attitude, Rockwell."

"It's Sheriff Rockwell. And if you don't like my attitude, that's just too bad. I'm sure you'll find my work satisfactory when we got some real lawbreakers in town. Good day."

Stoney shut the door and walked wearily back to the desk. Were all mayors puffed up windbags? Why the hell did perfectly sensible people elect them in the first place? Probably because no sane person wanted the job. Still, folk got pretty much what they deserved and if they couldn't get off their butts to look after their town, then they probably deserved Tandy.

He needed some coffee. There had to be somewhere he could get a cup of coffee until he fixed something up in the office. He was going to need a lot of coffee if he had to put up with the likes of Tandy.

The office door creaked open. His day wasn't getting any better because the Fancy Dan off the stage stepped into his office.

Stoney glared at him. "I've had a bellyful already this morning, so if you've come to complain, about Johnny Fierro or anything else, I suggest, Mr. Fancy Dan, that you take your complaints to the mayor."

The man raised an eyebrow in surprise. "I thought I'd just drop in to make your acquaintance and introduce myself."

He sure had a fancy way of speaking. "Well, that's right friendly but I'm very busy right now, so if you'll excuse me, I'll be getting on."

"Why did you think I'd be complaining about Johnny Fierro?"

"Because I've just had the mayor in demanding I get rid of Fierro. I guess you're another of those people who don't mind hiring a gun when it suits them and then wants to get rid of him as soon as he's done your dirty work."

The man fiddled with his gloves and looked like he was struggling to hold back a smile. "I assure you, Sheriff, I have nothing against Mr. Fierro."

Stoney narrowed his eyes. This fellow was way too sure of himself. Cocky, as if he was laughing at a secret joke. And he was so damn clean. How did people stay that clean and tidy — especially after a stage ride?

"So, can I assume, Sheriff, that as the personification of the law in these parts, you have no objection to Johnny Fierro staying in this vicinity?"

Stoney rolled his eyes. "If you're asking if I mind Johnny staying hereabouts, no, I don't mind. Johnny's fine."

"Johnny? Can I assume you're already acquainted with Mr. Fierro?"

Stoney rubbed his chin. He hadn't intended to let on that he knew Johnny. Still, he could cover the little slip. "I've run into Fierro a couple of times in the past. I've no reason to believe he's broken any laws here. Says he's settling down and hanging up his gun. So, providing he behaves like a law-abiding citizen, that's fine by me."

The fellow inclined his head in acknowledgment, and fiddled with his gloves again before shoving them in his belt. Stoney fought the urge to grab the things out of the man's hands and throw them out the window.

Stony eyed the fellow up and down. He wore his gun wrong. Too low for a dandy. It was almost like he'd copied someone without understanding the significance of a low gun. But dang, the fellow still looked like he was laughing at some private joke. Stoney waved a hand at the door. "Like I said, I've had a bellyful today, so if there was nothing else, Mr. Fancy Dan, good day to you."

"Fancy Dan?" The man said it like he was

weighing up the words. "I suppose that's slightly preferable to Soldier Boy."

What the hell was the fellow talking about? "Soldier Boy? I didn't mention soldiers, maybe you should get your ears looked at."

The man smiled. Took his gloves out of the belt and started smoothing them. "No, I assure you that there's nothing wrong with my hearing. I was just comparing the two soubriquets and trying to decide which was the least offensive."

Stoney rolled his eyes again and sighed deeply. "I just told you, if you'd pay attention, I didn't call you Soldier Boy. Don't look much like a soldier." He eyed the man's jacket with a dismissive eye. "Not like a soldier at all."

"No, it's what my brother called me." He paused. "When he first met me."

Stoney had a strange sinking sensation in his stomach. A Fancy Dan . . . Johnny's words echoed in his ears. "He looks a real dandy. His ma died when he was born. He was sent east and lived with his aunt and uncle in Boston. Went to some fancy school there. And he was in the cavalry in the war." The cavalry . . . soldier boy . . .

"Oh dang!" Stoney glared at him. "You're as devious as that damn brother of yours, you know that?"

The fellow gave a broad smile. "I'll take that as a compliment! Although, I confess that when it comes to deviousness, I'm not nearly as sneaky as my brother."

Stoney held his hand out. "Stoney Rockwell, Mr. Sinclair."

The fellow smiled. "Call me Guy. And do I take it that you've had something of a trying morning? A visit from the mayor? Did he really come here to complain about Johnny?"

Stoney sat down in his chair with a heartfelt sigh. "Silly old fool. Wanted to warn me about the desperado and stop him coming into town. I told him what he could do with that idea."

"How well do you know Johnny?"

The question caught him by surprise. Seemed Guy Sinclair was no fool. But he'd promised Johnny he wouldn't tell and he was a man of his word. "Like I said, I've run into him a couple of times over the years. He's no danger to people who mind their own business. Says he's trying to settle down and that's good enough for me. He ain't breaking any laws. My job is to uphold law and order, and Johnny ain't treading on my toes, so, it's not a problem."

"Someone tried to bushwhack him recently. People really resent his presence."

Stoney chewed on his lip. Couldn't say he was surprised. Sure didn't make it easy on Johnny though. He thought back to the pleading expression he'd noticed the previous evening. The look in Johnny's eyes when he'd said he was trying to settle. The gunfighter was going to have a tough time winning acceptance in a place like this. He tapped his fingers on the desk as he thought. "Johnny have any idea who this bushwhacker was?"

Guy nodded. "A local rancher. Johnny thinks he put the fear of God in the man and he won't try anything else. But . . ."

"Yeah, I got you. Still, if Johnny's scared him off, that's a good thing. And let's face it, some folks talk tough but when push comes to shove, most of them don't want to get their hands dirty. I figure if Johnny keeps himself out of trouble and nobody comes looking for him, things should settle. The main thing is he ain't wanted anywhere. If someone turned up with a wanted poster on him, things would be different. But as it is, everything should settle down and work out just fine."

CHAPTER THIRTY-FIVE

The stone skimmed across the sparkling water. Five bounces. Good with stones, good with guns and good with women. But pretty much rotten at everything else. Johnny sank down against a tree and gazed over the peaceful stretch of water, which reflected the mountains rising steeply up behind it.

He should've known this life wasn't going to be easy. Nothing ever was. And now the past had crept up on him and that worried him. Even if it was good to see Stoney, the man knew way too much. And Stoney's arrival brought back too many memories of things he'd rather forget.

Johnny took a small stone and hurled it into the water. Damn it. Of all the people to be sheriff, it had to be Stoney . . .

But maybe it would be OK. Maybe he was worrying needlessly. Fierro always worried over everything. He was constantly planning, scheming and always at least two jumps ahead of everyone.

And at the moment it seemed Fierro was being a right bastard to everyone. He'd even threatened Stoney. Stoney, of all people. He knew he could trust him, so why'd he threaten him? And why was he sitting here fretting over it?

He'd threatened Ben, too. Ben, who spent his life trying to help people. But he had threatened the doc. And he didn't know why he did it. Wasn't like he was scared of anything. Johnny Fierro wasn't scared of nothing. Was he? Except maybe hanging. Not dying. That held no fears. But he didn't want to hang. When Mama died, it was the thought of hanging that had scared him most of all. People gathered round watching that short drop and then poking the body with sticks and jeering.

He'd hang for Utah. And here he was, fretting over whether he'd covered his tracks well enough. He knew he'd been seen. And now, the more people who knew Fierro was alive and close by, the greater the odds of someone coming looking for him. And if they did, Stoney would hand him over. Because Stoney would follow the law — he wasn't a lawman who could be paid to look the other way. Shit.

Maybe nobody would come looking. It was quite a while ago now. And he sure as hell wasn't running. He'd never run from nothing and he wasn't planning on starting now.

But they'd all hate him if they knew about Utah. All of them. The old man, Harvard, Stoney, Ben, Delice. And he could never tell them why he did what he did. Never drop your guard. And even if they knew it all, they'd probably hate him even more. All he could do was cover his tracks.

Because he didn't want to leave here. He loved it. He'd loved it in the summer when the mountains seemed to shimmer in the heat and now, during the Indian summer, it was even more beautiful. The lengthening shadows, golden leaves and the smell of wood smoke in the air heralded the distant approach of winter. Even though he hated the cold, he was looking forward to seeing the ranch in the winter. Maybe he only hated the cold because he'd never had a refuge from it before. Somewhere warm and safe. Maybe the land would be covered in a snowy mantle, like the lace that Mexican women covered their hair with in church. He could imagine long evenings in front of a roaring fire, after a good meal. Beating Harvard at chess. He grinned. He loved

442

beating Harvard at chess. And just about everything else. Guy might have read an awful lot of books but when it came to things that mattered, Johnny knew he could more than hold his own against his older brother. Had to because he always had to win. Fierro always had to come out the winner.

He picked up another stone and sent it skimming across the water, watching the ripples spreading out from each bounce. Life was like that. You did something and the ripples spread out, affecting lots of other things. There'd been a time when, if he'd died, nobody would have cared. But if he died now, would things be different? Funny, but he thought maybe they would now. Even the old man. But they wouldn't care if they knew about Utah.

Strange how he'd managed to push it to the back of his mind for so long. But now, maybe because of Stoney's words, it was back, filling his dreams and every waking thought. Maybe it was an omen. Maybe someone was coming and it was his sixth sense that told him trouble was on its way. Damn it. More likely it was just him fretting. Like a dog with a fucking bone. Best check anyway that he'd covered his tracks. Same as he'd covered them after Mama died.

He sat and replayed the whole thing in his head. Every single action in Utah. Every move he'd made. And then he hauled himself to his feet and went and checked his saddlebags. Checked that he'd still got the slip of paper that could save his life. There was maybe one other thing he should do to cover his tracks. Couldn't be too careful.

And he should deal with the other thing plaguing him. He should put things right with Ben. Hated himself for leaving things hanging with the man. Hanging. Yeah. Maybe he could kill two birds with one stone. He knew Ben had thought he'd been helping by pushing Johnny. But shit, he wasn't talking about the past to nobody and Ben should have taken the hint and backed off. Still, the man had been a good friend since Johnny came to Sinclair. He knew Ben cared about him. He'd seen it in his eyes. And even seeing that, he'd still threatened him. Because he didn't want anyone to get too close. Because he'd end up letting them down. Like he always had with everyone. And he'd let his mother down most of all.

He picked up another stone. Smooth and flat. It should skim real good. Maybe six bounces. With a flick of the wrist he sent it skimming across the water, counting each bounce. He grinned. Six. It was all in the wrist action.

He dragged his mind back to the job at hand and started hunting for a suitable piece of wood. He grinned again. Yeah. Back to covering his tracks. He wasn't going to rest easy till he knew he'd done all he could.

Johnny bent and slipped the knife from his boot and went and sat back against the tree. And set about covering tracks.

Fuck. It hurt. A wave of nausea passed over him as he watched the blood spreading over his arm. An awful lot of blood for one simple cut. He shut his eyes and waited for the dizziness to pass. And hoped he wouldn't puke. Felt like everything was swimming round him so he bent farther forward, so his head rested between his knees. Stay like that until the dizziness passed. He knew the drill. He'd had enough injuries over the years to know what to do.

The sound of wheels and hooves echoed along the road above the lake. He tried to struggle to his feet, didn't want to be seen looking weak. Hopefully, whoever it was would just drive on by and not even notice that he was there.

"Hello, down there. Are you injured?" A woman's voice.

Shit. Not only had the person not driven past, she had obviously seen him stumble.

And the voice sounded horribly familiar. Of all the people . . .

"Are you all right . . . ?" Her voice trailed off as she clambered down to check on him. "Oh. It's you."

Holding the bandanna tightly to the wound, he nodded, as politely as he could, seeing as how he couldn't tip his hat with his hands full. "Mrs. Walsh."

Her gaze was fixed on his arm, a faint look of horror on her face. He glanced down. Hell, there really was a lot of blood. "It's not as bad as it looks." He didn't sound very convincing. And judging by the look on her face, she wasn't buying it.

She swallowed and then walked forward briskly, like she wanted to take charge. "What happened? Let me have a closer look. It looks a very bad cut. It's very deep."

He shrugged, and held up the piece of wood. "I was whittling. I lost my concentration, I guess. The knife slipped."

She gave him a look which said she didn't believe him. "Whittling? Johnny Fierro whittles?"

Why the hell shouldn't he whittle? He hadn't been, but that was neither here nor there. "Yeah, whittling. I was thinking of maybe making Guthrie a pipe rack." That should impress the old cow. "I don't spend all my time shooting people." It was childish, he knew, but he couldn't resist the dig at her.

"Oh, yes, I seem to recall that you told me you had some redeeming features." She didn't sound like she believed that either. Well, Mama always said she was a fucking bitch.

She took a large handkerchief from her pocket. "Hold still while I tie a tourniquet."

"A what?" He winced as she set about tying the cloth tightly above the cut.

She looked at him, like he was a dumb kid or something. "A tourniquet." She said it real slow like he was dumb or something. "To stop the bleeding. And then we'll get you to town to see Ben. That cut will need stitches."

He glared. "I can get myself to town. I ain't shot full of holes."

She raised an eyebrow. "No, I suppose a cut must seem quite a novelty. Certainly different from the injuries you must have suffered in your previous occupation."

He bit back a sharp retort. Damn woman. Like he'd accept any help from her. But he'd be polite. Didn't want to piss off Guthrie. And, hell, the woman was a friend of his or had been until the old man realized what a bigot she was.

447

"Ma'am, like I said, I'm fine to ride." The words almost choked him. "But thanks for the tourniquet. Much appreciated."

"You look as white as a sheet and are certainly not fit to ride. We'll tie your horse behind my buggy and I'll drive you to town."

"There's no need, ma'am, like I said, I'm fine." He spoke the words through clenched teeth, struggling to remain polite. How many times did he have to tell the damn woman? Still, it did no harm that she'd seen him. She'd be a very reliable witness, if he ever needed one. So maybe he should accept the ride with good grace. Went against the grain, though. Being pleasant to the woman who'd made his mother's life so unbearable. Poor Mama, no wonder she'd hated Edith Walsh. Not only didn't she like Mexicans and half-breeds, she was bossy, interfering, rude and smug.

Johnny grinned to himself. Actually it would be a pleasure to make use of Mrs. Walsh. He'd felt guilty about the prospect of using Ben, but hell, a doctor sure made a reliable witness if he ever needed someone to testify about the cut on his arm. This way, he'd have two. And a man couldn't be too careful when it came to witnesses.

He allowed the smile to appear on his

face, just a small one. "Sorry, Mrs. Walsh, I reckon you're right. Ben would be mad at me for refusing when I've got a bad cut, so, yeah, thanks. It's very obliging of you, ma'am."

She narrowed her eyes slightly, like she didn't trust him, but gave him a curt nod and turned to fetch Pistol.

"I'll get my horse, ma'am . . ."

She sighed. "You were always willful. Even as a two-year-old. For heaven's sake, go and sit in the buggy. I'm quite capable of leading your horse up to the road but I can't carry you if you pass out."

He opened his mouth to protest but to his surprise Pistol followed her meekly up the slope. Normally the horse wouldn't oblige anyone other than him. Damn woman.

He scrambled into the buggy, wincing as he did so. Couldn't believe he was allowing himself to be driven into town by any woman, let alone Edith Walsh. Still, it served his ends.

Luckily she didn't seem inclined to talk. They drove more than half the distance in silence. She could handle the buggy well, though. He had the uneasy feeling that she could probably handle a lot of things well and was nobody's fool. She certainly looked like she was deep in thought. Well, that suited him just fine. Much easier if he didn't have to try to talk to her.

"What did your mother tell you about me?"

The sudden question rocked him. Fuck. How could he answer that one? "Oh, I don't really recall, ma'am. It was a long time ago."

"You told me that I was exactly how she'd described me to you."

Why did the damn woman have to remember that? "Oh, I just meant how you look . . ."

It sounded feeble and he could tell she didn't believe him.

She swallowed hard. "Your mother and I did not get along. I'm sure she told you that." She gave him a piercing look and he found himself giving a reluctant nod.

"For what it's worth, I did try and welcome Gabriela to the neighborhood when she arrived. She was very young." Mrs. Walsh faltered. "And very beautiful." She cracked the whip to make the horse trot on faster. She had flushed a dull red. "This isn't an easy thing to admit, but all the men were very taken with her." She paused and bit her lip. "Including my husband."

She turned and looked at him. He could have sworn there were tears in her eyes. "I was very jealous. And, for what it's worth, so were all the other women in the area. We couldn't compete, and so we were not as kind as we should have been. I'm sorry."

She urged the horse on faster, avoiding his eyes now. He felt an unexpected wave of sympathy. Yeah, Mama had sure known how to turn heads. She wouldn't have hesitated to flirt with every man in the neighborhood. And she sure wouldn't have cared if the men were married. It was simply the way she was. But maybe if people had been nicer, Mama wouldn't have left. And he could have grown up at Sinclair. He sighed. Life really was a crock of shit. Everything hung on what hand you were dealt.

He knew he should say something. But he was so fucking useless with words. He shrugged. "I guess we're all sorry 'bout things we've done. All we can do is move on and live with it. Can't undo things."

"And you are trying to move on?" She was looking at him hard. "Put the past behind you?"

He nodded. "Yeah, ma'am, I am." Right now, he was trying to put his biggest sin behind him and she was playing a part in it. If only she knew. Trouble was, now, using her seemed cheap. Before it had felt like a victory.

They drove into town in silence and she

drew the buggy to a halt outside Ben's house.

His arm was throbbing as he jumped down, but he managed to tip his hat to her. "Thanks for the lift, ma'am."

He watched in silence as she unhitched Pistol and tied him to the rail outside Ben's office. As she went to climb back into her buggy she paused. "Oh, by the way, tell Guthrie I took his advice and hired some Mexican vaqueros. Tell him he was right. They've been a huge success."

Johnny smiled. "I'll tell him. And thanks again for the lift." He waved his good hand as he watched her drive away up the main street.

He tried to drag his mind back to what he had to do next and his stomach clenched. How to make things right with Ben. Get things back like they had been — if Ben was willing to forgive him. He should never have spoken to Ben the way he had, even though Ben had been pushing way too hard. He stared at the big door and then reluctantly, and oh so slowly, made his way up the steps to it. He was lifting his good arm to knock when the door swung open and he came face-to-face with the doctor.

CHAPTER THIRTY-SIX

Johnny swallowed hard as he tried to meet Ben's eyes — eyes that were wide with surprise. And something else. Suspicion? Supposed he couldn't blame Ben for that, what with him showing up on the doctor's doorstep like this. Must have been the last person he expected. He felt the heat rush to his face as he opened his mouth to try and say something. Anything. But he couldn't think of a damn thing, especially once he saw Ben's eyes focus on his arm.

"You're hurt. Again! What the hell happened?" Ben stood back to let him into the house.

Johnny shrugged. "Cut myself, whittling."

"Whittling?" The way Ben said it sounded like he didn't believe it. Hell, what was it with people? Why didn't they think he would whittle?

"Yeah. Whittling." It came out snappier than he'd meant it to, but shit, he whittled sometimes, better than most people. Ben just raised an eyebrow. A disbelieving eyebrow. "I was thinking of making Guthrie a pipe rack . . ." Stop trying, Fierro, nobody's gonna believe it.

Ben looked at him. "A pipe rack? That's a hell of a bad cut for the sake of a pipe rack. You're bleeding like a pig. Come on through and let's get it cleaned up. It's going to need several stitches."

Johnny followed Ben to his office, and perched on the edge of a high leather couch as Ben started searching through a cupboard. Johnny was already feeling bad about using him. Fierro really was a bastard. Using Ben, using Edith Walsh . . . How much lower could he sink? Where was rock bottom?

"Let me have a look at it. I need to ensure it's clean before we stitch it up."

Why did doctors always say "we" like the patient was gonna help? It was like "and how are we feeling today?" Nothing was more fucking irritating than that. Always made him want to say that he was fine but how was the doctor feeling. He bit his lip. Didn't want to start things off by irritating the hell out of Ben.

Ben was daubing at the cut with something. Shit, it made it sting, like a fucking snake bite. Maybe the cure was worse than the cut . . .

"So, how've you been, Johnny? I haven't seen you recently." Ben's voice was kind of level, no expression. The sort of thing he'd say to any patient . . . not one who'd threatened him?

Johnny sighed. Tried to look at Ben, but shit, he felt bad. Still didn't know what to say. Guy would know what to say. He always knew what to say. Guess that's the sort of thing they taught a fellow at school. "Ben . . . ouch . . . careful! That fucking hurt." He tried to wrench his arm free but Ben was holding on tight. Getting his own back, maybe.

"Ben. I'm sorry. I was a real idiot the other day."

"Oh? When was that, Johnny?" The man sounded casual, like he wasn't even interested.

Seemed Ben wasn't going to make this easy. Johnny shook his head, had to smile. He didn't deserve easy, after all. "I'm sorry, Ben, OK. Really." He hesitated, hated letting his guard drop. "I felt bad about how I left things. But I still ain't talking about the past to nobody. It's best left alone. I know you reckon I'm wrong but that's how it is."

Ben didn't say anything. He carried on

455

swabbing at the wound. And then Ben paused and peered at it, really close. Too damn close. What had he seen? "It's odd, this cut. It's almost as if there was another old scar exactly underneath it. Have you cut your arm before?"

Johnny swallowed hard, tried to ignore the tight sensation in his gut. Just sound casual. "No. It was a dumb thing to do. Like I said, I was . . ."

"Whittling." Ben's tone still sounded like he didn't believe it. "If this is an example of your whittling, I suggest you give it up. Buy Guthrie a pipe rack."

Johnny shut his eyes briefly, feeling relief flood through his body that Ben was so easily distracted. "Yeah, good advice, Ben. Anyway, are we good now, Ben?"

Ben shot him a sharp glance before looking back down to where he was starting to stitch. "We always were, Johnny. I can't force you to talk to Guthrie. You thought I was poking my nose in where it wasn't wanted. I was, but you're my patient and I think it's something you should talk about. But if you don't want to take my advice, that's up to you. I'm not about to hold a gun to your head."

He felt another twinge of guilt. "I am sorry, Ben." Johnny found his voice was little more than a whisper. He really was a total bastard using Ben this way. "I didn't mean to sound so . . ." Hell, he couldn't even think of a way to describe his behavior.

"Petulant? Childish? Bad tempered?" Ben sounded amused. In fact, Johnny would have sworn the man's shoulders were shaking.

"Are you laughing at me, Ben? Because if you are, could you stop stitching until you're done laughing?"

Ben leaned back, laughing openly now. "It might be for the best. Otherwise my stitches will be all over the place." Ben frowned suddenly. "Has it really been bothering you that much? You actually felt you had to apologize?" Ben was looking at him thoughtfully. "I wasn't angry at you, just a touch disappointed. I hate to disillusion you, Johnny, but oddly enough I am not in the least bit scared of you and I'm afraid you totally failed in your attempt to intimidate me. I imagine that was what you were trying to do that day."

Johnny stared at Ben, opened his mouth to say something, but hell, what could he say? He gave a snort of laughter. "Failed, huh? Must be losing my touch, then. But for what it's worth, I felt bad about it."

Ben raised an eyebrow in a kind of questioning way. "You know, you're not nearly as bad as you believe yourself to be. You really need to start letting up on yourself. You're your own worst enemy. And your own biggest critic."

Not as bad as he believed himself to be? But it still felt good to have someone believe in him. Maybe he really could just put things behind him. Get on with his life now. But he didn't want to let himself believe that. It would hurt all the more if it all blew up in his face. Just take each day as it comes. And cover tracks.

Ben put the final stitch in with a grunt of triumph and then reached for some cream that he smeared over the stitches. "Hold still while I bandage it up. And as long as you're careful with it . . . Did you hear that? Careful with it." He said the words slow and loud, like he was trying to make some kind of a point. Or talking to an idiot. "It should heal up in no time." He tilted his head to one side and shot Johnny a kind of fierce look, but sort of joking too. "Remember, as long as you're sensible, it will heal quickly." He gave a brief shake of his head. "Who am I trying to kid? Sensible? You? That'll be the day."

Johnny grinned. "I'll be good, Ben, I promise. Leastways this won't interfere with other activities. I can ride one-handed, so I'll be able to go and pay Delice and her girls a visit."

Ben smiled and shook his head. "Do you ever think of anything other than sex?"

Johnny scratched his head, tried to look like that was a tricky question. "Well, now you come to mention it, no." He grinned. "I got real healthy appetites you know."

"So you keep telling me. Frequently. I'm starting to feel sorry for Delice's girls."

"Hell, why? I'm their favorite customer."

Ben gave a snort of disbelief as he finished clearing up his equipment. "I see that modesty is not your strongest suit. Now, promise me you won't do any more whittling. You really shouldn't be allowed out without supervision. I don't know why people worry about you being dangerous. Seems to me you do yourself more damage than you ever do to anyone else!"

Johnny started laughing. It felt so good to know that things were back to normal with Ben. "So, how much do I owe you, Ben?"

The doctor shook his head. "Nothing. Guthrie's opened an account with me since you came home. Seemed to think it would be simpler. I can't imagine why."

"Kind of forward thinking of the old man, really."

The sound of galloping hooves in the street drew both of them to the window. Three men on sweating horses were reining in outside Stoney's new office. Ben peered through the glass, trying to see who the men were. "Well, they seem to be in an awful lather about something. Rushing to see our new sheriff." He half turned toward Johnny. "You did know the new sheriff has started?" Then Ben laughed. "Old age. Of course you knew, since Guthrie chose him and the ranch is paying his salary. Have you met the man yet?"

"Yeah, I met him. Seems nice enough." Johnny avoided Ben's eyes. Kept looking out of the window. Didn't want to get into any talk about how he already knew Stoney. Ben was way too good at reading him.

Ben nodded. "I met him very briefly outside the gunsmith's. Seemed a capable fellow. I know Guthrie had high hopes of him after receiving his letter." Ben struck his forehead like he'd forgotten something. "But you know that, too. Sorry." Ben rubbed his chin, like he was thinking about something. "I hope nothing's wrong. Those three men seemed in an awful hurry. They certainly don't look like they're dropping in to pass the time of day with the new sheriff."

Johnny shrugged. He really didn't care. If

folks round here had trouble, they had nobody to blame but themselves. Damn gringos. Thought they were so much better than other people, just because of the color of their skin. Or because they had money. Or shoes . . . They'd use Fierro and then treat him like shit. They'd treated Mama like shit. The resentment was starting to well up in him, choking him with its acrid, bitter taste, just like it always had. He turned away. "I'd best be getting back to the ranch. Thanks, Ben."

Ben raised his eyebrows, looking surprised. "Aren't you going to find out what's got those three" — he jerked his head toward the window — "so riled up? I thought you'd be interested."

"Nope. Ain't interested. I don't care. They got trouble, that's their problem. I've done enough for this town and I ain't lifting a finger in the future."

"My, that does sound bitter. Not like you."

Johnny gave a slight shake of his head. "Not like me? You don't know what I'm like, Ben, and I sure as hell don't feel inclined to do any more for this town. You got any idea how many of these folk would lift a finger to help you, Ben, if you were in trouble? Not one."

"You sound very cynical."

"Yeah, well, I learned my lessons the hard way and I know what gringos are like."

Ben gave him a piercing look and tilted his head to one side, like he was considering some problem. "Gringos? Does that include me?"

Johnny gave an exasperated sigh. Why did people have to take things personally? "No, Ben, it doesn't include you. But I've had enough trouble from this town, so, if you don't mind, I'm heading home."

"Take it easy with that arm, Johnny."

Johnny raised his thumb in acknowledgment and headed out to Pistol. He paused momentarily to listen to the sound of raised voices coming from Stoney's office. He grinned. Yeah, seemed the town had got itself more trouble. Served 'em all damn well right. Still, it was a shame that Stoney hadn't even had a chance to settle in before trouble came calling. Poor old Stoney. But what the hell, it was what he was getting paid for. He grinned again and spurred Pistol out of the town and toward home. The town's problems were no concern of his. He was much more concerned about explaining away the cut on his arm, seeing as how nobody believed the whittling story.

He still hadn't come up with a better story when he reached the ranch. But seeing as how that was the line he'd fed Mrs. Walsh and Ben, he'd have to run with it. Really was losing his touch. Getting soft. He'd failed to scare the shit out of Ben and nobody believed his whittling story. He was losing his edge. He'd have to start getting tougher again. Never could tell when it might be needed.

He tied Pistol to the rail outside the main door of the hacienda. He'd stable him later. It would look better if he went and explained about his arm first. It seemed that was the sort of thing they'd expect him to do. Family. He shook his head slightly. Couldn't figure it at all.

He was about to push open the door when it swung open and he almost collided with Guy.

"Johnny! I was looking for you. We're getting together a posse."

It was his lucky day. If posses were uppermost in Guy's mind, he wouldn't be asking too many questions about whittling. "A posse? What the hell d'you need a posse for?"

CHAPTER THIRTY-SEVEN

"You mean you haven't heard?" Guy stared at him like Johnny must have been lost in the desert for years or something.

Johnny eyed him thoughtfully. Guy sure looked riled up over something. He was fiddling with his damn gloves and he had his hat on the back of his head. Johnny tried to squash the smile that threatened to break out. Always made him smile when Harvard put his hat on like that. It made him look like an Arkansas farm boy. He resisted the urge to set the hat straight, square on his head, the way a man like Guy should wear his hat. Trouble was, he still looked like a man who hadn't quite settled to the ways of the west. He would in time. Johnny could picture Guy when he was older, wearing his hat just right with a plump wife and a whole parcel of kids. But would Johnny Fierro live long enough to see that?

He tried to push past Guy to go inside.

"No, I ain't heard nothing, so maybe you'd best start explaining."

"Well, it's like . . ." Guy paused, his brow suddenly furrowed with concern and he blanched as he stared down at Johnny's bandaged arm. "What happened to you? Did someone try to bushwhack you again? God. Come in and sit down."

Johnny grinned. "Yeah, well, that's what I was trying to do except you're standing in the middle of the door. Like to let me in?"

Guy moved rapidly to one side, and half pulled Johnny inside. By his good arm, luckily. "So, what on earth happened? Did someone shoot you? A bushwhacker? Oh hell, it wasn't another gunfight, was it?"

Johnny felt a pang of disappointment. Would he ever reach a stage where if he was injured, his family wouldn't just assume it must have been a gunfight or someone hunting him down? He glared at Guy. "No it wasn't another fucking gunfight." He held up his hand, hoping to quell Guy's flood of questions. "I cut myself whittling."

Guy opened his mouth to say something. Then closed it again. Then opened it again. Looked like a fish. "Whittling?" He didn't sound like he believed it either. "Whittling? You whittle?"

What was it with everyone? Did they really

465

think he spent every spare second fiddling with his gun and practicing his draw? Sure, he practiced his draw but even he had to have a break sometimes. Hell, he could play a guitar too, but they probably wouldn't believe that either. Maybe he should have just said . . . Hell, there wasn't any sort of excuse that could explain the cut other than whittling. Run with it, Fierro, you ain't got no choice.

"Yeah, whittling. You got a problem with that?"

Guy lifted an eyebrow and gave him a strange look. "So, you were whittling? What happened?"

Johnny sighed. "Well, like I said, I cut myself. Ben stitched it up, and it's fine. But that don't explain why you're all fired up and hell-bent on forming a posse."

Guy stared at him, still looking kind of confused. "It must have been a hell of a cut if you went to Ben for stitches. Are you sure it's all right?"

"Just tell me about the posse. My arm's fine. Now what the hell's been going on here?"

"It's the Cattlemen's Association, you see."

Johnny sighed. Would Guy ever get to the point? He sure did know how to drag things out. "You mean you're rounding up a posse to go after the Cattlemen's Association? You must be real pissed off with them." He couldn't help grinning at the prospect of a posse hunting down all those pompous ranchers. The thought of it improved his mood instantly.

Guy glared and started fidgeting with his damn gloves. "Don't be obtuse, Johnny."

Obtuse? What the hell did that mean?

"The man they entrusted with the task of overseeing the movement of funds has absconded with all their money."

"Can you say that in English?"

Guy rolled his eyes. "The man they put in charge of moving the money has disappeared with it all. Stolen it and vamoosed. Skedaddled. Or any other word you care to use."

Oh boy. This was too good to be true. Johnny could feel the broad smile spreading, just couldn't stop it. And the laughter was bubbling up now.

Guy fixed him with one of those looks, like he didn't think it was something to laugh about. "You find this funny, Johnny? Would it be funny if it was our money?"

Johnny shook his head in exasperation. "Oh, come on! This wouldn't have happened if they'd kept on doing it the way it was always done. It's only because they didn't trust me that they started making their own arrangements. Johnny Fierro ain't to be trusted but if you're a gringo rancher, well, that's just fine. Wouldn't catch no gringo making off with their money, just Mexicans or breeds — that's the way they think. Well, I tell you, it serves the whole bunch of gringo ranchers right."

Guy didn't say nothing. Just stood there, giving him a strange look. "Gringo ranchers? You mean like Guthrie and me?"

Johnny perched on the edge of the old man's desk. Stared down at his boots and could feel the heat flushing his face. He shot Guy a quick glance before staring at the floor again. He shrugged. "You know what I mean."

"I know it sounds insulting the way you said it." Guy sounded real pissed off.

Johnny shuffled the papers around on Guthrie's desk. And then repositioned the inkwell, anything rather than look at Guy right then. "Well, you are a gringo." Damn. Somehow he didn't think he'd said the wisest thing. "What I mean is . . ."

"That I'm just a gringo rancher." Guy sure didn't sound happy.

Johnny ran his fingers through his hair. How could he fix this? Trust him to put his foot in it. "No. That ain't what I mean."

Guy folded his arms and leaned against the fireplace. "Well, pray, do tell me, just what did you mean? Because from where I'm standing it sounds like you lump me in with all the other white ranchers you so resent."

"Oh, for God's sake, of course I don't. I just meant . . ." Damn! He wished he was better with words. He was fucking useless at explaining things. "I just meant . . ." He shook his head in exasperation. "Well, it's easy for you to stand there. You don't know what it's like having folk look down on you because of the color of your skin. All my life I've had that, Guy. All my life. I ain't good enough in Mexico and I ain't good enough here because either my eyes are the wrong color or my skin is. And I tell you, I get sick of it. Just like I get sick of being used. One day I ain't fit to walk the streets of town, the next day they want me to sort out their trouble because they don't want to risk their precious white skins, not even to protect their own families. But hell, they think they can toss me some money and then treat me like dirt. And you know something else, they treat me different to a white gunfighter too. I've seen enough gunfighters hired and fired to know they treat me different."

Johnny paused, took a deep breath. "So, yeah, I'm glad they've lost their money. Serves 'em right. Maybe next time they won't be so quick to judge someone because of the color of his skin."

Guy shook his head, still giving him a piercing look. "But don't you see, that's exactly what you're doing?"

It stopped him in his tracks. Couldn't think of a damn thing to say to that. Dios. Was that what he was doing? No. He wasn't like that. Was he? He couldn't be like that. He hated people who thought like that. No, it was just that . . . just what? He tried to meet Guy's eyes. "I didn't mean it to sound the way it did. But fact is John Dove was the only one of those ranchers willing to give me a chance. The rest of them just want me out of here." He shrugged. "So I guess I'm just calling it as I see it. And no, I don't see you as a gringo rancher. I know there's white folk who don't care what color someone is." He paused. "I just don't seem to have met many of them."

Guy looked at him, and frowned. "And of course, you never noticed that the association members are gringos, and judged them for it."

He felt like throwing a punch at Guy's face, but then figured maybe it was just as

470

well he didn't, because a smile spread across Guy's face. "Sorry," Guy said. "Couldn't resist that one, just too good an opportunity to miss."

Johnny grinned. He could give as good as he got. "Gringo."

"But not a gringo rancher who deserves to lose his money to a thief?"

Johnny paused briefly. Timing, after all, was everything. "Well," he drawled, "fact is, Guy, you are a gringo and you do own a third of a ranch. If you'd learn where your hat should sit you might even look like a rancher, but for now, I reckon you look more like a gringo farm boy." He ducked to avoid the mock punch that Guy aimed in his direction. And felt a surge of relief that Guy wasn't still pissed.

"So, who made off with the money?"

Guy sighed, slapped his leg with his gloves. "Seth Turner. Have you met him? Short, balding, skinny sort of face." He paused as though trying to recall the man. "He always looked hungry."

Johnny gave a short laugh. "No, ain't many of 'em wanted to meet me. I don't recall meeting him." He smiled coolly. "Wish I had though. Some sort of hombre, making off with their money like that. Hell, makes me look like an angel." He paused.

"And that takes some doing! So, how much they lose?"

Guy shrugged and perched on the edge of the old man's desk. "About seven thousand dollars, I believe. The small ranchers certainly can't afford it."

Johnny gave a low whistle. That was a hell of a lot of money. Served 'em all damn well right, but he didn't say it aloud. Didn't think Guy would agree with him. Still, he didn't fancy Turner's chances if some of those ranchers found him before the posse. He had a gut feeling that it wouldn't take much to turn them into a lynch mob. "So, where's Guthrie? Has he heard about it yet?"

Guy nodded. "He's gathering some men from the bunkhouse and then we'll join the posse. Some of the ranchers went into town to alert our new sheriff."

Johnny smiled. "Yeah, I saw them tearing into his office and raising a ruckus."

Guy tilted his head to one side, kind of thoughtful. "And it didn't occur to you to find out what the fuss was about?"

Johnny shrugged. "Like I said, Guy, I really ain't too interested in the ranchers hereabouts." He held his left arm out. "And I'd cut my arm, so I guess I was thinking of that."

Guy raised an eyebrow and gave him a look which said he sure didn't believe that. "So, Johnny, will you be joining the posse?"

"Well, much as I'd love to help, my arm's real sore, so I guess you'll all have to manage without me." He could feel Guy's eyes boring into him as he sank down and stretched out on the couch. But he was damned if he'd lift a finger for those ranchers. This time they could deal with their trouble themselves.

Footsteps echoed down the hallway. Heavy footsteps. He tensed as he waited for the next load of questions that would be fired in his direction. Somehow, he didn't think his father would accept a sore arm as a good enough reason not to ride. But he wouldn't join that fucking posse if his life depended on it.

"Guy, I've got together some men. Maybe we'll run into Johnny on the way to . . ." The words died as his father saw him lying on the couch.

"This is no time to be lying around, John. Surely Guy's told you we're forming a posse." He sounded real snappy, no surprises there.

"I'm afraid, sir, that Johnny won't be able to join us. He's injured." Guy sounded very smooth. And calm. Calm enough to keep the old man from laying into him?

"Injured?" Guthrie looked at him, real hard. "Injured how?" And then he saw the bandages. "What have you done to your arm? Not a bushwhacker . . ." Leastways he sounded concerned. That wouldn't last.

"No." It came out snappier than he meant it to. But hell, he was sick of people thinking he must have been shot, like that was the only thing that could ever happen to him. "I cut my arm. Ben stitched it up."

His father looked puzzled, was looking at Guy now, like it was only ever Guy who could answer questions. "What happened? How did he do it?"

"I ain't lost my voice, Old Man. I can answer questions for myself."

The old man's expression grew harder. His jaw clenched and his eyes narrowed. Probably wasn't the most sensible thing Fierro could have said right then. "Look, I cut it whittling, but like I said, Ben's stitched it up. It was a real deep cut." Would that win him a little sympathy? Maybe make the old man ease up?

"Whittling? What the hell were you doing whittling? This is a working ranch, and there is too much to do to spend our days sitting around whittling."

So much for the sympathy. "I'd been

474

working on fence lines since dawn and it was my lunch break. Or aren't I allowed to stop for chow? Maybe you'd rather I work myself to death." Johnny bit his lip, trying to stem the angry words. Why did he keep pushing and pushing? And yet things had been going better of late — they hadn't been fighting as much. But right now it felt like Fierro was back in control and Johnny Sinclair had gone missing. His father paced angrily around the room. His fists were clenched tight like he was trying to keep his temper under control. But his eyes never left Johnny.

"A sore arm doesn't preclude you from getting off your backside and joining the posse. We need to get going. We don't want Turner building up too much of a head start."

Johnny held his gaze, determined to keep his temper in check. Even so, nobody was fucking well giving him orders. "Like I said, it's a real deep cut. Ben said to take it easy."

Guthrie snorted. "I can't believe Ben told you not to ride. And since when did you ever take any notice of what anyone suggested when you're injured?"

The man had a point. "I lost a lot of blood. In fact, your friend, Mrs. Walsh, took me to Ben's, I was in such a bad way."

That stopped him in his tracks. Briefly —
but not long enough. "Well, I'll remember
to thank Edith when I next see her. But you
look fine now. I believe that's your favorite
expression, isn't it? And I see no reason why
you can't ride. We need all the men we can
muster."

Johnny shook his head and narrowed his
eyes. Kept his voice soft. "I ain't coming."

The pulse was going now at the side of
his father's head. Just like it always did when
he got real mad. And Guy gave a soft sigh,
shut his eyes briefly and shook his head.

"Are you refusing to help? Did I hear you
right?" The old man had gone a funny color
too and the pulse was going faster.

"Yeah, you heard right. I ain't coming."

"Sir, don't you think we should get a move
on . . . ?"

At least Guy was trying to help, but
Johnny suspected it wasn't going to work.

"So you're happy to go into town for a
gunfight, but not to join a posse. A crime
has been committed and it's your duty to
join a posse, if you know the meaning of the
word duty. Demonstrate that you're a law-
abiding member of this community."

"I ain't lifting a finger to help your rancher
friends. An' I tell you something else, Old
Man. If some of your so-called friends get

to Turner before the posse, they'll turn into a lynch mob. That's the sort of people they are. So I suggest you get moving."

Guthrie took a step forward. Hell. Was his father going to hit him? But no. The man was fighting to control himself. Breathing hard and his hands were balled into fists.

"You might not like some of the local ranchers, but whatever their failings they're decent men. You're living amongst civilized people now, not the rabble you're used to."

Guy gave another exasperated sigh. "I really feel this is Johnny's choice. If he doesn't feel up to coming, or chooses not to, it's his affair. We need to get moving." Guy pulled Guthrie's arm. "Come on."

The old man shot Johnny another furious glare. "You and I aren't done here, boy. I'll continue this discussion later." He turned and followed Guy to the door, banging it hard as they left the room and making all of Peggy's little ornaments rattle and shake.

Johnny huffed out a sigh. Why did he do these things? He always seemed to end up pushing the old man to breaking point. It was like he couldn't stop himself. Hell, he was losing his grip on everything at the moment. And now his arm was throbbing. Probably hadn't even been necessary to cut it. If only Stoney hadn't gone on about wanted posters. It was so long ago now. But . . . He shivered, and the hairs on his neck stood on end. Oh shit. He was just imagining things. Relax, Fierro. Ain't nobody coming. Not now. But if they did, at least he'd covered his tracks as best he could.

CHAPTER THIRTY-EIGHT

They rode in silence toward Cimarron, slightly ahead of the hands Guthrie had rounded up to join the posse.

Wisps of smoke drifted into the sky from the vaqueros' small settlement on the eastern boundary of the ranch. A horde of young, dark-eyed Mexican children, distracted from some game, ran to watch the group of somber-faced men riding past.

Guthrie's face might have been cast in stone but his lips were compressed in a thin line. Guy sighed. Truth be told, he was tired of acting as a buffer between his father and brother. But it seemed the task was falling to him yet again. Sometimes it felt it would be easier to return to Boston. To a world where he could predict, with reasonable accuracy, what each day might bring. He could return to a life where he could enjoy theaters, music and long leisurely evenings with friends, and formal dinners which stretched into the early hours of the morning while they debated politics and business. A place where a man wasn't measured by the speed of his draw or his ability to ride out the bucks of a young horse. A place with more civilized modes of behavior.

So, yes, it would be easier to return to that life, but it no longer interested him. He wasn't sure if it had ever interested him. He knew if he returned he would grow bored very quickly. And even if he wanted to, how could he leave when he knew that it would be tantamount to signing his brother's death warrant? Because he was certain of one thing: if he left it would only be a matter of time before Johnny and Guthrie fell out and Johnny stormed off, back to his old life and an early grave. Guy couldn't live with that on his conscience. He already had too many sins from the war to trouble him, without adding to the litany.

So it looked as though he'd have to accept the role of peacemaker. At least it was preferable to that of warmonger. He glanced across at Guthrie, who was still tight-lipped and angry, and wondered if the man would ever come close to understanding Johnny. Understanding Johnny. Never mind whether Guthrie would! Would he ever understand his own brother? Sometimes he felt he was making headway. Johnny would throw out some snippet of information about his past, and Guy savored each morsel. But then, at other times Johnny seemed to retreat out of reach, a menacing stranger from a different world. A very dangerous stranger who shouldn't be underestimated and who would probably never give away any information that he didn't want to give. He always tried to control every situation, and manipulated everything for his own ends. And that was what it boiled down to. Johnny played them all, an affectionate smile for Peggy; cheerful teasing for Carlita, particularly when he wanted to wheedle a Mexican meal out of her; an occasional story for Guy; and lighthearted banter for Ben. It seemed the only person he wasn't playing was Guthrie. Or maybe he was. The taunts, the swearing, the constant challenge to their father's authority, perhaps it was just another of Johnny's games, albeit a dangerous one.

He pushed his hat back and looked once more at Guthrie. "Why do you do it?"

His father gave a slight start, looked at him in confusion. "Do what? What are you talking about?"

"You and Johnny. Why do you keep pushing him? Do you want him to leave?"

"Don't be ridiculous. Of course I don't want him to leave. You know that. He knows that. But he does need to be reminded of his responsibilities as he seems totally unaware of how he should behave." Guthrie settled himself deeper in his saddle, pulling his coat around him in an effort to block the wind. "And I don't think now is the time to discuss this."

Guy bit back a smile. "You'll never think there's a right time to discuss it. But I disagree. I think his attitude over this is understandable. In the light of the way the ranchers have treated him, can you really blame him for not coming along?"

Guthrie was silent for a moment, as though trying to decide how to frame an answer to the question. "My point is that this is precisely why Johnny should have joined the posse. It's an opportunity for him to show he's a responsible member of this community, but that would be too easy for him." Guthrie's voice started to rise as he voiced his frustration. "Why couldn't he just do this one thing for me? Is it really too much to expect?"

"He's just had several stitches in his arm. Riding must be difficult and you need your wits about you on a posse." Guy kept his tone mild, hoping that Guthrie would calm down.

"Stitches!" Guthrie sounded scornful. "You know as well as I do that a few stitches wouldn't stop him from doing anything he wanted to do."

Guy grinned. The man had a point. Guthrie glared at him. "This is not funny, Guy. And whittling? What the hell was he doing whittling? He was meant to be working. And since when does he whittle? I've never seen him do anything except clean those damn guns."

Guy shrugged. "Who knows? I'd have thought you'd be pleased he had a hobby."

Guthrie snorted derisively. "A hobby. There isn't time for hobbies during the day. He needs to keep his mind on his job and put in a good day's work."

"He does. And you know it. He works very hard. Harder than I do, if I'm honest. He works longer hours than pretty much anyone else on this ranch. He regularly works through meal breaks and he drives himself hard. He obviously feels he has something to prove." Guy paused. "To you."

Guthrie turned sharply to look at him. "I don't need him to prove anything. I just want to see a good day's work."

Guy sighed. "That's not true. You ride him

harder than anyone else on the ranch. And let's be honest, if it'd been me sitting there with stitches in my arm, you wouldn't have asked me to join the posse. You'd have wanted to check that I was all right. But because it was Johnny, you got angry, as though you weren't concerned at all." He knew his words were harsh, but Guthrie needed to hear a few home truths before the situation could deteriorate further.

"Of course I was concerned . . ." Guthrie paused and chewed on his lip for a moment before sighing heavily. "You're right. I did fly off the handle. But I was frustrated because I really did think it was a good opportunity for him to —"

"Behave like a civilized person?" Guy couldn't resist finishing the sentence. Guthrie nodded.

Guy shrugged. "The ridiculous thing is that we can't need a posse like this for just one thief. Anyone would think the man was some desperado on a killing spree." He felt a cold sensation in his stomach as Johnny's words of warning came back to him. "You don't think that Johnny's right, about the posse turning into a lynch mob?"

Guthrie shook his head vigorously. "No. I've known these men for years. They wouldn't behave like that."

"You didn't think they were the sort of men who would bushwhack someone, but one of them tried to bushwhack Johnny. And I don't suppose you'd ever have thought Seth Turner could be a thief. I wonder whether we ever really know anybody."

Guthrie frowned and then nodded slowly. "I have to admit that people have certainly surprised me recently. I knew Johnny wouldn't be welcomed but some of the comments . . ." He trailed off with a sigh. "And the bushwhacking . . . But no, I can't believe they'd lynch someone. Anyway, it can't happen because we'll be riding in a group with the sheriff."

"And speaking of our new sheriff, there he is." Guy pointed at a small group of men riding toward them in tight formation.

The men reined in as they met on the trail. Stoney tipped his hat and cast a quick eye over the group from Sinclair. "Thought we'd come and meet you. We believe Turner's heading east, toward Bitterville. He probably figures we'll think he's headed south to the border and hopes to throw us off. We'd best get going." He looked again at the group, as though puzzled, a small furrow forming between his eyes. He glanced at Guy. "Where's Johnny? I thought he'd be with you."

Guthrie gave a grunt of irritation. Guy ignored it and smiled blandly. "Johnny couldn't come. He's got stitches in his arm. He cut it very badly."

"Cut his arm? How did he do that?"

"Whittling. The boy was whittling. Now can we get on?" Guthrie glared at Stoney, who had a slightly bemused expression on his face.

"Whittling?" A big smile spread across Stoney's face. "Johnny Fierro whittling?" He shook his head as if in disbelief. "Dang! Now I've heard everything."

Guthrie narrowed his eyes. "Can we get on? We don't want Turner to get away. Where are the others anyway?"

Stoney turned his horse toward the pass leading to Bitterville. "Some of them went ahead. They hoped to cut Turner off before the ground changes and it gets trickier to track him. Pity Johnny couldn't come. Arrogant son of a bitch is always saying he's a mean tracker. Must be that Apache blood of his."

Guthrie grunted and turned away, raising a gloved hand to greet Henry Carter and Matt Dixon as they eased their horses alongside Guy. But this was no time for pleasantries and by some unspoken agree-

486

ment the party surged ahead, with Stoney out front and the rest of them fanning out behind him.

Guy urged his horse on to ride alongside the sheriff. He had no desire to be with Carter and Dixon, suspecting they'd use the opportunity to make barbed comments about Johnny.

Stoney glanced over as he drew level with him. "Johnny is OK, ain't he? It's not his gun arm is it?"

Guy shook his head. "He'll be fine, and no, it's not his gun arm."

Stoney frowned. "Seems odd then, him letting a few stitches stop him from joining us. I reckon he's ridden with worse than that in the past."

Guy gave him a rueful smile. "I think you can probably guess why he didn't want to help this lot."

Stoney shrugged down deeper into his tartan wool jacket. "He was always one stubborn son of a bitch. He sure hasn't changed any."

Guy studied Stoney thoughtfully. How did the sheriff know Johnny? There was quite a difference in age between the two of them, but he felt certain that Johnny would call the shots in just about any situation and that Stoney would defer. He knew he shouldn't ask but he couldn't deny his need for information, any information, about his brother. He still feared he could lose Johnny again at any moment. Lose him to a gunfight, a bushwhacker or have him walk out because Guthrie pushed too hard, or maybe just because Johnny was too set in his ways to make the change to responsible rancher and perhaps didn't have the stomach for the challenge.

He shivered in the biting wind. The weather had changed so quickly from the sweltering heat of merely days ago. If it was this cold this early in the fall, God alone knew how cold the winter would be. It was as well Johnny hadn't come. He'd have hated it.

Stoney just hunched his shoulders up against the wind and pulled his hat down further. He had the look of a man who'd done a lot of solitary riding in his time, who'd take anything that came. Where the hell had he met Johnny? And when?

"You say he hasn't changed. When did you first know Johnny?" Well, he'd never find out if he didn't at least ask. No harm in asking.

Stoney stared straight ahead. "Don't recall. Best you ask him, he might remember."

Guy gritted his teeth. He didn't intend for the sheriff to get off that lightly. "Well, you must recall roughly how old he was. Was he established as a gunfighter when you first met him?"

Stoney shrugged. "I really don't recall. I only ever met him a couple of times. A few years apart." The sheriff clamped his jaw tight, like he regretted saying what he'd just said. Almost like he felt he'd given something away.

Guy pursed his lips thoughtfully. A few years apart. So Johnny must have been a lot younger when they'd first met. And obviously Stoney remembered the meeting. So where could it have been? And why would he have remembered Johnny? The man certainly wasn't very forthcoming. His memory couldn't be that bad. Had Johnny told him not to say anything?

Guy decided to go out on a limb. Try a bluff and see if Stoney would fall for it. "Yes, Johnny said he was just a kid when he first met you."

It wasn't going to work. The look the sheriff gave him said it all. He was not a man to fall into such an obvious trap. "Well, I figure if Johnny said that, he remembers better than me. Like I said, you'd best ask him." The man urged his horse into a faster lope, making it impossible to carry on the conversation.

Guy shook his head in frustration. Was it so unreasonable that he should want to learn more about his newfound brother? He gave an exasperated sigh. Whatever the reason for Stoney's reticence, now wasn't the time to pursue it. He glanced up at the gray sky. A bank of ominous clouds was building on the horizon and he could see rain far off. Damn. It was going to be a wet ride as well as a cold one. He envied Johnny, back at the ranch, doubtless curled up sleeping in front of the fire or scrounging cookies in the kitchen, making the most of his injured arm to win sympathy from Peggy and Carlita. Strange how he'd managed to cut himself so badly whittling on some wood. Johnny was very adept at all manual tasks and was blessed with quick hands. Somehow, it didn't ring true. And there was something niggling away in his memory if only he could remember what it was, something to do with his brother's arm.

He glanced back at the group riding behind him, still in a tight formation. Guthrie was sandwiched between Carter and Dixon. The other ranchers had ridden out earlier in search of Turner, anxious that the man shouldn't get too big a head start while the posse was formed. Maybe they'd all get lucky and catch up with him before nightfall. Guy certainly didn't relish a night on the trail in these conditions. There might be some shelter in the pass, which was narrow with rocky overhangs, but it wouldn't make for a comfortable night. Few trees grew there, though occasionally it opened out allowing a few stunted oaks to survive in the thin soil.

He urged his horse onward to join Stoney, who'd slowed as the ground became more rocky and uneven. Progress here would be slow as the horses picked their way through the pass. The first drops of rain were carried in the wind, which funneled them through the steep pass to sting the men's faces. Stoney cursed, wrapping his bandanna to cover his chin and pulling his hat lower on his head. Guy rode close alongside, reminded of his days in the cavalry when men rode closer together to ward off the worst effects of bad weather. The pass narrowed ahead, bending sharply to the left. In other circumstances Guy would have thought it a good place for an ambush, but at least that wasn't a concern today.

As he and Stoney rounded the sharp bend their horses spooked, digging their hooves in, refusing to carry on. And there, hanging from a gnarled oak tree, stirring in the quickening wind, was the body of a man.

CHAPTER THIRTY-NINE

Stoney smothered an oath as he slid from his horse and strode toward the body, unsheathing a bowie knife from his belt. Guy hurried to Stoney's side and steadied the swaying form while the sheriff made a savage cut at the rope. Despite the blue, contorted face, and swollen, protruding tongue, he could see that, in life, it had been Seth Turner.

"Bastards." Stoney spoke quietly. He seemed to be shaking with barely controlled rage.

"Johnny was right." Although Guy spoke more to himself, Stoney turned toward him.

"Right about what? A lynch mob?"

Guy nodded somberly. "Johnny said it wouldn't take much to turn a bunch of angry ranchers into a lynch mob. It's the only explanation, isn't it?"

Stoney nodded. "I reckon so. I guess Johnny judged 'em well. Even though the man stole their money, wasn't no cause to do this. They should have brought him in for trial."

Guy turned as Guthrie and the rest of the posse picked their way over the rocks and into view. Even though his father's face was half hidden by his hat, Guy could see his expression harden and his skin pale at the sight of Turner's body. He stumbled from his horse, closely followed by Dixon and Carter, and came to Guy's side. "God Almighty. That things should come to this."

Henry Carter shook his head. "Guess he felt guilty and hung himself."

Stoney's face was a picture. Guy put out a restraining hand thinking that Stoney was about to hit Carter.

"You blind or something? He didn't hang himself, he's been strung up. No way did he do that himself."

Matt Dixon nodded agreement. "Sorry, Henry, but I have to agree with Sheriff Rockwell. No way Turner did that himself." He paused before adding in a dismissive tone, "Turner wouldn't have had the guts anyhow."

Carter nodded. "Aye, that's true enough. Guess he ran into some outlaws."

Stoney made a sound which could only have been described as a derisive snort. Guy felt maybe it was prudent to keep his restraining hand on Stoney's arm.

"You really are a couple of dumb asses, ain't you? Seems to me it's far more likely he ran into some ranchers who didn't bother waiting for us. Outlaws my ass." Stoney threw them a ferocious glare, shaking his head in disgust.

Carter puffed out his chest, stepping forward aggressively. "No need to take that sort of tone, Sheriff. And you've no call to accuse local ranchers. They're all good law-abiding people." He turned angrily toward Guthrie. "But talking of outlaws, where was that other boy of yours today? Far more likely to have been the work of someone like Fierro. I told you he's scum, not fit to be with decent folk."

Guy didn't know his father could move so fast. Before he could intercede, Guthrie's fist flew out and connected with Carter's face with a resounding thud, sending Carter sprawling. Spitting dirt from his mouth, Carter scrambled to his feet and threw a punch at Guthrie's stomach. Guthrie side-stepped neatly and caught the man a glancing blow to the chin, hurling him back to the ground.

Bending to grasp the rancher by the front of his jacket and haul him to his feet,

Guthrie hissed, "Don't you dare say things like that about my son. My God, Johnny's done so much for this community since coming home. Put his life on the line more than once, but that's not good enough for the likes of you, is it? Well, I tell you, I'm sick of you all. Sick of the way you've been treating him. Hell, one of you even tried to put a bullet in his back, but you're quick enough to use him aren't you? You're a bunch of hypocrites, the whole damn lot of you. You make me sick to my stomach. To think I thought I knew you. All these years but I didn't know you at all." He thrust his hands into his pockets, letting Carter fall back to the ground.

"Guthrie. You gone crazy or something?" Dixon grasped his arm, pulling him to face him. "It's a fair question. Where was Fierro today? Not unreasonable that we want to know. I know he's your son, and you wouldn't be human if you didn't feel some loyalty, but nobody else wants him here, and if someone tried to put a bullet in his back, good riddance. The boy's no good, and you just don't seem to see it."

Guy winced as Guthrie's fists flew again. He turned toward Stoney, expecting the sheriff to say something, but the man was looking intently at the ground, and his shoulders were shaking. Guy bit back a smile. He had to admit Guthrie had surprised him. He just wished Johnny had been with them to see it. He'd never believe this.

Guthrie stood over the two ranchers who were sprawled on the ground. His face had a scarlet tinge, and he had his fists clenched tight, as though trying to stop himself striking out again. "If you must know, Johnny was out on the south range this morning. He cut himself badly and Edith Walsh drove him to town to see Ben, who stitched him back together and sent him home, which is where he is now. Plenty of witnesses can vouch for his whereabouts today — enough even to satisfy the likes of you two. And let me tell you, he's worth more than the whole pack of you put together. You didn't have the guts to straighten out the trouble in town by yourselves but you didn't hesitate to ask my son to do it for you. And then you treat him like dirt, just like you did after he risked his life to get rid of Wallace and his men."

"Are you going to stand there, Sheriff, and let Sinclair treat us like this?" Carter staggered to his feet. "The man assaulted us. You're a witness. You should arrest him."

Stoney scratched his head thoughtfully. "Witness to what? I didn't see anything.

Reckon you tripped, Mr. Carter."

Carter clenched his jaw, a vein pulsing in the side of his head. Blood oozed from a cut under his eye, and his lip was already starting to swell. Guy couldn't help thinking Ben should have joined the posse. At this rate there'd be all manner of ailments for him to treat from heart attacks to cut lips.

Carter puffed his chest out, his face a mottled red. "Easy to see who's paying your wages, Rockwell."

Guy flinched. It hadn't been a wise thing to say.

Stoney swung round aggressively and, pushing his face close to Carter, he hissed, "It's Sheriff Rockwell to you. If Guthrie Sinclair commits a crime, I'll throw him in jail, and it won't make no difference who pays my wages. I'm here to uphold the law and that's what I'll do. But right now I'm more interested in who did this to Seth Turner than fussing over your injured pride because you got exactly what you asked for, so get out of my face."

Stoney turned back to look at Turner's body again. "Damn it! If I find out who did this, I'll make sure they hang."

Guthrie, looking rather shamefaced now, crouched over the body. "It's not going to be easy. Without witnesses . . ." His voice trailed off as the sound of hooves echoed around the narrow pass. Turpin, on a skinny mare, and another rancher, Burton, riding a big barrel-chested sorrel, approached from the east.

"Thought we heard voices . . ." Burton paused, as he took in the scene in front of him. "Hell, is that Turner?"

Stoney eyed them suspiciously. "And where have you two been?"

Burton's face was a picture of innocent surprise. "What d'you mean, Sheriff? Will and I covered one side of the pass and Donovan and his men covered the other side." He paused, a furrow between his eyes as he screwed up his face as though puzzled. "What happened to Turner? You shoot him, did you?"

"I'd say even a jackass could tell he's been hanged." Stoney scowled at them. "So, somebody got to him first and I'm real eager to find out who."

Turpin shrugged. "Well, whoever it was, they did us all a favor. We won't have to drag our asses any farther from home. He probably ran into some outlaws."

"That's what we said." Dixon looked full of his own importance now. "And what I want to know is, where's our money?"

"Aye. What about our money, Sheriff?" Carter's words were muffled as he dabbed at the blood on his face with a large spotted handkerchief. "Instead of worrying over Turner, you should be looking for our money."

"Anyway, where's Fierro? For all we know, he's responsible for this . . ." Burton got no further before Stoney interrupted, even as Guy shot his hand out to restrain Guthrie, who had stepped forward with clenched fists.

"Johnny ain't got nothing to do with all of this and there's a whole passel of people who'll vouch for him, so leave him out of this." Stoney paused as Donovan and Porter rode into view. Carter and Dixon hurried over to them and started talking in low voices, but their agitation was clear to all as they gesticulated wildly and pointed toward Guthrie and Stoney.

"Stoney." Guy spoke quietly. "What do we do next? Take Turner's body back, or start hunting for the money? Always assuming that whoever did this didn't take it for themselves."

The sheriff rubbed his chin and squinted at the sky. "I guess we could have a quick scout around for the money, but it'll be dark soon and this ain't good ground for tracks.

One thing's for sure, ain't no way we're going to find out who did this unless someone comes over feeling guilty and wants to confess. And somehow I don't see that happening. Did Turner have a wife or family?"

Guy shrugged. "I really don't know anything about him. I haven't been here long and I'm still getting to know everyone. But my father will know." Turning, he beckoned his father over and couldn't help but think that the farther away Guthrie was from Carter and the rest of the ranchers, the better. "Did Turner have a wife or any other family?"

Guthrie shook his head. "No, it was all rather sad. His wife died giving birth to their second child, and the first child was taken by the measles. He was a rather lonely man. I think he'd lost the will to carry on and his ranch was becoming very run-down. I guess he saw the opportunity of some easy money and maybe a fresh start. But to end up like this . . ." Guthrie trailed off, the sadness in his face plain to see. "It's a hard life out here and better men than Turner have gone under." He glanced at Guy. "You'll find out for yourself how hard life out west is, not an easy ride for anyone. Never mind fighting Indians and outlaws to build what we have, the weather, long hours and backbreaking work take their toll on everyone." He looked at Stoney with a somber expression. "I've asked my segundo to search the outlying rocks for any sign of the money. If we find that, it'll put an end to the idea of Turner running into a band of outlaws. They'd have taken the money with them."

He'd barely finished speaking when Alonso called out from a crevice in the rocks a few feet from the ground. "Patrón. The money, it is here." He held up some saddlebags and tossed them down to one of the hands. Carter, on still shaky legs, hurried over to grab the bags before opening them and counting the money with Dixon and the others, as if to reassure themselves there wasn't a single dollar missing.

Guthrie looked at them with disgust. He shook his head. "To think I thought I knew these men. Look at them! I know it's their money but they're like a pack of jackals."

Stoney pulled his coat tighter, and pushing his hat forward to keep the driving rain out of his eyes, called out to the group. "Never mind that money. I got something to say to you all, so drag your sorry asses over here, now." The tone of his voice got their attention, and Guy smothered a very brief smile at the sight of the group of bedraggled ranchers walking slowly to join the sheriff.

"Now, I think we need to get things straight. First off, it's obvious Turner weren't killed by no outlaws. Any self-respecting outlaws would have taken your damn money, not left it for you to find . . ."

"Maybe someone came along and surprised the outlaws and they took off."

Stoney glared at Porter. "I'm cold and wet and my temper is wearing thin. Don't piss me off any more than I am already. So, like I was saying, it wasn't no outlaw who did this to Turner. More likely that one of you hid it so you could rejoin the posse and come back for it later. At least one of you is a killer. And I'll wager that he, or they, are very pleased with themselves right now, thinking they've made fools of the rest of us and had their revenge on Turner. But I warn you if I find out who was responsible for this, I'll charge you with murder. Seems you've had things your own way for too long, using the law when it suits you and ignoring it when it don't. Well, things are gonna change. I'm sheriff now, which means there'll be some law around these parts and I swear, I will enforce it and you'd best remember that. Now all of you get the hell out of here."

Guy couldn't help smiling. Stoney had

taken the wind out of their sails completely, because the other ranchers shuffled off, mounted up and rode out. He and Alonso hefted Turner's body across one of the packhorses and tied it down while Guthrie stood with a bowed head, seemingly lost in thought. Guy touched him gently on the shoulder. "Are you ready? We're riding back now, sir."

Guthrie gave a heavy sigh. "Aye, I'm ready." He mounted up and the party retraced their tracks toward Cimarron and home. They rode in silence. Stoney still looked furious about the turn of events and Guthrie seemed sunk in gloom and not inclined to talk. Even the ranch hands riding behind were silent. Turner's body struck Guy as a savage reminder of what a wild place the west still was. The wild west — they'd named it well.

They took their leave of Stoney a few miles outside Cimarron, where the path forked. Guthrie instructed a couple of hands to accompany the sheriff on to town with the body, while the rest of the party turned toward Sinclair.

Looking at Guthrie's drawn face, Guy felt a stab of concern for his father. He'd taken events badly and perhaps the time had come to lighten the situation. "Johnny'll be sorry to have missed this."

Guthrie turned sharply in the saddle to look at him, his brow furrowed. "I'm sorry? I don't get your drift."

Guy's mouth quirked with amusement. "Well, seeing his old man in a fistfight. He's never going to believe it."

For a moment he thought Guthrie was going to snap at him, but then, reluctantly almost, the man smiled. "Probably not! I suspect he'll never let me hear the end of it."

"Could you blame him? Given how hard you are on him?"

Guthrie shook his head. "Am I really that tough?"

Guy paused, weighing his reply carefully. Maybe this once his father would listen, really listen. "Yes, sir, I'm afraid you are. I have to admit, I regularly ask myself why he stays."

It got a response. Guthrie paled. "That bad? I'm that hard on him?"

Guy nodded. "And the sad part is he really doesn't expect much. Hell, who am I trying to kid? He doesn't think he deserves anything. But even the odd word of encouragement from you makes all the difference to him. If I'm honest, it seems to mean the world to him. It makes me wonder if anyone has ever been kind to him in his whole life. I keep telling you, he's a good man but this life is a big adjustment for him. It's different from anything he's ever known before but he's trying, really trying to fit in. Can't you meet him halfway and ease up a little? If you don't, I fear he'll leave."

Guthrie shifted in his saddle. "I've told him I don't want him to leave, you know that. I've told him more than once. And I told him how proud I was when he sent the ranchers packing when they first tried to hire his gun." Guthrie paused, lost in thought again. "It was odd, I heard him whistling that day. I've never heard him whistling at any other time."

Guy smiled. "Well, doesn't that tell you something?"

Guthrie looked across at him. "No need to sound so smug. But I have a nasty feeling I'm never going to hear the end of my fistfight! Come on, son, let's go home." And spurring his horse on, he raced ahead and left Guy in a cloud of dust.

CHAPTER FORTY

Life could be a hell of a lot worse. Johnny stretched out on the couch and lit one of Guthrie's best cigars. There was nothing quite like extra spicy tamales for putting him in a good mood. His injured arm had worked a treat on the women of the house. Peggy had rushed around with lemonade and cushions for him, while Carlita set to in the kitchen to make something special for poor Juanito. And knowing what his favorite meal was . . . well, the day had turned out just fine.

Even better, Peggy had turned in early, so he'd been able to enjoy his meal in peace, without having to worry about making conversation. And no disapproving looks when he drank tequila with it. No, all in all, it had been a pretty good day. Leaning forward, he topped off his glass with another shot of tequila — 100-percent blue agave. Not rotgut. He sighed contentedly before taking a long drag on the cigar. Damn, it was good.

He blew some perfect smoke rings, which drifted up before dissolving into nothingness. Smoke rings always made him grin. Yeah, it had been a real good day. And with a bit of luck, the posse might be away for some time. Maybe, by the time they got back, the old man would have calmed down and not still be mad at him. Hell, wasn't like they needed Fierro — not for hunting one dirt-poor rancher who'd made off with his neighbors' money. If it had been a bunch of outlaws it would have been different. He'd have gone, if only to keep an eye on his father and brother. But shit, not for one inexperienced thief. Why did they need a big posse for that? All fired up because someone had stolen their money. But the same bunch of men hadn't been prepared to risk an ounce of their blood to protect their womenfolk. Cowards, the whole fucking lot of them. The only reason they formed the posse was because there was no risk to their precious gringo blood. And God help poor Seth Turner, whoever he was, if the ranchers found him before Stoney did.

But the old man couldn't see what they were like. He'd have figured Guthrie to be a better judge of men. What was it Harvard had said? Something about not wanting to believe such things of people you thought you knew well? Something like that. Maybe he was right. Seemed that discovering Mrs. Walsh was a bigot had shaken the old man. Besides, she'd been fine earlier in the day. He'd actually felt some sympathy for her, when she'd said how jealous she'd been of Mama. Sounded honest. Kind of brave, really, to admit that. And the local women would've been jealous of Mama. Hell, she'd been a looker.

He leaned forward to pour another drink, but hesitated as the sound of hooves signaled the arrival of the men back from the posse. He resisted the urge to fill his glass. If the old man was still mad at him, he'd need his wits about him. He put the stopper back in the bottle but he was damned if he'd hide the cigar. He took an extra-long drag on it and then exhaled slowly, hoping the smoke would hang in the air. Show Guthrie Sinclair that he did as he damn well pleased. Including smoking his father's best cigars if he felt like it.

But his gut was already feeling tighter. How pathetic was that? Getting on edge just because his father was back sooner than he'd hoped. He was too tired for another fight. Maybe the old man wouldn't start in on him. Maybe he'd leave it to the morning. His father's parting words were ringing in his head — that their discussion wasn't over. And he could still see the anger in his father's eyes.

He could hear their voices now. Guthrie and Guy joshing each other about something. Leastways his father sounded in a good mood. That wouldn't last. He took another drag on the cigar and leaned back like he hadn't a care in the world, just as the door opened.

He had to bite back a smile. They sure looked wet. And cold. But they were still smiling about whatever they'd just been talking about. He envied Guy that, if he was honest, just to be able to relax and talk like it came easy.

Guthrie sniffed the air, looking like a dog on the scent of a bitch in heat. "Is that one of my best cigars?"

Johnny shrugged. "Yeah. You got a problem with that?"

Guthrie held his gaze, his face giving nothing away. "No, Johnny, I don't have a problem with that. As long as you left one for me too."

Johnny nodded toward the box, sitting open on his father's desk. "Plenty there."

Guy grabbed a bottle of whiskey and a glass as he moved to stand in front of the fire. If he got any closer he'd catch fire. "I'll have a cigar too, please. I think we deserve one."

"So? Catch up with Turner, did you?" Their smiles disappeared as fast as a rattler striking. Johnny narrowed his eyes and waited, figuring things had not gone well for the posse.

"Not soon enough, I'm afraid." Guy spoke softly as he poured himself a generous measure of Scotch.

Johnny raised an eyebrow fractionally. "You mean someone got to him first?" He paused, gave a slight shake of his head. "I'm guessing he was dead."

Guthrie bowed his head and sighed. "Yes. Seems you were right about a lynching."

"Didja find out who did it?"

"No. It could have been Turpin and Burton, or Donovan and Porter. We can't prove anything." Guthrie shuffled his feet like he was embarrassed. "Johnny . . ." The man hesitated, chewed on his lip and scratched his ear. Real fidgety, like he didn't know how to say something. "Son, I owe you an apology. You're a far better judge of men than I am."

Johnny almost choked on his cigar. Started

511

coughing and then damn near dropped the thing. The ghost of a smile crossed his father's face. "Having a spot of trouble with that cigar, Johnny? Too strong for you, maybe? Or was it something I said?"

The queasy feeling in his gut had gone. He laughed softly. "Well, it sure wasn't the cigar, Old Man. Just wondered if I ought to get my hearing checked."

Guy nodded. "Yes, it's a well-established fact that cutting your arm badly very often affects your hearing."

Johnny grinned at the jibe. "And you'd know, seeing as how you've been to that fancy school an' all."

Guthrie poured himself a drink and raised his glass to Johnny. "You were right about them all. And quite justified in not wanting to join a posse to chase after their money. I'm truly sorry, Johnny. They've behaved appallingly to you. Quite frankly I'm amazed that you've put up with it and even more surprised that you haven't walked out on us."

Johnny stared down at the floor, couldn't look at the man while he tried to figure out what to say. Surprised he hadn't walked out? Hell, nobody was more surprised about that than him. "Hell, I guess I'm used to it, Guthrie. If a man chooses to make his living with a gun, well, ain't nobody going to be too happy to have him around. Except when it suits them. Folk don't like gunfighters. It scares them. I don't expect nothing different, it's just the way things are. I'm sorry about the lynching, but I can't say I'm surprised. I bet Stoney's steaming over it."

Guthrie tilted his head to one side, a small crease between his eyes, like he was thinking over a problem. "Does nothing ever surprise you? The things people do to each other . . . It's like you've seen it all before. But then, maybe you have."

Johnny kicked at the rug, staring into the bottom of his glass before looking at Guthrie. "No, I guess nothing ever surprises me. I reckon people are pretty much shit everywhere. But sometimes you meet someone better than the rest." He shrugged again. "Just the way things are. For what it's worth, Stoney's a good man. He'll be a damn good sheriff, I reckon."

His father nodded. "Yes, I have to say, he impressed me today and I think he'll prove to be an excellent sheriff. Like I said, Johnny, you're a good judge of men." He paused briefly, looking kind of puzzled again. "I don't remember you saying how and where, exactly, you knew him."

He'd been expecting the question from the old man. The only surprise was it had taken him this long to ask it. Johnny screwed up his eyes, like he was trying to remember, before shaking his head. "Around. Our paths crossed a couple of times if I remember right."

Guy was giving him a sharp look, like he didn't believe a word of it, but Johnny stared right back at him, all innocent. No way was he admitting how he'd met Stoney. That would be a step too far. Never let your guard down.

Guthrie stood up, stretching his back out with a slight groan. "I think I'm turning in. Is there anything in the kitchen to eat or did you charm Carlita into cooking some incredibly spicy food that nobody else can eat?"

Johnny grinned. "Tamales and beans."

Guthrie grimaced. "I think I'll pass on that. How you don't have chronic indigestion, I'll never know. I will take my whiskey to bed. Good night, boys." He moved toward the door but slow, like he was aching bad.

"You OK, Guthrie? You look real sore. Getting too old, maybe, for riding out on posses?"

A muffled snort of laughter erupted from

Guy, and Guthrie shot him a strange look. "Don't say a word, Guy. At least, leave me the dignity of being able to leave the room first before you have a good laugh at my expense."

Guy was laughing even harder now, like he was gonna bust. Something had happened on their trip that they hadn't shared with him. Johnny quirked an eyebrow. "Am I missing something here?"

"Guy! Not a word . . ." His father didn't get any further as Guy cut across him.

"Johnny, our esteemed father has been brawling." Guy snorted with laughter again and the old man flushed.

"Brawling?" Johnny couldn't help but raise an eyebrow at the unlikely picture it conjured up.

"Yes, brawling. Fighting. Fisticuffs."

Johnny gave an exasperated sigh. "I know what brawling means. I just can't picture it . . ." He stared at Guthrie. "Who the hell were you brawling with?"

"Henry Carter and Matt Dixon. You should've been there. It was a sight to behold." Guy started laughing again.

Johnny fixed his father with a fierce look. "Fighting? Now a man your age should know better. And they're both skinnier than you. Didn't your mother ever tell you to pick on people your own size?"

"He couldn't find anyone his own size. That's why he took on two of them." Guy started laughing again and Johnny couldn't hold back his own laughter any longer.

"I am going to bed." Guthrie tried to sound offended but it didn't quite work.

"Hey. What were you fighting over?" Johnny couldn't imagine anything that would cause his father to get so angry with people he'd known for years.

Guthrie paused in the doorway, didn't answer for a second, like he couldn't decide quite what to say. "You, Johnny." He smiled. "I'll leave Guy to fill you in on the details. I'm sure he's relishing the prospect. But I think I can safely promise you that your old man won't be doing any more fighting. I'm getting far too old for it. Good night, boys."

Johnny turned to Guy, who was still smiling broadly. "What the hell did he mean? He was fighting over me?"

"Carter and Dixon dared suggest you might have had something to do with Turner's death. And they compounded their mistake by saying some rather unpleasant things about your character. Father did not take it well."

Couldn't think of a damn thing to say. His brain felt foggy and muddled. His father fighting? None of this made sense. Why would the old man fight 'cos of what some ranchers had said? He tried to speak, but the words didn't seem to come out. He ran his hand through his hair. And Guy was standing there looking as happy as a dog when it makes off with the Sunday dinner.

"You ain't kidding? He really had a fist-fight?" Somehow, this didn't seem real. Hell, if Johnny had been fighting, the old man would have given him hell.

Guy nodded. "Yes, he really did. He flattened Carter. Twice, actually. And then Dixon tried to intercede, but made the mistake of saying something else about you, so Father punched him too."

Shit. Just because they'd made a few comments about Fierro? Didn't make no sense. Guy was watching him, smiling like at some private joke.

"You don't get it, do you?" Guy spoke soft.

"I can't see why he'd hit them, just because they said what everyone thinks." Johnny shrugged. "What people say, it don't bother me none. I'm used to it."

"He was defending you. Told them how much they owed you for everything you've done since you arrived. He told them you're worth more than all of them together. I confess I think he was going to hit Donovan, too, but I restrained him at that point. He was going a very odd color and I was a little worried about his health. I felt that bringing back another body would be too much to cope with!"

Johnny smiled briefly at that. But he still couldn't figure any of this. "But what did Stoney do while all of this was going on? I mean, did he just stand there and let the old man fight?"

"He stood staring at the ground with his shoulders shaking. Poor Stoney was having great trouble controlling his laughter. And when Carter asked him to arrest Father, Stoney acted like he didn't know what Carter was going on about and said he assumed Carter must have tripped."

Johnny snorted with laughter. "Hell, I'd love to have seen that!" Johnny shook his head. "But the old man had a fucking fist-fight over me?" He paused, trying to picture it. His father all stoked up and wanting to defend his son. "Holy shit."

Guy raised an eyebrow. "Very eloquent. You have such a colorful vocabulary."

"Well, it is kind of a surprise, ain't it? I mean, the old man, fighting?"

"I think we could call today a milestone. And I suspect he might ease up on you from now on. He obviously wants you here.

Despite what you seem to think. If only you'd stop pushing him so hard, maybe things can improve. The ridiculous thing is how alike you are and neither of you seems to realize it."

Alike? Him and the old man? But then the old man was pretty good at hiding what he thought. A bit like Fierro. Except Fierro was better at it. And the old man was proud. Like Fierro. Maybe, just maybe, Guy had a point. And it felt good. Maybe life could be better. Maybe he really could have a future here. As long as the past didn't come back to bite him. He grinned across at Guy. "Want some tamales?"

He and Guy were leaning on the corral fence watching a vaquero trying to break a sorrel gelding when a bunch of the local ranchers rode in. What the fuck did they want? Whatever it was, it was bound to spell trouble. He wouldn't trust 'em an inch.

Guy raised an eyebrow as he nudged Johnny in the ribs. "I wonder what the deputation is for?"

"Maybe they want my head. On a platter. Like in that bible story."

Guy's eyes widened. "You never fail to surprise me. Where on earth did you learn about that?"

Johnny rolled his eyes. "Right now, I'm more interested in what those ranchers want." He turned toward the hacienda before glancing back at Guy. "Coming?"

Guy nodded. "I wouldn't miss this for the world."

The ranchers were in the living room and judging by their faces they were spoiling for trouble. Guthrie stood at the window, ramrod straight and scowling. "Well? What brings you all here? I've a lot to do so make it quick."

Turpin clenched his jaw, looked very pissed off. "We want to settle unfinished business, Guthrie. Fact is, someone killed Turner, and we've been talking it over and we reckon your explanation of Fierro's whereabouts was a little too pat. Like you had your speech all ready. None of us would've killed Turner, which leaves one obvious choice. Fierro." He turned, meeting Johnny's eyes. "So, where were you, Fierro?"

Johnny smiled coldly. "Well, I don't know what my old man told you, but that was the day I cut my arm. Ben Greenlaw stitched it up, and he'll vouch for me. Unless you're calling him a liar."

Donovan stepped toward him. "That don't explain where you cut your arm. You might have cut it fighting with Turner. You can't prove anything, Fierro."

Kind of funny really. He'd been setting up Edith Walsh to say when he'd cut his arm if he ever needed it, but it seemed she'd come in useful right now. "If you ask Mrs. Walsh, she'll tell you when I cut my arm. She was there. Tied something round it to stop the bleeding. Ask her. She'll tell you the same."

Some of the other ranchers shuffled their feet and looked embarrassed, but not Porter. Piece of shit.

"Edith Walsh." He sneered. "She's a good friend of Guthrie. She'll say whatever he tells her to say. You're scum, Fierro, and everyone in this room knows it."

Guthrie lurched forward, like a charging bull. Shit! The old man could move real fast when he had a mind to. His fists were out and he landed a heavy punch in Porter's gut. "The only scum around here is you, Porter. How dare you come here and accuse my son."

Porter reeled backwards, crashing against the bookcase. Guthrie, breathing hard, had his fists clenched. He wasn't done fighting yet.

But even as his father drew back his fist to strike again, Johnny saw Porter pull a gun from inside his jacket.

The explosion from the Colt shook the

room as Porter fell back, blood pouring from the wound in his side. Johnny kept his gun aimed at him until he'd kicked the rancher's gun clear. Not that it looked like Porter was going anywhere fast. Except, maybe, to hell.

It seemed like forever before anyone moved. Or spoke. Guthrie was deathly white and the other ranchers stood rooted to the floor. Any moment it would change and the old man would start yelling at him. Shit. Should have just winged the bastard. But his instincts had taken over and now Porter was bleeding out all over the rug.

Turpin was the first to move, bending over Porter, his fingers searching for some sign of life. Porter's jacket splayed open and a wallet fell from the inner pocket. The rancher examined it before turning to face them all. "This is Turner's wallet. I know, he showed it to me once. It was a gift from his wife. And now it's in Porter's pocket . . ."

It seemed to take a second for them to figure it out. They didn't seem none too bright.

Guthrie, still red and breathing heavy, glared round at them all. "I think you all owe Johnny an apology. If Porter's got Turner's wallet, it proves who the guilty man is. And it sure as hell isn't my son. So, get off our land."

Our land? That was a first. It was always his ranch. His land. Must have been a slip of the tongue. Yeah. Just a slip.

"Hold on, Guthrie." Matt Dixon frowned, holding his hand up. "Think on it. This doesn't make sense. It would have taken more than one man to string up Turner. Porter would have needed help."

Guthrie scowled. "Well, how d'you explain the wallet? Are you trying to tell me Porter wasn't involved? Are you accusing my son . . . ?"

Dixon huffed out a sigh. "Damn it, man! Let me finish." He shot Donovan a sharp glance. "Donovan, you were riding with him that day. The two of you were in a tearing hurry to split off from the rest of us."

"That's right!" Carter stepped forward. "You were the one suggested we should split up. And you were hell-bent on sticking with Porter."

Donovan snorted. "What are you accusing me of? I'm a law-abiding man, you know that. But none of us knows Fierro, there." He pointed at Johnny. "He just killed a man, in front of all of us. What does that tell you about him?"

Guy shook his head. "It won't work, Donovan. All you're doing is trying to divert attention from yourself. My brother's done nothing wrong. But Dixon's right, Porter couldn't have hung Turner by himself. And you were the one riding with him. What did you do? Hide the money once you strung him up, planning to split it between the pair of you later?"

"Aye," Carter spluttered. "That's right. Our money was hidden away in those rocks. And like young Sinclair says, Donovan, you were with Porter."

Donovan sucked in a breath, the tips of his ears turning bright red. "This is all nonsense. It's nothing to do with me —"

"Tell it to the sheriff," snapped Dixon. "I'm taking you in. Who's going to help me?"

A couple of the other ranchers stepped forward and, ignoring Donovan's protests, hustled him out the door.

Carter sighed heavily. "Seems we got things wrong. We were out of line. Sorry." He stared down at Porter's body. "Perhaps we should go back to our old ways of doing things. I reckon we've made fools of ourselves. And Porter and Donovan made fools of us all."

Guthrie bowed his head, as if lost in thought. The big old clock by the door was ticking real loud. How would this pan out?

Guthrie raised his head. "Just like that, Henry? Forget all the things you've said about Johnny? When I think how he's conducted himself in the face of all this prejudice and antipathy, it's made me realize I've misjudged you all over the years and I've misjudged him. Johnny's behaved with dignity and restraint, while you've shown yourselves to be cowards and bigots."

Johnny's blood was pulsing fast. Surely they must hear his heart thumping? He could barely believe his ears. Hell, he'd just shot a man, and his father didn't seem bothered about it.

"So, quite frankly, Henry, whether or not Sinclair returns to the original arrangements isn't really my decision." He gestured toward Johnny. "My partner calls the tune on this one." Guthrie looked hard at Johnny. Shit. Was that a wink? "In his own good time. But for now, like I said, get off our land."

EPILOGUE

Life was looking up. Johnny was going to enjoy making the ranchers sweat while Sinclair pondered its decision to join forces with them. They would, eventually, if only to save the ranch money, but it wasn't something to rush into.

He leaned back in his chair at his usual corner table in the bordello. Yeah. Life really was looking up. Delice was doing a roaring trade too, judging by the crowd this evening. The girls looked real pretty, their colorful dresses rustling as they moved between the tables, hips swaying in time to the music. Delice was moving among the customers, pausing for friendly banter with her regulars. He'd caught her emerald-eyed gaze earlier and she'd mouthed something at him but he hadn't a clue what. She'd get to him eventually, pushing through the throng. In the meantime he just enjoyed watching everyone. A huge bearded cowhand, all muscle and brawn, who headed upstairs with Susie, looked like a lamb for slaughter. And some skinny runt was hauling three girls up there, even though he looked like a good puff of wind would knock him sideways. Didn't look like he had the energy to deal with one girl, let alone three.

"Johnny." Delice placed a bottle of decent tequila on the table. Not the rotgut she served to most of the customers. "How've you been? Arm all healed up now?"

He poured himself a large shot. "Yeah, I'm fine. It sure is hopping in here. Don't recall ever seeing it so busy."

"They're mainly drovers. We've had a lot in over the past few days. I guess the fall drives are over now and they're making their way home for winter. Their pay seems to be burning holes in their pockets." She shrugged. "I'm not complaining. It's good business and mostly they're good tippers so the girls are all in good moods."

Johnny grinned. "So long as Sadie ain't taken and can squeeze me in."

Delice raised an eyebrow, her lips twitching. "In more ways than one, I take it."

"Well, far be it from me to brag . . ."

Delice gave an exaggerated sort of a sigh. "To change the subject totally, I wanted to let you know someone was in here this week showing a lot of interest in your where-abouts."

Johnny tensed, every nerve suddenly on edge. "What did he look like? A gunhawk?"

She shook her head. "No, he looked like a drover. But he heard your name mentioned and that's when he started asking questions. I didn't get the impression he was looking for you when he first arrived."

The fingers of his gun hand drummed on the table as he considered her words. A drover. Might not mean anything. Lots of people were interested in Fierro. It went with the territory. People were excited by the thought of seeing a famous gunfighter.

"Anything special about him? Anything at all?"

She looked at him hard, like she could sense his unease. "Is there something in particular you're worried about, Johnny?"

He shrugged and laughed, real easy. "Nope. Just curious. I like to know if someone's likely to be calling me out, that's all."

"Like I said, he looked like a drover, not a gunfighter. He seemed to think you were dead but heard your name mentioned in town so he started asking questions. Sadie!" She beckoned to Sadie, who was walking past with a tray of glasses and a bottle of bourbon. "That man who was asking about Johnny, do you remember anything special about him?"

Sadie placed the tray down and then leaned forward over the table to him, almost pushing her breasts in his face.

"Sadie." Delice sounded kinda bored. "Just answer the question. You can show him those later."

Sadie screwed up her face, like she was trying to remember. "He weren't nothing special. Just a drover, passing through."

He pushed his glass around in neat circles; it left damp marks and his fingers of his gun hand continued to tap. Didn't sound like anything special. Probably just someone who'd heard his name.

"I do remember one thing." Sadie beamed like she'd won a prize. "I remember where he was going home to."

Johnny inclined his head. "Yeah? And where was that, Sadie?"

"Utah."

ABOUT THE AUTHOR

Adventurer and journalist **JD March** has tracked leopards in the Masai Mara, skied competitively, ridden to hounds, paddled dugout canoes on the Indian Ocean, and is an accomplished sailor. JD has lived in a series of unusual homes, including a haunted twelfth-century house in Cornwall in Britain and a chalet in the French Alps. But a lifelong passion for the old West means JD is happiest in the saddle, rounding up cattle on the Bighorn Mountains in Wyoming.

www.jdmarch.com

THE

VOCABULARY

OF PEACE

Other books in English translation
by Shulamith Hareven

City of Many Days
The Miracle Hater
Prophet
Twilight and Other Stories

SHULAMITH HAREVEN

THE
VOCABULARY

Life, Culture, and Politics

OF PEACE

in the Middle East

MERCURY HOUSE
SAN FRANCISCO

United States Constitution, First Amendment: Congress shall make no law
respecting an establishment of religion, or prohibiting the free exercise
thereof; or abridging the freedom of speech, or of the press; or the right of
the people peaceably to assemble, and to petition the Government for a
redress of grievances.

Mercury House and colophon are registered trademarks of
Mercury House, Incorporated

Designed by Thomas Christensen
Printed on recycled, acid-free paper
Manufactured in the United States of America

Library of Congress Cataloging-in-Publication Data

Hareven, Shulamith. [Essays. English. Selections]
The vocabulary of peace : life, politics, and culture in the Middle East /
Shulamith Hareven.
p.   cm. Translations from Hebrew.
ISBN 1-56279-072-2 (pbk)
1. Jewish-Arab relations — 1973–   2. Peace movements — Israel.
3. National characteristics, Israeli. I. Title.
DS119.7.H3625   1995
956—dc20   94-23851
CIP

FIRST EDITION
5 4 3 2 1

Contents ━━━━━━━━━━━━━━━━━━━━━━━

Preface

surprisingly sunny, and the brisk walk to City Hall, where the Nobel Prize
for Peace ceremony took place, had an air of exhilaration. But the three
laureates were not smiling. To many it seemed that the greatly coveted
prize was perhaps premature; intention had been proclaimed, mutual
recognition was there for all to see and applaud, but the real work still lay
ahead.

Chairman Arafat's limitations and constraints came to light soon
enough: Moslem fundamentalist organizations carried out several bloody
attacks in Israel, unhampered by any loyalty to the PLO leaders or to the
peace process. Mr. Rabin, in a precarious political situation at home,
seemed unable to put a full stop to all construction in the territories, at
least until final borders could be demarcated. The expected period of
mutual trust-building had not started well. It seemed that two parallel
fears, the Jewish fear of being wantonly killed, and the Palestinian fear of
losing land, were not allayed, and were perhaps even exacerbated. Any
changes brought about by the accords were not yet visible, the new economic structure seemed to exist on paper only, and patience was running
short.

One essential thing did change: from now on it is not automatically
Jew against Arab and Arab against Jew; it is the Jews and Arabs who
support peace, and those, Jews and Arabs both, who oppose it—not one
nation against another, but two bi-national coalitions.

That in itself constitutes the greatest change in the Middle East, perhaps the only one that might succeed, indeed, perhaps a last chance. All
of us, Israelis and Palestinians, writers, academics, doctors, close friends
who had kept meeting during past years, openly and clandestinely, in
good days and bad ones, talking, listening to each other—perhaps the first

bi-national coalition preceding the political one—felt vindicated after Oslo.

I believe in this peace. I believe that any other way would sooner or later lead to slow deterioration into dirty, mindless belligerence. I also know that there is no simple solution to suicidal, fundamentalist terror, because the promise of eternal bliss and paradise is, to the religious killer, a greater incentive than any political compromise the leaders might achieve. On the other side, a rabbi in a settlement might tell his disciples in the course of a lesson that "thou shalt not kill" (actually, "murder" in the Biblical original) does not pertain to Gentiles; thereby legitimizing whatever the result might be. Nationalism reinforced by fundamentalist religion equals conflict.

In this region, we are drugged on man-made drama; on a perpetual high of violent politics. It will take more than a few men signing a paper to make people realize the strength of the ordinary; to feel that sanity can be exciting. Only visible, everyday change can, gradually, with great patience, make it happen.

A few hours before the ceremony in Oslo I came down to the hotel reception desk, wearing my Israeli delegation tag, and saw one of Arafat's security men, loaded with all his paraphernalia, standing there, unable to explain in his nonexistent English to the Norwegian receptionist what it was he required. Both men looked frustrated and unhappy. I asked, in Arabic, whether help was needed. For the next few minutes there was some earnest talk back and forth, writing names down in Arabic script and in English, until the matter was settled, and the beaming receptionist handed him the required key. Grateful to tears, the man shook both my hands fervently, repeating, "Thank you, Madame, thank you a hundredfold, may God bless you."

It was all very normal and I hardly thought about it; until hours later, the realization came: a few weeks before, we might have been completely —even violently—hostile. Now, without giving it a thought, we spoke in a different vocabulary—that of peace.

APRIL 1995

THE

VOCABULARY

OF PEACE

Words

Beginnings ━━━━━━━━━━━━━━━

OUR CONTACT WITH A BOOK
is determined by the first sentence. Every author knows that the entire
book hangs on the first diction, as on a hook; if you have the right opening sentence, then the book already exists somewhere, and all you've got
to do is not let it down.

The literary community—that is, good writers and good readers—
acknowledges with some amusement the various literary mannerisms that
at times determine beginnings, letting us guess what comes after. A thick
novel of the satisfying kind will usually begin something like this:

> In M., a small, gray industrial town in the north of the country
> of A., one Sunday, the day all are exempt from work, Mr. L. left
> his house on prosperous N. Street, his hat on his head, with-
> out bidding his extensive family farewell. His countenance
> was darkened with worry.

By the time Mr. L. returns to his home and his extensive family we will
have traversed with him at least three hundred pages of social and semi-
historical plot, a little comedy of manners, and a little tragedy of the inevitable—in any case, we will not be bored before the end of vacation.

Alas, the same cannot be said of contemporary books, which frequently begin with sentences like:

> The young man flung his duffel bag up onto the shelf, took a
> seat on the bus crammed with soldiers, spat out his chewing
> gum, and promptly fell asleep.

Where is the small gray industrial town? Where is the prosperous N.
Street, the exemption from work on Sunday? Where is the extensive family? Where is the hat?

I confess: I have had enough of thin content, paltry language, and antiheroes. I want important content, interesting language, and a hero. All my life I have loved magical beginnings, those that hint of momentous events and vicissitudes of fate and upheavals in the world. I confess I have had enough of trivial prose. From among the hundreds of thousands of books that are published, I seek the very interesting.

Admittedly, it is difficult to compete with

> In the beginning God created the heaven and the earth.

But that was hardly the final word in great beginnings. Take for example Henryk Sienkiewicz's *With Fire and Sword,* which begins:

> The year 1647 was a strange year, in which various portents in the heavens and on earth heralded unnatural events. In the spring locusts alighted on the fields in quantities never seen before and devoured all the grasses and seedlings—a portent of the Tartar raids. In the summer there was a great eclipse, and then the appearance of a comet. The people of Warsaw saw in the skies above the city a grave and a cross of flame; this caused them to fast and give alms, for they feared it meant a plague would descend upon the earth and eradicate the human race.

Sienkiewicz goes on to describe a strange spring that begins in December with the thawing of the snows and first sprouting, as if the seasons—nay, the very order of creation—had reversed themselves; by this point the reader is assured that this is not going to be a *petit bourgeois* book. Here he will find no Madame Bovary and her peccadilloes, but some fundamental metamorphosis. This particular metamorphosis was known as the Chmielnicki Rebellion.

A portent of the reversal of world order can also be found in the beginning of Barbara Tuchman's book *The Guns of August:*

> So gorgeous was the spectacle on the May morning of 1910 when nine kings rode in the funeral of Edward VII of England, that the crowd, waiting in hushed and black-clad awe, could not keep back gasps of admiration. In scarlet and blue and

green and purple, three by three the sovereigns rode through
the palace gates with plumed helmets, gold braid, crimson
sashes and jeweled orders flashing in the sun.

A book that begins with nine kings escorting a tenth to his rest could
hardly be about Mr. L., the merchant from the small, gray industrial town.
Indeed, it is about the First World War, that great upheaval of the start of
this century that marked the end of an era and the end of world order; this
glorious beginning records their last appearance on the face of the earth.

There are also sensational beginnings that instantly stun the reader,
such as the paragraph with which Heinrich von Kleist began "The Marquise of O——." He placed almost the entire story in the first paragraph, as
is the practice in modern newspapers:

In M——, a large town in northern Italy, the widowed Marquise
O——, a lady of unblemished reputation and the mother of several well-bred children, published the following notice in the
newspapers: that, without her knowing how, she was in the
family way; that she would like the father of the child she was
going to bear to report himself; and that her mind was made
up, out of consideration for her people, to marry him.

Only a great artist like Kleist could permit himself to begin in this way
a story that develops into one of the most delicate in all literature.

In the same tradition, if much less sensationally, Leslie Epstein, a talented contemporary writer, begins his book *King of the Jews:*

In the winter of 1918–19, on a day when the wind was blowing,
I. C. Trumpelman arrived in our town. He was wearing a
brown overcoat and a brown hat, and had a large suitcase in
each hand.

The continuation does not fall from the beginning. *King of the Jews* is
one of the greatest of all the books about the Holocaust; the intriguing
Trumpelman is modeled after M. C. Rumkowsky, the leader of the Jews
in the Lodz Ghetto. This opening sentence should be taught as an example in every writers' workshop; indeed, it is not surprising that Epstein is
among the few authors who teach the craft of writing. First, the hero

arrives on "a day when the wind was blowing"—in other words, here, too, we have the participation of the forces of nature, or the forces that control nature, in the plot. If the author had wanted to say that it was just plain windy, he would have concentrated on the hero and not on the wind, writing that he was bundled up against the wind, or had wrapped his neck in a scarf because of the wind. Yet he chose to write, "in the winter of 1918–19, on a day when the wind was blowing"; that is, we prepare ourselves for an epic plot of cosmic significance, a plot with a hero. From here on, the magic goes to work on us.

Huge historical plots often receive a lyric beginning, such as the unforgettable one of *A Tale of Two Cities:*

> It was the best of times, it was the worst of times, it was the age
> of wisdom, it was the age of foolishness, it was the epoch of
> belief, it was the epoch of incredulity, it was the season of
> Light, it was the season of Darkness ...

There is no doubt about the source of this opening of Dickens's. He belonged to a generation that knew the Bible by heart; it flowed in his blood. Doubtless he saw before him the model of "a time to be born, and a time to die; a time to sow, and a time to reap; a time to kill, and a time to heal; a time to cast away stones, and a time to gather stones together." We can see just how well Dickens knew the Bible, for example, in the marvelous scene in *The Pickwick Papers* in which they call the man who has been driving his carriage recklessly—that is, a dangerous driver—by the name Jehu, "for he driveth as though he were mad." How many contemporary Israeli writers could come up with such a name, and how many readers would understand it? In the last century the entire literary community instantly understood the allusion. Perhaps the Ministry of Police ought to issue "Jehu certificates" to certain Israeli drivers, if only to bring this fantastic name back to life.

The generation that knew the Bible by heart was also the one to which Herman Melville belonged; he begins *Moby Dick* with the famous sentence

> Call me Ishmael.

He ends it on the ship *Rachel,* which, weeping for her sons, crosses the breadth of the ocean to seek survivors. Between Ishmael and *Rachel* the whole terrible plot unfolds, the tale of Captain Ahab's vainglory.

Compared with Melville, Gabriel García Márquez is a blithe and uninhibited pantheist, a master of the mythological plot in which miracles happen in the course of birth and death, between the cooking pots and the sheets; from here springs the well-remembered beginning of *One Hundred Years of Solitude:*

> Years later, when the Colonel Orleano Buendía stood before
> the firing squad, he would remember that faraway evening
> when his father took him to see ice.

In contrast, Leo Tolstoy is hardly the best writer of beginnings. All of us remember the opening sentence of *Anna Karenina:*

> Happy families are all alike; each unhappy family is unhappy
> in its own way.

It is a nice sentence, but it deliberates; actually, it is what we would today call a "pensée." Like many other Russian writers, Tolstoy thought like both an author and an essayist, and neither he nor his literary community saw any fault in this. I imagine that his hapless wife, Sofia, who copied *War and Peace* in its entirety seven times from Lev Nikolaevich's illegible handwriting, did not see any fault in it either. Something of the "pensive" tradition can also be found in English literature—but what a difference! Let us see how T. E. Lawrence begins *Seven Pillars of Wisdom:*

> Some of the evil of my tale may have been inherent in our
> circumstances. For years we lived anyhow with one another in
> the naked desert, under the indifferent heaven. By day the hot
> sun fermented us; and we were dizzied by the beating wind. At
> night we were stained by dew, and shamed into pettiness by
> the innumerable silence of stars. We were a self-centered army
> without parade or gesture, devoted to freedom, the second of
> man's creeds, a purpose so ravenous that it devoured all our
> strength, a hope so transcendent that our earlier ambitions
> faded in its glare.

The first sentence is, indeed, a "pensée," but one that refers to a personal plot. Lawrence tells a story; Tolstoy, as usual, prepares a great moral sermon.

A moment ago I mentioned poor Sofia Tolstoy, and this reminds me of an anecdote connected with feminism. Not long ago there was a conference of feminist women writers in Jerusalem; all sorts of theses were presented with which I found it hard to agree, because I believe the distinction between women's literature and men's literature is a valid sociological and political one, but has nothing to do with art. A well-known feminist author from the United States stood on the podium and argued fervently that women are never, ever as egocentric as men, and that consequently not one single literary work written by a woman could begin with the word "I." Then a voice called from the audience: "Like—'I had a farm in Africa?' "

That is the sentence with which Karen Blixen—or Isak Dinesen, her pseudonym—begins her book, beautifully preserved in spirit and letter in the film *Out of Africa.* So much for generalizations.

On the subject of feminism, we ought to ask why, of all places, we often find completely authentic women in books that are considered so-called light reading—that is, detective stories, or comedies, or comedies of manners. Moreover, many women write detective novels, particularly in English, and lately in Hebrew as well. The mean-spirited want us to believe that this is female sublimation: she wants to kill somebody; rather than do it like a man, in real life, she does it in a novel.

It seems to me there is another reason. The detective story is, in essence, the classic fairy tale. The hero is in danger; for a while the forces of evil hold sway, but in the end the hero—the wise detective or the good police officer—comes through; justice triumphs and evil is punished. This is the classic recipe for a legend, and women are accustomed to inventing and telling legends with happy endings, as they have done since the children were three and four.

Let us recall the clever beginning of one of the more brilliant detective stories, one in a series penned by authors Caryl Brahms and C. J. Simon. I mean *A Bullet in the Ballet.* By the time they wrote this book the authors knew that they were old hands and their readers were old hands, and so they immediately reduced the distance between book and reader:

Since it is probable that any book flying a bullet in its title is going to produce a corpse sooner or later, here it is.

Some beginnings belong to what is called collective culture—that is, the culture and education that are supposedly the common denominator of those who take the same matriculation exams. Reality, of course, is different. Culture, in its narrow definition as education, is something we are meant to learn thoroughly, be examined on, and promptly forget. That is, we are meant to internalize it. How much education and culture, though, does the average high school graduate internalize, and how many words from the vast corpus of words does he remember by heart; words he would never get wrong even if awakened at three in the morning; words he would recite to himself, over and over, to preserve his sanity if he were in prison or captivity? If it were up to me, I would not award a certificate of education to anyone who declaimed theories; but I would award one immediately to anyone who was able at three in the morning, drunk or sober, to quote the grand opening of Dante's *Divine Comedy:*

> In the middle of the journey of our life
> I found myself in a dark wood,
> Where the straight way was lost.

This is undoubtedly one of the foundations of culture. Dante was an expert at grand openings. I have always seen the beginning of Canto III as an unseverable, almost prophetic link to the feelings of all those who survived the Holocaust:

> I am the way to the city of sorrow:
> I am the way to dolor eternal;
> I am the way to the people lost.

It is not difficult to find great beginnings in poetry; that is what poetry is for. We are affected by opening lines that have permeated our memories, our very bodies, and have become part of the stuff of which we are made. Personally, the opening sentence that has touched me more deeply than any other is the one that begins *The Sibyl* by Pär

Lagerkvist, who, to my mind, ranks with the greatest of all writers. A Swede, he won the Nobel Prize, and he wrote very thin books in very aristocratic prose— quite unlike the prevailing fashion of fat books in plebeian, "hey-buddy" prose. Lagerkvist never thought the reader was his buddy or that he needed to lure him. If someone were to have told him that he had to choose between bringing the reader closer to literature and bringing literature closer to the reader, he would not have understood what they were talking about. This man, who for decades influenced the best literature, was thought of us avant-garde many years after his death. He maintained absolute independence, without affiliating himself with any literary clique. He had artistic uniqueness, a brilliant intellect, and a metaphysical and theological background; the smarter critics claimed that there was practically no aesthetic problem in the area of writing and literature that Lagerkvist did not succeed in solving—not just in theory, but in his writing. His book *The Sibyl* opens with a line that is among the most wondrous in all literature:

> In a little house, on the mountain slope above Delphi, lived an
> old woman with her witless son.

This is how truly great legends begin. This woman has already been through it all; in her day she was the sibyl in the temple, the one from whose throat God speaks, the one whom God chooses and torments, until she is no longer of use to Him. A straight line can be drawn from here to the Book of Job. Many scholars have interpreted God's answer to Job out of the whirlwind as if it were no answer at all; as if it were a way of saying, "You are insignificant and I am great; do not question what is beyond your comprehension." Other scholars have seen the answer to Job not as an ethical one, but as a kind of aesthetic attitude: "I am making wondrous things, and this has a price, and the price happens to be you." This perception jibes with that in our midrashic literature, according to which God in effect abandoned Job to Satan, who toyed with him for a time, during the Exodus, so he wouldn't interfere until the Children of Israel had crossed the Red Sea safely.

In all humility, I would like to suggest a different interpretation. When God answers Job out of the whirlwind—pelting him with questions, all pertaining to the great Beginning, like

Knowest thou the time when the chamois of the rock bring forth? Or markest thou when the hinds do calve? Who hath sent out the wild ass free? Or who hath loosed the bands of the wild ass? Hast thou given the horse his strength? Hast thou clothed his neck with fierceness? Canst thou send forth lightnings that they may go, And say unto thee: here we are? Knowest thou the laws of heaven or dost thou appoint its rule on earth? Didst thou ever, in all thy days, command the morning; didst thou ever assign the morning-dawn its place? Where wast thou when I laid the foundations of the earth? Declare, if thou hast the understanding.

What does He really want from Job? His submission? His acquiescence to what has been ordained? Or perhaps curiosity, the mother of creation?

It seems to me that what Job should really have answered, if he had stood the test, was, "No, Lord, but I'm dying to know; please, please, share with me."

To my mind, the whole world is nothing more than an invitation to take part in creation. Literature, at least—or at least the magic of opening sentences—answers this need.

What Should We Do about Myth?

THE EASIEST THING THAT CAN be said about myth is that most of us have an ambivalent attitude toward it. Myth has a negative, derisive connotation, suggesting superstition in which no logical and enlightened person believes, as reflected in the adage, What *I* believe is a well-formed idea, what *you* believe is dogma, and what *he* believes is myth. As we all know, myth cannot be proven and does not stand the test of criticism—evidence of inferior intellectual development. Myth is that somewhat disgraceful part of the human constitution that enlightened people simply and benevolently ignore, since there is no enlightenment greater than elegant skepticism. Even the ancient Greeks asked themselves what to do about myth. Aristophanes came up with an answer in his play *The Frogs:* there, in the last act, a son who has come up in society chides his father, a common man, saying to him, "Father, for heaven's sake, in cultured circles one does not discuss myths at the dinner table."

A myth is first and foremost a story that is not meant to be founded in reality, or rationality, and to which is ascribed a degree of sanctity, or at least a degree of ancestral reverence. I say ancestral because it is a familial story, one that determines in large degree affiliation, solidarity and the codes of solidarity, the collective cultural text, and, to a great extent, cultural patterns. It is customary to think—following the Greek idea—that the antithesis of myth is historical criticism; the word "history" in Greek means investigation, learning through examination. Some claim to this very day that were we to break down myth into its historical components—that is, its "real" elements—we would find ourselves freed from myth, which binds us and stifles our thinking, and we would become more enlightened, more worthy of being counted among the civilized. According to this approach, it is important for us to know, and bear in mind, for example, that when the Bastille was stormed, it housed all in all about five pickpockets and two prostitutes, or vice versa; and this knowledge would all at once dim the mythological glitter that European thought attaches to the symbolic act of the storming of the Bastille.

Certainly the use of the testimony of history to explode myth is an important component of a human cultural pattern. Both history and myth are legitimate; remove either one, and no culture is possible. A large component of the phenomenon of social protest is the shattering of existing myths for dynamic purposes, to effect change, because myth can indeed block development. The Protestants, for example, turned to history to prove publicly just how illegal the roots of the Pope's absolute authority were; to do so, they pored through archives and brought out old documents and writings that limited the papal institution and that were deliberately "forgotten" by the Catholic Church as it created the myth of absolute papacy. Luther said in his day that "history is the mother of truth"—a particularly apt aphorism, given that the word "truth" in Greek is *alethea,* or *a-lethea,* the removal of oblivion. That is, through history, investigation, we arrive at *alethea,* truth, the removal of forgetting—a distinctly Greek concept. Protestantism, as a protest movement, really did see the world as "the site of God's trial," the site of a recorded and documented historical inquiry into justice and truth. One could say that protest in general requires knowing and publishing the historical truth, that protest frequently discovers and reveals historical truth, and that in this lies its principal strength. George Santayana said that the demand for the absolute and the need for its delegitimization are both components of culture.

The shattering of myth by enlightened historians who come bearing testimonies is, then, an idea beloved by historians. There are, however, several essential problems with it. First of all, it is reductionist and diminishing, and somehow misses an important point—perhaps even the most important point—which I will discuss presently. But the essential problem is that what is called "the historical perspective" is *also* not absolute truth, and is in any case subordinate to and reflects the thought and the world view of a given generation. Herodotus, for example, as befits a professional historian, made a thorough investigation of the cult of Heracles in Egypt, and arrived at the somewhat condescending conclusion that this cult relied on a great deal of fallacious myth that only a gullible fool would believe. Why? Because those who practiced it attributed to

Heracles the man all sorts of miracles, when any child knows that Heracles could not have performed miracles as a man, but only once he had died and become a god. We should remember that in its day, Herodotus's antimythological perception of history was the most enlightened and scientific one imaginable. This is reminiscent of the famous warning made by an enlightened missionary to the members of an uncivilized tribe: "My poor brethren, please, you must not believe in superstitions—it brings bad luck."

If we are going to be skeptics, then let's also be skeptics regarding the seemingly redemptive power of history. There is something about the perception of history as refuting myth that is itself myth: the promise of instant catharsis. We'll just learn a few facts, and abracadabra—the myth will vanish, never to return. This, too, is naive thinking, perhaps even magical to a certain extent; I have nothing against magical thinking if it helps someone feel less helpless at a given moment, but I would be very cautious about using it as a precise scientific tool. Cognitive dissonance, contradiction through proven facts, does not always force people to draw new conclusions or change their way of looking at things; the dissonance remains dissonant and the ways of the world remain as they were, as anyone who has ever studied the habits of the Israeli electorate surely knows.

Why is it so difficult to combat myth through proof and contradiction?

Something in the mythical tale is connected to the beginning, to genesis, to the prehistoric chaos before orderly thought, before God said, "Let there be light." Most people are willing to accept myth as the Siamese twin of genesis, of creation, of the beginning of the history of the tribe or the town. In the beginning the she-wolf suckled Romulus and Remus, and then there was history and caesars and a senate. An uninterrupted continuation runs from legendary oral culture through written and recorded culture. Indeed, patriarchs and matriarchs naturally invite a mythic approach—how much more so ancient patriarchs and matriarchs. For the moment it is not important—and here the historians err—whether people believe their myths or not; people are prepared, made, for this duality of thinking. The talent for myth is inborn, perhaps because myth, associated with early history, somehow parallels the experience of early childhood. The early childhood of each of us has its mythology, both because we had no possibility of arranging experience in an ordered conceptual design and because we lacked the ability to conceptualize and criticize and synthesize. Moreover, for the little boy and girl, mother and father and indeed all adults are all-powerful mythological creatures, in whose hands are life and death; everything can be made to happen by them and because of them. Mothers and fathers are great witches, miracle workers for good and ill, because everything they do the child cannot do, and therefore it is a wonder and a miracle and a legend and a myth. Apparently, mythical thinking is our first thought pattern.

In fact, it appears the very ability to think mythologically is inborn, part of our constitution, like the ability to walk and talk and the ability to acquire language; here lies its strength. Thus, whoever accepts myth as it is, without argument, is in essence saying to all the historians and all the protestants who ever were or will be: I live with the fact that I do not know; I have the innate ability to live with mystery. "I do not know" means that I also feel I have no way of knowing, or perhaps have no right to know. A man knows that it was his parents who put ten cents under his pillow in exchange for the baby tooth he lost, yet at the same time he also believes that the tooth fairy came at night and took the tooth and replaced it with a coin. There is duality here without contradiction, because not so long ago every man was a small child, and grown-ups were mythological creatures that could make miracles happen, and you had no right to know. Do not investigate things that are beyond your comprehension. The Rambam said that one shouldn't question legend too deeply.[1] Thus, we all have at least an ambivalent attitude toward myth, precisely because we all were once children, and it is no more possible to eradicate the child in us, and his abilities, than it is to eradicate the adult in us. A person is more than one persona; under the best of circumstances, we grow up not at the expense of the child within us, and not in its stead, but rather alongside it, each of us completely legitimate.

Moreover, because the mythical perception is somehow related to our origins, to the beginning of our lives, to our prehistoric period, it is usually a static, closed perception, because childhood ends at some point

---

1. Moses Maimonides (1135–1204), rabbi, physician, philosopher and one of Judaism's greatest scholars, published a great many works in Hebrew and Arabic on Jewish law, ethics, and conduct in daily life. *Trans.*

and does not continue. We usually do not expect myth to continue in the present. The French philosopher Paul Veyne asks whether the Greeks really believed in their myths and responds that they did indeed believe in everything that was related to the past: once upon a time Athena really did spring out of Zeus's head and become the goddess of wisdom. But if someone were to tell them that yesterday at 4 P.M. Athena had had enough and jumped back into Zeus's head, or that Zeus again turned into a swan and came down to earth to pay an adulterous visit to a nymph until her husband came home—this they would not have believed, because they were not suckers. The gods sat in their celestial realms, where they lived; but, in Veyne's words, the average Greek would have been quite surprised to lift his head and find all sorts of gods floating in the sky. Myth is always a story; it always takes place within language and will not become real. A myth that has become real, that has "come true," is history.

Many years ago an Israeli academic who was living in Accra, the capital of Ghana, told how when she asked to place a call to Jerusalem, the operator thought she was making fun of her, because there was no such city as Jerusalem. Jerusalem was a city in the sky—Heavenly Jerusalem—like everything else in the Bible. The Israeli woman had to go all the way to the central post office and ask for the person in charge, who checked in a book and found that, indeed, there was a city of Jerusalem on earth, and it had telephones and area codes; only then was it possible to place the call.

Nevertheless, we feel that we must somehow confront the matter of myth, if only because it is so often used to manipulate political power. We may consider myth in another way, asking not how to negate or kill myth, but how to develop the tools that will let us live well with myth without becoming enslaved to it, without letting it become the sole determinant of our lives and our fates; in other words, how to live with myth with minimal damage.

Judaism has confronted myth more successfully than has any other group, simply because from the start it has rarely produced it. There is no need to shatter the myths of our patriarchs and matriarchs and judges and kings because no such myths ever existed in the first place; the Bible describes them as flesh-and-blood people, mortals who sin and who are certainly not perfect. On the face of the biblical text, Abraham our father was a lousy husband and a lousy father who sent one son out into the desert, nearly sacrificed the other, abandoned his wife in various and sundry kings' courts, and in general causes us to raise many questions; none of this contradicts the fact that he was the father of monotheistic faith. David sinned with Bath-Sheba, caused the death of her husband, Uriah, on the battlefield, and commanded his son to murder Saul's descendants because he was prevented from doing so himself. Rachel not only believed in household idols, but also stole them from her father's house; and so on. If we compare biblical characters, not to mention kings, to the godlike ones that other peoples created for themselves, all of them flawless, none of whom ever needed to relieve himself, then Judaism clearly is on the side of the grown-up, nonmythic persona. It is sufficient to recall that in the whole Passover Haggadah,[2] which is devoted to the story of the Exodus from Egypt, the name of Moses—who commanded the Exodus—is mentioned only once. There is no myth of Moses in the Bible, and certainly not in the Haggadah. He is a stutterer, he is not charismatic, he is a man of many infirmities who cannot control his anger or his moods, and yet he is the man who brought Israel out of Egypt and brought it the Law: a man and not a god, and therein lies his greatness.

Nevertheless the Bible, which is almost not mythic at all—certainly not in its descriptions of people—did not eradicate the need for mythology. Whoever prostrates himself on the grave of Rachel our mother and asks for a living and health and good marriages for his children is not turning to the Rachel of the Bible, stealer of household idols, but to another Rachel, a mythological one who is a symbol of mercy and intercession—characteristics not even hinted at in the Bible. All that is written is "Rachel wept for her sons." This merges with an ancient myth known throughout the Mediterranean Basin as the mourning of Tammuz, of Demeter for Cora, of Mary for Jesus, beside her son's corpse. *Stabat mater dolorosa.* But mourning is not exactly mercy, nor is it intercession; the bereaved, weeping mother is not the person we would expect to effectively intervene and intercede on our behalf for income and health and good marriages. As far as efficiency is concerned, Leah was a much more effective character, but she was never included in the myth of *mater dolorosa,*

2. The Haggadah is a compilation of literatures that retell the story of the exodus from Egypt; it is chanted at the Passover seder, or service. The word *Haggada* in Hebrew means "narration." *Trans.*

apparently because she had more sons and less influence on Jacob. There is in the myth of Rachel, as in all prostration on graves, a beseeching for assistance and empathy and justice that is undoubtedly an echo of the childhood plea for empathy and assistance that was sometimes answered and sometimes not, because the mythological mother and the mythological father of childhood were perhaps not always available to answer us, perhaps we could not always depend on their being responsive—sometimes yes and sometimes no and sometimes they were too busy—and maybe that is why we pray and beseech and placate. The utterly nonbiblical myth of Rachel is thus a functional matter, just like the prostration on the graves of other righteous or holy people, a way of escaping helplessness, of finding hope, personal consolation, or emotional strength, and it should not be dismissed.

So even Judaism, which is so amythic and has a Bible that is so amythological, has not succeeded in routing myth, because it is a built-in component of our early perception of the world. What we must defend ourselves against is not myth itself, which is an inseparable part of our constitution; rather, we must learn how not to be victims of the manipulations of myth, how to preclude myth from being forced on us as individuals or populations, and how to protect ourselves from the artificial creation of myth. I am not now speaking of deep, primordial myth, but of new myth that has just now been made up.

We know, for example, that totalitarian regimes manufacture and use mythology, not the deep layer of mythology, but myth portrayed in the present, which is always the very incarnation of kitsch—usually deadly kitsch. We remember the use the Nazis made of myth—both ancient myth and modern, instant myth, such as the repugnant myth of Horst Wessel. Horst Wessel was a young hooligan, a violent drunk who was killed in a drunken brawl in a beer cellar, and who the Nazi regime turned into an official martyr. The official hymn of the Nazi Party organizations was the Horst Wessel song: "With us march comrades killed by the Red Death" —that is, socialism. This is a kitschy, cheap, instant connection to the myth of the good brother who is betrayed by his wicked brothers; it is Joseph sold by his brothers, it is Jesus turned in by Judas Iscariot. Practically, it is myth fabricated artificially, in the present. It didn't help that people knew about the charming Horst Wessel—and they knew—just as it didn't help to know about the pickpockets and the prostitutes who were inhabiting the Bastille when it was stormed. People believed in one as in the other, because of their ability to believe two different things. Similarly, we read in Joseph Goebbels's memoirs about the discussion in Hitler's headquarters at which the suggestion was made to use "The Protocols of the Elders of Zion" for propaganda purposes, as proof of the Jews' desire to take over the world. Goebbels said: "But Mein Führer, we actually know that the Protocols are a lie," and Hitler replied, "Yes, they are a lie, but they are also the truth." Hitler recognized the human ability to grasp both layers at the same time.

Every totalitarian regime knows how to confront our preadult persona with the mythic world, so that we will feel like children with a great savior, a redeeming father: he decides, he is the strong man, we have no responsibility for our actions whatsoever. Let us recall that communism, however antifascist and rational it has been during most of its existence, could not forfeit the cult of a mummified Lenin on display in a mausoleum, for all to see; the Chinese, too, with their tradition of common sense, did not forfeit the huge picture of Chairman Mao. What characterizes this particular kind of mythology is not only its creation in the present—a manipulative creation—but also the resulting need to guard it, jealously, through punishment and incarceration, from every fact and every criticism. Here historians are correct; a new myth created in the present may indeed be supported or contradicted by fresh facts, for it has not yet acquired sufficient prestige. The examples are well known to all of us. A god created in the present for political purposes stands on feet of clay; modern history is full of accounts of such instant gods who crumbled.

Until we become attuned, then, to when myth is being manipulated by those in power or those who would like to be in power, it may be worth our while to decide that, more than we must separate myth from state, we must separate myth from policy. Myth can certainly be neutral when related to a culture; it becomes deadly when it is used deliberately as a policy tool. Immediately after Israel's War of Independence, nay, while it yet raged, a man from the Ministry of Religion traveled the country marking supposedly holy spots—as a policy measure—in order to foster local cults; it did not help that historians and archaeologists said this was hogwash. The cults sprang up quickly and for the most part died out quickly; yet they were created at the time as deliberate policy. Perhaps it was to such things that Lawrence Durrell referred in the *Alexandria Quartet* when he described how the bathtub of Scobie the police officer became an object of the local cult of a holy man called "al-Scob."

Such instant myths, myths created in the present, are often manufactured by regimes to cover up error or oversight: for example, the site of a superfluous, badly fought battle becomes a monument to heroism, a site of pilgrimage. Several years ago a volcano erupted in Colombia; the story is one long list of mistakes made by the government: there were warnings but no preparation; people were not evacuated; there were no helicopters; medical supplies did not arrive where needed. Some 20,000 people were buried in the mud because of a roaring blunder.

What did the government that was responsible for all this do? What else could it do? It declared the area a holy site. As someone said, look how much effort people will invest in ignorance, when the need for illusion is great enough.

Another source of manipulative myth is the fallacious need to see flesh-and-blood people as flawless monuments—that is, to deprive them of their human significance. But if they have no human significance, it means there is no chance we could ever be like them, consequently it is not worth trying. When journalist Hanna Krall interviewed Dr. Mark Edelman, the last remaining survivor of the Warsaw Ghetto uprising, he told her that Mordechai Anielewicz grew up in the worst slum in Warsaw. Mordechai's mother was a fishmonger, and when she couldn't sell all her fish in a given day, little Mordechai would have to take a paintbrush and a tin of red paint and paint their gills so they would appear to be fresh the next morning. When the story was published, many in the Jewish community in the United States indignantly insisted: It can't be! Such things shouldn't be printed! How will we teach our children about Mordechai, that exemplary figure! In the end, a compromise was reached: it was not Mordechai but his mother who painted the fish gills red. Ironically, the really moving story is of course that the kid from the tough neighborhood who had had to paint fish gills in his youth—he was twenty-one—became the commander of the Warsaw Ghetto uprising: a man and not a god, a man and not a myth, a man and not kitsch, a man whom some of us may even have the chance to emulate.

What complicates the picture is that we have myths not only from the past, but also ones that relate to the future: the messianic age, the return of Jesus, the return of Arthur, the Once and Future King. Future-myths certainly cannot be refuted with history because they have not happened yet. As someone said, historians prophecy the past. The Rambam, an outstanding representative of the *logos,* or *Wort* as they say in our yeshivas, a man of written culture, the most antimythological man to have come from our midst, clearly warned us not to get caught up in myths that relate to the future. He took care to tell us that there would be no difference between the messianic age and our own, except freedom from the nations—that is, even then everything will be nearly the same as it is now. But how many people in distress actually look to the Rambam? And how many people see the messianic age with the same sobriety and sanity with which he viewed it?

But let us come back from the instant myth, an abomination, to the deep myth that determines patterns over time, and to our original question: what should we do about myth in order not to become its victim? The question concerns matters of life and death: myth has the power to execute people; people sacrifice themselves and are sacrificed in the name of and because of myths. I would like to suggest several ways of confronting myths without killing myth, several ways of reinforcing our adult selves—not at the expense of, but alongside of, in addition to, our earlier selves.

The first way is to attempt to understand the story behind the story—that is, the myth that preceded the myth at hand. I will present an example.

We all know the Oedipal story; we know precisely when and how the incest is discovered. In Thebes a plague breaks out, killing many people. Those who remain ask the soothsayer Tiresias what fatal flaw was found in the city, what the punishment is for. Then the story of the marriage between mother and son, Jocasta and Oedipus, comes to light. The principal elements are a holocaust, or a plague, or killing, that is somehow connected to incest; these are familiar elements of myths worldwide. In biblical sources it exists after the destruction of Sodom: in a cave in Zoar, Lot's daughters decide that there are no men left on earth; to perpetuate the human race after this total destruction, they have intercourse with their father. Anthropologists tell us of a myth in New Guinea according to which all the inhabitants of a village are buried in a rock as punishment for something they have done. Only a brother and sister, whom the tribe had cast out earlier because they were dirty, remain alive. They are the ones who perpetuate the race through incestuous relations. We thus have a clear connection between a tale of incest and destruction—it does not matter at this point which comes first; the connection is strong and outstanding. If we take a detour for a moment to the realm of literature, we may recall the story by Thomas Mann about the narcissistic, spoiled twins Siegmund and Sieglinde, who began having incestuous relations after a visit to the opera where the myth of the *Nibelungen* was presented, but also, and mainly, following the growing sense that they were alone in the world. Loneliness and destruction are the accepted background in most stories of incest.

We must now ask not only if there is not some story that predated the myth, but also if there is some strong basis in reality underlying the story; were there not in the ancient world many instances of the annihilation of villages or tribes due to war or natural disaster or plague, when all that remained were two members of the same family to perpetuate the tribe? In other words, it is not the incest that brought about the destruction, but the destruction that brought about the incest; in the myth, an inversion was made. For a later generation, a generation that began to recognize concepts of sin and punishment, the destruction ceased to be a cause and became a punishment. The story of the flood, for example, which appears in a great many cultures, apparently has some basis in objective reality; there is a great flood in human memory. But the story of the flood as punishment for the deeds of men was apparently conceived in a much later period, at the beginnings of morality. For example, Mircea Eliade claims that the myth of expulsion from the Garden of Eden refers to the ending of the Ice Age, because the Ice Age was apparently a Garden of Eden for hunters, a period of satiety; with the melting of the icebergs, fauna and flora dwindled, and it became necessary to invest a great deal of effort in getting them. The story of disobedience and punishment was invented later. In any case, we may find a kernel of truth behind the tenacious myth; perhaps it is what makes the myth so very tenacious. This is no Horst Wessel—the very comparison is sinful. This is a very deep memory indeed.

The same story may also appear in different forms in two different societies. Polish history tells a story from the days of the Turkish invasion of Europe: the Muslim armies reached Cracow and laid siege to it. One day, at noon, the Polish bugler came out on the tower and blew his bugle to declare it was noon, and perhaps also to tell the army cooks to begin passing out the afternoon's K rations. A Turkish soldier shot an arrow from his bow, and the arrow lodged in the bugler's throat, cutting off the melody in mid-note. Not only is the story well known to every Polish schoolchild, but the interrupted melody was for years the signal of the Polish radio station, a part of tradition.

Years later I was leafing through a collection of Turkish stories in translation, and came upon the following tale: many years ago the sultan's army set out to conquer nations across the sea. Allah delivered many nations into the hands of the Turks, because they harkened to His voice. Their path was most successful, until one day the armies of the faithful fell upon a large and fortified city. There one afternoon the muezzin came out on the balcony of the minaret to sound with a ram's horn the call of the faithful to prayer. One of the Turkish soldiers who was not respectful of the faith shot an arrow that hit the throat of the muezzin and cut off the holy prayer in the middle. From that moment, Allah was angry with the faithful for the desecration of His holy name and turned their luck to a curse. They retreated from the siege and continued to retreat until all the armies had returned to their country, and the great conquest was as if it had never been.

I have no doubt that the story is a true one, witnessed by two armies with their very eyes, except that on one side the story stated a factual account of something that happened, without an interpretation of sin and punishment, and on the other side what remained was a story of punishment, perhaps because there had been a defeat for which the regime had to make excuses. I have no difficulty with either the myth of punishment for desecration of God, or the bugler who calls for the cook to pass out lunch to the army. We must remember that the myth is a story, which takes place within language; and even the most ancient myth is nothing more than a midrash, a story, and we are dealing with a midrash on a midrash on a midrash, in each and every generation, as far as memory reaches, backward and forward.

The concept of myth as midrash is a concept that needs no explanation in the world of artists, because all art is a type of midrash. Not a semantic midrash, but one that takes place in the language of the given art. And I mean not just creative art, but performance art as well. Not long ago Professor Baron of the Juilliard School taught a master class at the Jerusalem Music Center, and conducted The Art of the Fugue according to his adaptation—a difficult and wonderful adaptation. He reported that most of the musicians studying at Juilliard today are Asians, and that they have their own interpretation, or midrash, of the accepted European classics. For example, Mozart becomes a Japanese Mozart; the emphases are different, the content is different, the phrasing is different. These interpretations were always in the notes, but we never saw them. And this, too, is of course a midrash.

In this case the constant, never-ending midrash is one of the strongest and most important ways of overcoming the damage caused by static, sanctified myth. Perhaps one of the most important things we can impart through education is the sense that all of us are free when it comes to myth, that we all have the freedom of midrash, of interpretation, that myth in our hands is as clay in the hands of the potter. All of us may add to it because there is nothing more dead and stifling and blocked than static myth, the cult that is not followed by a midrash, the cult that has an injunction against midrash.

But this interpretive approach alone is not enough. Another healthy addition to myth is the realization—the anthropological, if you wish, but not merely anthropological realization—that there is not one myth, but many myths. For example, in the story of the binding of Isaac as it is told in the Book of Genesis, we learn that human sacrifice, the sacrifice of the first-born son, was replaced by the sacrifice of a ram sent for this purpose from the heavens; according to a very early interpretation, this myth symbolizes the transition from human sacrifice to animal sacrifice. It is worth our knowing, then, that we are not unique. Agamemnon, in Greece, made a vow that he would sacrifice his daughter Iphigenia to the gods; but the goddess Artemis took pity on the girl and sent a ram to be sacrificed in her place, and in a storm swept the girl heavenward to be her priestess. Then we also have the Greek story of Phrixus, the first-born son of Athamas. During a drought the people asked to sacrifice Phrixus to change their ill luck, but the gods sent a ram to save Phrixus and carry him away from the sacrificial altar. Phrixus seems a tad ungrateful in the end; once he arrives at a safe haven he sacrifices the ram who brought him there, instead of ensuring it a ripe old age. There are many similar stories throughout the Mediterranean; in all of them, a ram is sent by the gods to take the place of man on the altar. It is true that the Jewish myth of the binding of Isaac is the richest of all in cultural meaning—and most of us don't even know that in Hebrew thought there is much doubt as to whether Isaac was indeed saved from the sacrificial knife. The authors of the Talmud asked several pointed questions: Why did Abraham, according to the Bible, come down from Mount Moriah alone, and where was Isaac? Why did Abraham mourn Sarah alone, and where was Isaac at his mother's funeral? Many *midrashim* tell us—for example, the *Book of Hadar Zekenim* and *Yalkut Reuveni*—that Isaac was indeed slaughtered and sent heavenward so the angels could treat his wounds, or his trauma, and there he stayed for several years, studying in the Beit Midrash[3] of Shem and Ever, until he was returned to earth to marry Rebecca. In the popular consciousness Isaac is indeed slaughtered; we talk about the actual sacrifice of the son and not only about his salvation through this ram that apparently the whole Mediterranean Basin knows about.

Tangentially, it is interesting to wonder why Isaac, who was not slaughtered in the end, is perceived as if he were slaughtered by his father; while the story of the daughter of Jephthah, who was indeed sacrificed and for whom no ram was sent, is not recorded in any particular myth.[4] The important thing behind the whole story is that even one of our most important myths is not unique. The explanations about the "test that God gave Abraham" in all the midrashim that have come after are from other generations, generations that searched for an ethos of faith behind the story. Each generation and its particular ethos.

There is no sense in shattering myth; there is a lot of sense in opening it, in learning it, in adding more and more knowledge to the existing story, just as there is no point in eradicating our childlike, early persona, but there is sense in gaining maturity by adding more and more layers of knowledge and organization and construction and differentiation. Certainly nothing may be added to several very beautiful myths of ours, such

---

3. Talmudic school. *Trans.*

4. Jephthah vows to God that if he is victorious over the Ammonites, he will make a sacrifice of the first thing that greets him on his return. His hapless daughter, his only child, is the first to come running out of his house when he returns from battle (see Judges 11:30–40). *Trans.*

as the legend of the thirty-six unknown righteous people on whose existence the existence of the world depends, a legend so beautiful that I find it difficult to see any need for an instructive midrash. Even if we know that the holiday of Chanukah comes at the winter solstice, the shortest day of the year after which the days begin to lengthen; even if we know that nearly all peoples have at this time a tradition or ritual of fires and candle lighting and torches, it need not change one whit our connection to *these* candles and to the very beautiful story that goes with them, the ancestral story of the jar of oil.

As I write, Chanukah is approaching: let us look at one more story connected with this holiday. We have been taught that the evil Greeks contaminated the Temple by sacrificing unclean animals in it, and that the Temple Mount was captured and the Temple purified and a new altar built just like the first one—the whole familiar myth, which is easily manipulated for reasons of politics or power in any age. Given that we retell this closed, finalized story year after year without change or fail, perhaps we should open it from a different angle, the angle of another story.

It appears that the members of the ancient empires, Romans and Greeks, knew that when they arrived in a conquered country it was polite to come to the local temple and make a goodly sacrifice of the best and most fatted animal they had to the local god, because it would ensure peace—and might find favor in the eyes of the local god, just to be on the safe side. Since for the Greeks the animal of choice for sacrifices was the pig, we can easily imagine the possibility that along came a group of well-mannered Greek soldiers who after having been taught to follow custom, prepared to sacrifice the best pig they could find; suddenly all the Jews came running, as the one-time comedian Uri Zohar once called us, *Judaicos problematicos,* and fell upon the Greeks with cries of anger and insult, and beat them without their knowing exactly why. That was an intercultural encounter of the least successful kind.

This, at any rate, is the answer to the question we posed, what should we do about myth: tell it from generation to generation, love it, and, in some part of ourselves, even believe it a little; but also open it, and add to it another midrash and another interpretation and some more knowledge, ours and that of others. There is no contradiction to them; "all are words of the living God," and the ability of man to contain different things is limitless. We may discuss myth at the dinner table, and say the blessing over these candles without any difficulty, and know and tell our children that the jar of oil, as a metaphor for continuous culture, will never be lacking.

Literature in the Age of Masses ——————

a few years ago, not far from Auvergne, we saw a road sign saying: "Breathe the air of la vieille France—its chateaux, its forests, its snack bars."

In a nutshell, there lies our problem. The individual undertakes an adventure, a quest, to look for the private fantasy of a castle, a forest. The great mobile masses look for the snack bar.

We live in a world of huge masses of people. Some of us wonder why, if there are so many of us, we are so lonely. Why is Western society so atomized? Where is the old neighborhood, where everyone knew everyone else?

The neighborhood probably still exists: our real neighbors are the people with whom we are connected by phone: we chat on the phone as we used to chat on the porch. The neighborhood spread, geographically speaking; in the physical sense many of us do not experience it anymore, being crowded by lots of unknown individuals. Our primary cultural experience, our lowest common denominator, is now mass produced by the media, and not provided by the particular village or neighborhood. The telephone-neighborhood is sometimes supportive, but it is not productive of culture, perhaps because the contact is so limited in space and in time.

We live in a world of huge masses of people. This is an entirely new phenomenon, and nobody quite knows how to handle it. In many places in the world this means a breakdown of services—and anyone who has ever suffered from nondelivery of mail knows what I am talking about. In other places this means breakdown of bureaucracy, in spite of—or perhaps because of—computers. In many places this means severe ecological crises.

Writing today becomes not only an act of faith, but also an act of courage. Why courage? Because, in a world of huge masses of people, it becomes increasingly hard to differentiate between feeling and pseud-ofeeling. Conditioned by so many "others," we sometimes cannot identify what we really feel, and substitute what we think we *ought* to feel in a given situation, what we are expected to feel. Surrounded on all sides by newspaper words, broadcast words, advertisement words, we seem to have ready-made words and phrases for every occasion. Few of us bother to check what we really feel, still less to find our own words and phrases for it. A personal, unique expression is sometimes met with the hostility that so often greets the unknown, the unfamiliar. People often rely, nowadays, on the spheres of reference with which they are familiar, at least verbally, and far less often on direct confrontation of personality and feeling. Familiar phrases are sometimes comforting in unfamiliar situations, but new situations should create new phrases and new references. Now the media, with their huge reservoir of verbiage, create whole ready-made spheres of reference; they actually create our associations a priori. We hear of a certain person or event, and we already have a slot for it in our media-conditioned thought; we know who the good guy and the bad guy are and what to expect of them. Now writing, real writing, has very little to do with so-called typical behavior. It must be whittled down from our familiar spheres of reference to what the person actually is and does; in good writing, no person is "typical."

Was it easier to be a writer in the past? In many respects, yes. Writing in an ancient language resembled cutting into stone (incidentally, Hebrew is written from right to left because it was originally carved in stone; the man held the chisel in his left hand and the hammer in his right, working from right to left). To this day our language has kept its stony, concentrated, concise character, striving for the essential. This makes Hebrew practically untranslatable; a phrase of three words in Hebrew becomes a phrase of eighteen words in French, so you can imagine what it does to poetry. There is a famous phrase in the Book of Kings, when King Ahab is threatened by the king of Syria who gathers "all his host together, thirty and two kings with him, and horses, and chariots," and he sends messengers to King Ahab to yield. So Ahab answers, in four resounding Hebrew words, "Al ithallal hogger ki-mephateah." In English Ahab's answer comes out as follows: "Let not him who putteth on his armor boast himself as he who taketh it off." Sixteen words to the Hebrew four.

Our language is still, in spite of aberrations, more concise than any language I know. It is true that Hebrew developed and changed and added words, but all the structures were familiar in older days; they carried in themselves the full weight and full prestige of tradition. To a certain extent, all writing is working within tradition: we use idioms, linguistic connections, and associations known to our tribe, because we cannot go outside language, and languages are tribal affairs.

In our generation, we are witnessing what some people call the barbarization of language, and what others prefer to call the common language of the global village, in Marshall McLuhan's famous phrase. C. P. Snow spoke of two separate cultures, technological and humanistic, and the chasm between the two. At a recent PEN Club meeting in Jerusalem we remarked that if it had been a gathering not of authors but of engineers and technicians from thirty countries, they would probably have been able to maintain communication in a kind of "universalese," broken and para-aesthetic, but factual, while we writers, who live within the semantic limitation of our art, needed simultaneous translation.

Yet C. P. Snow probably missed the greatest danger of all, which is not so much the chasm between the technological and the humanistic type of culture, but the development of the tourist mentality. If people visit books as they do tourist sites, looking for the famous passages they have heard about, looking for the best-seller they were told about, just to be able to say "I was there," then we have missed the whole point of literature.

There are other chasms, other gaps, as well. A person's age is also his culture. A group of people sixty or seventy years old treat language and linguistic forms in a completely different way from a group of high school kids. This gap has nothing to do with general education: often the high school kids will have had a very good education indeed.

This may be one of the reasons an author may feel so helpless when faced with translation. How is translation possible when people read different meanings into the written word, according to place, culture, age, idiosyncrasy? In huge masses of people this is not a stable structure any longer; it is a kaleidoscope. "Universalese" may be the lowest common denominator between cultures, and it is our greatest danger. In the most romantic mountain regions of Spain, Navarre and Aragon, paradors are named "California," "Hollywood," or "Miami."

Those who write in Hebrew are fortunate in several respects. One is the fact that the language has existed close to four thousand years. If a shepherd of Abraham's time, around the end of the Stone Age and the beginning of the Bronze Age, could come here today and address us, we would in all probability understand him with ease. The main structures of the language are still the same. But the visiting shepherd would not understand us, except for basic words, and no translation would be of help, because the language grew and expanded to an unbelievable extent. Our history is not only the history of a people, but also the history of a language.

Some parts of our tradition are widely known; others are less known because it is so difficult to translate from Hebrew. Whole theories were built upon incorrect translations from Hebrew. The commandment "Thou shalt not kill," as most translations have it, does not exist in the Bible. The original commandment is "Thou shalt not murder," which is entirely different. A whole ethos has been created in other cultures because of a fallacious translation of a commandment written originally in Hebrew. By the way, in the United States some years ago, I was addressing a group of students and told them about the two versions of the commandment. One of the students asked a question: he had a personal problem, he said, and he wanted to know urgently whether the commandment "Thou shalt not commit adultery" was also wrongly translated. I was sorry to be unable to help him: the commandment stands as written.

The very ability to differentiate between "Thou shalt not kill" and "Thou shalt not murder" is an ability our generation still has because of certain moral structures we have all absorbed from our literature. I should like to offer a theory—or perhaps a deep anxiety—that just as in mathematics, in which certain laws of behavior apply to small numbers and other laws apply to infinite numbers and the two are not always identical, it may be so with people as well. At this moment no one can foretell the possible structures—moral, literary, linguistic—in huge masses of people, that keep on growing. So far most of us have been reacting to what is taking place around us, rather than creating new structures relevant to the new situation. It was one thing to give the Ten Commandments to a few thousand people, it was one thing to write in *Vanity Fair* for what was once a limited number of educated readers—perhaps a few hundred thousand in the enlightened world, at best—and it is another thing to create a comprehensive literary structure for nearly four billion people, who are not closed in their townlets any longer, who are mobile, on the roads, and most of whom prefer television to books anyway.

One example of our inability to cope with large numbers is our lack of comprehension of the magnitude of the Holocaust. During the Adolf Eichmann trial in Israel, it was the individual murders that registered in our memories and our senses rather than the descriptions of mass murders. For many of us who attended the trial, Eichmann had to answer for personally whipping to death a fifteen-year-old Jewish boy who stole an apple. Large numbers tend to become abstract, too abstract to identify with. No writer can write about the six million of the Holocaust; we must write about individuals, about families. The writer of the Bible described Noah and his family on board his ark; even he did not attempt to describe what was happening on shore when the flood came.

As writers, we are indeed increasingly helpless. We write of what we know, but a large part of our local culture—not all but a large part—tends to lose its significance in transposition. I am told that *Romeo and Juliet* was completely misunderstood in Japan: they failed to see the problem. There are huge associative gaps between nations brought up on the Bible and nations who do not know the Bible at all. Were it not for their being well versed in the Bible, one could perhaps expect a different political stand from both Mr. Churchill in his time and Mr. Carter in recent times.

It is probable that the time of governments' wishing to control literature is past. What we are faced with now is the frightening authority of great, terrifying masses of people who hardly ever read, who prefer television and the movies, and who carry the terrible weight of sheer huge numbers.

What can we do? Essentially, what we have been doing so far: write of what we know, our places, our environment, our families. Tribal literature, if you wish. All the world understands families. A family contributes to the understanding of people as people. Some time ago we had a meeting in Haifa between Jewish and Arab writers, and I asked my Arab colleagues whether any of them had every tried to describe a Jewish family *as a family* in their work. The answer was an unequivocal no. In their literature, the Jew is still a stereotype, an abstract figure, never a living person who has a mother, uncles, a baby. In literary terms, this is demonization: a demon, a lone operator, a sinister figure, has no family. James Bond cannot have mother-in-law trouble, or a teething baby. Conversely, several of us Jewish writers in Israel have indeed described normal Arab family life in our work.

So the description of what we know will continue, probably much shortened, because no one has the time or inclination to read long-winded literature anymore. Have you noticed how much thinner books are in this century? No one can read the Russian-style novel anymore; it went out with trains, and can anyone imagine Anna Karenina meeting Vronsky in the baggage-claim area of a crowded flight? So we shall continue our tribal writing, telling of our human experience, which is all we have. In any form, it is an act of faith.

As structure and form become more concise, more concentrated every year, I am reminded of the Hassidic sage Rabbi Mendel of Kotzk, who once said, "All my life I have regretted one thing: being unable to write a book consisting of a single page."

The Limits of My Language
Are the Limits of My World ────

THE TITLE OF THIS ESSAY,
a quote from Wittgenstein, indicates its direction. Let me say right away
that this will not be an essay in linguistics; I am not a linguist. I shall write
as a craftswoman thinking about the tools of her craft, first, about language as a normative system; second, about the special nature of Hebrew
as a normative system; and third, about what has happened to this system
in our society over recent years and what possibilities are open to us in
the future.

Language has two functions. One is to make communication between
people possible. The other is the preservation of knowledge. Without
language it would be impossible to prove any scientific truth or to learn
from the experience of the past. All languages fulfill these two functions.
And yet different languages have developed in such ways that each one
represents the peculiar mind-set of those who speak it.

A child who learns a language—that is, learns to speak at about the age
of one—is already learning subconsciously the system of thinking peculiar to his language, and also its mental categories. If we assume that the
mental structures of a language in the process of its creation are not accidental, then they certainly are increasingly less so over the centuries, as
succeeding generations are intellectually formed in that thought system
and, indeed, contribute to its development. If this were not the case, we
would be able to translate from one language into another with the utmost
ease—which clearly doesn't happen. Many think that translation works
only at a very low level of precision. Generally, we translate only one level
of a language, the top of the pyramid, leaving very different levels concealed below.

Ancient languages are synchronic languages. Every moment in their
present time comprehends all the past and all forms of thought that existed in the past. Hebrew, which is about four thousand years old, is un-

doubtedly a comprehensively synchronic language with characteristics unlike any other spoken language.

What do we mean when we speak of a normative system? As von Humboldt put it, "Man lives in a world presented to him by his language," meaning that the characteristics of a language lay down the categories of thought. I am told that Chinese has no verb "to be." Therefore it is impossible to translate into Chinese not only *Hamlet,* but also the sentence *"Cogito, ergo sum"*—I think therefore I am. It is not only that verb that is missing in Chinese, but the parallel concept. Can we imagine Western culture or philosophy without the verb "to be?"

Western European languages are much concerned with time. They deal with time in many different aspects, a factor that has certainly had its effect on Western philosophy. But in the Hopi language, I am told, there are no times or tenses, only completed actions, and those not yet completed. In Hopi there is hardly any speculation about action in the future. In the African Muntu language the words for "wet stone" and "dry stone" are totally different, there being no single word in that language for the common denominator—stone. What we have here is clearly a category of sensual expression, not a synthesizing thought process. This has nothing to do with the comparative richness or poverty of languages. The Inuit, for example, lack abstractions, which are so important to the tradition of Western thought. But they do have twenty words for different types of snow. These are evidence of an exactness of sensual comprehension and an experience of life of which we are ignorant. As for the fact that French lacks the simple verb "to stand," what is one to make of that?

Wittgenstein was right when he said that the limits of our world are identical with the limits of our language, and, I would add, there is on an everyday level clear interaction between one's language and one's patterns of thought.

It is not only vocabulary that orders a language's normative system. Other features we often take for granted are influential and worth thinking about. Syntax, for example, sets up a linguistic normative system and a cultural hierarchy. So does the sound pattern, and the relative weight a language gives to noun, verb, and adjective in a sentence. For example, when Jorge Luis Borges visited Israel, he complained to me about what he thought was a basic failing in the sound pattern of Spanish and of all the Romance languages. What worried him was the adverb. When one uses the adverb in English—for example, eff*ectively*, *slowly*—the accent is on the action, the verb. In Spanish, on the other hand, and in French, the emphasis is on the formal final phoneme: lente*ment*, effective*ment*, lenta*mente*. According to Borges, this stress pattern posits a false hierarchy that values form and formula over the action itself. The emphasis is formal rather than actual, a characteristic fairly true of Latin cultures. It is of course difficult to prove what is cause and what is effect. Does the formal preference take precedent to the culture's character, or does the kind of culture lead to a preference for a certain sound pattern? In biblical Hebrew many adverbs have no formal ending at all, like *maher or le'at* not *bim'hirut* or *be-itiyut,* which is a latter-day preference, and we may conclude that in the Hebrew of the Bible it is the action that counts and not the formal marker.

Syntax also lays down hierarchies of value. Jacob Bronowski found that in all languages the order of words in a sentence corresponds to what is thought to be the natural order. At a certain age a child understands the sentence "The boy chases the cat," but not "The cat is chased by the boy." If the cat comes first (goes this logic), it has priority and initiates the action. One of the great advantages of Hebrew lies in its flexible syntax. In English you can say "The King went" but not "Went the King," except in very special usage. In Hebrew, if we rearrange the unit "The King fell on his sword"— "Fell the King on his sword," "On his sword fell the King," "Fell on his sword the King," "The King on his sword fell"—we find that all permutations are absolutely correct, allowing the writer to choose which hierarchy best suits his purpose. This syntactical flexibility is not accidental. One of the salient features of a Hebrew text is that the language never impedes the flow or the independence of thought. More of this later.

The value system of a language is also determined by the greater or lesser use of adjectives. Early Hebrew makes little use of them, in comparison with classical Greek for example. The *Iliad* and the *Odyssey* give us "fleet-footed Achilles," "anger-browed Zeus," "the rosy-fingered dawn," "the sly Odysseus," and many more. But when we open the Bible to Genesis I, we find: "In the beginning God created the heaven and the earth: And the earth was without form, and void, the darkness was on the face of the deep (in Hebrew this word is a simple noun, *tehom*): And the spirit of God moved upon the face of the waters. And

God said Let there be light. And there was light. And God saw the light that it was *good*."

It has taken six sentences to reach the first adjective. In the style of Homeric poetry the passage might have looked something like this: "In the beginning the great God, he of the pelting hail, created the blue-eyed heaven and the fair-mounded earth." As Auerbach observed in *Mimesis,* there is not a single adjective in the whole binding of Isaac narrative, which gives the language immense power. In fact, every reader adds his own adjectives to the story—awesome, frightening, horrible, pathetic— but such expressions are not present in the text, and for a reason. Hebrew's distaste for adjectives is just one feature in a system defined by its conciseness, which is perhaps Hebrew's distinctive quality.

The laconic manner is characteristic of early Semitic languages in general. We have the possessive suffix form without the word "of" or the possessive pronoun—*shulhan* (table), *shulhani* (my table). We may conjugate the verb in past and future tenses, without employing the pronouns "I" or "you" or "he," by changing the suffix: *asiti ve asita halahti.* As a result, a three-word sentence in Hebrew becomes twelve words in French, enough to deter any translator. A Hebrew proverb of four words becomes sixteen words when translated into English: "Let not him who putteth on his armor boast himself as one who taketh it off." This gift of compression makes Hebrew a very algebraic language, a language of concrete concepts and codes that allow for intense abstraction. It is a language that, if taught correctly, can educate its speakers toward intellectual categories that are simultaneously concentrated, abstract, and flexible. Such linguistic achievements have certainly contributed to intellectual advance.

Here we touch on another dominant characteristic of Hebrew. The most ornate phrases began life as concrete terms. The modern cliché *betza keseph* (material greed) meant originally a coin cut in two, each part called *betza*. So *betza keseph lo lakahu,* "they took no gain of money" in Deborah's song, means more or less "They did not take half a coin, or the King's shilling; they were not mercenaries, but fought as volunteers." Similarly, the word *mal'ah* means simply "messenger," and not "angel," which in the Christian tradition conjures up an innocent blue-eyed child with wings. Finally, the word *nephesh,* commonly translated as "soul," originally meant "throat," so the expression *ba'u ma'im ad nephesh* (water has risen up to the soul/throat), meaning a desperate state of affairs, has its origin in the body.

Perhaps the most important feature of Hebrew has to do with value concepts. Every language is replete with such concepts, which are linked to a system of associations. In Polish there is a root form meaning "to conceal." Add a prefix, and it becomes "to take out of hiding," "to uncover," and "to bring up" (a child). This is no accident, but implies a whole pedagogic outlook. Add another prefix, and the word means "to preserve." In Chinese, we are told, "teacher" and "doctor" are represented by the same ideogram. This implies a view of the teacher's function that involves curing the patient of his disease, ignorance. Also, I am told, in China much of medicine is preventive, so doctors in China spend much of their time teaching people rules. The Hebrew word *le-hitbonen* (to observe), contains the concept *bina*, wisdom. The word "illusion" contains the Latin *ludere*, "to play." Clearly, then, each language contains its own value system deriving from the special patterns of association that help to construct it. Hebrew, a synchronic language, holds certain precise ethical and philosophical value concepts that belong only to Hebrew and to Judaism and that are really untranslatable. Such words cannot be learned simply as words, without their philosophical context. Some are whole teachings. Thus the concept *teshuva* (repentance) is not what we think of today as repentance, or more commonly, becoming religious. In Judaism it covers a process involving a complete change of personality—sometimes even a change of name, work, and address. This significance is all but lost in its modern usage. The word is still there, but, wrongly used, is bereft of its philosophy. Another example is the term *malhut shama'im* (Kingdom of Heaven). In Judaism this is a value concept signifying the acceptance of God as king, here, now, and every day; but we use this expression now with its Christian coloring of the kingdom to come in messianic times, which is a distortion of the Jewish vision of the messianic period. Hebrew readers wrongly use the expression *dereh eretz* (way of the world) as a synonym for manners or politeness, when this term originally implied a whole ethical system of behavior. Then we misuse the word *emuna* (faith, belief) when we say "I believe it is late," thus jettisoning the central Jewish concept of faith as trust in God. Perhaps the worst offense of this kind is the political use of the Jewish value concept *z'hut avot* (merits of the fathers). Traditionally this means the righteousness of our patriarchs, which is thought to protect us their sinning children. It never meant the right of their children to settle in certain territories.

Such expressions, then, are like algebraic signs or codes, for complete cultural concepts. If we lose their original meaning, or at least the knowledge that there is such a meaning, and use them to translate alien expressions, then we have erased one of the components of our culture. We end up speaking English or German in Hebrew words.

Why is Hebrew like this? Where did this concision and urge for laconism derive? How did the language become one of codes and associative headings? Perhaps the cause lies in Hebrew's very early move from an oral to a written language. Oral cultures have special ways of preserving knowledge, by aids to memory, for instance. Hebrew poetry and prophetic rhetoric do make use of devices such as parallelism and the alphabetical poem, but not of rhyme. Elsewhere the repeated adjective is a mnemonic device. Achilles is always fleet of foot, Zeus is always the thunderbolt hurler, and that is how we remember them.

In Hebrew, writing arrived very early, and the effect on the nature of the language was immense. What do you write down, especially if you have to carve in stone? Whatever is most worth preserving. And you do it concisely. Hebrew, remember, has very few vowels, especially in non-plene or unvocalized spelling. It is as if the writer was not concerned with the phoneticization of the word, its vocalization in speech, but did care about the root and the associations that grow out of that written root. We were always very text oriented. Hebrew writing was then meant not for reading pleasure, but for the notation of essentials. What is worth preserving are those concrete things that supply the need of the tribe's code of knowledge. As a written language Hebrew is basically a skeletal, shorthand structure, in which the main process takes place in thought. Such are the substantive features of Hebrew. Should we lose them, an entire culture is lost.

This is the language that we inherited and that has preserved our culture and our selves for two millennia. During that period—in the Diaspora—the language has been a preserved language, without much development of vocabulary, with little adjustment to the changes taking place all around.

What happens to a language that serves as a cultural safe deposit alone? One might say that, like Latin, from the Renaissance onward, Hebrew became a language of men, used only outside the domestic scene. Women learned Torah less and were not expected to preserve the language and its values. The popular woman's Bible companion, *Tsena Ur'ena,* is full of Yiddish. The Sephardi woman prayed in Hebrew in the synagogue, but her private prayers at home were whispered in Ladino. The formal language of men was used essentially for purposes of rhetoric and dispute, two areas then foreign to women. Historically, one should add, the end of the teaching of rhetoric in European schools coincided with the demise of Latin as a school subject and the entry of girls into the classroom. So the connection is not accidental.

A preserved language also serves as a tribal code. When Sholem Aleichem's hero, Mottel, son of Peissy the Cantor, is caught by a policeman, a bystander whispers a phrase to him in Hebrew meaning "Free your hand from the Greek (that is, Gentile) and get thee hence, beloved," and the child understands. He would have understood not only in Sholem Aleichem's fictional *shtetl Kasrilevke,* but in Baghdad or Saloniki. When Yaakov Sapir, an Ashkenazi Jew from Poland who lived in Safed, arrived in San'a, Yemen, in the middle of the last century, he had no problem talking to the Yemenite Jews. Hebrew was their common tongue. Professor Ze'ev Ben Haim, a senior at the Academy of the Hebrew Language, states that in every generation, until about half a century ago, the majority of men in any Jewish community in the world could read and understand a Hebrew text.

Until about seventy years ago, Hebrew had all the structures necessary for communication, but lacked so many words that such communication was difficult. The effective date for the change of Hebrew into a language of everyday communication may be 1889, when Eliezer Ben-Yehuda and his associates founded the Clear Language Society for the Propagation of Unity and Amity in Israel. It is probably true that the generation born in Palestine sixty years ago was the first since the Dispersion whose parents spoke Hebrew as an *everyday* language. Also, for the first time in two millennia, there was no longer a division between the mother tongue spoken at home and the male language of study and ritual. This is no minor matter, for from a psychological point of view, Hebrew at that point stopped being only a language of learning and ideas and became a language of feeling. Let's not forget that this was a generation that grew up largely without grandparents, who stayed behind in the old country. We might put the question this way: Can such a laconic, reserved language be made to contain the myriad shades of a language of feeling, a gentle language of mothers and grandparents? One ought to remember that in Hebrew there were hardly any soft, playful words of a childish mode.

The simplest method of renewal was the coining of new words out of old words, structures, and emphases that had, before the Dispersion, served as means of communication. There are many curiosities here, including the coining of modern Hebrew words for common things such as "doll," "brush," and "tomato."

Only fifty years ago we used foreign words like "problema," "initsiativa," and "taxi," whereas today we use the Hebrew *b'aya, yozma, monit.* We had to invent the Hebrew equivalents of "involvement," "frustrations," "ambivalence," "pacemakers," "devaluation," and "linkage." So with many other words, including most of the military ranks, which are revivals of old Hebrew expressions and roots. For "rookie," however, meaning a new recruit, we have kept the Roman "tyro," in *tiron*—and the Hebrew *b'sis tironim* would be readily understood by the Roman Tenth Legion, who presumably had their Basis Tyronum. Such innovations and coinages, some of them euphemisms, can almost be read as chapters in the history of our country, so closely do they document social processes. Words are indeed renewed at a quick pace. And renewal is perhaps only a minor problem, as it is guided by a competent authority—the Academy. More than 80 percent of our innovations are accepted by the general public. But when there is such a flood of new words to meet new needs, many of them turn out to be artificial and unnecessary improvisations. They are coined simply because they exist in English, and not even in good English, but in the jargon of bureaucracy and the social sciences. With such a wealth of neologisms, the miracle is not that some bad or silly words get through, but that there are so few of them.

The real problem is not words, but what Noam Chomsky calls the deep structure of the language, and the sentence, a structure that is part of the intellectual development of the group. If language is indeed a form of behavior, deep structure is the form of behavior of the language, and of whoever thinks in it. Single words are the variable factor in a language's basic formal system. Proof of this lies in stories written by computers. In a western written by a computer, the sheriff draws the girl out of his holster, shoots the outlaw with elephants and tundra, and the outlaw falls dead bleeding a pool of whiskey. Here the structures are logical, but the words are variable. About Hebrew, then, we should ask not what has happened to single words, but what has happened to the deep structures of the language these last fifty years? For while a language can bear the burden of unsuitable words, absorb them, and eventually eject them, it cannot suffer too many deep injuries to its very anatomy.

My answer is not a positive one. Bad things have happened to form and also to the transformation of concepts. I will try to explain some of these changes.

Hebrew is getting long winded, which is against its nature. Who uses the short form when a longer form of words can be found? So instead of *im* (if) we use the deplorable *be-mida ve*—not "if" you get to Tel Aviv, but "in the measure that, to the extent that," you get to Tel Aviv. Today, who would use a simple Hebrew phrase like that of Cain in Genesis, *gadol avoni mi-nso*—"My crime is greater than I can bear"? The King James Version translates this, erroneously, as "my punishment." We would say something like "The crime to which I readily admit in so many words is greater than my personal ability to cope with it adequately." Could anyone think this an improvement? Similarly, we make wise language look foolish, saying "Rise *up*" and "Descend *down*," when the verb alone indicates the movement. Then there is the matter of propriety. False propriety is one of the injuries we have inflicted on the language in the last fifty years; a kind of linguistic Victorianism has spread. The more permissive society becomes, the more prudish its language. A man does not have a mistress, but "his publicly known person." In the lonely-hearts columns we do not find a married man willing to pay cash for sex, but a nonfree man seeking intimate friendship and willing to offer financial support. One may imagine this nonfree type looking at his watch while engaged in intimate friendship, and discovering not an "obligation" to go home, but certain "constraints." This is the jargon of sexual bureaucracy. The word we use for "pimp," *sarsur,* is the same as that used until recently for any go-between, or business agent. In older sources a brothel madam was called *k'lonit,* an "ignominous woman," with all the moral stress of the word for ignominy, *kalon.* Ignominy must be treated sternly. "Agent," *sarsur,* however, is a neutral, anemic term. He will get away with a few months in prison.

When we sterilize language, we sterilize its values. When children were left to their fate in a terrorist attack at Ma'alot some years ago, it wasn't their "teachers" who abandoned them, but their "education agents."[1] We have no "poor," only the "weaker strata," or lower echelons. That is somehow less demanding, for the Torah commands us to succor the poor, but is silent about lower echelons. We have no "rich," but "the top ten percent." We have no "luxury," but a "high standard of living"; no "apartments," but "dwelling solutions"; no "homes," but "housing." We must not ignore the emotional and practical significance of such changes. There is an immense difference between a home and housing, as there is between luxury, *motarot,* which in Hebrew signifies superfluous things, and a high standard of living, which is attractive. This illusory refinement is essentially crude. It sterilizes the language by creating distance between speech and the heart. No one dies today; they pass away. No one thinks, but is of an opinion. A woman doesn't conceive, but "enters into pregnancy," and apparently never gets out. Once pregnant, women give birth not to sons or daughters, but to age groups. If this goes on, we will have no hospitals in twenty years' time, but "temporary shelters for the unwell." Even today, they are called "medical centers," which are sometimes less hospitable than research oriented.

These false linguistic norms are the fault partly of our politicians and partly of social and behavioral scientists. Social scientists ruin many languages when they do such things as calling sleeping people "populations in a nonawake state."

Then there is the Hebrew of politicians. For linguistic features, single out the ambitious members of that breed. They love "parameters" and "constraints." They find themselves constantly "impeded" from doing things, and the minute they are appointed to high office they lose the ability to say "I hope," *ani m'kave,* preferring the stuffy formulation, *ani tikva,* "I am of the hope that. . . ." Add to this the psychological significance of the increase in the use of passive forms. We don't go to a reading but to a "being read to," *hakra'a.* Perhaps there is a connection between this and the fact that no one any longer fires shots. Instead shots are fired. Measures are taken. One does not simply do something. Something is done to one. A whole nation is acted upon.

Another curious feature of our recent speech is its turn from feminine

---

1. "Teacher" in Hebrew is synonymous with "one who points out" or "shows" or "instructs."

to masculine sound. Words with feminine endings are giving way to those with masculine endings. Meanwhile there is increasing confusion over the gender of words, and I confess that I do not know what this means. It may have something to do with the modern distaste for clearly defined sexual bipolarity.

Modern formulas of circumlocution abound. In the early years of the state people avoided the use of biblical or mishnaic formal phrases. They wanted to write what they felt, exactly, without recourse to ancient formulations. But recently phraseology and circumlocution have enjoyed a comeback—by the back door. These new forms are not the biblical kind, the use of which would at least show the writer's knowledge of the sources, but a modern type. Such expressions are both imprecise and betray the writer's laziness. For example, the whole scale of warnings and alerts has all but disappeared, to be replaced by the ubiquitous "blinking of a red light." We no longer speak angrily but "in high tones," erroneously from an acoustical point of view, as there is no connection between height of tone and power of sound. No one exploits an opportunity, but everybody hurries "to climb on the bandwagon." There is no majority, but "the lion's share." The worst thing about this imprecision and lack of imagination is that circumlocution multiplies and mixed metaphors feed on each other. This kind of language is certainly not worth preserving.

Every generation has its ignorant language. But what are we to make of the prevalent distaste for Jewish time, which for various philosophical reasons does not have a present tense for the verb "to be"? People apparently long for alien time structures and need a substitute for "is" to place before the adjective and even before the verb. Thus they do not say *ha'aretz yapha* (the land beautiful) but *ha'aretz hi yapha*—"the land she beautiful," where the "she" stands for the nonexistent "is."

Rabbi Adin Steinsaltz has already expanded on the subject of Jewish time with great authority. Suffice it to say that the lack of "is" in the present tense is no accident, but is part of the deep structure. Hebrew allows us a choice between saying "disappointment hard," *ha-ahzava kasha*, meaning "the disappointment is hard," and "hard disappointment," *kasha ha-ahzava*, meaning "hard is the disappointment." It all depends on the nuance, the shade of our meaning. But to insert the pronoun he or she is totally foreign. Examples like this of a turn toward European linguistic forms are more worrying than the misuse of individual words. As a result of this turn to alien forms we end up spreading our bread "with" marga-rine, *im margarina,* which in Hebrew means that we, together with the margarine, are spreading the bread. Or we mistakenly work "with" *im,* tools, giving equal status to man and tool, which is alien to Jewish hierar-chies of values, and also a breakdown in functional thinking.

These are not just errors of language. They reveal our inability to adapt ourselves to the real Hebrew structures, and they show our appetite for alien forms. In this way we actually do injury to the deep structures of our language, or to its anatomy, and we are likely to pay dearly for this in the impoverishment of our culture.

Here I would like to return to the distinction I made earlier between the two roles of language—that of preservation and that of communica-tion. We may well be entering a new oral age, for we now have the means to preserve information possessed by no previous generation. We have audio and video cassette libraries, computers, memory banks—every-thing is taped and recorded. Immediate communication fills our space now more than the function of preservation. Who writes a letter, when you can phone? The air is full of sound—from transistors, cassettes, and TV sets. It is full of music and songs and various forms of oral communi-cation, often of a low common denominator.

True, the technical possibility of transmitting such sounds has created new borders. Our real neighbors are those we speak to on the phone, so much so that we have a phone-call neighborhood at hand in our own house. We know more about a foreign politician or entertainer than we do about the man across the road. Such orality has rules and codes of its own, and its influence on all languages is immense. Yet, together with this apparent expansion of the limits of communication, an opposite process has occurred. Our cultural and cultural-geographic borders have shrunk. We have exchanged the long-term for a short-term, impoverished code. Once upon a time the Jew from the *shtetl* could rely on a Hebrew refer-ence to the Song of Songs, and the ancient tribal code would be immedi-ately understood by a Jew in Baghdad; today an Israeli Jew cannot use his local slang or jingle and be understood by an American Jew. The tribal code has shrunk and become short-term and expendable. It is not orality itself we should fear, but how we use it and how it could transform us.

What happens to Hebrew in the next thirty years will not be so dif-ferent from what may happen to highly developed written cultures in general. Some of them are already reeling under the burden of the new Western orality. At some point we will have to decide whether Hebrew in the next thirty or three hundred years will serve merely as a channel of immediate and basic communication, as a language at the top of a pyramid, without any pyramid beneath it, a claustrophobic language not much different from Esperanto, or whether it will embody an entire non-Western culture that we know is worth preserving.

Since language shapes us more than we shape it, this decision will be essentially about our own identity. It seems more and more certain that this will be a matter of a conscious decision.

For the writer, that decision is an easy one. Writing in Hebrew means first and foremost that the writer is using tools—words, structures, and norms—that have been in existence for between four and five thousand years, many of which still serve us today. The good news is that in theory at least you can delve into any linguistic layer to make your meaning or nuance more precise—an immense richness of possibilities. Second Temple, mishnaic language or idiom would serve, for example, a more legalistic, rational style, the style of discourse and argument; this would include some use of Aramaic, the way an educated person would use Latin or Greek expressions in a Western language discourse. The use of First Temple, biblical idiom, or syntax, or even a single significant word, would denote a much more emotional stand. The choices are almost unlimited.

The bad news, though, is that this and other factors make Hebrew —good Hebrew—nearly untranslatable. A Second Temple Hebrew proverb says that anyone who translates a sentence literally is a cheat and a fraud. They must have had painful experiences with Aramaic and Greek. The reason we authors consent to being translated, and quite often collaborate with the traitors—*tradittore traduttore*—is that although much gets lost in the translation, even more gets lost if you are not translated at all.

This brings us to the existential problems of writing in Hebrew. First, Israel is a country of about five million inhabitants, in which more than half of all adults are immigrants and one-fifth are Israeli Arabs, not all of whom have internalized Hebrew to the extent of reading good literature. It is true that in book publication, in relative numbers, Israel is second in the world after Iceland—but the Icelanders have such long nights. The

United States, incidentally, is number twenty or so, relative to the population. A runaway best-seller in Israel, however, would sell only about eighty to one hundred thousand copies, and that's very rare. Since readers of Hebrew outside Israel are not very numerous, we must be translated, or transplanted, into other languages, other cultures.

For some of us the wish to have one's work widely read generates a kind of impatience; one wants to be translated quickly and not create too many problems for the translator. The result, in many cases, is impoverished Hebrew.

The other danger to the original culture is secularization, which in Israel has taken the form of rejection, in many cases, of the Sources, so that not only much of the cultural idiom is lost, but also much of the deep structure. The result is that a great number of young people today simply do not understand the old cultural idiom, and not everyone is willing to look it up in the dictionary.

Finally, at the present stage of the conflict, it is easy to forget that Hebrew is a Semitic language, belonging wholly to this part of the world. We are exposed to American idiom much more than we are to Arabic. Peace with our neighbors will enable us to return to our common roots, vastly improving the parlance and style of both.

Writing in Hebrew, then, involves a great many decisions, most of which are unconscious. I would feel a bit claustrophobic in any other language, where I could not delve so deeply into time and nuance. In any other language I would miss the laconism, the almost plastic feeling of working in stone. And if the limits of my language are indeed the limits of my world, I cannot think of a world more open to exploration and discovery, more intriguing and satisfying, than Hebrew.

Knowledge —————————

God Is the Other Language ═══════

QUESTION: What is the Divine Plan?

ANSWER: I am not sure the question is relevant. If we accept God as a supremely exalted figure, relative to ourselves, undefinable save for a few attributes and their opposites, which we can identify—irreconcilable opposites, like merciful and compassionate versus vengeful and vindictive—then in order to understand an act or an omission of God we ourselves must *be* God, or something similar. We do not have a common language with this other Being, who is so very different from ourselves that He is, by definition, unfathomable. To me it seems that if human beings have created the concept of God, they have conceived this persona precisely to explain all the things they do not understand. If we do not understand the fairness of something that happens, for example, it is a sign that God wanted it that way. We say it was a higher power, or fate; or what man proposes, God disposes. So how can we possibly know what the Divine Plan is, or if there even is a Plan, or if each and every word in this parlance has any meaning? God is first and foremost another language. Perhaps *the* other language.

You will probably say that all religions deal with the dialogue between God and man; true enough, but that is precisely the argument I have with all religions. Nothing they say about God, none of the excuses they make for God, can answer the fundamental questions. The bottom line is always the same: do not question the unfathomable. At most, they throw you a few chance crumbs of information.

Here is an example. When my daughter was a young child, about five or six, she expressed the opinion that there was much evil in the world—for example, the death of little children. And then she came to the conclusion that perhaps God Himself is not all-powerful and cannot do everything He wants, because God has another God over Him, and that One has another God over Him, and so on, ad infinitum. This is a very modern model, a lovely model; at least it parcels out the responsibility. Moreover, it lets us out of the trap of the relationship between God and man, whose nature no one has been able to determine since the day human beings created God. That is, we know how we relate to God, but we do not know and cannot know what His attitude is toward us. And it is not certain that it matters.

When we speak of the Divine Plan, or what God has planned for us, it seems to me that we confuse God with a parental figure. Parents—the first authority—want us to be one way or another; they demand certain behavior of us. In psychological parlance this demand is the superego, the internalization of the authoritative parental plan. After all, it is they who gave birth to us, or, to use a different phrase, created us, led us through the amniotic waters, provided for us when we were helpless in the desert of infancy, and then gave us all sorts of rules of behavior, "do's" and "don'ts." I think all parents want their children to live in a better, more perfect world. If we like, we could also call this plan "perfecting the world." Ask any parent how to improve the world: he will be certain he knows. Whoever wants to can, instead, ascribe this to the concept of God. Practically speaking, it makes no difference. However, I would like to release God from His parental duties, and divorce parenthood from the divine, because the confusion between the two is driving the world mad.

QUESTION: What does it mean to "repair the world" in our time?[1]

ANSWER: The level of consensus concerning what a perfect world would be like is astounding. Almost anyone on earth will say the same thing. All people want health, peace, long and dignified lives; they want their needs met without suffering too much to attain them; they want homes; they want decent food; they want freedom from fear, freedom from oppression, freedom from violence; opportunities for their children; love, friendship, the chance to grow, the chance to learn and to satisfy their curiosity. These goals are so widely shared that we can only

---

1. The concept of "repairing the world"—*tikkun olam*—comes from the *kabbalah*, Jewish mysticism. The *kabbalah* uses the metaphor of God's luminescence having been scattered when the clay vessel in which it was contained was shattered and instructs that it is man's task to repair the vessel and gather God's light into it again.

wonder why it is that they have yet to be attained universally—as goals of the first priority should have been.

The truth is that there has been improvement in the world, but it is very slow, and we can speak of it only in statistical terms. In other words, more people today than in the past have a chance for or access to a better life. Of course, by saying this we have said very little. For example, in the Western world, the average intake is a great many calories, and the big problem there is dieting, not lack of food; but this does not solve the problem of hungry children and adults in other parts of the world, where population is rapidly increasing. The fact that quite a few countries respect minimum civil rights is no solace to those who live under occupation or oppression and whose lives are fair game. Statistics are only a partial answer; where morals are concerned, it is doubtful whether statistics are really an answer. In terms of health, our situation is better—statistically—than it was in any previous generation: babies do not die like flies; women in most areas no longer die in the throes of childbirth. In contrast, however, we are capable of wiping out millions of people with modern weapons and transportation accidents. So I am not quite sure what statistics teach. In the seventh century a man may have been able to live a long and good life in his village, while in the twentieth century a man can live very badly, can really suffer; an answer that involves the statistical majority is no answer at all, because it is immoral.

During the Second World War more than sixty million people were killed—and this in a generation that knew Pasteur and inoculation and penicillin; a generation that nearly routed tuberculosis; a generation that knew how to save and indeed saved millions of people, and yet at the same time, through war, killed more than sixty million people. This was man, all by himself, not God. Where is the "repair" here? Since we value human life highly, we send helicopters and rescue teams and who knows what, at enormous cost, to save one tourist who has lost his way in the desert; but since we also do not value human life highly—or, at least, not always—hundreds of Israelis are killed in car accidents every year. In other words, repair, to the extent that it exists, is erratic; if we look at the whole picture, it is not so clear where or how much we are progressing.

There is the repair that human beings have tried to do themselves, and there is the repair or change that takes place without our knowledge, through genetic development. The repair of the world that men have invented and are inventing may be divided into two principal categories: group repair, such as through the change of a political regime or social order; and individual repair, through improvement of one's personal attributes—through education, psychology, and so forth. We all agree that the lives of people living in a country that observes civil rights are better than those of people who live under despotism. And yet New York, in many respects the capital of Western democracy, is today one of the most violent cities in the world, the most unsafe to the man in the street, with an enormous number of homeless people. In Israel every woman has the right to study and work outside the home, but a woman cannot walk alone at night through the Valley of the Cross—here below us—or take a sleeping bag and spend the night in Sacher Park, eight hundred meters from here. Liberation from one type of fear and violence is not necessarily liberation from all types of fear and violence. A perfect country frees you from the terror of a tyrant and his henchmen; that is a lot, but it is not everything. Many other threats remain. And almost every revolution succeeds at the expense of something, or someone.

What about individual salvation? Education and psychology can improve the quality of some people's lives, but they cannot solve real existential problems. If there is a real conflict between Israel and Palestinians over land, it will not help if a psychologist comes along and tells me it is a matter of sibling rivalry. He may be right, within his discipline, and such an awareness might help a great many of his clients, but it cannot solve the problematic relations between Israel and the Palestinians. There are limitations to individual perfection, as well as to group perfection. Many improvements are merely apparent, and an improvement in one area may cause injury or harm in another.

This leaves us with the development that is *not* dependent on us— genetic, evolutionary development, which is very slow and very wasteful. Millions of sperm are wasted when one sperm fertilizes one ovum. Thousand of generations passed before man began to walk on two feet and grasp a tool. If there is any kind of plan here, first, it is astonishingly wasteful, and second, it is an example of absolute disregard for the individual. In nature, neither an individual nor generations of individuals are important; if this is supposed to be a model of our thinking, our ethics, then it is a poor one, because we want the individual to be important. A microbiologist friend says that all the troubles in the world are caused by too much DNA, the biological foundation of the universe. Yet the whole concept of the individual is based on uniqueness, on the fact that there is *not* too much DNA and that therefore every individual is important. In essence, every admission of the existence of God means disdain for the individual and makes the individual cower. If we are not willing to accept this situation, we must cease guessing what God does or does not want, we must cease seeing Him as a factor in our daily lives, with or without a plan; otherwise there is no way out of this. Repair of the world concerns us. It is not commanded from the heavens, but by us and for us, so that things will be better for all of us. I suggest we not mix God up in this. I suggest we work on horizontal, not vertical relations.

QUESTION: How do we set our priorities regarding the 613 commandments?[2]

ANSWER: This is a much more relevant question, because it leaves choice in our hands and does not guess at what God prefers. The 613 commandments are a base from which every generation chooses the commandments that have meaning for it at the time, during its era. Your question is directed, then, at this generation: what is its commandment of the hour? This commandment is not an absolute and eternal dictum, but rather relates to what present hardships we need to respond to. The rule is that each generation tries to rectify what it thinks was wrong with, or what most disturbed, the previous generation; it tries to overcome the most conspicuous hurdles or hindrances it grew up with. I am referring to the commandments that address the relationship between man and his fellow men, as in our day there is practically no need to address matters of man and God.

I believe we are in the third era of Judaism. During the first era, we made the transition from human sacrifice to animal sacrifice, symbolized by the story of the binding of Isaac; this transition was accompanied by a routine, defined cult ceremony and created an entire class of people—the priests—who carried out this ceremony. Later, after the Temple had been

---

2. The total number of precepts listed in the Torah, which Jews are expected (some believe, commanded) to observe is 613. Addressing all aspects of life, some are affirmative (thou shalt) and some are negative (thou shalt not). They are categorized as addressing the relations between man and God and between man and his fellow men. *Trans.*

destroyed, the second transition took place: prayer and tradition and custom replaced sacrifice. It became clear that it was possible to get along without sacrifice, without a lamb and a pigeon and honey and wheat and tithes, and without priests. For two thousand years the Jews existed as a nation without this ceremony, and found alternatives for it; rabbis and scholars sprang up—people who without a doubt had an advantage over the priestly cult. Rabbis, unlike church clergy, did not constitute a hierarchy; they did not acquire wealth; their reputation depended on how learned they were. The central lesson here for me is that our people continued to exist and to maintain its culture—even to flourish during certain periods—without an altar and without sacrifice and without the cult that made its living from these.

Now we are in the third era of Judaism—an era in which knowledge and learning are replacing—or should be replacing—ritual, custom, and prayer. We should all be familiar with our sources; every individual among us should know them, because they are our cultural code book. Without them, there is no Judaism at all. Yet I see no reason to keep the commandments regarding man and God; we should be focusing on the relationship between man and his fellow men. For example, a Jew who asks today, "What is Judaism without *kashrut,* the dietary laws, or without the sabbath?" is like the Jew who asked two thousand years ago, "What is Judaism without sacrifice?" It turns out that there can be Judaism without dietary laws and the sabbath; it turns out that we can make these large transitions and stay within the framework of basic Judaism. The reasons for the commandments are stronger than the commandments. Judaism is stronger than all of its would-be custodians.

To which commandments would I give primacy today? What oppressed us in previous generations and threatens to oppress us today is the patriarchal establishment, which contains hierarchies, holds ceremonies, and sanctifies the past. Like every patriarchal establishment, it foments feelings of ownership, of nationalism, of condescension toward anyone who is not like me, as well as fanaticism. I prefer the commandments that are based on personal righteousness and doing justice—that is, everything concerning the dynamic between people—over every commandment dealing with place and land and ownership. Every time the group that calls itself "The Temple Mount Faithful"—the very designation smacks of idol worship—goes up to rant and rave on the mount, to pray there and to fan the flames of hostility and discord and hatred, I want to shout in their ears: "When ye come to appear in my presence —who hath required this of ye, to tread down my courts? . . . incense of abomination it is unto me. . . . Yea, when ye make many prayers, I will not hear; your hands are full of blood. . . . Cease to do evil; learn to do well; seek justice, relieve the oppressed, do justice for the fatherless, plead for the widow." Are any words clearer than these? "Do justice for the father-less and plead for the widow," even if they are not of the people of Israel. One justice for the stranger and the dweller. All these, according to the ethics of the prophets and to their image of God, are a thousand times more important and powerful than sacrifice and prayer and ceremony. But there are people in this generation who have decided for some reason that the values of the Book of Joshua take precedence over the morals of Isaiah and the prophets; this is their order of primacy in keeping the ·commandments, and it is far from mine. In other words, their God is far from my God. According to their model, God is cruel and human beings even crueler. According to my model, very often human beings are better and have a greater sense of justice than does the God that people fash-ioned for themselves in ancient times, when they were young and He was young and everybody lacked experience.

At the top of my scale are the same three things on which the world is said to stand: justice, truth, and peace, and all the affirmative and negative commandments addressing these. I am not talking about sacrifice or cere-mony or the priestly crown,[3] nor about fasts or tithes or dietary laws or the sabbath or unleavened bread. I am talking about precepts that obli-gate the whole world, not just Israel. I have nothing—not a thing—against prayer and ceremony and dietary laws if they are meaningful to someone; I am even willing to remember, now and again, what Amalek did to our people.[4] But someone who raises these to a level of importance above that of justice, truth, and peace has set a different order of primacy; his priorities are so different from mine that there is absolutely no common language between his Judaism and mine.

---

3. This refers to both the crown once worn by the *cohens,* or caste of priests, and the name of a modern-day fundamentalist yeshiva, located in the Old City of Jerusalem, which recreates ritual items from the Temple.

4. An enemy of the ancient people of Israel, "Amalek" has come to symbolize all of Israel's enemies. *Trans.*

Beautifying Reality ═══════════════════

Theater was presenting a play in a city on the coastal plain. According to the papers, a few teachers tried to stop the show, claiming it was "neither educational nor moral." A junior high school principal summed up their sentiments, saying, "There is no need to actually show reality; instead, it should be beautified." End of quote.

At this point, some pedagogic figure should step in. Some pedagogic figure *must* step in, and fast, because it turns out there are teachers who are willing to send children out to navigate reality with fallacious maps.

The word "teacher" does not mean a person who "presents" a lesson (what an awful expression!), who is responsible for the pupils' being able to quote a few details and dates. A teacher—if he or she is also an educator—is responsible for seeing that most of the pupils in his or her class leave school as autonomous individuals, capable of independent thinking and decisive and discriminating behavior. For a person to be able to make autonomous decisions (read: to be a proper citizen), he needs to have as much information as possible. Not myths. Not legends. Not lies. Information.

To be able to one day change a harsh reality, we need to know how to define what needs to be changed and how to effect change. To cope with situations in life—both personal and public—we need to have a real picture of these situations and of their possible outcomes. We need to know the price of each and who will pay it in the end. To know that every act and every error has consequences. To reduce to a minimum the possibility that someone—the regime, or the press, or the local leadership—will deceive us, cram us with false "facts" that are appropriate to whoever is making use of them. To make quite sure that, in the highest possible percentage of cases, we can make our own decisions and not let someone else think for us.

All these things require a constant and precise mapping of reality. In other words, they require information about what exists and what is possible.

Whoever wants theater to "beautify" reality, the papers to "beautify" reality, literature to create "positive" heroes, and the nightly news to be "constructive" is raising loyal subjects, not citizens.

The "ornamental" perception of life, as the junior high school principal presented it—and it appears she is not the only one of our teachers—has no place in an education system whose goal it is to raise citizens and autonomous adults. And if a teacher does not have the courage to look reality in the eye as it is, together with her pupils, and to think with her pupils, the education of pupils should not be placed in her hands. It is not them but herself that she shields from reality; it is she, in essence, who does not have the strength to cope with reality. And self-pity has little to do with education.

Anatomy of a Deviation ════════

in religious circles, "Where did we go wrong?" it does not concern the questioners only. The Jewish terror-group affair, the manifestations of extremism in Gush Emunim (Bloc of the Faithful), the obscurantism of Rabbi Meir Kahane, and many of the words and acts proliferating in the streets today—all these seem to point to a new Jewish norm, liable to push a considerable section of the Jewish people toward a complete severance from the sources of Judaism, not as the result of legitimate controversy, but out of feelings of outrage and revulsion. Increasingly, one hears, "If these are Jews, then count me out." Those Israelis who had placed their Judaism in trust with the religious authorities—the putative custodians of Jewish tradition, enjoying special privileges as a result—now feel they have been cheated. A whole culture, an entire world, the accumulated wisdom of generations has gone off the rails before our very eyes and overturned in a fatal accident, while those at the wheel insist that they have been following perfectly valid Jewish road signs. If this is the case, then all of us are implicated.

The calamity was caused by a deviation among the religious—both in their thinking and education. It appears to center on four main points: (1) subordination of the rule of law to the principle of faith; (2) the assertion that the redemption of the people (or "the End of Days") exempts the individual from normative Jewish standards of behavior; (3) the conferring of excessive authority upon the rabbis at the expense of individual judgment; and (4) abrogation of the sense of sin and "fear of Heaven," causing severance from simple morality and the spirit of the Bible itself.

Faith Above All?

Both faith and law are basic elements of Judaism, but the subordination of law to faith is a continually recurring deviation in our history, which has always brought disastrous consequences and has proven itself alien to the essence of Judaism. It is rather difficult to understand why neither the secular nor the religious educational systems teach the history of these traumatic historical deviations, if only for their cautionary value. We are all familiar with George Santayana's admonition that he who does not remember his past is doomed to repeat it. But how short people's memories are! This very conflict between the principle of faith, or redemption, and the principle of law, or justice, took place here in Jerusalem one thousand nine hundred and fifty-two years ago, when the trial and death of Jesus, the Jew of Nazareth, represented the dramatic incarnation of this essential schism within the Jewish people itself.

The main teaching of Christianity (less so in the preachings of Jesus himself, who apparently had no intention of breaking away from Judaism and was cautious in his choice of words, and more in the writings of his pupil Saul of Tarsus, or Paul, who perpetrated the actual split) is that the principle of faith is incomparably more important than the rule of law, and takes precedence over it. This postulate is explicitly stated in Saul of Tarsus's Epistle to the Romans and Epistle to the Hebrews. Christian dogma, which deliberately defies logic and the accepted order of the world (such as Jesus as the Son of God, the Virgin Birth, and the Resurrection) is intended to create linchpins of total, unquestioning messianic faith, and to accord it precedence over the essentially legal principle of Judaism. Judaism obviously could not accept this, and Christianity became a dissident religion. That was the core of the controversy. In fact, the major confrontation between the two conflicting approaches began with the trial of Jesus as recorded by his disciples (a somewhat biased description). In this scenario, Jesus appears as the man of pure faith through which he works miracles, who comes to redeem the world (there was no room for doubt that the world was indeed redeemed by Jesus, and that his times were really "the days of the Messiah"), and he stands fast against the priests—or in another version the Sanhedrin—who try him for heresy and condemn him. Judge Chaim Cohen has already shown in his book, *The Trial and Death of Jesus of Nazareth,* that the story cannot be true, especially with regard to the "seder night" since the Sanhedrin would not sit in judgment on Seder night (Passover Eve), but historical exactitude is not the point here; it is the way in which events have been presented by the disciples and the underlying ideology.

Thus, according to the New Testament account, the Roman governor "washed his hands" of the affair, having no jurisdiction over Jewish legal authority. Jesus was crucified, and legality (that is, Judaism) triumphed. But then, say the Christians, through divine intervention a miracle was wrought, and Jesus arose from the dead and sat beside his Father as Messiah, or as King of the Jews. In the fundamental Christian story, in the quasi-historical scenario—where Christianity broke away completely from Judaism, out of which it grew—sheer unswerving faith in salvation triumphed over mere mortal judgment. This, in the most dramatic manner, was the turning point determining the future course of Christianity. Christianity, the dissident creed, subsequently became the leading opponent of Judaism and its tenets. From the Middle Ages up to the Protocols of the Elders of Zion, Christianity's great enemy was the Sanhedrin, the Jewish legal authority, and the text most abhorrent to it was the Talmud, the essence of the Jewish legal system. Christianity took its own faith-oriented path, and the central stream of Judaism, although shaken by the split, also continued on its own way, maintaining Law, not faith, as the main navigational system of human life, in the harsh realization that "grass will grow out of our bones and the Son of David is still not come," and meanwhile life must go on.

The difference of emphasis between these two bases is what distinguished Judaism from all other religions. Faith is not only the basis of all other theistic religions, but also of secular religions, or nondemocratic political movements that call upon the individual to believe that their way is the only path to salvation. Faith is an overwhelming principle, and it becomes gravely dangerous when it overrides the rule of law or natural justice. Many regimes have swayed the masses by deliberately encouraging them to uphold the principle of faith above all others. Already in the early 1930s, well before the Holocaust, Nazi ideology was very much based on the faith principle, and in their promotional material the Nazis made much use of terminology such as "absolute faith in our sacred rights," the belief that "what is taking place before us is indeed a miracle," and credence in "the exaltedness of the state and national and racial rectitude." In 1938, the SS organ Das Schwarze Korps posited three interconnected ideas: "Faith-Movement-Action: the three terms defining for us the path of true dedication." In 1927 Hitler had declared that "with us, faith holds first place and not only knowledge. . . . What makes people go out and struggle and die for ideas whose origin is in religion itself? Not knowledge, but absolute faith."

Any number of such examples could be cited from the various existing "secular religions" and dangerous ideologies. Those we have provided have been quoted not to equate them, mutatis mutandis, but to show that in the absence of drastic legal restrictions, faith can swiftly deteriorate into absolute evil, all the more because of its power to incite. The young are especially eager for great deeds and sacrifices, only awaiting a leader to authorize them. The uniqueness of Judaism lies precisely in the fact that at all times it was completely law-oriented, barring the way to brutalization. The only exceptions were, of course, the periods of the false messiahs. But they are the exception to the rule, providing a harsh lesson on the difference between the principle and the deviation.

Out of a misguided sense of priorities in certain circles, an exaggerated ethnocentricity has grown up. The belief in imminent redemption is always the concern of a particular religious or ethnic social group, while the principles of law and justice are always universal. Anyone who accords priority to the principle of faith will always, by definition, be ethnocentric.

Our second subject I believe to be one of the principal causes of the contemporary derailment of religious Judaism, and that is the idea that the redemption of the whole exonerates the individual from normative Jewish standards of behavior.

When the Messiah Is Nigh

The End of Days has often been perceived in Judaism as the redemption of the Jewish people rather than universal salvation. Space does not permit me to quote all or even part of the sources, but it would seem that the most vulgar conception of the days of the Messiah is the one in which the Jewish people achieve redemption through domination and the indiscriminate use of force, becoming a holy people living under a monarchical regime in which the prophecy "nations will bow down to you" is fulfilled. Roughly, this is the conception prevalent today in the circles responsible for the present catastrophe, and it cannot be described merely as a manifestation of incipient ethnocentricity, but one of rampant, megalomaniacal ethnocentricity. Such an attitude could be ascribed to a sense of inferiority, insecurity, and confusion, but it would be simplistic merely to define this fantasy-view without drawing attention to its inherent danger—namely, that the individual Jew ceases to be accountable for his actions.

This conviction that "we are at the Beginning of the Redemption, and that makes us all holy," this "instant sanctification" that seems to have descended upon us miraculously in the Six-Day War, grew out of the thought of Rabbi Zvi Yehuda Kook in Yeshivat Merkaz Harav. At its source, as the late Uriel Tal pointed out, are the ideas expressed by Rabbi Haim Bar-Abba in the name of Rabbi Yohanan in the Talmud, in Tractate *Berachot,* concerning a too-literal interpretation of some words of the prophets. From this fundamentalist interpretation it was only a short step to the contemporary opinion of Rabbi Arieli and of Rabbi Hadaya that war (!) redeems us from defilement and demoralization, so that from now on we all live in the realm of absolute sanctity. From this postulate it was an even shorter step to the thesis of Rabbi Shlomo Aviner that the Jews were commanded to be holy, but they were not commanded to be moral; ordinary human morality does not apply to the Jews, who are above humanity.

Certainly, sanctity is beyond good and evil and beyond the whole system of law and judgment, and anyone who claims to have been made holy "through the purifying power of war" (terminology known to us from European history) or "through the sanctity of the land" (this, too, is known to us from the same source, the well-known unholy faith in the mystical power of "blood and soil"), such a person does not have to account for his actions to anyone who is not part of his people and who consequently is not holy. There are many other principles involved: the "instant sanctification" school of thought says, in effect, to each individual: "The government is not so important. There is no need for law; there is no need for democracy. In any case, we are on the way to the great promised Kingdom and we have no more need for such laws as we have learnt from the Gentiles." Dr. Avi Ravitzky has correctly remarked that monarchy, too, is a form of government "like unto the nations," one we have learned and acquired exactly like democracy. But, even worse—if the government is not important and the law is immaterial, the result is a lack of trust in all organs of governance, and that lack of trust gives rise to rampant extremism and violence. To have a well-ordered life in a well-run state some degree of trust in the institutions and administration of the state and in the law of the land is necessary. If one severs that reliance, as certain religious elements have done systematically, one provides an alternative authority for many actions that are outside the law, thereby justifying not "taking the *law* into one's own hands," in Gush Emunim parlance, but taking *contempt of the law* into one's own hands. I shall quote only one of many examples.

During the election campaign of 1984, Rabbi Eliezer Waldman, in an address to his political supporters, suddenly said—to the astonishment of the radio reporter present—"Gentlemen, the time has come for morning prayers" (literally, "the time has come to recite the *Shema of Shacharit*"). Neither the reporter nor many of the secular listeners caught the allusion, but the cognoscenti among Rabbi Waldman's supporters were certainly aware that these words (quoted from the Passover Haggadah) were the call to revolt of Rabbi Akiva's students in A. D. 132. Indeed, the leadership of Gush Emunim in recent years has played many such dangerous games, disseminating hints and cryptic code words to its youth, giving it license for acts that go far beyond what is openly stated. When such messages are spread continuously, in both speech and actions—in Sebastia, in violence against the Israel Defense Forces (IDF) in Yamit, in the arson and plunder of the Hebron market, all done under the auspices of certain rabbinical authorities, and in such statements as "So let all thy enemies perish, O Israel!" (which of course is a deliberate falsification of the verse "So let all thy enemies perish, O Lord!")—a thousand admonitions to be loyal to the state and its laws will be to no avail. Cryptic messages and secret code words will always overshadow the verbal warnings, which will then be interpreted as mere lip service to law and order. The quasi-underground quality, the coded message, the feeling that "the secular authorities are stupid and don't understand," are the stock-in-trade of the mystics. Only those in the know were aware, for instance, that the halfhearted censure of the Jewish terror organization by Gush Emunim officials was not a condemnation at all. It opposed taking the law into one's own hands, a relatively venial offense not condemned by the Torah, and avoided mention of the main offense, the shedding of blood, which is expressly prohibited. One group in the large ethnicity called Judaism has arrogated to itself the right to abolish individual responsibility before the law, and to tell the individual that even his direst actions are unimportant because redemption is at hand. This is a reinterpretation or disintegration of individual responsibility in favor of the "instant sanctification" of the whole. Nothing could be more alien to the ethics of the prophets, or, indeed, the Ten Commandments, each one of which deliberately speaks in the singular, addressing the individual. As Samuel Taylor Coleridge said, "He who begins by loving Christianity better than truth, will proceed by loving his own sect better than Christianity, and will end in loving himself better than all." The inference is obvious.

Are Rabbis Infallible?

This question has preoccupied Jews ever since rabbis existed: namely, how far should their authority encroach on the independence of mind and judgment of the individual? As an educational question it is of the utmost importance, and it is hardly surprising that the leaders of the B'nai Akiva religious youth movement are trying to grapple with it today. Its secretary, Yohanan Ben-Ya'akov, recently published an instructional pamphlet discussing the *halachic* interpretation of the concept "Turn neither . . . to the right, nor left"—a clarification that chiefly concerns the authority of the Sanhedrin in questions about which there is "a certainty that an error was made in *halachic* judgment."

The booklet discusses the various existing interpretations of the following passage: "If there arise a matter too hard for thee in judgement . . . and thou shalt come unto the priests, the Levites, and unto the judge that shall be in those days" (this also applies to the secular Israeli courts of our time!), "thou shalt do according to the sentence which they shall shew thee . . . thou shalt not decline from the sentence which they shall shew thee, to the right hand, nor to the left." Rashi[1] interprets this as meaning that one should adhere to the rabbinical scholars, "even if they tell you that right is left and left is right," but the opinion of other rabbinical scholars is divided, and, for lack of space, I shall confine myself to the opinion of Rabbi Naphtali Zvi Yehuda Berlin of Volozhin, who stated that these things apply only when the Temple is standing, and of some other sources, according to which these rulings are invalid when there is a clear error of judgment on the part of the scholars. These are the Tractate *Horayot* in the Jerusalem Talmud and *Yad Ha-Melech,* where it is specifically stated that "if one knows in one's heart that it is contrary to what is specifically stated in the Torah, one is forbidden to listen to them," especially if the rabbinic authorities tell one "to kill an innocent person"

---

1. He was then a member of Knesset. *Trans.*

or to perform some action that obviously entails a transgression of the explicit commandments of the Torah. This limitation remarkably resembles the legal restriction accepted by the army, after the Kafr Kassem massacre (1956), where a similar question was asked about how far a soldier should go in obeying his commanders' orders and at what point he must use his own judgment. In the Kafr Kassem case, it was ruled that a soldier not only may, but ought to, disobey an order when it is "obviously unlawful."

Both these decisions—the religious and the secular—allow wide scope for individual morality and judgment concerning what "one knows in one's heart," or, in other words, for individual conscience when it senses a contradiction of the basic ethics of the Torah. Without this limitation there is no possibility of educating people in individual responsibility, ergo, there is no hope of educating them at all. If, for instance, we suppose (on the basis of the evidence) that rabbis and *halachic* scholars gave their blessing to the murders at the Islamic College in Hebron, we must assume that those who listened to them blindly obeyed what they saw as an infallible "papal" authority, clearly transgressing the caution in Judaism against blind obedience, the proviso that disobeying what "one knows in one's heart" is a clear case of sin.

Such a charge of "popery" may readily be advanced against this phenomenon of blind obedience when it is found within Judaism itself, as in the case of the distortion that has taken place, notably within Agudat Israel, with regard to the concept *da'at torah*. The concept itself is found in Tractate *Hullin* of the Babylonian Talmud, and it originally meant a clear idea that could be generally taught—in contrast with *de'a nota*, which is a reasonable and attractive idea, but unclear, and therefore unsuited as a basis for teaching. *Da'at torah* is akin to what the army calls "the school solution," and its main purpose is to allow continuity in carrying on a common language and a common teaching. Agudat Israel, especially in pre-Holocaust Polish orthodoxy, attached to this concept a meaning it had never possessed, as though to claim: the Torah sages have a special degree of discernment and knowledge that permits them to adjudicate on every subject in the world, including subjects of paramount importance in the world such as economics and politics and medicine, and their opinion is to be regarded as *da'at torah*, therefore infallible and indisputable. This is an unequivocal preference for *rov binyan* (the scholars' majority) over *rov minyan* (an ordinary majority) and *rov kinyan* (the majority of wealthy leaders of the community), all of which are legal in Jewish tradition; and it apparently invests anyone steeped in Torah with an authority that cannot be questioned. Strangely enough, this Agudah-Orthodox point of view has been accepted as a principle by the National Religious Party, which has begun to defer to its rabbis, or at least to some of them, in an unacceptable manner, allowing no margin for error or deviation from the morality of the Torah or the ethics of the prophets.

This attitude, too, is a major departure from the basic values of Judaism, which is essentially a culture of disputation and controversy, involving acceptance of the principle of nondecision ("Both these and those are the words of the living God"). It is sufficient to recall in this connection the well-known Midrash concerning Moses, who came to Rabbi Akiva's academy and could not understand a single word that was being said until he heard "This is a *halacha* from Moses on Sinai"; in other words, everything is given up to disputation and modification on the common basis of the Torah. From any point of view whatever—*halachic*, traditional, educational, psychological—the bestowal of absolute authority on rabbinical responsa and jurisdiction at the expense of the judgment and conscience of the individual, is not only a deviation, it is almost a heresy, and obviously an additional factor contributing to the catastrophe overtaking Judaism in our time, the import of which cannot be overstressed. The responsibility of the Jewish individual, even when he "receives an order" or follows a rabbinical decision, is unquestionable. It was not a Jew but the Nazi Adolf Eichmann who justified himself at his trial by saying that he "merely carried out orders."

When Fear of God Is Abolished

Several people, including this writer, have asked what would happen when the authority of the rabbis nullified a man's natural sense of sin and "fear of Heaven," assuring him that the performance of this or that mitzvah in itself makes him "a good Jew," so that he need not have scruples about his other deeds and transgressions. Such an assurance leaves the individual wide open to the manipulations of unscrupulous politicians who will not hesitate to use the obliteration of the sense of sin for their own purposes. But in this context I would cite an example from outside the sphere of politics to illustrate what can happen when a man's sense of sin is nullified by what appears to be the observance of the commandments.

Not long ago, an Orthodox rabbi in Jerusalem, who had apparently carried out all the commandments of the Torah, bar one that had not come his way, decided to carry out the remaining one: the mitzvah of letting the mother bird go. The Torah places a clear restriction on hunting birds, saying that if a hunter happens to find a nest with a mother bird sitting on its young, he is permitted to take the young, but "thou shalt . . . let the mother bird go" (Deuteronomy 22:6). The intention of this commandment should be clear to anyone with any sense: it is a limitation of cruelty, and obviously not a deliberate invitation to it. What did the rabbi do? He went out with the deliberate intention of finding a nest with a mother bird sitting on its young, took the fledglings, and let the mother bird go. His pupils saw this and followed suit, and a frantic hunt began for nests containing birds sitting on their young, with a complete disregard for the suffering caused to the birds, until the Society for the Protection of Nature intervened for fear that certain species of birds might be exterminated. The law was brought into action, and the scandal was more or less terminated. Fortunately, said the man from the Society who dealt with the matter, the yeshiva students were not particularly skillful at climbing trees or rooftops, or else the survival of some species might really have been endangered.

This is a graphic example of a disregard for the reality of the world in which we live, a disregard that comes about as the result of the so-called performance of a commandment without any understanding of the spirit of that commandment. For a long period, the pupils of this particular yeshiva had indulged in deliberate cruelty toward birds, and all in the name of a mitzvah they yearned to perform—something done "for the sake of heaven," without the slightest trace of the "fear of Heaven," without any relation to one's natural scruples, and, even more, to the spirit of the mitzvah itself. And, if this is the case with birds, how much more does it apply when one is concerned with men, who only have to be described as "Amalek" (once again, with a complete disregard for present-day reality), and a number of commandments can readily be found to justify exterminating them or expelling them and depriving them of their rights, all without the slightest sense of sin. This is a most dangerous negation of the moral side of man by certain religious groups who are supposed by their very definition to be preoccupied with developing man's consciousness of his own morality. Unscrupulous political groups are ever willing to take advantage of it.

All the deviations I have discussed have one obvious factor in common: their herd quality. All of them conceive of people not as individuals who have personal responsibility and personal moral standards, but as a herd that can be subjected to authority. And if we are a herd, then so are the Arabs, and all the rest of the world without distinction, without differentiation, without any difference not only between the righteous and the wicked, but between truth and falsehood, between one intention and another, between good and evil. Obviously, according to this approach, there is no value to the rights of the individual, and even less to the rights of a minority, because in a herd there are no rights: there can only be constant fighting between herds. Quite obviously, here there can be no concept of reward and punishment, of retribution, of reward according to effort or any other method of recognizing the guilt or merit of the individual, but only a totality of "instant sanctification" that absolves each individual in the holy herd of minimal responsibility.

When there is a deviation of such magnitude, there ought, on the face of it, to be a leadership capable of analyzing the deviation and of delineating the mainstream. From the days of David Ben-Gurion, there has been an understanding about the absolute necessity of a common language between the secular and religious, to avoid producing a split in a people whose members faced many heavy challenges. The religious leaders of today have for the most part abandoned the attempt to find a common language and have encouraged precisely the deviation (or heresy, as some think) that makes such a common language between different sections of the people impossible, and no one has been able to cry "Stop!"

It was Rabbi Hazon-Ish who once said, "Fanaticism is an alarm clock." Indeed, it awakens us all to the question of how we arrived at the clear split we have today, at a point seldom paralleled in the history of the Jewish people, at the feeling that we are no longer one people but at least two, and that Judaism as we knew it has been lost. If religious Judaism is not able to correct itself thoroughly, the present split will become a permanent fact. No "unity of land" will be of any avail if the unity of the people is lost, and lost without redress for generations.

Knowledge and Arrogance ━━━━━━

PEOPLE WHO ACQUIRE ACADEMIC diplomas are one of the smallest minorities on earth. All in all, less than 6 percent of mankind has had some academic education; and about 1 percent, or less, has a master's degree. The fraction of people who acquire a university degree in the humanities is too small to calculate, and belongs to the branch of statistics known as small-fraction number groups. The statistical chance of being hit by lightning is not very far from the chance of becoming an accredited dealer in the humanities. Those of us who do become such dealers, need every bit of luck we can get, because there is nothing in the world as morally binding as belonging to a minority.

Semantically, there is some problem with the word "humanities." If by the word we mean disciplines having to do with human thought, as opposed to the sciences, which deal with exact science, or social studies, which are interested in the workings of societies, then both mathematics and law should be included in the humanities. Mathematics are an invented science, a creation of the mind, an area of thought arrived at by sheer reasoning, not pre-existing information discovered by observation. Legal thought, too, is often a highly intellectual form of reasoning—for example, the legal differentiation between intentional and unintentional crime is an intellectualization of an existing human condition.

And yet, in most universities neither law nor mathematics is taught among the humanities. This is a pity, because it would benefit the so-called human spirit to move a little horizontally, not just perpendicularly, so that people could learn a few intellectual languages in addition to those they know. Perhaps this has something to do with the theory that one knows one's own language thoroughly after one has learned another, foreign language equally thoroughly.

The humanities do include, though, philosophy, history, language, education, comparative literature, and so on, all of them dealing with ideas, all of them supposed to confer upon us a complete freedom of thought, even if our thought is sometimes quite remote from what we call reality. It is exactly for this purpose that the term "intellectual" was invented. It is a highly problematic term, to be sure, difficult to define, more general than "an erudite" or "a scholar." Our intellectual is, it seems, the only one who is allowed to create models, the connection of which to any kind of reality he is not required to prove. It would be poor law indeed were it removed from human reality; there would be something very wrong if psychology acted outside reality; anthropology of course, deals with an existing human reality all the time—and I am quite aware that reality keeps changing all the time. But our intellectual does not have to adhere to those limits, strictly speaking, and this is as it should be, in the name of complete freedom of thought. Benjamin Disraeli's father once defined an intellectual as a man who, given the choice of going to paradise or reading a book about paradise, will choose the book. Poor man, some of us would say.

Sir Isaiah Berlin has always been unhappy about the possibility of a lack of connection between the intellectual and what is actually happening, and he made a beautiful differentiation between intellectuals and the intelligentsia. The intelligentsia of a country (and the whole definition flourished in Russia), is the community of enlightened people who display a high moral concern with what is happening around them. A member of the intelligentsia does not have to be an intellectual or a scholar, says Sir Isaiah. One can be an enlightened plumber, if one's principles are developed and truly enlightened, just as, theoretically at least, one can be a wholly obscurant intellectual.

This is an obvious differentiation, and would hardly be worth mentioning were it not for the fact that it concerns the root of one of the greatest perils facing free intellectuals: the danger underlying the fact that intellectuals are really not limited by anything, not even by existing social realities, not even by the price that others may have to pay for their brilliant models when someone puts them into practice. It is a familiar sight: an intellectual so sure of his thesis or model that he pesters the powers that be to put it into practice. Accountability, however, will always fall on the person who acted on the theory, not the person who invented it. We confer upon the intellectual—by definition—the full and complete freedom to create a theory and to build an abstract model without any responsibility for the results, and this is indeed one of the most difficult problems to be pondered on in the humanities. The jurist is limited by the reality of crime or the deterioration of the system of governance. The psychologist who sticks to a certain model and whose patients go from bad to worse is limited by the actual state of his patients. The freedom of the man of ideas is not limited by anything at all, and we oppose political systems that seek to limit that freedom, because there are no limits to the human spirit. And this is where arrogance lies in wait.

When does a group of thinking people become a sect, a kind of clergy, characterized by arrogance? It becomes a sect when time passes and the group fails to modify its vocabulary, instead retaining the words and concepts they started with. A discipline, any discipline, that works within the same vocabulary all the time, soon becomes a sect, and the people working within it become a kind of priesthood that conducts ceremonies, often without a shred of creative prophecy. Any given discipline contains a majority of priests and a minority of prophets, and the eternal question is who prevails.

A group that feeds on the same terminology all the time may develop habits contrary to intellectual mores and reflexes: it will not welcome too much openness—and what is too much openness is for the group to decide. It will discard or ignore or censor anything not like itself, anything not hitherto known to the group, or anything unfamiliar to its conceptual world and its binding use of words. Moreover, such a group might reject out of hand any information or idea coming from a noncanonical source, not from "one of us"—and this group arrogance may well lead the group to miss the most essential developments of the moment or the generation. Intellectuals usually analyze change, sometimes they are lucky enough to foretell it, and occasionally they are instrumental in causing change. In the usual situation the intellectual becomes a kind of ornament to a revolution, if it likes to pride itself on its intellectuals.

It is not the sovietologists who brought about the upheaval in the communist world, and it is not the art or literary theorists who bring about the most profound changes in the art and literature of a generation. The greatest danger to any discipline is the creation of a static model that keeps the same vocabulary for any length of time. In such a case, the intellectual becomes an ex-intellectual in no time. Thus, the criterion of vocabulary and word-concept—does it adjust itself or not? does it change with time or does it remain the same? — can serve as a measuring stick for the index of arrogance of a given discipline or group. By a change in vocabulary, I mean a complete change of all that had been thought of as basic or indispensable terms. Illustrations abound.

The disciples of Plato considered terms such as "possible," "probable," "may be," and "uncertain" unserious terms, the opposite of "true" or "scientific" in modern usage, not to be part of any serious thought process. Today the words "possibility" and "probability" are an inseparable part of the central epistemic and scientific body of knowledge of this generation.

At the end of the last century and the beginning of the present one, the concept of a "final solution" was widespread in world thought. In the name of a final solution, drugs were developed to eliminate certain diseases "once and for all." Freudian theory includes the same concept; the patient finds the "bad" or "pathogenic" source, the root of the disturbance, and analyzes it permanently out of the system. The final solution, as the Jewish people learned in the living flesh, was also a part of the social and political thought of the period. Only now, less than a century afterward, is the realization beginning to dawn that there are no final solutions, and that "once and for all" does not exist. The notion of killing "it" once and for all is no answer at all, but rather the continuation of a disturbance in other ways.

Today, we do not speak about "killing" or "squashing" conflicts; we speak about resolving them, diminishing them below the level of danger. We speak about conflict control, a term that would have been inconceivable in previous centuries. Our perception today is much less radical and much more ecological.

Thus, a group of intellectuals can unwittingly become an arrogant anti-intellectual group if it does not give a good shake once in a while to itself and its vocabulary, from the bottom up. It can become anti-intellectual if it is no longer able to live with ambiguity and cannot bring itself to say "I have no answer," "We do not know." The greatest arrogance is probably that in which a person thinks that he must provide an answer or a solution to all, that everyone expects him to have the answer and pressures him for a solution, because then, in no time, such a person will find himself bending the facts just a little to gloss over conflict or refutation and to canonize what is already known. Language becomes not a human language, but rather an esoteric professional slang, or lingua franca, losing the living significance at ultrasonic speed.

Of course, there is nothing intrinsically negative in being an erudite scholar in one's area. It is only, when all is said and done, very poor nourishment to comprehensive intellectual curiosity. Western thought, for instance—beginnings of the omission were in ancient Greece—had very little curiosity about Eastern thought and Eastern concepts, which in many cases were far less categorical and far more ecological than the concepts of the West.

Today we recognize that there are many lacunae in many fields of the previously hallowed Western mode of thought, from surgery to psychoanalysis and even history, and sometimes we witness real confusion. Were the West more able at the start to accept the foreign, the "not of us," what is so often called "unscientific," and to check all its stances vis-à-vis that which is strange and surprising, we might in many fields be in a far better position today, certainly in a more progressive one.

The most important intellectual question today is not *what* we know, but *how* we know the things we know and accept as given. What shaped our prevalent image of knowledge, and is the spirit or method that shaped it originally still valid, still relevant vis-à-vis reality, or do we need a new vocabulary?

It is easy for a writer to speak about the danger that knowledge will become arrogant because a person who writes books is probably the greatest individualist of all, and does not belong to any institutional engagement. But academics belong to a great structure, a great establishment that deals with many fields and many aspects of those fields. Surely there are great blessings in what they do, otherwise they would not be where they are, or pride themselves on being a minority of mankind, and such a small minority to boot. I will dwell a little on the blessings.

We live today, to a great extent, in a commercial culture, where everything has its practical purpose and its price. Under these circumstances our political culture, or great parts of it, is characterized by values of commercial expediency. We know the price of everything, sometimes before we know the value of it.

We stick to what we have and are afraid to let go, because every time we share material things with others, we find that our share has diminished. If we share a fortune, we have less of it; if we divide territory, less remains for us; if we share with others honors or positions of authority and rule, we have less. This situation does not make for greater peace in the world.

But there is one field that lies completely outside this category: the realm of knowledge. The more one shares knowledge, the more of it one has, and the more complete it becomes. Moreover, it is the sharing of knowledge that brings about greater knowledge and inspires more and better thought. Knowledge is not subject to purely commercial considerations, just as good books are not subject to the prevalent economy. Perhaps this is the true interpretation of the midrash according to which all of us in all generations were, are, and will be present at Mount Sinai—not Sinai as a sound-and-light production or a single pyrotechnical happening, a spiritual stock exchange in which those who were present gained and those who were absent, or not yet born, lost. Not even Sinai as territory, which may be ours today and under the rule of others tomorrow. In the Sinai of knowledge there is room for all of us, friends and enemies, opponents and admirers, all of us who populate the earth, without any limitation at all, in a different ecology yet unknown to us in most other fields. Perhaps, very slowly, we shall come to know it.

Place ═══════════════════════════════════════

On Being a Levantine ━━━━━━━━━━

I AM A LEVANTINE.

Born in Europe, all my days there passed in an obscure impatience, as if it were all a mistake, a confinement, like a wretched marriage—until I first saw strong light on rocky hedges on a mountain, a stooping summer olive tree, a well carved in stone—and I knew that was it. I had arrived at some deep, palpable ancientness, the womb of the world, where virtually everything was and will be created. Here were the right light, the right smells, the right touch. "A taste older than meat, older than wine. A taste as old as cold water," as a famous Irish Levantine, Lawrence Durrell, once wrote about the flavor of olives.

Levantinism is a slowly acquired trait. Not everything Mediterranean is Levantine. Lebanon, for example, as a real Levantine from Cairo once told me, behaves like scores of European tribes in the sixth or seventh century and heaps ignominy on our region.

One can be an excellent Levantine, or one who does not do the profession particularly proud. At his worst, the Levantine is one of Eric Ambler's unheroic characters, a petty smuggler, a crook, madly intelligent with the moral principles of an alley cat, who lives in the perpetual hope that the law will acquiesce, if not to bribery, then at least in deference to a good joke. At his best, the Levantine is a retired diplomat, seasoned, with an incomparable cultural patina, who will unfailingly prefer life experience to any theory and will always be right. He is the one with the perfect score in his assessment of the strengths and weaknesses of others, no matter what they say. In his flippant way, the Levantine is the man in the market who can talk to you in five languages, fluently, simultaneously, and ungrammatically. At his best, he is the man who knows five languages and their literature to perfection, because his part of the world has seen a host of conquerors speaking a multitude of languages, and suddenly you begin to have doubts about a world power that speaks one language only. For the Levant is the embodiment of synthesis and its essence, the opposite of all aggressive, crass single-mindedness. It is the color-blind pluralism that sees no racial, ethnic, or religious differences. The Levant hardly goes anywhere: everyone comes to it, and the blazing sun smooths and molds everything.

When the Levantine is feckless, he's an irredeemable layabout, a bungler who is incapable of—and not much interested in—organizing three telephone calls to pin down three people to a particular appointment, a charming "Never mind" on two feet. In his beauty, he's easy to be with, mindful that pressure and haste are bad manners. You can hear the Levant in the well-formed, lovely voices, never raised, always politely hesitant so as not to sound offensive. A girl from a kibbutz who married an Arab said that the first thing she learned to do in his village was to lower her voice. She had never been aware that most of the time she had been shouting.

Admittedly, the Levantine at his worst is wholly inconsistent, not bound by any particular principle, cynical—but always with humor. At his best, he is the man who does not believe in "isms," hierarchies, bureaucracies, organizations. His relation to all declarations is ironic from the outset, but he's too polite to say so. When he's not so good, he easily forgives himself and others for all kinds of transgressions, which he calls "human frailty." What can you expect from mere flesh and blood? At his best, nothing human is alien to him.

We are speaking about an entirely different kind of communication. Authentic Levantinism means the third eye and the sixth sense. It is the keen sensitivity to "how," the knowledge that "how" is always more important than "what"; therefore, every true artist is a kind of Levantine. It means a perpetual reading between the lines, both in human relations and in political pronouncements—an art no Israeli political leader has yet succeeded in acquiring. That is why we are always surprised in our part of the world—surprised by war, surprised by peace.

Levantinism is the tragic sense of life. It is tolerant humor. It is total sobriety. It is the knowledge that not everything has a solution; it is the basic awareness of human helplessness. Of course, at its worst, it can be translated into fatalism and inertia. But at its best it is the ability to live for long periods of time with opacity and ambiguity without denying weakness. It is the difference between maturity and sophistication. It is the great patience. It is the tacit knowledge that different nations live at different ages, and that age is culture, and that some nations are still adolescent, among them, quite often, Israel. And it is the bitter experience that knows that everything—every revolution, every ideology—has its human price, and there is always someone to pay it. It is the discerning eye, the precise diagnosis, that sees the latent narcissist in every ideologue. It is the joke at his expense, and the forgiveness.

The Levant is also that quality that knows there is no great art, no serious literature, without a hidden theological background to give it the dimension of depth. I am talking about theology, not a code of religious behavior—theology as distinct from sociology. Not by chance, all the monotheistic religions were born here, and all their heresies, too: all the serious systems by which man navigates his life, including Hellenism and its skepticism. Science, which cannot survive without monotheism and doubt, the absolute and the contradiction, was born here too. Certainly, the Levant still bears the vestiges of idolatry, but these are small and homey: a pilgrimage to the grave of a holy man, small village spells and exorcisms. Essentially, here man always deals directly with his god, with no mediation of clergy. Here religion was created; there clericalism grew up. There the all-devouring, giant hierarchies were created, all larger than life, all geared to intimidate and astound. Not the Levant, but Europe engendered the maculate conception of all those pure blue-eyed angels, as opposed to black devils who roast sinners in hell fire. Here angels are simple, prosaic messengers, and the devil is one of the nameless attendants. Here, not one of the prophets threatened sinners with a perpetual inferno of fire and brimstone. This paranoid polarization was created, not by chance, in Europe. Here in the Levant images have always been human, for better or worse. This human image applies even to the Greek gods. The God of Israel, too, is depicted with glaring inconsistency, now as jealous and vengeful, now as merciful and forgiving—just like the mortals He created in His image, in His likeness. The Manichaean heresy, which sees everything as totally good or totally evil, god or devil, the same outlook that is the original sin of stereotype and of totalitarianism, was created not in the Levant but in Iran, and it reached its religious and political apogee—naturally—in Europe.

Because there has always been here a direct, prosaic, and simple contact with the unknown, an everyday affair, it is not surprising that in our

Holy of Holies, as in Islam, as in early Christianity, there were no statues. We needed no intermediaries. We walked barefoot with our God. And when the vast, daunting temples of the ancient Near East had crumbled to heaps of ruins and became imprinted in people's minds as irretrievably destroyed, perpetual, lived-with reminders of the transience of pride, only then did the Europeans begin to build their towering cathedrals and constructing their own vast system of idolatry, sometimes known as hierarchies of saints. There, not here, men erected in every town square a bronze statue on a pedestal, depicting the idealized, larger-than-life image of a conqueror mounted on his charger, brandishing his sword at some unseen enemy—its only redeeming feature the unequivocally expressed opinion of the local sparrows and pigeons.

In the Levant humanism was created—gradually, over a long, long time—except that nobody called it by that name. The Levant is everything that was learned and created on the ruins of hubris, both personal and public. The arrogant Tower of Babel was erected here long ago, and the lesson was learned. Since then, building has been suited to the landscape, with which it lives in peace; there originated the listless little boxes and the aggressive skyscrapers. Here was never that schmaltzy crudeness, that eternal traffic to and fro between institutionalized sentimentality and institutionalized brutality, which is the very crux of the European experience. Santa Claus and Auschwitz. Gemütlichkeit and racism. Viennese operetta and Sieg Heil. Wig, minuet, and the Night of the Long Knives. Kalinushka and gulag.

And this food. Contrary to whatever a few diligent Tel Aviv or New York housewives may think, the regional food is not one Middle Eastern dish or another. It is a way of life. It is a vegetable in its time and season, a tomato ripened in a great sun, olive oil from the press, seasoned with basil and thyme from the early morning mountainside. It is the end-of-summer grapes, awaited all year, and it is the fig that has absorbed all the light. It is the fish caught in the bay, eaten without any special purpose or bottom line or haste, washed down with a drink made of anise that grows nearby. It is soul food; it is the basis. On this basis it is also possible to enjoy well-prepared Western dishes, but not the reverse.

A Levantine from France, Marcel Boulestin, said that peace and happiness begin, geographically, where garlic is used in cooking. But Golda Meir relates in her memoirs that when she arrived at the newly established Kibbutz Merhavia, she found the members eating what she called "terrible food": vegetables that "weren't even cooked" in "some awful green oil," spicy olives "that are bad for you, as everyone knows." She took over with a firm hand, and from the day she entered the kitchen she "forced" (as she put it) her companions to desist from their wayward "native" habits, and to start their day with good, hot, cooked mush. Their feeble protests were soon stilled, and they adapted. No wonder it was Golda who later declared that there was no such thing as a Palestinian (by her lights, there wasn't) and that the palm of her hand would sprout hair if Anwar Sadat really came to Jerusalem. Food is a world view. It is the real relationship between man and his environment; it is enjoying all this bounty, or forcing and being forced.

I am a Levantine, because life in the claustrophobia of the present bores me, and I yawn in the thin air of European existentialism. I am a Levantine, because houses festooned with multicolored laundry flapping in the breeze don't bother me, and I like human habitations that are manageably sized and don't try to intimidate me, and I am not totally bound to the clock, and I like to talk to people who are different from me without being obsessed about "the bottom line" and without asking "What's the point?" and I won't miss a trip to Cairo because they haven't yet found a way of controlling sanitation in the streets (the last time you loved a woman, my agitated friend, was it because she showered twice a day?). But it bothers me no end to see a man fall down in the street, and go unnoticed for hours in a big Western city, clean, bustling, built in big verticals and big egos. Because at the base of my soul are stone, dome, and arch, not block, brick, and rectangle. What was that old Israeli song of the 1930s? "We shall cover you with concrete and cement!" Truly a curious desire! A Zionism depicted from the outset as an unaesthetic conquest.

I am a Levantine because I prefer summer to winter, and the happiness of date palms to the dusk of pine and fir. If I absolutely had to choose between two perversions of justice, I'm quite sure that bribery (God forbid!) is much more egalitarian than nepotism. I am a Levantine because I am certain that murders, little or big, perpetrated in the name of an ideology, are no better than those that are not, and socialism alienated from basic humanity is just another "ism."

I am a Levantine because I'm language-struck, and the rocky, sensuous, luminous languages of the Levant took root in me far more naturally than the languages of the West, which sometimes sound too soft for my ears. I am a Levantine because I write Levantine books. Because when I go to Egypt, I suddenly understand a great number of scriptural and linguistic concepts that were closed to me before, and this is happiness. Peace with our neighbors is the lifeblood of language-struck types like me, because we wish to return the language to its Semitic roots—in other words, rescue it from extinction. For us, as secularization progressed, our Hebrew deteriorated and became shallow and devoid of cultural resonance, a language out of context. Here, because of our exposure to the West rather than the Levant, people sometimes write American books in Hebrew, or Russian books in Hebrew, or French feuilletons in Hebrew. We have come to accept the fact that our newspaper articles contain ten measures of linguistic and cultural ignorance; that our educated class, which in every civilized country is the standard bearer of language, prefers to write in English—not even good English, but sociologese. And because the boundaries of man's language are also the boundaries of his world, it will soon be unclear which world we're talking about and whether it is worth perpetuating.

It is doubtful whether the Arab citizens of Israel can help us grapple with this problem, because they are now learning Hebrew (and often their Hebrew is better than ours), and they are becoming westernized. We need direct contact with the Arab world to finally reach a true linguistic confrontation with ourselves, far beyond the words themselves. Otherwise good, idiomatic Hebrew will become the exclusive domain of a few rabbis, yeshiva students, writers, and eccentrics, while most of the language will become a basic regional dialect—simplistic, bereft of associations, useless beyond the level of simple communication and technology.

I am a Levantine because I see war as the total failure of common sense, an execrable last resort. And because I am a Levantine, all fundamentalists on all sides, from Khomeini to Kahane, will always want to destroy me and all Levantines like me, here and in the neighboring countries.

A Levantine Nobel Prize laureate, Georgis Seferis, a Greek who lived for many years in Egypt, wrote:

> And things that came later had the self-same
> calmness which you see here,

they had this calmness because no soul
was left to us to think about,
none except the strength to carve some signs in stones
that touched now more deeply, beneath remembrance.

Thus wrote Georgis Seferis, a true Levantine. And the strength to carve signs in stones is for me the Levant, and is what makes it all worthwhile.

Strange Siwa ═══════════════════

TO REACH SIWA, AN OASIS IN Western Egypt, it is first necessary to cross a sea and a desert. The sea is the sea of permits required. The oasis is just forty-five kilometers from the Libyan border; it's a closed area, and the Egyptians are loath to allow unwarranted visits to it. The desert is a real one: hundreds of kilometers of a flat sand table, *musattaha* in local parlance, which caravans once took nine days and nights to cross before they reached Siwa and feasted their eyes.

But it is very much worth reaching Siwa, if only to see one of the places in the world where our myths were concocted. True, Egypt has other oases: Harga and Farafra and Dahla and Bahriya. But Siwa is unique; once the site of a *ma'abad*—a temple, literally a place of worship-work—it is as old as human memory.

So one morning you set out from the pure turquoise beach of Mersah Matruh, leave behind El Alamein and all the other places that have become markers of World War II, of the battles of Rommel and Montgomery, and, only a few kilometers south, come to another world, another history. A history that makes even World War II seem like just another episode in time, soon to be forgotten.

A desert then, sandy, vastly empty. Here and there are a few sparrow-wort shrubs, the ones whose branches you can peel down to green cords to make rope, as the Philistines did to tie Samson. Then the sparrow-wort gets sparse and disappears; all that remains is sand from one horizon to the other, and here and there a herd of thin, small camels, darker than the species we know.

The journey is hours long, and barren, until suddenly, practically without warning, the road comes to a kind of crater; a sheer drop to the bottom, and a world is revealed: forests of palm, a blue and white plain of lakes and salt flats, a sunburnt-brown town that sends forth a braying of asses, a sound that accompanies the sojourner all the days of his stay here.

What a lot of water! Siwa sits in a huge basin below sea level; beneath it in the depths of the earth is an ancient fossil sea. In essence, it is a water park full of burbling springs around which large, round pools were constructed; you can see the swell of the water, bubble by bubble.

There are great salt flats, too, some of them marshy, some of them hardened so you can walk across them, like in some science fiction landscape. There is also an artesian well from which the water shoots thirty meters into the air with ten-force atmospheric pressure; bits of pipe and hollow barrels bobbing on top of the fantastic flow are used to fill containers, wash beasts, and shower off fully dressed, laughing children. Amazing water. This is not the familiar house pet, the one that succumbs to the turn of a tap. This is an immense, wild beast that cannot be tamed, that no faucet can contain.

Water, tanned mud, salt, palm trees: all of them large, all of them in huge quantity, all of them in the heart of an empty desert. Is it any wonder that all who have come here, in every generation, have seen this as a special place, the home of a very great God?

Once upon a time there was an oracle here, *lux et veritas,* which people came from around the world to consult. The first name known to us is the Oracle of the god Ammon. Later the name was changed to the Oracle of Zeus, of Jupiter. It makes no difference. Alexander the Great came to consult it and, enlightened as he was, did not dispute the customs of the place or dishonor a soul. The oracle answered, bestowing upon him the title "Son of Ammon." Cymon of Athens sent his men here, and the oracle told them to leave. Pindar the poet asked for happiness and was rewarded with death. Lysander of Sparta tried to bribe the oracle and failed. Cambyses, son of Cyrus, came as a haughty white conqueror and did not get very far: his entire army was buried in a sudden sandstorm.

We did not see a sandstorm, such as historians tell us about. There were only a few of the usual columns of rising dust—"Satan's farts," as they are called here. Perhaps Ammon has lost his power. In his temple on the hill of Agurmi—that is, ancient Siwa—I try to contact him, but he is cosmic miles away. Perhaps it is monotheism—ours, Islam's—that has driven him so far away.

The 800-year-old city of Shali stands in its ruined entirety high above Siwa's shanties. Its skyline is very like curlicues of Arabic script, written on downward slants. Whoever ascends to the heights of Shali at sunset sees all around him the tanned houses and the sea of palms bathed in magenta light, and suddenly feels strange vibrations under his feet and through his body; he won't know what is happening until he hears, long and low, the *Allahu akbar*—"God is great"—that resonates sonorously in everything, in the deep-red air and the tremulous walls. Here and there is a door. One is open a crack; it seems there's a scent of hashish wafting from it. More is concealed than revealed.

Several hundred years ago only 600 people lived here. Today, about 11,000 do. They are not Egyptians. They are, and since the days of the pharoahs they have been, far from the center of government. They are Berbers; their origins are in North Africa; their language is Berber. Arabic is for the outside world, and for school.

It is quite obvious that this is not the Nile Valley. Unlike the Egyptians, whose openness and hearty affability are unparalleled, the residents of Siwa do not really want others to take any special interest in them—and they have their reasons.

All the wayfarers who ever were tell of the homosexuality practiced in Siwa. Britain's Belgrave, once governor of the region, wrote: "They are not immoral. They simply have no morals." In his day it was a matter of morality. As recently as 60 years ago formal homosexual marriages were held, complete with ceremonies and certificates, until King Fuad came along and said, "Enough." It seems they haven't invented anything new in San Francisco.

Some say the custom developed because of the *zaggala*, the caste of young men who for generations have composed Siwa's work force and nighttime civil defense. They come and go in the local homes, but do not own them. The *zaggala* have their own songs, their own customs. Years ago a Bedouin "madam" arrived with a few girls, prostitutes. Before long she had earned such influence that the sheikhs were afraid of her: all the *zaggala* supported her. The parties of the *zaggala*, attended by the other local young men, are known far and wide for their dances that are erotic to the point of ecstasy.

In Siwa you won't see a woman outside. In three days in Siwa we saw one woman walking briskly, and another group of four women, all cloaked in gray *milayas* from head to toe, four cloth cones sweeping quickly from house to house. Siwa is a man's world.

Children, however—both boys and girls—are completely free, outside and on the carts. Siwa's transportation is ass-drawn carts. One of our drivers, who sits behind the wheel of a cab in Alexandria every day of the year, says, "In this Siwa, every ass is a Mercedes." The braying can be heard everywhere, day and night. A band of toddlers aged three and four and five swarm the cart, bridle the ass with ten pairs of tiny hands, and off they go, a row of ten pairs of eyes peeping over the side of the cart.

There's also a place to rent bicycles, for the few tourists who come here. And indeed. between two salt marshes we stumble upon four young men, two Englishmen and two Germans, lying around doing sweet nothing, their bicycles parked among the palms. We tell one of them he'll be missing the reunification of Germany that night. He responds, "They can get reunified without me; it's more important that I be unified." He's right.

What can one say of the palms of Siwa to convey the color of their shade, the taste of their dates? The dates are smaller than those we know; their taste is that of a ripe tropical fruit, not at all sinewy. The fan of the palm glimmers, like real gold. Everything is made out of these palms: beams for the houses, shutters, thatch for the roofs, fences, mats, and baskets.

The houses themselves are made of mud. Not bricks fashioned from mud—just mud. And when once in a blue moon a stiff rain falls, all day and all night, the houses simply melt. They have just begun to bring in ugly, white commercial blocks for building. They are hardly the real thing, but at least the houses won't melt in the first rain.

Monotheists or not, it appears that we haven't disturbed the local gods, because that very night we learn we have fallen, by great good luck, on Siwa's principal festival: three days of celebration on the plain outside the city. What's the festival for? They don't really want to say. A local saint? No. A celebration commemorating a truce between two rival families? No. "Just a local party," they say, evasive. What's clear is that this is the start of the date harvest. The moon, too, cooperates: it is full.

When they say "festival," they mean a festival for men only. The women, as usual, stay home. Children up to age twelve—girls, too, who get betrothed on this occasion—do attend; they run around the plain in pink and blue sequined dresses, each with her own parasol. Fathers come, or uncles, leading ten or twelve girls in a row, just like in a class, all of them decked out, shyly coquettish, twirling their parasols.

An Egyptian television crew also shows up: unlike us, they knew about the festival. What happens next is a struggle between local custom, better left obscure, and the television crew, which, it seems, has paid the local notables and wants its money's worth. The residents do not quite cooperate.

What is kept from us we cannot know, but it is difficult not to feel the excitement. On the first day of the festival all the ass-drawn carts, decorated, trundle through the palm forest to the plain. Here outside the city, beneath a high mountain, the sacrifices are made. In the local language, the word for sacrifice is *kurban*—so it is pronounced.[1] Sheep and goats are brought one after another to the slaughterer on a ridge on the mountainside. Near the site of the sacrifice, groups of men pray ceaselessly. After a sheep is slaughtered according to ritual law, young men flock to the carcass and use sharpened sticks to separate the flesh from the hide, blowing furiously under the skin to make the skinning easier. The skinned carcass is then hung on the handlebar of a cart. upended for the occasion; it is rinsed thoroughly with water and separated into three parts, one of which will be consumed on each of the three days of the festival.

In the meantime the families build themselves booths, that's right, booths, *succot*,[2] at the edges of the plain. We don't yet know what purpose they serve. For a whole day sheep are slaughtered; the smell of their blood fills the area around the mountain. There isn't much compassion: not all of the sheep are completely dead when skinning begins. A runaway ewe gets no sympathy: she's pushed back in line, bleating fearfully.

All the next day, from early morning, carts keep flowing down the palm avenues, and the plain fills with people. Thousands of men take their places at the base of the mountain, children scurrying among them, everyone waiting. For what? We stand high up on a ridge; not one of us

---

1. The Hebrew word for sacrifice is *korban*. *Trans.*

2. Such booths, or *succot,* are built by Jews during the harvest festival of *Succot,* the Feast of Tabernacles. *Trans.*

fails to see the most explicit similarity between this and what took place at Mount Sinai: a mass of people, washed clean, wearing blue or blue and white *galabiyas,* stands on a plain below a mountain, stares at the mountain, and waits. But Moses is late in coming; he does not come; one hour passes, two hours, three. Instead, the television crew comes, and it's the people against the media; they shove a little, there's a lot of anger.

Finally, someone gives an order to break it up. A loudspeaker blares the command: every man to his tent. Those who have been standing facing the mountain go back to the booths they had prepared the day before. Row after row of boys carrying laden trays on their heads comes from the slaughter site, bringing meat to each man in his booth. The plain empties until evening. We rub our eyes, incredulous: after all, this week we celebrate the festival of Succot.

The meat left over from the festival, salted and dried for the days to come—there is no lack of salt in Siwa; a large white mound of salt sits between every three or four houses—is called *kadid.* This meat is eaten during the date harvest. We wonder if our *gadid*[3] is just the name for the activity of harvesting the dates, or if it implies the festival and its foods —that is, eating the fruit of the harvest. Here's another one for linguists: before the circumcision of a male child in Siwa, there is a ceremony of decorating his bed, and this ceremony is called *kashata.*[4]

The evening after the gathering is the most mysterious of all. It is the night of the *zikr,* a recalling of the names of God in rhythmic declamations and dances in circles to the point of ecstasy. This ceremony is for men only. Nary a girl child will be seen here once darkness falls. Whoever wishes can ponder the similarity between the primal word *zachar*[5] and this custom. Such was apparently our own ancient custom: a ceremonial recalling of the name of God, and not only in the sense of remembrance.[6]

As a group we decide not to go to this ceremony, to avoid provoking

---

3. *Gadid* is the Hebrew word for date harvest. *Trans.*
4. The Hebrew verb for decorating is *kashet. Trans.*
5. *Zachar* is the Hebrew word meaning "male." *Trans.*
6. "Remembrance," *zchira* in Hebrew, is based on the same root as is *zachar,* male. *Trans.*

unnecessarily. But Osnat, our woman-photographer, dresses up as a boy and, swift as a sprite, runs there without asking.

Apparently the negotiations with the Egyptian television crew ended well; maybe they simply paid more money in the end. As a result, the plain is floodlit, unnaturally, inauthentically. Ultimately, all the strangers retreat, leaving the men of Siwa on the plain alone with the full moon and their God, whom they call repeatedly by all the known names until dawn's light, until the words run out, and all that remains is the ecstatic, rasped call, Allah, Allah, Allah. Perhaps thousands of years ago it was Ammon, Ammon, Ammon.

The dawn breaks, innocent. The bus, which comes twice a week, is only a few hours late. Siwa closes up again, showing only her public face: a market, a gas station—actually one broken pump—a breakfast of wedges of cheese and broad beans at the dinky hotel.

We load up and set out to cross the *musattaha* back to the seashore, trying to recreate conversations, sights. Actually, no one knows if we really were in the depths of Siwa, and if we really understood everything coursing under the surface of this strange place, which celebrates a date harvest and Succot and the giving of the law at Mount Sinai, which makes sacrifices at the altar and, maybe, unlike us, can still make contact with the local prophecy.

Israel: The First Forty Years ══════════

Genuine and Less Genuine Tensions

A few years ago, an English tourist visited the zoo in an Arab capital. He was appalled at what he saw: the animals were neglected, the cages filthy; obviously, the denizens of the zoo were not being properly looked after. In the best English tradition, the tourist sought out the director of the zoo and asked him for an explanation of this scandalous state of affairs. The director sighed, rolled his eyes heavenward, and said, "What can we do, sir, it is all because of the Struggle."

For a generation, the struggle, or the war, or the possibility of war, or the existential conflict, or security, or the tension—everyone has his own favorite term—has served as an excuse for everything under the sun in Israel, for whatever is done or not done, whatever should be done but is not; it has wormed its way into everyday life. Ask the Israeli-in-the-street what he thinks the reason is for the bureaucracy, the high rate of road accidents, the rudeness one encounters from cab drivers, on the street, in offices; ask what the reason is for the decline of professionalism in almost every domain, for the growing tendency to "fake it," for the increasing negligence and indifference, the inability to tell the essential from the trivial, to distinguish between fact and mood, between quality and dilettantism; ask what the reason is for the Israeli's perpetual shortsightedness and impatience; for the almost obsessive covetousness, the xenophobia, the constant scowl—ask and you will be told, What can we do, there are security problems, there is tension, people are edgy.

Really?

Let's take a look at a few facts.

Between the War of Independence, which was genuinely a life-or-death conflict, a war for survival in every sense of the word, and the Lebanon War, which even according to Mr. Begin was an optional war—in this period of thirty-four long years we had only *five weeks* of all-out war involving the bulk of the IDF; and the individual soldier experienced far fewer combat days than that. Between the two events, during one thousand seven hundred and sixty weeks, we raised children, watered the plants, worked, studied, bought appliances for the house, ate, hiked, and paid income tax, some more and some less. None but we ruled the country: we were subjected neither to occupation nor to air raids. Our skies were and remain defended. In Israel today there are three times as many families that have lost their dear ones in traffic accidents as there are bereaved families from all the fighting and hostilities in the entire period. In the more intensive bloodshed, that on the roads, there has not been a single week of respite. When Ariel Sharon, attempting to justify the Lebanese adventure, spoke of "over one thousand victims of terrorism," there was, as one had come to expect with him, a considerable disparity between what he said and the truth. According to the IDF spokesman, terrorism had been on an absolute decline: in the three years preceding the Lebanon War, thirty-seven persons were killed in all hostile actions, and, in the year preceding the war—one. Surely even one is too many, and every person killed is a heartbreak. But let us bear in mind that in the Lebanon War, fought at Sharon's initiative, more Israelis were killed in two weeks than fell at the hands of the terrorist organizations in Israel's harshest security periods, including the periods of pursuit operations and massive IDF offensive actions against terrorists. The upshot, then, of presenting things as though Israel faced a threat to its existence, the danger of a holocaust, is that by our own talk and with our own hands we generate situations in which dozens or hundreds of times as many of our people fall as are killed in all the acts of terrorism combined, and without an iota of justification.

The truth is that despite the threatening rhetoric our politicians choose to employ—and Mr. Begin was apparently a past master at this—the state of Israel, since the War of Independence, has never faced a situation even remotely approaching a holocaust; and its strength today, including its nuclear strength, precludes such a situation for the foreseeable future. It was precisely to fulfill this mission that Israel was established, and to date it has done so admirably. The country's wars were fought not on our land, but on enemy territory. Our homes were not captured and our families were not herded onto trucks. When in the Yom Kippur War two neighboring states launched a major thrust against us, that war terminated not in our territory, but forty kilometers from Damascus and a hundred kilometers from Cairo. No one seized our lands: we were the ones who expropriated lands of others.

Terrorism, too, in the perspective of forty years, has failed. It dealt us a few severe blows, particularly in the state's first decades. But it proved absolutely unable to disrupt life in the country. Most terrorist attempts are discovered. Half an hour after the explosion of a bomb, or the dismantling of a bomb, life is back to normal. Not a single person refrains from taking a bus, or decides not to shop in the market, for fear of a bomb. If anyone intended to disrupt life completely in Israel, to create an atmosphere of fear in schools and public institutions to the point of their closure, to bring travel on the roads to a standstill, he has failed abysmally. And even if the overall security burden was quite heavy throughout, and will probably remain so for a long time to come, the vast majority of Israelis did not bear that burden on an everyday basis, with the exception of the tax burden, or the burden of reserve duty, which for the most part was not combat duty and was not even especially difficult. Soldiers maintain close contact with their families and get plenty of leave. The connection between the fighting echelon and the rear was never snapped. Our mode of life, for the most part, remained unaffected.

Perhaps we will gain a better perspective if we recall that in World War II there were soldiers and units who accumulated hundreds of combat days. Some did not see their families for five full years, while those families suffered under the burden of a horrific occupation or bombings on a scale that wiped out whole communities. Here, with the exception of five weeks in the course of thirty-four years, Israelis went about their affairs almost completely normally—and for this we all owe a debt of gratitude to the IDF, which, notwithstanding its mistakes and despite various hitches, has for forty years fulfilled its mission as the Israel *Defense* Forces.

This, together with the solid international sympathy Israel enjoyed in its early days, proved highly effective. True, the generation of Arab leaders in the 1950s and 1960s still thought and spoke in terms of eradicating Israel, throwing the Jews into the sea, and the like; and the Palestinian Covenant of 1964 well reflects that spirit. Let us not forget that the Palestine Liberation Organization (PLO) was founded by the Arab states three years *before* Israel occupied the territories; then it really wasn't Hebron or Nablus they were talking about, but Jaffa.

Had someone been able, in those first years, to foresee the future, and reveal to that generation of Arab leaders that they were destined to fail; that in the 1980s Israel would enjoy contractual peace with the largest Arab country, Egypt; that a quarter of a million Israelis would visit Egypt as tourists; that Israelis would visit Morocco officially and unofficially; that there would be open bridges and trade and thousands of hours of negotiations with Jordan; that for years not one shot would be fired on Israel's southern and eastern borders; and that the PLO itself, which for years spoke of liquidating Israel, would, having exhausted the operational option, speak of readiness for territorial compromise based on United Nations resolutions—those Arab leaders would surely have refused to believe it. What began as the insoluble Israeli-pan-Arab conflict split into elements, each different from the others, and all that is now left is the Palestinian problem, which is solvable. Of the Khartoum Conference's three "no's"—no to recognition of Israel, no to negotiations, no to peace—only the paper they were written on remains: we now have recognition, negotiations, and peace, whether de facto or de jure. The "fundamental, eternal and total conflict" has been reduced to one single issue. There is no arguing with reality, and even if one sometimes hears echoes of that thirty-four-year-old rhetoric, in this generation no one doubts the fact of Israel's existence, or that it will continue to be a part of the region. Some may accept this with gritted teeth, but there is nothing they can do about it. So it's a bit ridiculous to keep hearing—from our side—the old anxieties: "But they want Jaffa." Even if "they want," they won't get; besides which, the very point of negotiations is to get them to forgo their dreams of Jaffa, while we forgo our dreams of Hebron, and all of us start living normal lives. One can visit the Cave of the Machpelah (Tombs of the Patriarchs) in Hebron or Joseph's Tomb in Nablus with a visa, just as Israelis today attend the festivities at Damanhur, in Egypt. Israel is simply not targeted for destruction. Here there are no compromises. Where compromises can be made is in the matter of territories.

My contention is that the primary tension in Israel is not security tension. What generates the oppressive atmosphere is societal tension, or, more accurately, an array of societal tensions. Security tension has become a kind of emblem, or projection, of a great many other, but totally different, tensions within Israel; consciously or unconsciously, we are using what in an imprecise generalization is termed the "Arab-Israeli conflict," however undesirable and problematic it may be, as a projection, if not an excuse, for other unresolved conflicts within society and within individuals. These other, uniquely Israeli tensions, which have nothing to do with security, seem to exercise a deeper and more lasting influence than security tension—which has been exaggerated out of all proportion in our everyday life and in our rhetoric.

It is not my wish to understate the security tension. It exists, and with a good deal of objective justification. Some of the Arab states have not yet accepted our existence, and our northern border still bears a high potential of danger. Failure to solve the Palestinian problem is definitely liable to trigger a war, perhaps the most devastating we have known. Even if there have been only five weeks of full-scale combat in thirty-four years, in the other 1,760 weeks the next war was "with us," at least metaphorically. And there were periods of attrition, or pursuit operations, and there are the front-line settlements and bombs on Jerusalem buses and stones thrown at vehicles, though these are not war. But, really, does the rampant disrespect for the individual have anything to do with the shell fired during the night at northern Galilee? Is the fact that a large part of our intelligentsia does not speak Hebrew properly the result of the bomb planted at a bus stop? There have been societies, there have been intelligentsias, there have been social organizations in the world that functioned effectively even under occupation. There have been nations that returned to a quality-laden life, to creativity, courtesy, concern for the individual, almost immediately after calamitous destruction. There is an immense disparity between metaphor and fact, and anxiety about war is not the same as war itself. And when we are preoccupied with just one kind of tension—and not the principal kind, at that—we ignore other tensions in our society that are immeasurably more harmful than the tension and the anxiety entailed in security; and it is precisely those tensions that determine our everyday image. In the following paragraphs I shall attempt to analyze those tensions.

Land of Immigration

It is impossible to discuss today's Israeli society without taking into account the relevant facts and the social history of the past twenty years.

Some of the basic data are immutable. We live in a small country, lacking the sense of security provided by a broad continent. We have no great rivers, or vast deserts, or endless forests; our population is small and is for the most part concentrated near urban centers. We have few natural resources; and the level of the Sea of Galilee—and with it the entire quantity of water at our disposal for all our needs—is beyond our control.

With these data for openers, the society itself becomes immensely important. People are extremely interdependent: they must find ways to live together, talk to one another, solve problems together. The resilience of an orderly society lies in its ability to imbue each of its members with a sense of security: in their work, in their contact with institutions, in their economic expectations, in their opportunities of study and advancement.

The major contours of Israeli society were determined in the 1950s and 1960s, years in which the country's population doubled almost overnight. Overwhelming historical circumstances made Israel above all a land of immigration, or *aliyah* (literally "coming up," "ascending" in Hebrew). This is of crucial significance. A country of which the majority of the inhabitants are immigrants is a country where large numbers of the population underwent a total change in their lives at one age or another, a complete change, sometimes a traumatic one, of country, language, customs, climate, culture. Moreover, many of those who experienced this change were unable ever to see their land of birth again; their past was virtually obliterated in one fell swoop, wiped out as though it had never been. A country predominantly made up of immigrants is also a country in which most of the inhabitants cannot point to a normal sense of continuity in their lives, in contrast to other countries where the history of the inhabitants residing in the same place goes back hundreds, if not thousands, of years. One visits a village in Egypt and sees men and women with facial features remarkably similar to drawings that have survived from the ancient Nilotic culture; after at least seven thousand years of continuous habitation in one place, Egypt is, for good and for ill, a total culture.

By contrast, Israel is a collection of people most of whom, in spite of their likenesses, have undergone an uprooting. Some of us also went through the most shattering experience, the Holocaust, and then hardly said a word about it. Some of us still add up the grocery bill in Arabic;

others dream in Yiddish, or sing their children lullabies in English or Russian. Few among us can speak of a commonly experienced childhood. The *Song of the Neighborhood* sung by the legendary Israeli group, the Roosters, did not in fact evoke the childhood of most Israelis. Influences are passed on to the second generation, too. Clear and distinctive traits, for example, have been found to characterize children whose parents survived the Holocaust; clear and distinctive traits have also been found in children whose parents came from a specific Arab state. The patterns of the past—a person's wellsprings—are not easily expunged, and not in a single generation. Even if Ben-Gurion thought that "the very air of Eretz Israel produces wisdom," apparently by osmosis, and even if Golda Meir said patronizingly that "we will bring them here and turn them into human beings," reality proved them wrong. People do not "become Israelis" the moment they receive their immigrant's card and have their name changed arbitrarily by someone in school. (Incidentally, I was told by a social worker who worked with the recent Ethiopian immigrants that the Israeli educational system has still not learned the lesson. Ringing and flowery Israeli names are still being foisted on Ethiopian children in their new schools, much to the displeasure of both the children and their parents: a totally vacuous attempt at "instant socialization.")

Immigrants arriving in a long-established country possessing a clear identity and rooted cultural patterns, can, apparently, be easily absorbed. But in Israel things were never like that. Here the immigrants—and I am still speaking about the years of mass immigration, the 1950s and 1960s—encountered very few clear and rooted social, civil, or cultural norms to be ingested and emulated. We live in the midst of such a diversity of norms, beliefs, rules, and customs that it seems doubtful whether full social integration will be feasible even in the course of several generations. Perhaps the best reflection of this is the political atomization in Israel, which, more than it attests to academic differences regarding society, economy, and state—such differences are to be found in every country—is intimately related to the question of identity. Our vaunted melting pot did not do much melting after all. In England no great personal and cultural difference existed between Whigs and Tories. In the United States today, after two hundred years of independence, no salient and unequivocal differences can be found between Republican and Democratic voters (and the roots of many of them lie in different countries; some are secular, some are believers of differing degrees). In Israel things are different: immense basic differences exist between various groups of voters, and those disagreements go well beyond political outlook. A society of immigrants, particularly immigrants who lacked a clear role-model, is a society destined for group polarization and political violence. When personal identity is not sufficiently defined, politics, too, can become a characterizing and identifying competitive factor—it's like backing your home soccer team, whether it wins or not.

If so, our ingrained, everyday tension, the tension that is always with us, at home, in the street, on the bus, in offices, is societal tension; it is the most direct tension, and it affects Israeli life most forcefully. A large percentage of Israelis from all ethnic groups live with a feeling of social dissatisfaction, a feeling of incomplete or uncompleted absorption, under the impact of a socialization process that was not properly internalized and in some cases involved a fairly brutal shattering of cultural patterns, parental authority, religious and cultural authority, and the authority of the community. All this is true without anyone's being able to say precisely what, at the individual and family level, constitutes "correct Israeliness."

All this happened not only because in Israel of the 1950s and 1960s, as elsewhere, the concept of the social melting pot was still prevalent. It happened because Israel took on itself, in the 1950s especially, the impossible task of immigrant-absorption at a 1:1 ratio—one absorber per one immigrant. Within a brief period the population was more than doubled, in a country that had been in existence for only a few years, a country with no economy to speak of, without natural resources, besieged by hostility, immediately after a Holocaust that ravaged its sources, and following a war in which one out of every hundred Israelis was killed. The inevitable result was that beyond the most elementary material absorption, there was no absorption. By comparison, many Australians complain about an excessive immigration rate that is untenable in a properly run state—they are talking about 2 percent a year!—and Australia is a rich country, blessed with plentiful natural resources, boasting an enviable economy, and facing no security problems. To be sure, the professionals disagree about the feasible pace of social absorption, one that does not erode the established patterns of society and does not perpetuate the classic problems of a country made up entirely of immigrant groups; but there is no disagreement that the rate of absorption (or quasi absorption) in Israel in the 1950s and 1960s was impossible, and entailed a very heavy price in sharing and sense of sharing. Under these conditions, one must ask what remains that is shared. Israeli youth point to military service as virtually the only saliently Israeli experience (and therefore hate Arabs and the ultra-Orthodox because they do not serve), but patently, this is not an experience on which a total identity and culture can be built. But under the law this is the shared experience of all groups, dating back to the 1950s and 1960s. This fact, too, has far-reaching ramifications.

We live, then, in a country that for years was subject to the constant shock of sweeping and too-rapid changes, on every street, in every settlement, in every school, leading to a pervasive sense of transience, instability, and discontinuity. These phenomena generated profound unease not only among immigrants vis-à-vis absorbers, but also among absorbers vis-à-vis immigrants—the anxiety of the veteran population in Israel, which is not talked about enough. Every wave of immigration was greeted by someone who said, *Yin'al din al-babour illi jabhoum* (Curse the name of the boat that brought them).[1] But few among us suspected that a situation of this kind almost invariably creates group stereotypes regarding everything that is strange and foreign. In the 1950s and 1960s it was the stereotype of "the Poles," "the Yekkes" (German Jews), "the Moroccans," "the Iraqis," followed by "the Anglo-Saxons" (Americans and other English speakers), "the Russians," "the Georgians," "the Persians." This stereotypic thinking seems to have become more sophisticated over the years, as it is no longer saliently ethnic and communal, although it remains resolutely groupthinking: "Laborites, Likudniks, religious, reporters, PLOniks, feminists, Nazis, leftists, bleeding hearts," and so on. No perception of the individual exists; there is a group label for everything and everyone. Apparently, there is a limit to a person's ability to withstand deep social change over many years.

This can be exemplified by a totally different sector: cab drivers. Alongside the courteous and correct driver, there is also the cabbie who is rude and who never stops cursing and complaining, who tries to cheat on the meter and who makes the ride a nightmare even for Israelis, let alone

---

1. A popular curse in colloquial Arabic.

tourists. Yet this very driver, if he happens to have regular passengers and gets to know them, that is, knows something about them, where they live, what they do for a living, their regular destinations, whether they like the air conditioning on or not—this same driver will become one of the boys; the driver will speak politely, be convivial, and wouldn't think of coming on aggressively. It emerges that there is a fairly intense cumulative effect to the whole situation of high turnover in conditions of personal anonymity, and not everyone can cope with this. That unpleasant cab driver will function far better socially in a situation where a certain closeness has been established, a kind of expanded "familiality," than that driver will in a situation in which the traveling room (which is what a taxi is) is constantly being invaded by strangers with whom the driver has little prospect of social interplay even when a common interest exists, and even that little is probably being constantly eroded.

This, in a nutshell, is the situation in a land of immigration in which the changes were too deep and too fast.

Social Overload

What I have described thus far is a given situation, historically and otherwise immutable. Israel was obliged to absorb every one of the waves of immigration at the pace dictated by events and without any predetermined order: this was the country's raison d'être. Despite all the vexations, people had a fierce desire to create something shared here, something they could identify with, proudly, in a good spirit. Nor can it be denied that something began to gel in the 1950s and early 1960s—I need but mention entertainers such as Hagashash Hahiver,[2] the Roosters, *Shlomo and Shalmai*,[3] or the new homegrown slang. And even if Israelis lived with an unviable economy, outside help and support were constantly pouring in, in the form of Jewish fund raising, foreign aid, German reparations. People worked. Something new was being created. Factories were set up. The new society began to coalesce. No longer the old Yishuv[4]: something Israeli, something new.

But the nascent sense of continuity and the feeling of partnership and

---

2. Israel's most popular and longest-surviving comedy trio.
3. A very literate musical produced by the Cameri Theatre.
4. The Jewish community in Palestine before 1948.

of a shared culture were abruptly snapped in the summer of 1967 with the conquest of a large swath of land in the West Bank and the Gaza Strip, an unplanned occupation, encompassing a sizable population that within a dozen years would constitute almost half the total population of this region.

No one had any illusions about the possibility of absorbing these people in the emerging Israeli society. That was never in the cards. The country was supposed to be a Jewish state with a population sharing a common, fundamentally Jewish background, but receptive to the absorption of a not-too-large minority. It is almost certain that if in 1967 it had been put to Israelis that the country should absorb the entire Arab population of the territories, as the new immigrants were absorbed, the idea would have been rejected out of hand. The tendency was to see the territories, but to close one's eyes to the people there. The country's leaders at the time, and the overwhelming majority of its inhabitants, who had just been released from a period of great anxiety, did not look on the territories as something permanent, but as a bargaining card in future negotiations; hence the situation of the Arab residents there became "permanently temporary," and therefore—presumably—no decision was required. Immediately after the Six-Day War, I heard Chief of Staff Moshe Dayan say in the Tel Aviv Press Club that "the present borders of Eretz Israel may be ideal borders, but it is unrealistic to think that we will be able to maintain them indefinitely." The concern was for ensuring the security of the young country, no more. Certainly there was no talk of prolonged rule over another people.

The expected phone call from Jordan's King Hussein did not materialize, as everyone knows, and twenty years went by without anyone making a concrete and binding decision concerning the fate of the population in the territories, whose numbers had greatly increased in the meantime. It is a fruitless exercise to speculate today what could have happened if we had left the territories immediately, while still crowned with the victor's glory, and what kind of relations would have formed, in a slow process, as measured as the flow of Siloam's waters, between two neighboring populations interdependent in affairs of work and welfare and trade, but not in a situation of occupier and occupied, without military rule. Without detentions, without deportations, without settlements, without the deep residue of bitterness left by the relations of the past twenty years.

In reality, of course, it didn't happen that way. Instead, an administrative vacuum was created, a decision-making void, into which leaped opportunists with ideas of establishing a Greater Israel now, right away, by exploiting Israel's strength, and with no hesitation about undercutting both the rule of law and the IDF itself. No political decision was made. The situation that emerged on the ground, even without the annexation of the West Bank, was one in which the inhabitants of the territories, in practice, entered our social fabric without having been incorporated in a political settlement; and that development undermined the entire social infrastructure that had just begun to exist. One hundred and twenty thousand or more laborers enter Israel every day to do work that Jews no longer do. Industries set up cheap-labor plants in the territories, generating a backward colonial economy. We live side by side with people who not only do not share our identity and culture—not to mention our language and traditions—but who are subject to a law different from that to which Israeli citizens are subject; indeed, they are at the whim and mercy of every policeman or soldier manning a roadblock. In the area controlled by Israel, half the population are citizens in a reasonably functioning democracy, while the other half, who are not citizens, live under occupation. The two groups share nothing in the way of identity, principles, expectations, laws, rights, hopes. A sense of alienation holds sway, compounded by an almost polar political interest. There is no possibility, let alone desire, to find a common social-national denominator, a universally acceptable identity.

Moreover, the situation profoundly modified the newly emergent Israeli identity. From being freedom fighters who had successfully defended ourselves, we became overlords, and lately also oppressors. David became Goliath, without anyone deciding so, without a national consensus, without planning; the country careened downhill, out of control.

Even societies larger and stronger than our own could not have coped with an upheaval of this magnitude. Israel, a problem-riddled nation of just over four million inhabitants, is almost buckling under it, and not from the security viewpoint: we can very likely hold the West Bank for some time to come, despite the constant harm caused the IDF in training and in the feelings of its soldiers. The collapse is entirely social.

Some people believe that the recent events in the territories prove, to whoever still needed proof, that the status quo cannot be maintained indefinitely, without political movement toward a solution. I believe that

Israel should get out of the territories even if not one more stone is thrown, for the simple reason that 55 percent cannot rule 45 percent who are not citizens, neither with a strong hand nor with a soft hand, not with a hand outstretched in force and not with a hand bearing gifts, not by fear and not by trembling, because the consequence is the destruction of the society and its identity. This is a permanent no-win situation in which we have placed ourselves for the past twenty years, one that bears permanent potential for war, a war that Israel will win militarily, but in which seven thousand Israeli soldiers will be killed, according to estimates of the *minimalists* in the IDF. Militarily, Israel can sustain that result. Socially, it cannot. Israeli society's ability to cope with attrition is high; it is not unlimited. To cure itself of its ills, which have multiplied alarmingly in recent years, Israel requires calm and quiet, not the occupation of a population almost its own size that it can neither spew out nor swallow, and most certainly not another war. Under a social overload of this scale a society inevitably bursts apart at its seams, as a society, as a culture, as an entity.

Individual versus Society

At the end of the 1960s and in the early 1970s the territories did not yet constitute the permanent cause of societal tension that they do today. A sense of anticipation prevailed; the IDF did not sit in the midst of population centers, indeed it refrained from entering such areas. Jewish settlement commenced only in the late 1970s and was not yet a numerical or political provocation, although there were some prescient enough to understand that the clashes of newly-born Gush Emunim with the law of the land and the IDF in their first attempt to settle at Sebastia were an indicator of that body's future course of action.

Moderate Palestinian leaders in the West Bank, such as the late Kadri Toukkan, spoke appreciatively of the authorities' "kid-gloves" policy—an approach that defused all desire to revolt. The population of the West Bank was far smaller than it is today—about half the size—and the numerical disparity between the refugees and the indigenous inhabitants, particularly in the Gaza Strip, was much less significant.

True, already then workers from the territories streamed into Israel, usually through the brokerage of *ra'isim* (bosses) and the disgraceful exploitation of workers of both sexes. But relatively speaking, this was a limited phenomenon, still accompanied by a feeling of shame on the part of the Israeli who had been raised to do his own work, steeped in the ethos of manual labor. At the same time, a kind of slumber set in, a freeze in the political process that was of course illusory, but contributed much to the pervasive feeling among Israelis that all was for the best, and that since nothing succeeds like success, Israel need do nothing, for its future was assured for a century at least.

This sense of victory, which was permeated with considerable arrogance —an understandable human reaction, perhaps, to the former sense of fear —certainly did nothing to ameliorate, and in fact undoubtedly exacerbated, one of the most acute of the tensions in Israeli society: the tension of the individual versus the society. Any prospect of mitigating this tension that may have existed grew more difficult after 1967: dialogue becomes all but impossible in a community so strong, so supercilious, and so successful. It doesn't hear.

With the wisdom of hindsight, it now seems possible that some of Israel's unremitting and alienating changes could have been overcome (I refer to the tension analyzed in the first section of this essay) if Israeli society, at bottom, showed concern and care for individuals and was genuinely attentive to their needs, if it established a relationship of dialogue and not of patronizing dictates from above. Patently, every group undergoing a socialization process consists of a certain number of individuals, each of whom is being socialized or absorbed at a personal level.

Israeli society, however, in which each and every individual is exhorted to participate maximally in the life of the commonality, in body and in capital, and is called upon to demonstrate a feeling of involvement with events around him (where else in the world do people listen to the news every hour on the hour but in Israel?), that society never learned to treat the individual respectfully and honorably, in a relationship of true dialogue. Israelis always absorb immigration but disregard the immigrant ("Don't let them tell you otherwise, we gave them"); talk about the underprivileged but don't know how to deal with one low-income family ("Don't let them tell you otherwise, there's a welfare-allowance law, and that's that"); educate, optimally, a class, or a youth group, but the teacher often has no idea about the stresses of the individual pupil ("He saw I was busy, he could have approached me later").

Cogent historical reasons brought about a situation in which not only are the individual's needs ignored and his stresses unnoticed—not to mention his uniqueness, including his criticism of ourselves—but in which a constant process is at work that relentlessly represses the individual's needs and feelings. We behave as though only the plural exists, completely oblivious of the fact that the plural is made up of a great many singulars, and when things are bad for each of them, they aren't good for the whole either.

This situation did not come about in the 1960s or even the 1950s; its origins greatly predate the state. Its roots are to be found in the generation of the founding fathers, who determined the patterns of life here for many decades, perhaps having no other choice at the time. The roots of our group-thinking, which was greatly reinforced by the immigrant society, actually lie in the founding fathers' ideology of "the submergence of the individual."

That generation consisted overwhelmingly of people who themselves performed the most difficult surgery in their own lifetime—and did so voluntarily. That generation cut itself off completely, as an ideology, from their past background—not only as a necessity but also as a world view.

The move from "an inhabited country to a backward land," as the song went, was an almost violent passage for the individual and his sensibilities, and it entailed the forfeiting of individuality, to be "born again" within a group. There were some who, ashamed of their origin, placed a heavy emphasis on the new group identity they had chosen. The price was prodigious, even at the time: the early years of Zionist settlement in Palestine are replete with stories of suicide, collapse, bodily and mental anguish; the sound of weeping at night is an almost permanent counterpoint to the refrain of pioneering Zionism.

There was a tremendous desire to submerge the "I." Individuation was nearly tantamount to a sin. For a time, in the first kibbutzim, it was thought undesirable for a child to know who its biological parents were, the better to enable the group framework to succeed the individual family and its role.

Much has changed since then, and recent studies have demonstrated the overriding influence of the biological family in the kibbutz. But the attempt to expunge all individuation for the sake of the group was typical

of the founding generation, and "we," "the whole," "the group" solidi-
fied into a virtually unbreakable mold.

It is quite possible that given the huge, unprecedented tasks that faced
the founders, the group pattern was a proper working instrument for the
time; without it, the Zionist revolution might never have occurred. This is
retrospective wisdom.

But harshness toward the individual became a fact of life, a fact of
existence, and today no one can say whether things could have been done
a little better, a little more considerately: to allow the mother to visit her
sick child in the hospital and not make do with a visit by the class nurse;
to be a little more attentive to personal predilections, to softer feelings. It
is not at all certain that Zionism would have collapsed. But this, too, is the
wisdom of hindsight.

Let us not forget that the first generation of children who grew up in
Palestine was in large part a generation without grandparents, of whom
the great majority remained in the Diaspora, outside the pioneering
framework. This fact, too, brought about a harsher outlook on life, less
pampered, less compassionate. The young, inexperienced parents had to
deal with the business of life and the family without the possibility of
turning to their old people for help—so they became more severe and less
empathic than was needed.

And when the families who had remained abroad perished in the
Holocaust, all these feelings were overlaid with a sense of guilt—the Guilt
of Noah, it can be called, for Noah, too, according to Scripture, did not
take his parents on the Ark. In the diary of one of the founding fathers, I
came across a bitter, self-lacerating poem. I quote one stanza:

> Perhaps between one burning village and the next
> You cried out there, my brother, when your heart's blood
>   poured:
> "You forgot my life. To you I was expendable.
> "You threw my body to its death in a foreign land."

As required by the ethos and the era, the poem remained hidden in the
personal diary. The hardness toward the individual, which was not only
an ethos but almost a religion, required of the individual absolute silence
regarding his own hardships. That ethos ensnared Holocaust survivors,

who for a long time said nothing about their experiences; it ensnared parents and their children, disadvantaged youth, persons caught in insensitive surroundings, soldiers who suffered horrors no one knew about. Almost until the past decade, Israel was not only a society of immigrants, it was also a society of persons who had undergone dreadful experiences—but were silent.

Under these conditions, it is not surprising that a deep need was created—fundamentally defensive—to justify everything done in Israel unreservedly, for good or for ill, accompanied by an ingrained intolerance of criticism (for otherwise, if things are bad, why did we suffer and endure guilt—and how we suffered!). This incapacity manifested itself in its most acute form during the period of immigrant absorption after the establishment of the state, when we turned a deaf ear to the new immigrants' needs. The criticism they voiced, which was unquestionably a form of social participation, was ignored: Do what you are told—or be silent. After all, we, too, were silent.

The unstated rationale was: If I could effect a great change in my life and become an instant Israeli, "one of the boys," so can you. And because this model worked in my generation and in the struggles of my period, don't argue with success; get used to it.

The trouble is that this recipe didn't work for the waves of immigration after the establishment of the state, for they had very different, and perhaps saner, ideas of what it meant to be an Israeli. I refer to the immigrants from North Africa as well as the immigrants from North America and England—communities for whom the suprapersonal, suprafamily group recipe was neither a Zionist nor a personal ideal.

The result is visible to this day. Israel, despite all its shared, binding elements, is a country full of angry people, harboring longstanding resentment and insult, never resolved.

Instant Israelization

From this perspective the absurdity of positing Israel as a country of Western culture becomes strikingly apparent. Axiomatic in Western culture is the attitude toward the individual, his expectations, and rights. Israel is, apparently, the only country in what is called the West that to this day lacks a constitution assuring the elementary rights of the individual. Even if, technologically, in sophisticated industry, we can compete with some Western countries, the fact is that computers, Danish furniture, and VCRs do not make a society and a culture, and cannot assuage the salient Israeli tension: that of the individual against the society.

This state of affairs is still reflected in the relations between the individual and what the public regards as the representatives of the community: the bureaucracy and the police. Forty years after the establishment of the state, the violence of the security forces or the arbitrariness and officiousness of the bureaucrats do not trigger the appropriate protest. In the confrontation between the individual and the community, or its representatives, apparently individuals are not really in the right; anyhow, they're not going to be pampered, especially if they are Arab. This is the polar opposite of Western culture, and it leads one to suspect that perhaps our vaunted Westernness is really only a form of anti-Easternism or anti-Arabism—unabashed racism.

What happens, then, when socialization is insufficient, integration incomplete, when there is so much repression in a family or a group or among individuals in which cultural continuity, tradition, and emotional feelings are relentlessly dislocated?

In the first place, people, despite everything, want to belong, to be partners, to feel that they are part of a whole society. The quickest—and most dangerous—way to achieve this is by identifying with a common myth. The myth need have no connection to reality. Its function is different. It is an instant answer to a subjective need, not a substantive entity. It is a tribal code that can also serve as a form of tribal drug, concocted by the tribe's various witch doctors.

If the individual feels weak and helpless, the Holocaust is made into a universal, pan-Israeli symbol of a sense of helplessness; and every fear that has a real or imaginary cause immediately becomes Holocaust anxiety. This is what we were raised on. Every ten-year-old in a refugee camp who throws a stone becomes a symbol of Auschwitz; it threatens us. Everyone knows and identifies this collective code immediately.

If the individual feels neglected, discriminated against, and unprotected as a person, as an individual, as a personality, the Arab-Israeli conflict becomes the all-embracing symbol of his plight. One can always be an "Israeli patriot," as part of a group, and curse "the Arabs" as a whole, as a group, indiscriminately.

Such attitudes are speedily rewarded in the form of an immediate feeling of identification and partnership with the society and its myths—a kind of instant belonging and more, instant identity, at least for a short time. Many of the Jews who came to Israel from the Soviet Union took as their symbol of Jewish identity Messrs. Kahane and Sharon without knowing the first thing about them. The reason: Radio Moscow was always flaying them, and these Jews genuinely thought that espousing the opposite of whatever Radio Moscow said would transform them quickly into authentic Israelis, make them more Jewish. Only after a lengthy period in Israel, with incipient socialization, does Radio Moscow cease to exert an influence, and the true picture begin to come clear.

Why must we oppose so resolutely these tribal codes, together with the marginal interest they may hold out? Why should it concern us if people forge symbols and a mythology for themselves, if these play some kind of functional role in the socialization process?

Because this Israeli mythology, even if it affords a momentary sense of belonging, an Israeli "trip" at cut rate, twists and distorts reality. And if there is one country in the world that can't afford to eschew reality, even for a minute, it is Israel.

It is a safe assumption that many readers of this essay were surprised by the figure with which it opened: only five weeks of war in thirty-four years. Recent years have witnessed a growing reliance on emotional knowledge as a substitute for hard facts; what the average Israeli sees as a known fact, a hard given, on the country's fortieth anniversary, is very often false.

Ask anyone on the street how many mixed marriages, between Jews and Arabs, are performed in Israel. There must be quite a few thousand, will come the reply. Actually, since the establishment of the state, the percentage of such marriages stands at 0.0004! A youth group asked by its leader not long ago how many Jews and how many Arabs live within the Green Line, replied that there were about 3 million Jews and 12 million [sic] Arabs.[5] In the same way, "everybody knows" that Sadat was assassi-

---

5. The Green Line is synonymous with the borders of Israel before the Six-Day War, i.e., Israel not including the territories. Arabs living within those borders are full citizens of Israel, who number at the time of publication about 800,000. Since no Israeli government ever annexed the territories, their Arab inhabitants are not citizens of Israel. In 1995, their number is estimated at close to 3 million.

nated because he signed a peace treaty with Israel (whereas he was actually gunned down by fundamentalists because of his attitude toward Islam, which included derision of traditional customs).

Others "know" that Neville Chamberlain was a bleeding-heart compromiser, a naive peacenik, who went to make peace with Hitler and became a symbol of Europe's surrender. The historical truth is that Chamberlain set out in full knowledge of the situation, his government having assigned him the task of delaying Hitler for a year or two, after the Cabinet had been informed that it would be two years before Britain's aircraft industry could supply the Royal Air Force with fighter planes to defend England's skies. Following Chamberlain's death, Churchill lauded him profusely for having accepted the thankless task of becoming the butt of the free world's vilification—and the savior of England.

Thus also, during the recent events it was the less-sane left, who "knew" that "Israel is burning"—referring to Israel inside the Green Line —whereas in fact fewer than one-tenth of one percent of all Israeli Arabs took part in the disturbances of the intifada.

Under these conditions, with this disparity between "public knowledge" and the truth, in a climate where what counts is not the facts but the mythology, we can go on talking about a "total conflict for our very survival with twenty-two Arab states" even in the reality of the late 1980s, when that notion has been completely expunged from the rhetoric and politics of the majority of the region's states, and when peaceful relations, whether de jure or de facto, exist with many of them.

Nor is this myth the exclusive purview of the Israeli right. Not long ago a kibbutznik from the Hashomer Hatza'ir movement, replying to a young Arab woman who asked why Arabs were refused membership in kibbutzim, said that the kibbutzim wanted to refrain from placing the Arabs in an untenable situation, since Israel was involved in a "total conflict for our very survival with twenty-two Arab states." This is absolute nonsense, unless the kibbutznik couldn't come up with something better to tell his interlocutor, who was an Israeli Arab, with whom he certainly was not involved in a conflict for survival, total or otherwise.

A typical example of how all-pervasive the mythology is was provided by a well-known journalist who, on the day of the general strike by Israeli Arabs in December 1987, wrote that "this is the end of education for democracy, this is the end of [Jewish-Arab] teachers' encounters." On that same day Tel Aviv University held a special study day for Jewish and

Arab teachers, and not one was absent. Indeed, not only are such encounters continuing, but part of the fact that 99.9 percent of Israel's Arab citizens have never violated the law or standing of the state by one iota, not even on the day of the general strike, can apparently be credited to education for democracy and the approach it stands for. So why expend emotions?

The price of these mythologies, all of which are verbal and around which all the self-excitation is also primarily verbal, lies not only in the loss of credibility of media people or politicians. Their credibility is problematic in other countries too. In Israel the price is far higher. He who sows myth, reaps hysteria; and when it is hysteria and not facts that dictates our actions, it is here that the danger to Israel's survival lies.

Only against this background can Sharon hold up the threat of "Katyushas hitting Ashkelon" if, heaven forbid, the Gaza issue is resolved; only against this background could Mr. Begin, the high priest of fear, liken Arafat to Hitler; and only against this background can Kahane and the leaders of the ultranationalist Tehiya Party—there is no longer much to differentiate between the two groups—evoke Auschwitz every time a stone is thrown at a bus.

The nondifferentiation between Israel of the 1950s and Israel of the 1980s—the it's-all-the-same-stew syndrome—is our prevailing hysteria. The inability to grasp that the Arab leaders of the 1980s are not those of the early 1960s is hysteria. To think that Egypt's Husni Mubarak wants to throw us into the sea, and that King Hussein wants to set up gas chambers for us, and that King Hassan is just waiting for the chance to conquer Jaffa, and that all of them are one endless Amalek—that is hysteria and that is the danger.

This writer said in October 1967, in an article in *Ha'aretz,* that if we hold on to the territories, the first consequence will be that we will start lying to ourselves. That is exactly what happened, very rapidly, and that is what is happening today, when a weak population, deprived of citizenship and rights, lacking arms and the means to defend itself, is claiming its rights —a claim that is consonant with the Israeli social interest itself—but is reflected in our warped mirror as actually threatening the existence of the state. Not only an outsider will have trouble understanding this; so will the historian of the future.

The worst of it is that these tribal mythologies leave us with no alternative, no scale of possibilities, no prospect of culture, no choice of identity—except to be either murderers, the murdered, or both. As though Israel had no other identity. As though this were the essence of being Israeli. As though, in the biggest lie of all, this were Judaism.

Myths inherently block any possible change; that is evidently their raison d'être. Certainly they are utilized for this purpose. After all, it is far easier to point to the security situation as the root of all our troubles, and thereby shift the responsibility from ourselves to others ("the Arabs," "the region") than to admit that the dominant Israeli tensions, including the tension of holding on to territories containing a million and a half people, are basically social tensions, and hence their solution depends on us.

As that zoo director put it: "Everything is neglected—it is because of the Struggle." He probably knew he was reciting a well-worn excuse. He winked as he spoke. Here, we have forgotten the difference.

Thus is a disorderly society created.

The State as a Perennial Dilettante Show

On the face of it, there are at least three elements around which a continuous and more complete social and cultural model can be built, even in a society of immigrants with a traumatic past. These elements are the rule of law as a nondiscriminatory universal authority that guarantees individual rights; language, which is a normative system accessible to everyone, with all its richness and pleasures; and a knowledge of the common sources and traditions.

A society can indeed rest on these three qualitative foundations. The United States, for example, also a country of immigration, albeit under nothing like Israel's conditions, from the outset took great care to institute the rule of law and adopt an exemplary constitution. Language has throughout constituted the cornerstone of cultural absorption in America—even if reservations are perhaps in order about the required level.

The ethnic groups in the United States that were not adequately socialized did in fact produce organizations and subcultures like the Mafia or the hate groups, which do not accept the prevailing rule of law. By behaving in this manner they demonstrate their nonabsorption and nonbelonging; most of them remain outside the law, largely outside the language, as it were (by using their former language or creating a distinctive vernacular), and outside the common tradition as well—the three socializing elements in an immigrant society.

In its early days, Israel, despite the insecurity about survival and the prevailing social disarray, did manifest an intuitive tendency to maintain these three norms; people tended to view them as solid props even when problems of socialization exceeded the personal capacity to cope with them. Here a contribution was made by personalities and whole groups from virtually all the waves of immigration. Even those consumed with personal resentments, and there are many such in our midst today, considered the norms of the rule of law, language, and knowledge of the Tradition in the most general sense a source of social pride. The national consensus upheld all three. Azulai the Policeman, as portrayed in the film of the same name by the late beloved comic actor Shaike Ofir, was a salient cultural entertainment model of this shared approach in the state's early years.

In the 1980s, all three norms are showing signs of erosion and disintegration. Cracks have appeared in the rule of law, which was supposed to be a normative common denominator, transcending all differences of culture, identity, and customs. These cracks are caused by consistent assaults, principally from one end of the political spectrum and because of party and political considerations.

Expertise in language did not become a challenge for those who should have been its main exponents, our educated class, and certainly not for the media or the street. Our language is becoming impoverished and unidiomatic, and in part it is simply translated from English.

For certain circles, knowledge of the Tradition became a demand to practice traditional customs, and the majority, in consistently rejecting this demand, has also turned its back on knowledge of the Tradition itself.

What happens when a relatively small immigrant society, insufficiently socialized and living in a small country; which has accustomed itself to thinking in group terms and subsuming the individual; which from the outset has a deep residue of concerns and social erosion—what happens when this society is told that its problems are insoluble and that it is caught up in a hundred-years war for its very survival?

The first thing that emerges is a growing sense of transience, of uncertainty, a feeling that in any case there is no point in being industrious, in investing for the long term, in seeking quality, excellence, professionalism, doing something serious. Everything becomes a momentary fling. Numerous domains in Israel in which the standard of professionalism has declined and is continuing to decline are gradually, inevitably, becoming areas of dilettantism for which professional training is no longer required —at times one has the impression that the only required document is a birth certificate.

In the realm of politics, where no great importance is attached to a purely professional expertise and where power struggles are the name of the game, the majority of appointments are made not on the basis of merit or professional ability, but according to intergroup power politics.

This kind of compromise between groups is not confined to Israel and is not always a negative phenomenon. When a country has a large population that recognizes a certain professional ethos, every political group will be found to contain, and select, at least a few serious politicians who are also professionals in their fields. In our small and fractious population not every group contains professionals, for the simple reason that there are not enough professionals in every field—the country is simply too small. The upshot is that selection becomes a raucous power game that has nothing to do with substance and merit: it comes down to a contest between dilettantes from one group against dilettantes from another group.

Few of our cabinet ministers are professionals. The number of Knesset members who have even the faintest notion of what strategic thinking means, of a proper decision-making process, of how and from whom information should be obtained and accountability demanded is negligible. Decisions that determine the course of our life are frequently made at the dilettante level. The decision to launch the Lebanon War is a scandalous example of this kind of amateurishness: it was not preceded by any kind of professional thinking, and all the Cabinet ministers knew was that they were supposed to raise their hands in favor.

It is similarly unclear what prior level of factual information, and what level of professional political assessment of the anticipated consequences, preceded the government's "hard-line decision" regarding the territories, a decision taken when the riots had already been going on for a week and the only response available to the small groups of soldiers was to open fire. It is extremely doubtful that this subject underwent any comprehensive prior study. All that was left was to improvise, as it were, in the worst Israeli tradition.

Almost everyone knows that at the political level in Israel things are not as professional as they might be. Few understand that the dilettantism runs from top to bottom: the political unprofessionalism and the substandard level of people on our key committees are merely a reflection of an overall social malaise.

Year by year Israel looks more like a dilettante state. Thousands are killed on the roads because of dilettante drivers, whose number is legion. Dilettante contractors build construction hazards; a dilettante plumber "releases" a drain blockage by blocking the neighbor's pipes; a dilettante clerk shifts a citizen's problems from one department to another instead of solving them by his own authority. We have dilettante department heads and dilettante therapists. Dilettante journalists fail to check facts, paraphrase instead of quoting interviewees, are incapable of writing or speaking a single foreign-language term without a mistake or of pronouncing people's names correctly (Ulmert or Olmert? Nehamkin or Nehemkin? concensus or consensus?), and have the effrontery to ask what difference it makes anyhow. We have bookshop proprietors who have long ceased to be literate—dilettantes who could just as easily sell soft drinks or tampons.

In Gush Emunim and its periphery we have dilettante rabbis for whom any profundity of Jewish thought is remote, as are fundamental Jewish values such as individual accountability, the rule of law, or equality before the law. Not to mention their deliberate forgetting that the Torah completely rejects collective punishment or that midrashim enjoins us to respect the rights of non-Jews (such as the midrash that says Esau was engaged in fulfilling the precept of settling the Land while Jacob spent long years abroad).

In the absence of any social continuity or continuity of identity, when there is no hope of release from the existing dejection, since the "total conflict for survival" is a permanent fixture, you bet the pot. The predominant feeling is one of transience, and if everything is temporary, there is no value in a profession or in a serious approach to a profession—it's all dilettantism, it's all one big gamble. Here today, gone tomorrow. "What will be? What will be? The lottery."[6] The first school in Tel Aviv, the Herzliya Gymnasium, was demolished to build a shopping mall; thus did the decision makers determine the scale of priorities, according to which the *shmatte* business and its attendant fashions take precedence over a historical educational institution. A value scale like this, when determined by a leading group such as the city fathers, sets the tone for generations to come.

By comparison, immediately after World War II, the city fathers of Warsaw, which lay in ruins, decided that their first task was to restore, stone by stone, the historic ancient quarter. That, too, was a normative value decision.

But even if unremitting dilettantism works in various domains, such as commerce—exemplified by the unending series of shops that open and close down, not one of them run by professionals—there are two realms in which a level of makeshift dilettantism is out of the question, and not just in politics. The spheres that are immediately and directly harmed by provisionality and by a decline in professionalism are education and the arts. Both are by definition based on quality, professionalism, knowledge, and continuity. And as for the arts, their basis is not a group of one sort or another, but the unique work of the individual, for which there is no substitute.

In the Israel of the 1980s it is very difficult to find serious preoccupation with the quality of artistic creation; indeed, the criteria for determining quality are not even on the agenda, are not the subject of debate, and the result is that their value is constantly declining. Before our eyes struggles are waged over theater productions because of their group-political world view, and the truly important issue in art—the quality of the production—is pushed to the sidelines.

Nowhere else in the world does this happen to the same extent. At La Scala, for example, a singer whose coloratura is not up to par is not allowed to continue; no one knows, or cares, what her political views are. In Shakespeare's time an amateur actor was sometimes whistled off the stage not because of the text, but because of his unprofessional performance.

---

6. This is a popular jingle promoting the buying of lottery tickets as a universal panacea.

In Israel there is hardly a writer or other creative artist who cannot regale you with opposite examples. Some years ago, dissatisfied with the previous translation, I retranslated Adam Mickiewicz's classic *Konrad Wallenrod.* As it happened, the previous translator was apparently from a certain political party, because a cultural arbiter from that party immediately told the newspaper *Ma'ariv* that Mapam[7] had instructed the writer to retranslate *Wallenrod.* But why stop at Mapam? Why not the trade unions, or the United Nations Security Council, or the Flat-Earth Society?

And when my book, *The Miracle Hater,* whose literary criteria definitely do not resemble our group norm, first appeared, the critics said they found it hard to believe that no political point had been intended; the "truth" was that "she was talking about Sharon, Uri Dan, and Gush Emunim."

These are two examples from my own experience, examples of the obloquy resulting from the decline in cultural standards and their supersession by a stereotypic group standard steeped in the current political scene. Our best-seller (another dubious artistic concept) is not necessarily the best book; it is a topical book whose characters are ostensibly "recognizable," and in fact tally with some deep social stereotype. The issue of good writing versus bad, the central question of this art, has been shunted aside. Lately we have even seen the awarding of literary prizes based on a left-right political "balance."

The universities, too, are not immune from these baneful influences. The literature departments like to classify texts and writers into groups or periods or even sexes ("women's literature") without the graduates of the departments having the slightest inkling about artistic criteria or what constitutes the craft of good writing. In other words, instead of dealing with literature, they engage in sociology.

The primary objective of a university is to engage in thought, to increase the world's wisdom, to educate a generation of students to pursue these goals. All too frequently, however, we are witness to the encroachment of the group-power attitude even in these citadels, which become assembly lines of conceptually worthless research, laden with statistics of dubious value, often written in dreadful Hebrew beyond the ability of the

---

7. A left-wing political party.

academic adviser to correct. The entire point of the exercise is to magnify the quantitative strength of one department or another, while suppressing the intellectual and professional curiosity of good students.

I need not pursue this subject further, because there are people far more competent than I am who have plenty to say about it. The examples are meant only to indicate concretely how Israel's deficient social norms in the 1980s exert an influence in some areas that is tantamount to ruin, and certainly causes major anatomical and systemic damage that will take years to correct.

The Price of the Deadlock

This, then, is the situation in education and the arts, once saliently areas of Jewish excellence. And this is also the situation as regards the most significant decision awaiting us in the coming year, perhaps the most important since the establishment of the state: territories or peace. That decision will be made by voters who for the most part haven't the remotest idea what they are voting for, since no official body (as distinct from extragovernmental research institutions) has taken the trouble to draw up a judicious balance of scenarios and their prices. People will vote without any information, according to groups and the political slogans they are familiar with.

And if anyone thinks that even if the people don't know the ramifications of their decision, at least the Knesset and the cabinet do, he is wrong. Never has a serious, professional, multidisciplinary, supragroup and supraparty discussion been held concerning the price to be paid for retaining the territories versus relinquishing them. It is to be feared that as with the Lebanon War, here too the decision will ultimately be made at the level of absolute dilettantism. A neighborhood grocery store run with the same degree of information, price assessment, and judiciousness wouldn't last two months.

These are the prices we have paid, and continue to pay, for Israel's being—in its first forty years—an impressive success story. The state was established; the immigrants arrived, even if in disappointing numbers; basic security has been maintained.

Almost everything else is wobbly. Our form of social organization

—democracy, which cannot withstand even one more year of the load imposed by our rule in the territories—is wobbly. The supremacy of the law—no longer self-evident because of our rule in the territories, and not supported unreservedly by all those in government—is wobbly. Education, health, and public services are all in decline and have all had their value hierarchies badly shaken. Also in decline are interpersonal relations, the use of language, education, the economy, labor relations—in other words, all the elements of identity that transcend mere subsistence. One can state without hesitation that the Israeli society of the 1980s is a very sick society.

Anyone who doubts this would do well to look at what is happening in emigration. It no longer consists of what prime minister Yitzhak Rabin called "the bottom of the barrel." Nor does emigration today necessarily entail the permanent abandonment of the country; there is also contextual, practical emigration, even if it is partial—people who spend many months of the year abroad and conduct the bulk of their commercial, economic, educational, or scientific business there. For them, Israel is increasingly becoming a place to live for a few months of the year. Since not all of them return even to vote, the question arises of what makes them Israeli.

Youth is also seeking a more solid environment, surroundings possessing greater cultural clarity, even if it is a totally foreign culture, but at all events one more comprehensive and less atomized than Israel's is nowadays. There are people who under the Israeli social overload—not the security burden, despite what we're told—simply blew a fuse.

A recent study that examined the causes of emigration came up with a finding that surprised many Israelis, particularly those who perfunctorily cite "security, army, reserve duty" as the prime causes of tension. It emerged that so-called security tension was very low on the scale of the causes of emigration. The highest places were occupied by feelings of disappointment and frustration, defined as dissatisfaction with and a sense of not belonging to Israeli society, a feeling that they had not found their place, an inability to influence events—all social causes par excellence.

Is it really feasible to tell a society undergoing such intense social erosion that there is no solution, that we are fated to live by the sword, that we will not concede one inch and will not solve the Palestinian problem for another hundred years? Can such a group of people reasonably be told that there is no alternative, that every few years quantities of blood will be shed—and, as mentioned, according to IDF estimates, at least seven thousand Israelis will be killed in the next war, and over thirty thousand on the other side?

How far, and at whose expense, can the defense budget be inflated beyond its already monstrous proportions; how long can we go on purchasing armaments costing hundreds of millions of dollars? At the expense of the elderly who are rotting in their own feces in the hospitals? At the expense of schoolchildren? At the expense of research and development and growth, and all that differentiates us from a backward society? At the expense of quality?

By the end of its first forty years, Israeli society has no choice but to examine its priorities for the coming forty years. Does it want to remain in its current state of social malaise—a situation that will perhaps enable it to carry on its existence from one war to the next, but only as a small, violent, compulsive, and unsympathetic state that the best talents and minds will ultimately find inhospitable—or will it prefer a situation in which the society, as in the *Shemone Esrei* prayer, will retreat three steps while intoning the "He who makes peace" benediction, and relinquish the major source of its malaise: control of the territories? Then we will be able to devote our best efforts to healing, urgent healing, so that we can once more become a good people, a good society, a good place to live.

And perhaps, if we can get by this critical juncture safely, pride, too, will return.

People

Portrait of a Terrorist ═══════════

Abu-Nasser for the first time when he was standing on my doorstep.

Slightly stooped, visibly excited, he stood behind the tall back of Dr. Iyad el-Sarraj, a Gazan psychiatrist and an old friend, who came to have lunch with me and take me with him to Gaza. Those were the first months of the intifada, and I wanted to be there, see with my own eyes, and report in my paper.

"Meet Mohammed Abu-Nasser," said Dr. Iyad. "He drives my car. He threw a hand grenade on a queue of hitchhiking soldiers when he was seventeen years old, spent thirteen years in jail, and was released under the Jibril agreement."[1]

Conflicting thoughts churned in my head. True, I am going to Gaza to meet the people there, the reality of it—but here, in my home? On the other hand, Dr. Iyad brought him, and Dr. Iyad is not an irresponsible person, nor an insensitive one. He must have a reason.

I groped quickly for some kind of acceptable limit, some norm of behavior.

"Mohammed," I asked sternly, "did you kill people?"

He went very red. Tears stood in his eyes. He spoke with much inner pressure.

"No, no, no, *wallahi* (by God), *wallahi,* by my children's life, I never killed anyone, I just wounded, upon my life, upon my life."

A strange terrorist indeed, I thought, and glanced at Dr. Iyad. He stood aside, listening and not interfering, as behooves a psychiatrist, but

---

1. An agreement between the Israeli government and the Ahmad Jibril group, made in April 1985, under which seven Israeli soldiers held by terrorist groups were exchanged for 1,150 condemned terrorists incarcerated in Israel.

there was some tension in the way he held his shoulders. Now, to my mute question, he responded with a nod: Yes, that's true.

A week later the security people confirmed he was telling the truth.

"Sit down," I said to Mohammed, and added a plate to the table.

Later I learned that I was the first Israeli Mohammed had ever met who was neither a jailer nor a soldier, and that Dr. Iyad brought him intentionally: see each other, form your own impressions.

It was a strange meal. Mohammed was so excited that he could not touch a thing. It turned out that he spoke fluent Hebrew—a kind of jail-bird Hebrew. Once he said, with his shy smile, "I am a saboteur (*hablan*)," and I had to remind myself that by the time he went to jail, at the age of seventeen, we still said *hablan* and not *mehabel* (terrorist), as the current terminology goes. His face was broad, open, ingenuous, all his emotions immediately apparent. He certainly did not fit the stereotype of a terrorist you can see in children's drawings: no mustache, no burning eyes, no clamped mouth, no keffiah on his neck. He might have been an Egyptian fellah from the Delta.

Then we drove to Gaza, and Dr. Iyad said: If you want to understand what is going on, take the car, take Mohammed, go wherever you see fit, and come back to Gaza in the evening.

Thus I came to spend three-and-a-half days in the refugee camps of Gaza and between them, in many meetings, expected and unexpected, all of them in the company of Mohammed, whose presence opened all doors. A hard talk with an author who lived in Gibalia.[2] A meeting with a group of women. A conversation with a gang of stone-throwing children, who would have stoned us too, were it not for Mohammed, who signaled an agreed pattern with the car lights, and they apologized. A meeting with the headman of a village on a dust road between two orange groves. An unplanned meeting with young men who had some unusual ideas. A huge overflow of impressions. But most of all, it was a full three-and-a-half-day seminar on what it was like to be a child of Gibalia.

Mohammed was born in Gibalia, on the eternally damp concrete floor of a two-meter-by-two-meter room with a thin mattress and some old cushions; between the never-ending laundry in the window at right, and thick whorls of barbed wire marking the IDF encampment through

---

2. The Gibalia refugee camp, near Gaza City, is where the intifada originated in December 1987.

a breach in the wall on the left; in a cloud of mosquitoes and smells from the great sewage pool in the heart of Gibalia camp. Everything there is hard, harsh, loud. Not a whit of beauty or tenderness. Speech means shouting, sights are harsh, smells are a heavy stench. Even a table to work on is a daydream, and here there have been no daydreams for a long time.

The family came from the village of Masmiya. The people of Masmiya were not deported back in the 1948 war; they panicked and escaped for their lives.

In the words of David Karon of Kibbutz Kfar Menahem, a Hagana[3] veteran: "That was the beginning of harvest time, I don't remember the exact date, but part of the crop was still in stacks, and part of it in silos, so it must have been the beginning of May. The Masmiyya people sent a delegation to Egypt and bought firearms. They were very scared. So a delegation from the Hagana came to Masmiyya, a few people from Gedera, the headman of Kfar Menahem, some more from the neighboring villages; they sat down with the Masmiyya people and told them: We cannot tolerate an arsenal of arms. We suggest that you hand over the weapons to us and trust us. The Masmiyya people thought it over and decided that the best idea for them would be to run away for a time, until the crisis was over. All of them evacuated the village: old men, young, women, children. They packed for a few days' absence, locked their houses, and ran. And they swept some other villages with them as well, those who decided to abide by what Masmiyya was doing."

So, from one day to another, in one disastrous decision, they became refugees, people without citizenship or nationality, with no state in the world responsible for them. Dwellers of Gibalia, a huge slum from which it is almost impossible to extricate oneself. The one to two weeks became forty-five years. And no solution yet.

Mohammed's father was killed by Israelis. I do not know the circumstances. His mother, one of those panther-women, raised the children with her own hands, all responsibility, fanaticism, and anger, and taught them to take revenge. She gave them, as their daily bread, her hatred and dreadful rage, her only identity on earth. She was their home, their heaven and earth, their law and religion, their faith and their existence.

---

3. The main pre-state Jewish underground organization, later transformed into the IDF.

No tenderness, no sympathy. A harsh and demanding symbiosis between her and her children, a love that does not protect: Grow up quickly and face your destiny, for your destiny is already foreordained.

Mohammed's way was mapped out for him. At the age of seventeen, he proudly joined a group of followers of George Habash.[4] They gave him a hand grenade to throw. They told him he would become a hero, a great man; they kept saying how noble it was to sacrifice yourself for the cause and that everyone would admire him. They said they would give him money, support his family; his mother would be proud of him. And he, preening inwardly like a young cock, went to throw the grenade at the queue of soldiers on the road to Jericho, as if he was going to carry out the most glorious deed of his life.

He did not remember the sights, later on, only the screams. There were quite a few wounded. He ran without looking back. For a time he was hiding in the orange groves of Gaza, on the thin, sandy dust, lying low on dry leaves and a shriveled castor bush. They caught him soon enough. He told me later that he could still remember how he lay there, trussed, and how an Israeli officer who seemed to be a giant stood there and looked at him from above.

He thought they would kill him. They did not kill him. He was sentenced to twenty years in jail.

He told a little about his jail experiences. He was seventeen years old when he went in, thirty when he came out. A few times they moved him from one place to another. In the end, he was incarcerated in the Ashkelon prison. The only time, he said, that his violent image of Jews, the eternal enemies, was cleft occurred with the Peace Now demonstration of 400,000 Israelis after the massacres at the Sabra and Shatila refugee camps. This new perception filtered into the minds of Mohammed and his cell mates as a dissonant notion. They were much disturbed. They talked it over a lot, maybe for weeks. Maybe there was someone there that they could talk to after all. But it was not an upheaval. Reality always prevails, and reality was jail, the guard who often humiliated and insulted. Mohammed told proudly that he once raised his hand to a jailer.

He finished a few grades of elementary school in Gibalia, the same school that at the beginning of the intifada was taken over from the IDF by two hundred screaming women, who became heroines of the day, until

4. Leader of the Popular Front for the Liberation of Palestine.

the men put them back in their place, to wash and cook. He finished his high school studies in jail.

Then the Jibril agreement materialized, and he was suddenly free.

He came back to Gibalia to find a horrible reality. The shock of freedom was impossible to bear. The organization he had belonged to had forgotten him, or maybe he could not find the right people. No one was grateful to him. The promises they gave him were never fulfilled. The girl he had loved before his arrest married someone else and lived now a few blocks away, not his. They are all strangers, he said, all materialists, everyone is after "the dinar and the dollar and the shekel." All his heroism, all his sacrifice, thirteen of his best years in jail, did not count for much in the everyday stock exchange of Gibalia and Gaza.

"He went in seventeen years old, and walked out seventeen years old," said Dr. Iyad. "He was and remained an adolescent. In the isolation in which he lived, he did not develop a mature personality."

The indifference he met with was too much for him. He wanted to run after people, to shout, But I'm a hero, look, I'm a hero, look at me, please accept me as an important person, a leader. And people slapped his shoulder, said, "Well-done, Mohammed"—and went about their tasks.

With the hurt feelings of a seventeen-year-old, he did something impulsive: he asked to be returned to jail. There at least he knew how to live. They laughed at him. He went to everyone he knew in Gaza and asked them to intercede for him to go back to jail. No one took him seriously.

Embittered, humiliated, he gave in at last. He asked his mother to find him a wife to take the place of his old love. She went about and found him a woman, with some disdain, which later turned into complete rejection: no woman was worthy of her heroic son.

They married quickly, a Gibalia wedding. Someone brought a straw stool. Someone else got a few glasses that did not match, and woe to the child who breaks one. The family managed to get a mattress. No one spoke about happiness.

At first he worked in a small videocassette shop in Gaza, gave a hand here and there in the used-car business, got a little money from those who had mobilized him, until they broke contact. Three children were born in quick succession, the third generation with refugee status and living in poverty. He whistled up some childhood friends and formed a street gang to scare the rich of Gaza, to blackmail them a bit, to provoke them. He would enter an orange grove, fill up crates, and walk out arrogantly.

People shrugged. No one wanted anything to do with him. He did not achieve anything, just deepened the alienation. The gang disintegrated.

At this stage his wife broke down and was taken into psychiatric care, and that was how he met Dr. Iyad.

"He came," said Dr. Iyad, "because he began to understand the misery his family lived in. He entered the house, saw a chess table near the sofa, and asked to play. We sat there and played chess. Slowly, he began to talk. He said his life was dreadful. He is a stranger to all and all are strangers to him. He said that most of all he hated the Gazan well-to-do people. He uttered sentences like 'I sacrificed my life for you, so that you can live happily in your villas'; 'I went to die for the Cause, and you reap the fruits of my sacrifice.' I listened. Later, too, when he was having a hard time, we would play chess and talk. He thought his only place in the world was by way of violence. He said that he was fed up with the Habash people; they'd let him down. He asked me to arrange a meeting with someone from Jibril's organization. Jibril was all right, Jibril got him out of jail.

"I refused," said Dr. Iyad. "I tried to convince him, slowly, gradually, that he would not repair the mess of his life in that way. That he had to do something constructive, for himself and for others. That this struggle would not help. I saw a fluent man, an intelligent one, very emotional and completely lost. I asked him how he felt about some higher studies. He did not believe at first: how could he, a Gibalia child, study any more. I arranged for a small scholarship and rooming at Bir Zeit University. Slowly, it penetrated. He said that he would like to study political science."

"And then?" I asked.

"And then," said Dr. Iyad equably, "the Israeli authorities closed down Bir Zeit University."

Mohammed clung to Dr. Iyad. He became part of the household: running errands, driving the car, bringing in pitas with kabob in the evening to eat with his patron in the clinic.

He met people of a different kind: worldly, educated people who spoke nicely to him, people who would pick up a phone and call colleagues and friends in London, Chicago, Israel. He was flabbergasted. Once there was a sudden curfew in Gaza, and he stayed the night at the el-Sarraj home. He was a bit confused in the morning. He, who only knew nights spent in Gibalia and in jail, had for the first time in his life slept in a room by himself.

Now the psychiatrist was his authority figure, the man whose word was law, perhaps the father he had never known. Slowly, things penetrated. Now he doubted that the intifada could be the only solution. In one of those days we spent together, he brought me in contact with some of his friends at the outer edge of a southern refugee camp. All of them had ideas about peace—perhaps naive, perhaps not feasible, but that was their current hope. Now he would say, with a shy smile, "I used to be a saboteur."

Once Dr. Iyad was invited to dinner at a colleague's home in Jerusalem, and booked a room at the American Colony Hotel for himself and Mohammed. All at once, a beautiful hotel, a restaurant with well-appointed settings, a soft bed where they changed the bedclothes every day. His hungry senses almost drove him crazy in this place. He was in a palace, a fairy tale. He asked Dr. Iyad, humbly, to let him stay in the hotel, to take the wheel on his own, just this once. He never dreamed such things really existed. No one could converse with him for a few days afterward: his eyes were veiled as he walked.

"He was a refugee born in a refugee camp, the family household existed no more, he had no citizenship," said Dr. Iyad. "He could just as well have become a war-person as a peace-person; all he wanted was to be recognized as someone, a man, a Palestinian, a person who made a sacrifice. Since he could not attain any achievement, he looked for a misachievement. And I hoped to wean him away from that."

You don't know Jews, the doctor would say to him; go out and meet some Jews. That's not the enemy you have in your head. That's something different. And Mohammed was scared. Thus was the meeting on my doorstep born, and that was the beginning of my long journey with him in Gaza and the camps and the dust roads between them.

After three-and-a-half days, a curfew was imposed on Gaza. It was to start in the evening, and no one could tell when it would be over. There was no sense in my remaining there, immobilized in a curfew. I called Jerusalem and ordered a cab to pick me up at the Erez checkpoint.

Mohammed was deeply hurt. We spent so much time together, he said, and now you don't want me to drive you back to Jerusalem. You are my mother, you are my elder sister, it is out of the question that you go with a strange driver in a cab.

I explained to him that he would not be able to get back to Gaza before the curfew began and that he had to obey the law. Parting at the gas station of Erez checkpoint was a repetition of our meeting: again, tears in Mohammed's eyes, fists rubbing the tears, an honest emotion. Nothing helped: he had to check out, personally, whether that cab driver from Jerusalem was dependable. Then he stood waving for a long time.

Back at home, I wrote for hours impressions of the days and nights in Gaza. I mentioned Abu-Nasser casually, in half a phrase, his name withheld, for fear of bloody revenge on the part of the radicals. The relationship did not continue, and my next entry into the intifada was in the Jerusalem area, in other circumstances, with other people.

Dr. Iyad told me later how Mohammed brought the car back from the Erez checkpoint, but instead of going home he paced up and down, very agitated, telling about the hours he had spent with the Israeli who could have been his mother. Later, when the article appeared in *Yediot Aharonot,* he sat happily in the garden for hours, learning it almost by heart, translating bits and pieces to anyone willing to listen: Look, they wrote about us in the paper, my friend Shulamith wrote about us. Dr. Iyad still smiles when he recalls that childish pride. But it was a different pride from the one he had been raised on.

Were we in the realm of fairy tales, one could have stopped here, in the atmosphere of a happy ending. But our world is not like that, and the rest of the story was not a legend, but a gray horror.

Dr. Iyad's wife is English, and the moment came when she made up her mind that Gaza was not the best of places for her and for the children, and she went back to England. For a long time Dr. Iyad stayed on by himself, caring for mental patients whose number was increasing. Finally he missed his family too much; he packed and went to England without any notion when he would come back.

Mohammed Abu-Nasser was left alone. Completely alone. The good father and instructor disappeared, in an ultimate betrayal. From now on he could not depend on anyone. He fell back into terrible rage, into alienation. The loss was total, and the rest of the story was inevitable.

In the first months he was still visibly oscillating. Since he no longer believed in the various terror organizations, he tried to establish his own group and become its leader. Then he became friendly with people from the international organization Save the Children, which has an office in Gaza. One day we learned in the press that a member of the organization, an American, was kidnapped in circumstances that were not clear. After a short time, he was inexplicably released. The kidnapped man refused to talk, and the whole event was never explained. To this day they think in Gaza that the kidnapping was a put-up job, that the American who befriended Abu-Nasser wanted to give him "an achievement," to give him credit with the organizations—exactly the kind of misachievement from which the doctor was hoping to wean him. Only one thing is certain: that the kidnapper was, indeed, Mohammed Abu-Nasser.

Then he was interviewed by David Shipler of the *New York Times* for a film called *Arab and Jew: Wounded Spirits in a Promised Land.* I saw the film. Eloquent, convincing, Mohammed Abu-Nasser spoke about the need of Palestinians for an identity. Almost there. Almost a leader. And still not violent.

Then one day someone gave him a gun—and that was already in another category, something decisive. Mohammed Abu-Nasser fell back into the only identity remaining to him—that of a terrorist. In any case, there was no one left to make him feel ashamed.

At this point any possibility of a connection between the two of us was over. The border had been crossed. One day we read in the paper that a terrorist tried to murder, with an ax, a Jewish truck driver at a gas station in the south. He did not succeed in killing the man, but he did inflict a severe wound. And the truck driver also has a name, and a family, and an identity, perhaps a story, too, because there are very few Israelis who do not have a story of their own in this country, and in that gas station in the south two stories, completely blind to one another, met and clashed. At this point one cannot be understanding any longer, certainly one cannot condone.

Now he was wanted. He hid in various miserable hiding places in Gaza. The family disintegrated completely. They saw him, they did not see him. Like every wanted man, he acquired a mysterious quality: they swore in Gibalia that he killed a lot of Jews, a lot of Arabs. But these were just stories. A senior person in the security services, whom I asked about it later on, made light of them.

The end was sordid. Our forces noticed him in a small street near the Shif'a hospital and shot him down. He was pulling out a gun.

I heard, and found no pity, only a sad knowledge that it could have worked out differently. As if a gravestone was put in place. His mother said later that his body was returned to her with the head missing, but that, too, is probably just a story. Enclosed and sealed within her fanaticism, in her black clothes, she now has another reason to hate, and the family has one more myth, harsh and ineluctable.

Days went by, and Dr. Iyad returned to Gaza, by himself. He had spent eighteen months abroad with his family and could remain there no longer. The decision must have been very difficult, but he was sure they needed him in Gaza. He was right. Apart from his medical duties, Dr. Iyad el-Sarraj is now a member of the Palestinian delegation to the peace talks, working slowly, with great inner strength, toward the goal he believes in—peace.

We met for the first time after his return at an international conference on Mount Scopus, and the first subject we discussed was Mohammed. Dr. Iyad said he felt very guilty about being busy with his private affairs and letting Mohammed down unintentionally. He said things could have turned out differently. Both of us thought that if any of his authority figures had been present at that gas station, if only to say, "Mohammed, what are you doing with that idiotic ax? Drop it right now," he would have dropped it.

And it makes no difference. "If only" has no validity: people are judged by what they actually do, not by other possibilities. The life of Mohammed, which lacked any continuity, started badly and ended badly, thirty-three or -four years that made no sense. A person in the security services told me later: We have not forgotten him, either, there was something special about him. We knew that there was a rapid, inexplicable deterioration. There is no doubt that he was a very complex man.

This story has no moral, it is not a parable, no lesson can be drawn from it. Mohammed Abu-Nasser does not exemplify anything or anyone except himself alone. He was not a psychopath; some of the terrorists are. He was not a fanatic, religious or otherwise; many of them are. He did not have the profile of a murderer, a killer; some of them do. Each man and his circumstances. His case does not teach very much, except maybe that there is no such thing as a single motive, the motive of eternal hatred of Israel, as the more paranoid among us would like us to believe; rather, that there is a cluster of motives; that there are moments when everything can still happen, the good or the bad, for nothing is predestined; and that where norms are absent, the demarcation line can be hair thin.

This, perhaps, is the only conclusion to be drawn from the story of Mohammed Abu-Nasser, a child of Gibalia, in whose life all windows were barred.

Reflections in a Dark Mirror ━━━

EIGHTEEN YEARS AGO, DAVID
Ben-Shimol of Katamon was born. Several years earlier, Issa Jebrin of
Dahaisha was born.[1]

Both of them belonged to families with many children. Both of them
had parents who kept their traditions. Both of them were thought of at
home as rebels whose parents had lost all control over them and their
actions.

Both of them were small-timers with a history of crime, of getting
mixed up with the law, of having tempers.

Issa Jebrin walked around with a belly full of vengeance against the
Jews: his family tells that his cousin was killed by the gunfire of the Border Police during a demonstration in Hebron; ever since, he has been a
ball of rage.

David Ben-Shimol walked around with a belly full of fury at the Arabs:
his family says that his woman friend was killed in the terrorist bombing
of the number eighteen bus in Jerusalem; ever since, he has been a ball of
rage.

When in Jordan, Issa Jebrin asked to join the Palestine Liberation
Organization. The organization did not accept him. They said that he
was just a dumb kid. Apparently he wanted to prove he was not just a
dumb kid, like they thought. That he could kill defenseless people.

When on leave from prison, David Ben-Shimol asked to join Kach.[2]
They took their time answering him. After he had admitted to firing a
"Lao" missile at an Arab bus, the people at Kach called him a courageous

---

1. Katamon is a poor neighborhood of Jerusalem; Dahaisha is a Palestinian refugee
camp south of Jerusalem. *Trans.*
2. Kach is a violent, extremist right-wing movement founded by Meir Kahane, and
one-time political party, now outlawed. *Trans.*

Jew and welcomed him to their ranks. He proved he knew how to kill defenseless people.

Issa Jebrin was accused of stealing weapons from the IDF and of the cold-blooded murder of two young people in their twenties, people described by their friends as "flowers." He laid an ambush for them in one of the loveliest spots outside Jerusalem.

David Ben-Shimol was accused of stealing weapons from the IDF and of the cold-blooded murder of a young man in his twenties, a man described by the members of his village as a "flower." He laid an ambush for him in one of the loveliest spots outside Jerusalem.

A mirror image.

How long will our lives, our feelings, our consciousness, our security, and our anxieties—our very policy—be conducted according to these dark images, reflecting each other in this dark mirror with such chilling exactitude?

The Man Who Descended
into Inferno

I am the way to the city of sorrow:
I am the way to dolor eternal;
I am the way to the people lost.
 — Dante, *Inferno,* Canto III

THIRTY YEARS AGO THE POST
of Attorney General was filled by a forty-five-year-old man named
Gideon Hausner. Like every Attorney General, he handled both important and less important cases: from closed espionage files to minor squab-
bles over land to decisions over whether to open or close cases in which
corruption was suspected — and in those days, corruption meant someone
had built an ostentatious villa of three whole rooms, and no one could
figure out how he had financed the construction.

Like every Attorney General, Hausner was ambassador of the rule of
law in a country where actions speak; he represented the norm of law and
justice — that which is meant to govern each of us without exception, that
which is perhaps man's most earnest attempt to settle his disputes without bloodshed.

A man can live out his life without thinking about such things even
once; between one case and another, contesting an issue, deposing a re-
calcitrant witness, all the stores of minutiae that only rarely add up to
something substantial. A man does his part, an Attorney General does his
part, day in and day out, making order of those matters where it is in a
man's power to make order — that is, any matter that may be adjudicated.
No more. And one day Gideon Hausner was listening to a special edition
of the news on the radio and, like all of us, heard Ben-Gurion announce
to the Knesset that Adolf Eichmann had been caught and would be

brought to trial. In an instant he realized that it was he, in his capacity as Attorney General, who would be called upon to represent the state of Israel in its suit against Eichmann. In other words, he was the man who, together with his staff, would have to prosecute Eichmann in the name of the entire people of Israel, item by item, testimony by testimony, for deeds involving the murder of six million men, women, and children.

The principle itself was not new to him. In Judaism, there is no criminal act, however dark and unfathomable, to which the framework of the law does not apply. According to *The Kkabbalah,* even the dead are called from their graves to stand earthly trial, because the law is one in both this world and the world to come. The verdict of an earthly court outweighs even a hint from heaven.

But here a unique kind of courage was required: the courage to say to ourselves first, and then to the whole world, that even the Holocaust with all its atrocities is bound by the seemingly prosaic definition of a criminal act and is therefore subject to jurisdiction; that therefore those responsible for it are accountable to an ordinary court of justice and will stand trial.

Courage was needed—and in those days, the government of Israel had courage—to say that beyond all the pain, beyond the demonization, beyond the tempest of emotions, acts had been committed that could be defined as murder. Not natural catastrophe: murder. And that he who had committed the murder, or who had personally authorized it, would personally stand trial. Not Satan or Amalek, neither a demon nor a beast, but a man born of woman, named Adolf son of Adolf-Karl Eichmann. And a man of flesh and blood is subject to jurisdiction.

Eichmann could have been shot down on the spot. Such things have happened. One bullet and the murderer is no more. Except that, actually, there is nothing in such a deed. Murder a criminal in secret, and it is as if nothing has happened. No hearts are opened. No facts come to light. No lesson is learned. In essence, nothing changes.

But when a criminal stands trial, a great deal happens. A lead bullet fired by a professional cannot really be a counterweight. The only possible counterweight is trial in a court of law, with all its calm, due process: prosecution, testimony, defense, cross-examination, debate, verdict, appeal. Only within this orderly framework, this rigid framework that is precise almost to the point of boredom, can a great personal and public

catharsis take place, like the one that indeed took place during the Eichmann trial, the like of which has not often occurred in history.

Not everyone understood this, and not immediately. A great many
wanted vengeance, and right away. Many asked why bother with details,
when everything is already known. Many wanted instant justice, which is
no justice at all. Rankled newspapers in Israel and abroad asked what all
the show, all the theatrics, were about. He, they said, does not deserve a
trial. He should be lynched, not tried. A great many people thought in
terms of revenge, weapon of the weak, the powerless, the dispossessed,
and of which those innocent of any crime are also, and always, victims.

The principle of statehood embodied in trial, as opposed to the ghetto
mindset behind revenge, has never been taught in our schools. Every
Israeli schoolchild knows the desperate acts of our history by rote. In
how many Israeli schools are court rulings taught?

Then came the wave of disbelief. There is no court in the world, they
said, and certainly not in Israel—are the judges not Jews?—that can try
him objectively, justly. Besides, they said, it is not at all clear whether a
court in Israel has jurisdiction over a man kidnapped and brought from
afar. Neither is the state of Israel's status clear regarding deeds committed
before it existed. There is no way this can possibly be a fair trial, they said.
A performance, at most.

But Ben-Gurion understood. He understood that one cannot confront a murderer with an avenger, another murderer, a petty hired gun
who would kill him, him or some other handy German, what difference
does it make, they're all animals. Eichmann, the human being who murdered many human beings, must be confronted by the state of Israel in all
the might of its sovereignty: Israel as the heir of those murdered, not as a
pathetic little terrorist.

Thus it came to pass that the Attorney General came to represent the
state of Israel as representative of the entire Jewish people in its case
against Adolf, son of Adolf-Karl Eichmann, Criminal Case Number
40/61.

And in those days, the Attorney General was a modest and most humble
man named Gideon Hausner, who had assumed the post only a year

before; and Gideon Hausner thought he did not have the right. After all, he wasn't there. How could he?

For first and foremost, he had humility in the face of the *Shoah*. Unlike politicians who take the name of the Holocaust in vain. Unlike the arrogant hacks who were not there but who have no qualms about manipulating the Holocaust, using it as a political ploy or as an excuse to turn others into victims. Unlike those *Shoa*logists who milk it for all it's worth, using it to make names for themselves and get funding—in what some have called "*Shoah* Business"—those who talk about the Holocaust with habitual bathos, but without a hint of sorrow, a whit of humility.

He had humility regarding the Holocaust. He made his ego very, very small. He had questions. He did not have answers. It seems sometimes in our world that those whose grammar consists of question marks and those whose grammar consists of exclamation points do not speak the same language.

He brought his questions before those with whom he sought counsel. He did not ask whether he would or would not succeed—an opportunist's question, no matter what the issue. Clearly, he was bound to succeed; after all, the whole world was on his side. But whether he did or did not have the right. Just this. He knew that first he had to face the Holocaust by himself, as an individual; only then could he speak in the name of society.

He didn't want to star. Not he. He was not interviewed by any newspaper. He did not stand in front of spotlights and flashbulbs to answer the inevitable foolish question, "How did you feel when you learned. . . ." He never dreamed of "telling all," nor did he see in the situation the chance of a lifetime.

In the end he went to Kibbutz Lohamei HaGettaot[1] and sat with its members until the wee hours of the morning. He aired his doubts. Over and over, he said: But I was not there. How can it be that I have the right? Who could grant me such license?

Between three and four in the morning Antek and Zvia[2] said to him: Gideon, you talk just as we do; go out there and represent us. Only then,

---

1. Kibbutz Lohamei HaGettaot is a kibbutz founded by Holocaust survivors. *Trans.*
2. These were surviving leaders of the Warsaw Ghetto uprising. *Trans.*

knees weak, did he make up his mind that he would. He gathered the vast amount of material and holed himself up in a hotel for two-and-a-half months, not even going home in all that time. Then, like Dante, he descended into Inferno. And through him, we all descended to the city of sorrow, and to the people lost in it.

On one of those nights I met him on a Tel Aviv street. He had left his room, the chamber of agony in which he had locked himself, wrapped in a coat and deep in thought, to breathe a little night air. We stopped to talk for a moment. He told me that, technically, he could not grapple with all of the material and that he was presently taking a course in rapid reading. We discussed some minor details. I didn't dare ask him how he was bearing up. Down such a path a man walks alone. Everything was gray, painstaking, step by step.

Then he wrapped himself in his coat again and went on his way, back to his chamber of agony, to be the family lawyer for us all. The lawyer who would represent so many people who not only died in the industry of death, but first of all lived and worked, spoke and read and joked, loved and hated and studied and stole and went on picnics and celebrated and felt and consulted physicians and argued and wrote letters, until other people came and murdered them. Not Satan's progeny murdering the saintly. People murdering other people.

Within a few weeks it became clear to Gideon Hausner, as to the whole team of capable prosecutors who were called to the task, that it was possible they would not have witnesses. People refuse to come and testify, he told his wife.

There were those who said, I don't want to, I can't, I won't reopen old wounds. Others said, I've built myself a new life; why take on the stigma of "Holocaust survivor" again? Still others said, My own children don't believe me, why should the judges? They were afraid to confront again the icy disdain of Israelis toward all those who "went like sheep to the slaughter." To confront their absolute lack of understanding of what had happened.

It was necessary to convince people to come; a great many said no. The dead can't testify, he told his wife, and the living won't testify. I'll be left without witnesses, he said sadly. Never had he imagined how great the gulf was between those who were there and those who were not: in the street, at the grocery store, at work, everywhere people come together, seemingly one nation, seemingly not so different. Two hundred thousand Holocaust survivors were then in Israel, and most of them did not have the strength.

In the meantime the wheels were turning rapidly: Dr. Robert Servatius, the German defense attorney, arrived, as did his deputy and his secretary; the hall was prepared. Gideon, an honest and thorough jurist who had never been much of an orator, wrote his speech for the prosecution, today considered a classic, as if inspired. Only deep humility can produce such a speech.

Another man might have said: "Honorable Judges, I, Attorney General of the government of Israel, stand here in the name of six million murdered Jews." He said: "Standing before you, Judges of Israel, to argue the case against Adolf Eichmann, I do not stand alone."

Another man might have said: "The great honor and great obligation have fallen upon my shoulders. I am humbled before the task." He said: "Their voices can be heard no more; therefore I speak for them, and in their name will make the terrible indictment." Because they cannot speak. Then, and only then, will I be their mouthpiece. A world of difference in phrasing.

And the process began. An entire nation went to work with the radio on. A bank clerk counted money and brushed back tears. A housewife stirred dinner and sobbed. A bus followed its route, its passengers sitting in hushed silence, hanging on every word without a moment's letup, listening to the careful, polite, orderly voices that represented sanity where there was no sanity, that spoke stability and order where there was nary a hint of either, voices from the courtroom. Whole classrooms sat at attention and listened.

Some fainted on the stand. Some were rushed to intensive care while listening in their homes. Some spent all of the long weeks of the trial in unending tears. Perhaps it is just as well there was no television then. The radio enabled each person to retreat into himself, to close his eyes, to connect.

So above all, through it all, from morning until night, no voice was heard in the land, no bird chirped, save those grave voices like a sane, steady, solid frame around the tales of atrocity, originals and translations told slowly, painstakingly, clearly, according to procedure, order, and law. The opposite of pandemonium. The opposite of hysteria. A trial according to law.

And all at once things began to happen. Suddenly many people wanted to come and testify. They recognized themselves in what was happening. They heard on the radio about incidents at which they themselves had been present. Dams burst, and suddenly had the legitimacy to burst. After the testimony of Judge Moshe Beisky, who related the horrible incident of the hanging of a child, a woman came, trembling, and said, choked with emotion: "I was there, I stood by it all, I want to come testify, I *must* testify."

By then it was impossible to stem the torrent of people who came under terrible emotional pressure, pleading that they, too, be allowed to testify. To tell. To say in public. If, before, the prosecution had feared it would remain without witnesses, now it had to sift and sort, and turn away many deserving people.

All at once it became clear that not only the dead were represented by the prosecution, but the living as well. As if the prosecution had enabled them to live. Enabled them to breathe.

A great many hearts opened. People spoke in a different manner. There was a certain gentleness in the way they approached one another. The members of the prosecution team, who performed a legal task unlike most others, often talked among themselves frankly about their emotions. One, then a senior member of Bureau 06, the office established to conduct the investigation, and today a senior judge, told me how he was sent in the middle of the night to the place in northern Israel where Eichmann had been incarcerated, to question him for the first time. This was also the first he knew of Eichmann's being in Israel. Before dawn he went and sat in the grayish cell in the grayish light, a soldier with an Uzi in the corridor, another armed soldier inside the cell. From far off, from the end of the corridor, he suddenly heard the sound of approaching footsteps and manacles: they were bringing Eichmann. And I—this man told me— I, a native-born Israeli, coming in the name of the state, one soldier guarding me outside and another inside, I heard that sound and I shook with fear.

All at once it became permissible to talk about fear. All at once it was all right to admit many things. Once, during a recess, I heard two members of the prosecution team debate quite candidly, whether they, too, would have knuckled under and collaborated with the Nazi regime if Hitler had not been against the Jews but, say, against some obscure tribe of Uzbeko-Etruscans. They spoke with utter sanity about the temptation to collaborate with an apparently rational abomination. About the menace that always lies in wait. These words were not spoken theoretically. This was a serious probing of personal conscience.

And again and again it became clear that there is no barricade, no insurance against such things save a fair trial, a trial according to law. A trial to which every other consideration is foreign. A trial that is a statement. Blind to all secondary outcomes, yet the only thing that can bring them about. Nearly dissociated from human emotion, yet the only thing that can give expression to human emotion. Boring, pedantic—as many journalists and guests in the balcony would comment, surprised—yet the only thing that makes change happen.

Eichmann was found guilty and put to death by hanging. His claim that he was only following orders, that everything was the fault of the statesmen and commanders, that he was only the victim of a misguided concept, of the drawing of mistaken conclusions, did not help him at all. The journalists drew lots to see which few of them would be present when the sentence was carried out. The lots fell to Aviezer Golan of *Yediot Aharonot* and Shmuel Shnitzer of *Ma'ariv*. Later they would attest to feeling nothing, to feeling hollow at the sight. They did not feel vindicated: a guy with a crooked mouth and a crooked soul had been hanged—so what. It was in no way proportionate to what he had done. Neither did it bring a single person back to life.

We knew: the man wasn't the main thing, and his death wasn't the main thing. We sensed that only fools would demand vengeance. The most important thing, the decisive thing, the thing that had brought about real change, was the trial itself.

There was no drama. The closing statements of the judges in Criminal Case Number 40/61 dealt with documents and references. Everyone who had taken part in the trial rose up out of the Inferno and went on his way.

The prosecution team turned to other matters, other tasks. The judges turned to property and bribery trials. Gideon Hausner, too, went back to his files; even before the Eichmann trial had concluded, the infamous Lavon Affair[3] was awaiting him. One thing followed another.

When brutality and ignorance in Israel increase; when fools talk about a "juridical mafia" or a "dictatorship of the law"; when petty murderers take the law into their own hands and spiritual and political leaders incite them to it; when there is more and more talk of revenge and less and less talk of law and justice; when the arm of a child is broken, though he was not the one who threw the stone; when two old people in an Arab village are killed, though they were not the ones to murder Kahane in New York —when these things happen, perhaps we need to remind ourselves of the sentence with which Gideon Hausner closed his great speech for the prosecution. He said: "Adolf Eichmann will be granted a right he did not grant a single one of his victims. He will be able to defend himself before a court of law. His fate will not be sealed, except by law and evidence beyond any doubt; and the burden of proof is on me and my colleagues."

Even he.

---

3. The Lavon Affair ultimately brought about the resignation of then Prime Minister David Ben-Gurion. *Trans.*

Identity: Victim ====================

that when Israeli schoolchildren are asked to name the most important events in the history of the people of Israel, they answer thus: the destruction of the First Temple; the destruction of the Second Temple; the expulsion from Spain; the Holocaust; the establishment of the state; the Yom Kippur War. Pupils in state religious schools sometimes add the Exodus from Egypt and the giving of the Law on Mount Sinai, but they are not the majority.

Not the building of the First Temple, but its destruction. Not the existence of the Second Temple, but its destruction. Not the magnificent, lengthy construction of the Mishnah and the Talmuds. Not the Golden Age of Spain, but the expulsion. To these children, the people of Israel was not the cradle of monotheism, with all its complex implications far beyond religion. There is nothing to be proud of: there has been no development of a people, its thought, its social organization, its systems of navigation and justice. The people of Israel has no cultural and social history; even if it had, that is not its uniqueness. There is only one history: that of destruction; there is only one identity: that of victim. There is no individuality, only Fate.

To many people in Israel, myself included, because of their personal history, there is no need to call the Holocaust to mind; only a complete fool would infer that this article is a willful attempt to forget or to dwarf the most monstrous tragedy experienced by the people of Israel. This is not the question at hand. The question we must answer is whether it is possible to raise a generation on nothing but traumas that were caused by others, exclusively on a sense of perpetual destruction and deterministic hatred, or whether there are some other things about Judaism, not necessarily related to victimization, that define us both as a people and as individuals. Does being a Jew only mean being a victim, defined by the actions of others? Or does it also mean being a people that established an elaborate judicial system, created a language to be proud of, built a state and established a social order (not only fought for their existence!), and developed demands and expectations for perfecting the world and the individual, expressed in various phenomena throughout history, that no other people did? In other words, are we willing to accept Jean-Paul Sartre's definition of Judaism, "anti-semitism makes Jews" (that is, he even denies us the right of self-definition)? Or are there also things about us that have nothing whatsoever to do with the acts and attitudes of others?

By their nature, traumas leave deep and painful residue for a long time. Plastic surgeons tell us of a study conducted among people whose limbs were amputated in accidents and ligated back to the body in the hospital. Several months after the event, the people were asked to draw a picture of themselves; almost all of them drew themselves missing an arm or a leg. In other words, the trauma of the loss was greater and more definitive than the relief of regaining the limb and the use of it. Yet we may say with a great degree of certainty that were these people to continue to draw (that is, to see) themselves as amputees ten years hence, we would think there was something pathological about their perspective, that they had turned themselves—whether because of a lack of ability or because their surroundings reinforced their behavior—into people whose only identity was that of a victim.

In the short run, the identity of victim does, indeed, pay off. Sholem Aleichem recognized this in his story "Lucky Me, I Am an Orphan." Anyone who is a victim and nothing but a victim—in the sense of "deserving" compensation and forgiveness for everything—usually milks this position for all it is worth, through the end of the generation that witnessed the tragedy. In the longer run, the perpetuation of the victim identity causes complete severance from reality, utter dependence on the past and the past alone, and distortions of all proportions and emphases to the point of warping the personality.

We do not lack examples. Not long ago, Rabbi Haim Druckman[1] objected to the passage of a law against incitement to racism, on the astonishing grounds that only Jews could be victims of racism. Apparently Rabbi Druckman had never heard about blacks, for instance. Mr.

---

1. He was then a member of Knesset. *Trans.*

Begin tried to excuse the violent invasion of Lebanon in 1982 with symbols from the Holocaust. Every seizure of Arab property in the West Bank is made under the banner and in the name of the victim identity, which many of us abhor. Even the late Golda Meir, in a meeting with writers that I attended, made a strange excuse for the failure to return lands to the villagers of Ikrit and Baram: "True, there is justice, but then there is Jewish justice." Why? Because we are the victim. Even relative to the villagers whom we divested of land, we are victims. It is no wonder that the commander of one of the units that participated in the 1956 War ended his briefing to his men with the cynical words, "So, men, we're still chasing Trumpeldor's murderer—go!"[2] In truth, a time comes when it is no longer possible to use this victimhood as an excuse for everything. As every educator knows, it creates a great residue of cynicism, if only because of the obvious gap between what children are taught by rote and what they see with their own eyes.

If I am a victim—and not just any victim but an eternal victim—then I am excused from many things: from having pride in what I am, for example; from exploring and studying my real identity; from looking in the mirror; from a sober look at my surroundings to see what is in it and what is not; and from any possibility of empathy for another. Semantic clichés, whose truth no one questions, arise and are parroted, such as "the whole world is against us," when in reality we have both enemies and friends, and the majority of nations and people take no interest in us at all. Or "all the Arabs want to throw us into the sea," with no realistic discernment of our actual, diverse relations with each Arab country separately. Or "the world was silent while we were slaughtered." Nations do not usually hasten to the military aid of other nations in distress. Neither did we send our air force to fight the Khmer Rouge in Cambodia when they were systematically murdering and burying alive infants and adults of the professional classes. During the Second World War, however, not only did the world not remain silent, it lost more than sixty million men fighting Hitler. True, they were not fighting because of us, and certainly they would not have offered aid for our sakes only. They were fighting against fascism in general, against its deeds and beliefs and aggression. But the

---

2. Joseph Trumpeldor was a Russian Jew who came to Israel early in the century and died fighting. *Trans.*

loss of more than sixty million men in a war does not exactly mean that the world sat by with its arms crossed. And our emotional outburst— while understandable given our terrible feeling of having been utterly for- saken by God and man—is not the entire truth. The world fought against Hitler and defeated him. Sixty million families suffered losses, and those of us who survived, including the small numbers of us then inhabiting Israel, survived because of them.

If I am the sole and eternal victim, then I create around and within myself and raise my children to an inability to see anyone who is not me. If I and only I occupy the throne of the victim, then no stranger can occupy it. This blindness reaches proportions that distort reality. I am not talking only about right-wing Jewish settlers, professional blind men who never see the residents of the West Bank. I am talking about our media, too. Some time ago a few settlers murdered innocent students at the Islamic College in Hebron. How many of us knew then—not to men- tion know today—the names of the victims? Knew anything about them? How many journalists clamored to visit the families and detail their grief, as they are wont to do when Jews are killed? We all saw the names of the murderers and pictures of their wives and children. But what about the victims?

If I am the sole and eternal victim, then of course I refuse to accept any information that is liable to ruin my self-image. My receptors simply do not pick it up. I have no need of it; I already have a map, with one marker on it only: I am a victim, and everyone is against me. I refuse to hear not only about the Arabs, but also about myself. I break the mirror.

At the base of this attitude is a dangerous thing: it is as if all of Zionism, as if the fact of our living in Israel, is dependent on our not knowing and not wanting to know. Those who hold this attitude do not see the Israeli who gets up in the morning, goes to work, pays taxes, waters plants, raises his children, and does reserve army duty. Rather, they see the eternal victim, alone in the world, who sits upright on his throne with his eyes closed, smothering all other peoples (especially Arabs), and is always, always right, right with the blind, cold righteousness of the victim above whose head flutters the banner, "Vengeance is mine!"

How many of us, today, see ourselves in this picture?

There is a certain coldness, a certain frightening passivity in this atti- tude of "justification at all costs" (even if the cost is truth) of our inhabiting this land. People do not actually live anywhere as a result of justifications or the lack thereof. They live in the realm of the humanly possible. What happened to concepts like love, for instance—a totally possible concept? Or caring? Or involvement, engagement? Or belonging? A deep sense of belonging, which keeps a person from sitting on his backside, which gets a person up and working to fix what is broken, heal what is sick, act to make things better? A love for which people will fight to make a present as good as it can be, if not better—not to mention a future?

Not long ago, at a meeting of people involved with social policy, Mr. Shimon Peres said that there are two things in the world that have no lobby: the weak and the future. I would recommend that we all adopt this diagnosis. We have too big a lobby for the past and not a big enough one for the future. If we look at the past only, there is practically no possibility of talking about absolute justice vis-à-vis the situation between us and the Arabs. They did terrible things to us, and we did terrible things to them. They refused to recognize us and our identity for a very long time, and we refused to recognize their identity for a very long time. There are those among them who claim ownership of Jaffa, and there are those among us who claim ownership of Hebron. The Palestine Liberation Organization has not been able so far to arrive at any kind of peace, for existential and political reasons (loss of support and budgets among them), and our right wing is not capable of negotiating peace, for mythological and political reasons ("not one inch"). If we insist on absolute justice, the reckoning of lives will never end. All we can talk about is beneficial justice, beneficial for both sides—that is, a territorial compromise and the continuation of the conflict at the negotiating table.

This undoubtedly brings us back to the question of our identity. If my only identity is that of the victim, the world's deterministic and doomed victim, I may (or so it seems) commit any atrocity, including exiling Arabs from their homes (excuse me, dear hawks, "relocating" them) and taking possession of their land, because I am the victim and they are not; because this is the only way I define myself and my identity—forever. But if I also define myself as the son, or daughter, of a people with a splendid four-thousand-year history of responsibility, of conscience, of repairing and improving, of appealing for social order and justice, of a legal system nearly unparalleled in the world, and of the protection of these traditions; if I have indeed learned and internalized all these, so that they define my identity; then even if often in history I have been the victim of others, I will never oppress those weaker than myself and never abuse my power to exile them (excuse me, dear hawks, "bus them out"). I will not have to define my uniqueness in terms of the past alone. People established a state, despite all opposition; people absorbed immigration at a ratio of one to one, and, in spite of horrendous errors, did it; people defended themselves from within the narrow borders of the Green Line and achieved their greatest victory in 1967; people, who were caught by surprise on Yom Kippur, made it to within kilometers of Cairo and Damascus. People founded a great legal system, despite antagonists; they created a system of democratic government, despite those who fought against it; they recently were smart enough to turn back from the road to economic suicide. There is a state, there is industry, there is agriculture. Day by day, hour by hour we create Hebrew, Israeli culture, and we take it for granted—not because we wonder whether or not it is "justified," but because this is our existential circumstance. Every day children are born here whose right it is to live, and in peace. Is not all this reality? Surely we commit many wrongs and take great risks. But, as one young man said on the eve of his induction into the IDF, "Sure, this country is sick, but that's no reason not to defend it." How much less so to abandon it. For there is no other place, and moreover there is no other tree and no other stone; there is nothing to do but to fix and fix and repair and repair all the time, every day, all our lives.

Where, then, in the final analysis, does our identity and our uniqueness lie? Certainly not in our being victims; there have been and are victims, including whole peoples who were wiped out without a trace and not compassionately. We have existed as a people for a very long time, and during this time we have indeed amassed a difficult and tortuous history, and very often we were victims. But our uniqueness lies not in what others do to us, but in ourselves alone, in our selfhood, our character, and our culture. It lies in our reality, which is, perhaps, different from that of others. How is it different? In our "who," in our "how." Not what was done to us, but who we are. The uniqueness of a Jew is not in his being a victim. It is in his being a Jew, a proud son of a people at least four thousand years old, who built a humane present and ask for an attainable future. Not a future of messianic proportions, but one of human dimensions.

We read in the Passover Haggadah, "Pour thine wrath out upon the gentiles, who know thee not." What we did not read is a piece not included in the Haggadah—and not by accident. It was written in Worms in 1521 by Rabbi Yehuda Ben-Yekutiel, a descendent of Rashi himself. He wrote, "Pour thine love out upon the gentiles, who know thee, and upon the nations that call thy name, because of the righteousness they do unto the seed of Jacob, protecting thy people Israel from its enemies." During his life, Rabbi Yehuda Ben-Yekutiel had no need to pay lip service to the ruling powers. He wrote ingenuously. But the Haggadah, completed during a trying time for Israel, did not include anything that did not smack of our being victims. The Haggadah is symptomatic of many of our scholarly writings and of our conception of ourselves as victims—notwithstanding reality.

No, under no circumstances are we to forget our tragedies. But whoever bases our identity on them and them alone, distorts the greatness of this people and keeps from its sons not only pride, but sanity itself.

Conflict

Eyewitness ═══════════════════════

In the autumn of 1982, during the war in Lebanon, Christian Phalangists burst into two Palestinian refugee camps near Beirut, Sabra and Shatila, killing several hundred people. No Israeli participated in the deed; but since the area was under Israeli army rule, public opinion in Israel was outraged. A Peace Now demonstration of 400,000 people in Tel Aviv demanded a legal investigation into the question of responsibility for letting the slaughter happen. A high-level judiciary commission was set up, headed by Supreme Court Judge Kahn.

On Monday evening, last week, the Kahn Commission presented its findings on the events leading to the Sabra and Shatila murders to the prime minister. One of its statements was that Mr. Ariel Sharon was no longer fit to be minister of defense. The following day Mr. Sharon announced that he refused to accept the commission's recommendations pertaining to him and would not resign. Until Thursday, the government of Israel dithered, and did not come up with the unambiguous declaration that it accepted the commission's report and its conclusions. Between Monday and Thursday, Israeli society went through the three most critical days of its existence as a democracy. The issue has not yet been resolved. Perhaps it has just begun.

Let me say, first, that the dividing line was not ethnic. Adi Levi, a Yemenite, now hospitalized for wounds caused by that hand grenade, was cursed and called "Ashkenazi." Marchers from underprivileged neighborhoods suffered as many blows as anyone else. Nor did the dividing line run between the religious and the secular. Professor Avi Ravitzky of the religious dovish movement Netivot Shalom, most of whose members are yeshiva students, testified that many members of the group were badly beaten up that evening. The rift was clearly political, between two opposing views.

By Thursday evening the government was still silent. Peace Now *decided to hold a protest march from Zion Square in midtown Jerusalem, to the prime minister's office, demanding the immediate implementation of the commission's conclusions.*

This, then, was the picture on Thursday in Jerusalem:

Right from the start, as soon as the marchers set out from Zion Square and travel up Ben Yehuda Street, they realize this is not an ordinary clash of ideas, nor the familiar level of marginal violence. Even before the demonstrators arrive, organized groups of violent hooligans have been waiting for them, and now they repeatedly burst into the lines of marchers with great force, wedging deliberately into the procession. Next to me are shouts, whistles, blows. A great many blows.

The police do not seem prepared for so much violence. Here and there a lone policeman attempts, in vain, to fight off an oncoming wave of roughnecks. I see, to my right, a kindly policeman who looks like a pater familias about to collect his children from an afternoon movie, trying to stop the surging throng bodily—to no avail.

The din is deafening. Begin, Begin, Begin. PLO, PLO, PLO, PLO. Arik king of Israel, Arik king of Israel, Arik, Arik.[1] You won't succeed, you PLO supporters, you're trash, trash, trash, your commission is trash, you set up a commission against Arik, you did this against Begin, we will kill you all, we will do a Sabra and Shatila on you, we will make a holocaust on you, you trash, you trash, trash, trash. Arik is the king, Arik.

The march moves on among the blows and curses, a slow, large, ponderous body. Next to me I recognize a sixteen-year-old boy, not an Ashkenazi, now pale as a sheet. This is the first demonstration he has ever taken part in, his first encounter with this kind of mob. He came to stand up for the law, as they taught him in school. The poster he is holding is torn; his shirt is torn; already he has been punched in the face. We tell him to keep cool, to smile; we are stronger, democracy shall win; and if they yell "Begin" at him, yell a little louder: "Go home."

Now there is a very large number of demonstrators, but I, too, feel my guts churning when I see three goons beating Alon in the face. Alon was with the rescue unit at Entebbe and fought in other antiterror operations that have never been made public. They yell at him, as they punch him

---

1. "Arik" is Ariel Sharon.

hard: "Were you ever in the army, you PLO? Did you ever do a day's army service in your life?"

Slowly, the march advances. Incessant blows. Spitting. Stones. Someone throws a burning cigarette in Amiram's face. Anat is beaten up. Later, one of the mob tries to hold a burning torch in the face of Tala Ziv, an artist from the Israel Museum. This is not a chance street mob: someone has organized them. They hit—methodically—Mordecai Bar-On, former chief education officer in the IDF. A man in city clothes, certainly not the average hooligan, shouts at Naftali, who blocks the thugs with his body in the first row, "Say, say, you traitor, what's the difference between you and the PLO?" And Naftali replies quietly, "The difference is that I have been fighting the PLO for the past seventeen years." But the man is not listening at all. He keeps shouting: "Phooey, shit, traitors! PLO!"

The marchers show restraint. They are not hitting back, though the temptation is great. The strongest feeling that we share here today is that the street is on the verge of a civil war, and that must be prevented at any price. I see Yarom and Zohar and Alon and Emil and Amos Arieli and Ofer and Shaul, paratroopers in the reserves, linking arms and forming a tight human wall, facing the violent mob, so that the demonstration can continue on its way; actually, so that Israeli democracy can continue on its way. The incensed mob has now reached the stage of sexual invective: "Arafat will caress your asses, go fuck with Arafat, you maniacs, you transvestites, you gays, you're trash. Begin Begin Begin, Arik Arik Arik king of Israel."

We now march along the mall. Whenever I pass this spot, there is a second of stillness: thirty-five years ago, in the Hagana, I helped bandage the wounded from a car bomb at this very spot—my baptism as a teenage medic. Now, in exactly the same place, I get kicked in the knee by a disheveled young woman. I feel no anger, only a great, sad bewilderment: was it for this we fought to have a state? Someone behind me says that tomorrow we shall be summoned to return our identity cards as citizens and to stand in line to get our subject-certificates. The responding grin is a little crooked: it doesn't even sound funny. In the line behind me, Professor Hava Lazarus, a well-known orientalist, is trying to calm her young daughter, who is very frightened. No one expected so much violence.

Slowly, we arrive at the square of Hamashbir department store. Here the hooligans are reinforced by Rabbi Meir Kahane's men. I see him borne high on the shoulders of a young supporter. This man, never legitimized by Israeli society, is now whipping his men to a frenzy, yelling that the marchers are traitors, a knife in the back of the nation. To me it seems that a great many of the marchers are the backbone of the nation, not the knife; but any idea of a discussion here is a daydream. A moment later, a highly symbolic scene: some of Kahane's men, who were not in the Holocaust and always try to preempt the Holocaust argument, are punching—in front of my eyes—a couple of elderly people on the fringe of the procession, both of them Holocaust survivors. I try to find a cameraman to record this, but they are all on the other side of the street. The single policeman on my side cannot leave his post, either. He looks at me helplessly, and I do not press him.

Begin Begin Begin Begin. Arik Arik Arik king, Arik king. Two high school girls now pass under a veritable rain of spit, one can see the gobs of spit flying, and their mouths quiver. Democracy has some strange front lines these days, and it seems that standing fast under a rain of spit is one of them, but no one prepared them for this experience, and they are certainly having a bad time. A towering goon bursts into my field of vision in the thick crowd, prancing like a mad dervish, and yells, "Ashkenazis! Laborites! Trash! Arik king of Israel!" and the marchers chant in unison, "Arik, resign and go, you're not greater than the law!" I see a big red bruise under Alon's eye and know it was only his iron discipline that stopped him from retaliating. Some hours later, after the murder, I hear him say in a bewildered voice: "Until now I knew that the PLO was my enemy. I fought them. Now these people are fighting me—can you tell me who my enemy is?"

At this point I leave the march for half an hour to make some calls from the Plaza Hotel lobby, and when I rejoin it at the top of the Kirya Road, marchers tell me what happened in the meantime: they got to the end of Bezalel Street, slowly, but they made it, then halted at the entrance to the underground pass. There was no way they could move ahead. The police were losing control. Suddenly, a hail of stones came down from one of the roofs above—a classic ambush. Through great bodily pressure and perseverance they managed to break through and pass through the tunnel, but a few people were badly bruised by the stones and had to be helped to leave.

Night falls. Near Sacker Park, the marchers now light torches and sing the Chanukah song: "We Came to Banish the Dark." The stones still keep flying, but desultorily: we are now out of range. Things seem quieter; only a single hoodlum comes running and tries to push the arm of Eitan Shashinsky, a senior economist, so that his torch would inflame the windbreaker he is wearing. Eitan holds fast. The goon escapes.

I say to myself: These are your supporters, Mr. Begin. Your supporters. You cannot write them off, or perhaps you don't want to. Did you really not realize, Mr. Prime Minister, what three fatal days of indecision would do to the street, and how the street would interpret them? You, the expert on swaying the street, did not understand that you did not have the time to hesitate? Yet Minister Aharon Uzzan, and Knesset member Abu-Hatzeira, who know the grass roots well, told you in no uncertain terms that the government must make up its mind quickly, otherwise the street will try to decide for it. Under no circumstances, Mr. Prime Minister, should you have passed the decision to the mob, not for three long days, not even for a single hour: the duty of an immediate decision was yours, and yours only, and you failed to make it. This is not the way to govern. This is not the way to command, either. Any young second lieutenant marching here tonight can tell you that.

We arrive at our destination: the square outside the prime minister's office. The Israeli cabinet is in session inside the building we are facing.

The shouts "Begin-Begin, Arik-Arik" now become mad whirls of dancers, but not in our immediate proximity; the presence of police and border police is strong here, and the violence is restrained by a buffer of barriers. It is still hard to make oneself heard: the noise is overwhelming. Opposite, in the dark, a murky mass of Tehiya Party youngsters, this time not armed with bicycle chains, as they were last time at the Hebrew University, but holding slogans: Peace in Vain, PLO Peace Now. The face of Tzahi Hanegbi, one of their leaders, is lit for a moment, and I see his mouth move; he is probably shouting slogans, but one cannot hear a single word. Tzali, the Peace Now spokesman, plants a microphone in front of me and says urgently, "Speak." I say, and probably no one can hear me in the deafening din, that the government is not above the law; that a minister of defense who evades responsibility will not be able to demand responsibility from a single officer or a single soldier; that a government that does not recognize the supremacy of law cannot demand of its citizens that they obey the law. I say the government is duty bound to implement the findings of the Kahn Commission, and may the arm of law pierce the minister's defense.

Now Uri Simon takes the microphone and reads a text. I think I recognize Jeremiah, but I cannot be sure, because the shouts of "Arik king of Israel" drown out the Bible, too. On the steps of the Bank of Israel edifice in front of me I see, in the torchlight, Emil, who had sustained a great many blows in the procession through town. Just this week he came back from Lebanon: he was doing reserve duty as a paratroop officer. Now he exchanges jokes with a friend. He looks relaxed. He decided to come on the spur of the moment; his original intention was to stay at home and finish a long-overdue paper on the nature of democracy. At this moment, he has about eight, nine minutes left to live.

The anthem. Attention. "To be a free people in our land." Dispersal. The huge crowd and the police mingle, in the dark, as the barriers are dismantled. Police car lights flicker. Members of the Peace Now secretariat are asked by megaphone to remain and collect any trash we may have left in the square. I move down toward the Ministry of Finance parking lot, passing by a group of crazily dancing dervishes, and one of them yells in my ear from behind, "Hey, lady, lady, we're going to do you a Sabra and Shatila!" Amiram, who comes close behind, tells me that from one such group someone screamed at him, "Hey, Peace Now, this is the last time you demonstrate without some grenades flying." I see the cigarette burn on his face, or perhaps it is from another blow. Amiram gets into his car, I wait for friends—and the night air is rent by a muffled, vicious explosion.

Milly Raphaeli says a few minutes later that she saw some men standing on the slope near the bank steps and heard the shout "Now!" She thought they were going to spit at her, and ducked. Not long afterward the explosion was heard. A little later the police find a grenade pin on the slope. It is a shrapnel grenade of standard IDF issue.

They carry away Emil, hit just above the heart and in the throat. There is no breath left in him. More wounded are evacuated in Galia's van, all pock-marked now by splinters, to Sha'arey Tzedek hospital. The bearers are all battle veterans; they have carried the wounded and the dead more than once. But this time it is different: this time they are attacked at the very entrance to the emergency room, on the hospital premises. Five thugs jump on Naftali and ruthlessly bash the head of Dr. David Gild, a physician who participated in the march and escorted the wounded to the hospital, administering first aid on the way. Naftali, with Yarom and Shaul who come running, shakes off the goons—for the present. At the same time the group realizes that Avraham Burg,[2] who helped carry the wounded, has a fragment of shrapnel lodged in his back and requires treatment. Yehoshua Shkedi, badly wounded, is taken into emergency surgery. All this—to the sound of threatening voices: "Next time we'll finish you off, next time we'll kill even more, Arik king of Israel, too bad it was only one."

The next day, during the funeral in Haifa, a young man leans out of a car passing the procession and shouts at the mourners, "That one was just the first!"

I love and admire the president, Mr. Itzhak Navon. I have much esteem for Deputy Prime Minister, Mr. David Levi, who is very sane. I respect the sangfroid of Mr. Peres. They, and many others, have stated publicly that we need to calm the tensions and have issued the call for national reconciliation. No doubt they are right. Reconciliation is an excellent thing; we all need it as we do the air we breathe. But those who understand the importance of national reconciliation were not among the mob last Thursday, and those who used their fists on Thursday do not want reconciliation: what they want is power. I am afraid that those leaders who were alarmed and spoke out as they did are fighting a war long past. Since last Thursday, the rules of war adopted by the Arik-king-of-Israel people have undergone a radical change, and it is not reconciliation that will restore their sanity. Those who do not grasp this have failed, I am afraid, to understand what really happened last Thursday, in the heart of Jerusalem, and outside the seat of government in session.

---

2. Today a member of the Knesset (Labor).

Four Bus Stops Away ═══════════════════

The Other Intifada

Ask an average Israeli what the intifada is and he'll answer: stones, Molotov cocktails, roadblocks, chaos.

There is also another intifada. When schools are closed by order of the authorities and children study regularly, clandestinely, in private homes that have been organized as classrooms, this, too, is intifada. When a person plants ten eggplant seedlings by the side of his home so that he will not be dependent for vegetables on stores that are ordered to close almost daily, this, too, is intifada. When suddenly people stop obeying the *mukhtar* (village headman), the perennial traditional servant of all powers that be, and just ignore him, this is intifada. And when instead of the *mukhtar,* an active and industrious village committee is elected, one that goes into people's homes, deals with welfare, food supplies, all the current problems, and the entire committee is made up of women— this is a very interesting facet of the intifada.

The violent part, the part aimed directly against the occupation, with bottle and stone, is a very small part of what is happening. Some claim here maybe 5 to 10 percent. But it is the only part that is known and heard about in Israel. It provides food for the media: there's action, occasional blood, something to photograph. The rest of it doesn't reach us. Children learning a chapter in geography is not news.

But this profound change, which is taking place before our eyes, is perhaps the most important thing that is happening today among the Arabs of the territories.

The book-filled house of an educator, who wishes to remain nameless since he engages in illegal activity these days. He is one of several thousand unemployed Palestinian academics, and he teaches today in this alternative educational system, which we Israelis have forbidden, known here as *a-ta'alim a-sha'abi,* "people's education." Everything going on here within the wide parameters of discovering and establishing self-identity, is called *sha'abi,* "people's." Even the eggplant and the tomato plant by the side of the house are *bitinjan sha'abi* and *bandora sha'abia* (people's eggplant and people's tomato). The day will come, they say, when everything that today is *sha'abi* will be *watani* (national). After we have a state. From a people to a state.

The very same expression that we once used.

The educator is worried. We've lost a year, he says, with a lot of pain. At first the schools were closed by the Palestinians themselves. The Israeli authorities were interested in seeing the children studying and not wandering around the streets. Now it is the authorities that close the schools. Pressure started coming from the parents not to lose another year. The neighborhood committees began to organize classes inside homes and to mobilize teachers, especially among university students. A complete system of "gray" education was created—and it is clandestine. The apartments are secret, the names of teachers and meeting places are secret. Apartments are changed from time to time.

What do they study? In part, the official study program; although, says the educator, how can you study chemistry in a private apartment, without laboratories? The other part is so-called intifada studies, subjects that strengthen national identity.

Is it successful? It depends on the neighborhood. It is very successful in places like Ramallah, Beit Sahur, in the villages. Less so in the refugee camps, where life is transparent, like an aquarium; and even less among the upper classes, the rich, where the parents are in any case afraid of any contact between their children and "people's" children. Among this class, whoever is able sends the children abroad to study, in Amman or in Europe. But this is a minority.

Would you like to see? my host suddenly asks. We get into his car and travel to a nearby village, very close to Jerusalem. It is almost noon. A group of pupils spills out from one of the stone houses that cling to the mountain slope, their school bags in their hands. They surround us, very suspicious, especially at the sight of the guest taking notes.

"Who's she?" they ask the educator, with grave expressions. He reassures them there's nothing to worry about. But they—eleven-year-olds, twelve-year-olds—adhere to secrecy more religiously than he.

"You shouldn't have brought her," they say. "Don't believe anyone. They are all *muhabbarat*" (intelligence; that is, General Security Services).

"I understand that school was closed today," says the educator.

"Yes, but tell the *Hukkuma* (government) that it was open," they reply, sullenly and with not a little hostility, scattering in every direction. One of them blurts over his shoulder, in an ironic tone, "We thought you were settlers."

There is much more secrecy, much more suspicion than before. This, too, is a unifying factor. "I have a secret leadership" is a unifying factor.

I can see this clearly as I sit in another home, in another village. It is a pleasant-looking quarter, red bougainvillea surrounding the houses, a strongly colored pomegranate tree, fuchsia. A well-to-do quarter. Only the sewage overflows on the badly paved roads. West Bank residents pay taxes, even social security, but do not receive services for their money.

Here we sit, a few people, over the eternal Coca-Cola, and because of their tangible suspicion, I don't ask their names, even though the host has vouched for me. Actually, I'm waiting for a woman who is supposed to come, too, a member of one of those emergency neighborhood committees, to tell me about their activities. At the last minute she telephones my host, notifying him that she has decided not to come. She has opted for secrecy.

"Our committees," says my host, "have created great decentralization, and that is their purpose: after years of total dependence on the authorities—never mind at the moment which authorities—people are discovering that there is another way. For example, we've established a legal committee, so that we would not be dependent on the Israeli courts. Today there is an internal judiciary system, and all problems must be dealt with on the spot. There is internal agricultural aid, local guidance."

"For example?"

"For example, raising rabbits in homes as a source of cheap meat. Or vegetables by the side of the house. Not to be dependent on a store that is closed most of the time."

"The Popular Front,"[1] interrupts someone, "opposed this at one time: what will ten eggplant seedlings achieve? We told them, it won't bring independence, and it won't create an alternative to the Israeli market, but people will learn that they can live without being dependent. Before that our self-esteem was too low. Now we've learned that we can depend on ourselves. This is the great success of the intifada."

And, of course, there is also a medical committee. So as not to be too dependent on the hospitals. A hospital, too, is transparent, a public realm.

"So far, there have been three stages of the intifada," says the host. "At the beginning it was sheer protest against the occupation, without a thought ahead, what to do next, or the consequences. Later, people saw that they felt better personally, that it was possible to resist, and that led to hope that something political would change. There was a lot of naiveté in this. We thought a Palestinian state would rise up overnight. Now we are in the third stage, which began around May or June 1988; people began to think that it would take many years, that things would not ripen quickly, that the immediate task was to build the Palestinian identity."

"Things will get worse," says someone. "There are those who hope for more Israeli cruelty, which would lead to deterioration and world pressure on Israel. Hope that you Israelis, by your own actions, will cause such a state of affairs that no one will want you in the Middle East, not even Hussein and Saudi Arabia. We will sacrifice, but we will make you into the monsters of the world."

But the others shake their heads in doubt.

"A pipe dream," they say. "No one will send in an army to defend us. Not even the Soviet Union. That particular dream is over. What the Palestinians will not do for themselves, no one else will do for them."

"What part does the PLO play as a factor in the intifada?"

"The PLO tried to buy people with money, just like Jordan and Israel," answers one of them. "And the refugees suffered the most, because no one wanted to buy them."

The host interrupts: "Every child knows that the PLO was very problematic in the distribution of resources, in its use of money. A large chunk

---

1. This is the Popular Front for the Liberation of Palestine, led by George Habash.

never reached the needy, the refugees, the workers, the poor. There was also the paternalism of the PLO—and part of the intifada is a protest against them too, although they are still the official representatives. The fact of the matter is that we are at last learning to be ourselves, to depend only on ourselves. Hussein felt this too. Today people feel as though Hussein doesn't exist—maybe from a lack of political consciousness. His key figures are silent, and we ourselves are changing. One village was under curfew for thirty-five days and lost its entire agricultural output; the damage was some $150,000. The authorities called in the two *mukhtars,* demanded that they turn in six wanted people, and said they would then receive compensation. Before the intifada they would definitely have turned them in. Today they said no."

"Sometimes we even say no to offers of financial assistance," says someone. "American artists came, they wanted to donate money, to make a big thing of it. We weighed one thing against another—the money against the secrecy—and told them thank you, no. A year ago something like that would have been unthinkable."

Through the window one sees the writing on the walls of the houses. A lot of graffiti. "Close Ansar 3."[2] "There is no alternative to a Palestinian state." "Brothers, beware of drugs." "Congratulations to the striking merchants."

"Hamas, the fundamentalist organization, erases what others write," they say, with displeasure. "They are known to be violent. Sometimes they demand that stores be closed. The first time we listened to them, because we were afraid; the second time we resisted."

When my host accompanies me outside, I ask him about all the small fruit and vegetable stalls that have sprouted like mushrooms in the heart of the quarter. He shrugs his shoulders.

"The merchants closed the stores and set up stalls. It's easier for them, with either Israel or the fundamentalists coming along and closing the stores all the time. Anyway, it wasn't worth keeping fruits and vegetables in the stores, because it's impossible to sell all the stock in three hours

---

2. Ansar 3 is a detention center in the Negev Desert, established during the intifada to hold the scores of Palestinian detainees who wouldn't fit in the already-overfilled prisons.

and it rots.[3] And besides, the merchants have had it hard for a long time. Taxes are high, prices are beginning to equal those in Israel, the regular customers are disappearing. Even in Nablus, the traditional commercial artery of the West Bank, there were fears of bankruptcy even before the intifada, because the stores are just not making money. So the merchant prefers to be a 'negative merchant.'"

"How do they live?"

"You know you'll lose a year, two years. There are other sources of income, from abroad as well. There are chains that have branches in Amman. You get by. And besides, since the intifada, there's a lot of mutual aid. People are no longer embarrassed to go to a neighbor and ask for help, and this is new."

How do you break this? With rubber bullets, or plastic?

In Kalandiya, after the Curfew

"Curfew has been imposed today on the Kalandiya Camp."

How many times have we heard this sentence on the news? It barely registers, we are so used to it. Recently there was an extended curfew, because of rioting: the anniversary of Sabra and Shatila. The memorial services, like our own, have become a means to increase national feeling. Someone offered to get me into Kalandiya during the curfew, but I refused: I will fight against the laws of my country in the Knesset, I told him, but I will not break them. He agreed: yes, you really have a democracy. We know this. Your newspapers are all right. Our press is castrated.

Now that curfew has been lifted, I enter with a young friend who works in a well-known office in East Jerusalem. A group of soldiers lean idly against a vehicle. Voices on the walkie-talkie: the battalion commander said this, said that. We ask if we can enter the narrow opening to the left of the wall of barrels, and they raise their hands: go ahead. There is no tension, no helmets or visors. They crack sunflower seeds. Someone reads a newspaper.

Perhaps because my friend has come directly from work and carries a

---

3. With the beginning of the intifada Palestinian stores remained open only from nine to noon.

James Bond briefcase, a group of youths stands opposite us saying, "*Muhabbarat, muhabbarat.*" They don't know what to make of us.

"That's right," I tell them, "this is James Bond and I'm his mother."

Our entry, amidst the general, liberating laughter, is made much simpler.

Kalandiya is a veteran camp, relatively clean, certainly compared to the camps in the Gaza area. It is a mountain-area camp: there are no stagnant sewage swamps, there are no flies. Most of the inhabitants came from the Lydda-Ramle area forty years ago. Their children were born in the camp and grew up in it. A United Nations Relief and Works Agency branch overlooks the entrance, a brand on the camp's forehead.

We sit on couches in a small family house where several young men have gathered. It is a small place, but compared with Gibalya, for example, it is a palace. Most of the men work: one in a restaurant, one as a porter, one lays pipes. One twenty-two-year-old does not work. "I live with my father," he says with a dash of bravado. As the conversation continues, there are communication problems with him.

One has already been in jail four times, the first time when he was fourteen and sentenced to two years. They've all taken their share of beatings. One received hard club blows on the head, and since then "I wander about at night, can't sleep." Even during a curfew. His family runs after him and brings him back home. On the way they get beaten too. After the grenade was thrown following the swearing-in ceremony of the paratroopers at the Western Wall before the intifada, the beatings here were indiscriminate. All the men present in the little room, without exception, were hit. In the stomach, in the testicles, and after being arrested, with their hands tied. One was arrested while transporting guests to his brother's wedding: what was he doing driving back and forth all the time? He was brutally beaten up.

"What has the intifada done for you?" I ask, meaning the violent intifada. But for them it is really only a very small part of what is happening, even though here I am in the center of potential disturbances: the violent trend was born and thrives in the refugee camps. They answer: Hope. Mutual aid. People feel that they are one nation. Consideration, sensitivity. Doing much less "for show": the extravagant weddings have come to an end. There is a big change in customs, much less class differentiation, for example. We no longer observe the religious commandment of charity by giving to the mosque, but to the needy. We send food during curfews. We're happy to share with a neighbor, even olives. Homes have opened up, people talk more to one another, live the problems together.

"What about schooling?"

There is no people's education here. Things are too transparent; it's hard to maintain secrecy. The one who did time in jail when he was fourteen left prison at sixteen and wanted to continue studying, but a representative of the military government came to the prison and told him not even to dream about it. So now he works as a porter for a Jewish contractor. Yes, they curse him a lot. What can you do?

All the young men sitting before me have been cursed and beaten since their early youth. And the hands are the hands of Jacob.

But still, what about the violent aspect of the intifada?

The violence, they say disparagingly, is only our loudspeaker. Before it there was a media blackout over everything we were and did. Throwing a bottle opens the news media all over the world to you. In our era, violence raises the volume; there is no other way.

And what would happen if the national leadership made a decision to stop the violence for a certain period—would you accept this or not?

Opinion is divided. One says yes. Another says that throwing a stone is not violence.

"Anyway, with you everything we do is called violence. If we raise a flag, to you that's violence. A flag is not a stone or a bottle, it doesn't hurt anyone."

And a third adds: "Look, one of you went to Tunis and met with Abu Ammar (Arafat) and suggested a period of quiet for one hundred days, and Arafat said to him: 'We'll consider it. There are disagreements among us, but we'll consider it.' He made some concessions. It's just that your government is not credible."

"In what?"

"Look, the one that was in Tunis, that pilot (Abie Nathan), when he got back from there, they demonstrated against him."[4]

I explain to him that in a democracy it is permissible to demonstrate

---

4. Abie Nathan is an Israeli pilot and professional peacenik who violated an Israeli law forbidding Israeli citizens from meeting with terrorists (i.e., the PLO) and was sent to prison for a four-month term, having refused to appeal the sentence.

for any point of view. But he will have none of it: "It's a fact that the government, the police, permitted this. And now you're investigating him. That means you're credible?"

"What about Hussein's disengagement?"

"Let him keep himself distant. That whole connection—Israel and Jordan and the Palestinians—the refugee camps never benefited from it."

"Thatcher's his mother, Reagan's his father, and when you step on his tail he barks in New York and London."

"And you should know that we hate the Arab states even more than we hate you. Hussein slaughtered more than 50,000 of us." The king of Jordan does not have many fans in the refugee camps, and we didn't expect to find any. For the record, he killed some 3,000 Palestinians during "Black September" and afterward.

"You," says one of them, "made the mistake of your lives when you started relying on our labor and stopped working. You've become a spoiled people. You won't last. If you show an even stronger hand, we'll make a Beirut here, car bombs and all."

I put down my writing pad and tell them as a private person that not a single man or woman from any party would permit the situation they are describing, and it will not come about. And as to being spoiled, they don't know us: we are ready to return to a low standard of living overnight if need be.

Now it is their turn to ask: "Tell us, why is Israel afraid of peace? Both sides will receive international guarantees, there will be security for everyone, what are you afraid of?"

I didn't come here to argue—and it was certainly possible to present entirely different facts as to what Arafat did and did not say of late. I make do with a short answer that a nation that has lost one-third of its people, six million, is very cautious about its security.

The youth who doesn't work glances sideways with contempt: "What six million? We learned in history that there were maybe half a million."

The others are sensitive to my reaction. One of them says to me on the way out: "It isn't right what he said. We know very well that you lost six million. But why should we be the victims?"

Later, outside, they admit that they were being, deliberately, "a little provocative."

Children play outside: the IDF against their forces. Some of them have cut the bottoms off large plastic bottles and are using them as visors. A stick serves as a rifle. Make no mistake: the "soldiers," too, play their roles with enthusiasm. At least when they are playing, they identify with the stronger.

A man who accompanies us along the pathway tells us that during the last curfew soldiers stole from houses. What did they steal? In one place cash, in another gold jewelry, in a third a watch. At the moment I have no possibility of checking. I hope that someone, somewhere, will investigate. Maybe it's a naive hope. Whoever goes into a refugee camp comes out a lot less naive.

We're sitting in the house of a young man who was deported to Lebanon a few weeks earlier. He was accused of incitement and decided not to appeal to the High Court of Justice for reasons of principle. His parents show me photographs of him, among them a photograph from the front page of an Israeli newspaper that shows him getting out of the helicopter, handcuffed. His name is Mursi. They keep these photographs in a drawer, because if soldiers come in and see the photographs "they make trouble."

Umm Mursi (Mursi's mother) has a hard time doing the housework: her hand is very swollen from a club blow. Twelve days ago, she says, they came in, mixed kerosene into their rice. Just like that. There is no running water in the house, only an outside faucet, and to this day Umm Mursi calls it, after the custom of the fellaheen, *el-ayin,* "the spring." The eight-year-old son went out to bring water from the "spring" during a curfew, and a soldier fired a rubber bullet. That was a good soldier, she says, he didn't want to hurt the boy, he fired to the side. But the bullet entered the house. They make me a gift of the bullet.

What has the intifada done to them, personally?

First of all, they say, it has strengthened our identity. Encouraged local produce. Now far fewer go out to work in Israel. People have become closer to each other. Even the slumbering have awakened. We also "accumulate accounts," are in no hurry to pay taxes. There is a change in our relations to institutions, to the banks.

Umm Mursi: "How would you hear us otherwise? We weren't born bad. No one is born with a stone in his hand. The stones are not an end in themselves, only a means."

The son, Suheil: "The young boy doesn't see it that way. The child sees the soldiers beating—and he hates. Wants to express his anger. We older ones know how to differentiate, but it will be difficult to wean the children from hatred."

As if on signal, the children playing soldiers outside throw a bottle filled with sand, pretending it is tear gas. They cover their nostrils and run away. One of the adults goes out to chase them away and when he returns says smilingly, "We are from the UN, separating between your forces and ours."

The father: "What bothers us most is that you always want to connect us to the Arab countries, as if we didn't have our own identity. We are not them, we have a long list of grievances with the Arab states. We don't want to be dependent, neither on them nor on Israel."

How do they see peace?

The mother: "First of all you should return the deportees. You should stop deporting. And I say, when we have our state, there will be peace. When we get a bit of homeland, we'll forget everything. We'll cooperate."

"Could you really forget this whole period?"

Umm Mursi: "I will forget that Mursi was deported. The bereaved parent will forget. The injured will forget. The only thing is to gain a little homeland of our own, and no one to rule over us. My dear friend, we'll even cancel the memorials."

Suheil: "If there is a solution, and it is implemented with international guarantees—and at this stage it is I who am first of all in need of international protection—let them come in and protect us; then there is a possibility that the problem will be solved. The next stage will be negotiations. And when there is a solution, and there is a state, we will obligate ourselves before the entire world to observe the decisions made at the international conference. We weren't born bad. I'm like a cat, when you put him behind bars he becomes a lion. After the agreement, I'll go back to being a cat."

As I leave, one of them says to me: "Why do you consider us lawbreakers? We didn't vote for your government, or your Knesset. How can you break a law that someone else forced on you?"

On the way home I hear the news on the radio: a Molotov cocktail was thrown in Nablus. A soldier was seriously burned.

View from This Side

Shmulik is a platoon commander in a "good" unit, and comes to tell me about his three weeks alongside the Jelazoun camp.

"As soon as we arrived the company commander called us together and said: 'I don't care who you vote for. In the Lebanon War they shot at us and we shot at them, but no one said "Arab son of a whore." It will be the same way here. Don't get into anything personal.'

"And the company commander was 100 percent right. Company X had been here before us; they told us, Learn from us, every day you go down to the camp, rough up a few of them, go back and there's quiet. And they had incidents all the time. We didn't do any roughing up, 90 percent of us didn't even carry a club, and it was quiet. Even during a curfew we let those who really went out to work pass. A forty-year-old comes along with pita in a plastic bag, he's going out to earn a living, not to make trouble. And the people here know exactly who they're dealing with.

"The settlers drove us crazy. At the beginning they came from Shiloh, Beit El, with coffee and cakes. They began to brainwash the soldiers. At first they said that the Arabs accepted our presence, afterward it turned out that they really wanted to expel them. Once when I was standing at a roadblock, a hysterical settler came and started screaming: 'A boy threw a stone at me, go catch him, in a yellow shirt.' I said to him, 'Sir, there are 7,000 people in this camp, and the boy has already changed his shirt ten times. I'm not running after him.' He began to shout, 'You're whores, leftists, we know your unit, get out of here, we don't need you here.' I told him to go. We had a hard time getting him into his car. He was really hostile.

"Another time, at a different village, there was a curfew, and we brought a tractor to remove iron nails from the road. A settler with an M-16 rifle and a pistol passed by, raised his weapon, and began shooting, just like that, into the village. We were hard-pressed because we also had to concentrate on our work, and how to avoid getting a building block on the head. The officer got angry, threw him out of there. Then this settler raised his weapon again and shot into the village—and there were soldiers in the village too, it's a miracle that no one was hurt—and wrecked eight solar water heaters, just like that.

"Once, during a curfew, they brought lists of names from the Shabak (General Security Services), and we had to arrest people at night. I'm from a right-wing family myself, but to go into houses like that at night, with the children crying, I said to myself, My God, we're already South America. That whole bit stinks. It's bad enough for the reservists, but they drive the regular army completely crazy. They've all become policemen, they do the work of the police. It's not being a soldier at all."

Of course this is not being a soldier. Some two hundred and fifty people have been killed during the intifada; of these more than fifty were small children. Two school classes. Seven people, and perhaps even twelve, were definitely shot by settlers, one of these in the Kalandiya camp.

The intifada, in all its forms, already has one important achievement to its credit: the image of the Palestinian has changed. He is no longer the terrorist who comes from outside, his face covered with a stocking, a Kalashnikov in his hand; now, the Palestinian is the boy who lives four bus stops from your house, wears a school bag on his back, and throws stones.

I'm beginning to think that our fear of a Palestinian state is not a fear of them. No sane person in Israel thinks in terms of missiles in Jelazoun. Their weakness is clear and evident. Our fear is that somehow our eyes are deceiving us, that somehow we cannot rely on what we see. It is still an image from the past. Millions of European Jews did not foresee that there would soon be a holocaust and that six million would be brutally murdered. The error in judgment preceding the Yom Kippur War also increased our lack of confidence in ourselves. Something deep in the heart won't let us rest: it's true, everything is true, but what if we're making another mistake. What if everything we know and see turns out to be wrong. What if, in spite of everything, they could destroy us. And politicians come along, and instead of reinforcing sanity, they work on our fears, play up everything that is not rational.

The Palestinians have a very big story now. But this story still does not connect with our story, as if we and they were in fact close, but living in different time spheres. A person leaves the West Bank; across from him in the bus sits a religious man, entirely absorbed in the *Tikun* prayer, mouthing a psalm—and there is no way at all to connect the two stories. Further on one sees a class outing to Ammunition Hill. And here too there is no way to connect the stories. Later still, one arrives in the city, sees families, children, housewives, purchases in the corner grocery store —and here some kind of connection simply must be found.

A few bus stops away there is a child with perhaps only two or three days left to live. It could be the fifty-first child.

And I can still hear the voice of Umm Mursi, the sentence that sent chills down my spine: "My dear friend, if we have a little bit of homeland, we'll even cancel the memorials."

Eyeless in Gaza ———————————

ON THE OUTER WALL OF ONE
of the Israeli administration buildings in Gaza, a section painted in white
stands out. On it—in gay colors—are the words "Love, Brotherhood,
Peace, Friendship." Beautiful words. There is just one problem: they are
written solely in Hebrew.

Gaza. A chilly night, under curfew, in the home of a friend, a Gazan psychiatrist, in the well-to-do A-Rimal residential quarter. This quarter is
inhabited, as they say here, by "refined people, the kind who throw
stones wrapped in Kleenex." A quiet neighborhood. One can hear the
sea murmur nearby. A vagrant camel ambles by, slowly chewing the leaves
of the mulberry tree outside. Only Israeli security vehicles travel on the
faulty roads, carrying soldiers wearing helmets with visors. Were anyone
from my own family to pass by in a vehicle, I would not recognize him.
Some of these vehicles are traveling to a nearby structure called Ansar II
(the coastal detention compound). Others are out enforcing the curfew.

Earlier, my hosts had collected a number of small stones that were
lying in the road, "so that the soldiers won't break into the house at two
o'clock in the morning, get us up in our pajamas, and order us to clear."
At the moment it is very quiet. The nearby Arab police station was completely vacated in less than an hour. In the evening, a single police officer
could still be seen there, speaking nervously on the telephone; later, only
the great lights remained, illuminating the empty building. The Palestine
Liberation Organization's Leaflet No. 10 called on all employees of the
Israeli administration to resign. To drive the point home, a police officer
was assassinated—an intimation of things to come.

The PLO game is obvious: as the anarchy in the territories increases,
internal pressures increase, and there is a greater chance of trapping Israel into taking stronger and stronger measures until the world will be

forced to intervene. But the police officer I meet the next day, who has been made to resign, is not responsible for the PLO's games. He is very sad, for if there is no work, there will be nothing to live on. The transition from eking out a living to near-starvation is a very short one in the refugee camps of Gaza. But they obey. They have no choice.

The curfew is due to end at three o'clock in the morning, to enable Gazan workers to go to work in Israel. Gaza, much more than the West Bank, is economically dependent on Israel. At three or four o'clock in the morning they will slowly shuffle their way to the collection points—if they are not pelted with stones, if the bus that has come to collect them has not been set on fire by extremists, if there is not yet another general strike. Afterward they will commute to the restaurants of Tel Aviv, to the construction scaffoldings of Ashkelon, to sanitation work in the sewers of Gush Dan. Someone will say, Dirty Arab. Someone will mutter, We ought to kill the lot of you. At the end of the day's work, they will return home to sleep, to a few square meters of damp, gray concrete with a mat and a worn-out mattress, dead and drained after fifteen hours on their feet.

But in A-Rimal quarter no one has to get up at three o'clock in the morning. Only in one house does a light burn all night: one of their sons did not know about the curfew and has not arrived home. They worry: perhaps some soldier got jumpy and opened fire. It turned out that the son had remained in his car at the Erez checkpoint with a number of latecomers like himself, waiting out the end of the curfew. Not so terrible. Just another inconvenience, and by no means the worst.

For twenty years the Gazans, who today number more than 650,000 persons, have been living with what we call harassment and the Arabs call humiliation. Not only in big things. Not only in the fact that 1,800 people live here per one square kilometer of land—one of the highest population density quotients in the world. Not only in the fact that one-third of the lands of the Gaza Strip have been expropriated for some two thousand settlers, including a large part of the water. It is not expressed merely in the need to "request ten licenses for every carton of eggs," as they say, but also in agricultural restrictions, marketing restrictions, the cutting of exports, budget delays, restrictions on fishing and fishing hours. Not only in unjustified taxation, or the prohibition on working the land, which has left them no alternative but to go out and do blue-collar work in Israel, or the thousand-and-one prohibitions and restrictions we have imposed here.

We are talking about twenty years of regular, daily, stupid harassment; harassment for the sake of harassment, malice for its own sake. Malice to which all the governments of Israel, irrespective of person or party, have been silent partners. A person goes out in his car in the morning and does not know what will happen along the way. It is very likely that he will be stopped, ordered to remove all four wheels of the car and then reassemble them. In the beginning they said it was a search. Later, even the excuse of a search disappeared. If you are lucky, they'll tell you to remove one wheel only. What do you have in the bag back there? Pitas? They take them and throw them in the garbage can. You have no idea when you will reach your destination. Even if you are a doctor rushing to the hospital. Even if you are taking a family member to the airport to catch a plane or are a teacher on the way to class.

No one thing is terrible in and of itself. In Gaza City they used to say it was a six-day-a-week occupation, because very few soldiers were seen in the streets on the Sabbath. There is one thing only: for twenty-four hours, day and night, on the road and at home, you are at the arbitrary mercy of every official, every soldier at a roadblock.

Moshe Dayan, with all his drawbacks, knew the importance of contact between residents and the authorities. In the beginning he personally interviewed and selected every candidate for a senior position in the administration. Later on things deteriorated. A corporal in charge of transport in some small village became a deputy commander in a larger village, in the Civil Administration, and afterward, out of inertia, a top person in the entire region. No one knew what his education was or what training he had received for such a sensitive job. In the eyes of the residents, he is Israel. They have no other Israel. Except, perhaps, the merchant who comes to buy goods at a cut price, the contractor in search of laborers, the settler. Today settlers also serve in the administration.

The harassments accumulate. One family scrimped and saved to send their only daughter to study at Cairo University. The girl was not particularly talented, and several years passed until she succeeded, with much hard work and financial contributions from the entire family, in getting her degree. The family dressed up in their best clothes, traveled to Cairo, and proudly photographed the graduation ceremony—so that they would have something to brag about to the neighbors. On their return, at the border, their camera was taken from them and the film burned in front of their eyes. Why? That's the way it is.

A woman student, who was returning from the United States by way of Egypt, received an interesting welcome from a woman soldier at the border crossing. The latter took all her clothing out of the suitcase, and, calling out to her friends, held the blouses against her chest: "Come on everybody, come and see what expensive clothes this one has." When the student, the daughter of a well-known figure, remarked that, in her opinion, this was not the place for a fashion show, she was insulted. She shouldn't be impertinent, the Arab. Shouldn't get so high-handed here.

A person in the street is called to: "Come here, donkey." Someone who doesn't please the local official is expelled from work for a week, returned for a week, and then the cycle begins again. When the head of the Civil Administration assembled the staff of the Gaza health services, and one of the doctors stood up and requested that people be treated with more equality, more respect, he was immediately shut up—he must not speak politics. For a week afterward he was called up for investigations. He should be thankful that he didn't spend a few months in administrative detention. They were doing him a favor.

No, this is not the worst. Of course, there is greater suffering than this. They themselves say, Hussein killed more of us than you do. I am sitting in the home of a Gazan family whose four children are studying in universities abroad; the authorities will not permit them to return home because "they have been abroad too long." The father says, You are Nazis. Both I and my friend the psychiatrist protest immediately. My friend explains, sensitively, earnestly, that there is no comparison. But this father is retired and lives on 200 shekels (about $135) a month, not a budget that allows him to purchase a plane ticket and see his children. He has not seen the oldest for fifteen years. Here, he shows me, last month he was barely able to buy a pair of pants made in Israel, which were sewed by cheap labor in Gaza but bought at the steep Israeli price—an example of the colonial economy we have set up here. So what can they do? They sit at home and cry and kiss the photographs their children send them. Family reunion is not one of the things our administration encourages here.

And another story: five people, one after another, tell me with great emotion about Mr. Shamir's visit to Gaza a short while before the uprising broke out. He had convened the community leaders and notables for a meeting. Intentionally or not, they were made to wait for twenty minutes in the street, facing locked doors. Afterward, when they entered and said what they had to say, Shamir paid no attention to their words, saying only that Israel would never leave Gaza. Even if the story is exaggerated, the shame remains. "Why did he assemble us?" they ask. "What are we, a herd of sheep?" All swear that this event influenced the escalation of the intifada, the uprising. This time it was not a question of an administration official's abusing his elders and betters. It was the prime minister in person. Humiliation from that quarter has intentional political significance.

No one understood that every act has a consequence, that for every harassment, whether at a basic-training camp or in the territories, there will, in the end, be a reaction.

It did not take much—one road accident, one rumor, one funeral—and the intifada broke out.

It has many faces. Not only a protest against Israeli rule, although this is the principal and most open component. There is a note of rebellion against the established, traditional leadership, which has not succeeded in changing anything in twenty years. There is a rebellion of women and children against patriarchal rule, which has existed since time immemorial. There is a shade of protest—still covert—by the residents of the camps against the wealthy old families of Gaza, who have connections in Israel and around the world. Their voices are being heard, while the paupers of the camps are living in mute and rebellious poverty.

Two hundred women broke into the school building in Gibalia, had a harsh collision with the army, and returned home hurt by rubber bullets and coughing from tear gas—but every one of them returned to launder and cook and wash the dishes, because this is women's work. Youths from the Nuseirat camp and from the villas of Gaza discuss the intifada with one another, and the social aspect is only hinted at here and there, in a statement like, "Actually, I should be throwing the stones at your windows." But all these currents will be apparent in the future, because this is a society undergoing significant changes before our eyes, and even if the present riots are quelled, the process will continue. Only we stand immobile, like Lot's wife looking back at past destruction, turned into a pillar of salt.

Outside guidance? You have to be here to see what nonsense this is. An incident begins like this: three children stand and taunt soldiers. Ten more join them and they begin to throw rocks, and the rocks are big and damaging. Fifteen women come out of their homes to protect the children and to curse. Behind their backs two teenagers set fire to a tire. The soldiers begin to respond. The situation escalates. It becomes an "incident." There was no guiding hand here. But the terrorist organizations understood immediately that they had to jump on the bandwagon, as if they were in control.

This is a grass-roots war, way below the level of the IDF; therefore, it is doubtful whether it was wise to deal with it by means of the army. So far it has been a very restrained war, a war with brakes on; no one has yet used his full force, and everyone knows this. These relatively contained rules of the game are broken by two parties only: the PLO, which hits and attempts to hit in order to escalate, and our crazy right wing, which shoots on sight and also demands an escalation. In the meantime, this is a war without organization and without a budget, and therefore it can continue, in one form or another, for a long time to come.

I pose the same question to everyone I meet here: suppose the administration behaved humanely, suppose there weren't so many restrictions and harassments, would the intifada still have broken out? The answer is astonishingly uniform: It would have been delayed for a while, it would have been much less violent, but in the end it would have broken out, because no one wants to live without an identity.

My friend the psychiatrist testifies that people's pride has returned. The incidence of depression has decreased significantly; conflicts within families and between families have diminished; daily anxieties have gone down; the use of drugs has greatly declined. After twenty years of fear, the pendulum has swung in the opposite direction. The people have lost all fear. Everyone is on a "trip," which is sometimes exaggerated.

An officer friend of mine confirms this: "That's exactly the way it is. They sing *shu el huf, shu el huf* (what is there to be afraid of), and come as close as twenty to thirty meters from our weapons."

There is a whole spectrum of views here, just as there is among Israelis. There are pro-Jordanians and anti-Jordanians; separatists and those who seek partners; those who are for George Shultz and those who are against him; those who want social reformation first and those who want national identity first; people who are more religious and those who are less so. The religious are also divided: some are Jihad and some are the Islamic Opposition Movement. The latter was one of the worst mistakes that Israel made in the Gaza Strip. Someone had the idea that the movement would be something like Agudat Israel, that it would concern itself with religious matters and not interfere too much in politics. The authorities supported them vis-à-vis the left wing. At present, the Gazans tell me, "They are our Kahane, the craziest of all." They are the ones who write on the walls not to forget Acre and Jaffa. They are the ones who write "Muhammed Is Coming"—something like "Messiah Now." In Israel it is erroneously thought that religion fans the passions here. From within Gaza, things seem the other way around: the existing euphoria finds, in part, a means of expression in religion and religious slogans.

They asked if I wanted to see the real extremists. Even the refugee camps are not all of one mind. Gibalia is of Marxist persuasion. Sejiya—fundamentalist. Gaza City itself—the Jihad.

The Gibalia refugee camp is one of the most shameful spots in the entire world. Israel certainly does not bear the sole culpability for this. The Arab states, especially *al nafti'in*, "the oil-rich," have not contributed a thing to solve the problem. Egypt, which controlled the area until 1967, kept the people in tents and forbade building permanent structures. None of this changes the fact that we are not entitled to wash our hands of the matter. This is not some distant crown colony, out of sight, out of mind. This place is in our very midst, and the thousands of people crowded within it are part of our social fabric. As long as this place is under Israeli control, even if we are not wholly guilty, we are responsible.

To enter Gibalia you have to pass a formidable roadblock of children aged nine to twelve. The man who brought me to the camp, himself a resident of Gibalia, is much respected here—he has done time in an Israeli prison (see also page 127). The children check who is with him in the car, and only when he vouches for the guest do they let us pass. One girl runs after us and throws a stone, but they apologize immediately: she's a silly girl. One of them, at the request of my host, opens his shirt and shows me his scar—he had caught a bullet in the chest during the first month of the uprising. Make no mistake about it: if the children had not given their permission, we would not have passed.

Here, in a tiny concrete room that makes an Israeli slum look like a palace, the most difficult conversation of this visit takes place. Within these few square meters lives an educated man, a teacher and writer, who is currently host to two West Bank students; according to a new prohibition, they are unable to travel home from the Gaza Strip. There are a lot of children. A round-faced, pleasant woman holds an infant in her arms. There is no table on which to write, only a drawer filled with books and journals. He was born here, a refugee son of refugees. In his eyes, and in the eyes of his young friends, all Israelis are the same. There is no difference between Shamir and Peres. Shultz has come to kill us. Peace Now is interested only in philanthropy, not a political solution. Hussein has killed us already (here he makes the same gesture I saw countless times in Gaza when Palestinians spoke of killings—a kind of karate chop of the right hand on the left palm), and now he will kill us again. There is only one party they would like to see in power in Israel—Rakah (the Communist Party). This isn't realistic? They shrug their shoulders. Only Rakah. And Arab Jerusalem is ours.

I ask: Do you believe that the PLO will solve your problems? The terrible social conditions? Before the establishment of the Jewish state, we already had a prepared infrastructure; does the PLO have any kind of social program? Any kind of an infrastructure? They are silent for a moment, and then answer: "In your Knesset there are also differences of opinion. But we authorize Arafat. He is a good man, dedicated, never married, never raised a family, works only for the people. We have nothing to lose. We will have a state, not in your stead, but alongside you." These last qualifying words sound as if they were said out of a sense of social obligation.

Someone whose physical world, from the day he was born, begins and ends in a few meters of damp concrete on which are thrown a thin mattress and a few old pillows—with the eternal laundry at the window to the right and the IDF camp seen through a hole in the wall to the left; plagued by mosquitoes from the large cesspool in the center of Gibalia —someone who was born here, studied here, fell in love here, brought forth children here, who writes here in the evenings, without hope, without opportunity, and now without electricity as well, because the authorities have shut it off at night—maybe he really doesn't want to distinguish between people, parties, and opinions in Israel. He will not come to terms with us of his own free will. His is a great and blinding anger.

When I depart, he says: "The occupation has built both of us. We built the houses for you, and you have built us into a people."

A few hours later, in other company, an intelligent group seeking a way to come to terms with us, but not interested in revealing itself, I pose the same question: Is the PLO the one that will solve your problems?

Because trust has been established, they answer candidly: "We'll tell you what we would never say to any stranger, certainly not a foreign journalist. No, the PLO will not solve anything. Everyone here knows that. Where does Arafat live? Where are his men? At the casino. But what alternative have you left us? Every time a leader has sprouted up among us, you have immediately deported him. So what is left?"

At the other end of the political spectrum: a young teacher, the daughter of friends, emotionally tells me about an argument in the teachers' room concerning the terrorist hijacking of the "mothers' bus" on the road to Dimona.[1] Some thought this was good, that it showed "how strong we are," that extremism was good and would advance the goal. Others said it was a mistake, that nothing useful would come from terrorism, violence would only lead to more violence, and then the present situation would never end. Some teachers said that the Jews only understood force. Maybe, in the end, a few were convinced, or at least spoke with less acrimony. A mirror image of the arguments in some of our own teachers' rooms.

Later on, a similar story from a doctor, an educated and pleasant man. Like many of his class here, he was educated in England. Sometimes I feel he should be introduced to all those fools and boors among us who say "too bad we gave them an education"—as if *we* had given it. He, too, has argued with his friends about the use of violent measures. This doctor, despite the harassment of *el manganon,* (Hebrew word) as he calls the Civil Administration's bureaucratic machine, despite the insults he has

---

1. The bus, called a "mothers' bus" because it left at an hour convenient to mothers of small children, was carrying workers to a plant in Dimona. It was hijacked on the road by Arab terrorists, who shot three of the hostages, two women and one man. An Israeli army unit managed to free the rest, most of them women, without casualties.

borne, holds a positive image of Israel. He has friends among the Jews who receive him with open arms. It turns out that in 1967 this man was abroad, afraid to return home to what suddenly became occupied territory. At the border crossing a soldier—the first Israeli he had ever seen— spoke to him politely and in good English: "Why are you sad? Don't worry, you'll soon meet your family and you'll see that everything will be all right." Since then, no power in the world has been able to convince him that all Israelis are bad. The ability to differentiate is there.

El manganon is not the only Hebrew word he knows. He also knows how to say "You're all thieves and crooks," which he and his household have heard so many times. They once called his sister, in the middle of the night, kicking on the door, to come out and read the inscription on the wall. His sister, a graduate of an English university, said she didn't know how to read. There were two graffiti: "Yes to a Palestinian state" and "O, you rich ones of Gaza, pay attention to your poor brethren."

He is not blinded by anger, like the wretched of the earth in Gibalia. His is a balanced anger. But he too, like the teacher, is part of the intifada. "We are like what the Hagana was for you," they say, "opposed to violence, opposed to terrorism, but we want our nationality. And you would be amazed how many there are like us. If only the government of Israel would give us, just once, a positive sign, a sign that it is interested in a solution. As a government, not as this party or that. So that there would also be hope."

A sentence that is heard over and over again: "The intifada is our 'crossing of the canal.' Just as Sadat was able to come to you and make peace only after he had crossed the canal, so will we be able to talk peace only after we have shown ourselves, after we have proved our resistance."

The story of an IDF officer who has just finished an extended service in Gaza, vis-à-vis a refugee camp. Let us call him Rami.

"For the life of me I can't understand why they had to bring the army into the camps. They want to burn tires—let them burn them; they want to raise the Palestinian flag—let them raise it. No sweat. You just need to keep the main routes open, and that's it. But they became hysterical, juggernaut style. Someone decided that this was a war against the people of Israel; for all I know, maybe they want to conquer the whole state of Israel.

What nonsense. They are fighting against the forces stationed among them. We stood facing the camp, and we would say into the walkie-talkie: 'Attention, men, the third grade is coming out for a recess in the school-yard.'

"In general, all the casualties, both theirs and ours, were caused by lack of discipline and loss of control. We also had a bad incident. Two soldiers entered the camp without an officer present—the battalion commander was not around—and they lost their bearings. The *shabab* (PLO youth) drew them on in the direction of the mosque, the muezzin began to call out, and they started throwing stones, nails, everything at them. One soldier opened fire, without an order, and killed a youngster. There was an investigation. Since then we have learned a lesson. We enter only in large numbers and definitely do not overdo it. I, personally, did not walk around with a club; I went with tear gas, and that was enough. But I know another unit who were really barbarians, they and their officers. Here, all decisions are made at company level. If the company commander is okay, then the soldiers stand up well to pressure. And if he's an animal, then they break hands and legs and heads without a second thought. I saw this happen.

"In the beginning, no one talked to the soldiers at all. We practically never saw the big shots. They just didn't know what to do, so they didn't come. Everyone here is an authority unto himself. It took ages before we received any instructions about how to behave. I also know one senior commander—I think he's a Kahanist—who walked around with a sniper. Shooting at the legs, all very precise, according to the law. Then you face this poverty here, see how people live here, and it's not pleasant at all to crack down on them. In time, we also came to recognize them by face. We knew who the village lunatic was and didn't get excited about him."

Lieutenant Lior: "In the camp where I was stationed there was one incident where we'd really had it. We said to the demonstrating kids: 'That'll do for now, kids, we want to go home.' So there was a bit of laughter. And another time they said to us in Hebrew: 'We're going away now for a while, we'll be back in half an hour.' But most of the time we were under pressure, running after them. They scamper like little mice, and if you catch one then it's a ball, you beat him for all the pressure. The next day one came up to one of our soldiers and said, 'By God, you hit hard, you do.' "

Rami: "Certainly the police are more restrained than we are, because they know how to deal with civilians. We acted as if it were a built-up area combat situation, walking along the sides of walls, because that's what we were taught. I know a unit that went into a camp to look for someone, and when they didn't find him got nervous and smashed the headlights of all the cars on the road. Now I hear that the IDF has bought something new, a vehicle that throws gravel." (In Gaza they are already joking about this: "Look at those lazy Jews. They won't even throw a rock by hand; they had to invent a machine to throw it for them.")

Lior: "We had a story right out of the movies. We found a method, smoke and tear gas together, a kind of cocktail, very efficient. One day there emerges from all this smoke a guy dressed to the hilt, white shirt, cuff links, and says to us, 'Please, men, let me pass, I have to get to Ramat Gan.' 'What do you have to do in Ramat Gan?' 'I work at the Bon-Ton wedding halls.' So we let him go. If it had been X's unit, they would have broken all his bones for sure. They are all barbarians, each and every one, from the officers on down."

Rami: "The truth is that there has been a lot of lack of discipline in the army, a lot of covering up, totally incorrect reports, and this is all because no one knew exactly what to do. I don't think that this was a business for the IDF. The men drew all kinds of conclusions. As for me, my personal conclusion is that there is nothing for us there. I never want to see Gaza again in my life. Not as a volunteer, you can bet on that."

It is a waste of time now to mull over what was done in the past, to ask what we could have done that we didn't do, where we went wrong. This won't change a thing as regards the future. Even if the present wave subsides, the process is irreversible. Sooner or later, these people will acquire for themselves some form of national identity. There is not one who is not involved in the intifada, through a son, a wife, cousin, neighbors. There isn't one who has not suffered shame and humiliation at our hands.

If we continue being obtuse, like a stupid colonial regime, the process will be a bloody one for all of us. Geographically, too, it will not remain limited to what stands between us and them.

Not being obtuse means we have to start talking. Perhaps not apart from the entire peace process, but to talk. How to talk? Two societies, both of them very wounded, very overwhelmed, carrying past traumas, full of anxiety for the future, stand facing one another. Instead of talking, they present each other with lists of grievances, and God knows the accounts are long: killing, abuse, casualties, humiliation—page after page, and all of them true. How many of us, on each side, have the strength to emerge from the present entrenchment, to try for a new start? How many have the wisdom to make distinctions, how many have the ability to differentiate, to listen as an individual? To give up the tense, despairing conception—ours and theirs—that "they are all the same"? When will we both be able to decide, knowingly, intentionally, to refrain from the image of ourselves as each other's eternal victim? "To wipe up the blood," as one Gazan who did time in prison said to me, "and look forward to the future"?

But perhaps the most important sentence was the one I heard from the woman student who was subjected to the "fashion show" at the border crossing: "Understand, you must understand. In order to coexist with you, we first have to exist."

No One Asked the Medics ══════════

THE HISTORY OF THE ISRAELI-
Palestinian conflict is the history of two societies in extreme distress: anyone who speaks only of the anguish of the Israelis is not telling the whole
truth, nor is anyone who speaks only of the misery of the Palestinians.

It may very well be that the conflict itself was unavoidable under the
conditions that existed since the beginning of the century. Both sides
were seized by intense anxiety and were therefore entrenched in their
positions. "Final solutions" of one kind or another were still dominant in
the *zeitgeist;* the concept of "negotiating conflict" was not as prominent in
international dialogue as it is today, and certainly had not been internalized. A spirit of "it's either us or them," which precluded compromise,
prevailed in Europe as in many parts of the world. The decisive events
were the First World War, during which tens of thousands of men were
killed pummeling each other on three meters of land; the Bolshevik Revolution, which knew no compromise; and, of course, the rise of Nazism
and the Second World War. The phantom of the "final solution" hovered
over all of the thinking of the first half of the century.

Perhaps our region could have freed itself from this prevailing mode of
thinking; perhaps not. One cannot play the game in retrospect. Neither
can one talk about statistics and numbers without addressing the entirety
of human misery, or, by extrapolation, without asking the medics.

To what extent—if at all—is a history of documents the history of war?
The question remains open. Historians will ask, justifiably, on what they
should rely if not on written documents, since "oral history" is often a
story someone told himself—he has convinced himself of its truth, even if
it does not correspond with other known details.

However, the use of documents in itself also requires a cautious approach and a careful, methodical examination of every event separately.
Did the documented order obligate anyone; did it reach commanders in

the field? Did anyone act in accord with it? Israel's War of Independence, with all the chaos that characterized it, is a striking example of a historical event in which there was little correspondence between what was written in documents and what was known in the field. It was a diffuse, decentralized war, completely chaotic, in which people improvised, as well as they could, within a very small radius around themselves. There were instructions from the minister of defense that not even the chief of staff was aware of. The chain of command was frequently problematic. Most certainly, things were said in meetings of the Jewish Agency that obligated no one but the pompous men who said them; if known in the field at all, they aroused only scorn. What Yitzhak Grünbaum, one of the heads of the agency, said about immigrants—that Oriental Jews could have less comfortable lodgings, not being accustomed to luxury—was translated in the field in more or less the same way as what Begin wrote about the "conquest" of Bevingrad[1] by his underground: both were figments of the writers' imaginations. Often it was a place-specific war, a war of high school kids whose commanders were only a year or two older than they were (I am talking about the Israeli side at the moment). Ambiguity—and worse —reigned. To this day people argue over the meaning of David Ben-Gurion's hand gesture in response to the question of what to do with the Arab inhabitants of the captured cities of Lod and Ramle: did he really mean to exile them all, or was it only a local commander who chose to interpret the gesture that way? There was also an argument over how our forces in the case of the Kafr Kassem curfew should have interpreted Colonel Yiska Shadmi's unfortunate *"Allah Yerahmum."*[2] In fact, Inspector Frankenthal, who refused to harm an Arab boy out in the curfew, and Gabi Dahan, the lieutenant who opened fire on a truck entering the village, which was carrying women laborers, interpreted these two words in opposite ways. Who was right?

---

1. Bevingrad was the British compound in the heart of Jerusalem.

2. *Allah Yerahmum* may be translated roughly as, "God have mercy on them." *Trans.* The Kafr Kassem area commander, when asked how to deal with those who broke the curfew, gave this unclear answer. One of the platoon commanders present took it to mean "shoot them" and subsequently a truckload of laborers returning from the field were massacred. He was subsequently tried and found guilty of carrying out what would be an obviously unlawful order.

At this point the historian will say, Right, that is why I examine documents and certificates and protocols of meetings—in order to know what the intention was, what the policy was that guided most, if not all, of the people.

This is precisely where the danger of error lies. Once a large, difficult, bloody conflict with many losses has begun, it is not the guiding policy of politicians that determines what happens in the field, but rather the ordeal, the sense of distress, the feelings of weakness at each and every spot. In a war, it is not papers that do the fighting, but people—people who are scared, stunned, sometimes hungry and sometimes desperate for vengeance; people who often make bad mistakes. Only now, on the fifty-year anniversary of the Allied invasion of Normandy, are we told that the number of Allied forces killed by friendly fire during the first days of the invasion was far greater than that killed by enemy fire. This is not surprising, if you think about it: all at once a huge number of people landed on a beach; there was crowded movement of more than one million men; shooting at one another was inevitable. No historian will call into question the actions of the commanders then: fifty years after the fact, the difficulty of that situation is completely clear. Only one revisionist historian, none too bright, blamed Churchill for not reaching a compromise with Germany that would have prevented the war. This historian did not seem interested in what would have happened to the world had Churchill done so.

Another problem is the retrospective use of statistics to understand situations. Statistics are often the last refuge of the antihumanist. When told that during the Israeli War of Independence the Jewish and Arab forces were almost equally matched, that toward the end of the war the Jews even had a slight numerical advantage, one does not know whether to laugh or cry. If we in Jerusalem were shelled heavily, were made thirsty and starved by forces far greater than we in men and weapons, what did it matter to us if on the coastal plain the Jews had a statistical or numerical advantage? The same was true in Negba, in Kfar Etzion, in Galilee, and in the tens of places where the war actually happened in all its horror—in each spot, to each person.

By the way, the whole idea of statistics is inapplicable to that war: there is absolutely no way to examine the balance of forces in the field, because the Arab countries sent expeditionary forces only, and had the potential and the hinterland to recruit an increasing number of people and re-sources as the war continued. The Jews had no hinterland, our potential resources were destroyed in the Holocaust only three or four years ear-lier, and the contribution of volunteers from overseas was insignificant.

Certainly we would not and could not divest historians of their profes-sional tools, which have often proven themselves effective and efficient. But the question remains: aside from a great writer, or a writer-historian of Barbara Tuchman's stature, who can draw an accurate picture of the situation and not enrage those who were there? Who can highlight the distress of both sides, without betraying either one?

It is possible to call Zionism "colonialist." Zionism is not sacred, nor is it beyond criticism. Some of the deeds done in its name—like using cheap Arab labor or practicing political protectionism—do smack of co-lonialism. What is inane is to apply the concepts of one period to another period, like the historian who is angry with Churchill for not finding a way to compromise with Hitler. Colonialism is a broad concept—from the colonialism of the Romans, who hardly interfered with local customs and never destroyed local gods, to Islamic colonialism, which was essen-tially religious, as was Spanish colonialism, which imposed on its sub-jects a cruel regime and a foreign religion. True, Ben-Gurion once vented an idea of converting the Negev Beduin to Judaism, but as it was only one of many ideas the man dreamed up, no one ever tried to implement it. So, yes, it is possible to call the awful stress of saving people from the inferno and bringing them to Israel, in spite of the inhabitants of that land at that time, a form of colonialism. But this concept is multifaceted, and in to-day's terms, many nations may be retrospectively thought to have been more or less enlightened colonialists.

It seems that the right way to understand events is not through "isms" with mutable definitions, but through what I earlier called "asking the medics." Medics see victory and defeat from a completely different per-spective than do politicians or researchers, among others. We must ask the medics what the particular distress was at a given time in a given place. We must understand both what it is to see the corpses of friends left to die with their cut-off penises in their mouths; and to see an infant thrown out of his village, collapsing with thirst and fatigue, his mother tearing her hair because she has nowhere to go, all the while screaming, *Bidnash nihgar* (We do not want to be evacuated). We must understand both the terror of the people trying to climb into a lifeboat that still has empty places in it, and the shock of the people sitting in it, who fear the newcomers will throw them overboard. We must try to understand the level of fear. What it leads to. Whether it was at all possible to do things otherwise. Whether, in a conflagration this extreme, things could have happened any other way. We must weigh the fear of physical extinction, of mass slaughter and rape, against the fear of disenfranchisement from land and home, of becoming a refugee, of the loss of identity. More than anything, we must understand that this was not a battle of strength against strength, but of weakness against weakness; throughout the whole Arab-Israeli conflict, each side has felt itself to be far weaker than its opponent, and acted accordingly. We must understand that there was no "Jewish justice," as Golda Meir said in one of her less sterling moments, nor was there "Arab justice," a claim that also has proponents; rather, there were two deep traumas, on which a completely new life, a different world, new hope must be built.

Who should take an interest in what befell the other side in this historical "Rashomon"? Certainly, historians should. But, as they deal with power, not with what ails people, there is not much catharsis in their work. The best encounter is not between Jews and Jews, or between Arabs and Arabs. The best encounter—and such things have happened—is between Jews and Arabs who know one another personally, intimately, and who can tell each other honestly what their anxieties and fear were, what they and their families felt when things happened as they did. The shock of such encounters is great. People learn things they did not know or had repressed, or that their leaders or teachers did not tell them because they did not dare break the silence—not necessarily because they had evil intentions. A different truth is revealed, and not through documents: documents do not talk; a person talks, a family talks. Then something happens: people who have recognized each others' anguish are people who are capable of making peace. People who know the anguish of one side remain stuck in the past, which becomes less and less relevant as the years pass.

The Cuban writer Alejo Carpentier wrote a book called *The Harp and the Shadow;* in it, in the finest revisionist-historical tradition, he describes Christopher Columbus as a vile courtier and cruel schemer, a colonialist whose only goal was profit, a man who brought tragedy to every place he set foot. This book has everything save one thing: the ocean. Not one drop of salt water. There is no mention of a voyage unlike any other in history, no mention of brilliant navigation, of control over a mutinous crew, of Columbus's specific order to treat the "natives" with respect. No weight is given the possibility that Columbus, turned against his will into a governor of remote islands—a role for which he was singularly unsuited—and at a loss about how to act outside his private realm of the ocean, became paranoid.

Columbus without the ocean is like the Israeli-Palestinian conflict without the distress: an attempt to apply to one period and to one set of circumstances the concepts of another. Moreover, it is a futile attempt. These two societies do not need any more probing of their pasts; they do not need to be shown what "really" happened, nor do they need a painstaking examination of protocols and documents. They need only one thing: healing. Anyone who does not bring them succor, or balm, who does not help them bind their wounds and find common ground, would do best to keep his silence.

Peace ═══════════════════════

Against Charisma

THE THEME OF THIS ESSAY IS four types of leadership and their distinguishing characteristics. Readers should bear in mind the following parameters:

First, in speaking about leadership I am not referring to leadership in an hour of extreme crisis as in battle. At such times, I have no doubt that what is needed is charismatic leadership, or whatever we wish to call it: that is, someone we would follow through fire and water, for whom we would temporarily renounce our autonomy and judgment and critical faculties, lest each of us sink into his own fear and never climb out. The distinctions I will make will have bearing, then, not on a temporary, extreme crisis, but on leadership for the long haul: first and foremost, political leadership.

Second, this essay concerns individuals who have the ability, in one way or another, to lead others and who have proven this ability in the past. I am not talking about people in general; I have made a preliminary selection. Potential leaders, who have not yet fulfilled their promise, and bureaucratic leaders—these, too, exist—are not the issue here.

Third, the model propounded here of four types of leadership is not a closed one. In fact, there is no pure model; the types overlap and share some basic elements.

The four types of leadership are, then, the charismatic leader, the authoritative leader who is not necessarily charismatic, the role model, and the facilitator.

I will first discuss charismatic leadership. It is reasonable to ask if there is any leadership in the world that is not charismatic to some extent; I would therefore presume that each type of leader has some measure of charisma. When I say charismatic leader, however, I mean a leader who stacks his whole appeal on charisma, which is the basis of his relationship with his public.

There is an odd word in Russian, *cheramizhnik,* which means a miserable beggar, the most wretched of those who hold out a hand for charity. The word is not originally Russian. It came into the world during the retreat of Napoleon's *grande armée* from Russian soil. Thousands of French soldiers, wounded, crippled, with limbs amputated, cut off from units that no longer existed, forgotten by man and God, dragged themselves along the roads, frozen and hungry, thrusting out their hands to the Russians whose lands they had set out to conquer, begging, "*Cher ami, cher ami,* give me a piece of bread." The Russians named them *cheramizhniks.* It is this picture we should keep in mind as we consider charismatic leadership and its demise, to remind ourselves that history is almost always told from the perspective of those who commanded, not from those who suffered its outcome.

Charisma is catastrophic. It is a relationship—a sick one, and to a great extent symbiotic—between a man who is very, very much in need of applause and constant reinforcement, and a public that seeks a hero to whom it may attribute all sorts of mythological virtues. Once it has found such a hero, this public disclaims all responsibility, as long as the leader endlessly excites and entertains it. A charismatic leader forges an unholy alliance with his public; he becomes a kind of national drug pusher, a provider of constant thrills in return for the vocal adoration he craves. He cannot manage without his public, and his public cannot manage without him: there is a kind of unchecked, mutual, constant high. A leader of this type does not have a normal public; he has groupies. It is difficult to understand what this kind of relationship has to do with leadership, since a leader's role is to define real problems and solve them. Throughout history charismatic types have led people to disaster. Once they have vanished—and they vanish in the blink of an eye—a mere decade or fifteen years later, no one can understand wherein lay their power. In retrospect they usually look ridiculous, their speech and movements laughable, like those of bad actors. There is nothing less comprehensible than the frenzied excitation of yesterday.

Perhaps we should make the first distinction here by saying that the greatest leaders the world has known were never charismatic or dependent on their public's falling in love with them. Moses, the greatest leader of all generations, who led the Hebrews out of Egypt, wandered with them in the desert for forty years, made them into a nation, and gave them the Torah, the law whose principles bind us to this very day, was not a charismatic personality. He was the most humble of men, a stutterer, inelegant of speech, who needed an interpreter; he was a man with whom the people were most certainly not enthralled, calling him "that man Moses," complaining without cease, barely accepting his rule over them.

The first things that get lost in charismatic leadership are facts. In this situation, people are not in the least interested in assessing reality, so in need are they of the giddy symbiosis with their leader, which he readily encourages, like Abimelech King of Shechem, who said, "I am your bone and your flesh." And yet many of the greatest of charismatic leaders were not even of the nations they led. Hitler, who hypnotized Germany, was Austrian; Napoleon was Corsican. To overcome just such a contradiction, before the 1977 elections in Israel, a rumor was spread in Nahlaot[1] that Mr. Begin was actually a native of Morocco who had been sent to study in a yeshiva in Poland. People need to see their leader as a familial figure, one of "our crowd," a figure they can merge with, never mind the facts.

In fact, Hitler, who was so wound up in his theory of the Aryan race, was himself the antithesis of the Aryan type: dark, not very tall, narrow-shouldered, hysterical, nervous; had he met himself, who knows where he would have sent such a suspicious character. Not to mention Minister of Propaganda Josef Goebbels. But no one in Germany was willing to see this. It was also a fact that Napoleon, beloved of the troops, hated his soldiers; he visited the recruits as infrequently as possible, and then only with a scented handkerchief over his nose. First and foremost, then, this familiality, this symbiosis—like all symbioses—dismisses the facts. The aura surrounding the leader generates a mythological reality, a world outside of reality. The groupies of Mr. Ariel Sharon, for example, believe to this day that he conceived the plan of crossing the Suez Canal during the Yom Kippur War, thereby saving the people of Israel; they refuse to hear that Mr. Sharon merely implemented a plan decided upon by headquarters, that he was following orders, some say less than perfectly. The desire to merge with the leader is stronger than any reality.

---

1. Nahlaot is an older, somewhat run-down neighborhood in western Jerusalem, then inhabited mainly by Sephardi Jews, Begin's most ardent supporters. *Trans.*

Perhaps the aspect of charismatic leadership that causes the most diffi-
culties is the charismatic leader's sloughing of all responsibility when
defeat comes—if he is still alive. It is as if he were saying: What do you
want? You wanted me to play a role, so I played a role; you got what you
asked for. Now the show is over and I am going home. What do you want
from me? I'm through. What stands out is the strongly theatrical basis of
charismatic leadership. The leader is constantly on stage, and his public
(his audience) applauds him because he acts precisely according to their
expectations. But plays end; the question then is. what becomes of
responsibility? Any volunteers to stop the buck? The *cheramizhniks* remain. What often happens then to the followers of such a leader is cognitive dissonance: it is inconceivable that he has abandoned us; he is all
right, he is one of us; therefore there must have been traitors. All of the
fury that should have been turned on the leader is then turned on these
traitors, imaginary or real. Father Stalin was all right, but those Jewish
physicians betrayed him. Jesus was all right—he nearly saved the world
—but that bastard Judas Iscariot turned him in. Begin (the "Moroccan")
was all right—he almost finished off the PLO—but the left and all those
kibbutzniks stabbed him in the back. The fall of the leader is a terrible
disappointment, because a charismatic leader's public is always consumed with longing for purity, faith, soul, absolute justice, the whole
truth—and it thinks its leader is delivering or has promised to deliver all
these things. Charisma is at base a promise never fulfilled. So what went
wrong? Those traitors ruined everything; were it not for them, we would
today be living in a perfect world.

Tangentially, perhaps it is this longing for purity and faith that makes it
so difficult to come up with a hermetically sealed definition of the charismatic leader's public; after all, they are not only people from the lower
socioeconomic strata. A significant portion of the British aristocracy was
fascinated by Hitler, whom it regarded as the personification of personal
purity and innocence—inconceivable as that sounds today. An extreme
always appears more pure than a compromise.

Perhaps there is one context in which we may conceive it: wherever a
great promise is not and cannot be fulfilled, the resultant empty space is
filled in by fantasy. Such is the case with leaders and followers, with parents and children, and between spouses; who knows better than psy-
chologists or writers how difficult it is, then, to confront that fantasy with
reality.

It is most desirable that the charismatic leader not have a family or, if he does, that it remain in the shadows: an instant support group, a moving background, like the doo-wop girls who back a singer. The man who trades in demonics had best remain a lone figure. A demon has no family. The minute there is a family, everyone becomes more human. If the charismatic leader has a family, then perhaps he does not belong wholly to us, to our imagination; perhaps he belongs to his family—a thought too disturbing to contemplate. As T. S. Eliot wrote, "Go, said the bird, mankind cannot bear too much reality." In any case, it is a literary rule that if you create a mythological hero, you do not give him a family.

It is interesting to compare the charismatic leader with the authoritative leader who is not necessarily charismatic. The example that first springs to mind is that of Charles de Gaulle. He was thoroughly unpopular, particularly when he decided, to a great extent on his own. that France would leave its territories in Algeria; at that time, nearly the entire army was against him. Their bitterness was even greater because de Gaulle had attained the presidency largely thanks to the support of the army, and now he was overriding it. I was in France at that time and can attest to what transpired then, in the midst of what was practically a mutiny. President de Gaulle came to confer rank on a class of cadets that had completed officers' training at Saint-Cyr. He spoke to the three. flanks of soldiers assembled before him; you could have cut the animosity with a knife. When he finished his speech, he began singing the "Marseillaise," and no one joined in. He stood there, this old man, facing the microphone, facing the silent parade, and in his old, raspy voice sang three whole stanzas of the "Marseillaise," all alone. I have seen few such displays of courage in my life. Behind that courage, of course, he was setting things straight: I am France; I am the legal authority; and you are petty insubordinates.

But de Gaulle was authoritative and his histrionic pose never impugned his authenticity. He never went over well with crowds; he needed a director to prepare him for his press conferences, which were disastrous. De Gaulle's authority was not derived from popularity or from a desire to be popular; rather, it was normative, it grew out of public order, from social organization, from *étatism*. He goaded the people, he scolded them, he called them to order. In his way, he represented norms; he was an educator who said: this is the book, and you will go by the book. He was a teacher, a guide. To project this successfully, a man must have a great deal of personal integrity and prestige, which he had. He was an elitist leader, in no way "the bone and flesh of the people," and with no intention in the world of being so.

Let us go back to the uncharismatic figure of Moses; without a doubt he was most authoritative, without ever being popular. He, too, chided the people. His authority grew out of the power of norms, the power of the law that he gave; it grew out of the role he played as educator—at times, a petulant educator. The authoritative leader usually takes seriously the norms of law, of government, of statehood; in this way he delineates boundaries of some sort for the ego. The charismatic leader first destroys the boundaries of the ego in his relationship with his public: I am you and you are me; eventually, norms vanish and obedience to the law becomes unimportant. The examples are too numerous to count. In one of the last Apocryphal books, King Ahashuerus tells Queen Esther she should not fear the law, because "the law is for the masses"; that is, all those who are not of the masses are exempt. The prophet Samuel warns the people against the transition from judge to king in Israel, because a king will do whatever he pleases, will take your property and your wives; while a judge obeys behavioral norms that are an outgrowth of the social order. Moshe Dayan was greatly indulged in his day because as far as some people were concerned, he was the epitome of the mythological *sabra,* our bones and our flesh. This inexplicable indulgence cost us the heavy price of the Yom Kippur War.

Not by chance have I used the word "mythological," because the charismatic leader trades in amorphous myths, ancient myths, before the existence of law and social order and democratic organization. His leadership is unbridled, his audience trusts him to somehow lead this wild spontaneity; after all, he is a good driver, one can press the gas pedal to the floor, nothing will happen, yippee. Anyway, in an accident no one will be to blame. Accidents come from God; they are fate.

Let us recall the precise role myth plays in society: it inhibits change. Perhaps that is its raison d'être.

The extent to which myth can be an obstacle to change may be inferred from the story of the cargo cult, a story anthropologists tell. It turns out that the Second World War—a near-holocaust for entire peoples —was a virtual paradise for the residents of several islands in the South

Pacific where landing fields were built to accommodate American cargo planes. From time to time a plane would come out of the sky and unload all sorts of wonderful things. Then the war ended and the cargo stopped coming. The elders of the tribe sat down and decided that if the cargo was not coming, perhaps it was angry with them; therefore, they would make the cargo come to them. For years they went out to the abandoned and neglected airfield and lit candles in tins for landing lights; in place of a control tower they erected a booth where a man sat, coconut shells over his ears, waiting to hear that the good cargo was on its way, and not quite comprehending why it wasn't coming—after all, they were doing everything just right.

I have no idea how many years passed before at least some of the island people began to realize that the cult would not bring them the fruits of the earth, and that they would have to do something if they wanted to attain them. But to my mind, the story symbolizes the role of myth as a barrier to change, or at least as a means to postpone change for a very long time.

When a government, or a military command, or any authority errs on a grand scale, there is a tendency to sanctify the error with myth. We, too, have several such "sanctified" places. Mythology prevents real confrontation with the regime because it creates a situation of no doubts, no criticism. It belongs to the social climate of what I once defined as a "society of sons," a filial society in which the source of authority is vertical, hierarchical, as opposed to a "society of brothers," an autonomous, democratic fraternity where the source of authority is horizontal and grows out of societal agreement, and therefore includes the concept of responsibility. The word "responsibility" in Hebrew, *achraiyut,* comes from the root *acher,* "other," someone who is not me. Responsibility presupposes a response. In charismatic relationships there is no responsibility, only guilt; in more developed relationships, responsibility is present. With charisma there is no "other"; everyone is part of one familial porridge, a *publis pabulum.* Anyone outside of it is an enemy.

Of course the authoritative leader also makes some use of myth; de Gaulle's "La France" is no less a myth than our "David, King of Israel, Lives."[2] There is apparently some overlap in these two forms of leadership, but it is primarily in the public and not in the leader. Just as the

---

2. A popular song. *Trans.*

charismatic leader has a nonautonomous public, the authoritative leader, the teacher, may have a group of devotees who are not autonomous. A friend of mine went to Germany immediately after its defeat in the Second World War; when he returned, I asked him how the Germans were. He replied: "Democrats. They were told to be."

Nevertheless, I would not recommend confusing the two types of leader. Since their sources of authority are very different, their behavior is also very different. Unlike the charismatic leader, the teacher-leader sets limits and determines some kind of social norm; while it is true that both of them rule and that both of them represent authoritative leadership, what each rules is very different. Take Harry Truman, for example, who from a historical perspective is considered a very good president. He fired General Douglas MacArthur, national hero and decorated victor, at the height of his fame, because MacArthur was guilty of slighting the president. Truman forced an issue, but by doing so he set a norm according to which a democratically elected president is more important than any heroic general. That was more educational than a thousand speeches pontificating on the importance of democracy. There is quite a difference between that and a system that claims a hero is above the law.

The two types of leader, authoritative and charismatic, are prone to being disrupted from within; in fact, they are constantly threatened and usually need a group of "faithful," a Praetorian guard that surrounds and protects them from attempted coups, which often end in executions. That is the price of overweening, hierarchical leadership: there will always be those who will challenge it and want to be free of it. That is why it is in need of immense defense mechanisms.

The two remaining types of leader, the role model and the facilitator, are far less threatened by violence, because neither generates violence; if they are defeated, it is usually as a result of democratic process, because others do not agree with them or their way. An example of a role model is Nahman Shai, IDF spokesman during the Gulf War. He was the man who said, "Watch me and do as I do." He did not promise anything. He said, "Let us go into our sealed rooms, let us don our gas masks—don't forget to open the filter—and, as my daughter Dana said yesterday, it is always a good idea to drink a glass of water." Everything was very familial, very close. In this way Nahman Shai entered the homes and sealed rooms of every family, became a part of each small group; this is one of the characteristics of the role model. Had Nahman Shai stood on a balcony and spoken to a mass rally in the town square, his type of leadership would not have caught on. But, as it happened, it caught on so well that several years hence Nahman Shai (temporarily) found himself a candidate for mayoralty of Jerusalem.

The attitudes of women and men toward this type of leader, as toward the facilitator, described later, differ significantly. I know of no studies on the subject, so I speak from personal observation. Since women usually work better in networks than in large hierarchies and since women usually prefer small and individually focused identity groups, it is not surprising that role models have a striking effect on women. A woman is very likely to see leadership qualities in another woman who is her role model, and to react with skepticism to the exalted demagogue in the town square. Not long ago in Jerusalem, Dr. Ada Avraham presented the results of a study in which boys and girls were asked to draw a group (of which they were not a member). The girls drew small groups with individual figures distinguishable from one another in form and dress, without leaders. The boys drew large, anonymous groups with leaders.

This anecdote indicates that a role model is dependent on the type of society he leads. He or she has practically no place in a large, hierarchical society, but has a respectable place in a society composed of networks, small groups, families. Sometimes a person will choose a teacher or authoritative educator as a role model in his life, but this usually happens on an individual basis or within a small group—not in the town square. I have always felt that if the feminist movement had done its job well, it would not have tried to force women into large, hierarchical frameworks that do not suit them; rather, it would have done its utmost to change society from a largely vertical construct, with authority descending from the top down, as it is today, to a horizontal construct, with autonomous networks and cooperating groups.

It would seem, then, that the model of "watch me and do as I do" is acceptable to women not because they are women, but because it suits the small group, and women prefer small identity groups. I would like to qualify the examples I have used. Nahman Shai was a successful role model during a period of acute crisis; it is not at all clear how this model would work in the long run and in ordinary times. Nahman Shai was a good candidate for the mayor's office, but not necessarily for the command of a military brigade. We are familiar with the role models of advertisements, where the advertiser hopes that the famous basketball player will draw people to a given brand of beer or cigarettes. We are somewhat familiar with the role model that is used to convince women to go for a breast examination twice a year; it is usually a figure accepted by the female public who says that she, too, goes for mammography twice a year. By the way, the agencies fighting cancer through early diagnosis have found that it is best to be positive in these public service announcements, to say that nothing was found; if they say that there was something suspicious,that a leading figure was diagnosed with a malignant growth, women get so frightened they stop coming.

Naturally, role models do work in small groups that are completely male: e.g. the military unit in time of battle. Often, the role model here is created instantly, by personal example—if he advances, I'll advance, too; if he charges, so will I—by a positive and providential mixture of charismatic leadership and role model. But what we are looking for is leadership for the long haul, where matters are much more complicated. In his day, Ben-Gurion tried to be a role model by going to Sde Boker;[3] he did not draw a single soul after him to the Negev Desert. Mr. Begin promised he would build his house near Yamit, on the northeast coast of the Sinai Peninsula, but nothing came of it. It seems it is very difficult to make the transition from the existing, hierarchical mode to that of the real role model who says "watch me and do as I do," follow my example. People expected Ben-Gurion to decide on various matters of policy; no one asked him to go to the Negev himself, and his act had no resonance. Some things work in hierarchies, and some things are the province of small groups, and the passage between them is difficult. Even India's Mahatma Gandhi, revered for his faith in nonviolence, did not have many followers clamoring to imitate his abstention from sex. For some reason, Jesus did not do well in this matter either.

In this context it is worth recalling the great metamorphosis that the British royal family has undergone. Its beginnings were in absolute mon-

---

3. Sde Boker is a kibbutz in the Negev Desert. It was Ben-Gurion's vision to settle and cultivate this large, arid region of southern Israel. *Trans.*

archy; when constitutional limits were set for it, it became a role model, plain and simple. During the Second World War, while Churchill was providing military leadership, the royal family provided a role model for every family in England: grandmother, father, mother, and two small girls who bore up and did not leave London—a classic example of "watch me and do as I do."

It is difficult to scrutinize the leadership of the role model, as we have very little experience with it; and we have little experience with it because history is the written and recorded story of hierarchical rulership. The experiences of small groups are not yet significantly on record.

The polar opposite of the charismatic leader—and I mean completely antipodal—is the facilitator. This, too, is a new type of leadership. I do not mean the group facilitator who enables the members of a therapy group to express themselves. I am speaking about a leader, a figure who steers toward a defined goal, but in a totally new and different way. He is far from being close to his public, let alone merging with it, and he seeks no symbiosis with the crowd; on the contrary, he creates space between himself and the public—that blessed space in which things may happen. Those who do not understand that they have been given the great gift of space are liable to be disappointed by this type of leader. He seems to them too distant, not emotional enough; they feel they are not being supported, or "held," in the Winnicottian phrase; it seems to them that this man is not really a leader; he is disappointing; perhaps he is not even trustworthy. That longing for fusion, for merger, for shared glory, has nothing to cleave to. Those who do not recognize space and the need for space are liable to think they are being cheated. A contemporary example of this type of leader is Shimon Peres. If you are looking for symbiosis, he is not the man for you. But this is the type of leadership that leads least often to bloodshed.

The charismatic leader says, "I know what is best for the people" (or "we know what is best for the people") and reaps applause. The authoritative teacher says, "There is a book; in it is written what is best for the people; you will follow me and go by that book, even against your will, so that things will be best for the people." The role model says, "Do as I do, because I have the knowledge and personal experience to know what is best for the people." But the facilitator says, "I have come to the conclusion that this is what is best for the people; let's sit down and discuss it, and I will try to convince you." Since this leader says "come let's sit down" and not "run after me," he has no chance of garnering rhythmic applause in the town square. It is difficult to ask people to sit down and think a minute. It is thought to be practically unleaderly. As if a leader, like a gym instructor, must always make people run.

But if we ask ourselves what a leader should do, especially a facilitator-leader, the answer is fairly clear: a leader must first correctly define his nation's goals. Then he must put them in order, according to the correct priorities. Once he has done this, he must attain the maximum agreement for both the definitions and the priorities. After he has attained reasonable percentages of agreement, he must solve the problems one by one, in order, and with determination. At each and every stage, before he gets to the point of action, he must attain some consensus, because there is no fusion or identity between him and his public, or the members of his party, but there is a space in which people can agree or disagree. He is a leader-manager, even a great manager, not a macho commander.

The facilitator is also the only one of the four types who holds discussions; all the others hold monologues. We may say that the facilitator is first and foremost a leader of adults, of autonomous people. He listens to them. If he hears that a certain goal of his does not appeal to them, he can rescind it or retreat; if he hears that his public insists on a different goal or a different set of priorities, he listens to them. He changes his mind more than once, not because he has no opinion, but because he listens to other opinions, and without consensus he cannot move forward. Certainly he must lead in order to achieve consensus, and here we may measure his personal influence. What he cannot do, however, is force his opinion on the public at the outset—at least not according to this model. The facilitator is basically a man who has internalized the limitations of a democratic society and takes them seriously.

Since this type of democratic leader is so new, we know little about him. We know much more about the former two conservative types, because we have a wealth of observations. The latter two types are still at the stage of trial and error.

Nonetheless, there are one or two things we may already say about the role model and the facilitator. Unlike the charismatic leader, the facilitator calculates the cost and consequence of each act and every error, as well as who will ultimately have to pay the price. With the facilitator, there are no *cheramizhniks*. It's not part of the scheme. Charisma, whose connection to the reality principle is feeble at best, does not want and is not able to calculate costs and consequences. When the decision was made to start the war in Lebanon, the government did not ask for, and in any case did not receive, any estimate of casualties, of how many would be killed and wounded: that is, the ministers made their decision and voted without knowing its cost. In other instances the minister of defense claimed that an estimate of lives lost would have a negative effect on morale. Charisma hates to be reminded of the cost, because cost belongs to reality, responsibility, facts—and charisma's mind is made up; don't confuse it with facts.

If we look at the leaders of Arab countries in our times, Gamal Abd el-Nasser suited the charismatic type to a T; the man was one of "our crowd" who spoke a peasant's Arabic, not the Arabic of the educated. Jordan's King Hussein is the model of an authoritative leader, speaking and acting in the name of the state and statehood, and he most certainly does not draw thunderous applause. He speaks a classical Arabic. Mubarak is an interesting blend of the facilitator and the authoritative leader, the man of statehood. He speaks an average modern Arabic.

In a very rough way, perhaps even a very inexact way, we can divide our four basic types according to male perceptions and female perceptions—and I am quite aware of the problematic nature of these terms. There is a clearly machoistic, hierarchical, patriarchal basis to the first two types. In contrast, there is a pragmatic approach to relations and a stress on individuality at the base of the latter two types, and those qualities are more characteristic of women; it is no wonder that in opinion polls both Adlai Stevenson and Shimon Peres always enjoyed more massive support from women. We all recall this graffito from the Gulf War: "Nahmanize my husband." Now, at the end of this century, it is possible to make such a distinction, since part of the spirit of the times is that women have become sensitive to the issue of personal autonomy. Certainly, at the beginning of the century it would have been much more difficult to talk about feminine versus masculine characteristics; back then, a woman supposedly did not have the right to an independent viewpoint. Women adored Hitler no less than men, just as, in contextual contrast, Jesus was surrounded by adoring women who wiped his feet with the hair of their heads. Today, though, it seems to me that the woman who has achieved autonomy will not relinquish it so quickly; she will be very cautious about being conned. The modern woman is not an adoring woman, and she is certainly critical.

Whether we divide the types this way or that, the issue of criticism provides an important distinction between the first two and the last two types. Charisma must not be criticized—certainly not out loud; criticism is immediately interpreted as disloyal, even threatening. Only the charismatic leader knows just how easy it is to topple him. In the relationship between a charismatic leader and his public, there is no way to distinguish between legitimate, focused criticism and an emotional issue; the response is always one of "you hate him," even when it is a matter of presenting cold facts.

This is where the crucial question comes up: how does it happen that the charismatic leader overcomes society's checks and balances, its mechanisms of criticism, such as the elites, the courts, the press, academia, and the professional intelligentsia? How does he silence them utterly?

The answer is that more than he silences them, they silence themselves, and gladly; and that is the greatest danger of charisma. Dr. Arie Carmon's study on the collapse of Heidelberg University, the pride of German universities, showed that within a very short time it became a vassal of the Nazi regime—without inducement from any leader. The collapse was absolutely and entirely internal. No charismatic leader will openly demand the complete silencing of academic or journalistic criticism—at least not at the outset. Sometimes his advisers will. In totalitarian states, the press usually relinquishes its freedom of criticism all by itself, sometimes through a complete staff turnover, to become the trumpet of the ruling regime. That same urge that grips the public rallying in the town square, to cling to a leader and believe in him, sometimes also takes hold of the elite, the press, even the courts, as occurred in Europe in the 1930s; they cancel themselves out before the leader has a chance to say a word. This self-abnegation, usually undertaken with glee, and not only for opportunistic reasons, takes place with awesome speed. Because of it the personal characteristics of the leader have no great importance; he might be a psychopath or merely a charlatan. The minute the agents of check and balance, caution and criticism, neutralize themselves, as if hypnotized, the departure from reality becomes total.

The authoritative teacher does permit criticism, but without much enthusiasm; this type of leader fears for his prestige. He will never accept criticism from below; he will accept it, infrequently, from the mouths of those whom he reveres—that is, people in his league. A mere citizen could not have criticized de Gaulle and expected the criticism to be taken seriously. De Gaulle would have immediately made him aware of his insignificance: "Euh, Monsieur le Sous-Prêfet from the village of Turnipville has been so kind as to inform us of his thoughts upon . . ." The only one who could have criticized de Gaulle, and then only barely, was the likes of a world-renowned philosopher, on condition that he had won a Nobel Prize.

It goes without saying that the last two types, the role model and the facilitator, being democratic, are not only exposed to criticism but are wide open to criticism; often we witness a virtual inundation of the democratic leader with criticism, if only because no one fears him. There is a saying in Russian that a czar whom no one fears is no czar. We have seen the extent to which Gorbachev was no czar; people did not know whether this was good or bad, because according to their tradition, a leader is someone you fear.

Gorbachev was an out-and-out facilitator. He facilitated the passage from the centralism of communism to the Commonwealth of Independent States, for better or worse, and he did it without the shedding of one drop of blood. It is almost certain that no charismatic leader could have accomplished such a swift revolution without leaving hundreds of thousands dead in the streets.

It also goes without saying that the qualities of facilitator with which Shimon Peres is endowed are what have led to the current agreements.

From friends who work as group instructors I have learned that group interactions, whether the group is small or large, are always regressive compared with interactions between two or at most three people, because in a group everyone behaves with less maturity and exercises less judgment than they do in a personal interaction. From psychologist friends I have learned that wherever there is regression, we must ask how far back the regression goes. Permit me, then, to hazard a guess.

It seems to me that with the charismatic leader we see the most deep, most distant regression, going back to the youngest age. With the authoritative leader we witness a regression to a later period, one in which there is already socialization, a social conscience, consciousness—however reluctant—and a sense of social obligation. With the role model we see an imitation, though not an automatic one, as there is a certain degree of choice: we choose whom we wish to imitate, and we reserve the right to stop imitating that person if we think he is not taking the right tack. We may not yet be original, but at least we have the ability to choose or reject.

As for the facilitator, I am not sure we are in any regression at all; perhaps even the opposite. The facilitator demands that we be independent, think autonomously, be critical, have an open mind. In other words, he demands that we be not subjects in a more or less enlightened regime, but citizens; this is sometimes a painful process, because knowing the difference between good and evil also means expulsion from the Eden of childhood. But if we do not leave this Garden of Eden, we will never be able to mend or change anything about our reality—and ultimately, will not be very different from the people on that South Pacific island, who to this day place candles in tins on the runway and hope for the best.

Life Is Now, Mr. Shamir ══════════════

MR. SHAMIR RECENTLY DECLARED
that the conflict is but a passing phase. Mr. Shamir is right: recent events really are no more than a passing phase. What isn't a passing phase, Mr. Prime Minister?

You, us, life itself.

After this passing phase there will be another passing phase. One era follows another, and it is good or bad not according to any decree of fate, but according to what people who live during that era do or do not do. We don't make the phases of the moon or ocean squalls, and we are not responsible for them. But we do make the era we live in, for better or worse. This is our life. We are responsible for it. We are responsible for its quality.

This is our life, Mr. Prime Minister, and in this phase of our limited lifetime, we have already wasted more than twenty years—and for nought. Twenty years in which we have not solved the problem of our occupying territories with a large population that does not want to live under occupation. We have solved many other problems; this is one we have not solved.

Of these territories and their population we must take leave. Even if not a single stone is thrown, even if men and women are not stabbed to death on street corners, we must take leave of these territories. We must leave them—we can leave them—because we cannot ride on people's backs forever. Every time they try to shake us off their backs, we in our blindness search for "instigators." There are no instigators, Mr. Prime Minister; there are just people who do not want a foreign occupation. Let me ask you: did you do what you did in the underground in the 1940s because of "instigators," Mr. Shamir?

Anyone who didn't understand this in 1967, and who still doesn't understand it now, is shaping our current quality of life—one in which, now and again, parts of this country, street corners in these cities become unruly islands beyond the pale of the law. A quality of life in which people are searched for weapons before they go into a store, in which people scour the landscape for trouble when they escort their small children to school. A quality of life in which hundreds of thousands of children watch their fathers being humiliated, and other children watch their fathers turn into humiliators. A quality of life in the infamy of the occupation. Of a "nasty little Sparta" as we were once called, years ago. Day-to-day depression. Day-to-day anxiety. One long battle shock for two nations.

Is it impossible to stand this? It is possible. It is also possible to stand the intifada, the current bloody uprising. The price is high, but it is possible. We aren't whiners.

The question is not whether it is or is not possible, but whether it is or is not worthwhile. Is it worthwhile for us to live like this for much longer? Is this really our life? Is there really no way out? Is there really no other way?

One of the things Zionism was meant to make from scratch was a Hebrew present. Not only in reality; in the language, too. In ancient Hebrew, there was very little grammatical present. There was a past and a future—that is, memory and longing. We almost never said "I go," "I do." It was necessary to make the present a linguistic habit, a routine part of life. Perhaps Zionism came into being primarily to create for us a present tense. To say at long last that the Jews, too, have a present.

Whoever now denies this present has forgotten the whole lesson of Zionism; he would send us back to the days of remembering and longing of the Diaspora. We came to Israel so as to *not* wait for a messiah who is yet to come; rather, we came to be here now, today. That is Zionism in a nutshell.

Rabbi Mendel of Kotsk, a wise man, once said: See how strange human beings are: a man suffers his whole life for the sake of his child, and his child in turn suffers his whole life for the sake of his child, and so on and on for generations. When, at long last, will there be a real child?

Life is now, Mr. Prime Minister. Our children are children now. They have the right to live as human beings, not just as links in the never-ending "chain of generations," part of the never-ending "Jewish destiny." Yet for some reason they are always the excuse used by those who don't want to do anything to change the situation.

If there were no choice, we would defer. But there is a choice. It is a diplomatic solution based on leaving the territories. There is no point and no hope in continuing the present situation, Mr. Shamir. If there is no diplomatic solution, then there is no "better future." There is only a continuous and most unpleasant present. Another passing phase and yet another passing phase. Until the next time. Or until someone gets up and gathers the courage to make the change, to say there is no one house in Kedumim (a West Bank settlement) that is worth the price of our present, because life is now, and it is up to us to determine whether it is good or bad.

Are not leaders supposed to lead?

Without Love

A CAB DRIVER ADVISES: "LADY, you take it from me: What we gotta do is grab those Arabs, and get a big stick, and hit them over the head but good—hit 'em and hit 'em until they quit hating us."

The sentence quoted here—only one of many of this ilk—is much less amusing than it first sounds. You don't have to be a psychologist to hear the despair behind it: they don't love us. We want them to love us, we want them to see how nice we are—but they refuse to cooperate. So we'll do what any disturbed child would do: we'll hit them, hard, so they'll learn we won't stand for their not loving us.

If only we were talking just about cab drivers. But in Israel, whole groups get stuck on this point—groups of people who are supposed to be more sophisticated than cabbies. Not long ago an Arab poet wrote a poem that, to say the least, did not express any great love for Israel. He said what was in his heart: that he would be very happy to see us get the hell out of here.

Some of us read it and didn't get excited; others responded with anger—both completely legitimate.

Yet others, from what are called "leftist circles," ironically, responded as if their whole world had caved in: How dare he—our friend—not love us? Where does he get the gall not to see how nice we are? If this is the case, then *all* is lost—woe to us all!

It seems that the right to hate—so well understood in these parts—is a right not granted the Arabs. We may hate them. In parliamentary elections we may grant legitimacy to individuals and movements that talk of deporting the Arabs, if not worse; but they may not hate us. Even if their houses and property are laid bare to any who would break down their doors. Even if any sadist and sicko can kick their shackled sons.

At a meeting of Jewish and Arab senior educators—one of those meetings that are like a ray of hope just now—an Arab educator proclaims his position openly. He says he is a citizen of the state of Israel, recognizes all of its laws and statutes, both the serious and the trifling, and is committed to upholding them to the letter. He admits, however, in light of all that has been happening lately (the word "light" is most ironic in this dark context), he does not feel any great love for us.

Several Jewish educators jump up out of their chairs: Is this possible? Can this be? If so, there's nothing to talk about! This meeting is a waste of time! All Arabs—men, women, and children—must love us, and right away! If not, they are not our partners.

And here I thought, ingenuously, that the commitment made in public to uphold the laws of the state was the most important and monumental thing we could have heard at that meeting, because it is the greatest test of citizenship.

What is the difference between these two approaches?

The first approach, the one that demands love, that is so panicked by any expression of anger or hatred, is native to a minority in a diaspora. An exiled minority's existence is entirely dependent on the love, or absence of hatred, of the majority, particularly of the ruling powers. If the majority loves you, you can live in reasonable security. If they hate you, you're in a bad way: they will harm you, physically and materially; you may even find yourself threatened by pogroms. If you're lucky, you live among "good gentiles," gentiles who love Jews, and your existence is secure. If you're not lucky and they hate you, there are edicts and pogroms and holocaust situations.

That is the essence of the Diaspora.

Sovereign states are not at all dependent on love or hate. These concepts are simply not in their lexicon. Sovereign states sign agreements in accordance with their best interests, and they uphold these agreements; if they do not, a new military and political situation is created. Accords and agreements have been and are being signed between countries whose populations hate each other fiercely. That is precisely what agreements are for: so that hatred won't become war. Between two nations that love each other (and who knows of many like that?) the signing of agreements and accords carries little weight. Accords normalize relations—such is the usual way of things—when there is conflict and when mutual feelings are not particularly exalted. As a solution, an accord does not deal with emotions at all. It determines the existentialist situations: how both sides will live from now on; according to what rules life, heretofore lawless and violent, will be conducted.

Never has a nation been more hated than was the Germany of the Second World War—and justifiably so. Yet before long Germany became a member of the European Economic Community; its sons now engage in joint military exercises in various European frameworks with French and Belgians.

These accords were not concluded out of love. We can probably say they were concluded without love. They were concluded with maturity: in order to determine safe zones and secure borders and a way of life from now on. Today, war is inconceivable between Germany and, say, France. After undergoing training exercises with them, a young French soldier was asked by an interviewer how he felt about German soldiers. His answer was, "I don't love them and I don't hate them—but they sure are nicer than the guys in my unit from Marseille."

There are no guarantees for love. There is no guarantor for emotion. However, when dealing with accords and not emotions, we may—perhaps must—ask what the guarantees are. Indeed many ask, If we do come to any sort of agreement with the Arabs, how do we know they'll be satisfied with what is determined by the signed accord? How do we know they won't pull one over on us in stages, like slicing a salami?

How, in fact, do we know?

Well, I don't know of any salami in possession of nuclear arms, not to mention the best and strongest army in the entire region. We are neither a minority, nor a salami, nor a potential victim of a pogrom. Israel's real, deterrent power is the best guarantee possible. Even if they "want" to, they can't. Period.

Another important consideration is the record, the history of whether accords between us and neighboring countries have been kept. To this day all of our neighbors have kept their agreements with us, both written and oral. Egypt, chief among these sovereign states, has kept the peace agreement in letter and spirit, even when the pressure of other Arab countries caused it great damage and financial loss, even when Israel, by invading Lebanon, turned its back on the stated agreement: "no more war, no more bloodshed." If Egypt had sought an excuse to break its agreement with us, it had no better one than June 1982: Arab television nightly showed our air force pummeling civilian neighborhoods in Beirut in saturation bombings. Israel, not Egypt, is the one that did not keep the agreement for even two months. But Egypt, with its diplomatic maturity, with its serious "stateness," behaved as expected of a respected partner, and kept the agreement. It kept the agreement because the desirable policy for Egypt is indeed one of "no more war." It is diverting the vast resources needed for modern warfare to other, constructive channels.

For years Syria has been careful—punctilious, even—in keeping an informal agreement with us to prevent terrorists from crossing its borders into Israel. For years, Jordan has been wary of same. That's why we can travel safely on the roads along Israel's borders with Jordan and Syria. Israel, not Syria, violated this informal but most binding agreement when, under Ariel Sharon's command and without government approval, the IDF provoked the Syrians during the Lebanon war.

Even the Palestine Liberation Organization carefully kept the Begin-Arafat agreement that was concluded through an intermediary in 1981. For a whole year all was absolutely quiet on the Lebanese front, then the PLO front, until the government of Israel, latching on to a deed perpetrated by Abu Nidal for the express purpose of breaking this agreement, invaded Lebanon. Ambassador Shlomo Argov, the attack on whom was the excuse for the invasion, made no secret of his opinion: Israel should never have done it.

If we leave aside Israeli self-pity and examine the facts, we'll see that it is Israel, not its neighbors, that, to date, has broken all of the agreements made through various intermediaries since the Yom Kippur War in 1973; that it is the Arab states, not Israel, who greatly need guarantees that Israel will keep its agreements. Not out of love or hate, but for reasons of "stateness"; to abide by matters that have been agreed upon. Perhaps the most tragic joke of our generation is the saying "the Likud brought peace." It is the Likud Party that missed the opportunity for peace—scandalously so. It was the Likud that thwarted this opportunity with the wretched Lebanon War, with its unwillingness to uphold the agreement, with its lust for annexation and its opposition to the agreements made between Shimon Peres and King Hussein, known as "the London Paper." As if someone had given birth to a beautiful child, then denied it food until it nearly starved to death. All that is left are photographs. Beautiful photographs, really; but where is the baby?

We are living in an age of peacemaking. Not peace through love. Peace through accord. The Soviet Union and the United States, the two great powers and, currently, the powers that be, are destroying vast quantities of offensive weapons, not because they've suddenly fallen in love with one another. Communism and capitalism are still diametrically opposed, as before. But there is an accord. After eight years of horrific war with practically a million dead on both sides, Iran and Iraq are signing an accord; journalists report that all along the border soldiers are embracing those who only yesterday were their enemies. Not because they've fallen in love with one another; because they're overjoyed that they won't be killed. The so-called Arab-Israeli conflict—that is, the problem of the territories and their population—is one of the last remaining conflicts, and one of the most superfluous. It can be resolved. Not by love: by accord.

An accord means new borders. Anyone who declares he is not willing to alter his borders through negotiation thereby declares he will not be party to an accord. He will be party to the next war. Anyone who wants to maintain the current situation, the so-called status quo, lays the groundwork for the next war. In fact, the term "status quo" is only part of the phrase "status quo ante bellum": the situation as it was before the war. There are no static situations in the world, least of all in the roiling Middle East. Anyone who thinks it is possible to arrive at peace through continued force—without accords, without rules, avoiding the determination of new and secure borders—misleads people. Anyone who thinks the policy of "nary an inch" will bring about an accord is a deceiver. No one will come to talk to him seriously.

If Israel wants at long last to join the twentieth century as it draws to a close, to join the ranks of those making accords around the world, it must begin to think like a mature adult. It can afford to: it has more than enough defensive power and all sorts of weapons not currently possessed by any of its enemies. This is the ideal time for Israel to announce its readiness for an accord that will alter its borders and liberate it from the constant burden of one and a half million people—a great deal of excess weight for Israel.

Love cannot be ensured. Maximal security can. No one can promise that the day the accords are signed will be a wedding day. Statesmen do not come out of love; they come because it is the right thing to do. There will be no heartfelt embracing. There will be excitement. There will be the sense that a historic act has taken place. Not the Messianic Age. Just mothers who will get up in the morning and know that their sons have a chance, a very good chance, of leading their lives as they should be led in a sane country—of not being killed. Little by little. No one will get carried away with joy. This country, which has never known complete peace, will not immediately sense it fully. The change will be so great that it will be difficult to assimilate all at once.

But a year will pass, and then two, and the agreement will be kept. We'll begin to have regional industry—water plants, electric plants, agricultural and industrial ventures. Three years will pass, and the women of Jerusalem will go shopping in Amman, just as they now buy leather goods in Cairo's Talaat Harb Street. Young people will travel to Petra as they now do to Luxor. Young couples from Basra and Damascus will come to be married in Jerusalem's hotels, and their fathers to consult physicians at Tel Hashomer and their mothers to try on clothes in Tel Aviv's Kikar Hamedina. Agricultural technicians from development towns will teach irrigation practices in the deserts of Jordan.

And we'll walk down the street and see all this, and suddenly, out of the blue, we'll sense that we are very happy indeed.

The Vocabulary of Peace ═══════════

cultural change that enables people to think in terms of cooperation, rather than enmity and strife, is the conceptual change from the language and state of mind of a closed agrarian society, the forerunner of the nation-state, to that of an open technological one. In the agrarian society we usually witness an extended family or tribe that works its land and must defend it from enemies outside who covet the land. The more land you have and are able to defend, the better off you are, a simple equation. But in the United States today, only 3 percent of the land is used for agricultural purposes; modern methods of cultivation enable that 3 percent to feed all of the United States as well as a few other countries. So much for Lebensraum.

Not only has land and its defense lost a great deal of its former vital significance. The transition from accumulation of land to accumulation of knowledge has brought about an even more important change in our state of mind. Material possessions, like land, cannot be shared with others without experiencing loss, or deprivation. If you share your land, you have less of it. On the other hand, knowledge can be shared with as many people as possible without any loss; on the contrary, sharing knowledge often brings about pollination, or fertilization of minds, and we end up having more knowledge than we had before. The citizen of today's world will want to acquire more and more knowledge, including information and know-how, rather than feddans of land. In other words, sharing, not only within the tribe but also quite often outside, is now considered desirable and good, which in turn makes for a less belligerent disposition.

Closed agricultural societies are usually also patriarchal ones, where the wise fathers are the source of wisdom, of information, of understanding, and are hallowed as such, they and their sanctified graves. Today young people are not dependent on their father or grandfather for knowledge and advice on forming an intelligent opinion; they acquire good information from other sources, like world media, like computerized stores of knowledge on particular subjects, and chances are that these sources are far more extensive than what the local patriarchs knew. Their sources know no borders; the whole world village sees the same event in real time on television. This fact does not assure wisdom. But it does permit a flow of data.

Not only the local patriarch, but also the local god belongs to the agricultural society: when you are wholly dependent on weather, on water resources in times of drought, your vision concentrates on the local, tribal, ethnic powers that be to whom you can pray for local grace to be granted. The very secular ability to flip the air-conditioning switch, or to lay an international pipeline hundreds of kilometers long, may be interpreted as an act of defiance against the jealous local god on whom we need no longer depend, at least not totally. And for modern engineering we need broad cooperation. In general, the modern technical project knows no national borders; its engineers, scientists, and workers can come from many countries, many ethnic identities, to work together. The prevalent words around such a project would be "cost estimate," "energy sources," "input and output," "research," "environment," rather than "destiny," "sin," "expiation," "grace," and "salvation."

So, with this most important change, our concepts and our vocabularies have undergone a significant transformation. As Wittgenstein said, the limits of my language are the limits of my world. Almost imperceptibly, our concept of national borders has lost importance; today we fly not from Egypt via Denmark to Canada, but from Cairo to Copenhagen to Toronto, because an aircraft transcends national borders easily, and the world becomes one connected world containing various cities, rather than countries. Air-travel agencies realized this long ago. Borders are easily crossed, often with no more than a wave of "move on" from the guard; what matters is what goes on within borders rather than the borders themselves, which are in most cases open, a far cry from the hermetically closed national boundaries of previous times. Communicating across borders and distances, once a big production, has ceased to be a problem when we can, in our slippers, with a cup of coffee nearby, send a fax from home to China and get a response within minutes.

When a shipwrecked English sailor, many years ago, was washed ashore in faraway Japan, he had no way of returning home, and remained there to become a shogun. The reasonable expectation that in our time this sailor would be brought home within a day illustrates the change not only in fact, but also in concept: distance is no longer a threat, and does not by itself constitute destiny. The fact that everyone knows what I am talking about illustrates the fact that nearly all of us read the same books, another reminder of how the importance of borders has diminished.

Not only new technical skills but also new terminology is aiding us in the present climate of cooperation rather than strife. Today we know that there is no final solution, ever; that if there is a conflict, it has to be managed—another modern term, management of conflict, management of crisis—rather than impose a final, violent solution. We speak about localizing a crisis or a conflict, describing its parameters. Modern psychology, too, taught us how to "work on the problem" peacefully, using awareness and caring rather than sheer force, which aims "to end it once and for all"—an unattainable goal.

Access to information, previously the closely guarded privilege of governments, has also enabled us to give an entirely new meaning to the concepts of just and unjust war. The terms were known to the ancient Romans and Greeks and to later philosophers like Erasmus. The phrases usually referred to offensive versus defensive war. But the data that could enable individuals to decide for themselves whether a war was in fact defensive or not were not made public.

Today the distinction between a just, or justified war, and an unjust war is made by the individual, who regards it as his right and his duty to be critical of the government. Criteria are now far more sophisticated. With a free and informative press, we are able to judge for ourselves and do not have to depend blindly on what the ruler tells us. A well-informed citizen may well oppose a war over an issue that seems to him, or her, not to justify a war situation, and such a citizen may demonstrate against the war—a stance synonymous with high treason not so long ago. The antiwar vocabulary would include the "price of war" in human terms, including a count of casualties, or even "unnecessary casualties"—a far cry from the fatalistic attitudes of the first half of this century, when millions died in world wars. Words like "responsibility" or "incompetence" would be used more than the word "tragedy." The result is that a modern ruler must be very careful of the opinion of the citizens and what they would regard as an unjust war and unnecessary casualties; they are in possession of information and are therefore not automatically the loyal subjects of past centuries.

In short, in an era when patriarchal, hierarchical, patronizing attitudes have lost their importance, when we do not accept the patronage of one culture over another, when women are no longer treated as inferior beings, and when children have their legal rights, management and cooperation are prevailing over war. The horizontal society of equals rather than one of perpendicular hierarchical groups, a society that creates worldwide networks, is the society of peace. Minorities struggling for recognition have taught us that assertiveness is good, while aggression is dangerous; that empowerment is good, while the abuse of power can be catastrophic; that discrimination is not to be tolerated. We now describe situations rather than groups at fault. All these constitute a modern dictionary of terms unknown to our grandparents.

Modern life has also brought about the legitimization of the present tense. More and more literary works throughout the world include scenes written in the present. This change may be due in part to the influence of television, which portrays events in real time, that is, the present. But it probably goes deeper than that. With the waning of the patriarchal society, we have also freed ourselves from the tyranny of the past and do not feel obliged to prefer that tense over our present, here and now. In Hebrew, writing in the present tense was considered bad form only half a century ago; now it is prevalent, almost as a kind of protest language. But other languages have undergone the same process: the present, previously used mostly in slang and street parlance, is now completely legitimate in literature, and not by accident. We are important; the here and now is important; we need no more obey blindly the supremacy of the past. We need not accept the supremacy of the locus, either; our real neighborhood is the circle of friends with whom we converse by phone rather than our physical neighbors across the street. In other words, we can choose not to be limited by the tyranny of the past, or the tyranny of our particular location, which was previously almost synonymous with destiny. We are free of phrases like "eternal conflict," and "eternal hate"; free trade and the general wish for a high standard of living have freed us from much of the burden of such dire eternity. Group stereotypes are simply not acceptable anymore in polite society, the more so as the phenomenon of extensive world travel has brought us in contact with more and more "others," who thereby have lost much of their otherness.

One of the consequences of the emergence of cross-border economics and the superseding of the nation state is the political typology of certain words and the frequency of their usage. A conservative person is likely to use the terms "national" and "patriotic"; a more modern person will frequently use words like "environmental," "interacting," and "dialogue." Today, we can discern from the vocabulary the underlying ideology of a text or a speech. No self-respecting liberal would freely use the terms "enemy," or "annihilate," or "avenge," which no fundamentalist can do without. We have developed a kind of self-consciousness about the use of certain words, which influences our choice of vocabulary. And ungendered languages, like English, have a hard time adjusting to feminist demands concerning a word like "chairman," which has become "chairperson." Gendered languages, like Hebrew, or Arabic, or Spanish, have no such problem, at least not a verbal one.

Another cultural term that has lost significance is "absolute justice." Heinrich von Kleist had made us aware of the price of *fiat iustitia* (let justice be done) which is precisely that of *peraeat mundus* (the world perishes). His Michael Kohlhaas was the incarnation of many historical grievances, lasting to this day even in parts of Europe, all of which are based in a demand for absolute justice, which we know now is a non-starter. After Auschwitz, absolute justice has no meaning; the Nuremberg trials did not bring a single murdered child back to life. We do not expect absolute justice today, perhaps not an absolute anything. The preferred term now is "beneficial justice," one that would do most reasonable good to all parties concerned. Conflict management has taught us that presenting each other with lists of grievances will not bring about any justice at all, and that it is the feasible, rather than the absolute, to which we should aspire. The astute listener will of course understand that the moment we use terms like "cooperation" and "conflict management" we have given up the old or neo-Marxist vocabulary of power struggle as the sole human motivation.

Thus do linguistic changes, new semantic habits, usher in a different era. It is not free of possible tragedies and errors. It is not ideal or faultless. In the era of the market economy and intense privatization, we still do not know what will happen to altruism, to individual excellence, to heroism, to pity and cultural depth and the tragic sense of life; to emotional continuity and perseverance; to languages and local cultures, some of them highly developed. In the era of market demand, how do we assure the survival and esteem of the person whose artistic and personal values are not necessarily dictated by those of the market? How do we avoid banality at a time when normative standards are dictated by popular demand? How do we recognize, let alone praise, the outstanding? How do we listen to that suspicious individual who does not, in the Latin phrase, frequent "the marketplace, the theater, and the temple?"

Francis Fukuyama wrote about the end of history—and he may have had in mind the end of historical narrative consisting of war and conquest, victors and victims, the kind of history that has been dictated by the patriarchal hierarchical society and that seldom took into account ordinary life, creation, culture at all levels, literature, ideas, everything that happened between wars. But the end of history means the beginning of ecology, both in the broad sense and in the primary sense of the word, which comes from the Greek *oikos,* meaning "home." In the present era we concentrate on the home and its environment, in networks and partnerships and cooperation, for the benefit of all. The moment people realize that war is not only cruelty, brutality, and the complete failure of human common sense, but also the most antiecological act possible, we are on the way to the most beneficial and the sanest possible peace. Our semantics already enable us to take this road. Politics would be well advised to follow.

Translation and Source Information

WORDS: "Beginnings" translation © 1995 Marsha Weinstein. From *Yediot Aharonot*, Rosh Hashana Eve, 1991; "What Should We Do about Myth?" translation © 1995 Marsha Weinstein. From the Van Leer Chanukka lecture, published by *Yediot Aharanot* in December 1989; "Literature in the Age of Masses" presented by the author at the International PEN Congress in Jerusalem, 1974; "The Limits of My Language Are the Limits of My World" translation © 1977 Malka Jagendorf and Shulamith Hareven. From the Van Leer lecture, May 1977. First published in a slightly different form in a collection of essays, *The Dulcinea Syndrome*, by Keter Publishers in 1981.

KNOWLEDGE: "God Is the Other Language" translation © 1995 Marsha Weinstein. From an interview for Voice of Israel Radio conducted by Benny Hendel, Shavuot 1991. Published by *Yediot Aharonot*, March 15, 1991; "Beautifying Reality" translation © 1995 Marsha Weinstein. From *Yediot Aharonot*, December 2, 1985; "Anatomy of a Deviation" translation © 1985 Malka Jagendorf. From *Yediot Aharonot*, November 12, 1984; translated in *The Jerusalem Quarterly*, No. 36, Summer 1985; "Knowledge and Arrogance" is from a lecture in English to new graduates of Hebrew University in Jerusalem, June 21, 1990. Published in *Yediot Aharonot*, July 1990.

PLACE: "On Being a Levantine" English translation © 1985 Malka Jagendorf. From *Al Hamishmar*, April 5, 1985; "Strange Siwa" English translation © 1995 Marsha Weinstein. From *Yediot Aharonot*, October 26, 1990; "Israel: The First Forty Years" English translation © 1988 Malka Jagendorf. Serialized in *Yediot Aharonot*, February 1, 12, and 26, 1988.

PEOPLE: "Portrait of a Terrorist" translation © 1995 Shulamith Hareven. From *Yediot Aharonot*, January 29, 1993; "Reflections in a Dark Mirror" translation © 1995 Marsha Weinstein. From *Yediot Aharonot*, November 12, 1984; "The Man Who Descended into Inferno" translation © 1995 Marsha Weinstein. From *Yediot Aharonot*, December 14, 1990, on the death of Gideon Hausner; "Identity: Victim" translation © 1995 Marsha Weinstein. From *Yediot Aharonot*, May 13, 1986.

CONFLICT: "Eyewitness" translation © 1995 Harriet Lewis and Shulamith Hareven. From *Yediot Aharonot*, February 14, 1983; "Four Bus Stops Away" translation © 1991 Harriet Lewis. From *Yediot Aharonot*, February 26, 1988. English translation originally published in *New Outlook*, by Dvir Publications, 1991; "No One Asked the Medics" translation © 1991 Harriet Lewis. From *Yediot Aharonot*, July 29, 1994. English translation originally published in *New Outlook*, by Dvir Publications, 1991.

PEACE: "Against Charisma" translation © 1995 Marsha Weinstein. From *Yediot Aharonot*, October 1 and 6, 1993; "Life Is Now, Mr. Shamir" translation © 1995 Marsha Weinstein. From *Yediot Aharonot*, October 28, 1990; "Without Love" translation © 1995 Marsha Weinstein. From *Yediot Aharonot*, August 19, 1988; "The Vocabulary of Peace" was presented by the author in English at the Israeli-Arab meeting, sponsored by UNESCO, Granada, December 1993. From *Yediot Aharonot*, January 1994.

SHULAMITH HAREVEN has written fifteen books; her work has been translated into fourteen languages. She was the first woman admitted as a full member to the Academy of the Hebrew Language. Her works in English include *City of Many Days* and *Twilight and Other Stories*. The first two volumes of her historical trilogy, *The Miracle Hater* and *Prophet*, were published by North Point Press; the trilogy will be completed and published in full by Mercury House in the near future.

MARSHA WEINSTEIN received a B.A. magna cum laude in English and American literature from Brown University. In 1985 she left the wilds of New England for Israel, where she has worked as a park ranger, an English teacher, a magazine editor, and a family-planning counselor. A perpetual student, she has dabbled in literatures, Middle Eastern history, philosophy, and several languages. In addition to her work with Shulamith Hareven, she has translated the fiction and nonfiction of Albert Swissa, David Grossman, Meir Shalev, Yitzhak Ben Ner, Ronit Matalon, Amira Hess, and others. She lives in Jerusalem.